THE ANNOTATED DRACULA

"THE SLEEP OF REASON PRODUCES MONSTERS," *CAPRICHIO #5* BY GOYA

THE ANNOTATED DRACULA

Dracula by BRAM STOKER

Introduction, Notes, and Bibliography by

LEONARD WOLF

Art by SÄTTY

With Maps, Drawings, and Photographs

Clarkson N. Potter, Inc./Publisher NEW YORK

DISTRIBUTED BY CROWN PUBLISHERS, INC.

This edition of *Dracula*
is dedicated to Bela Lugosi

PUBLISHER'S NOTE

Through the years the popularity of Bram Stoker's Dracula *has brought many editions into print. Inevitably this has resulted in some text variations. In order to insure the authenticity of the text, we arranged with the Yale University Library to microfilm a copy of the second printing of the first edition. That text has been reproduced in this volume by the photo offset process.*

PHOTOGRAPH CREDITS: frontispiece, courtesy The Aschenbach Foundation, San Francisco; p. xvi, courtesy Cleveland Public Library; p. viii (left), copyright Universal Pictures; p. viii (right), copyright American International, 1970; p. 58, courtesy Hal Jacques; p. 66 (bottom), courtesy The Mansell Collection, London; p. 107, courtesy Triplex Holdings, Ltd., from *British Architect*, 1893; p. 172, courtesy Masson & Cie, from George Guillain, *J. M. Charcot: His Life–His Work.* Translated by Pearce Bailey. Paul B. Hoeber, Inc.; p. 126, courtesy the Berkeley Hotel; p. 214, courtesy The British Museum; p. 256, courtesy Prana Studios, 1922. Photographs by Leonard Wolf appear on the following pages: 5 (top and bottom), 9, 11, 12, 44, 65, 66 (top), 123, 177, 180, 330.

 Inquiries should be addressed to Clarkson N. Potter, Inc., 419 Park Avenue South, New York, N.Y. 10016.
Published simultaneously in Canada by General Publishing Company Limited
First edition
Printed in the United States of America

Designed by Shari de Miskey

Library of Congress Cataloging in Publication Data

Stoker, Bram, 1847-1912.
The annotated Dracula.

Bibliography: p.
1. Stoker, Bram, 1847-1912. Dracula. I. Wolf, Leonard, ed. II. Title.
PZ3.S8743An4 [PT6037.T617] 823'.8 75-4544
ISBN 0—517—52017—6

ACKNOWLEDGMENTS

A great many people deserve my thanks for their help in the preparation of *The Annotated Dracula*. What follows is a by-no-means-complete list of persons who have given me more of their time and attention than I had any right to expect and to whom I am grateful:

Alex Besuan, Senior Lecturer of the Institutul Agronomic, "Dr. Petru Groza," Cluj, Romania; Lynne Billes, Publicity Department of Triplex, London; Charles M. Collins; Professor Frank Dollard, California State University, San Francisco; Robert Doucet; Pamela Edwards; Valerie Eliot of Faber and Faber, London; Radu R. Florescu, coauthor of *In Search of Dracula;* Charles Fornara, General Manager of the Berkeley Hotel, London; G. Graham of the Whitby Literary and Philosophical Society; Virginia Hayes; Mr. Horne of *The Whitby Gazette;* Professor Kay House, California State University, San Francisco; Lawrence Kayton, M.D., of the Institute for Psychosomatic and Psychiatric Research and Training, Chicago; Nadine Kenney; Professor Daniel Knapp, California State University, San Francisco; Monsignor Richard S. Knapp, *Officialis* of the Archdiocese of San Francisco; Professor R. Macgillivray, Department of History, University of Waterloo, Ontario; Raymond McNally, coauthor of *In Search of Dracula;* David O'Dell; Professor Jan Perkowski, University of Texas; Dorothee Perloff, M.D., and Phillip Perloff, M.D.; J. H. Price, Editor, *Cooks Continental Time Tables;* Ioan Puia of the Institutul Agronomic, Cluj, Romania; Father William Quinn of the Archdiocese of San Francisco; Charles C. Raether, Executive Director, The National Funeral Director's Association of the United States; Professor David Renaker, California State University; Nancy Ritter; Professor Bill Robinson, California State University, San Francisco; Herman Schwartz, M.D.; J. D. R. Sheldon, Managing Director of W. Garstin and Sons Ltd., Funeral Directors, London; Peter Suttle; Professor Christy Taylor, California State University, San Francisco; Godfrey Thompson, F.L.A., Librarian, Guildhall Library, London; Frank Tumminia, American Consul in the United States Embassy in Bucharest; David Webb, A.L.A., Librarian, the Bishopsgate Foundation, London; Professor Daniel Weiss, California State University, San Francisco; Judith White; Professor James Wilson, California State University, San Francisco; Professor William A. Wimsatt, Professor of Zoology, Cornell University.

Finally, I want to thank literally scores of students who for more than a year and a half in my various courses on *Dracula* brought me tough questions and hard data with equal enthusiasm.

CONTENTS

CHRISTOPHER LEE AS DRACULA.

BELA LUGOSI AS DRACULA.

INTRODUCTION

Dracula, the book you are about to read, or reread, is one of the most terrifying in the world. It is also, as a literary experience, one of the strangest since it gives wildly contradictory signals about what kind of a work it is. Certainly it is a horror tale in which there is plenty of that fearful, grisly, wonderful, and sometimes silly stuff that we count on finding in our blood-and-gore late-bedtime reading. On the other hand, from its pages there rise images so dreamlike and yet so imperative that we experience them as ancient allegories. Everywhere one looks, there flicker the shadows of primordial struggles: the perpetual tension between the dark and the light; the wrestling match between Christ and Satan; and finally, the complex allegories of sex: sex in all its unimaginable innocence, or sex reeking with the full perfume of the swamp. And all these urgencies are seen or sensed through a hot wash of blood which, deny it though we will, fascinates us very nearly to the point of shame.

This book, this *Dracula*, has, since 1897 when it was written, managed to interject into the culture of the West the image of a creature of such symbolic force that he has become something like a culture hero whom our first duty it is to hate even while we have for him a certain weird admiration. What an elegant monster he is! How strong, how graceful, how lonely, how wise. And above all—and here is his central mystery—how deadly . . . and erotic.

Everywhere one looks, the power—or the legacy—of the book is felt. The film industry in a dozen countries inexhaustibly reinvents the adventures of the Count or his various semblables: Baron Latoes, Count Alucard, Count Yorga, Blacula. Because there are more than two hundred Draculoid titles (and the rate at which new ones appear is accelerating), it is nearly impossible to make a sensible filmography. The old Hamilton Deane–John Balderston stage version of the play is a staple of provincial and repertory theatres; musical Draculas occasionally make their appearance. There are Dracula dolls, Dracula comics (in which, notably, Dracula is a "good guy"). With all of that—no doubt because of that—Bram Stoker's splendid fiction *Dracula* is not yet a thoroughly respectable literary work.

Cultivated readers of the book, like Anthony Boucher who obviously loved and appreciated it, are willing to concede that "it is . . . a masterpiece of a kind, if not a literary one." Montague Summers, nearly forty years before Boucher, would concede to Stoker only brilliantly selected subject matter and occasionally "admirable" writing.

Summers, himself an exhaustingly copious writer on anything to do with vampires, and author of the book *The Vampire: His Kith and Kin*, admired the first four chapters of *Dracula* but wished that "the whole story [could] have been sustained at so high a level." "Then," says Summers, "we should have had a complete masterpiece [p. 333]."

Let me say at once that we *have* a complete masterpiece, flawed here and there, as the Chinese insist masterpieces should be, but, nevertheless, the real thing. What those flaws are will be readily apparent. Stoker was a hasty writer with the habits of a hack. He was, too, overendowed with the sensibility of his age, which means that every so often passages, even whole chapters, grow soft or moist with too much feeling or insufficient characterization; but to dwell on the book's flaws in a brief introduction to the *Annotated Dracula* is as much a critical error as it is a bad tactic. More to the point is a short overview of the literary context in which *Dracula* appears and then some comment both on Stoker himself and on the way his great fiction sustains its power.

Dracula is a Gothic romance, a species of writing that first appeared in England in the mid-eighteenth century and which flourished in the late eighteenth and early nineteenth centuries. The typical Gothic romance has a beautiful young woman in it, who is pursued by wicked, dark, usually Italian, men whose intentions are strictly dishonorable. Her flight takes her to a variety of dismal or dangerous places: subterranean corridors, vaults, crypts, ruins, caves, secret rooms, graveyards. Usually the young woman is well-bred, sensitive, frail. Clearly, she deserves a better fate than the one that threatens her, and it almost goes without saying that she is rescued from it (sometimes repeatedly) by a handsome but sexually unthreatening young man with whom, as the book closes, she settles down to live happily ever after. It is a genre of fiction easy enough to poke fun at, but its finest practitioners have produced works that have either endured or that are frequently rediscovered.

The great authors of Gothic fiction before Stoker mostly lived in the eighteenth century. Robert Walpole's *The Castle of Otranto,* which was published on Christmas Eve in 1764, is usually credited with being the "first" Gothic romance. *The Castle of Otranto* is the work of an antiquarian with a feverish brain, "who"—as I say in *A Dream of Dracula*—"could imagine for himself (and build) a stone and plaster castle jam-packed with medieval scraps of glass, statuary and armor. It was called Strawberry Castle, and was a quaint structure with towers, battlements, and saints in imitation Gothic windows, vaulted roof, balustrades, stairways [pp. 153–54] . . ." Walpole tells us that his book had its origin in a dream "of which all I could recover was that I had thought myself in an ancient castle . . . and that on the upper most bannister of a great staircase I saw a gigantic hand in armor. In the evening, I sat down to write. . . ." *The Castle of Otranto* is hardly a moving work, but it does have the ambience and the machinery that were to characterize Gothic fiction in the years to come. Harry Ludlam, Stoker's biographer, who likes *Otranto* more than I do, says that it

> had doors with rusty hinges, a trapdoor, and lamps extinguishable in a wink. It had a superb villain in Manfred, who, discovering his only son dead on his wedding morning—dashed to pieces beneath an enormous helmet—determined to marry his son's bride, Isabella, so that his line should not become extinct. His own wife, Hippolita, he planned to confine in a convent [p. 181].

For Ludlam, the novel ends in a "roaring climax in which a hundred men appeared bearing a huge sabre, and a portrait walked out of its frame." I am myself fond of *Otranto* without being either moved or surprised by it. It seems precisely the sort of novel a neurasthenic antiquarian with bad dreams and plenty of time on his hands would write in two months time "without knowing in the least what [he] intended to say or to relate."

With Ann Radcliffe's *The Mysteries of Udolpho* (1794), we have the first fully realized Gothic romance in the history of the genre. Despite its sometimes endless descriptions of places to which its author had never been; despite lapses into fifth-rate poetry; despite even its author's insistence on demystifying her first-rate mysteries, the work has a compelling fascination that commands respect. And if in *Udolpho*'s genteel certitudes about terror we care what happens to Emily St. Aubert as she is pursued by Montoni the tyrant, how much more avid is our interest in the heroine of Ann Radcliffe's even more successful *The Italian* (1797). That young woman's enemy is fouler, blacker, and more consummately evil than Montoni, with the added horror that the monster turns out to be (and then not to be) her father.

If there is a hint of incest in *The Italian*, it appears *in flagrante* in Matthew G. Lewis's *The Monk* (1796). Lewis, at nineteen, as Walpole did at forty-seven, wrote his book at top speed, finishing it in the space of ten weeks. *The Monk* is a work of wonderful adolescent gusto. The young Lewis intensely enjoyed the lustful and violent extravagances of his villain, Ambrosio, and devoted himself to giving them to us in every macabre and delicious detail. Since Ambrosio is made to begin his career of villainy after having led a life of blameless chastity for thirty years, one is right to suppose that the long-banked fires of evil that the seductions of the beautiful Rosario-Matilda cause to flame up in him will blaze with an especial heat. And so they do. Before his career of iniquity is done, Ambrosio, once the saint of Madrid, has surrendered (one might better have said "squandered") his virginity and become a practiced, if insatiable satyr. Inflamed, always inflamed by beauty, he murders what turns out to be his mother so that he can enjoy what turns out to be his sister. That frenzied consummation with an unconscious fifteen-year-old girl takes place "by the side of three putrid half-corrupted bodies" in a charnel house beneath a Capuchin monastery in Madrid.

Charles Maturin's *Melmoth the Wanderer* (1820), a work of greater depth, though not greater intensity, has probably the most sustained, and certainly the most complex vision of any Gothic fiction—not excepting *Dracula*. *Melmoth* is a vast work of nearly unrelieved somberness that follows the adventures of Melmoth who, at the cost of his own soul, purchases a one-hundred-and-fifty-year life-span only to learn in the most bitter way that he has only purchased an opportunity for more and more loathsome experience in a world that was monstrous from the start. *Melmoth* is replete with Gothicisms: dungeons, whips, cannibalism, and truly monumental instances of personal dismay. What gives profundity to the fiction is the way in which Melmoth's long adventure into the abyss that is the world becomes an apparently accurate chart of the cost to mankind of original sin.

So far, the works talked about have been those that helped to establish the Gothic tradition in English. It remains to notice a couple of books in the vampire vein to which Stoker undoubtedly paid some attention: John Polidori's *The Vampyre* and Thomas Presket Prest's *Varney the Vampyre*. Since neither of the stories, except as they relate to *Dracula*, have much to recommend them, one may pass over them quickly. John Polidori's *The Vampyr* is, like *The Monk*, a young man's book. Polidori wrote *The Vampyre* when he was twenty-four as a consequence of what Anthony Boucher called "that same splendid brainstorming session that also produced Mary Shelley's *Frankenstein*." On that famous summer evening in 1816, Byron suggested to the two Shelleys, to Polidori, and to "Monk" Lewis, who were all there in Geneva keeping out of the rain, that each of them write a horror tale in imitation of some "German stories of ghosts, which happened to fall into their hands." The eighteen-year-old Mary Shelley and John Polidori were the only members of the group that followed through. Here, our interest is only in Polidori's *The Vampyre* (1819), which introduced to English literature the suave, wicked, and bloodthirsty Lord Ruthven whose "dead grey eye" fascinated his victims. *The Vampyre* is a work almost without merit, having neither memorable characters, a plot worth pursuing, nor any noticeable style. Its subject, on the other hand, made it a success, and the deadly hued Lord Ruthven, pursuing first the evanescent, beautiful Ianthe and later the good-looking Aubrey's sister, became well known in England and on the continent, particularly in one of the many stage versions of the story that appeared.

Varney the Vampyre (1847), a work that has no literary pretensions, is for that reason much more fun to read. The book is an enthusiastic potboiler whose energy almost never lags. A couple of paragraphs from the first chapter of *Varney* convey almost everything one needs to know about the work except the vicissitudes of the plot, which are constructed on the same organizational principle as a mad seamstress's workbasket. Here, then, are some passages from *Varney.* After that, each reader's own taste—and endurance—must come into play. Prest writes:

> . . . A shriek bursts from the lips of the young girl, and then, with eyes fixed upon that window and with such an expression of terror upon her face, she trembled, and the perspiration of intense fear stood upon her brow.
>
> A tall figure is standing on the ledge immediately outside the window. . . . The lightning has set fire to a mill, and the reflection of the rapidly consuming building falls upon that long window. There can be no mistake. The figure is there, still feeling for an entrance, and clattering against the glass with its long nails. . . . A small pane of glass is broken, and the form from without introduces a long gaunt hand, which seems utterly destitute of flesh. The fastening is removed, and one half of the window, which opens like folding doors, is swung wide open upon its hinges.
>
> . . . The figure turns half round, and the light falls upon the face. It is perfectly white—perfectly bloodless. The eyes look like polished tin; the lips are drawn back, and the principal feature next to those dreadful eyes is the teeth —the fearful looking teeth—projecting like those of some wild animal, hideously, glaringly white, and fang-like. It approaches the bed with a strange, gliding movement. . . .
>
> With a sudden rush that could not be foreseen—with a strange howling cry that was enough to awaken terror in every breast, the figure seized the long tresses of her hair, and twining them round his bony hands he held her to the bed. Then she screamed . . . Shriek followed shriek in rapid succession . . . Her beautiful rounded limbs quivered with the agony of her soul. The glassy, horrible eyes of the figure ran over that angelic form with hideous satisfaction . . . He drags her head to the bed's edge. He forces it back by the long hair still entwined in his grasp. With a plunge he seizes her neck in his fang-like teeth—a gush of blood, and a hideous sucking noise follows. *The girl has swooned, and the vampyre is at his hideous repast* [pp. 3–4]!

The villain making that hideous sucking noise is Sir Francis Varney whose deeds and misdeeds race on and on over 220 chapters distributed among 868 double-columned closely printed pages. Though Stoker took hints here and there from *Varney*, particularly for the great Lucy-staking episode in chapter XVI, *Dracula* and *Varney* have almost nothing but their vampire theme in common.

What distinguishes *Dracula* from the vampire fictions that preceded it, as well as from those that subsequently appeared, is the way in which folklore and authentic history merge to give Stoker's tale the texture of something long known or naturally remembered. How did he find what he used? Harry Ludlam, his biographer, tells us that the impetus for the making of the book came to him in a nightmare brought on "from a too generous helping of dressed crab at supper one night. . . ." In that dream, we are told, Stoker saw "a vampire king rising from the tomb to go about his ghastly business." But a private British dream is not enough foundation on which to build a master work of fiction—as *The Castle of Otranto* ought to prove. Evidently Stoker's genius, which had been in hiding for so many years, also knew this and sent him to the British Museum where, following a lead provided him by a Hungarian friend, Arminius Vambery, he found what he needed: first, an authentic vampire folklore; second, a dreadful historic figure named Vlad

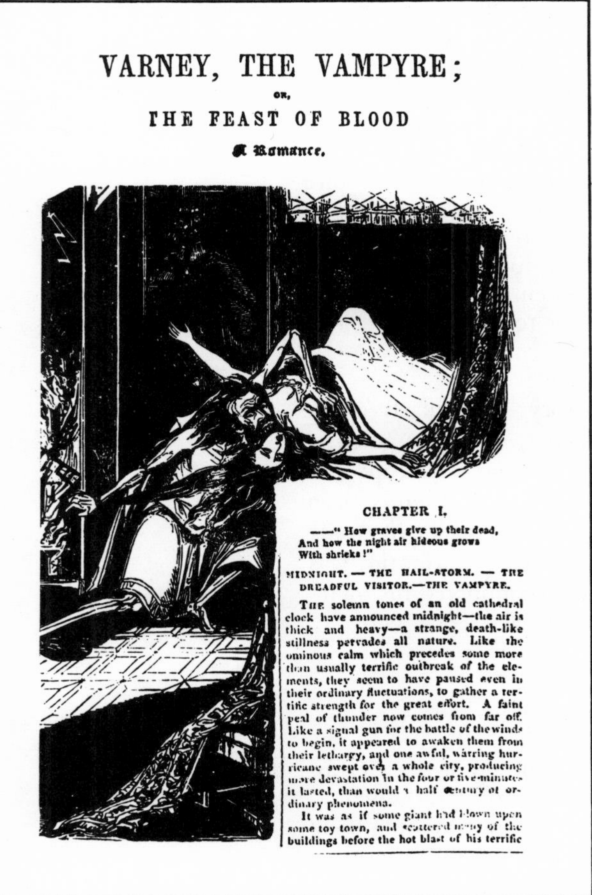

VARNEY, THE VAMPYRE;

OR,

THE FEAST OF BLOOD

A Romance.

CHAPTER I.

——"How graves give up their dead,
And how the night air hideous grows
With shrieks!"

MIDNIGHT. — THE HAIL-STORM. — THE DREADFUL VISITOR.—THE VAMPYRE.

THE solemn tones of an old cathedral clock have announced midnight—the air is thick and heavy—a strange, death-like stillness pervades all nature. Like the ominous calm which precedes some more than usually terrific outbreak of the elements, they seem to have paused even in their ordinary fluctuations, to gather a terrific strength for the great effort. A faint peal of thunder now comes from far off. Like a signal gun for the battle of the winds to begin, it appeared to awaken them from their lethargy, and one awful, warring hurricane swept over a whole city, producing more devastation in the four or five minutes it lasted, than would a half century of ordinary phenomena.

It was as if some giant had blown upon some toy town, and scattered many of the buildings before the hot blast of his terrific

OPENING PAGE OF *VARNEY THE VAMPYRE.*

THE FEAST OF BLOOD. 83

A great many efforts were made to get him to say more, particularly with reference to the case under consideration, as being no common one, but the octogenarian had made his effort, and he only replied to the remonstrances of those who, alternately by coaxing and bullying, strove to get information from him, by a vacant stare.

"It's of no use," said the butcher, "you'll get nothing more now from old Timothy; he's done up now, that's quite clear, and ten to one if the excitement of to-night won't go a good way towards slaughtering him before his time."

"Well, it may be so," cried the blacksmith, "but still it's good advice, and as I said before it comes to this—is we to be afraid of lay down in our beds at night, or isn't we?"

Before any reply could be made to this interrogatory, the old clock that was in the public-house parlour struck the hour of eleven, and another peal of thunder seemed to be answering to the tinkling sounds.

"It's a rough night," said one, "I thought there would be a storm before morning by the look of the sun at setting—it went down with a strange fiery redness behind a bank of clouds. I move for going home."

"Who talks of going home," cried the blacksmith, "when vampires are abroad? hasn't old Timothy said, that a stormy night was the very one to settle the thing in."

"No," cried another, "he did not say night at all."

"I don't care whether he said night or day; I've made up my mind to do something; there's no doubt about it but that a vampyre is about the old church. Who'll come with me and ferret it out? it will be good service done to everybody's fireside."

ILLUSTRATED PAGE FROM *VARNEY THE VAMPYRE.*

Dracula, or, as he was also called, Vlad Ţepeş, the Impaler; and third, a place that incorporated them both—Transylvania, The Land Beyond the Forest.

Vampire lore, one must insist, is not restricted to Transylvania. As Dr. Van Helsing properly says in his ridiculous English:

> Let me tell you, he is known everywhere that men have been. In old Greece, in old Rome; he flourish in Germany all over, in France, in India, even in the Chersonese; and in China, so far from us in all ways, there even is he . . .

And in Tibet, North Africa, Borneo, North and South America, Polynesia, Australia, and Nepal. In short, as I like to say, vampires have appeared almost everywhere that men have bled. It is true, however, that in Central Europe, and particularly in Transylvania, which was for centuries a battleground between Turks and Christians, there is a heavy Christian overlay on the pagan content of vampire legendry, a fact that Stoker seized upon eagerly and exploited well.

Probably the richest single source of folklore information for him was Emily Gerard's fine travel book, *The Land Beyond the Forest*, which, in addition to giving him a lively and extraordinarily circumstantial account of daily life in Transylvania *circa* 1888, is crammed with information about its history and folkways. In Miss Gerard's book he could read that:

> More decidedly evil is the *nosferatu*, or vampire, in which every Roumanian peasant believes as firmly as he does in heaven or hell . . . even a flawless pedigree will not insure any one against the intrusion of a vampire into their family vault, since every person killed by a *nosferatu* becomes likewise a vampire after death, and will continue to suck the blood of other innocent persons till the spirit has been exorcised by opening the grave of the suspected person, and either driving a stake through the corpse, or else firing a pistol-shot into the coffin . . . In very obstinate cases of vampirism it is recommended to cut off the head and replace it in the coffin with the mouth filled with garlic, or to extract the heart and burn it, strewing its ashes over the grave [pp. 185–86].

If Transylvanian folklore is already Gothic enough, its history, particularly of the fifteenth century, is even more so. Vlad Ţepeş, voivode of Wallachia, which he ruled briefly in 1448, from 1456 to 1462, and for two months in 1476, was one of Europe's bloodiest tyrants. His life and character (if that is the right word for it) have recently been the subject of a popular study, *In Search of Dracula,* by Professors Raymond T. McNally and Radu Florescu, in which Vlad's life and cruelties are probed. Ţepeş, it is certain, was a boundlessly dreadful man. What else can one think of a prince who conducted his own St. Bartholomew's Day Massacre in the course of which "some 30,000 persons were probably killed." Florescu and McNally tell us that Vlad's

> crimes, the refinements of his cruelty . . . deserve a chapter unto themselves. Impalement, hardly a new method of torture, was his favorite method of imposing death. A strong horse was usually harnessed to each leg of the victim, while the stake was carefully introduced so as not to kill instantly. . . . Such quick deaths would have interfered with the pleasure he sought in watching their agonies over a period of time, as the stakes were propped in the ground. This torture was often a matter of hours, sometimes a matter of days. . . .
>
> There were also various geometric patterns in which the impaled were displayed. Usually the victims were arranged in concentric circles, and in the outskirts of cities where they could be viewed by all. There were high spears and

VLAD THE IMPALER.

> low spears, according to rank. There was impalement from above—feet upwards; and impalement from below—head upwards; or through the heart or navel. There were nails in people's heads, maiming of limbs, blinding, strangulation, burning, the cutting of noses and ears, and of sexual organs in the case of women, scalping and skinning, exposure to the elements or to the wild animals, and boiling alive [pp. 45–46].

And that list of Vlad's abominations neither exhausts their number nor includes all their varieties. And yet there have been historians like Colonel Leon Lamouche who can write that "Vlad was, nevertheless, an energetic, skillful prince, and his cruelty, which certainly was not always understandable, had at least the result that it made order reign in Wallachia and it completely suppressed brigandage, which before him was commonplace." One thing must be granted to him—if it matters. Vlad Ţepeş was not a vampire. That attribute was given him by Bram Stoker who, it seems to me, saw the proper metaphor lurking in the man. Taking his cue from the European lore of the vampire in which the vampire is seen as having a tainted soul, Stoker invested Vlad Dracula with it for the sake of his fiction. In the circumstances, it hardly seems libelous.

How often is a mother's estimate of her son's achievement confirmed by history? Rarely, one may be certain, and yet, here is Charlotte Stoker writing to her son Bram on the occasion of the publication of *Dracula*, as quoted in Ludlam's biography:

> My dear, [*Dracula*] is splendid, a thousand miles beyond anything you have written before, and I feel certain will place you very high in the writers of the day . . . No book since Mrs. Shelley's Frankenstein or indeed any other at all has come near yours in originality, or terror—Poe is nowhere [pp. 108–9].

Mrs. Stoker was right on target. Her son had indeed written a uniquely terrifying book. And one would like to know a great deal about the sort of person he was. Unfortunately, a full discussion of Bram Stoker's life is not yet possible.

Harry Ludlam's *Biography of Dracula*, whose subtitle is *The Life Story of Bram Stoker*, while it is useful enough as a sort of public record of the events in which Stoker was involved, leaves essentially unexplored those aspects of his private life about which we are likely to be most curious. Ludlam's bias is in favor of what is immediately visible to a not very scrutinizing eye. As a result, in Ludlam's pages, Stoker comes across as part boy scout, part Horatio Alger hero, and more than a small part Victorian boor. All the crucial questions that are raised by the recorded facts of Stoker's life as well as those raised by his work, Ludlam is unwilling either to notice or to answer. For example, the most enigmatic relationship of Stoker's life is, presumably, the one he had with the actor Henry Irving who was both his employer and his friend. Though that complex and charged friendship is touched upon, it is not explored beyond the banalities of true-blue loyalty and devotion. Stoker's relationships with his wife (about whom one would also like to know a great deal), his mother and father, and his son are similarly left politely unexplored. There is reason to hope that a biography of Stoker by his great-nephew, Daniel Farson, which is scheduled for publication in England late in 1975, will fill in the gaps left by a too-respectful Ludlam.

Meanwhile, we must be grateful to Ludlam for having assembled the public facts of Stoker's life, which, briefly, are as follows: Stoker was born in 1847 in Dublin, the third son of seven children. His father, Abraham Stoker (for whom Bram was named), was an Irish civil servant who worked in the Chief Secretary's Office at Dublin Castle. Bram was a sickly child who was not able to stand upright, as he tells us, until he was seven years old. He recovered from his childhood illnesses and grew into such vigorous, athletic young manhood that he could later claim of himself, "in fact I feel justified in saying I represented in my own person something of the aim of university education *mens sana in corpore sano* . . . ." Stoker graduated with honors in mathematics from Trinity College, Dublin, but when he left school he pursued a longtime interest in writing and the theatre by taking on an unpaid job as drama critic for the Dublin *Mail* while, at the same time, he followed in his father's footsteps in the Irish civil service.

Then, in his twenty-ninth year, he met Henry Irving. The meeting changed both their lives. Stoker followed the famous actor to London and not long afterward he became Irving's confidante and the actor-manager of his theatre, a job he held for twenty-eight years, until Irving's death. For Stoker, they were years of extraordinary busyness in the course of which, he tells us, he wrote in Irving's name "nearer half a million than a quarter of a million letters." The quality of Stoker's life in Irving's service is perhaps conveyed in the following description given in *A Dream of Dracula*:

> The tall, handsome, vigorous Irishman was henceforth a familiar figure before the doors of the Lyceum theater. Maybe what drew Stoker to the task (in addition to Irving) was the opportunity it gave him to move about in the cosmopolitan ambience of the glittering London that whirled around Irving. For a provincial young Irishman, not thoroughly convinced of his own talents, there

BRAM STOKER, A SKETCH BY W. W. DENSLOW.

BRAM STOKER, AN 1885 SKETCH.

ELLEN TERRY WITH SIR HENRY IRVING.

ELLEN TERRY AND SIR HENRY IRVING IN TENNYSON'S *BECKET.*

> may have been some psychic nourishment in being always within sight and sound of greater men than himself. Irving's son Laurence writes that "to Stoker, these illustrious patrons, whom he welcomed on their arrival in the foyer, were the breath of life; Irving, who dismissed them with his blessing from the stage, found that they made him depressed and nervous." Or, in addition to the excitement of the life of the theater, Stoker was pleased to find an outlet for the bureaucratic and organizational talents [he had]. . . . Laurence Irving tells us that the great actor's "retinue of fifty-four included the players necessary for these productions and the key men in all the departments of stage management. The organization of this imposing caravan was left to Bram Stoker; it was the kind of work he thoroughly enjoyed and at which he excelled" [p. 253].

That fascination with small detail also shows up in *Dracula* where both Jonathan and Mina Harker have railroad timetables much on their minds.

On October 13, 1905, Sir Henry Irving died in the hall of the Midland Hotel, London. Two minutes later Bram Stoker arrived to do his friend one last service—he closed the dead man's eyes. In the seven years that remained of Stoker's life, he produced *The Personal Reminiscences of Sir Henry Irving*, a two-volume work, as well as two novels, *The Lady of the Shroud* and *The Lair of the White Worm*, plus a volume of short stories, and some periodical writing. *The Lady of the Shroud* has a seven-foot-tall hero and some fake vampirism in it, but mostly the book is a sort of Tom Swift-and-His-Private-Ruritania fiction set in the Land of the Blue Mountains where both the good guys and the villains speak elevated prose and where, very likely, the first airplane bombardment in literary history takes place. *The Lair of the White Worm* is not much better as fiction, but the novel's plot and tone give one a good deal to think about regarding those of Stoker's perplexities that his biographer Ludlam avoided confronting. Ludlam summarizes the *Lair* as follows:

> The White Worm of the story was one of those monsters which had secreted itself for thousands of years in a well of uncommon depth . . . The creature had so developed its brain and powers as to be able to project itself in the form of a woman, a woman in white with low and sibilant voice and long, flexible hands, from whose path all common snakes fled.
>
> So far so good. But the plot that resulted in the snake woman Lady Arabella, being unmasked and her lair dynamited by a resourceful young hero, introduced a number of other weird, incredible characters that moved through the story like evil cardboard figures in a macabre toy theatre [p. 149].

Harry Ludlam, commenting on *Dracula*, has written:

> Critics, psychologists and others have laboured over earnest examinations of suspected deeper, hidden meanings behind Stoker's chilling horror. The genial, red-bearded giant would have laughed loud at such high-flown nonsense [p. 8].

The trouble is that this very same genial red-bearded giant wrote both *Dracula* and the *Lair of the White Worm*. In *Dracula* the fear of and fascination with women is a pulsating theme of the fiction. In the *Lair of the White Worm* the fear and fascination are writhing, horrid presences. Both books, earnestly examined, make one wonder just how genial Bram Stoker's inner life could have been.

Anthony Boucher, in his introduction to the Heritage Edition (the only one ever illustrated, incidentally) of *Dracula* asks: "How did the most successful horror novel in the English (and possibly in any) language come to be written by a man whose first published book was entitled *The Duties of Clerks of Petty Sessions in Ireland*?" One might extend the question to inquire how *Dracula* came to be written by the same man who wrote such arch fictions as *The Snake's Pass*, *The Watter's Mou'*, *The Shoulder of Shasta*, *The Mystery of the Sea*, and *The Lady of the Shroud*. Anthony Boucher, shrewdly, did not try to answer his question, and I have no intention of answering mine. Literary greatness is easier to acknowledge than to explain. It is enough that the world was lucky; that something gathered in Bram Stoker that made it possible for him to make one—and only one—work whose central figure could become an overwhelming symbol of the crimes and temptations of the twentieth century. As I said in my *Dream of Dracula:*

> . . . Dracula. Our eidolon . . . He is huge, and we admire size; strong, and we admire strength. He moves with the confidence of a creature that has energy, power, and will. Granted that he has energy without grace, power without responsibility, and that his will is an exercise in death. We need only to look a little to one side to see how tempting is the choice he makes: available immortality. He has collected on the devil's bargain: the infinitely stopped moment [p. 302].

For this, Faust was willing to risk damnation. Here, then, is the figure that Bram Stoker created—a figure who confronts us with primordial mysteries: death, blood, and love, and how they are bound together. Finally, Stoker's achievement is this: he makes us understand in our own experience why the vampire is said to be invisible in the mirror. He is there, but we fail to recognize him since our own faces get in the way.

DRACULA

BY

BRAM STOKER

WESTMINSTER
ARCHIBALD CONSTABLE AND COMPANY
2 WHITEHALL GARDENS
1897

HALL CAINE.

1 *Hommy-Beg*. A Manx name of endearment for Hall Caine, the English novelist and Stoker's very close friend. Caine dedicated his own *Cap'n Davy's Honeymoon* (1893) to Stoker. The words "Hommy-Beg" mean "little Tommy."

TO

MY DEAR FRIEND

HOMMY-BEG [1]

How these papers have been placed in sequence will be made manifest in the reading of them. All needless matters have been eliminated, so that a history almost at variance with the possibilities of later-day belief may stand forth as simple fact. There is throughout no statement of past things wherein memory may err, for all the records chosen are exactly 2
contemporary, given from the standpoints and within the range of knowledge of those who made them.

2 *are exactly contemporary*. This technique Stoker borrowed from Wilkie Collins who used it in his novel *The Woman in White* (1860).

"THE MOST WESTERN OF SPLENDID BRIDGES."

DRACULA.

CHAPTER I.

Jonathan Harker's Journal. 1

(Kept in shorthand.) 2

3 *May.* *Bistritz.*—Left Munich at 8.35 p.m. on 1st May, 3
arriving at Vienna early next morning; should have arrived at
6.46, but train was an hour late. Buda-Pesth seems a wonderful place, from the glimpse which I got of it from the
train and the little I could walk through the streets. I feared
to go very far from the station, as we had arrived late and
would start as near the correct time as possible. The impression I had was that we were leaving the West and entering the
East; the most Western of splendid bridges over the Danube, 4
which is here of noble width and depth, took us among the
traditions of Turkish rule.

We left in pretty good time, and came after nightfall to
Klausenburgh. Here I stopped for the night at the Hotel 5, 6
Royale. I had for dinner, or rather supper, a chicken done
up some way with red pepper, which was very good but thirsty.
(*Mem.*, get recipe for Mina.) I asked the waiter, and he said
it was called "paprika hendl," and that, as it was a national 7

1 *Jonathan Harker.* According to Harry Ludlam (p. 98), Stoker's biographer, the source for Jonathan's name was a Joseph Harker, a stage scenic designer with whom Stoker worked.

2 *shorthand.* As far as can be determined Stoker had Harker use the Pitman method of shorthand that had only recently come into general use.

3 *8.35 p.m.* The clock is the unacknowledged monitor of the action to come. Stoker was obsessed by time, and in *Dracula* he uses it to good effect to put his larger theme of Life-in-Death into sharp relief.

4 *the most Western of splendid bridges over the Danube.* Count Széchenyi's great bridge over the Danube linking Buda and Pest took nearly twenty years to build, from 1854 to 1873, and was considered a marvel in its day.

OLD TOWER AT KLAUSENBURG WITH LEITERWAGON.

8 dish, I should be able to get it anywhere along the Carpathians. I found my smattering of German very useful here; indeed, I don't know how I should be able to get on without it.

Having some time at my disposal when in London, I had
9 visited the British Museum, and made search among the
10 books and maps in the library regarding Transylvania; it had struck me that some foreknowledge of the country could hardly fail to have some importance in dealing with a noble of that country. I find that the district he named is in the extreme east of the country, just on the borders of three
11, 12 states, Transylvania, Moldavia, and Bukovina, in the midst of the Carpathian mountains; one of the wildest and least known portions of Europe. I was not able to light on any map or work giving the exact locality of the Castle Dracula, as there are no maps of this country as yet to compare with
13, 14 our own Ordnance Survey maps; but I found that Bistritz,
15 the post town named by Count Dracula, is a fairly well-known place. I shall enter here some of my notes, as they may refresh my memory when I talk over my travels with Mina.

16 In the population of Transylvania there are four distinct nationalities: Saxons in the south, and mixed with them the Wallachs, who are the descendants of the Dacians; Magyars in the west, and Szekelys in the east and north. I am going among the latter, who claim to be descended from Attila and the Huns. This may be so, for when the Magyars conquered

5 *Klausenburgh.* A city and department in central Transylvania. Modern Cluj. At the turn of the century, Klausenburg had 34,500 inhabitants. (See map, p. 335.)

6 *Hotel Royale.* Not shown in Baedeker. Though why Harker, as a patriotic Englishman, did not stay in the Königin von England (Queen of England) is a puzzle.

7 *"paprika hendl."* Marcia Colman Morton's recipe for this well-known dish in her book, *The Art of Viennese Cooking* (p. 60) follows:

PAPRIKA CHICKEN (*Paprikahendl*)

1 young fowl, about 4 pounds	2 tablespoons Hungarian sweet paprika
2 tablespoons fat	½ cup tomato juice
2 large onions, chopped	2 tablespoons flour
	½ cup sour cream

Cut chicken into serving pieces, and salt. Lightly brown onions in fat. Blend in half the paprika. Add tomato juice and chicken. Simmer, covered, 1 hour or until tender. Remove chicken. Add remaining paprika to sauce, then add the flour beaten into sour cream. Simmer, stirring, 5 minutes or until well blended. Put sauce through sieve, food mill or blender. Heat chicken and puréed sauce together over low flame. Arrange chicken on warm platter. Pour half the sauce over; pass the rest separately in a sauceboat. Serve with Flour Dumplings.

6 servings

Paget (p. 261) gives a more charming recipe: "I do not think I have yet enlightened the reader as to the mystery of a *paprika hendel*; to forget it would be a depth of ingratitude of which, I trust, I shall never be guilty. Well, then, reader, if ever you travel in Hungary, and want a dinner or supper quickly, never mind the variety of dishes your host names, but fix at once on *paprika hendel.* Two minutes afterwards, you will hear signs of a revolution in the *basse cour*; the cocks and hens are in alarm; one or two of the largest, and probably oldest members of their unfortunate little community, are seized, their necks wrung, and, while yet fluttering, immersed in boiling water. Their coats and skins come off at once; a few unmentionable preparatory operations are rapidly despatched—probably under the traveller's immediate observation—the wretches are cut into pieces, thrown into a pot, with water, butter, flour, cream, and an inordinate quantity of red pepper, or paprika, and, very shortly after, a number of bits of fowl are seen swimming in a dish of hot greasy gravy, quite delightful to think of."

8 *Carpathians.* A mountain range extending 800 miles from northeast Czechoslovakia to northern Romania. The highest peak is 8,737 feet.

9 *British Museum.* According to Stoker's biographer, Harry Ludlam: "Restoring Dracula to a natural home in Transylvania, in a vast ruined castle perched on the edge of a great precipice, took Bram many hours of research among books and maps in the British Museum. Most of his information about the country was gleaned from an old guide book; but when, after publication of *Dracula*, he was congratulated by all sorts of people on his first-hand knowledge of Transylvania, and the settings so eerily true, he found it prudent not to spoil the illusion."

The reading room of the British Museum in Stoker's day accommodated 458 readers at a time who were watched over by a superintendent sitting "on a raised seat in the centre of the room." Every reader had a chair, a folding desk, a small hinged shelf for books, pens and ink, a blotting pad, and a peg for his hat.

One could not (and cannot) simply walk in and use the reading room. "Persons desirous of using the Reading Room," says a nineteenth-century Baedeker, "must send a written application to the Principal Librarian, specifying their names, rank or profession, purpose, and address, and enclosing a recommendation from some well-known householder in London."

10 *regarding Transylvania.* The name means "the Land Beyond the Forest," and refers to a high plateau in modern north and central Romania. Originally part of Roman Dacia, Transylvania became part of Hungary in the eleventh century. After the battle of Mohács in 1526 (see Chapter III, note 23), the voivode of Transylvania, under the instigation of Süleyman the Magnificent, claimed the throne of Hungary. Transylvania remained a semi-independent principality under the Turks until the beginning of the eighteenth century.

In Stoker's day it was a Hungarian province, chiefly a land of wheat fields, orchards, and vineyards, though sulfur, lead, timber, and iron were being exploited.

11 *Moldavia.* A district of Romania from 1861 to 1940, covering 13,000 square miles. Its capital was Kishinev. (See map, p. 335.)

12 *Bukovina.* A former possession of Austria, now a province in northeast Romania, covering an area of 14,031 square miles. (See map, p. 335.)

13 *Ordnance Survey maps.* A military map showing the topography of a terrain.

14 *Bistritz.* Modern Bistrita. (See note 22 of this chapter and map, p. 335.)

A POST STATION IN HUNGARY.

15 *post town.* A town that has a central post office or a town in which post-horses are available.

16 *distinct nationalities.* In 1888 Emily Gerard gave the population of Transylvania as "2,170,000 heads. . . . Of these the proportion of different races may be assumed to be pretty nearly as follows:

Roumanians	1,200,000	Gypsies	79,000
Hungarians	652,221	Jews	24,848
Saxons	211,490	Armenians	8,430

A Baedeker's *Austria* for 1900 gives a slightly different breakdown of Transylvania's population:

"The Magyars . . . including the Szeklers, number about 765,000 souls. The Saxons are about 222,000 in number. . . . Roumanians or Wallachians . . . are no fewer than 1,395,000. Armenians, 8,400. . . . There are also about 88,000 Gipsies in Transylvania.

"The other races represented are Jews (26,000), Slovaks, Ruthenians, Bulgarians, Servians, and Greeks—The total population [of Transylvania] is in round numbers 2,400,000."

A TRANSYLVANIAN WALLACH.

"THE HORSESHOE OF THE CARPATHIANS."

17 *"mamaliga."* The recipe for mamaliga follows:

3 cups water	½ cup sour cream
salt	4 slices feta cheese
1 cup corn meal	(or other sharp cheese)
2 tablespoons butter	

Bring salted water to boil and add the cornmeal. Cook like porridge while stirring frequently with wooden spoon for twenty-five minutes.

Grease a deep ovenproof casserole well with butter. Pour in the porridge, cover with the sour cream, and arrange the slices of feta on top. Put in a 400-degree oven for ten minutes. Serve when mamaliga is golden on top, garnished with one poached egg per person if you wish. Serves four.

18 *"impletata."* Stoker may mean *patlagele impulute*, a traditional dish, the recipe for which is:

Wash and cut one eggplant in half. Score the surface, salt well, and set aside for one-half hour, then gently squeeze excess moisture from halves.

Place eggplant halves face down in a buttered frypan and let them cook gently, covered, until tender. Scoop the center pulp out of each half, leaving one-half inch of meat attached to the skin. Mix the pulp with salt, pepper, onions, and any ground meat. Brown mixture in a frypan, then press gently into eggplant shells, sprinkle with bread crumbs and melted butter, and brown in a quick oven.

19 *an hour before we began to move.* Harker left at 8:30 A.M. The journey from Klausenburg to Bistrita, a distance of seventy-four miles, took four and

the country in the eleventh century they found the Huns settled in it. I read that every known superstition in the world is gathered into the horseshoe of the Carpathians, as if it were the centre of some sort of imaginative whirlpool; if so my stay may be very interesting. (*Mem.*, I must ask the Count all about them.)

I did not sleep well, though my bed was comfortable enough, for I had all sorts of queer dreams. There was a dog howling all night under my window, which may have had something to do with it; or it may have been the paprika, for I had to drink up all the water in my carafe, and was still thirsty. Towards morning I slept and was wakened by the continuous knocking at my door, so I guess I must have been sleeping soundly then. I had for breakfast more paprika, and a sort of por-
17 ridge of maize flour which they said was "mamaliga," and
egg-plant stuffed with forcemeat, a very excellent dish,
18 which they call "impletata." (*Mem.*, get recipe for this also.)
I had to hurry breakfast, for the train started a little before
eight, or rather it ought to have done so, for after rushing to
the station at 7.30 I had to sit in the carriage for more than
19 an hour before we began to move. It seems to me that the
20 further East you go the more unpunctual are the trains. What
ought they to be in China?
21 All day long we seemed to dawdle through a country which was full of beauty of every kind. Sometimes we saw little towns or castles on the top of steep hills such as we see in old missals; sometimes we ran by rivers and streams which seemed from the wide stony margin on each side of them to be subject to great floods. It takes a lot of water, and running strong, to sweep the outside edge of a river clear. At every station there were groups of people, sometimes crowds, and in all sorts of attire. Some of them were just like the peasants at home or those I saw coming through France

"THE WOMEN LOOKED PRETTY, EXCEPT . . ."

and Germany, with short jackets and round hats and home-made trousers; but others were very picturesque. The women looked pretty, except when you got near them, but they were very clumsy about the waist. They had all full white sleeves of some kind or other, and most of them had big belts with a lot of strips of something fluttering from them like the dresses in a ballet, but of course petticoats under them. The strangest figures we saw were the Slovaks, who are more barbarian than the rest, with their big cowboy hats, great baggy dirty-white trousers, white linen shirts, and enormous heavy leather belts, nearly a foot wide, all studded over with brass nails. They wore high boots, with their trousers tucked into them, and had long black hair and heavy black moustaches. They are very picturesque, but do not look prepossessing. On the stage they would be set down at once as some old Oriental band of brigands. They are, however, I am told, very harmless and rather wanting in natural self-assertion.

It was on the dark side of twilight when we got to Bistritz, **22**

three-quarter hours, and cost four *florins* thirty *kroners* first class (about $1.75 or seven English shillings). The slow speed of the train was not unusual. Austrian trains seldom went faster than twenty-five miles per hour.

20 *unpunctual are the trains.* Emily Gerard (p. 16) comments: "The railway communications are very badly managed, so that it was only on the evening of the second day (fully forty-eight hours later) that we arrived at Klausenburgh, where we were to stop for a night's rest."

21 *to dawdle.* Exceptionally. Harker tells us later that he arrived in Bistrita "on the dark side of twilight," which would be about 7:00 P.M. in that latitude. Even at the slow speed noted, that would mean a twelve-hour journey or nearly eight hours late!

"THE STRANGEST FIGURES WE SAW WERE THE SLOVAKS."

22 *Bistritz.* The 10th edition of the *Encyclopaedia Britannica* (p. 267) describes Bistritz in this way: "Bistritz (Hungarian, Besztercze), an ancient town (now corporate) of Eastern Hungary, 48 miles N.E. by E. of Kolosvar; capital of the county of Bestercze-Naszód, with 12,081 inhabitants. It is surrounded with the ruins of ancient bastions and towers; but in 1857 a great portion of the old town was burnt down."

Florescu and McNally (pp. 29–30) write:

"Castle Bistrita, located near the Borgo Pass, may have served as the model for the castle in Stoker's novel. It was John Hunyadi who actually completed Castle Bistrita around 1449, five years before the fall of Constantinople. . . . Hunyadi was the father of Mathias Corvinus, the Hungarian king who kept [the historical] Dracula imprisoned in his citadel on the Danube for some twelve years, from 1462 to 1474. . . . Not a trace of Bistrita Castle remains today—only legends. It is probable that Stoker heard of these legends connecting Dracula to this region. The Saxon population of Bistrita, who disliked the Romanians and the Hungarians, doubtless heard of Dracula's atrocities against their brethren farther south in the towns of Brasov and Sibiu, where most of the horrors were committed and recorded. . . . In any event, Bistrita Castle was attacked, ransacked, and totally destroyed by the German population of the city at the close of the 15th century, an apparent gesture of defiance against the Hungarian kings, who, as we know, were allies of Dracula."

23 *Borgo Pass.* Harker's coach probably took him from Bistrita to Jail, then Borgóprund, then Maros Borgo, then Tihucza where the Borgo Pass begins. The average elevation of the Pass is 1,227 feet above sea level.

The real landscape around Bistrita, though it is certainly mountainous, is hardly the crag-and-torrent-filled terrain of Stoker's description. Gustave Doré's illustrations of Dante's *Inferno* are pressing against his imagination more than any pictures of Transylvania he (or Harker) may have seen in the reading room of the British Museum. (See map, p. 335.)

24 *Fifty years ago a series of great fires.* A 1900 Baedeker speaks of "the Gothic Protestant Church, finished in 1563, and much injured by repeated fires." (See note 22 of this chapter.)

25 *Golden Krone Hotel.* There was no such inn in Bistrita in Stoker's day.

26 *too tight for modesty.* Harker's unseemly comment, besides what it betrays about his state of mind, is not surprising for a British male traveler. Paget (p. 85) describes an old Wallachian woman:

"I shall not easily forget the figure this woman presented. With no sort of covering save the linen shift, which was open as low as the waist, its whiteness strangely contrasting with the colour of the body it should have concealed,—the blear eye and vacant gaze of extreme age, the clotted masses of hair bound with a narrow fillet round the head, the fleshless legs, and the long pendulous breasts exposed without any idea of shame, presented a picture, the horrors of which I have rarely seen equalled. And to such a state is the Wallack woman, so beautiful in the freshness of youth, reduced before

which is a very interesting old place. Being practically on the
23 frontier—for the Borgo Pass leads from it into Bukovina—it has
had a very stormy existence, and it certainly shows marks
24 of it. Fifty years ago a series of great fires took place,
which made terrible havoc on five separate occasions. At the
very beginning of the seventeenth century it underwent a
siege of three weeks and lost 13,000 people, the casualties
of war proper being assisted by famine and disease.

25 Count Dracula had directed me to go to the Golden
Krone Hotel, which I found, to my great delight, to be
thoroughly old-fashioned, for of course I wanted to see
all I could of the ways of the country. I was evidently
expected, for when I got near the door I faced a cheery-
looking elderly woman in the usual peasant dress—white
undergarment with long double apron, front, and back, of
26 coloured stuff fitting almost too tight for modesty. When I
came close she bowed, and said, "The Herr Englishman?"
"Yes," I said, "Jonathan Harker." She smiled, and gave
some message to an elderly man in white shirt-sleeves, who
had followed her to the door. He went, but immediately
returned with a letter:—

"My Friend,—Welcome to the Carpathians. I am anxiously expecting you. Sleep well to-night. At three to-morrow the diligence will start for Bukovina; a place on it is kept for you. At the Borgo Pass my carriage will await you and will bring you to me. I trust that your journey from London has been a happy one, and that you will enjoy your stay in my beautiful land.

"Your friend,

"Dracula."

4 *May.*—I found that my landlord had got a letter from the Count, directing him to secure the best place on the coach for me; but on making inquiries as to details he seemed somewhat reticent, and pretended that he could not understand my German. This could not be true, because up to then he had understood it perfectly; at least, he answered my questions exactly as if he did. He and his wife, the old lady who had received me, looked at each other in a frightened sort of way. He mumbled out that the money had been sent in a letter, and that was all he knew. When I asked him if he knew Count Dracula, and could tell me anything of his castle, both he and his wife crossed themselves, and, saying that they knew nothing at all, simply refused to speak further. It was so near the time of starting that I had no time to ask any one else, for it was all very mysterious and not by any means comforting.

Just before I was leaving, the old lady came up to my room and said in a very hysterical way:

"Must you go? Oh! young Herr, must you go?" She was in such an excited state that she seemed to have lost her grip of what German she knew, and mixed it all up with some other language which I did not know at all. I was just able to follow her by asking many questions. When I told her that I must go at once, and that I was engaged on important business, she asked again:

"Do you know what day it is?" I answered that it was the fourth of May. She shook her head as she said again:

"Oh, yes! I know that, I know that! but do you know what day it is?" On my saying that I did not understand, she went on:

"It is the eve of St. George's Day. Do you not know that 27
to-night, when the clock strikes midnight, all the evil things in 28
the world will have full sway? Do you know where you are going, and what you are going to?" She was in such evident distress that I tried to comfort her, but without effect. Finally she went down on her knees and implored me not to go; at least to wait a day or two before starting. It was all very ridiculous, but I did not feel comfortable. However, there was business to be done, and I could allow nothing to interfere with it. I therefore tried to raise her up, and said, as gravely as I could, that I thanked her, but my duty was imperative, and that I must go. She then rose and dried her eyes, and taking a crucifix from her neck offered it to me. I did not know what to do, for, as an English Churchman, I have been taught to regard such things as in some measure idolatrous, and yet it seemed so ungracious to refuse an old lady meaning so well and in such a state of mind. She saw, I suppose, the doubt in my face, for she put the rosary round my neck, and said, "For your mother's sake," and went out of the room. I am writing up this part of the diary whilst I am waiting for the coach, which is, of course, late; and the crucifix is still round my neck. Whether it is the old lady's fear, or the many ghostly traditions of this place, or the crucifix itself, I do not know, but I am not feeling nearly as easy in my mind as usual. If this book should ever reach Mina before I do, let it bring my good-bye. Here comes the coach!

5 *May. The Castle.*—The grey of the morning has passed, and the sun is high over the distant horizon, which seems jagged, whether with trees or hills I know not, for it is so far off that big things and little are mixed. I am not sleepy, and,
as I am not to be called till I awake, naturally I write till 29
sleep comes. There are many odd things to put down, and, lest who reads them may fancy that I dined too well before I left Bistritz, let me put down my dinner exactly. I dined on what they call "robber steak"—bits of bacon, onion, and beef, seasoned with red pepper, and strung on sticks and
roasted over the fire, in the simple style of the London cat's- 30
meat! The wine was Golden Mediasch, which produces a 31
queer sting on the tongue, which is, however, not disagreeable. I had only a couple of glasses of this, and nothing else.

When I got on the coach the driver had not taken his seat, and I saw him talking with the landlady. They were evidently talking of me, for every now and then they looked at me, and some of the people who were sitting on the bench
outside the door—which they call by a name meaning "word- 32
bearer"—came and listened, and then looked at me, most of
them pityingly. I could hear a lot of words often repeated, 33

she has arrived at what we should call a middle age. . . . The Wallack woman is never by any chance seen idle. As she returns from market it is her breast that is bulged out with the purchases of the day."

ST. GEORGE AND THE DRAGON

27 *"It is the eve of St. George's Day. . . ."* Dragon slayers are to be found in the myths of peoples around the world—in China, India, and Japan. In the Christian world other saintly dragon killers besides St. George include St. Philip the Apostle, St. Martha, St. Florent, St. Cado, St. Maudent, St. Michael, St. Margaret, and St. Clement.

St. George, however, is clearly the star performer, and deserves some comment. Mrs. Cornelia S. Hulst (quoted in Ingersoll, p. 186) neatly summarizes the life story of this "essentially mythical saint" as follows:

"'According to legend [this Christian George] was born, about A.D. 285, of noble parents in Cappadocia, eastern Anatolia. As he grew to manhood he became a soldier; his courage in battle soon won him promotion, and he was attached to the personal staff of the emperor Diocletian. When this ruler decided to enter on his campaign of persecution, George resigned his commission and bitterly complained to the emperor. He was immediately arrested, and when promises failed to make him change his mind he was tortured with great cruelty. . . . At last he was taken to the outskirts of the city and beheaded [April 23, A.D. 303] . . . The earliest narrative of his martyrdom known to us is full of the most extravagant marvels: three times George is put to death, chopped into small pieces, buried deep in the earth, and consumed by fire, but each time he is resuscitated by God. Besides this we have dead men brought to life to be baptized, wholesale conversions, including that of the "Empress Alexandra," armies and idols destroyed simultaneously, beams of timber suddenly bursting into leaf, and finally, milk flowing instead of blood from the martyr's severed head.' "

In the more familiar dragon-slaying tale George comes to the town of Silene in Libya. Near the town there is a pond in which a dragon lives; for years it has exacted a dreadful toll, first of livestock, then of sons and daughters of the inhabitants. Finally, the king's daughter, chosen by lot, is turned loose near the pond where "dressed in her best, and nerved by high resolve" she waits for the dragon.

Fortunately for her, she meets George the valiant knight, and, though she warns him to "fly! fly! Sir knight," his only answer is the sign of the cross. Then he advances to meet "the horrible fiend . . ." First he transfixes it, then, when the princess passes her girdle around it, she is able to lead the monster "like a docile hound." With the tamed beast serving as a parable, George is able to convert twenty thousand people to Christianity, after which he cuts the dragon's head off.

In this tale, as in other Christian dragon tales, the dragon represents Satan. And he does in Stoker's fiction, as well, if we remember that *Dracul* in Romanian means both "dragon" and "devil."

Among other delightful things Stoker would have found in Paget's *Hungary and Transylvania* would be the information that near the village of Babakay, on the Hungarian side of the Danube, travelers were shown the very cave of "the Dragon slain by St. George, and where, they say, the foul carcass still decays, and, like Virgil's ox, gives birth to a host of winged things."

As for St. George's Eve, Montague Summers (1968, pp. 311–13) gives us Romanian lore about that occasion as follows:

"Throughout the whole of Eastern Europe, indeed, the feast of S. George, 23 April, is one of the most important celebrations of the whole year . . . upon the eve of the saint the power of vampires, witches and every evil thing is at its height. Among the Ruthenians of Bukowina and Galicia the farmer's wife gathers great branches of thorn to lay on the threshold of her house and every door is painted with a cross in tar to protect it from the witches. The Huzuls kindle large bonfires for their houses for the same reason whilst throughout Transylvania, Walachia, and Bulgaria precautions of various kinds are similarly taken. . . . On the morrow, 23 April, the house is garlanded with flowers, chaplets of roses decorate the stalls and the horns of the cows are wreathed with blossom in honour of the saint. . . . In Roumania upon these particular days when the vampire is most malicious the country folk anoint the windows with garlic, they tie bundles of garlic on the door and in the cow sheds. All lights throughout the house must be extinguished and it is well that every utensil should be turned topsy-turvy."

As for the buried treasure, that too is a standard ingredient of dragon lore. Beowulf, it will be remembered, killed a three-hundred-year-old serpent that guarded a great treasure. Apparently, the sources for this kind of legendry are to be found in the burial practices of precivilized tribes that often buried their important men (along with such treasures as their heroes might need wherever they were going) in caves or barrows in which, naturally, snakes also took refuge. (See chapter II, note 16, on "the blue flames.")

28 *midnight*. The witching hour around the world. In Meade's "Ghost and Vampire Tales of China" (p. 5), we find that the "appropriate setting for uncanny happenings should be the dead of night; the third watch, from 11:00 to 1:00 A.M., when Yin, the dark principle, reigns supreme."

A HUNGARIAN COACH.

29 *I am not to be called till I awake*. Who would do the calling and how the caller will know when Jonathan is awake is not made clear.

30 *London cat's-meat!* Cooked horse flesh, sold in the streets from a barrow.

31 *Golden Mediasch*. There is a town called Mediaş, in modern Romania (see map, p. 335), but the wine continues to elude research. Professor Ioan Puia and Senior Lecturer Alex Besuan of the Institutul Agronomic in Cluj in a personal communication write:

"We looked for it in the old viticultural literature both general and local and we spoke to some of the old generation viticulturists from Mediash (the town and the region), but nobody ever heard either of the vine or the wine called 'Golden Mediasch' . . . We suppose therefore that this name was either invented by the novelist or . . . was . . . a temporary trade name for some commercial product . . . with no special value . . . According to its description in the novel, it doesn't seem to have deserved special esteem, even by the author, since it 'produced a queer sting on the tongue' which is a characteristic mark of inferiority no matter what the wine."

Jonathan Harker, evidently not much of a connoisseur, seems to have been impressed. Paget, a contemporary traveler, is generally contemptuous of nineteenth-century winemaking in Transylvania. He writes (pp. 140–41): "Nothing can be more careless than the actual method of wine-making. All kinds of queer words, for there were many nationalities in the crowd; so I quietly got my polyglot dictionary from my bag and looked them out. I must say they were not cheering to me, for amongst them were "Ordog"—Satan, "pokol"—hell, "stregoica"—witch, "vrolok" and "vlkoslak"—both of which mean the same thing, one being Slovak and the other Servian for something that is either were-wolf or vampire. (*Mem.*, I must ask the Count about these superstitions.)

When we started, the crowd round the inn door, which had by this time swelled to a considerable size, all made the sign of the cross and pointed two fingers towards me. With some difficulty I got a fellow-passenger to tell me what they meant; he would not answer at first, but on learning that I was English he explained that it was a charm or guard against the **34**
evil eye. This was not very pleasant for me, just starting for an unknown place to meet an unknown man; but every one seemed so kind-hearted, and so sorrowful, and so sympathetic that I could not but be touched. I shall never forget the last glimpse which I had of the inn-yard and its crowd of picturesque figures, all crossing themselves, as they stood round the wide archway, with its background of rich foliage of oleander and orange trees in green tubs clustered in the **35**
centre of the yard. Then our driver, whose wide linen drawers covered the whole front of the box-seat—"gotza" they call them—cracked his big whip over his four small horses, which ran abreast, and we set off on our journey. **36**

I soon lost sight and recollection of ghostly fears in the beauty of the scene as we drove along, although had I known the language, or rather languages, which my fellow-passengers were speaking, I might not have been able to throw them off so easily. Before us lay a green sloping land full of forests and woods, with here and there steep hills, crowned with clumps of trees or with farmhouses, the blank gable end to the road. There was everywhere a bewildering mass of fruit blossom—apple, plum, pear, cherry; and as we **37**
drove by I could see the green grass under the trees spangled with the fallen petals. In and out amongst these green hills of what they call here the "Mittel Land" ran the road, losing

grapes are mixed indiscriminately; no care is taken to separate the over-ripe and those yet green from the others; and the process of pressing is, as I have described it, dirty and careless." But picturesque. He goes on to say: "In a number of large tubs we found a set of almost naked men dancing barefooted, with all their force, to the music of the bagpipes, on the heaps of fruit which the carriers were throwing into them. I did not wonder we were led to this place alone, for except in some of the Silenic processions of Poussin, I never saw so extraordinary a scene. And it is in this manner the whole wine of this country is prepared!"

32 *a name meaning "word-bearer."* None of my Romanian correspondents can identify the name of this bench. The Romanian word for bench is "banca." "Word-bearer," translated into Romanian, is "purtătorul de cuvînt."

33 *a lot of words often repeated.* Let's take this list of names in order:

ordog: Florescu and McNally (p. 181) write: "The link between Stoker's Dracula and the region of Bistrita is not wholly imaginary. There was an old Szeckler family in this region. The family was called Ordog, which is a Hungarian translation of the word *Dracul*, or devil."

pokol: A Hungarian word for hell.

stregoica: The feminine form of the word *strigoi*, Romanian for vampires, dead and alive.

vrolok and *vlkoslak:* "Vrkolak," says Dr. F. S. Krauss (p. 10), "is the Romanian form of the Serbian word *vukodlak*, meaning werewolf." And Montague Summers (1968, p. 306) calls the *vârcolac* "a third type of vampire . . . thought to be an extraordinary creature which eats the sun and moon and thus causes eclipses." In Serbia, Bosnia, Bulgaria, and Slovenia, says Dr. Krauss, the peasants beat on pots and pans to keep the dragon Vrkolak from swallowing the sun.

"WHAT THEY CALL HERE THE 'MITTEL LAND'."

34 *guard against the evil eye.* Which "guard" did Harker see? Was it the *mano fica*, the *mano cornuta*, or the *mano pantea*?

The *mano fica* is made by doubling together all the fingers and inserting the thumb between the forefinger and the middle finger. It is both a guard against the evil eye and an expression of indifference (I don't care a fig). It has, too, the implications of sexual insult, since in Europe the fig stands for the female genitals.

The *mano cornuta* is made by extending the forefinger and the ring finger, while keeping the thumb and the other fingers folded. On the one hand, the *mano cornuta* is useful against the glance of the Medusa; on the other, it is the notorious sign used to show that the person pointed to is a cuckold.

The *mano pantea* is made by extending the index and middle fingers, while holding the ring and little fingers close to the palm with the thumb.

That there *is* an evil eye, we learn from the Bible (Matthew 6:22–23), where we are told that "the light of the body is the eye . . . But if thine eye be evil, thy whole body shall be full of darkness."

Since eyes are "the windows of the soul," it has been easy enough to conclude that a strange-looking eye is an evil portent. The peacock, beautiful bird that it is, was suspect just the same because its tail throngs with eyes.

There are scores of ways to ward off the evil eye, in addition to the hand signs noted above: spitting, mascara worn on the eyelids, various stones, metals, and amulets. Certain shapes—crescent moons, rayed suns, wheels, swastikas—will deflect the power of a wicked glance. But the best way is to look the evil-looker straight in the eye.

35 *oleander and orange trees.* The oleander is a plant that arouses mixed feelings. For the Chinese it symbolizes beauty and grace. Because of its poison leaves, the Hindus call it "the horse killer," and yet decorate their temples with it and bind wreaths of it on the brows of their dead. In Christian lore it is a plant capable of producing health-giving miracles under the auspices of St. Joseph.

The orange is, of course, the golden apple that was given to Hera on her wedding day by Gaea, the goddess of earth and fertility. It is likely to have been the golden apple used by the crafty Hippomenes in escaping Atalanta. Orange blossoms are still popular at weddings as a symbol of happiness and fecundity.

36 *which ran abreast.* In no *Dracula* film yet made has anyone ever depicted the horses harnessed in this way.

37 *apple, plum, pear, cherry.* This springtime landscape is in sharp contrast to the wintry heights to which Jonathan is being borne.

38 *Hospadars.* The word is of Slavonic origin. The rulers of Wallachia and Moldavia were called hospodars from the fifteenth century to 1866.

"AN ENDLESS PERSPECTIVE OF JAGGED ROCKS."

itself as it swept round the grassy curve, or was shut out by the straggling ends of pine woods, which here and there ran down the hillsides like tongues of flame. The road was rugged, but still we seemed to fly over it with a feverish haste. I could not understand then what the haste meant, but the driver was evidently bent on losing no time in reaching Borgo Prund. I was told that this road is in summer-time excellent, but that it had not yet been put in order after the winter snows. In this respect it is different from the general run of roads in the Carpathians, for it is an old tradition that they
38 are not to be kept in too good order. Of old the Hospadars would not repair them, lest the Turk should think that they were preparing to bring in foreign troops, and so hasten the war which was always really at loading point.

Beyond the green swelling hills of the Mittel Land rose mighty slopes of forest up to the lofty steeps of the Carpathians themselves. Right and left of us they towered, with the afternoon sun falling full upon them and bringing out all the glorious colours of this beautiful range, deep blue and purple in the shadows of the peaks, green and brown where grass and rock mingled, and an endless perspective of jagged rock and pointed crags, till these were themselves lost in the distance, where the snowy peaks rose grandly. Here and there seemed mighty rifts in the mountains, through which, as the sun began to sink, we saw now and again the white gleam of falling water. One of my companions touched my arm as we swept

round the base of a hill and opened up the lofty, snow-covered peak of a mountain, which seemed, as we wound on our serpentine way, to be right before us:—

"Look! Isten szek!"—"God's seat!"—and he crossed himself reverently. As we wound on our endless way, and the sun sank lower and lower behind us, the shadows of the evening began to creep round us. This was emphasized by the fact that the snowy mountain-top still held the sunset, and seemed to glow out with a delicate cool pink. Here and there we passed Cszeks and Slovaks, all in picturesque attire, but I noticed that goitre was painfully prevalent. By the roadside were many crosses, and as we swept by, my companions all crossed themselves. Here and there was a peasant man or woman kneeling before a shrine, who did not even turn round as we approached, but seemed in the self-surrender of devotion to have neither eyes nor ears for the outer world. There were many things new to me: for instance, hay-ricks in the trees, and here and there very beautiful masses of weeping birch, their white stems shining like silver through the delicate green of the leaves. Now and again we passed a leiter-wagon—the ordinary peasant's cart, with its long, snake-like vertebra, calculated to suit the inequalities of the road. On this were sure to be seated quite a group of home-coming peasants, the Cszeks with their white, and the Slovaks with their coloured, sheepskins, the latter carrying lance-fashion their long staves, with axe at end. As the evening fell it began to get very cold, and the growing twilight seemed to merge into one dark mistiness the gloom of the trees, oak, beech, and pine, though in the valleys which ran deep between the spurs of the hills, as we ascended through the Pass, the dark firs stood out here and there against the background of late-lying snow. Sometimes, as the road was cut through the pine woods that seemed in the darkness to be closing down upon us, great masses of greyness which here and there bestrewed the trees, produced a peculiarly weird and solemn effect, which carried on the thoughts and grim fancies engendered earlier in the evening, when the falling sunset threw into strange relief the ghost-like clouds which amongst the Carpathians seem to wind ceaselessly through the valleys. Sometimes the hills were so steep

39 *". . . Isten szek!"—God's seat!"* Stoker's translation is correct. Otto Zarek (p. 48) writes of the Magyars: "The fact of their belief in one unique god, and consequently of their pagan monotheism, is proved by the language which already knew the word 'Isten' (God), having long used it in connection with such words as 'unique,' 'creator of all,' and so on."

A ROADSIDE SHRINE.

40 *goitre was painfully prevalent.* An enlargement of the thyroid gland that produces considerable swelling of the neck. The ailment used to be common in mountain regions, and is associated with lack of iodine in the diet.

41 *hay-ricks in the trees.* To this day farmers in Transylvania construct hayricks by throwing hay around two or three long stakes set into the ground. Illustrations of such hayricks, with the stakes protruding from them like branches, may have given Stoker the impression of "hay-ricks in the trees."

42 *a leiter-wagon.* Again, Paget is useful. He writes (p. 78): "for our carriage, we were glad to content ourselves with a Leiter-Wagon, so called

"HAY-RICKS IN THE TREES."

from the similarity which its sides bear to a ladder. In this part of the world, every thing is in so very primitive a state, that these carriages are not only deficient in springs, but they have often not even a particle of iron about them, so that it is impossible to conceive by what means they hold together. They are gifted, however, with the singular power of bending about like a snake; and as one wheel mounts a bank, while the other falls into a pit, the body accommodates itself . . ."

43 *when it grew dark.* Some three or four hours out of Bistrita.

44 *of an odd and varied kind.* What these gifts are we learn in chapter III, notes 3 and 4.

45 *thunderous one.* Stoker has been letting us know, a bit melodramatically, that Harker is passing from the civilized to the primordial; from the known to the unknown.

VIEW TOWARD BORGO PASS.

A MODERN LEITERWAGON.

that, despite our driver's haste, the horses could only go slowly. I wished to get down and walk up them, as we do at home, but the driver would not hear of it. "No, no," he said; "you must not walk here; the dogs are too fierce;" and then he added, with what he evidently meant for grim pleasantry—for he looked round to catch the approving smile of the rest—"and you may have enough of such matters before you go to sleep." The only stop he would make was a moment's pause to light his lamps.

43 When it grew dark there seemed to be some excitement amongst the passengers, and they kept speaking to him, one after the other, as though urging him to further speed. He lashed the horses unmercifully with his long whip, and with wild cries of encouragement urged them on to further exertions. Then through the darkness I could see a sort of patch of grey light ahead of us, as though there were a cleft in the hills. The excitement of the passengers grew greater; the crazy coach rocked on its great leather springs, and swayed like a boat tossed on a stormy sea. I had to hold on. The road grew more level, and we appeared to fly along. Then the mountains seemed to come nearer to us on each side and to frown down upon us; we were entering on the Borgo Pass. One by one several of the passengers offered me gifts, which they pressed upon me with an earnestness which would take
44 no denial; these were certainly of an odd and varied kind, but each was given in simple good faith, with a kindly word, and a blessing, and that strange mixture of fear-meaning movements which I had seen outside the hotel at Bistritz—the sign of the cross and the guard against the evil eye. Then, as we flew along, the driver leaned forward, and on each side the passengers, craning over the edge of the coach, peered eagerly into the darkness. It was evident that something very exciting was either happening or expected, but though I asked each passenger, no one would give me the slightest explanation. This state of excitement kept on for some little time; and at last we saw before us the Pass opening out on the eastern side. There were dark, rolling clouds overhead, and in the air the heavy, oppressive sense of thunder. It seemed as though the mountain range had separated two atmospheres, and that now
45 we had got into the thunderous one. I was now myself looking out for the conveyance which was to take me to the Count.

Each moment I expected to see the glare of lamps through the blackness; but all was dark. The only light was the flickering rays of our own lamps, in which the steam from our hard-driven horses rose in a white cloud. We could now see the sandy road lying white before us, but there was on it no sign of a vehicle. The passengers drew back with a sigh of gladness, which seemed to mock my own disappointment. I was already thinking what I had best do, when the driver, looking at his watch, said to the others something which I could hardly hear, it was spoken so quietly and in so low a tone; I thought it was "An hour less than the time." Then turning to me, he 46
said in German worse than my own:—

"There is no carriage here. The Herr is not expected after all. He will now come on to Bukovina, and return to-morrow or the next day; better the next day." Whilst he was speaking the horses began to neigh and snort and plunge wildly, so that the driver had to hold them up. Then, amongst a chorus of screams from the peasants and a universal crossing of themselves, a calèche, with four horses, drove up behind us, overtook us, and drew up beside the coach. I could see from the flash of our lamps, as the rays fell on them, that the horses were coal-black and splendid animals. They were driven by a tall man, with a long brown beard and a great black hat, 47
which seemed to hide his face from us. I could only see the gleam of a pair of very bright eyes, which seemed red in the lamplight, as he turned to us. He said to the driver:—

"You are early to-night, my friend." The man stammered in reply:—

"The English Herr was in a hurry," to which the stranger replied:—

"That is why, I suppose, you wished him to go on to Bukovina. You cannot deceive me, my friend; I know too much, and my horses are swift." As he spoke he smiled, and the lamplight fell on a hard-looking mouth, with very red lips and sharp-looking teeth, as white as ivory. One of my companions whispered to another the line from Burger's "Lenore:"—

"Denn die Todten reiten schnell"— 48
("For the dead travel fast.")

The strange driver evidently heard the words, for he looked up with a gleaming smile. The passenger turned his face away, at the same time putting out his two fingers and crossing himself. "Give me the Herr's luggage," said the driver; and with exceeding alacrity my bags were handed out and put in the calèche. Then I descended from the side of the coach, as the calèche was close alongside, the driver helping me with a hand which caught my arm in a grip of steel; his strength must have been prodigious. Without a word he shook his reins, the horses turned, and we swept into the darkness of the Pass. As I looked back I saw the steam from the horses of the coach by the light of the lamps, and projected against it the figures of my late companions crossing themselves. Then the driver cracked his whip and called to his horses, and off they swept on their way to Bukovina.

As they sank into the darkness I felt a strange chill, and a lonely feeling came over me; but a cloak was thrown over my

46 *"An hour less than the time."*—that it would normally take to reach the Borgo Pass.

A CALÈCHE.

47 *tall man.* No doubt this is a manifestation of Dracula himself, though the brown beard is wrong.

Throughout the fiction, Dracula's eyes are spoken of as having a red gleam in them. Though we are never told precisely what color his eyes are, it is worth noting that in Greece vampires were likely to have blue eyes. In Romania the cold gaze of a vampire looking at a pregnant woman could result in the birth of another vampire.

48 *"Denn die Todten reiten schnell"*—Bürger's poem "Lenore" has in it all the Gothic machinery of the German *Schauerroman:* the young woman waiting for her bridegroom Wilhelm who is away at King Frederick's wars. When he delays his return, she reproaches him with faithlessness. Suddenly there is the clatter of horse's hooves, and Wilhelm is there; he takes her up on his horse and they ride off at midnight on a strange wild ride. It takes the reader hardly any time at all to learn that Wilhelm, though he clasps his bride fiercely, is dead, and that he and Lenore will plight their troth only in the grave.

The line Harker is quoting is reiterated as a chorus line five times through the poem. The first time it reads: "We and the dead ride fast." Then, three other times, it is "Hurrah! The dead ride fast." And finally, the line is simply, "The dead ride fast." At no time is it "For the dead travel fast."

Bürger's poem was published in German in 1773 and was rendered into English in 1796 by William of Norwich. Montague Summers, in his *The Vampire: His Kith and Kin* (pp. 275–76), discusses the tremendous popularity the poem had among the Romantic poets. In Germany the poem became a household word.

shoulders, and a rug across my knees, and the driver said in excellent German:—

"The night is chill, mein Herr, and my master the Count
49 bade me take all care of you. There is a flask of slivovitz [the
plum brandy of the country] underneath the seat, if you should
require it." I did not take any, but it was a comfort to know
it was there all the same. I felt a little strangely, and not a
little frightened. I think had there been any alternative I
should have taken it, instead of prosecuting that unknown night
journey. The carriage went at a hard pace straight along,
then we made a complete turn and went along another straight
50 road. It seemed to me that we were simply going over and
over the same ground again; and so I took note of some
salient point, and found that this was so. I would have liked
to have asked the driver what this all meant, but I really feared
to do so, for I thought that, placed as I was, any protest would
have had no effect in case there had been an intention to
delay. By-and-by, however, as I was curious to know how
time was passing, I struck a match, and by its flame looked at
51 my watch; it was within a few minutes of midnight. This gave
me a sort of shock, for I suppose the general superstition
about midnight was increased by my recent experiences. I
waited with a sick feeling of suspense.

Then a dog began to howl somewhere in a farmhouse far down the road—a long, agonised wailing, as if from fear. The sound was taken up by another dog, and then another and another, till, borne on the wind which now sighed softly through the Pass, a wild howling began, which seemed to come from all over the country, as far as the imagination could grasp it through the gloom of the night. At the first howl the horses began to strain and rear, but the driver spoke to them soothingly, and they quieted down, but shivered and sweated as though after a run-away from sudden fright. Then, far off in the distance, from the mountains on each side of us began a louder and a sharper howling—that of wolves—which affected both the horses and myself in the same way—for I was minded to jump from the calèche and run, whilst they reared again and plunged madly, so that the driver had to use all his great strength to keep them from bolting. In a few minutes, however, my own ears got accustomed to the sound, and the horses so far became quiet that the driver was able to descend and to stand before them. He petted and soothed them, and whispered something in their ears, as I have heard of horse-tamers doing, and with extraordinary effect, for under his caresses they became quite manageable again, though they still trembled. The driver again took his seat, and shaking his reins, started off at a great pace. This time, after going to the far side of the Pass, he suddenly turned down a narrow roadway which ran sharply to the right.

Soon we were hemmed in with trees, which in places arched right over the roadway till we passed as through a tunnel; and again great frowning rocks guarded us boldly on either side. Though we were in shelter, we could hear the rising wind, for it moaned and whistled through the rocks, and the branches of the trees crashed together as we swept along. It grew colder and colder still, and fine, powdery snow began to fall, so that soon we and all around

49 *slivovitz.* A plum brandy famous as the national drink of the Serbs. It is made of sweet blue plums that produce a colorless aromatic brandy that is nearly 70 percent alcohol. Admirers of the drink consider it a cure-all.

50 *over and over the same ground.* The dreamlike mood of this journey serves a mythic purpose. Harker's passage from light to dark at the very beginning of the fiction will be replayed later as the book reaches its climax.

Stoker may also be remembering Mephistopheles's remark to Faust (p. 127) that "the fool who speculates on things is like some animal on a dry heath led by an evil fiend in endless circles."

For the moment it is enough to note that Harker's ascent to the castle is a sort of mirror reverse of certain classical descents into hell: Odysseus's, Proserpine's, Orpheus's.

51 *within a few minutes of midnight.* Harker is now some 8½ hours out of Bistrita.

"IT GREW COLDER AND COLDER STILL . . . ALL AT ONCE THE WOLVES BEGAN TO HOWL ."

52 *a faint flickering blue flame*. The lore of the blue flame is discussed fully in chapter II, note 16.

53 *the trap*. Here "trap" means the calèche.

us were covered with a white blanket. The keen wind still carried the howling of the dogs, though this grew fainter as we went on our way. The baying of the wolves sounded nearer and nearer, as though they were closing round on us from every side. I grew dreadfully afraid, and the horses shared my fear; but the driver was not in the least disturbed. He kept turning his head to left and right, but I could not see anything through the darkness.

52 Suddenly, away on our left, I saw a faint flickering blue flame. The driver saw it at the same moment; he at once checked the horses and, jumping to the ground, disappeared into the darkness. I did not know what to do, the less as the howling of the wolves grew closer; but while I wondered the driver suddenly appeared again, and without a word took his seat, and we resumed our journey. I think I must have fallen asleep and kept dreaming of the incident, for it seemed to be repeated endlessly, and now looking back, it is like a sort of awful nightmare. Once the flame appeared so near the road, that even in the darkness around us I could watch the driver's motions. He went rapidly to where the blue flame arose —it must have been very faint, for it did not seem to illumine the place around it at all—and gathering a few stones, formed them into some device. Once there appeared a strange optical effect: when he stood between me and the flame he did not obstruct it, for I could see its ghostly flicker all the same. This startled me, but as the effect was only momentary, I took it that my eyes deceived me straining through the darkness. Then for a time there were no blue flames, and we sped onwards through the gloom, with the howling of the wolves around us, as though they were following in a moving circle.

At last there came a time when the driver went further afield than he had yet gone, and during his absence the horses began to tremble worse than ever and to snort and scream with fright. I could not see any cause for it, for the howling of the wolves had ceased altogether; but just then the moon, sailing through the black clouds, appeared behind the jagged crest of a beetling, pine-clad rock, and by its light I saw around us a ring of wolves, with white teeth and lolling red tongues, with long, sinewy limbs and shaggy hair. They were a hundred times more terrible in the grim silence which held them than even when they howled. For myself, I felt a sort of paralysis of fear. It is only when a man feels himself face to face with such horrors that he can understand their true import.

All at once the wolves began to howl as though the moonlight had had some peculiar effect on them. The horses jumped about and reared, and looked helplessly round with eyes that rolled in a way painful to see; but the living ring of terror encompassed them on every side, and they had perforce to remain within it. I called to the coachman to come, for it seemed to me that our only chance was to try to break out through the ring and to aid his approach. I shouted and beat the side of the calèche, hoping by the noise to scare the wolves from that side, so as to give him a chance of reaching
53 the trap. How he came there, I know not, but I heard his

CHAPTER II.

JONATHAN HARKER'S JOURNAL—*continued.*

5 *May.*—I must have been asleep, for certainly if I had been fully awake I must have noticed the approach to such a remarkable place. In the gloom the courtyard looked of considerable size, and as several dark ways led from it under great round arches it perhaps seemed bigger than it really is. I have not yet been able to see it by daylight.

When the calèche stopped the driver jumped down, and held out his hand to assist me to alight. Again I could not but notice his prodigious strength. His hand actually seemed like a steel vice that could have crushed mine if he had chosen.
Then he took out my traps, and placed them on the ground 1
beside me as I stood close to a great door, old and studded with large iron nails, and set in a projecting doorway of massive stone. I could see even in the dim light that the stone was massively carved, but that the carving had been much worn by time and weather. As I stood, the driver jumped again into his seat and shook the reins; the horses started forward, and trap and all disappeared down one of the dark openings.

I stood in silence where I was, for I did not know what to do. Of bell or knocker there was no sign; through these frowning walls and dark window openings it was not likely that my voice could penetrate. The time I waited seemed endless, and I felt doubts and fears crowding upon me. What sort of place had I come to, and among what kind of people? What sort of grim adventure was it on which I had embarked? Was this a customary incident in the life of a solicitor's clerk sent out to explain the purchase of a London estate to a foreigner?
Solicitor's clerk! Mina would not like that. Solicitor,—for 2

1 *my traps.* My luggage. My bags.

2 *Solicitor.* In British legal practice there are two kinds of lawyers. The solicitor prepares cases for the barrister to try, and usually appears, if at all, only in the lower courts. The barrister may plead in any court.

"IN THE GLOOM, THE COURTYARD LOOKED OF CONSIDERABLE SIZE."

3 *a tall old man.* Stoker's portrait is an amalgam of Polidori's Lord Ruthven in *The Vampyre*, Prest's *Varney the Vampyre*, and an anonymous author's *The Mysterious Stranger*.

That Dracula is an old man at the beginning of the story has been persistently forgotten in all but one of the many film versions of the tale.

For his description of Dracula Stoker has added folklore material regarding the appearance of vampires. The traditional elements are summarized both in Montague Summers's *The Vampire: His Kith and Kin* and in Ornella Volta's *The Vampire*. Summers writes (p. 179):

"A Vampire is generally described as being exceedingly gaunt and lean with a hideous countenance and eyes wherein are glinting the red fire of perdition. When, however, he has satiated his lust for warm human blood his body becomes horribly puffed and bloated, as though he were some great leech gorged and replete to bursting. Cold as ice, or it may be fevered and burning as a hot coal, the skin is deathly pale, but the lips are very full and rich, blub and red; the teeth white and gleaming, and the canine teeth, wherewith he bites deep into the neck of his prey to suck thence the vital streams which re-animate his body and invigorate all his forces, appear notably sharp and pointed."

And Volta's composite portrait (p. 145) is no more enticing:

"Vampires differ according to regions in which they are found . . . but they all have certain characteristics in common such as an emaciated face, with a phosphorescent pallor . . . The vampire has many thick hairs on his body which are often reddish in colour, and often has hair in the palms of his hands . . . and blue eyes . . . The vampire also has swollen, sensual lips covering sharp canine teeth . . . Vampires also have extremely long finger nails, pointed ears like bats, foetid breath, and move jerkily, showing a tendency to suffer from epilepsy. Their bite has anaesthetizing powers."

One should take both of these descriptions with some caution. Volta and Summers occasionally use Stoker as their source for folklore. The "hair in the palms," for example, cited by Volta, is found, as far as I can tell, only in *Dracula*.

It is likely, too, that Stoker had read an anonymous German tale called (in English) *The Mysterious Stranger* (1860). The structural parallels between *Dracula* and the German tale are remarkable. There is no question of plagiarism. At the same time sheer coincidence isn't enough to account for the similarity of moments in the two stories. Perhaps "inspired borrowing" is one way to describe what happened.

4 *"Welcome to my house! Enter freely and of your own will!"* This is an interesting moment. Stoker is making use of the tradition that the Devil can only do his business with willing clients. In Coleridge's

just before leaving London I got word that my examination was successful; and I am now a full-blown solicitor! I began to rub my eyes and pinch myself to see if I were awake. It all seemed like a horrible nightmare to me, and I expected that I should suddenly awake, and find myself at home, with the dawn struggling in through the windows, as I had now and again felt in the morning after a day of overwork. But my flesh answered the pinching test, and my eyes were not to be deceived. I was indeed awake and among the Carpathians. All I could do now was to be patient, and to wait the coming of the morning.

Just as I had come to this conclusion I heard a heavy step approaching behind the great door, and saw through the chinks the gleam of a coming light. Then there was the sound of rattling chains and the clanking of massive bolts drawn back. A key was turned with the loud grating noise of long disuse, and the great door swung back.

3 Within, stood a tall old man, clean shaven save for along white moustache, and clad in black from head to foot, without a single speck of colour about him anywhere. He held in his hand an antique silver lamp, in which the flame burned without chimney or globe of any kind, throwing long quivering shadows as it flickered in the draught of the open door. The old man motioned me in with his right hand with a courtly gesture, saying in excellent English, but with a strange intonation:—

4 "Welcome to my house! Enter freely and of your own will!" He made no motion of stepping to meet me, but stood like a statue, as though his gesture of welcome had fixed him into stone. The instant, however, that I had stepped over the threshold, he moved impulsively forward, and holding out his hand grasped mine with a strength which made me wince, an effect which was not lessened by the fact that it seemed as cold as ice—more like the hand of a dead than a living man. Again he said:—

5 "Welcome to my house. Come freely. Go safely; and leave something of the happiness you bring!" The strength of the handshake was so much akin to that which I had noticed in the driver, whose face I had not seen, that for a moment I doubted if it were not the same person to whom I was speaking; so to make sure, I said interrogatively:—

"Count Dracula?" He bowed in a courtly way as he replied:—

"I am Dracula; and I bid you welcome, Mr. Harker, to my house. Come in; the night air is chill, and you must need to eat and rest." As he was speaking he put the lamp on a bracket on the wall, and stepping out, took my luggage; he had carried it in before I could forestall him. I protested but he insisted:—

"Nay, sir, you are my guest. It is late, and my people are not available. Let me see to your comfort myself." He insisted on carrying my traps along the passage, and then up a great winding stair, and along another great passage, on whose stone floor our steps rang heavily. At the end of this he threw open a heavy door, and I rejoiced to see within a well-lit room in which a table was spread for supper, and on whose mighty hearth a great fire of logs flamed and flared.

The Count halted, putting down my bags, closed the door, and crossing the room, opened another door, which led into a small octagonal room lit by a single lamp, and seemingly without a window of any sort. Passing through this, he opened another door, and motioned me to enter. It was a welcome sight; for here was a great bedroom well lighted and warmed with another log fire, which sent a hollow roar up the wide chimney. The Count himself left my luggage inside and withdrew, saying, before he closed the door :—

"You will need, after your journey, to refresh yourself by making your toilet. I trust you will find all you wish. When you are ready come into the other room, where you will find your supper prepared."

The light and warmth and the Count's courteous welcome seemed to have dissipated all my doubts and fears. Having then reached my normal state, I discovered that I was half famished with hunger; so making a hasty toilet, I went into the other room.

I found supper already laid out. My host, who stood on one side of the great fireplace, leaning against the stonework, made a graceful wave of his hand to the table, and said :—

"I pray you, be seated and sup how you please. You will, I trust, excuse me that I do not join you; but I have dined 6
already, and I do not sup.'

I handed to him the sealed letter which Mr. Hawkins had entrusted to me. He opened it and read it gravely; then, with a charming smile, he handed it to me to read. One passage of it, at least, gave me a thrill of pleasure :

"I much regret that an attack of gout, from which malady I am a constant sufferer, forbids absolutely any travelling on my part for some time to come; but I am happy to say I can send a sufficient substitute, one in whom I have every possible confidence. He is a young man, full of energy and talent in his own way, and of a very faithful disposition. He is discreet and silent, and has grown into manhood in my service. He shall be ready to attend on you when you will during his stay, and shall take your instructions in all matters."

The Count himself came forward and took off the cover of a dish, and I fell to at once on an excellent roast chicken. This, with some cheese and a salad and a bottle of old Tokay, of which I had two glasses, was my supper. During the time I was eating it the Count asked me many questions as to my journey, and I told him by degrees all I had experienced.

By this time I had finished my supper, and by my host's desire had drawn up a chair by the fire and begun to smoke a cigar which he offered me, at the same time excusing himself that he did not smoke. I had now an opportunity of observing him, and found him of a very marked physiognomy.

His face was a strong—a very strong—aquiline, with high bridge of the thin nose and peculiarly arched nostrils; with lofty domed forehead, and hair growing scantily round the temples, but profusely elsewhere. His eyebrows were very massive, almost meeting over the nose, and with bushy hair that seemed to curl in its own profusion. The mouth, so far as I could see it under the heavy moustache, was fixed and rather cruel-looking, with peculiarly sharp white teeth; these protruded over the

"Cristabel" the monstrous Lady Geraldine must be invited into Cristabel's ancestral home. In Goethe's *Faust*, Mephistopheles in the guise of a poodle is called by Faust to him and later is introduced into the scholar's home. See, too, *The Mysterious Stranger:*

> "You wish it?—You press the invitation?" asked the stranger earnestly and decidedly.
> "To be sure, for otherwise you will not come," replied the young lady shortly.
> "Well, then, come I will!" said the other, again fixing his gaze on her. "If my company does not please you at any time, you will have yourself to blame for an acquaintance with one who seldom forces himself, but is difficult to shake off."

Free will is of the essence in these implied contracts between good and evil.

5 *"Welcome to my house. . . ."* If this splendid greeting is based on a Central European formula, I have been unable to find its source.

6 *". . . I have dined already, and I do not sup."* To the British (and on the continent) dinner was formerly the large meal of the day taken at midafternoon. Supper was a light evening repast. There is no doubt some play on the words dine and, particularly, on sup as implying sip.

DRAWING OF A CHILD WITH HYPERTRICHOSIS.

lips, whose remarkable ruddiness showed astonishing vitality in a man of his years. For the rest, his ears were pale and at the tops extremely pointed; the chin was broad and strong, and the cheeks firm though thin. The general effect was one of extraordinary pallor.

Hitherto I had noticed the backs of his hands as they lay on his knees in the firelight, and they had seemed rather white and fine; but seeing them now close to me, I could not but notice that they were rather coarse—broad, with squat fingers.
7 Strange to say, there were hairs in the centre of the palm. The nails were long and fine, and cut to a sharp point. As the Count leaned over me and his hands touched me, I could not repress a shudder. It may have been that his breath was rank, but a horrible feeling of nausea came over me, which, do what I would, I could not conceal. The Count, evidently noticing it, drew back; and with a grim sort of smile, which showed more than he had yet done his protuberant teeth, sat himself down again on his own side of the fireplace. We were both silent for a while; and as I looked towards the window I saw the first dim streak of the coming dawn. There seemed a strange stillness over everything; but as I listened I heard as if from down below in the valley the howling of many wolves. The Count's eyes gleamed, and he said:—

8 "Listen to them—the children of the night. What music they make!" Seeing, I suppose, some expression in my face strange to him, he added:—

"Ah, sir, you dwellers in the city cannot enter into the feelings of the hunter." Then he rose and said:—

"But you must be tired. Your bedroom is all ready, and to-morrow you shall sleep as late as you will. I have to be away till the afternoon; so sleep well and dream well!" and, with a courteous bow, he opened for me himself the door to
9 the octagonal room, and I entered my bedroom. . . . .

I am all in a sea of wonders. I doubt; I fear; I think strange things which I dare not confess to my own soul. God keep me, if only for the sake of those dear to me!

7 *May*.—It is again early morning, but I have rested and enjoyed the last twenty-four hours. I slept till late in the day, and awoke of my own accord. When I had dressed myself I went into the room where we had supped, and found a cold breakfast laid out, with coffee kept hot by the pot being placed on the hearth. There was a card on the table, on which was written:—

"I have to be absent for a while. Do not wait for me. ---D." So I set to and enjoyed a hearty meal. When I had done, I looked for a bell, so that I might let the servants know I had finished; but I could not find one. There are certainly odd deficiencies in the house, considering the extraordinary evidences of wealth which are round me. The table service is of gold, and so beautifully wrought that it must be of immense value. The curtains and upholstery of the chairs and sofas and the hangings of my bed are of the costliest and most beautiful fabrics, and must have been of fabulous value when they were made, for they are centuries old, though in excellent
10 order. I saw something like them in Hampton Court, but there they were worn and frayed and moth-eaten. But still in none of the rooms is there a mirror. There is not even a

7 *hairs in the centre of the palm.* Very strange. There does exist a medical condition known as hypertrichosis, an excessive hairiness that may be purely localized or so extreme that sufferers from the condition may be exhibited as hairy monsters. There was a Peter Gonzales born with such long hair in 1556 in the Canary Islands. He was later sent to the court of King Henry II of France. Gonzales married, and several of his children, too, were hairy. Hypertrichosis is an exceedingly rare condition, occurring only once in a billion births.

Though Summers does not give other instances of palm hair, he does quote the Frenchman Venette as saying that very hairy men are "usually amorous."

One wonders whether Stoker knew the American boys' entrapment game in which one boy says "If you masturbate, you'll grow hair on your palms," and watches to see which of his listeners looks guiltily down at his hands.

Finally, following this lead a moment longer, it is worth noting that the description of Dracula given here has certain similarities with the standard nineteenth-century image of the masturbator. Wayland Young, in *Eros Denied* (p. 236), quotes from William Acton's *Functions and Disorders of the Reproductive Organs* (1857), in which Claude-François Lallemand's description of the effects of masturbation on children is given as follows:

toilet glass on my table, and I had to get the little shaving
glass from my bag before I could either shave or brush my
hair. I have not yet seen a servant anywhere, or heard a
sound near the castle except the howling of wolves. When I
had finished my meal—I do not know whether to call it
breakfast or dinner, for it was between five and six o'clock **11**
when I had it—I looked about for something to read, for I
did not like to go about the castle until I had asked the
Count's permission. There was absolutely nothing in the
room, book, newspaper, or even writing materials; so I
opened another door in the room and found a sort of library.
The door opposite mine I tried, but found it locked.

In the library I found, to my great delight, a vast number of
English books, whole shelves full of them, and bound
volumes of magazines and newspapers. A table in the centre
was littered with English magazines and newspapers, though
none of them were of very recent date. The books were of
the most varied kind—history, geography, politics, political
economy, botany, geology, law—all relating to England and
English life and customs and manners. There were even
such books of reference as the London Directory, the "Red" **12**
and "Blue" books, Whitaker's Almanack, the Army and
Navy Lists, and—it somehow gladdened my heart to see it—
the Law List.

Whilst I was looking at the books, the door opened, and the Count entered. He saluted me in a hearty way, and hoped that I had had a good night's rest. Then he went on:—

"I am glad you found your way in here, for I am sure
there is much that will interest you. These friends"—and he
laid his hand on some of the books—"have been good friends
to me, and for some years past, ever since I had the idea of
going to London, have given me many, many hours of
pleasure. Through them I have come to know your great
England; and to know her is to love her. I long to go
through the crowded streets of your mighty London, to be in
the midst of the whirl and rush of humanity, to share its life, **13**
its change, its death, and all that makes it what it is. But
alas! as yet I only know your tongue through books. To
you, my friend, I look that I know it to speak."

"But, Count," I said, "you know and speak English thoroughly!" He bowed gravely.

"I thank you, my friend, for your all too flattering estimate, but yet I fear that I am but a little way on the road I would travel. True, I know the grammar and the words, but yet I know not how to speak them."

"Indeed," I said, "you speak excellently."

"Not so," he answered. "Well I know that, did I move
and speak in your London, none there are who would not know
me for a stranger. That is not enough for me. Here I am
noble; I am *boyar*; the common people know me, and I am **14**
master. But a stranger in a strange land, he is no one; men **15**
know him not—and to know not is to care not for. I am content if I am like the rest, so that no man stops if he see me,
or pause in his speaking if he hear my words, to say, 'Ha, ha!
a stranger!' I have been so long master that I would be
master still—or at least that none other should be master of
me. You come to me not alone as agent of my friend Peter

"However young the children may be, they become thin, pale and irritable, and their features assume a haggard appearance. We notice the sunken eye, the long, cadaverous-looking countenance, the downcast look which seems to arise from a consciousness in the boy that his habits are suspected, and, at a later period, from the ascertained fact that his virility is lost . . . Habitual masturbators have a dank, moist, cold hand, very characteristic of vital exhaustion; their sleep is short, and most complete marasmus [wasting of the body] comes on; they may gradually waste away if the evil passion is not got the better of, nervous exhaustion sets in, such as spasmodic contraction, or partial or entire convulsive movements, together with epilepsy, eclampsy, and a species of paralysis accompanied with contraction of the limbs."

If this is a portrait that does not suggest the power that Dracula manifests, one needs only to remember the inert, pale cataleptic figure of the vampire in his daytime coffin.

8 ". . . *What music they make!*" This line, spoken by Bela Lugosi in the Tod Browning film version of *Dracula* (1931), has achieved something of a classic life of its own. There is hardly a schoolchild who does not achieve a moment's illusory greatness by imitating the inimitable Master.

9 *the octagonal room*. The octagonal room is, one suspects, a visual pun. Coffins, particularly nineteenth-century coffins, were frequently octagonal in shape. Poe, too, plays this game. See the five-sided room in *Ligeia*.

10 *Hampton Court*. Hampton Court Palace, situated between Bushy Park and Home Park about fifteen miles from London, was founded by Cardinal Wolsey in 1515. Wolsey later presented the palace to Henry VIII, his patron.

The tapestries Harker saw were probably those in the Great Hall of the palace, which contains tapestries representing scenes from the life of Abraham.

The castle, in Stoker's time (and today), was open to visitors daily from 10:00 A.M. to 4:00 P.M., though on Sundays it opened at 2:00 P.M. Admission was free, and visitors were "required to pass from room to room in one direction only."

Alexander Pope describes the ambience of artificiality and sexual frivolity for which Hampton Court was famous in the eighteenth century. For Pope, Hampton Court was the place where

". . . *Britain's* Statesmen oft the Fall foredoom
Of Foreign Tyrants, and of Nymphs at home;
. . . .
Hither the Heroes and the Nymphs resort,
To taste awhile the Pleasures of a Court;
In various Talk th' instructive hours they past,
Who gave the *Ball*, or paid the *Visit* last:
. . . .
. . . one describes a charming *Indian Screen;*

A third interprets Motions, Looks, and Eyes;
At ev'ry Word a Reputation dies.
Snuff, or the *Fan*, supply each Pause of Chat,
With singing, laughing, ogling, and all that."

As Pope saw it, Hampton Court was the appropriate setting for the heartless amatory war between the beautiful Belinda and the Baron who was to commit the Rape of the Lock.

11 *between five and six o'clock.* A.M.

12 *the "Red" and "Blue" books.* The Red Book, formerly published in England, listed all persons serving or pensioned by the state. A Blue Book is a British parliamentary or other publication bound in a blue binder.

13 *to share its life, its change, its death.* No doubt a horrific irony is intended here.

14 *I am* boyar. Originally a member of the old Russian nobility. In Romania a member of the privileged classes. A prince. Mrs. Walker in *Untrodden Paths in Roumania* says: "The Boyards were created a distinct class of nobility in the fifteenth century, when Radu, Voïvode of Wallachia, endeavoured to model them in imitation of the offices of the Court of Byzantium. The title of Boyard, if now used, merely signifies a person of fortune and position."

15 *a stranger in a strange land.* The devil, in this case, is citing Scripture. In Exodus 2:22 we learn that Moses' son by Zipporah was named Gershom, "for he said, I have been a stranger in a strange land."

16 *the blue flames.* Conveniently enough for Stoker, Emily Gerard (p. 230) neatly puts together St. George's Eve and the lore of the blue flame. It seems inconceivable that he did not see the following details in her fine book on Transylvania: "The night of St. George, the 24th of April (corresponding to our 6th of May), is of all others the most favorable for [the recovery of buried treasures] . . . For in this night (so say the legends) all these treasures begin to burn, or . . . 'to bloom,' in the bosom of the earth, and the light they give forth, described as a bluish flame . . . serves to guide favored mortals to their place of concealment . . . There is hardly a ruin, mountain, or forest in Transylvania which has not got some legend of a hidden treasure attached to it."

The blue flame is a fixture of the Gothic novel and makes its appearance in the romances of Ann Radcliffe and "Monk" Lewis. More than likely the lore of the flame is related to the fluorescence that is seen over marshes, sometimes called the *ignis fatuus*, or foolish fire. The flame is also called will-o'-the-wisp, corpse light (because, when the soul leaves the body, it is said to form a small flame), friar's lantern, elf fire, fetch light, and fire drake. Though *ignis fatuus* can appear in a variety of colors, its usual form is blue, as here.

Hawkins, of Exeter, to tell me all about my new estate in London. You shall, I trust, rest here with me a while, so that by our talking I may learn the English intonation; and I would that you tell me when I make error, even of the smallest, in my speaking. I am sorry that I had to be away so long to-day; but you will, I know, forgive one who has so many important affairs in hand."

Of course I said all I could about being willing, and asked if I might come into that room when I chose. He answered: "Yes, certainly," and added:—

"You may go anywhere you wish in the castle, except where the doors are locked, where of course you will not wish to go. There is reason that all things are as they are, and did you see with my eyes and know with my knowledge, you would perhaps better understand." I said I was sure of this, and then he went on:—

"We are in Transylvania; and Transylvania is not England. Our ways are not your ways, and there shall be to you many strange things. Nay, from what you have told me of your experiences already, you know something of what strange things here may be."

This led to much conversation; and as it was evident that he wanted to talk, if only for talking's sake, I asked him many questions regarding things that had already happened to me or come within my notice. Sometimes he sheered off the subject, or turned the conversation by pretending not to understand; but generally he answered all I asked most frankly. Then as time went on, and I had got somewhat bolder, I asked him of some of the strange things of the preceding night, as, for instance, why the coachman went to the
16 places where we had seen the blue flames. Was it indeed true that they showed where gold was hidden? He then explained to me that it was commonly believed that on a certain night of the year—last night, in fact, when all evil spirits are supposed to have unchecked sway—a blue flame is seen over any place where treasure has been concealed. "That treasure has been hidden," he went on, "in the region through which you came last night, there can be but little doubt; for it was the ground fought over for centuries by the Wallachian, the Saxon, and the Turk. Why, there is hardly a foot of soil in all this region that has not been enriched by the blood of men, patriots or invaders. In old days there were stirring times, when the Austrian and the Hungarian came up in hordes, and the patriots went out to meet them—men and women, the aged and the children too—and waited their coming on the rocks above the passes, that they might sweep destruction on them with their artificial avalanches. When the invader was triumphant he found but little, for whatever there was had been sheltered in the friendly soil."

"But how," said I, "can it have remained so long undiscovered, when there is a sure index to it if men will but take the trouble to look?" The Count smiled, and as his lips ran back over his gums, the long, sharp, canine teeth showed out strangely; he answered:—

"Because your peasant is at heart a coward and a fool! Those flames only appear on one night; and on that night no man of this land will, if he can help it, stir without his doors.

And, dear sir, even if he did he would not know what to do. Why, even the peasant that you tell me of who marked the place of the flame would not know where to look in daylight even for his own work. You would not, I dare be sworn, be able to find these places again?"

"There you are right," I said. "I know no more than the dead where even to look for them." Then we drifted into other matters.

"Come," he said at last, "tell me of London and of the house which you have procured for me." With an apology for my amissness, I went into my own room to get the papers from my bag. Whilst I was placing them in order I heard a rattling of china and silver in the next room, and as I passed through, noticed that the table had been cleared and the lamp lit, for it was by this time deep into the dark. The lamps were also lit in the study or library, and I found the Count lying on the sofa, reading, of all things in the world, an
English Bradshaw's Guide. When I came in he cleared the **17**
books and papers from the table; and with him I went into plans and deeds and figures of all sorts. He was interested in everything, and asked me a myriad questions about the place and its surroundings. He clearly had studied beforehand all he could get on the subject of the neighbourhood, for he evidently at the end knew very much more than I did. When I remarked this, he answered:—

"Well, but, my friend, is it not needful that I should? When I go there I shall be all alone, and my friend Harker Jonathan—nay, pardon me, I fall into my country's habit of putting your patronymic first—my friend Jonathan Harker will not be by my side to correct and aid me. He will be in Exeter, miles away, probably working at papers of the law with my other friend, Peter Hawkins. So!"

We went thoroughly into the business of the purchase of
the estate at Purfleet. When I had told him the facts and got **18**
his signature to the necessary papers, and had written a letter with them ready to post to Mr. Hawkins, he began to ask me how I had come across so suitable a place. I read to him the notes which I had made at the time, and which I inscribe here:—

"At Purfleet, on a by-road, I came across just such a place as seemed to be required, and where was displayed a dilapidated notice that the place was for sale. It is surrounded by a high wall, of ancient structure, built of heavy stones, and has not been repaired for a large number of years. The closed gates were of heavy old oak and iron, all eaten with rust.

"The estate is called Carfax, no doubt a corruption of **19**
the old *Quatre Face*, as the house is four-sided, agreeing with the cardinal points of the compass. It contains in all some twenty acres, quite surrounded by the solid stone wall above mentioned. There are many trees on it, which make it in places gloomy, and there is a deep, dark-looking pond or small lake, evidently fed by some springs, as the water is clear and flows away in a fair-sized stream. The house is very large and of all periods back, I should say, to mediæval times, for one part is of stone immensely thick, with only a few windows high up and heavily barred with iron. It looks like

Will-o'-the-wisp is mischievous and will delude travelers when it can. Its sudden appearance may presage the death of the beholder or of a loved one.

The blue flame has other associations as well. "The population [of Vienna in 1349] identified the plague as the *Pest Jungfrau* who had only to raise her hand to infect a victim. She flew through the air in the form of a blue flame, and in this guise was often seen emerging from the mouths of the dead," says Philip Ziegler (p. 258), while Anthony Masters, in his *Natural History of the Vampire*, cites Willoughby Meade's description of coffins in China that "whenever the year is rainy . . . the coffins are soaked and in a rotten condition, their wood decays [giving off phosphorescent lights] and the lights detach themselves from it and fly about. Being lights produced by Yin, they can endure no Yang (sun) light, and await the twilight after sunset to burst forth . . . The men who chase away these lights . . . fall upon them and beat them . . . When spectre-light sees lamp-light it vanishes of its own accord."

17 *Bradshaw's Guide.* A volume of comprehensive timetables for the English railway system.

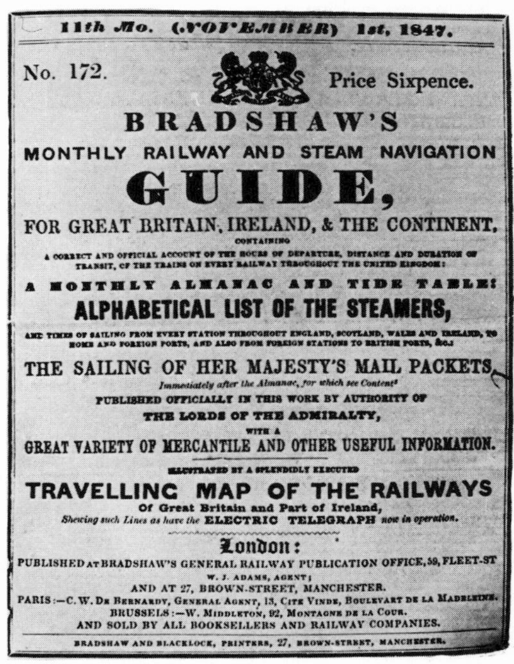

11th Mo. (NOVEMBER) 1st, 1847.

No. 172. Price Sixpence.

BRADSHAW'S

MONTHLY RAILWAY AND STEAM NAVIGATION

GUIDE,

FOR GREAT BRITAIN, IRELAND, & THE CONTINENT,

CONTAINING

A CORRECT AND OFFICIAL ACCOUNT OF THE HOURS OF DEPARTURE, DISTANCE AND DURATION OF TRANSIT, OF THE TRAINS ON EVERY RAILWAY THROUGHOUT THE UNITED KINGDOM:

A MONTHLY ALMANAC AND TIDE TABLE:

ALPHABETICAL LIST OF THE STEAMERS,

AND TIMES OF SAILING FROM EVERY STATION THROUGHOUT ENGLAND, SCOTLAND, WALES AND IRELAND, TO HOME AND FOREIGN PORTS, AND ALSO FROM FOREIGN STATIONS TO BRITISH PORTS, &c.;

THE SAILING OF HER MAJESTY'S MAIL PACKETS,

Immediately after the Almanac, for which see Contents

PUBLISHED OFFICIALLY IN THIS WORK BY AUTHORITY OF

THE LORDS OF THE ADMIRALTY,

WITH A

GREAT VARIETY OF MERCANTILE AND OTHER USEFUL INFORMATION.

ILLUSTRATED BY A SPLENDIDLY EXECUTED

TRAVELLING MAP OF THE RAILWAYS

Of Great Britain and Part of Ireland,

Shewing such Lines as have the ELECTRIC TELEGRAPH *now in operation.*

London:

PUBLISHED AT BRADSHAW'S GENERAL RAILWAY PUBLICATION OFFICE, 59, FLEET-ST

W. J. ADAMS, AGENT;

AND AT 27, BROWN-STREET, MANCHESTER.

PARIS:—C. W. DE BERNARDY, GENERAL AGENT, 13, CITE VINDE, BOULEVART DE LA MADELEINE.

BRUSSELS:—W. MIDDLETON, 92, MONTAGNE DE LA COUR.

AND SOLD BY ALL BOOKSELLERS AND RAILWAY COMPANIES.

BRADSHAW AND BLACKLOCK, PRINTERS, 27, BROWN-STREET, MANCHESTER.

18 *Purfleet.* A suburb approximately twenty miles east of central London on the north bank of the Thames. In Stoker's time a government arsenal was situated there. (See map, p. 337.)

19 *Carfax, no doubt a corruption of the old* Quatre Face. Carfax Road was and is located in the far west of London, while Carfax Square is in central London. But both are considerably removed from Purfleet, the site of Dracula's estate. Harker's etymology is not precise. *The Oxford Dictionary of Etymology* gives "Carfax: a place where four roads meet, especially as a proper name. Fourteenth century Anglo-Norman *carfuks* from Old French *carrefurkes* (Modern French *carrefour*)."

What makes this choice of a name for Dracula's later hideaway interesting is that suicides were buried at crossroads; and, according to folk tradition, suicides, among their other disabilities, risked turning into vampires. Later, it will be seen that Dracula finds shelter in a suicide's grave.

20 *a keep.* A keep is the strongest or innermost tower of a medieval castle.

21 *I found in certain places little rings marked.* London, Exeter, and Whitby (see map, p. 337). The point is at once clear and mysterious: clear, because we learn that Dracula has plans for England; mysterious, because, though we may later understand why he marked Exeter (because it was his solicitor's address) and London (because it was teeming with life), we are never clear as to why he marked Whitby.

Or did his hypnotic powers sort out his victims at long range?

20 part of a keep, and is close to an old chapel or church. I could not enter it, as I had not the key of the door leading to it from the house, but I have taken with my kodak views of it from various points. The house has been added to, but in a very straggling way, and I can only guess at the amount of ground it covers, which must be very great. There are but few houses close at hand, one being a very large house only recently added to and formed into a private lunatic asylum. It is not, however, visible from the grounds."

When I had finished, he said:—

"I am glad that it is old and big. I myself am of an old family, and to live in a new house would kill me. A house cannot be made habitable in a day; and, after all, how few days go to make up a century. I rejoice also that there is a chapel of old times. We Transylvanian nobles love not to think that our bones may be amongst the common dead. I seek not gaiety nor mirth, not the bright voluptuousness of much sunshine and sparkling waters which please the young and gay. I am no longer young; and my heart, through weary years of mourning over the dead, is not attuned to mirth. Moreover, the walls of my castle are broken; the shadows are many, and the wind breathes cold through the broken battlements and casements. I love the shade and the shadow, and would be alone with my thoughts when I may."

Somehow his words and his look did not seem to accord, or else it was that his cast of face made his smile look malignant and saturnine.

Presently, with an excuse, he left me, asking me to put all my papers together. He was some little time away, and I began to look at some of the books around me. One was an atlas, which I found opened naturally at England, as if that
21 map had been much used. On looking at it I found in certain places little rings marked, and on examining these I noticed that one was near London on the east side, manifestly where his new estate was situated; the other two were Exeter, and Whitby on the Yorkshire coast.

It was the better part of an hour when the Count returned. "Aha!" he said; "still at your books? Good! But you must not work always. Come; I am informed that your supper is ready." He took my arm, and we went into the next room, where I found an excellent supper ready on the table. The Count again excused himself, as he had dined out on his being away from home. But he sat as on the previous night, and chatted whilst I ate. After supper I smoked, as on the last evening, and the Count stayed with me, chatting and asking questions on every conceivable subject, hour after hour. I felt that it was getting very late indeed, but I did not say anything, for I felt under obligation to meet my host's wishes in every way. I was not sleepy, as the long sleep yesterday had fortified me; but I could not help experiencing that chill which comes over one at the coming of the dawn, which is like, in its way, the turn of the tide. They say that people who are near death die generally at the change to the dawn or at the turn of the tide; any one who has when tired, and tied as it were to his post, experienced this change in the atmosphere can well believe it.

All at once we heard the crow of a cock coming up with preternatural shrillness through the clear morning air; Count Dracula, jumping to his feet, said:—

"Why, there is the morning again! How remiss I am to let you stay up so long. You must make your conversation regarding my dear new country of England less interesting, so that I may not forget how time flies by us," and, with a courtly bow, he left me.

I went into my own room and drew the curtains, but there was little to notice; my window opened into the courtyard, all I could see was the warm grey of quickening sky. So I pulled the curtains again, and have written of this day.

8 *May*.—I began to fear as I wrote in this book that I was getting too diffuse; but now I am glad that I went into detail from the first, for there is something so strange about this place and all in it that I cannot but feel uneasy. I wish I were safe out of it, or that I had never come. It may be that this strange night-existence is telling on me; but would that that were all! If there were any one to talk to I could bear it, but there is no one. I have only the Count to speak with, and he!—I fear I am myself the only living soul within the place. Let me be prosaic so far as facts can be; it will help me to bear up, and imagination must not run riot with me. If it does I am lost. Let me say at once how I stand—or seem to.

I only slept a few hours when I went to bed, and feeling that I could not sleep any more, got up. I had hung my shaving glass by the window, and was just beginning to shave. Suddenly I felt a hand on my shoulder, and heard the Count's voice saying to me, "Good-morning." I started, for it amazed me that I had not seen him, since the reflection of the glass covered the whole room behind me. In starting I had cut myself slightly, but did not notice it at the moment. Having answered the Count's salutation, I turned to the glass again to see how I had been mistaken. This time there could be no error, for the man was close to me, and I could see him over my shoulder. But there
was no reflection of him in the mirror! The whole room 22
behind me was displayed; but there was no sign of a man in it, except myself. This was startling, and, coming on the top of so many strange things, was beginning to increase that vague feeling of uneasiness which I always have when the Count is near; but at the instant I saw that the cut had bled a little, and the blood was trickling over my chin. I laid down
the razor, turning as I did so half round to look for some 23
sticking plaster. When the Count saw my face, his eyes blazed with a sort of demoniac fury, and he suddenly made a grab at my throat. I drew away, and his hand touched the string of beads which held the crucifix. It made an instant change in him, for the fury passed so quickly that I could hardly believe that it was ever there.

"Take care," he said, "take care how you cut yourself. It is more dangerous than you think in this country." Then seizing the shaving glass, he went on: "And this is the wretched thing that has done the mischief. It is a foul bauble of man's vanity. Away with it!" and opening the heavy window with one wrench of his terrible hand, he flung out the glass,

22 *in the mirror!* Stoker has prepared us for this bizarre event on page 16 where Harker writes that "when he [Dracula as the coachman] stood between me and the flame he did not obstruct it, for I could see its ghostly flicker all the same."

The folklore of mirrors holds that the images people see of themselves in the glass are reflections of the human soul. Dracula, who is merely a corpse in motion is not, in a proper sense, *anima*ted, and therefore makes no reflection.

The custom of turning mirrors to the wall on the occasion of a death in the family, though it is said to symbolize that "all vanity, all care for earthly beauty are over with the deceased . . .", may also be an acknowledgment that the soul has fled.

Mirrors are naturally mysterious and have on that account their uses in magic and divination. A broken mirror, as everyone knows, is bad luck; and in northern England it was considered unlucky to see the new moon reflected in a mirror. Mirrors have figured largely in the destinies of people as various as Aristotle, Snow White's stepmother, Napoleon, and Lewis Carroll.

Lawrence Kayton, a contemporary psychiatrist, writing in the *Journal of Youth and Adolescence* (vol. I, no. 4, 1972, pp. 303–14), says "the vampire has been nicknamed the 'living dead,' which signifies his suspension between these two existences. This failure to be completely in either world is also exemplified in his not casting a reflection in the mirror . . . The failure of the vampire to cast a reflection in the mirror is seen homologously in the schizophrenic as feelings of invisibility or reduced visibility."

In Stoker's fiction, it seems to me, the invisibility of the vampire serves the larger Christian allegory by emphasizing that we cannot see vampires because (a) we tend not to believe in them and (b) we choose not to see those aspects of *ourselves* that are most like those of the vampire.

23 *razor*. A straight razor, one need hardly add.

which was shattered into a thousand pieces on the stones of the courtyard far below. Then he withdrew without a word. It is very annoying, for I do not see how I am to shave, unless in my watch-case or the bottom of the shaving-pot, which is fortunately of metal.

When I went into the dining-room, breakfast was prepared; but I could not find the Count anywhere. So I breakfasted alone. It is strange that as yet I have not seen the Count eat or drink. He must be a very peculiar man! After breakfast I did a little exploring in the castle. I went out on the stairs and found a room looking towards the south. The view was magnificent, and from where I stood there was every opportunity of seeing it. The castle is on the very edge of a terrible precipice. A stone falling from the window would fall a thousand feet without touching anything! As far as the eye can reach is a sea of green tree-tops, with occasionally a deep rift where there is a chasm. Here and there are silver threads where the rivers wind in deep gorges through the forests.

But I am not in heart to describe beauty, for when I had seen the view I explored further; doors, doors, doors everywhere, and all locked and bolted. In no place save from the windows in the castle walls is there an available exit.

The castle is a veritable prison, and I am a prisoner!

CHAPTER III.

Jonathan Harker's Journal (*continued*).

When I found that I was a prisoner a sort of wild feeling came over me. I rushed up and down the stairs, trying every door and peering out of every window I could find; but after a little the conviction of my helplessness overpowered all other feelings. When I look back after a few hours I think I must have been mad for the time, for I behaved much as a rat does in a trap. When, however, the conviction had come to me that I was helpless I sat down quietly—as quietly as I have ever done anything in my life—and began to think over what was best to be done. I am thinking still, and as yet have come to no definite conclusion. Of one thing only am I certain: that it is no use making my ideas known to the Count. He knows well that I am imprisoned; and as he has done it himself, and has doubtless his own motives for it, he would only deceive me if I trusted him fully with the facts. So far as I can see, my only plan will be to keep my knowledge and my fears to myself, and my eyes open. I am, I know, either being deceived, like a baby, by my own fears, or else I am in desperate straits; and if the latter be so, I need, and shall need, all my brains to get through. I had hardly come to this conclusion when I heard the great door below shut, and knew that the Count had returned. He did not come at once into the library, so I went cautiously to my own room and found him making the bed. This was 1
odd, but only confirmed what I had all along thought—that there were no servants in the house. When later I saw him through the chink of the hinges of the door laying the table in the dining-room, I was assured of it; for if he does himself all

1 *and found him making the bed.* There is something homey about this image of Count Dracula as chambermaid. He is also, as we have seen, a fine butler and first-rate cook—something of an accomplishment for a man on a liquid diet.

2 *the Count himself.* This suspicion occurred to Harker first on page 20.

3 *garlic.* Because this section of *Dracula* is heavily annotated, and because the lore of garlic is so rich and strange, I have deferred comment on this remarkable plant. (See pp. 123 and 213 for "the crucifix . . . the garlic . . . the wild rose.")

4 *the mountain ash.* According to Joseph Wood Krutch (p. 198), the mountain ash is "actually a member of the rose family and resembles an Ash in nothing save the shape of its leaves." Like the rose, it has its legendry, and Krutch cites Pliny reporting "that if a snake be confined with a circle composed in part of the branches of an Ash, it will escape across the fire rather than touch the Ash. . . . In England, children were passed through a cleft in an Ash to cure them of rupture or rickets."

5 *as idolatrous.* This comment lets us know that Harker is no Catholic.

6 *We Szekelys.* Emily Gerard in *The Land Beyond the Forest* says that the Szeklers "are fond of describing themselves as being descended from the Huns. Indeed one very old family of Transylvanian nobles makes, I believe, a boast of proceeding in line direct from the Scourge of God [Attila the Hun] himself." Miss Gerard (p. 43) quotes the following bit of popular doggerel that has in it much of Dracula's boastfulness:

> "A noble Szekel born and bred,
> Full loftily I held my head;
> Great Attila my sire was he,
> A legacy he left to me
>
> "A dagger, battle-axe, and spear;
> A heart to whom unknown is fear;
> A potent arm, which oft has slain
> The Tartar foe in field and plain.
>
> "The Scourge of Attila the bold
> Still hangs among us as of old;
> And when this lash we swing on high,
> Our enemies are forced to fly.
>
> "The Szekel proud then learn to know,
> And strive not to become his foe,
> For blood of Huns runs in him warm,
> And well he knows to wield his arm."

Dracula's claim that the Szeklers were entrusted with the guarding of the frontier is based on fact, but in Miss Gerard's account of the Szeklers their role as border guards acquires more prosaic dimensions. She writes (p. 149): " 'At the frontier' or 'beyond' is the signification of the Hungarian word Szekel, which, therefore, does not imply a distinctive race, but merely those Hungarians who live beyond the forest—near the frontier . . . One Hungarian authority tells us that the word Szekel, meaning frontier-keeper or watchman, was indiscrimi-

these menial offices, surely it is proof that there is no one else
to do them. This gave me a fright, for if there is no one else
2 in the castle, it must have been the Count himself who was the
driver of the coach that brought me here. This is a terrible
thought; for if so, what does it mean that he could control
the wolves, as he did, by only holding up his hand in silence.
How was it that all the people at Bistritz and on the coach
had some terrible fear for me? What meant the giving of
3, 4 the crucifix, of the garlic, of the wild rose, of the mountain
ash? Bless that good, good woman who hung the crucifix
round my neck! for it is a comfort and a strength to me whenever I touch it. It is odd that a thing which I have been
5 taught to regard with disfavour and as idolatrous should in a
time of loneliness and trouble be of help. Is it that there is
something in the essence of the thing itself, or that it is a
medium, a tangible help, in conveying memories of sympathy
and comfort? Some time, if it may be, I must examine
this matter and try to make up my mind about it. In the
meantime I must find out all I can about Count Dracula,
as it may help me to understand. To-night he may talk of
himself, if I turn the conversation that way. I must be very
careful, however, not to awake his suspicion.

Midnight.—I have had a long talk with the Count. I asked him a few questions on Transylvanian history, and he warmed up to the subject wonderfully. In his speaking of things and people, and especially of battles, he spoke as if he had been present at them all. This he afterwards explained by saying that to a *boyar* the pride of his house and name is his own pride, that their glory is his glory, that their fate is his fate. Whenever he spoke of his house he always said "we," and spoke almost in the plural, like a king speaking. I wish I could put down all he said exactly as he said it, for to me it was most fascinating. It seemed to have in it a whole history of the country. He grew excited as he spoke, and walked about the room pulling his great white moustache and grasping anything on which he laid his hands as though he would crush it by main strength. One thing he said which I shall put down as nearly as I can; for it tells in its way the story of his race:—

6 "We Szekelys have a right to be proud, for in our veins
flows the blood of many brave races who fought as the lion
fights, for lordship. Here, in the whirlpool of European races,
7 the Ugric tribe bore down from Iceland the fighting spirit
8, 9 which Thor and Wodin gave them, which their Berserkers displayed to such fell intent on the seaboards of Europe, ay,
and of Asia and Africa too, till the peoples thought that the
were-wolves themselves had come. Here, too, when they
came, they found the Huns, whose warlike fury had swept
the earth like a living flame, till the dying peoples held
that in their veins ran the blood of those old witches, who,
10 expelled from Scythia had mated with the devils in the
desert. Fools, fools! What devil or what witch was ever so
great as Attila, whose blood is in these veins?" He held up
his arms. "Is it a wonder that we were a conquering race;
that we were proud; that when the Magyar, the Lombard, the
Avar, the Bulgar, or the Turk poured his thousands on our
11 frontiers, we drove them back? Is it strange that when Arpad

SZEKLER PEASANT.

and his legions swept through the Hungarian fatherland he
found us here when he reached the frontier; that the Hon- 12
foglalas was completed there? And when the Hungarian
flood swept eastward, the Szekelys were claimed as kindred
by the victorious Magyars, and to us for centuries was trusted 13
the guarding of the frontier of Turkey-land; ay and more
than that, endless duty of the frontier guard, for, as the Turks
say, 'water sleeps, and enemy is sleepless.' Who more gladly 14
than we throughout the Four Nations received the 'bloody 15, 16
sword,' or at its warlike call flocked quicker to the standard of
the King? When was redeemed that great shame of my
nation, the shame of Cassova, when the flags of the Wallach 17
and the Magyar went down beneath the Crescent, who was
it but one of my own race who as Voivode crossed the Danube 18
and beat the Turk on his own ground? This was a Dracula 19
indeed! Woe was it that his own unworthy brother, when he
had fallen, sold his people to the Turk and brought the
shame of slavery on them! Was it not this Dracula, indeed,
who inspired that other of his race who in a later age again 21
and again brought his forces over the great river into Turkey-
land; who, when he was beaten back, came again, and again,
and again. though he had to come alone from the bloody field 22

nately applied to all soldiers of whatever nationality who defended the frontier of the kingdom."

With Dracula before us, it is intriguing to read John Paget's mid-nineteenth-century account (p. 192) of the Szekler character: "The Szeklers inhabit a mountainous country and are consequently poor; but it was easy to see they are far more industrious than any of the Transylvanians we had before visited. From all I heard of their character, they seem a good deal to resemble the Scotch. The same pride and poverty, the same industry and enterprise, and if they are not belied, the same sharp regard to their own interests."

Paget's Szeklers were more than poor, proud, and industrious. His journey among them took place during a cholera epidemic that had just taken its first victim whose "funeral had taken place the day we arrived; and, as it is a custom of the Szeklers to get especially drunk on these occasions, we found nearly the whole village as glorious in liquor as their friend could be in sanctity" (p. 193).

7 *Ugric tribe.* Ugric or Ugrian. An ethnological group that included Magyars and related peoples of western Siberia.

In ancient China, according to Meade (p. 4), "not only Europeans, but various Turkish and Ugrian invaders on the north-western frontiers of China [were] credited, at times, with certain diabolical powers . . ."

8 *Thor and Wodin.* See chapter XVI, note 9, for discussion of Thor. Woden—the Scandinavian Odin—is chieftain of the Norse gods.

9 *Berserkers.* Warriors of Norse mythology capable of assuming at will the shapes of bears or wolves. Ordinarily they appear as human beings and are no stronger than ordinary men, but in battle only their eyes are human. They go into savage frenzy, howling, barking, foaming at the mouth, and, invulnerable to fire or steel, they sweep their enemies before them.

Berserkers are frequently cited as sources for werewolf lore. Stoker is fond of the name and gives it to the wolf in the London zoo (p. 127).

Florescu and McNally (p. 180) write that "shortly before Stoker wrote his famous book, the British Museum had purchased one of the German pamphlets printed in 1491 which related horror tales about Dracula. Surely Stoker must have discovered it there, or been directed to it by Vambery, who was familiar with a similar pamphlet in the library of the University of Budapest. Although the pamphlet does not describe Dracula as a '*wampyr*' it does call him a cruel tyrant and *wütrich*, an old German term for 'berserker' or, more literally, 'blood-thirsty monster.'" Interestingly, though the *Oxford English Dictionary* acknowledges that the etymology of "berserk" is disputed, it nowhere translates the word as "blood-thirsty." I am fond of the etymology that suggests the word comes from "bear-sark," meaning a bear coat, or that it comes from the Norse warriors' practice of fighting without a shirt.

10 *Scythia.* The name given in ancient times to a region in southeast Europe and Asia lying north of the Black and Caspian seas.

11 *Arpad.* Arpad was the elected successor to Attila the Hun. C. A. McCarthy (p. 7) tells us that ". . . the seven chieftains elected the most powerful of their number, Árpád son of Álmus, to lead them swearing with ritual drinking of mingled blood to accept him and his male issue in perpetuity as heads of the nation." Arpad's "mystical identification" with Attila helped to inspire "the actual task of taking possession of Attila's land, so as to turn it into the country of Hungarians," says Otto Zarek (p. 44).

12 *Honfoglalas.* The word means "conquest of the Homeland."

In the year A.D. 895 a number of Magyar chieftains and their tribes followed Arpad (*see* preceding note) through the Verecski Pass in the Carpathians into the land that was to become Hungary.

The thousandth anniversary of the Honfoglalas was still being celebrated in Hungary, says Ronay (p. 56), "with great pomp and circumstance in 1896—the year when Stoker was writing *Dracula.*"

13 *victorious Magyars.* Because of the similarity of their language and origin.

14 *'water sleeps, and enemy is sleepless.'* So far, I have not been able to identify this proverb. But in Forster's edition of de Busbecq (p. 15), the following remark by Ogier Ghiselin de Busbecq, the ambassador of the Austro-Hungarian Empire to Turkey (1554–1562), is of interest. Describing the prowess of the Turkish armies, he writes: "The Turkish armies are like mighty rivers swollen with rain, which, if they can trickle through at any point in the banks which retain them, spread through the breach and cause infinite destruction."

It may be that Stoker had in mind the French proverb *"L'ennemi ne s'endort pas"*—one's enemy does not sleep.

15 *the Four Nations.* A turn of the century Baedeker's *Guide to Austria* gives three "privileged 'Nations' of Transylvania, the Magyars, Szeklers, and Germans . . ." who formed "in 1437 a 'fraternal union' for mutual protection." Presumably, by the Four Nations Stoker means these three plus the Wallachs.

16 *'bloody sword.'* The gauge of battle.

17 *Cassova.* In 1389 the Turks won the field at the first battle of Kossovo, thereby establishing their presence in Europe.

The battle was fought on the "field of the Blackbirds" beside the river Schinitza. The Turks, though outnumbered, were better disciplined and led than their Christian (Serbian) foes and won the day after a very long, very hard engagement.

The Turkish emperor, Murad I, who led his troops to Kossovo, was killed on the occasion, but not in battle. A Serbian nobleman named Milosh, pretending to be a turncoat, was ushered in to see Murad in his tent and there stabbed him.

William Stearns Davis (pp. 195–96) says that "the battle of Kossova had proved that it was beyond the power of the Balkan people to turn the intruders come out of Asia. The Turks would have to be halted by the men of Central and even of Western Europe if they were to be halted at all."

There was a second battle of Kossovo in 1448 in which John Hunyadi, the heroic voivode of Transylvania (see note 19 of this chapter), leading a Hungarian revolt against the Turks, was defeated.

18 *Voivode.* A Romanian word for "prince." Webster's defines it as a military commander or governor of a town or province.

19 *beat the Turk on his own ground.* Gabriel Ronay (p. 57) identifies this ancestor as "John Hunyadi, the Governor of Hungary. His victory over the Turks at Nándorfehérvár in 1456 stemmed the eastern threat to Europe for a hundred years and earned him the nickname 'Turk-beater.' "

20 *his own unworthy brother.* In 1462 Vlad the Impaler was finally driven from power, and, according to Franz Babinger (p. 222), his brother Radu, "a voluptuous weakling and famous for his beauty, which was in great contrast to the ugliness of his brother . . . ," was put on the Wallachian throne. Radu's beauty was said to have inspired lustful desires in Muhammad II.

21 *that other.* Ronay identifies him as "Vlad III *Dracul,* who distinguished himself in the battle of Varna in 1444."

22 *though he had to come alone from the bloody field.* Later, on page 300, this is interpreted by Mina to mean that "he fled back over the Danube, leaving his forces to be cut to pieces." Mina takes it for granted that "that other" was Dracula himself.

Florescu and McNally (p. 76) describe the historical Dracula's "scorched earth" retreat from the Turks in 1462: "Targoviste . . . had been stripped [by Dracula] of virtually all its holy relics and treasures; the palace was emptied of all that could be taken and the rest had been put to fire. Here, as elsewhere, all wells had been poisoned."

TURKISH WARRIORS.

where his troops were being slaughtered, since he knew that he
alone could ultimately triumph? They said that he thought
only of himself. Bah! what good are peasants without a
leader? Where ends the war without a brain and heart to
conduct it? Again, when, after the battle of Mohacs, we threw **23**
off the Hungarian yoke, we of the Dracula blood were amongst
their leaders, for our spirit would not brook that we were not
free. Ah, young sir, the Szekelys—and the Dracula as their
heart's blood, their brains, and their swords—can boast a
record that mushroom growths like the Hapsburgs and the
Romanoffs can never reach. The warlike days are over.
Blood is too precious a thing in these days of dishonourable
peace; and the glories of the great races are as a tale that is told."

It was by this time close on morning, and we went to bed.
(*Mem.* this diary seems horribly like the beginning of the **24**
"Arabian Nights," for everything has to break off at cock-
crow—or like the ghost of Hamlet's father.) **25**

A JINNI ASLEEP IN THE LAP OF A BEAUTIFUL DAMSEL.

23 *Mohacs.* The battle of Mohács was fought in 1526 between the troops of the great Turkish emperor Süleyman the Magnificent and the army of the Hungarian King Louis II. The result was a victory for the Turks and a disaster for the Hungarians who lost "their king, eight bishops, a great majority of the Hungarian nobles and twenty-four thousand men. . . . This decided the fate of Hungary" write Eversley and Chirol (p. 119).

The consequences of the Turkish campaign in Hungary were dreadful. Some two hundred thousand men were massacred and a hundred thousand captives taken away into Turkish slavery.

24 *like the beginning of the "Arabian Nights."* Given the complex, if subvert, relationships that will develop between Jonathan Harker, Harker's wife-to-be, Mina, and Dracula, this early reference to *The Arabian Nights* makes it worthwhile to recall that adultery is the framework in which that collection of tales is firmly set.

The Thousand Nights and One Night, as Sir Richard F. Burton called his 1885 translation of *The Arabian Nights*, begins with the story of two brother kings, Shah Zaman and Shah Sharyar, who are respectively betrayed by their wives. The two monarchs then set out to inquire whether it is indeed true that "all do it and there is no woman but who cuckoldeth her husband . . ." (p. 7). After much wandering, Sharyar and Zaman come upon a Jinni asleep, with his head in the lap of a beautiful damsel who contrives, nevertheless, to compel the kings to her lustful service: "Stroke me a strong stroke," she insists, "without stay or delay, otherwise will I arouse and set upon you this Ifrit who shall slay you straightway" (p. 12). The reluctant monarchs finally do as they have been told. For their reward the damsel shows them her collection of five hundred and seventy seal rings—and collects two more from her chagrined new lovers—telling them meanwhile that "these be the signets of five hundred and seventy men who have all futtered me upon the horns of this foul, this foolish, this filthy Ifrit . . . Of a truth this Ifrit bore me off on my bride-night, and put me into a casket and set the casket in a coffer and to the coffer he affixed seven strong padlocks of steel and deposited me on the deep bottom of the sea that raves, dashing and clashing with waves; and guarded me so that I might remain chaste and honest, quotha! that none save himself might have connexion with me. But I have lain under as many of my kind as I please, and this wretched Jinni wotteth not that Destiny may not be averted nor hindered by aught, and that whatso woman willeth the same she fulfilleth however man nilleth" (pp. 12–13).

After such a wrenching lesson on the power of female lust, Shah Zaman and Shah Sharyar return to their kingdoms, but Sharyar "also swore himself by a binding oath that whatever wife he married he would abate her maidenhead at night and slay her next morning to make sure of his honor" (p. 14). It took more than three years of such bedding and beheading before the learned, brilliant, and beautiful

Shahrázád, at her own instigation, became King Sharyar's bride and brought an end to the cycle of love and death with her irresistible tales.

It is not cockcrow that breaks off Sharázád's stories. We are told throughout the tales that "Shahrázád perceived the dawn of day and ceased saying her permitted say."

25 *like the ghost of Hamlet's father. Hamlet*, Act I, Scene I, lines 146 et seq.:

"Bernardo: It was about to speak, when the cock crew.
Horatio: And then it started like a guilty thing Upon a fearful summons . . .
Marcellus: It faded on the crowing of the cock."

26 *Lincoln's Inn.* One of the four legal societies in central London that have exclusive right of admission to the bar. The other societies are Gray's Inn, the Middle Temple, and the Inner Temple. All date from before the fourteenth century, and are named after the buildings in which masters taught law to apprentices.

27 *Newcastle, or Durham, or Harwich, or Dover.* Of these port cities in England, Dover, Newcastle, and Durham have ancient castles, and would therefore be of special interest to Dracula. (See map, p. 337.)

12 *May.*—Let me begin with facts—bare, meagre facts, verified by books and figures, and of which there can be no doubt. I must not confuse them with experiences which will have to rest on my own observation or my memory of them. Last evening when the Count came from his room he began by asking me questions on legal matters and on the doing of certain kinds of business. I had spent the day wearily over books, and, simply to keep my mind occupied, went over some
26 of the matters I had been examined in at Lincoln's Inn. There was a certain method in the Count's inquiries, so I shall try to put them down in sequence; the knowledge may somehow or some time be useful to me.

First, he asked if a man in England might have two solicitors, or more. I told him he might have a dozen if he wished, but that it would not be wise to have more than one solicitor engaged in one transaction, as only one could act at a time, and that to change would be certain to militate against his interest. He seemed thoroughly to understand, and went on to ask if there would be any practical difficulty in having one man to attend, say, to banking, and another to look after shipping, in case local help were needed in a place far from the home of the banking solicitor. I asked him to explain more fully, so that I might not by any chance mislead him, so he said:—

"I shall illustrate. Your friend and mine, Mr. Peter Hawkins, from under the shadow of your beautiful cathedral at Exeter, which is far from London, buys for me through your good self my place at London. Good! Now here let me say frankly, lest you should think it strange that I have sought the services of one so far off from London instead of some one resident there, that my motive was that no local interest might be served save my wish only; and as one of London resident might, perhaps, have some purpose of himself or friend to serve, I went thus afield to seek my agent, whose labours should be only to my interest. Now, suppose
27 I, who have much of affairs, wish to ship goods, say, to Newcastle, or Durham, or Harwich, or Dover, might it not be that it could with more ease be done by consigning to one in these ports?" I answered that certainly it would be most easy, but that we solicitors had a system of agency one for the other, so that local work could be done locally on instruction from any solicitor, so that the client, simply placing himself in the hands of one man, could have his wishes carried out by him without further trouble.

"But," said he, "I could be at liberty to direct myself. Is it not so?"

"Of course," I replied; "and such is often done by men of business, who do not like the whole of their affairs to be known by any one person."

"Good!" he said, and then went on to ask about the means of making consignments and the forms to be gone through, and of all sorts of difficulties which might arise, but by forethought could be guarded against. I explained all these things to him to the best of my ability, and he certainly left me under the impression that he would have made a wonderful solicitor, for there was nothing that he did not think of or foresee. For a man who was never in the country, and who did not evidently do much in the way of business, his knowledge and acumen were wonderful. When he had satisfied himself on these points of which he had spoken, and I had verified all as well as I could by the books available, he suddenly stood up and said :—

"Have you written since your first letter to our friend Mr. Peter Hawkins, or to any other?" It was with some bitterness in my heart that I answered that I had not, that as yet I had not seen any opportunity of sending letters to anybody.

"Then write now, my young friend," he said, laying a heavy hand on my shoulder; "write to our friend and to any other; and say, if it will please you, that you shall stay with me until a month from now."

"Do you wish me to stay so long?" I asked, for my heart grew cold at the thought.

"I desire it much; nay, I will take no refusal. When your master, employer, what you will, engaged that some one should come on his behalf, it was understood that my needs only were to be consulted. I have not stinted. Is it not so?"

What could I do but bow acceptance? It was Mr. Hawkins's interest, not mine, and I had to think of him, not myself; and besides, while Count Dracula was speaking, there was that in his eyes and in his bearing which made me remember that I was a prisoner, and that if I wished it I could have no choice. The Count saw his victory in my bow, and his mastery in the trouble of my face, for he began at once to use them, but in his own smooth, resistless way :—

"I pray you, my good young friend, that you will not discourse of things other than business in your letters. It will doubtless please your friends to know that you are well, and that you look forward to getting home to them. Is it not so?" As he spoke he handed me three sheets of note-paper and three envelopes. They were all of the thinnest foreign post, and looking at them, then at him, and noticing his quiet smile, with the sharp, canine teeth lying over the red under-lip, I understood as well as if he had spoken that I should be careful what I wrote, for he would be able to read it. So I determined to write only formal notes now, but to write fully to Mr. Hawkins in secret, and also to Mina, for to her I could write in shorthand, which would puzzle the Count, if he did see it. When I had written my two letters I sat quiet, reading a book whilst the Count wrote several notes, referring as he wrote them to some books on his table. Then he took up my two and placed them with his own, and put by his writing materials, after which, the instant the door had closed behind him, I leaned over and looked at the letters, which were face down on the table. I felt no compunction in doing so, for under the circumstances I felt that I should protect myself in every way I could.

One of the letters was directed to Samuel F. Billington, No. 7, The Crescent, Whitby, another to Herr Leutner, Varna; the third was to Coutts & Co., London, and the fourth to Herren Klopstock & Billreuth, bankers, Buda-Pesth. The second and fourth were unsealed. I was just about to look at them when I saw the door-handle move. I sank back in my seat, having just had time to replace the letters as they had

28 *the case.* The window frame.

been and to resume my book before the Count, holding still another letter in his hand, entered the room. He took up the letters on the table and stamped them carefully, and then turning to me, said:—

"I trust you will forgive me, but I have much work to do in private this evening. You will, I hope, find all things as you wish." At the door he turned, and after a moment's pause said:—

"Let me advise you, my dear young friend—nay, let me warn you with all seriousness, that should you leave these rooms you will not by any chance go to sleep in any other part of the castle. It is old, and has many memories, and there are bad dreams for those who sleep unwisely. Be warned! Should sleep now or ever overcome you, or be like to do, then haste to your own chamber or to these rooms, for your rest will then be safe. But if you be not careful in this respect, then"——He finished his speech in a gruesome way, for he motioned with his hands as if he were washing them. I quite understood; my only doubt was as to whether any dream could be more terrible than the unnatural, horrible net of gloom and mystery which seemed closing round me.

Later.—I endorse the last words written, but this time there is no doubt in question. I shall not fear to sleep in any place where he is not. I have placed the crucifix over the head of my bed—I imagine that my rest is thus freer from dreams; and there it shall remain.

When he left me I went to my room. After a little while, not hearing any sound, I came out and went up the stone stair to where I could look out towards the south. There was some sense of freedom in the vast expanse, inaccessible though it was to me, as compared with the narrow darkness of the courtyard. Looking out on this, I felt that I was indeed in prison, and I seemed to want a breath of fresh air, though it were of the night. I am beginning to feel this nocturnal existence tell on me. It is destroying my nerve. I start at my own shadow, and am full of all sorts of horrible imaginings. God knows that there is ground for any terrible fear in this accursed place! I looked out over the beautiful expanse, bathed in soft yellow moonlight till it was almost as light as day. In the soft light the distant hills became melted, and the shadows in the valleys and gorges of velvety blackness. The mere beauty seemed to cheer me; there was peace and comfort in every breath I drew. As I leaned from the window my eye was caught by something moving a storey below me, and somewhat to my left, where I imagined, from the lie of the rooms, that the windows of the Count's own room would look out. The window at which I stood was tall and deep, stone-mullioned, and though weather-worn, was still
28 complete; but it was evidently many a day since the case had been there. I drew back behind the stonework, and looked carefully out.

What I saw was the Count's head coming out from the window. I did not see the face, but I knew the man by the neck and the movement of his back and arms. In any case I could not mistake the hands which I had had so many opportunities of studying. I was at first interested and somewhat amused, for it is wonderful how small a matter will

interest and amuse a man when he is a prisoner. But my very feelings changed to repulsion and terror when I saw the whole man slowly emerge from the window and begin to crawl down the castle wall over that dreadful abyss, *face down*, **29**
with his cloak spreading out around him like great wings. At first I could not believe my eyes. I thought it was some trick of the moonlight, some weird effect of shadow; but I kept looking, and it could be no delusion. I saw the fingers and toes grasp the corners of the stones, worn clear of the mortar by the stress of years, and by thus using every projection and inequality move downwards with considerable speed, just as a lizard moves along a wall.

What manner of man is this, or what manner of creature is it in the semblance of man? I feel the dread of this horrible place overpowering me; I am in fear—in awful fear—and there is no escape for me; I am encompassed about with terrors that I dare not think of. . . .

15 *May*.—Once more have I seen the Count go out in his lizard fashion. He moved downwards in a sidelong way, some hundred feet down, and a good deal to the left. He vanished into some hole or window. When his head had disappeared I leaned out to try and see more, but without avail—the distance was too great to allow a proper angle of sight. I knew he had left the castle now, and thought to use the opportunity to explore more than I had dared to do as yet. I went back to the room, and taking a lamp, tried all the doors. They were all locked, as I had expected, and the locks were comparatively new; but I went down the stone stairs to the hall where I had entered originally. I found I could pull back the bolts easily enough and unhook the great chains; but the door was locked, and the key was gone! That key must be in the Count's room; I must watch should his door be unlocked, so that I may get it and escape. I went on to make a thorough examination of the various stairs and passages, and to try the doors that opened from them. One or two small rooms near the hall were open, but there was nothing to see in them except old furniture, dusty with age and moth-eaten. At last, however, I found one door at the top of a stairway which, though it seemed to be locked, gave a little under pressure. I tried it harder, and found that it was not really locked, but that the resistance came from the fact that the hinges had fallen somewhat, and the heavy door rested on the floor. Here was an opportunity which I might not have again, so I exerted myself, and with many efforts forced it back so that I could enter. I was now in a wing of the castle further to the right than the rooms I knew and a storey lower down. From the windows I could see that the suite of rooms lay along to the south of the castle, the windows of the end room looking out both west and south. On the latter side, as well as to the former, there was a great precipice. The castle was built on the corner of a great rock, so that on three sides it was quite impregnable, and great windows were placed here where sling, or bow, or culverin could not reach, and consequently light and comfort, **30**
impossible to a position which had to be guarded, were secured. To the west was a great valley, and then, rising far away, great jagged mountain fastnesses, rising peak on peak, the

29 *face down*. This scene would be remarkable in any event, but when we are told that Harker could see the Count's "fingers and toes grasp the corners of the stones . . . ," it becomes positively uncanny.

Question: Was the Count in his stockinged feet or barefooted?

T. S. Eliot was so impressed with this head-down climb that he tried the image out in his drafts of *The Wasteland*. In the first printed edition of the poem (Part V, "What the Thunder Said"), there is this stanza:

"A woman drew her long black hair out tight
And fiddled whisper music on those strings
And bats with baby faces in the violet light
Whistled, and beat their wings
And crawled head downward down a blackened
wall."

In an early draft of the last line Eliot had written, "a ~~man~~/form crawled downward down a blackened wall." Later he wrote:

Such a one crept } head downward down a wall.
I saw him creep }

Valerie Eliot, in a letter to the *Times Literary Supplement* dated May 18, 1973, writes: "What I regret omitting [from the notes to her facsimile edition of the manuscripts of *The Wasteland*] under the impression that it was known, is a reference linking the man ('bats' in the received text) who crept 'head downward down a wall' (p. 112) with the scene in *Dracula* where the Count crawls in a similar way."

30 *culverin*. In the Middle Ages a form of musket. Later, in the sixteenth and seventeenth centuries, the word designated a heavy cannon.

31 *even colours.* There is a wistfulness in this scene that comes, I think, from one's sense that Harker needs to get away from Dracula's stern, hard, "masculine" presence. Here, in this dusty boudoir, the harshness of the rest of the castle is mitigated a little. The yellow moonlight turned to colors by the windowpanes, the quietude, and the comfortable furniture together with Harker's passivity are skillful preparation for the extraordinary erotic scene that follows.

It is hard to shake the thought that Stoker had Keats's "Eve of St. Agnes" in mind as he was setting his stage. In Keats's poem we have the same cold corridors, impassive stones, and imminent danger surrounding Madeline's bedchamber where:

"A casement high and triple-arched there was,
All garlanded with carven imag'ries
. . . .
Full on this casement shone the wintry moon,
And threw warm gules on Madeline's fair breast,
As down she knelt for heaven's grace and boon;
Rose-bloom fell on her hands, together pressed,
And on her silver cross soft amethyst,
And on her hair a glory, like a saint:"

By comparison with Keats's scene, Stoker's is, as it were, out of focus and faded, but in both places the aura of sexual desire is strong. For the yearning Porphyro, it is love's own glory, while Jonathan Harker is assailed by it as by a taint.

32 *It is nineteenth century.* "It" refers to his shorthand.

33 *"My tablets! . . ." Hamlet*, Act I, Scene V, lines 107–8, actually read:

"My tables,—meet it is I set it down,
That one may smile, and smile, and be a villain;"

sheer rock studded with mountain ash and thorn, whose roots clung in cracks and crevices and crannies of the stone. This was evidently the portion of the castle occupied in bygone days, for the furniture had more air of comfort than any I had seen. The windows were curtainless, and the yellow moonlight, flooding in through the diamond panes, enabled one
31 to see even colours, whilst it softened the wealth of dust which lay over all and disguised in some measure the ravages of time and the moth. My lamp seemed to be of little effect in the brilliant moonlight, but I was glad to have it with me, for there was a dread loneliness in the place which chilled my heart and made my nerves tremble. Still, it was better than living alone in the rooms which I had come to hate from the presence of the Count, and after trying a little to school my nerves, I found a soft quietude come over me. Here I am, sitting at a little oak table where in old times possibly some fair lady sat to pen, with much thought and many blushes, her ill-spelt love-letter, and writing in my diary in shorthand all that has happened
32 since I closed it last. It is nineteenth century up-to-date with a vengeance. And yet, unless my senses deceive me, the old centuries had, and have, powers of their own which mere "modernity" cannot kill.

Later: the Morning of 16 *May.*—God preserve my sanity, for to this I am reduced. Safety and the assurance of safety are things of the past. Whilst I live on here there is but one thing to hope for: that I may not go mad, if, indeed, I be not mad already. If I be sane, then surely it is maddening to think that of all the foul things that lurk in this hateful place the Count is the least dreadful to me; that to him alone I can look for safety, even though this be only whilst I can serve his purpose. Great God! merciful God! Let me be calm, for out of that way lies madness indeed. I begin to get new lights on certain things which have puzzled me. Up to now I never quite knew what Shakespeare meant when he made Hamlet say:—

33 "My tablets! quick, my tablets!
'Tis meet that I put it down," etc.,

for now, feeling as though my own brain were unhinged or as if the shock had come which must end in its undoing, I turn to my diary for repose. The habit of entering accurately must help to soothe me.

The Count's mysterious warning frightened me at the time; it frightens me more now when I think of it, for in future he has a fearful hold upon me. I shall fear to doubt what he may say!

When I had written in my diary and had fortunately replaced the book and pen in my pocket I felt sleepy. The Count's warning came into my mind, but I took a pleasure in disobeying it. The sense of sleep was upon me, and with it the obstinacy which sleep brings as outrider. The soft moonlight soothed, and the wide expanse without gave a sense of freedom which refreshed me. I determined not to return to-night to the gloom-haunted rooms, but to sleep here, where of old ladies had sat and sung and lived sweet lives whilst their gentle breasts were sad for their menfolk away in the midst of remorseless wars. I drew a great couch out of its place near the corner, so that, as I lay, I could look at the lovely view to east and south, and unthinking of and uncaring for the dust, composed myself for sleep.

I suppose I must have fallen asleep; I hope so, but I fear, for all that followed was startlingly real—so real that now, sitting here in the broad, full sunlight of the morning, I cannot in the least believe that it was all sleep.

I was not alone. The room was the same, unchanged in any way since I came into it; I could see along the floor, in the brilliant moonlight, my own footsteps marked where I had disturbed the long accumulation of dust. In the moonlight opposite me were three young women, ladies by their dress **34**
and manner. I thought at the time that I must be dreaming when I saw them, for, though the moonlight was behind them, they threw no shadow on the floor. They came close to me and looked at me for some time, and then whispered together. Two were dark, and had high aquiline noses, like the Count, and great dark, piercing eyes, that seemed to be almost red when contrasted with the pale yellow moon. The other was fair, as fair as can be, with great, wavy masses of golden hair and eyes like pale sapphires. I seemed somehow to know her face, and to know it in connection with some **35**
dreamy fear, but I could not recollect at the moment how or where. All three had brilliant white teeth, that shone like pearls against the ruby of their voluptuous lips. There was something about them that made me uneasy, some longing and at the same time some deadly fear. I felt in my heart a wicked, burning desire that they would kiss me with those red lips. It is not good to note this down, lest some day it should meet Mina's eyes and cause her pain; but it is the truth. They whispered together, and then they all three laughed—such a silvery, musical laugh, but as hard as though the sound never could have come through the softness of human lips. It was like the intolerable, tingling sweetness of **36**
water-glasses when played on by a cunning hand. The fair girl shook her head coquettishly, and the other two urged her on. One said:—

"Go on! You are first, and we shall follow; yours is the **37**
right to begin." The other added:—

"He is young and strong; there are kisses for us all." I lay quiet, looking out under my eyelashes in an agony of delightful anticipation. The fair girl advanced and bent over me till I could feel the movement of her breath upon me. Sweet it was in one sense, honey-sweet, and sent the same tingling through the nerves as her voice, but with a bitter underlying the sweet, a bitter offensiveness, as one smells in blood.

I was afraid to raise my eyelids, but looked out and saw perfectly under the lashes. The fair girl went on her knees, and bent over me, fairly gloating. There was a deliberate voluptuousness which was both thrilling and repulsive, and as

34 *ladies by their dress and manner.* Harker's British (and genteel) class consciousness does not forsake him even in this most interesting of moments. Curiously enough, we never will meet a working-class vampire in this book.

35 *know her face.* This is a major mystery in the book. Whose face is it? There is the smallest hint that this blonde beauty may have something in common with Lucy, whom the reader will meet later. If so, then the plot is very thick, indeed. But see chapter XVI, note 3, where Lucy is described as dark-haired.

We have seen that Dracula has already marked on his map the town of Whitby, where Lucy is staying, along with Exeter and London (see chapter II, note 21).

36 *tingling sweetness of water-glasses.* The music is made by filling several glasses to varying levels with water, then striking them with a knife or spoon. Stoker is fond of the image and repeats it on pages 190 and 322.

37 *"Go on! . . . yours is the right to begin."* Apparently, she is the favored mistress of the vampire. (See p. 324 for further evidence of her distinction.)

Why these beautiful Transylvanian vampires speak English is not explained. Or are they speaking German, a language Harker has some knowledge of?

she arched her neck she actually licked her lips like an animal, till I could see in the moonlight the moisture shining on the scarlet lips and on the red tongue as it lapped the white sharp teeth. Lower and lower went her head as the lips went below the range of my mouth and chin and seemed about to fasten on my throat. Then she paused, and I could hear the churning 38
sound of her tongue as it licked her teeth and lips, and could feel the hot breath on my neck. Then the skin of my throat began to tingle as one's flesh does when the hand that is to tickle it approaches nearer—nearer. I could feel the soft, shivering touch of the lips on the supersensitive skin of my throat, and the hard dents of two sharp teeth, just touching and pausing there. I closed my eyes in a languorous ecstacy and waited—waited with beating heart.

But at that instant another sensation swept through me as quick as lightning. I was conscious of the presence of the Count, and of his being as if lapped in a storm of fury. As my eyes opened involuntarily I saw his strong hand grasp the slender neck of the fair woman and with giant's power draw it back, the blue eyes transformed with fury, the white teeth champing with rage, and the fair cheeks blazing red with passion. But the Count! Never did I imagine such wrath and fury, even to the demons of the pit. His eyes were positively blazing. The red light in them was lurid, as if the flames of hell-fire blazed behind them. His face was deathly pale, and the lines of it were hard like drawn wires; the thick eyebrows that met over the nose now seemed like a heaving bar of white-hot metal. With a fierce sweep of his arm, he hurled the woman from him, and then motioned to the others, as though he were beating them back; it was the same imperious gesture that I had seen used to the wolves. In a voice which, though low and almost in a whisper, seemed to cut through the air and then ring round the room as he said:—

"How dare you touch him, any of you? How dare you cast eyes on him when I had forbidden it? Back, I tell you all! This man belongs to me! Beware how you meddle with him, or you'll have to deal with me." The fair girl, with a laugh of ribald coquetry, turned to answer him:—

"You yourself never loved; you never love!" On this the other women joined, and such a mirthless, hard, soulless laughter rang through the room that it almost made me faint to hear; it seemed like the pleasure of fiends. Then the Count turned, after looking at my face attentively, and said in a soft whisper:—

"Yes, I too can love; you yourselves can tell it from the 39
past. Is it not so? Well, now I promise you that when I am done with him you shall kiss him at your will. Now go! go! I must awaken him, for there is work to be done."

"Are we to have nothing to-night?" said one of them, with

38 *the churning sound of her tongue*. I have tried, calmly as well as passionately, to reproduce this churning sound with my tongue but without success. It may be a noise that only a passionate vampire can make.

39 *I too can love*. After the ferocious speech Dracula has just made, this is a somewhat chastened reply, which has in it a certain tone of domestic guilt.

"IN THE MOONLIGHT OPPOSITE ME THERE WERE THREE YOUNG WOMEN . . . I THOUGHT AT THE TIME THAT I MUST BE DREAMING . . . I FELT IN MY HEART A WICKED, BURNING DESIRE THAT THEY WOULD KISS ME WITH THOSE RED LIPS."

a low laugh, as she pointed to the bag which he had thrown upon the floor, and which moved as though there were some living thing within it. For answer he nodded his head. One of the women jumped forward and opened it. If my ears did not deceive me there was a gasp and a low wail, as of a half-smothered child. The women closed round, whilst I was aghast with horror; but as I looked they disappeared, and with them the dreadful bag. There was no door near them, and they could not have passed me without my noticing. They simply seemed to fade into the rays of the moonlight and pass out through the window, for I could see outside the dim, shadowy forms for a moment before they entirely faded away.

Then the horror overcame me, and I sank down unconscious.

CHAPTER IV.

Jonathan Harker's Journal—*continued.*

I awoke in my own bed. If it be that I had not dreamt, the Count must have carried me here. I tried to satisfy myself on the subject, but could not arrive at any unquestionable result. To be sure, there were certain small evidences, such as that my clothes were folded and laid by in a manner which was not my habit. My watch was still unwound, and I am rigorously accustomed to wind it the last thing before going to bed, and many such details. But these things are no proof, for they may have been evidences that my mind was not as usual, and, from some cause or another, I had certainly been much upset. I must watch for proof. Of one thing I am glad: if it was that the Count carried me here and undressed me, he must have been hurried in his task, for my pockets are intact. I am sure this diary would have been a mystery to him which he would not have brooked. He would have taken or destroyed it. As I look round this room, although it has been to me so full of fear, it is now a sort of sanctuary, for nothing can be more dreadful than those awful women, who were—who *are*—waiting to suck my blood.

18 *May.*—I have been down to look at that room again in daylight, for I *must* know the truth. When I got to the doorway at the top of the stairs I found it closed. It had been so forcibly driven against the jamb that part of the woodwork was splintered. I could see that the bolt of the lock had not been shot, but the door is fastened from the inside. I fear it was no dream, and must act on this surmise.

19 *May.*—I am surely in the toils. Last night the Count asked me in the suavest tones to write three letters, one saying 1
that my work here was nearly done, and that I should start for home within a few days, another that I was starting on the next

1 *to write three letters.* Altogether, Harker writes five letters from Transylvania.

MODERN TRANSYLVANIAN GYPSIES.

2 *Hungary and Transylvania.* See chapter I, note 16, on Transylvania's population.

morning from the time of the letter, and the third that I had left the castle and arrived at Bistritz. I would fain have rebelled, but felt that in the present state of things it would be madness to quarrel openly with the Count whilst I am so absolutely in his power; and to refuse would be to excite his suspicion and to arouse his anger. He knows that I know too much, and that I must not live, lest I be dangerous to him; my only chance is to prolong my opportunities. Something may occur which will give me a chance to escape. I saw in his eyes something of that gathering wrath which was manifest when he hurled that fair woman from him. He explained to me that posts were few and uncertain, and that my writing now would ensure ease of mind to my friends; and he assured me with so much impressiveness that he would countermand the later letters, which would be held over at Bistritz until due time in case chance would admit of my prolonging my stay, that to oppose him would have been to create new suspicion. I therefore pretended to fall in with his views, and asked him what dates I should put on the letters. He calculated a minute, and then said:—

"The first should be June 12, the second June 19, and the third June 29."

I know now the span of my life. God help me!

28 *May.*—There is a chance of escape, or at any rate of being able to send word home. A band of Szgany have come to the castle, and are encamped in the courtyard. These Szgany are gipsies; I have notes of them in my book. They are peculiar to this part of the world, though allied to the ordinary gipsies all the world over. There are thousands of
2 them in Hungary and Transylvania, who are almost outside all

law. They attach themelves as a rule to some great noble or *boyar*, and call themselves by his name. They are fearless and without religion, save superstition, and they talk only their own varieties of the Romany tongue. 3

I shall write some letters home, and shall try to get them to have them posted. I have already spoken them through my window to begin an acquaintanceship. They took their hats off and made obeisance and many signs, which, however, I could not understand any more than I could their spoken language. . . . .

I have written the letters. Mina's is in shorthand, and I simply ask Mr. Hawkins to communicate with her. To her I have explained my situation, but without the horrors which I may only surmise. It would shock and frighten her to death were I to expose my heart to her. Should the letters not carry, then the Count shall not yet know my secret or the extent of my knowledge. . . . .

I have given the letters; I threw them through the bars of my window with a gold piece, and made what signs I could to 4
have them posted. The man who took them pressed them to his heart and bowed, and then put them in his cap. I could do no more. I stole back to the study, and began to read. As the Count did not come in, I have written here. . . . .

The Count has come. He sat down beside me, and said in his smoothest voice as he opened two letters :—

"The Szgany has given me these, of which, though I know not whence they come, I shall, of course, take care. See!"—he must have looked at it—"one is from you, and to my friend Peter Hawkins; the other"—here he caught sight of the strange symbols as he opened the envelope, and the dark look came into his face, and his eyes blazed wickedly—"the other is a vile thing, an outrage upon friendship and hospitality! It is not signed. Well! so it cannot matter to us." And he calmly held letter and envelope in the flame of the lamp till they were consumed. Then he went on :—

"The letter to Hawkins—that I shall, of course, send on, since it is yours. Your letters are sacred to me. Your pardon, my friend, that unknowingly I did break the seal. Will you not cover it again?" He held out the letter to me, and with a courteous bow handed me a clean envelope. I could only re-direct it and hand it to him in silence. When he went out of the room I could hear the key turn softly. A minute later I went over and tried it, and the door was locked.

When, an hour or two after, the Count came quietly into the room; his coming wakened me, for I had gone to sleep on the sofa. He was very courteous and very cheery in his manner, and seeing that I had been sleeping, he said :—

"So, my friend, you are tired? Get to bed. There is the surest rest. I may not have the pleasure to talk to-night, since there are many labours to me; but you will sleep, I pray." I passed to my room and went to bed, and, strange to say, slept without dreaming. Despair has its own calms.

31 *May*.—This morning when I woke I thought I would provide myself with some paper and envelopes from my bag and keep them in my pocket, so that I might write in case I should get an opportunity; but again a surprise, again a shock!

Every scrap of paper was gone, and with it all my notes, my

A GYPSY WOMAN.

3 *only their own varieties of the Romany tongue.* Stoker, and therefore Harker, is mistaken. Because they are always a minority in the countries where they live, gypsies are necessarily multilingual.

4 *a gold piece.* Harker, obedient to the suggestion of Baedeker's *Austria*, is no doubt carrying French gold pieces as a useful currency.

MONEY TABLE.

1897

Approximate Equivalents.

American Money		English Money			French Money		German Money		Austrian Money	
Doll.	*Cts.*	*L.*	*S.*	*D.*	*Fr.*	*Cts.*	*M*	*Pf.*	*Fl.*	*Kr.*
—	1 1/4	—	—	5/8	—	6 1/4	—	5	—	3
—	2 1/2	—	—	1 1/4	—	12 1/2	—	10	—	6
—	5	—	—	2 1/2	—	25	—	20	—	12
—	10	—	—	5	—	50	—	40	—	24
—	12 1/2	—	—	6	—	62 1/2	—	50	—	30
—	20	—	—	10	1	—	—	80	—	48
—	25	—	1	—	1	25	1	—	—	60
—	40	—	1	70	2	12 1/2	1	70	1	—
—	50	—	2	—	2	50	2	—	1	20
—	75	—	3	—	3	75	3	—	1	75
1	—	—	4	—	5	—	4	—	2	40
1	25	—	5	—	6	25	5	—	3	—
1	50	—	6	—	7	50	6	—	3	50
1	75	—	7	—	8	75	7	—	4	10
2	—	—	8	—	10	—	8	—	4	80
2	25	—	9	—	11	25	9	—	5	40
2	50	—	10	—	12	50	10	—	6	—
3	—	—	12	—	15	—	12	—	7	20
4	—	—	16	—	20	—	16	—	9	60
5	—	1	—	—	25	—	20	—	12	25
25	—	5	—	—	125	—	100	—	60	—
125	—	25	—	—	625	—	500	—	300	—

memoranda relating to railways and travel, my letter of credit,
in fact all that might be useful to me were I once outside
the castle. I sat and pondered a while, and then some
thought occurred to me, and I made search of my portmanteau
and in the wardrobe where I had placed my clothes.

The suit in which I had travelled was gone, and also my
overcoat and rug; I could find no trace of them anywhere.
This looked like some new scheme of villainy. . . . .

5 17 *June*.—This morning, as I was sitting on the edge of my
bed cudgelling my brains, I heard without a cracking of whips
and pounding and scraping of horses' feet up the rocky path
beyond the courtyard. With joy I hurried to the window, and
saw drive into the yard two great leiter-wagons, each drawn by
eight sturdy horses, and at the head of each pair a Slovak, with
his wide hat, great, nail-studded belt, dirty sheepskin, and high
boots. They had also their long staves in hand. I ran to the
door, intending to descend and try and join them through the
main hall, as I thought that way might be opened for them.
Again a shock: my door was fastened on the outside.

Then I ran to the window and cried to them. They looked
6 up at me stupidly and pointed, but just then the "hetman" of
the Szgany came out, and seeing them pointing to my window,
said something, at which they laughed. Henceforth no effort
of mine, no piteous cry or agonised entreaty, would make
them even look at me. They resolutely turned away. The
7 leiter-wagons contained great, square boxes, with handles of
thick rope; these were evidently empty by the ease with which
the Slovaks handled them, and by their resonance as they were
roughly moved. When they were all unloaded and packed in
a great heap in one corner of the yard, the Slovaks were given
8 some money by the Szgany, and spitting on it for luck, lazily
went each to his horse's head. Shortly afterwards I heard the
cracking of their whips die away in the distance.

24 *June, before morning*.—Last night the Count left me
early, and locked himself into his own room. As soon as I
dared I ran up the winding stair, and looked out of the
9 window, which opened south. I thought I would watch
for the Count, for there is something going on. The
Szgany are quartered somewhere in the castle, and are
doing work of some kind. I know it, for now and then
I hear a far-away, muffled sound as of mattock and spade,
and, whatever it is, it must be to the end of some ruthless
villainy.

I had been at the window somewhat less than half an hour,
when I saw something coming out of the Count's window. I
drew back and watched carefully, and saw the whole man
emerge. It was a new shock to me to find that he had on
10 the suit of clothes which I had worn whilst travelling here,
and slung over his shoulder the terrible bag which I had
seen the women take away. There could be no doubt as
to his quest, and in my garb, too! This, then, is his new
scheme of evil: that he will allow others to see me, as they
think, so that he may both leave evidence that I have been
seen in the towns or villages posting my own letters, and
that any wickedness which he may do shall by the local
people be attributed to me.

It makes me rage to think that this can go on, and

5 *17 June.* There has been a two-week lapse since the last entry in Jonathan's journal. One would like to know how he spent his time in the interval.

6 *the "hetman."* Polish, from the German word *hauptmann*, meaning chief man or captain.

7 *square boxes.* This is a strange shape for these boxes, considering the use to which they will be put.

8 *spitting on it.* The custom of spitting on money is common in various parts of the world. In England it was sometimes called "handsel" and was reputed to bring good luck. C. J. S. Thompson, in *The Hand of Destiny*, reports how the butcher women of London kiss the first money they receive in a morning and put it in a special pocket. And Frederick Thomas, in *The Evil Eye*, says that spitting is practiced in the hope of good fortune and also to avert the evil eye. In Germany the fishwives of Ellerbeck, says Thomas, spat on money as a way of keeping off witchcraft.

9 *which opened south.* This is the window mentioned on page 36, the one from which he first saw the Count crawling head downward.

10 *I had worn.* This fusion of identities marks the beginning of a sporadically developed subtheme of the novel. We will see later how Harker begins, physically, to resemble Dracula—and what else they will have in common.

whilst I am shut up here, a veritable prisoner, but without that protection of the law which is even a criminal's right and consolation.

I thought I would watch for the Count's return, and for a long time sat doggedly at the window. Then I began to notice that there were some quaint little specks floating in the rays of the moonlight. They were like the tiniest grains of dust, and they whirled round and gathered in clusters in a nebulous sort of way. I watched them with a sense of soothing, and a sort of calm stole over me. I leaned back in the embrasure in a more comfortable position, so that I could enjoy more fully the aerial gambolling.

Something made me start up, a low, piteous howling of dogs somewhere far below in the valley, which was hidden from my sight. Louder it seemed to ring in my ears, and the floating motes of dust to take new shapes to the sound as they danced in the moonlight. I felt myself struggling to awake to some call of my instincts; nay, my very soul was struggling, and my half-remembered sensibilities were striving to answer the call. I was becoming hypnotised! Quicker and quicker danced the dust, and the moonbeams seemed to quiver as they went by me into the mass of gloom beyond. More and more they gathered till they seemed to take dim phantom shapes. And then I started, broad awake and in full possession of my senses, and ran screaming from the place. The phantom shapes, which were becoming gradually materialised from the moonbeams, were those of the three ghostly women to whom I was doomed. I fled, and felt somewhat safer in my own room, where there was no moonlight and where the lamp was burning brightly.

When a couple of hours had passed I heard something stirring in the Count's room, something like a sharp wail quickly suppressed; and then there was silence, deep, awful silence, which chilled me. With a beating heart, I tried the door; but I was locked in my prison, and could do nothing. I sat down and simply cried.

As I sat I heard a sound in the courtyard without—the agonised cry of a woman. I rushed to the window, and throwing it up, peered out between the bars. There, indeed was a woman with dishevelled hair, holding her hands over her heart as one distressed with running. She was leaning against a corner of the gateway. When she saw my face at the window she threw herself forward, and shouted in a voice laden with menace:—

"Monster, give me my child!" **11**

She threw herself on her knees, and raising up her hands, cried the same words in tones which wrung my heart. Then she tore her hair and beat her breast, and abandoned herself to all the violences of extravagant emotion. Finally, she threw herself forward, and, though I could not see her, I could hear the beating of her naked hands against the door.

Somewhere high overhead, probably on the tower, I heard the voice of the Count calling in his harsh, metallic whisper. His call seemed to be answered from far and wide by the

11 *"Monster, give me my child!"* This accusation is directed against *Harker*, not at Dracula. Evidently the Count's ruse has succeeded in confusing the peasants who, having seen him in Harker's clothes, believe Harker is the vampire.

The child is Dracula's second child victim—a pretty poor showing for so practiced a monster. In England, as will be seen, Dracula fares better.

12 *and second father*. That is, Peter Hawkins, Jonathan's employer.

13 *I took off my boots*. Harker takes his boots off to climb down the wall. We are not told how Dracula did it. (See chapter III, note 29.) For the British the word "boots" more usually means shoes.

howling of wolves. Before many minutes had passed a pack of them poured, like a pent-up dam when liberated, through the wide entrance into the courtyard.

There was no cry from the woman, and the howling of the wolves was but short. Before long they streamed away singly, licking their lips.

I could not pity her, for I knew now what had become of her child, and she was better dead.

What shall I do? what can I do? How can I escape from this dreadful thrall of night and gloom and fear?

25 *June, morning*.—No man knows till he has suffered from the night how sweet and how dear to his heart and eye the morning can be. When the sun grew so high this morning that it struck the top of the great gateway opposite my window, the high spot which it touched seemed to me as if the dove from the ark had lighted there. My fear fell from me as if it had been a vaporous garment which dissolved in the warmth. I must take action of some sort whilst the courage of the day is upon me. Last night one of my post-dated letters went to post, the first of that fatal series which is to blot out the very traces of my existence from the earth.

Let me not think of it. Action!

It has always been at night-time that I have been molested or threatened, or in some way in danger or in fear. I have not yet seen the Count in the daylight. Can it be that he sleeps when others wake, that he may be awake whilst they sleep? If I could only get into his room! But there is no possible way. The door is always locked, no way for me.

Yes, there is a way, if one dares to take it. Where his body has gone why may not another body go? I have seen him myself crawl from his window; why should not I imitate him, and go in by his window? The chances are desperate, but my need is more desperate still. I shall risk it. At the worst it can only be death; and a man's death is not a calf's, and the dreaded Hereafter may still be open to me. God help me in my task! Good-bye, Mina, if I fail; good-bye, my faithful
12 friend and second father; good-bye, all, and last of all Mina!

Same day, later.—I have made the effort, and, God helping me, have come safely back to this room. I must put down every detail in order. I went whilst my courage was fresh straight to the window on the south side, and at once got outside on the narrow ledge of stone which runs round the building on this side. The stones were big and roughly cut, and the mortar had by process of time been washed away between them.
13 I took off my boots, and ventured out on the desperate way. I looked down once, so as to make sure that a sudden glimpse of the awful depth would not overcome me, but after that kept my eyes away from it. I knew pretty well the direction and distance of the Count's window, and made for it as well as I could, having regard to the opportunities available. I did not feel dizzy—I suppose I was too excited—and the time seemed ridiculously short till I found myself standing on the windowsill and trying to raise up the sash. I was filled with agitation, however, when I bent down and slid feet foremost in through the window. Then I looked around for the Count, but, with surprise and gladness, made a discovery. The room was

"THERE WAS NO CRY FROM THE WOMAN, AND THE HOWLING OF THE WOLVES WAS BUT SHORT."

14 *three hundred years old.* Harker shows unbelievable coolness in examining the dates of the coins at a moment like this.

empty! It was barely furnished with odd things, which seemed to have never been used; the furniture was something the same style as that in the south rooms, and was covered with dust. I looked for the key, but it was not in the lock, and I could not find it anywhere. The only thing I found was a great heap of gold in one corner—gold of all kinds, Roman, and British, and Austrian, and Hungarian, and Greek and Turkish money, covered with a film of dust, as though it had lain long
14 in the ground. None of it that I noticed was less than three hundred years old. There were also chains and ornaments, some jewelled, but all of them old and stained.

At one corner of the room was a heavy door. I tried it, for, since I could not find the key of the room or the key of the outer door, which was the main object of my search, I must make further examination, or all my efforts would be in vain. It was open, and led through a stone passage to a circular stairway, which went steeply down. I descended, minding carefully where I went, for the stairs were dark, being only lit by loopholes in the heavy masonry. At the bottom there was a dark, tunnel-like passage, through which came a deathly, sickly odour, the odour of old earth newly turned. As I went through the passage the smell grew closer and heavier. At last I pulled open a heavy door which stood ajar, and found myself in an old, ruined chapel, which had evidently been used as a graveyard. The roof was broken, and in two places were steps leading to vaults, but the ground had recently been dug over, and the earth placed in great wooden boxes, manifestly those which had been brought by the Slovaks. There was nobody about, and I made search for any further outlet, but there was none. Then I went over every inch of the ground, so as not to lose a chance. I went down even into the vaults, where the dim light struggled, although to do so was a dread to my very soul. Into two of these I went, but saw nothing except fragments of old coffins and piles of dust; in the third, however, I made a discovery.

There, in one of the great boxes, of which there were fifty in all, on a pile of newly dug earth, lay the Count! He was either dead or asleep, I could not say which—for the eyes were open and stony, but without the glassiness of death—and the cheeks had the warmth of life through all their pallor, and the lips were as red as ever. But there was no sign of movement, no pulse, no breath, no beating of the heart. I bent over him, and tried to find any sign of life, but in vain. He could not have lain there long, for the earthy smell would have passed away in a few hours. By the side of the box was its cover, pierced with holes here and there. I thought he might have the keys on him, but when I went to search I saw the dead eyes, and in them, dead though they were, such a look of hate, though unconscious of me or my presence, that I fled from the place, and leaving the Count's room by the window, crawled again up the castle wall. Regaining my own chamber, I threw myself panting upon the bed and tried to think. . . . .

29 *June.*—To-day is the date of my last letter, and the Count has taken steps to prove that it was genuine, for again I saw him leave the castle by the same window, and in my clothes. As he went down the wall, lizard fashion, I wished I

"I FOUND MYSELF IN AN OLD, RUINED CHAPEL."

Satt

had a gun or some lethal weapon, that I might destroy him; but I fear that no weapon wrought alone by man's hand would have any effect on him. I dared not wait to see him return, for I feared to see those weird sisters. I came back to the library, and read there till I fell asleep.

I was awakened by the Count, who looked at me as grimly as a man can look as he said:—

"To-morrow, my friend, we must part. You return to your beautiful England, I to some work which may have such an end that we may never meet. Your letter home has been despatched; to-morrow I shall not be here, but all shall be ready for your journey. In the morning come the Szgany, who have some labours of their own here, and also come some Slovaks. When they have gone, my carriage shall come for you, and shall bear you to the Borgo Pass to meet the diligence from Bukovina to Bistritz. But I am in hopes that I shall see more of you at Castle Dracula." I suspected him, and determined to test his sincerity. Sincerity! It seems like a profanation of the word to write it in connection with such a monster, so asked him point-blank:—

"Why may I not go to-night?"

"Because, dear sir, my coachman and horses are away on a mission."

"But I would walk with pleasure. I want to get away at once." He smiled, such a soft, smooth, diabolical smile that I knew there was some trick behind his smoothness. He said:—

"And your baggage?"

"I do not care about it. I can send for it some other time."

The Count stood up, and said, with a sweet courtesy which made me rub my eyes, it seemed so real:—

"You English have a saying which is close to my heart, for its spirit is that which rules our *boyars*: 'Welcome the coming,
15 speed the parting guest.' Come with me, my dear young friend. Not an hour shall you wait in my house against your will, though sad am I at your going, and that you so suddenly desire it. Come!" With a stately gravity, he, with the lamp, preceded me down the stairs and along the hall. Suddenly he stopped.

"Hark!"

Close at hand came the howling of many wolves. It was almost as if the sound sprang up at the raising of his hand, just as the music of a great orchestra seems to leap under the bâton of the conductor. After a pause of a moment, he proceeded, in his stately way, to the door, drew back the ponderous bolts, unhooked the heavy chains, and began to draw it open.

To my intense astonishment I saw that it was unlocked. Suspiciously I looked all round, but could see no key of any kind.

As the door began to open, the howling of the wolves without grew louder and angrier; their red jaws, with champing teeth, and their blunt-clawed feet as they leaped, came in through the opening door. I knew then that to struggle at the moment against the Count was useless. With such allies as these at his command, I could do nothing. But still the door continued slowly to open, and only the Count's body stood in

15 '. . . *speed the parting guest.*' How Count Dracula comes to be quoting Pope is one of the more charming mysteries of this work. The line is from Pope's translation of the Odyssey (Book XV, line 83), and is accurately quoted.

On the other hand, Pope's line makes aphoristic what in Homer is an extended courtesy on Menelaus's part. Menelaus, replying to Telemachus, who wants to be on his way, says (lines 68–74):

"Not in any way at all will I hold you here,
. . . .
It is equally wrong of one who speeds a guest
Who is loathe to go as it is wrong to keep back
A guest who is on his way. It is necessary to
Make welcome the guest who is present
And to send on his way the one who wishes to go."

the gap. Suddenly it struck me that this might be the moment and the means of my doom; I was to be given to the wolves, and at my own instigation. There was a diabolical wickedness in the idea great enough for the Count, and as a last chance I cried out:—

"Shut the door; I shall wait till morning!" and covered my face with my hands to hide my tears of bitter disappointment. With one sweep of his powerful arm, the Count threw the door shut, and the great bolts clanged and echoed through the hall as they shot back into their places.

In silence we returned to the library, and after a minute or two I went to my own room. The last I saw of Count Dracula was his kissing his hand to me; with a red light of triumph in his eyes, and with a smile that Judas in hell might be proud of.

When I was in my room and about to lie down, I thought I heard a whispering at my door. I went to it softly and listened. Unless my ears deceived me, I heard the voice of the Count:—

"Back, back, to your own place! Your time is not yet come. Wait. Have patience. To-morrow night, to-morrow night, is yours!" There was a low, sweet ripple of laughter, and in a rage I threw open the door, and saw without the three terrible women licking their lips. As I appeared they all joined in a horrible laugh, and ran away.

I came back to my room and threw myself on my knees. It is then so near the end? To-morrow! to-morrow! Lord, help me, and those to whom I am dear!

30 *June, morning.*—These may be the last words I ever write in this diary. I slept till just before the dawn, and when I woke threw myself on my knees, for I determined that if Death came he should find me ready.

At last I felt that subtle change in the air, and knew that the morning had come. Then came the welcome cock-crow, and I felt that I was safe. With a glad heart, I opened my door and ran down to the hall. I had seen that the door was unlocked, and now escape was before me. With hands that trembled with eagerness, I unhooked the chains and drew back the massive bolts.

But the door would not move. Despair seized me. I pulled, and pulled, at the door, and shook it till, massive as it was, it rattled in its casement. I could see the bolt shot. It had been locked after I left the Count.

Then a wild desire took me to obtain that key at any risk, and I determined then and there to scale the wall again and gain the Count's room. He might kill me, but death now seemed the happier choice of evils. Without a pause I rushed up to the east window, and scrambled down the wall, as before, into the Count's room. It was empty, but that was as I expected. I could not see a key anywhere, but the heap of gold remained. I went through the door in the corner and down the winding stair and along the dark passage to the old chapel. I knew now well enough where to find the monster I sought.

The great box was in the same place, close against the wall, but the lid was laid on it, not fastened down, but with the nails ready in their places to be hammered home. I knew I

"THEN CAME THE WELCOME COCKCROW."

"LONDON, WHERE . . . HE MIGHT, AMONGST ITS TEEMING MILLIONS, SATIATE HIS LUST . . ."

must search the body for the key, so I raised the lid, and laid it back against the wall; and then I saw something which filled my very soul with horror. There lay the Count, but looking as if his youth had been half renewed, for the white hair and moustache were changed to dark iron-grey; the cheeks were fuller, and the white skin seemed ruby-red underneath; the mouth was redder than ever, for on the lips were gouts of fresh blood, which trickled from the corners of the mouth and ran over the chin and neck. Even the deep, burning eyes seemed set amongst swollen flesh, for the lids and pouches underneath were bloated. It seemed as if the whole awful creature were simply gorged with blood; he lay like a filthy leech, exhausted with his repletion. I shuddered as I bent over to touch him, and every sense in me revolted at the contact; but I had to search, or I was lost. The coming night might see my own body a banquet in a similar way to those horrid three. I felt all over the body, but no sign could I find of the key. Then I stopped and looked at the Count. There was a mocking smile on the bloated face which seemed to drive me mad. This was the being I was helping to transfer to London, where, perhaps, for centuries to come he might, amongst its teeming millions, satiate his lust for blood, and create a new and ever-widening circle of semi-demons to batten on the helpless. The very thought drove me mad. A terrible desire came upon me to rid the world of such a monster. There was no lethal weapon at hand, but I seized a shovel which the workmen had been using to fill the cases, and lifting it high struck, with the edge downward, at the hateful face. But as I did so the
head turned, and the eyes fell full upon me, with all their
16 blaze of basilisk horror. The sight seemed to paralyse me,
and the shovel turned in my hand and glanced from the face, merely making a deep gash above the forehead. The shovel fell from my hand across the box, and as I pulled it away the flange of the blade caught the edge of the lid, which fell over again, and hid the horrid thing from my sight. The last glimpse I had was of the bloated face, blood-stained and fixed with a grin of malice which would have held its own in the nethermost hell.

I thought and thought what should be my next move, but my brain seemed on fire, and I waited with a despairing feeling growing over me. As I waited I heard in the distance a gipsy song sung by merry voices coming closer, and through their song the rolling of heavy wheels and the cracking of whips; the Szgany and the Slovaks of whom the Count had spoken were coming. With a last look around and at the box which contained the vile body, I ran from the place and gained the Count's room, determined to rush out at the moment the door should be opened. With strained ears, I listened, and heard downstairs the grinding of the key in the great lock and the falling back of the heavy door. There must have been some other means of entry, or some one had a key for one of the locked doors. Then there came the sound of many feet tramping and dying away in some passage which sent up a clanging echo. I turned to run down again towards the vault, where I might find the new entrance; but at the moment there seemed to come a violent

16 *of basilisk horror.* The basilisk, or, to give it its other name, the cockatrice, is a fearsome mythical beast hatched from an egg laid by a seven-year-old cock. The basilisk has such a dreadful stare that birds at which it merely glances fall down and are devoured.

Pliny describes the basilisk as a snake with a crown on its head. Later it was described as looking like a cross between a toad and a rooster.

The last recorded basilisk hunt took place in 1587 in Warsaw, but the creature, accused of killing two girls in a basement, was not found.

A BASILISK.

puff of wind, and the door to the winding stair blew to with a shock that set the dust from the lintels flying. When I ran to push it open, I found that it was hopelessly fast. I was again 17
a prisoner, and the net of doom was closing round me more closely.

As I write there is in the passage below a sound of many tramping feet and the crash of weights being set down heavily, doubtless the boxes, with their freight of earth. There is a sound of hammering; it is the box being nailed down. Now I can hear the heavy feet tramping again along the hall, with many other idle feet coming behind them.

The door is shut, and the chains rattle; there is a grinding of the key in the lock; I can hear the key withdrawn: then another door opens and shuts; I hear the creaking of lock and bolt.

Hark! in the courtyard and down the rocky way the roll of heavy wheels, the crack of whips, and the chorus of the Szgany as they pass into the distance.

I am alone in the castle with those awful women. Faugh! Mina is a woman, and there is nought in common. They are devils of the Pit!

I shall not remain alone with them; I shall try to scale the castle wall farther than I have yet attempted. I shall take some of the gold with me, lest I want it later. I may find a way from this dreadful place.

And then away for home! away to the quickest and nearest train! away from this cursed spot, from this cursed land, where the devil and his children still walk with earthly feet!

At least God's mercy is better than that of these monsters, and the precipice is steep and high. At its foot a man may sleep—as a man. Good-bye, all! Mina!

17 *hopelessly fast*. Dracula, though dormant, is not entirely helpless, as this sudden door-closing lets us know.

CHAPTER V.

Letter from Miss Mina Murray to Miss Lucy Westenra.

"9 *May.*

" My dearest Lucy,—

" Forgive my long delay in writing, but I have been simply
overwhelmed with work. The life of an assistant schoolmis- 1
tress is sometimes trying. I am longing to be with you, and by the sea, where we can talk together freely and build our castles in the air. I have been working very hard lately, because I want to keep up with Jonathan's studies, and I have been practising shorthand very assiduously. When we are married I shall be able to be useful to Jonathan, and if I can stenograph well enough I can take down what he wants to say in this way and write it out for him on the typewriter, at which also I am practising very hard. He and I sometimes write letters in shorthand, and he is keeping a stenographic journal of his travels abroad. When I am with you I shall keep a diary in the same way. I don't mean one of those two-pages-to-the-week-with-Sunday-squeezed-in-a-corner diaries, but a sort of journal which I can write in whenever I feel inclined. I do not suppose there will be much of interest to other people; but it is not intended for them. I may show it to Jonathan some day if there is in it anything worth sharing, but it is really an exercise book. I shall try to do what I see lady journalists do: interviewing and writing descriptions and trying to remember conversations. I am told that, with a little practice, one can remember all that goes on or that one hears said during a day. However, we shall see. I shall tell
you all my little plans when we meet. I have just had a few 2
hurried lines from Jonathan from Transylvania. He is well, and will be returning in about a week. I am longing to hear all his news. It must be so nice to see strange coun-

1 *an assistant schoolmistress.* Mina is a working girl, though her friend Lucy is not. This is appropriate, since later we will see that Mina can be an astonishingly competent young woman; clearly someone who has had to make her own way in the world. This letter, though dated, does not tell us at which school Mina is an assistant schoolmistress, though we may surmise from what we learn later that it is in Exeter.

2 *a few hurried lines . . . from Transylvania.* This letter from Jonathan, received on May 9, must have been posted by him in Bistrita or in Klausenburg *before* he reached Castle Dracula.

According to the May 8 entry, past midnight Jonathan was listening to Dracula's prideful lecture on the history of the Szeklers.

3 *"17, Chatham Street . . ."* A short street in south central London, joining Darwin Street to Rodney Road. Located on the south side of the Thames (see map, pp. 340–41).

4 *at the last Pop.* A popular concert. The *Oxford English Dictionary* quotes from George Eliot's *Life:* "We have been to a Monday Pop, to hear Beethoven's Septett." It cites the Newcastle *Evening Chronicle* (December 14, 1891) as observing that "the Saturday Pops in Newcastle are in a bad way." And, in Gilbert and Sullivan's *Patience* we hear of:

"An everyday young man:
A commonplace type,
With a stick and a pipe,
And a half-bred black and tan;
Who thinks suburban 'hops'
More fun than 'Monday Pops,' "

5 *That was Mr. Holmwood.* Arthur Holmwood. Holmwood's name refers to a type of wood that comes from a species of oak, *Quercus ilex*, or holm oak.

It may be, though I think it is not, a coincidence that the name Ringwood appears in Prest's *Varney the Vampyre.* In that book one of Varney's victims, Clara Crofton, has a fiancé named Ringwood. Lucy's fiancé lives in a family home called Ring.

6 parti. The *Oxford English Dictionary*'s first definition of *parti* is the one that fits here. It says that a *parti* is "a marriageable person considered in reference to means or position, or what kind of a 'match' he or she may be."

tries. I wonder if we—I mean Jonathan and I—shall ever see them together. There is the ten o'clock bell ringing. Good-bye.

"Your loving

"MINA.

"Tell me all the news when you write. You have not told me anything for a long time. I hear rumours, and especially of a tall, handsome, curly-haired man???"

Letter, Lucy Westenra to Mina Murray.

3 "17, *Chatham Street,*

"*Wednesday.*

"My dearest Mina,—

"I must say you tax me *very* unfairly with being a bad correspondent. I wrote to you *twice* since we parted, and your last letter was only your *second.* Besides, I have nothing to tell you. There is really nothing to interest you. Town is very pleasant just now, and we go a good deal to picture-galleries and for walks and rides in the park. As to the tall, curly-haired man, I suppose it was the one who was with me
4 at the last Pop. Some one has evidently been telling tales.
5 That was Mr. Holmwood. He often comes to see us, and he and mamma get on very well together; they have so many things to talk about in common. We met some time ago a man that would just *do for you*, if you were not already engaged to
6 Jonathan. He is an excellent *parti*, being handsome, well off, and of good birth. He is a doctor and really clever. Just fancy! He is only nine-and-twenty, and he has an immense lunatic asylum all under his own care. Mr. Holmwood introduced him to me, and he called here to see us, and often comes now. I think he is one of the most resolute men I ever saw, and yet the most calm. He seems absolutely imperturbable. I can fancy what a wonderful power he must have over his patients. He has a curious habit of looking one straight in the face, as if trying to read one's thoughts. He tries this on very much with me, but I flatter myself he has got a tough nut to crack. I know that from my glass. Do you ever try to read your own face? *I do,* and I can tell you it is not a bad study, and gives you more trouble than you can

WHERE CHATHAM STREET ONCE WAS.

well fancy if you have never tried it. He says that I afford him a curious psychological study, and I humbly think I do. I do not, as you know, take sufficient interest in dress to be able to describe the new fashions. Dress is a bore. That is slang again, but never mind; Arthur says that every day. There, it is all out. Mina, we have told all our secrets to each other since we were *children*; we have slept together and eaten together, and laughed and cried together; and now, though I have spoken, I would like to speak more. Oh, Mina, couldn't you guess? I love him. I am blushing as I write, for although I *think* he loves me, he has not told me so in words. But oh, Mina, I love him; I love him; I love him! There, that does me good. I wish I were with you, dear, sitting by the fire undressing, as we used to sit; and I would try to tell you what I feel. I do not know how I am writing this even to you. I am afraid to stop, or I should tear up the letter, and I don't want to stop, for I *do so* want to tell you all. Let me hear from you *at once*, and tell me all that you think about it. Mina, I must stop. Good-night. Bless me in your prayers; and, Mina, pray for my happiness.

"LUCY.

"P.S.—I need not tell you this is a secret. Good-night again.

"L."

Letter, Lucy Westenra to Mina Murray.

"24 *May.*

"My dearest Mina,—

"Thanks, and thanks, and thanks again for your sweet letter! It was so nice to be able to tell you and to have your sympathy.

"My dear, it never rains but it pours. How true the old proverbs are. Here am I, who shall be twenty in September, and yet I never had a proposal till to-day, not a real proposal, and to-day I have had three. Just fancy! THREE pro-

"HE HAS AN IMMENSE LUNATIC ASYLUM ALL UNDER HIS OWN CARE."

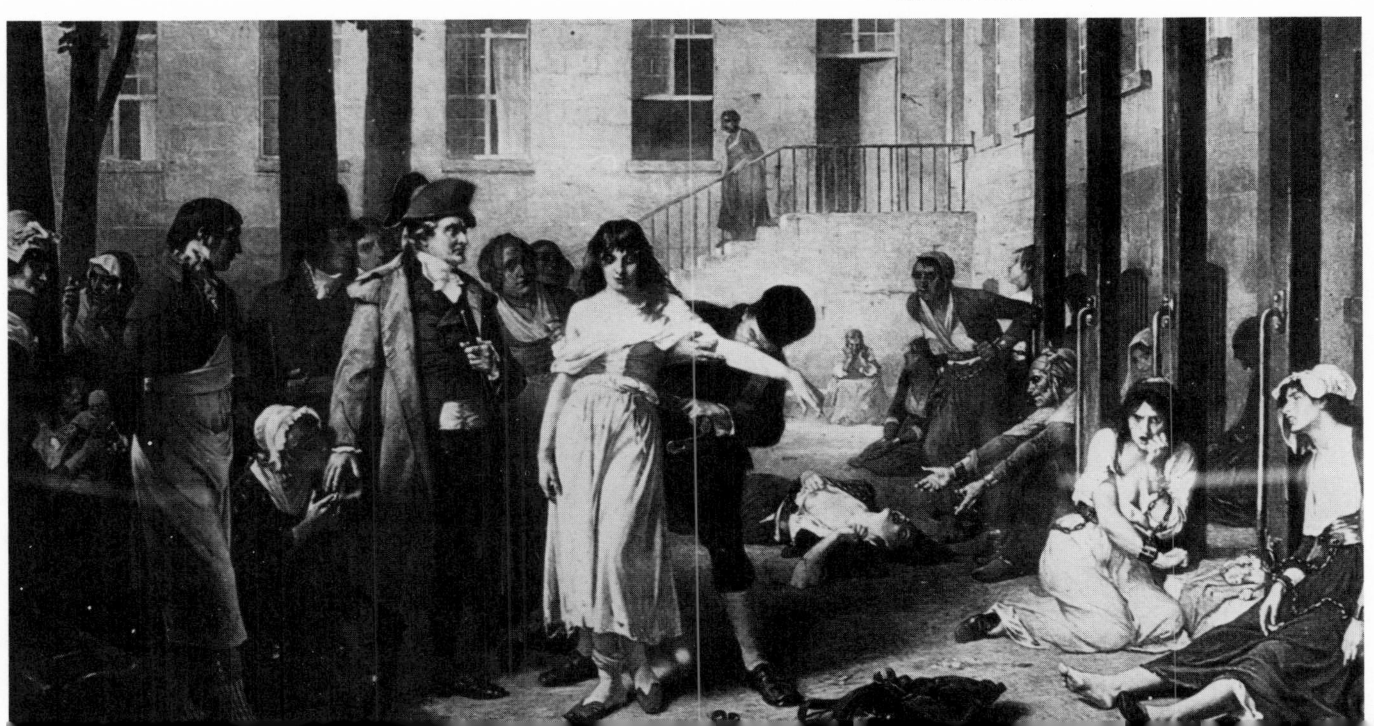

7 *sit down on his silk hat.* Seward's behavior is certainly flustered. How a Victorian gentleman dealt with his hat had significance. Edward Royston Pike (p. 37) tells us that a gentleman "should not put his hat on until the hall. . . . To leave his hat in the hall would be considered a liberty and in very bad taste." So that Seward was expected to hold the hat in his lap or set it down discreetly beside him.

8 *with a lancet.* A lancet is a two-edged, sharp-pointed surgical instrument, commonly used to open boils. Why does Seward, a psychiatrist, toy with a lancet? We will learn later (p. 110) that Seward is an experienced surgeon, too. But the question still remains: Why does he carry a lancet when he goes courting?

Sharp-pointed instruments seem to be sexually totemic for the men in this book. The weapons, in order of increasing size, are as follows: Seward carries a lancet; Quincey Morris will be armed with a bowie knife; Jonathan Harker with a kukri knife; and Dr. Van Helsing, their teacher, produces, when the time comes, the most formidable weapon of all—the stake.

posals in one day! Isn't it awful! I feel sorry, really and truly sorry, for two of the poor fellows. Oh, Mina, I am so happy that I don't know what to do with myself. And three proposals! But, for goodness' sake, don't tell any of the girls, or they would be getting all sorts of extravagant ideas and imagining themselves injured and slighted if in their very first day at home they did not get six at least. Some girls are so vain. You and I, Mina dear, who are engaged and are going to settle down soon soberly into old married women, can despise vanity. Well, I must tell you about the three, but you must keep it a secret, dear, from *every one*, except, of course, Jonathan. You will tell him, because I would, if I were in your place, certainly tell Arthur. A woman ought to tell her husband everything—don't you think so, dear?—and I must be fair. Men like women, certainly their wives, to be quite as fair as they are; and women, I am afraid, are not always quite as fair as they should be. Well, my dear, number One came just before lunch. I told you of him, Dr. John Seward, the lunatic-asylum man, with the strong jaw and the good forehead. He was very cool outwardly, but was nervous all the same. He had evidently been schooling himself as to all sorts of little things, and remembered them; but he almost
7 managed to sit down on his silk hat, which men don't generally do when they are cool, and then when he wanted
8 to appear at ease he kept playing with a lancet in a way that made me nearly scream. He spoke to me, Mina, very straightforwardly. He told me how dear I was to him, though he had known me so little, and what his life would be with me to help and cheer him. He was going to tell me how unhappy he would be if I did not care for him, but when he saw me cry he said that he was a brute and would not add to my present trouble. Then he broke off and asked if I could love him in time; and when I shook my head his hands trembled and then with some hesitation he asked me if I cared already for any one else. He put it very nicely, saying that he did not want to wring my confidence from me, but only to know, because if a woman's heart was free a man might have hope. And then, Mina, I felt it a sort of duty to tell him that there was some one. I only told him that much, and then he stood up, and he looked very strong and very grave as he took both my hands in his and said he hoped I would be happy, and that if I ever wanted a friend I must count him one of my best. Oh, Mina dear, I can't help crying; and you must excuse this letter being all blotted. Being proposed to is all very nice and all that sort of thing, but it isn't at all a happy thing when you have to see a poor fellow, whom you know loves you honestly, going away and looking all broken-hearted, and to know that, no matter what he may say at the moment, you are passing quite out of his life. My dear, I must stop here at present, I feel so miserable, though I am so happy.

"*Evening.*

"Arthur has just gone, and I feel in better spirits than when I left off, so I can go on telling you about the day. Well, my dear, number two came after lunch. He is such a nice fellow, an American from Texas, and he looks so young and so fresh

"I SYMPATHIZE WITH POOR DESDEMONA."

that it seems almost impossible that he has been to so many places and has had such adventures. I sympathise with poor Desdemona when she had such a dangerous stream poured in 9
her ear, even by a black man. I suppose that we women are such cowards that we think a man will save us from fears, and we marry him. I know now what I would do if I were a man and wanted to make a girl love me. No, I don't, for there was Mr. Morris telling us his stories, and Arthur never told any, and yet—— My dear, I am somewhat previous. Mr. Quincey P. Morris found me alone. It seems that a man always does find a girl alone. No, he doesn't, for Arthur tried twice to *make* a chance, and I helping him all I could; I am not ashamed to say it now. I must tell you beforehand that Mr. Morris doesn't always speak slang—that is to say, he never does so to strangers or before them, for he is really well educated and has exquisite manners—but he found out that it amused me to hear him talk American slang, and whenever I was present, and there was no one to be shocked, he said such funny things. I am afraid, my dear, he has to invent it all, for it fits exactly into whatever else he has to say. But this is a way slang has. I do not know myself if I shall ever speak slang; I do not know if Arthur likes it, as I have never heard him use any as yet. Well, Mr. Morris sat down beside me and looked as happy and jolly as he could, but I could see all the same that he was very nervous. He took my hand in his, and said ever so sweetly:—

"'Miss Lucy, I know I ain't good enough to regulate the fixin's of your little shoes, but I guess if you wait till you find a

9 *Desdemona*. Othello, the Moor, Shakespeare tells us, was a frequent guest in the home of the Venetian senator Brabantio and was by him often importuned to tell the story of his adventurous life. Othello complied:

"I ran it through [Othello says], even from my boyish days
To the very moment that he bade me tell it;
Wherein I spake of most disastrous chances,
Of moving accidents by flood and field,
Of hair-breadth 'scapes i' the imminent deadly breach,
Of being taken by the insolent foe
And sold to slavery, of my redemption thence
And portance in my travels' history;
And of the Cannibals that each other eat,
The Anthropophagi, and men whose heads
Do grow beneath their shoulders. This to hear
Would Desdemona seriously incline;"

So seriously that she rewarded the tale-teller with

". . . . . .a world of sighs:
She swore, in faith, 'twas strange, 'twas passing strange;
'Twas pitiful, 'twas wondrous pitiful:
She wish'd she had not heard it, yet she wish'd
That heaven had made her such a man; she thank'd me,
And bade me, if I had a friend that lov'd her,
I should but teach him how to tell my story,
And that would woo her. Upon this hint I spake."
(*Othello*, Act I, Scene III, lines 132–66)

The young men about whom Lucy is here prattling are hardly Othello figures, but later in our story, when Lucy's relationship to Dracula is more fully developed, we may recall that Brabantio, Desdemona's father, believed from the first that Othello's hold on her was the result of "some mixtures powerful o'er the blood,/Or with some dram conjur'd to this effect,/He wrought upon her." (Act I, Scene III, lines 104–6).

TEN VIRGINS.

10 *seven young women with the lamps.* Actually, there were ten young women with the lamps, and, says the New Testament, "five of them were wise, and five *were* foolish." All ten of them took their lamps and went forth to meet the bridegroom, but "they that *were* foolish took their lamps, and took no oil with them: But the wise took oil in their vessels with their lamps. . . . And at midnight there was a cry made, Behold, the bridegroom cometh; go ye out to meet him." The rest of the story is well known. The young foolish women were rejected by the bridegroom while the wise virgins "they that were ready went in with him to the marriage: and the door was shut" (Matthew 25:1–10).

Presumably, Quincey is suggesting that the bridegroom has come; and that the time is now.

11 *marry three men.* In one sense, Lucy will get her wish. (See the King Laugh episode on p. 158.)

10 man that is you will go join them seven young women with the lamps when you quit. Won't you just hitch up alongside of me and let us go down the long road together, driving in double harness?'

"Well, he did look so good-humoured and so jolly that it didn't seem half so hard to refuse him as it did poor Dr. Seward, so I said, as lightly as I could, that I did not know anything of hitching, and that I wasn't broken to harness at all yet. Then he said that he had spoken in a light manner, and he hoped that if he had made a mistake in doing so on so grave, so momentous, an occasion for him, I would forgive him. He really did look serious when he was saying it, and I couldn't help feeling a bit serious too—I know, Mina, you will think me a horrid flirt—though I couldn't help feeling a sort of exultation that he was number two in one day. And then, my dear, before I could say a word he began pouring out a perfect torrent of love-making, laying his very heart and soul at my feet. He looked so earnest over it that I shall never again think that a man must be playful always, and never earnest, because he is merry at times. I suppose he saw something in my face which checked him, for he suddenly stopped, and said with a sort of manly fervour that I could have loved him for if I had been free:—

"'Lucy, you are an honest-hearted girl, I know. I should not be here speaking to you as I am now if I did not believe you clean grit, right through to the very depths of your soul. Tell me, like one good fellow to another, is there any one else that you care for? And if there is I'll never trouble you a hair's breadth again, but will be, if you will let me, a very faithful friend.'

My dear Mina, why are men so noble when we women are so little worthy of them? Here was I almost making fun of this great-hearted, true gentleman. I burst into tears —I am afraid, my dear, you will think this a very sloppy letter in more ways than one—and I really felt very badly.
11 Why can't they let a girl marry three men, or as many as want her, and save all this trouble? But this is heresy, and I must not say it. I am glad to say that, though I was crying, I was able to look into Mr. Morris's brave eyes, and I told him out straight:—

"'Yes, there is some one I love, though he has not told me yet that he even loves me.' I was right to speak to him so frankly, for quite a light came into his face, and he put out both his hands and took mine—I think I put them into his—and said in a hearty way:—

"'That's my brave girl. It's better worth being late for a chance of winning you than being in time for any other girl in the world. Don't cry, my dear. If it's for me, I'm a hard nut to crack; and I take it standing up. If that other fellow doesn't know his happiness, well, he'd better look for it soon, or he'll have to deal with me. Little girl, your honesty and pluck have made me a friend, and that's rarer than a lover; it's more unselfish anyhow. My dear, I'm going to have a pretty lonely walk between this and Kingdom Come. Won't you give me one kiss? It'll be something to keep off the darkness now and then. You can, you know, if you like, for that other good fellow—he must be a good fellow, my dear, and a fine fellow, or you could not love him—hasn't spoken yet.' That quite won me, Mina, for it *was* brave and sweet of him, and noble, too, to a rival—wasn't it?—and he so sad; so I leant over and kissed him. He stood up with my two hands in his, and as he looked down into my face—I am afraid I was blushing very much—he said:—

"'Little girl, I hold your hand, and you've kissed me, and if these things don't make us friends nothing ever will. Thank you for your sweet honesty to me, and good-bye.' He wrung my hand, and taking up his hat, went straight out of the room without looking back, without a tear or a quiver or a pause; and I am crying like a baby. Oh, why must a man like that be made unhappy when there are lots of girls about who would worship the very ground he trod on? I know I would if I were free—only I don't want to be free. My dear, this quite upset me, and I feel I cannot write of happiness just at once, after telling you of it; and I don't wish to tell of the number three till it can be all happy.

"Ever your loving
"LUCY.

"P.S.—Oh, about number three—I needn't tell you of number three, need I? Besides, it was all so confused; it seemed only a moment from his coming into the room till both his arms were round me, and he was kissing me. I am very, very happy, and I don't know what I have done to deserve it. I must only try in the future to show that I am not ungrateful for all His goodness to me in sending to me such a lover, such a husband, and such a friend.

"Good-bye."

Dr. Seward's Diary.

(Kept in phonograph.) 12

25 *April*.—Ebb tide in appetite to-day. Cannot eat, cannot rest, so diary instead. Since my rebuff of yesterday I have a sort of empty feeling; nothing in the world seems of sufficient importance to be worth the doing. . . . . As I knew that the only cure for this sort of thing was work, I went down amongst the patients. I picked out one who has afforded me a study of much interest. He is so quaint in his ideas, and so unlike the normal lunatic, that I have determined to understand him as well as I can. To-day I seemed to get nearer than ever before to the heart of his mystery.

I questioned him more fully than I had ever done, with a view to making myself master of the facts of his hallucination. In my manner of doing it there was, I now see, something of cruelty. I seemed to wish to keep him to the point of his madness—a thing which I avoid with the patients as I would the mouth of hell. (*Mem.*, under what circumstances would I

12 *(Kept in phonograph.)* The phonograph was invented by Thomas A. Edison in 1877. What appears to be the first use of a phonograph in medical recordkeeping is described in *Science* (vol. 15, p. 43), where A. D. Blodgett, a Massachusetts physician, is quoted as follows:

"We got a record from an actual patient in an actual examination which was reproducible and could be understood. I am sure that anyone with a little practice could use this machine as a way to obtain durable and trustworthy records from the lips of the patients. Any instrument of this kind might be made portable, and a visiting physician in a hospital might give his directions into a funnel, when they would be recorded on a small cylinder, which can be put on another machine, and a physician's directions as to treatment can thus be accurately recorded. This record is got by means of the graphophone, which is used a great deal in conjunction with the typewriter. In medico-legal cases I think it would be of great service because the utterances of the patient could be reproduced at an indefinite period afterward."

ADVERTISEMENT OF THE PERIOD.

13 Omnia Romæ venalia sunt. All Romans are venal. In Sallust's *Jugurthine Wars*, chapter 35, paragraph 10, we read that "if anyone can find a buyer, the city [Rome] is for sale."

14 verb. sap. *verbum sapienti* [*est*]: a word to the wise [is sufficient].

15 *ætat.* Age. As in Julius Caesar, *ætat* 35 — Julius Caesar, age 35.

16 *balance it.* This is the first of Seward's introspective speeches. His point here is that a madman *with* a great cause is more dangerous than one who is merely self-absorbed.

17 *Titicaca.* A lake in the Andes between southern Peru and western Bolivia: the highest large lake in the world.

18 Hopwood. This is clearly a misprint for Holmwood and was so corrected in later editions of *Dracula*.

13 *not* avoid the pit of hell?) *Omnia Romæ venalia sunt.* Hell
14 has its price! *verb. sap.* If there be anything behind this instinct it will be valuable to trace it afterwards *accurately*, so I had better commence to do so, therefore—

15 R. M. Renfield, ætat 59.—Sanguine temperament; great physical strength; morbidly excitable; periods of gloom ending in some fixed idea which I cannot make out. I presume that the sanguine temperament itself and the disturbing influence end in a mentally-accomplished finish; a possibly dangerous man, probably dangerous if unselfish. In selfish men caution is as secure an armour for their foes as for themselves. What I think of on this point is, when self is the fixed point the centripetal force is balanced with the centrifugal; when duty, a cause, etc., is the fixed point, the latter force is paramount, and only accident or a series of accidents can
16 balance it.

Letter, Quincey P. Morris to Hon. Arthur Holmwood.

"25 *May.*

"My dear Art,—

"We've told yarns by the camp-fire in the prairies; and dressed one another's wounds after trying a landing at the
17 Marquesas; and drunk healths on the shore of Titicaca. There are more yarns to be told, and other wounds to be healed, and another health to be drunk. Won't you let this be at my camp-fire to-morrow night? I have no hesitation in asking you, as I know a certain lady is engaged to a certain dinner-party, and that you are free. There will only be one other, our old pal at the Korea, Jack Seward. He's coming, too, and we both want to mingle our weeps over the wine-cup, and to drink a health with all our hearts to the happiest man in all the wide world, who has won the noblest heart that God has made and the best worth winning. We promise you a hearty welcome, and a loving greeting, and a health as true as your own right hand. We shall both swear to leave you at home if you drink too deep to a certain pair of eyes. Come!

"Yours, as ever and always,

"QUINCEY P. MORRIS."

---

18 *Telegram from Arthur Hopwood to Quincey P. Morris.*

"26 *May.*

"Count me in every time. I bear messages which will make both your ears tingle.

"ART."

CHAPTER VI.

Mina Murray's Journal.

24 *July*. *Whitby*.—Lucy met me at the station, looking
sweeter and lovelier than ever, and we drove up to the house
at the Crescent in which they have rooms. This is a lovely 1, 2
place. The little river, the Esk, runs through a deep valley, 3
which broadens out as it comes near the harbour. A great
viaduct runs across, with high piers, through which the view
seems somehow further away than it really is. The valley is
beautifully green, and it is so steep that when you are on the
high land on either side you look right across it, unless you are
near enough to see down. The houses of the old town—the side
away from us—are all red-roofed, and seem piled up one over
the other anyhow, like the pictures we see of Nuremberg. Right
over the town is the ruin of Whitby Abbey, which was sacked by 4
the Danes, and which is the scene of part of "Marmion," where 5
the girl was built up in the wall. It is a most noble ruin, of
immense size, and full of beautiful and romantic bits; there
is a legend that a white lady is seen in one of the windows. 6
Between it and the town there is another church, the parish
one, round which is a big graveyard, all full of tombstones.
This is to my mind the nicest spot in Whitby, for it lies right
over the town, and has a full view of the harbour and all up
the bay to where the headland called Kettleness stretches out 7
into the sea. It descends so steeply over the harbour that
part of the bank has fallen away, and some of the graves have
been destroyed. In one place part of the stonework of the
graves stretches out over the sandy pathway far below. There
are walks, with seats beside them, through the churchyard; and
people go and sit there all day long looking at the beautiful

"THE HOUSE AT THE CRESCENT."

1 *in which they have rooms*. Number Four Crescent Terrace is now pointed out to *Dracula* pilgrims as the house in which Lucy and her mother lived. At the time Stoker was writing *Dracula*, the house was owned by a Mrs. Storm whose advertisement in *Horne's Guide to Whitby* (1897) is reproduced here.

Ronald Anderson, the present owner of the house, very kindly permitted me to inspect the room in which Lucy, had she been real, would have lived. Since the room was being used to store a variety of novelties sold by Mr. Anderson in his shop in Whitby, I was unable to form much of a judgment of it, beyond noticing that it was spacious, airy, and light.

Mr. Anderson tells me that previous owners of the house included titled aristocracy as well as Russell Bailly, the man who is famous for having invented the easily constructed army bridge that bears his name.

MRS. STORM,

4, Crescent Terrace, West Cliff, Whitby.

FURNISHED + APARTMENTS.

Uninterrupted Sea Views, close to the Saloon, Tennis Courts, Golf Links, and the Beach.
The House is certified as possessing perfect Sanitary Arrangements. Terms on application.

---

2 *This is a lovely place.* The description of Whitby given here, and later, is accurate enough to be used as a tourist guide to Victorian Whitby which, in 1891, had a population of 13,261 inhabitants. The town was, and is, both a fishing port, a vacation resort, and the center of a jet mining industry (see note 14 of this chapter).

3 *The little river, the Esk.* The Esk River flows, at Whitby, into the North Sea. The riverside houses along the Esk at Whitby are built as close to the water as possible.

At one time ships entering the harbor made by the mouth of the Esk were required to pay toll. The practice was abolished in 1861. (See map, page 338.)

4 *Whitby Abbey. Horne's Guide to Whitby* says that "the Monastery of Streonshalh, from which arose Whitby Abbey, was founded in the year 658, by Oswy, King of Northumbria. . . ." The *Guide* adds that "the whole of this district was destroyed by the Danes in the year 867. . . ."

5 *"Marmion," . . . built up in the wall.* Mina is remembering the fate of Constance de Beverley in Walter Scott's *Marmion* (1807). Constance, in love with the brave, but false, knight Marmion, forswore her nun's vows. She says that:

> "I listened to a traitor's tale,
> I left the convent and the veil;
> For three long years I bowed my pride,
> A horse-boy in his train to ride;"

Marmion, in turn, proved false to the vows he had sworn to Constance when:

> "He saw young Clara's face more fair,
> He knew her of broad lands the heir,
> Forgot his vows, his faith forswore,
> And Constance was beloved no more."
> (Canto II: xxvii)

For violating her vows Constance was condemned by the Benedictines to be bricked up, alive, in a dungeon of Whitby Abbey. Her judges, passing up the "hundred winding steps" that led from the dungeon to the daylight:

> ". . . ere they breathed the fresher air
> They heard the shriekings of despair,
> And many a stifled groan
> . . . .
> Even in the vesper's heavenly tone
> They seemed to hear a dying groan,
> And bade the passing knell to toll
> For welfare of a parting soul."
> (Canto II: xxxiii)

It is some comfort to know that the traitor Marmion, sorely wounded at the battle of Flodden field, later died a miserable death as well, his dying spasm brought on by the news of Constance's death, given to him by the injured but pitying Clare.

WHITBY ABBEY.

view and enjoying the breeze. I shall come and sit here very often myself and work. Indeed, I am writing now, with my book on my knee, and listening to the talk of three old men who are sitting beside me. They seem to do nothing all day but sit up here and talk.

The harbour lies below me, with, on the far side, one long granite wall stretching out into the sea, with a curve outwards at the end of it, in the middle of which is a lighthouse. A heavy sea-wall runs along outside of it. On the near side, the sea-wall makes an elbow crooked inversely, and its end too has a lighthouse. Between the two piers there is a narrow opening into the harbour, which then suddenly widens.

It is nice at high tide; but when the tide is out it shoals away to nothing, and there is merely the stream of the Esk, running between banks of sand, with rocks here and there. Outside the harbour on this side there rises for about half a mile a great reef, the sharp edge of which runs straight out from behind the south lighthouse. At the end of it is a buoy with a bell, which swings in bad weather, and sends in a mournful sound on the wind. They have a legend here that

WHITBY HARBOR, C. 1890.

when a ship is lost bells are heard out at sea. I must ask the 8
old man about this; he is coming this way. . . . .

He is a funny old man. He must be awfully old, for his 9
face is all gnarled and twisted like the bark of a tree. He tells me that he is nearly a hundred, and that he was a sailor
in the Greenland fishing fleet when Waterloo was fought. He 10
is, I am afraid, a very sceptical person, for when I asked him about the bells at sea and the White Lady at the abbey he said very brusquely:—

"I wouldn't fash masel' about them, miss. Them things be 11
all wore out. Mind, I don't say that they never was, but I do say that they wasn't in my time. They be all very well for comers and trippers an' the like, but not for a nice young lady
like you. Them feet-folks from York and Leeds that be 12, 13
always eatin' cured herrin's an' drinkin' tea an' lookin' out to
buy cheap jet would creed aught. I wonder masel' who'd be 14
bothered tellin' lies to them—even the newspapers, which is full of fool-talk." I thought he would be a good person to learn interesting things from, so I asked him if he would mind
telling me something about the whale-fishing in the old days. 15
He was just settling himself to begin when the clock struck six, whereupon he laboured to get up, and said:—

"HE IS A FUNNY OLD MAN."

6 *a white lady.* The shade of St. Hilda, the daughter of the abbey's founder. According to some versions of the legend, St. Hilda, carrying her lamp, showed herself, on particularly stormy nights, in the northern windows of the abbey to guide seamen safe to shore.

A more pragmatic explanation of the apparition in Charleton's *History of Whitby,* cited by *Horne's Guide to Whitby* (p. 14), is that "at a particular time of the year, namely, in the summer months, at ten or eleven in the forenoon, the sunbeams fall in the inside of the northern part of the choir; and 'tis then that the spectators who stand on the west side of the Whitby Churchyard . . . imagine they perceive in one of the highest windows there the resemblance of a woman, arrayed in a shroud . . . constantly believed among the vulgar, to be an appearance of Lady Hilda, in her shroud, or rather her glorified state."

7 *Kettleness.* Kettleness is the name given to the village in the rocky headlands to the north of Whitby. The cliff at Kettleness, which Lucy and Mina could see from the "suicide's seat," is 375 feet high. In 1829 the entire village of Kettleness slid slowly toward the sea, but no lives were lost.

8 *bells are heard out at sea.* There is a legend in Whitby about bells at sea. The story is that the bells of Whitby Abbey made such lovely sounds that they "excited the cupidity of some searoving free-booter" who stole them, but before he could get very far, his ship struck a rock and foundered. Since then, it is said, anyone who dares to sit on that rock and say his sweetheart's name will hear the ringing of the sunken bells.

9 *funny old man.* Two pages later, we are given his name—Mr. Swales. There is a Swales River that runs through Yorkshire, joining the Ure at Boroughbridge above York.

In 1897 there was a Granby Hotel on the West Cliff whose proprietor was a George Swales. Stoker's old pensioner is no hotelkeeper, but it seems likely that Stoker borrowed a highly visible name for his fiction.

10 *Waterloo.* The Waterloo Campaign—February 27, 1815, through July 14, 1815. The campaign ended in Wellington's defeat of Napoleon who abdicated the following week.

Since the action of the book is certainly after 1893 and Mr. Swales is said to be nearly a hundred years old, he would have been at least a twenty-two-year-old sailor at the time of Waterloo.

11 *fash masel'.* Wouldn't trouble myself.

12 *feet-folks.* Tourists.

13 *Leeds.* A city in the West Riding of Yorkshire; center of an industrial district and an important transportation junction. (See map, p. 337.)

14 *cheap jet.* "The name of Whitby," says the fifth edition of *Horne's Guide to Whitby,* is throughout the civilized world associated with jet and its manufacture, but there is considerable difficulty in explaining the origin of this substance. It was formerly thought to be entirely of vegetable origin, and somewhat of the nature of coal or lignite, but it is more probably bitumen, which has collected in a fluid condition."

One reason for the former prosperity of the jet industry at Whitby is that it was introduced to the Court of Queen Victoria on the occasion of a period of Court mourning. The *Guide* does not mention whose death it was that made the mourning necessary, but evidently it augured well for the black beads of Whitby.

15 *whale-fishing in the old days. Horne's Guide to Whitby* (fifth edition, 1897) reports proudly that in the years 1767 to 1816 Whitby vessels brought home "2,761 whales; besides about 25,000 seals, 55 bears, 43 unicorns, and 64 sea-horses." In 1971, when I visited Whitby, there was no trace of this picturesque catch, though I would have given much for a glimpse of the unicorns and sea horses.

16 *"I must gang ageeanwards home . . . sairly by the clock."* A translation of this paragraph follows: "I must go home again now, miss. My granddaughter doesn't like to be kept waiting when the tea is ready, for it takes me time to hobble about the grass, for there be many of them; and, miss, I'm very hungry according to the clock."

17 *how many.* In 1971, when I counted them, there were 199.

18 *Sir Oracle.* "Sir Oracle" appears in Shakespeare's *Merchant of Venice*, Act I, Scene I, lines 93–94. The lines are from Gratiano's "let me play the fool" speech. Gratiano, talking to Bassanio, says:

> "There are a sort of men whose visages
> Do cream and mantle* like a standing pond,
> And do a wilful stillness entertain,
> With purpose to be dress'd in an opinion
> Of wisdom, gravity, profound conceit;
> As who should say, 'I am Sir Oracle,
> And when I ope my lips let no dog bark!' "

*Cream and mantle—form a scum.

19 *"It be all fool-talk . . ."* A translation of this paragraph follows: "It is all fool's talk, lock, stock, and barrel; that's what it is, and nothing else. These curses and ghosts and apparitions and spirits and bogies and all such things are only fit to set children and dizzy women to wailing. They are nothing but

16 "I must gang ageeanwards home now, miss. My granddaughter doesn't like to be kept waitin' when the tea is ready, for it takes me time to crammle aboon the grees, for there be a many of 'em; an', miss, I lack belly-timber sairly by the clock."

He hobbled away, and I could see him hurrying, as well as he could, down the steps. The steps are a great feature of the place. They lead from the town up to the church; there are
17 hundreds of them—I do not know how many—and they wind up in a delicate curve; the slope is so gentle that a horse could easily walk up and down them. I think they must originally have had something to do with the Abbey. I shall go home too. Lucy went out visiting with her mother, and as they were only duty calls, I did not go. They will be home by this.

1 *August.*—I came up here an hour ago with Lucy, and we had a most interesting talk with my old friend and the two others who always come and join him. He is evidently the
18 Sir Oracle of them, and I should think must have been in his time a most dictatorial person. He will not admit anything, and downfaces everybody. If he can't out-argue them he bullies them, and then takes their silence for agreement with his views. Lucy was looking sweetly pretty in her white lawn frock; she has got a beautiful colour since she has been here. I noticed that the old men did not lose any time in coming up and sitting near her when we sat down. She is so sweet with old people; I think they all fell in love with her on the spot. Even my old man succumbed and did not contradict her, but gave me double share instead. I got him on the subject of the legends, and he went off at once into a sort of sermon. I must try to remember it and put it down:—

19 "It be all fool-talk, lock, stock, and barrel; that's what it be, an' nowt else. These bans an' wafts an' boh-ghosts an' barguests an' bogles an' all anent them is only fit to set bairns an' dizzy women a-belderin'. They be nowt but air-blebs! They, an' all grims an' signs an' warnin's, be all invented by parsons an' illsome beuk-bodies an' railway touters to skeer an' scunner h ffin's, an' to get folks to do somethin' that they don't other incline to. It makes me ireful to think o' them. Why, it's them that, not content with printin' lies on paper an' preachin' them out of pulpits, does want to be cuttin' them on the tombsteans. Look here all around you in what airt ye will; all them steans, holdin' up their heads as well as they can out of their pride, is acant—simply tumblin' down with the weight o' the lies wrote on them, 'Here lies the body' or 'Sacred to the memory' wrote on all of them, an' yet in nigh half of them there bean't no bodies at all; an' the memories of them bean't cared a pinch of snuff about, much less sacred. Lies all of them, nothin' but lies of one kind or another! My gog, but it'll be a quare scowderment at the Day of Judgment when they come tumblin' up here in their deathsarks, all jouped together an' tryin' to drag their tombsteans with them to prove how good they was; some of them trimmlin' and ditherin', with their hands that dozzened an' slippy from lyin' in the sea that they can't even keep their grup o' them."

I could see from the old fellow's self-satisfied air and the way in which he looked round for the approval of his cronies that he was "showing off," so I put in a word to keep him going :—

"Oh, Mr. Swales, you can't be serious. Surely these tombstones are not all wrong?"

"Yabblins! There may be a poorish few not wrong, savin' 20
where they make out the people too good; for there be folk that do think a balm-bowl be like the sea, if only it be their own. The whole thing be only lies. Now look you here; you come here a stranger, an' you see this kirk-garth." I nodded, for I thought it better to assent, though I did not quite understand his dialect. I knew it had something to do with the church. He went on: "And you consate that all these steans be aboon folk that be happed here, snod an' snog?" I assented again. "Then that be just where the lie comes in. Why, there be scores of these lay-beds that be toom as old Dun's 'bacca-box on Friday night." He nudged one of his companions, and they all laughed. "And my gog! how could they be otherwise? Look at that one, the aftest abaft the bier-bank; read it!" I went over and read :—

"Edward Spencelagh, master mariner, murdered by pirates off the coast of Andres, April, 1854, æt. 30." When I came back Mr. Swales went on :—

"Who brought him home, I wonder, to hap him here? Murdered off the coast of Andres! an' you consated his body lay under! Why, I could name ye a dozen whose bones lie in the Greenland seas above"—he pointed northwards—"or where the currents may have drifted them. There be the steans around ye. Ye can, with your young eyes, read the small print of the lies from here. This Braithwaite Lowrey—I knew his father, lost in the *Lively* off Greenland in '20; or Andrew Woodhouse, drowned in the same seas in 1777; or John
Paxton, drowned off Cape Farewell a year later; or old John 21
Rawlings, whose grandfather sailed with me, drowned in the
Gulf of Finland in '50. Do ye think that all these men will 22
have to make a rush to Whitby when the trumpet sounds?
I have me antherums aboot it! I tell ye that when they got 23
here they'd be jommlin' an' jostlin' one another that way that it 'ud be like a fight up on the ice in the old days, when we'd be at one another from daylight to dark, an' tryin' to tie up our cuts by the light of the aurora borealis." This was evidently local pleasantry, for the old man cackled over it, and his cronies joined in with gusto.

"But," I said, "surely you are not quite correct, for you start on the assumption that all the poor people, or their spirits, will have to take their tombstones with them on the Day of Judgment. Do you think that will be really necessary?"

"Well, what else be they tombsteans for? Answer me that, miss!"

"To please their relatives, I suppose."

"To please their relatives, you suppose!" This he said with intense scorn. "How will it pleasure their relatives to know that lies is wrote over them, and that everybody in the place knows that they be lies?" He pointed to a stone at our feet which had been laid down as a slab, on which the seat was

air bubbles! They, and all ghosts and signs and warnings, are invented by parsons and ill-natured pedants and railway touts to scare and disgust young boys, and to get folks to do something that they don't otherwise want to. It makes me angry to think of them. Why, it's they who, not content with printing lies on paper and preaching them out of pulpits, cut them on tombstones. Look here all around you wherever you choose; all those stones, holding up their heads as well as they can out of their pride, leaning to one side—simply tumbling down with the weight of the lies written on them, 'Here lies the body' or 'Sacred to the memory' written on all of them, and yet in nearly half of them there are no bodies at all; and the memories of them aren't cared for so much as a pinch of snuff, much less being [held] sacred. Lies, all of them, nothing but lies of one kind or another! My God, but it'll be a strange turmoil at the Day of Judgment when they come tumbling up here in their death robes, all splashing about and trying to drag their tombstones with them to prove how good they were; some of them trembling and dithering, with their hands so withered and slippery from lying in the sea that they can't even keep their grip on them."

20 "*Yabblins!* . . ." Those passages in Mr. Swales's speech, from here to the middle of page 70, which appear to need it, are translated here:

"It's all chatter! There may be a poor few that are not wrong, except where they make people out to be better than they are; for there are those who think a balm-bowl is like the sea, if it is their own. All of it is lies. You see this churchyard. . . . And you suppose that all these tombstones are above folk who are buried snug and tidy here? . . . Why, there are scores of these graves that are as empty as old Dun's tobacco box on Friday night. . . . Look at that one, the farthest one past that ridge . . .

Who brought him home, I wonder, to bury him here? Murdered off the coast of Andres! and you supposed his body lay under [this stone]!"

21 *Cape Farewell.* The most southerly point of Greenland. (See map, p. 336.)

22 *Gulf of Finland.* An arm of the Baltic Sea, south of Finland. (See map, p. 336.)

23 *I have me antherums.* More translation: "I have my doubts about it! I tell you that when they got here there'd be such jostling and shoving that it would be like a fight on the ice in the old days . . ."

24 *"Ye don't see aught funny! . . ."* The translation is: "You don't see anything funny! Ha! ha! But that's because you don't know that the sorrowing mother was a hell-cat that hated him because he was crippled—a regular lame one he was . . . [The musket] wasn't for crows then, for it brought the crows and flies to him. . . . won't it make Gabriel chuckle when Geordie comes panting up the grass with that tombstone balanced on his hump, and asks that it be taken as evidence!"

25 *getting scart.* Because it will be the Last Judgment.

"THE BAND ON THE PIER IS PLAYING A HARSH WALTZ."

rested, close to the edge of the cliff. "Read the lines on that thruff-stean," he said. The letters were upside down to me from where I sat, but Lucy was more opposite to them, so she leant over and read:—

"Sacred to the memory of George Canon, who died, in the hope of a glorious resurrection, on July 29, 1873, falling from the rocks at Kettleness. This tomb is erected by his sorrowing mother to her dearly beloved son. 'He was the only son of his mother, and she was a widow.'" "Really, Mr. Swales, I don't see anything very funny in that!" She spoke her comment very gravely and somewhat severely.

24 "Ye don't see aught funny! Ha! ha! But that's because ye don't gawm the sorrowin' mother was a hell-cat that hated him because he was acrewk'd—a regular lamiter he was—an' he hated her so that he committed suicide in order that she mightn't get an insurance she put on his life. He blew nigh the top of his head off with an old musket that they had for scarin' the crows with. 'Twarn't for crows then, for it brought the clegs and the dowps to him. That's the way he fell off the rocks. And, as to hopes of a glorious resurrection, I've often heard him say masel' that he hoped he'd go to hell, for his mother was so pious that she'd be sure to go to heaven, an' he didn't wan't to addle where she was. Now isn't that stean at any rate"—he hammered it with his stick as he spoke—"a pack of lies? and won't it make Gabriel keckle when Geordie comes pantin' up the grees with the tombstean balanced on his hump, and asks it to be took as evidence!"

I did not know what to say, but Lucy turned the conversation as she said, rising up:—

"Oh, why did you tell us of this? It is my favourite seat, and I cannot leave it; and now I find I must go on sitting over the grave of a suicide."

"That won't harm ye, my pretty; an' it may make poor Geordie gladsome to have so trim a lass sittin' on his lap. That won't hurt ye. Why, I've sat here off an' on for nigh twenty years past, an' it hasn't done me no harm. Don't ye fash about them as lies under ye, or that doesn' lie there
25 either! It'll be time for ye to be getting scart when ye see the tombsteans all run away with, and the place as bare as a stubble-field. There's the clock, an' I must gang. My service to ye, ladies!" And off he hobbled.

Lucy and I sat a while, and it was all so beautiful before us that we took hands as we sat; and she told me all over again about Arthur and their coming marriage. That made me just a little heart-sick, for I haven't heard from Jonathan for a whole month.

The same day.—I came up here alone, for I am very sad. There was no letter for me. I hope there cannot be anything the matter with Jonathan. The clock has just struck nine. I see the lights scattered all over the town, sometimes in rows where the streets are, and sometimes singly; they run right up the Esk and die away in the curve of the valley. To my left the view is cut off by a black line of roof of the old house next the Abbey. The sheep and lambs are bleating in the fields away behind me, and there is a clatter of a donkey's hoofs up the paved road below. The band on the pier is

playing a harsh waltz in good time, and further along the quay there is a Salvation Army meeting in a back street. Neither of the bands hears the other, but up here I hear and see them both. I wonder where Jonathan is and if he is thinking of me! I wish he were here.

Dr. Seward's Diary.

5 *June.*—The case of Renfield grows more interesting the more I get to understand the man. He has certain qualities very largely developed: selfishness, secrecy, and purpose. I wish I could get at what is the object of the latter. He seems to have some settled scheme of his own, but what it is I do not yet know. His redeeming quality is a love of animals, though, indeed, he has such curious turns in it that I sometimes imagine he is only abnormally cruel. His pets are of odd sorts. Just now his hobby is catching flies. He has at present such a quantity that I have had myself to expostulate. To my astonishment, he did not break out into a fury, as I expected, but took the matter in simple seriousness. He thought for a moment, and then said: "May I have three days? I shall clear them away." Of course, I said that would do. I must watch him.

18 *June.*—He has turned his mind now to spiders, and has got several very big fellows in a box. He keeps feeding them with his flies, and the number of the latter is becoming sensibly diminished, although he has used half his food in attracting more flies from outside to his room.

1 *July.*—His spiders are now becoming as great a nuisance as his flies, and to-day I told him that he must get rid of them. He looked very sad at this, so I said that he must clear out some of them, at all events. He cheerfully acquiesced in this, and I gave him the same time as before for reduction. He disgusted me much while with him, for when a horrid blow-fly, bloated with some carrion food, buzzed into the room, he caught it, held it exultingly for a few moments between his finger and thumb, and, before I knew what he was going to do, put it in his mouth and ate it. I scolded him for it, but he argued quietly that it was very good and very wholesome; that it was life, strong life, and gave life to him. This gave me an idea, or the rudiment of one. I must watch how he gets rid of his spiders. He has evidently some deep problem in his mind, for he keeps a little note-book in **26**
which he is always jotting down something. Whole pages of it are filled with masses of figures, generally single numbers added up in batches, and then the totals added in batches again, as though he were "focussing" some account, as the auditors put it.

8 *July.*—There is a method in his madness, and the rudimentary idea in my mind is growing. It will be a whole idea
soon, and then, oh, unconscious cerebration! you will have **27**
to give the wall to your conscious brother. I kept away from **28**
my friend for a few days, so that I might notice if there were any change. Things remain as they were except that he has parted with some of his pets and got a new one. He has managed to get a sparrow, and has already partially tamed

26 *he keeps a little note-book in which he is always jotting.* Along with everyone else in the book!

27 *unconscious cerebration!* Henry James is perhaps the most famous user of this phrase, and is sometimes credited with inventing it. In a passage of his Preface to *The American* (p. 9), James, discussing the progress of his idea for that novel, says that at one point he "must have dropped it for the time into the deep well of unconscious cerebration . . ."

The term was first introduced by W. C. Engledue, a physician-phrenologist, in 1842, though the principles implied by it were being developed earlier by Dr. Thomas Laycock (1812–1876) and William Benjamin Carpenter (1813–1885) working independently. Laycock's 1840 work, which helped prepare the way for Freud's discovery of the unconscious was, curiously enough, *A Treatise on the Nervous Diseases of Women.*

For Henry James the term "unconscious cerebration" has a somewhat wider meaning than that given to it by nineteenth-century physician-physiologists for whom it denoted the unconscious processes of "mentation." James, the novelist, it seems to me, links the concept to the creative imagination.

28 *give the wall to.* Defer to. The expression derives from the bad old days when pedestrians who did not walk close to the wall were in danger from debris that was tossed into the streets from the upper stories of houses.

Gentlemen "gave the wall to" ladies as a matter of course, but men often contended for it as a sign of their prestige or masculinity.

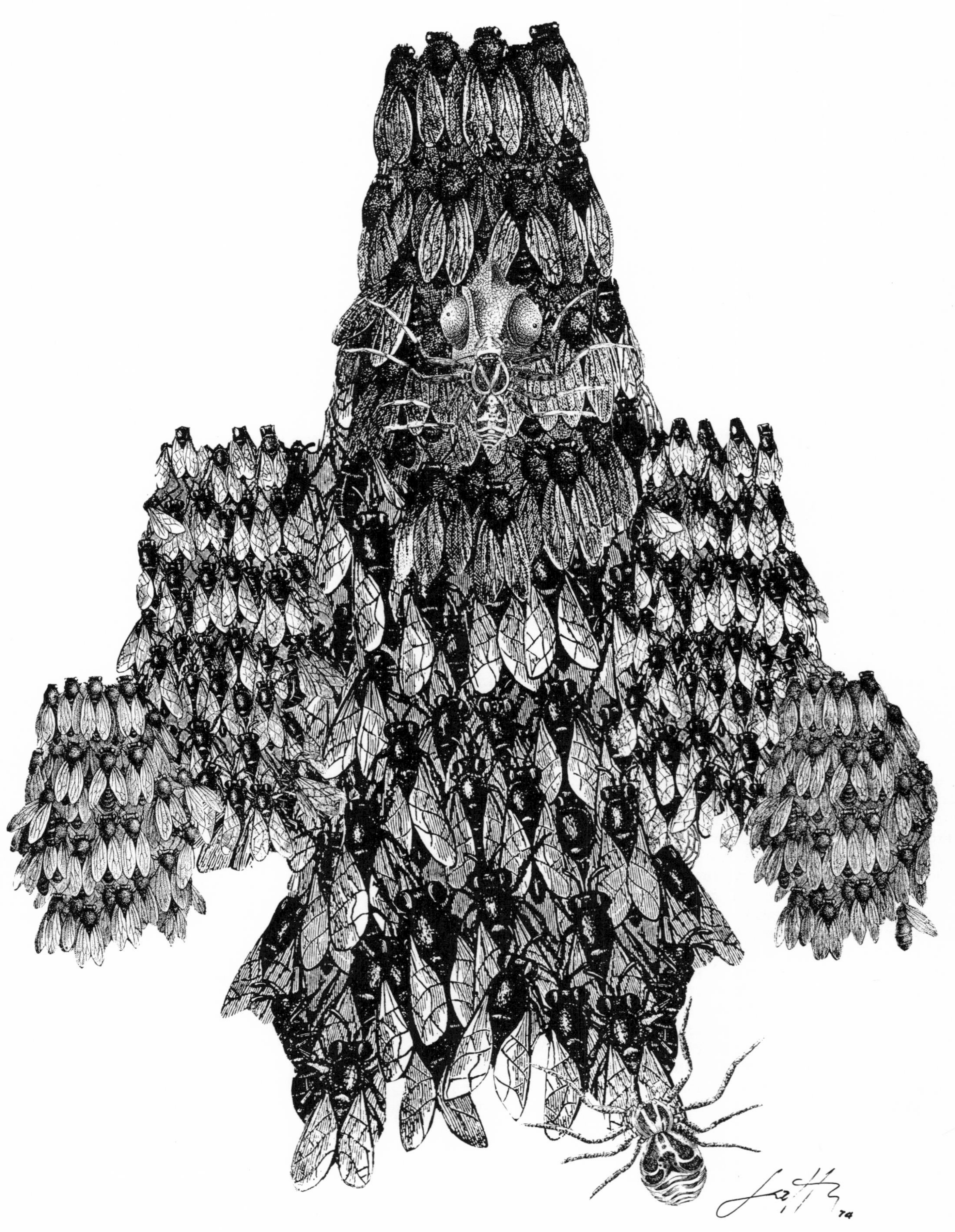

it. His means of taming is simple, for already the spiders have diminished. Those that do remain, however, are well fed, for he still brings in the flies by tempting them with his food.

19 *July.*—We are progressing. My friend has now a whole 29
colony of sparrows, and his flies and spiders are almost obliterated. When I came in he ran to me and said he wanted to ask me a great favour—a very, very great favour; and as he spoke he fawned on me like a dog. I asked him what it was, and he said, with a sort of rapture in his voice and bearing:—

"A kitten, a nice little, sleek, playful kitten, that I can play with, and teach, and feed—and feed—and feed!" I was not unprepared for this request, for I had noticed how his pets went on increasing in size and vivacity, but I did not care that his pretty family of tame sparrows should be wiped out in the same manner as the flies and the spiders; so I said I would see about it, and asked him if he would not rather have a cat than a kitten. His eagerness betrayed him as he answered:

"Oh yes, I would like a cat! I only asked for a kitten 30
lest you should refuse me a cat. No one would refuse me a kitten, would they?" I shook my head, and said that at present I feared it would not be possible, but that I would see about it. His face fell, and I could see a warning of danger in it, for there was a sudden fierce, sidelong look which meant killing. The man is an undeveloped homicidal maniac. I shall test him with his present craving and see how it will work out; then I shall know more.

10 *p.m.*—I have visited him again and found him sitting in a corner brooding. When I came in he threw himself on his knees before me and implored me to let him have a cat; that his salvation depended upon it. I was firm, however, and told him that he could not have it, whereupon he went without a word, and sat down, gnawing his fingers, in the corner where I had found him. I shall see him in the morning early.

20 *July.*—Visited Renfield very early, before the attendant went his rounds. Found him up and humming a tune. He was spreading out his sugar, which he had saved, in the window, and was manifestly beginning his fly-catching again; and beginning it cheerfully and with a good grace. I looked around for his birds, and not seeing them, asked him where they were. He replied, without turning round, that they had all flown away. There were a few feathers about the room and on his pillow a drop of blood. I said nothing, but went and told the keeper to report to me if there were anything odd about him during the day.

11 *a.m.*—The attendant has just been to me to say that Renfield has been very sick and has disgorged a whole lot of feathers. "My belief is, doctor," he said, "that he has eaten his birds, and that he just took and ate them raw!"

11 *p.m.*—I gave Renfield a strong opiate to-night, enough to make even him sleep, and took away his pocket-book to look at it. The thought that has been buzzing about my brain lately is complete, and the theory proved. My homicidal maniac is of a peculiar kind. I shall have to invent a

"RENFIELD . . . HAS TURNED HIS MIND NOW TO SPIDERS, HE KEEPS FEEDING THEM WITH HIS FLIES."

29 *We are progressing.* The progress is from lesser to greater creatures in a typical biological food chain, or food pyramid.

There is also the children's song:

"There was an old lady
Who swallowed a fly
I don't know why
She swallowed a fly,
I guess she'll die."

In the song it will be remembered, the progress is from the fly to:

"There was an old lady
Who swallowed a horse
She died
Of course!"

30 *for a kitten.* In the first of the Count Yorga films (1970), a young female vampire is actually shown drinking the blood of a kitten.

new classification for him, and call him a zoophagous (life-eating) maniac; what he desires is to absorb as many lives as he can, and he has laid himself out to achieve it in a cumulative way. He gave many flies to one spider and many spiders to one bird, and then wanted a cat to eat the many birds. What would have been his later steps? It would almost be worth while to complete the experiment. It might be done if there were only a sufficient cause. Men sneered at vivisection, and yet look at its results to-day! Why not advance science in its most difficult and vital aspect—the knowledge of the brain? Had I even the secret of one such mind—did I hold the key to the fancy of even one
lunatic—I might advance my own branch of science to a pitch
31 compared with which Burdon-Sanderson's physiology or
32 Ferrier's brain-knowledge would be as nothing. If only
there were a sufficient cause! I must not think too much of
this, or I may be tempted; a good cause might turn the scale
33 with me, for may not I too be of an exceptional brain, con-
genitally?

How well the man reasoned; lunatics always do within their own scope. I wonder at how many lives he values a man, or if at only one. He has closed the account most accurately, and to-day begun a new record. How many of us begin a new record with each day of our lives?

To me it seems only yesterday that my whole life ended with my new hope, and that truly I began a new record. So it will be until the Great Recorder sums me up and closes my ledger account with a balance to profit or loss. Oh, Lucy, Lucy, I cannot be angry with you, nor can I be angry with my friend whose happiness is yours; but I must only wait on hopeless and work. Work! work!

If I only could have as strong a cause as my poor mad friend there, a good, unselfish cause to make me work, that would be indeed happiness.

Mina Murray's Journal.

26 July.—I am anxious, and it soothes me to express myself here; it is like whispering to one's self and listening at the same time. And there is also something about the shorthand symbols that makes it different from writing. I am unhappy about Lucy and about Jonathan. I had not heard from Jonathan
for some time, and was very concerned; but yesterday dear
34 Mr. Hawkins, who is always so kind, sent me a letter from
him. I had written asking him if he had heard, and he
said the enclosed had just been received. It is only a line
dated from Castle Dracula, and says that he is just starting
for home. That is not like Jonathan; I do not understand
it, and it makes me uneasy. Then, too, Lucy, although she
35 is so well, has lately taken to her old habit of walking in her
sleep. Her mother has spoken to me about it, and we have decided that I am to lock the door of our room every night. Mrs. Westenra has got an idea that sleep-walkers always go out on roofs of houses and along the edges of cliffs, and then get suddenly wakened and fall over with a despairing cry that echoes all over the place. Poor dear, she is naturally anxious about Lucy, and she tells me that her husband, Lucy's father,

31 *Burdon-Sanderson's physiology*. Burdon-Sanderson (1828–1905) is the physiologist who, with J. R. Page, first measured the electrical impulses that emanate from the heart.

32 *Ferrier's brain-knowledge*. James Frederick Ferrier (1808–1864) was a Scottish metaphysician whose theory of knowledge assumed a unity between the knowing subject and the object known.

33 *of an exceptional brain*. There is a Nietzschean quality to Seward's speculations here that contributes to our sense of the murkiness of Seward's mind.

34 *letter from him*. This is one of those letters Harker wrote under duress, probably the one Dracula instructed him to date June 19 (see May 19 entry, chapter IV).

35 *walking in her sleep*. Lucy's sleepwalking has fascinating implications. Is she merely in the grip of a hypnotic trance imposed on her at a distance by Dracula or does it reflect something in her, something symptomatic? The fact that Lucy's father had the same habit suggests that there is more to Lucy and her family than meets the eye.

Writers on hypnotic states (which are defined as modes of somnambulism) recognize that the experience of the hypnotic is a form of hysteria. Robert Fliess writes that the hypnotic trance may be a form of evasion. In his *Ego and Body-Ego* (p. 7), he tells us "this often occurs when aggression is the object of evasion and the patient may be with the subject or the object of that aggression, or more frequently, hypnotic evasion evades an erogenic [sexual or infantile sexual] process, and the feeling [affect or impulse] that it might engender if it had been allowed to occur."

Jack R. Strange, in his *Abnormal Psychology* (pp. 174–75), remarks that "the typical hysterical personality is marked by immaturity, high suggestibility to suggestion, and in general a self-centered outlook on life."

had the same habit; that he would get up in the night and dress himself and go out, if he were not stopped. Lucy is to be married in the autumn, and she is already planning out her dresses and how her house is to be arranged. I sympathise with her, for I do the same, only Jonathan and I will start in life in a very simple way, and shall have to try to make both ends meet. Mr. Holmwood—he is the Hon. Arthur Holmwood, only son of Lord Godalming—is coming up here very shortly—as soon as he can leave town, for his father is not very well, and I think dear Lucy is counting the moments till he comes. She wants to take him up to the seat on the churchyard cliff and show him the beauty of Whitby. I daresay it is the waiting which disturbs her; she will be all right when he arrives.

27 *July*.—No news from Jonathan. I am getting quite uneasy about him, though why I should I do not know; but I *do* wish that he would write if it were only a single line. Lucy walks more than ever, and each night I am awakened by her moving about the room. Fortunately, the weather is so hot that she cannot get cold; but still the anxiety and the perpetually being wakened is beginning to tell on me, and I am getting nervous and wakeful myself. Thank God, Lucy's health keeps up. Mr. Holmwood has been suddenly called to Ring to see his father, who has been taken **36**
seriously ill. Lucy frets at the postponement of seeing him, but it does not touch her looks; she is a trifle stouter, and her cheeks are a lovely rose pink. She has lost that anæmic look which she had. I pray it will all last.

3 *August*.—Another week gone, and no news from Jonathan, not even to Mr. Hawkins, from whom I have heard. Oh, I do hope he is not ill. He surely would have written. I look at that last letter of his, but somehow it does not satisfy me. It does not read like him, and yet it is his writing. There is no mistake of that. Lucy has not walked much in her sleep the last week, but there is an odd concentration **37**
about her which I do not understand; even in her sleep she seems to be watching me. She tries the door, and finding it locked, goes about the room searching for the key.

6 *August*.—Another three days, and no news. This suspense is getting dreadful. If I only knew where to write to or where to go to, I should feel easier; but no one has heard a word of Jonathan since that last letter. I must only pray to God for patience. Lucy is more excitable than ever, but is otherwise well. Last night was very threatening, and the fishermen say that we are in for a storm. I must try to watch it and learn the weather signs. To-day is a grey day, and the sun as I write is hidden in thick clouds, high over Kettleness. Everything is grey—except the green grass, which seems like emerald amongst it; grey earthy rock; grey clouds, tinged with the sunburst at the far edge, hang over the grey sea, into which the sand-points stretch like grey fingers. The sea is tumbling in over the shallows and the sandy flats with a roar, muffled in the sea-mists drifting inland. The horizon is lost in a grey mist. All is vastness; the clouds are piled up like giant rocks, and there is a "brool" over the sea that sounds **38**
like some presage of doom. Dark figures are on the beach here and there, sometimes half shrouded in the mist, and seem "men like trees walking." The fishing-boats are **39**

36 *called to Ring.* Ring is the Holmwood family home.

37 *but there is an odd concentration about her.* What means this behavior? (See note 35 of this chapter on sleepwalking.)

38 *"brool."* A brool, according to the *Oxford English Dictionary*, is "a low deep humming sound; a murmur."

39 *"men like trees walking."* The phrase is not, as at first it seemed to be, a distorted line from Shakespeare's *Macbeth* where Birnam Wood, as we remember, comes to Dunsinane—much to Macbeth's confusion.

Stoker is quoting from Mark, Chapter 8, where we read that when Christ came to Bethsaida, they brought "a blind man unto him, and besought him to touch him. And he took the blind man by the hand, and led him out of the town; and when he had spit on his eyes, and put his hands upon him, he asked him if he saw aught. And he looked up, and said, I see men as trees, walking. After that he put *his* hands again upon his eyes, and made him look up; and he was restored, and saw every man clearly" (Mark 8:22–25).

Mina, quoting the Gospel at this moment, serves to remind us that soon Stoker's fiction will move more pronouncedly in the direction of Christian allegory.

40 *We aud folks.* A translation of Mr. Swales's more difficult passages follows: "We old folk that have grown stupid, and have one foot above the grave, don't altogether like to think of it. . . . I'm so near it that the Old Man is already whetting his scythe. You see, I can't get out of the habit of complaining about it all at once; jaws will wag as they are used to. Some day soon the Angel of Death will sound his trumpet for me. But don't you grieve and lament, my deary!"

racing for home, and rise and dip in the ground swell as they sweep into the harbour, bending to the scuppers. Here comes old Mr. Swales. He is making straight for me, and I can see, by the way he lifts his hat, that he wants to talk. . . . .

I have been quite touched by the change in the poor old man. When he sat down beside me, he said in a very gentle way:—

"I want to say something to you, miss." I could see he was not at ease, so I took his poor old wrinkled hand in mine and asked him to speak fully; so he said, leaving his hand in mine:—

"I'm afraid, my deary, that I must have shocked you by all the wicked things I've been sayin' about the dead, and such-like, for weeks past; but I didn't mean them, and I
40 want ye to remember that when I'm gone. We aud folks that be daffled, and with one foot abaft the krok-hooal, don't altogether like to think of it, and we don't want to feel scart of it; an' that's why I've took to makin' light of it, so that I'd cheer up my own heart a bit. But, Lord love ye, miss, I ain't afraid of dyin', not a bit; only I don't want to die if I can help it. My time must be nigh at hand now, for I be aud, and a hundred years is too much for any man to expect; and I'm so nigh it that the Aud Man is already whettin' his scythe. Ye see, I can't get out o' the habit of caffin' about it all at once; the chafts will wag as they be used to. Some day soon the Angel of Death will sound his trumpet for me. But don't ye dooal an' greet, my deary!"—for he saw that I was crying—"if he should come this very night I'd not refuse to answer his call. For life be, after all, only a waitin' for somethin' else than what we're doin'; and death be all that we can rightly depend on. But I'm content, for it's comin' to me, my deary, and comin' quick. It may be comin' while we be lookin' and wonderin'. Maybe it's in that wind out over the sea that's bringin' with it loss and wreck, and sore distress, and sad hearts. Look! look!" he cried suddenly. "There's something in that wind and in the hoast beyont that sounds, and looks, and tastes, and smells like death. It's in the air; I feel it comin'. Lord, make me answer cheerful when my call comes!" He held up his arms devoutly, and raised his hat. His mouth moved as though he were praying. After a few minutes' silence, he got up, shook hands with me, and blessed me, and said good-bye, and hobbled off. It all touched me, and upset me very much.

I was glad when the coastguard came along, with his spy-glass under his arm. He stopped to talk with me, as he always does, but all the time kept looking at a strange ship.

"I can't make her out," he said; "she's a Russian, by the look of her; but she's knocking about in the queerest way. She doesn't know her mind a bit; she seems to see the storm coming, but can't decide whether to run up north in the open, or to put in here. Look there again! She is steered mighty strangely, for she doesn't mind the hand on the wheel; changes about with every puff of wind. We'll hear more of her before this time to-morrow."

"SHE'S A RUSSIAN, BY THE LOOK OF HER; BUT SHE'S KNOCKING ABOUT IN THE QUEEREST WAY."

RIG MILL, 1897.

1 *Mulgrave Woods, Robin Hood's Bay, Rig Mill, Runswick, Staithes.* Mulgrave Woods, near Mulgrave Castle, in the environs of Whitby, are described by *Horne's Guide to Whitby* in lyric fashion: "For the artist, no lovelier bits of sylvan scenery can be found anywhere than among its secluded lawns, its rippling rivulets passing beneath spreading trees and its countless charms of grotto, glen and garnished hillsides . . ." The *Guide* adds the cheering note that "no cars are allowed in the woods" (pp. 117–18).

Robin Hood's Bay is still a very charming village some three miles south and east of Whitby. The place acquired its name, the story goes, because Robin Hood, looking for a place in the neighborhood where he might build a seaside home, shot an arrow into the air and let its fall decide the place where he would build. The arrow embedded itself in the cliff overlooking Robin Hood's Bay.

Rig Mill is a picturesque walk in the vicinity of Whitby. Runswick is a notable fishing resort about six miles north of Whitby on the coast.

Staithes, a fishing village some eight miles north and west of Whitby, is most famous, perhaps, for the fact that the great explorer Captain Cook spent some of his boyhood years here serving as an apprentice to a shopkeeper who sold both draperies *and* groceries. In 1740 the street in which the shop stood was washed away in a storm. (See map, p. 338.)

CHAPTER VII.

CUTTING FROM "THE DAILYGRAPH," 8 AUGUST.

(*Pasted in Mina Murray's Journal.*)

From a Correspondent.

Whitby.

ONE of the greatest and suddenest storms on record has just been experienced here, with results both strange and unique. The weather had been somewhat sultry, but not to any degree uncommon in the month of August. Saturday evening was as fine as was ever known, and the great body of
1 holiday-makers laid out yesterday for visits to Mulgrave Woods, Robin Hood's Bay, Rig Mill, Runswick, Staithes, and the various trips in the neighbourhood of Whitby. The steamers *Emma* and *Scarborough* made trips up and down the coast, and there was an unusual amount of "tripping" both to and from Whitby. The day was unusually fine till the afternoon, when some of the gossips who frequent the East Cliff churchyard, and from that commanding eminence watch the wide sweep of sea visible to the north and east, called
2 attention to a sudden show of "mares'-tails" high in the sky to the north-west. The wind was then blowing from the south-west in the mild degree which in barometrical language is ranked "No. 2: light breeze." The coastguard on duty at once made report, and one old fisherman, who for more than half a century has kept watch on weather signs from the East Cliff, foretold in an emphatic manner the coming of a sudden storm. The approach of sunset was so very beautiful, so grand in its masses of splendidly-coloured clouds, that there was quite an assemblage on the walk along the cliff in the old churchyard to enjoy the beauty. Before the sun dipped below the black mass of Kettleness, standing boldly athwart the western sky, its downward way was marked by myriad clouds of every sunset-colour—flame, purple, pink, green, violet, and all the tints of gold; with here and there masses not large, but of seemingly absolute blackness, in all sorts of shapes, as well outlined as colossal silhouettes. The experience was not lost on the painters, and doubtless some of the sketches of the "Prelude to the Great Storm" will

grace the R.A. and R.I. walls in May next. More than one 3
captain made up his mind then and there that his "cobble" or his "mule," as they term the different classes of boats, would remain in the harbour till the storm had passed. The wind fell away entirely during the evening, and at midnight there was a dead calm, a sultry heat, and that prevailing intensity which, on the approach of thunder, affects persons of a sensitive nature. There were but few lights in sight at sea, for even the coasting steamers, which usually "hug" the shore so closely, kept well to seaward, and but few fishing-boats were in sight. The only sail noticeable was a foreign schooner with all sails set, which was seemingly going westwards. The foolhardiness or ignorance of her officers was a prolific theme for comment whilst she remained in sight, and efforts were made to signal her to reduce sail in face of her danger. Before the night shut down she was seen with sails idly flapping as she gently rolled on the undulating swell of the sea,

"As idle as a painted ship upon a painted ocean." 4

Shortly before ten o'clock the stillness of the air grew quite oppressive, and the silence was so marked that the bleating of a sheep inland or the barking of a dog in the town was distinctly heard, and the band on the pier, with its lively French air, was like a discord in the great harmony of nature's silence. A little after midnight came a strange sound from over the sea, and high overhead the air began to carry a strange, faint, hollow booming.

Then without warning the tempest broke. With a rapidity which, at the time, seemed incredible, and even afterwards is impossible to realise, the whole aspect of nature at once became convulsed. The waves rose in growing fury, each overtopping its fellow, till in a very few minutes the lately glassy sea was like a roaring and devouring monster. White-crested waves beat madly on the level sands and rushed up the shelving cliffs; others broke over the piers, and with their spume swept the lanthorns of the lighthouses which rise from the end of either pier of Whitby Harbour. The wind roared like thunder, and blew with such force that it was with difficulty that even strong men kept their feet, or clung with grim clasp to the iron stanchions. It was found necessary to clear the entire piers from the mass of onlookers, or else the fatalities of the night would have been increased manifold. To add to the difficulties and dangers of the time, masses of sea-fog came drifting inland—white, wet clouds, which swept by in ghostly fashion, so dank and damp and cold that it needed but little effort of imagination to think that the spirits of those lost at sea were touching their living brethren with the clammy hands of death, and many a one shuddered as the wreaths of sea-mist swept by. At times the mist cleared, and the sea for some distance could be seen in the glare of the lightning, which now came thick and fast, followed by such sudden peals of thunder that the whole sky overhead seemed trembling under the shock of the footsteps of the storm. Some of the scenes thus revealed were of immeasurable grandeur and of absorbing interest—the sea, running

2 *mares'-tails.* The *Oxford English Dictionary* says that "mares' tails" are "long straight streaks of cirrus [clouds], supposed to foretoken stormy weather."

3 *R.A. and R.I.* Royal Academy and Royal Institute.

4 *"As idle as a painted ship upon a painted ocean."* These lines are from Coleridge's *The Rime of the Ancient Mariner:*

> "Day after day, day after day,
> We stuck, nor breath nor motion;
> As idle as a painted ship
> Upon a painted ocean."
> (Part II, lines 115–18)

It is well to keep Coleridge's poem in mind in reading *Dracula* since it will be seen that the vampire's bite turns Lucy into a version of the Specter-Woman, Life-in-Death, who in Coleridge's poem is described as:

> "Her lips were red, her looks were free,
> Her locks were yellow as gold:
> Her skin was as white as leprosy,
> The Nightmare Life-in-Death was she,
> Who thicks man's blood with cold."
> (Part III, lines 190–94)

5 mirabile dictu. Marvelous to relate.

6 *Tate Hill Pier*. There are two piers projecting into Whitby Harbor: the West Pier and the East Pier. East Pier, as Stoker writes, is known locally as Tate Hill Pier. The piers were a long time building. They are first mentioned in public documents in the reign of Henry VIII, and have been rebuilt at intervals since. (See map, p. 337.)

mountains high, threw skywards with each wave mighty masses of white foam, which the tempest seemed to snatch at and whirl away into space; here and there a fishing-boat, with a rag of sail, running madly for shelter before the blast; now and again the white wings of a storm-tossed sea-bird. On the summit of the East Cliff the new searchlight was ready for experiment, but had not yet been tried. The officers in charge of it got it into working order, and in the pauses of the inrushing mist swept with it the surface of the sea. Once or twice its service was most effective, as when a fishing-boat, with gunwale under water, rushed into the harbour, able, by the guidance of the sheltering light, to avoid the danger of dashing against the piers. As each boat achieved the safety of the port there was a shout of joy from the mass of people on shore, a shout which for a moment seemed to cleave the gale and was then swept away in its rush. Before long the searchlight discovered some distance away a schooner with all sails set, apparently the same vessel which had been noticed earlier in the evening. The wind had by this time backed to the east, and there was a shudder amongst the watchers on the cliff as they realised the terrible danger in which she now was. Between her and the port lay the great flat reef on which so many good ships have from time to time suffered, and, with the wind blowing from its present quarter, it would be quite impossible that she should fetch the entrance of the harbour. It was now nearly the hour of high tide, but the waves were so great that in their troughs the shallows of the shore were almost visible, and the schooner, with all sails set, was rushing with such speed that, in the words of one old salt, "she must fetch up somewhere, if it was only in hell." Then came another rush of sea-fog, greater than any hitherto—a mass of dank mist, which seemed to close on all things like a grey pall, and left available to men only the organ of hearing, for the roar of the tempest, and the crash of the thunder, and the booming of the mighty billows came through the damp oblivion even louder than before. The rays of the searchlight were kept fixed on the harbour mouth across the East Pier, where the shock was expected, and men waited breathless. The wind suddenly shifted to the north-east, and the remnant of the sea-fog melted in the blast; and
5 then, *mirabile dictu*, between the piers, leaping from wave to wave as it rushed at headlong speed, swept the strange schooner before the blast, with all sail set, and gained the safety of the harbour. The searchlight followed her, and a shudder ran through all who saw her, for lashed to the helm was a corpse, with drooping head, which swung horribly to and fro at each motion of the ship. No other form could be seen on deck at all. A great awe came on all as they realised that the ship, as if by a miracle, had found the harbour, unsteered save by the hand of a dead man! However, all took place more quickly than it takes to write these words. The schooner paused not, but rushing across the harbour, pitched herself on that accumulation of sand and gravel washed by many tides and many storms into the south-east corner of the pier jutting under the East Cliff,
6 known locally as Tate Hill Pier.

"PITCHED HERSELF ON THAT ACCUMULATION OF SAND AND GRAVEL."

rights of the owner are already completely sacrificed, his
property being held in contravention of the statutes of mort- 7
main, since the tiller, as emblemship, if not proof, of dele-
gated possession, is held in a *dead hand.* It is needless to
say that the dead steersman has been reverently removed
from the place where he held his honourable watch and
ward till death—a steadfastness as noble as that of the
young Casabianca—and placed in the mortuary to await inquest. 8

Already the sudden storm is passing, and its fierceness
is abating; the crowds are scattering homeward, and the
sky is beginning to redden over the Yorkshire wolds. I 9
shall send, in time for your next issue, further details of the
derelict ship which found her way so miraculously into harbour
in the storm.

Whitby.

9 *August.*—The sequel to the strange arrival of the
derelict in the storm last night is almost more startling
than the thing itself. It turns out that the schooner is a
Russian from Varna, and is called the *Demeter.* She is 10
almost entirely in ballast of silver sand, with only a small 11
amount of cargo—a number of great wooden boxes filled
with mould. This cargo was consigned to a Whitby solicitor,
Mr. S. F. Billington, of 7, The Crescent, who this morning
went aboard and formally took possession of the goods consigned to him. The Russian consul, too, acting for the
charter-party, took formal possession of the ship, and paid
all harbour dues, etc. Nothing is talked about here to-day
except the strange coincidence; the officials of the Board 12
of Trade have been most exacting in seeing that every com-
pliance has been made with existing regulations. As the
matter is to be a "nine days' wonder," they are evidently
determined that there shall be no cause of after complaint.
A good deal of interest was abroad concerning the dog which
landed when the ship struck, and more than a few of the
members of the S.P.C.A., which is very strong in Whitby, have
tried to befriend the animal. To the general disappointment,
however, it was not to be found; it seems to have disappeared entirely from the town. It may be that it was
frightened and made its way on to the moors, where it is
still hiding in terror. There are some who look with dread
on such a possibility, lest later on it should in itself become a
danger, for it is evidently a fierce brute. Early this morning
a large dog, a half-bred mastiff belonging to a coal merchant
close to Tate Hill Pier, was found dead in the roadway opposite its master's yard. It had been fighting, and manifestly
had had a savage opponent, for its throat was torn away, and
its belly was slit open as if with a savage claw.

Later.—By the kindness of the Board of Trade inspector, I
have been permitted to look over the log-book of the *Demeter,*
which was in order up to within three days, but contained
nothing of special interest except as to facts of missing men.
The greater interest, however, is with regard to the paper
found in the bottle, which was to-day produced at the
inquest; and a more strange narrative than the two between
them unfold it has not been my lot to come across. As
there is no motive for concealment, I am permitted to use

7 *mortmain. Black's Law Dictionary* tells us that mortmain is "a term applied to denote the alienation of lands or tenements to any corporation, sole or aggregate, ecclesiastical or temporal. These purchases having been chiefly made by religious houses, in consequence of which lands became perpetually inherent in one dead hand, this has occasioned the general appellation of 'mortmain' to be applied to such alienations."

8 *young Casabianca.* This is the young boy of Felicia Hemans's famous poem (1827), which begins "The boy stood on the burning deck." And although the dead steersman is pathetic enough, the thirteen-year-old boy of the poem, who perished, wrapped in flames, because he would not abandon his post without his father's express command, is still able to make some hearts quicken. As the flames leaped around him, the boy, not knowing his father was dead, cried:

" 'My father! must I stay?'
While o'er him, fast, through sail and shroud,
The wreathing fires made way."

Until, finally,

"They wrapped the ship in splendor wild,
They caught the flag on high,
And streamed above the gallant child,
Like banners in the sky.

"There came a burst of thunder sound;
The boy—oh! where was he?
Ask of the winds, that far around
With fragments strewed the sea,—

"With mast, and helm, and pennon fair,
That well had borne their part,—
But the noblest thing that perished there,
Was that young, faithful heart."

9 *wolds. The American College Dictionary* defines wold as "an open, elevated tract of country; especially applied (in plural) to districts in parts of England (as Yorkshire and Lincolnshire) resembling the downs of the southern counties."

10 *the* Demeter. Demeter was the mother of Persephone who was ravished from the face of the earth by Hades, the ruler of the underworld. Persephone was permitted to return to her mother one third of each year "when the earth shall bloom with the fragrant flowers of spring . . ."

Demeter is also a mother earth figure who controls the progress of the crops and represents, thereby, the fertility of woman.

In the story of *Dracula* Demeter is a coherent choice for the name of the ship that brings the vampire to England because of the goddess Demeter's connection, by her daughter's marriage, with the king of the underworld.

Though there is no record that a sailing ship named *Demeter* was ever registered with Lloyd's, there *was* a ship named *Demetra* that sailed out of the Norwegian port of Christiania throughout the 1890s. The *Demetra* was 133′ 4″ long, 29′ 4″ in breadth, and 16′ 8″ in depth. She weighed 405 tons. Her skipper in 1896 and 1897 was E. Jorgensen.

11 *silver sand.* A kind of sand used to polish stones. It is used in lithography.

12 *Board of Trade.* In 1897 there was no Board of Trade among the municipal organizations listed in *Horne's Guide to Whitby.*

13 cum grano. *cum grano salis:* with a grain of salt.

14 *Bosphorus.* A strait between the Black Sea and the Sea of Marmara, eighteen miles long. Famous in Turkish history as the place where the Turkish emperors disposed of their garroted wives, lovers, or political adversaries (see map, p. 336).

15 *Backsheesh.* A word well known in the Middle East where it signifies a money payment or other gift, usually in the form of a bribe or tip.

16 *Dardanelles.* A forty-mile strait connecting the Sea of Marmara with the Aegean Sea (see map, p. 336).

17 *Archipelago.* Another name for the Aegean Sea, particularly in the area of the Dardanelles (see map, p. 336).

18 *Cape Matapan.* The most southerly point of the Morea peninsula in Greece (see map, p. 336).

"WE WOULD SEARCH FROM STEM TO STERN."

them, and accordingly send you a rescript, simply omitting technical details of seamanship and supercargo. It almost seems as though the captain had been seized with some kind of mania before he had got well into blue water, and that this had developed persistently throughout the voyage. Of
13 course my statement must be taken *cum grano,* since I am writing from the dictation of a clerk of the Russian consul, who kindly translated for me, time being short.

LOG OF THE "DEMETER."

Varna to Whitby.

Written 18 July, things so strange happening, that I shall keep accurate note henceforth till we land.

On 6 July we finished taking in cargo, silver sand and boxes of earth. At noon set sail. East wind, fresh. Crew, five hands, ... two mates, cook, and myself (captain).
14 On 11 July at dawn entered Bosphorus. Boarded by
15 Turkish Customs officers. Backsheesh. All correct. Under way at 4 p.m.
16 On 12 July through Dardanelles. More Customs officers and flagboat of guarding squadron. Backsheesh again. Work of officers thorough, but quick. Want us off soon. At dark
17 passed into Archipelago.
18 On 13 July passed Cape Matapan. Crew dissatisfied about something. Seemed scared, but would not speak out.

On 14 July was somewhat anxious about crew. Men all steady fellows, who sailed with me before. Mate could not make out what was wrong; they only told him there was *something,* and crossed themselves. Mate lost temper with one of them that day and struck him. Expected fierce quarrel, but all was quiet.

On 16 July mate reported in the morning that one of crew, Petrofsky, was missing. Could not account for it. Took larboard watch eight bells last night; was relieved by Abramoff, but did not go to bunk. Men more downcast than ever. All said they expected something of the kind, but would not say more than that there was *something* aboard. Mate getting very impatient with them; feared some trouble ahead.

On 17 July, yesterday, one of the men, Olgaren, came to my cabin, and in an awestruck way confided to me that he thought there was a strange man aboard the ship. He said that in his watch he had been sheltering behind the deck-house, as there was a rain-storm, when he saw a tall, thin man, who was not like any of the crew, come up the companion-way, and go along the deck forward, and disappear. He followed cautiously, but when he got to bows found no one, and the hatchways were all closed. He was in a panic of superstitious fear, and I am afraid the panic may spread. To allay it, I shall to-day search entire ship carefully from stem to stern.

Later in the day I got together the whole crew, and told them, as they evidently thought there was some one in the ship, we would search from stem to stern. First mate angry; said it was folly, and to yield to such foolish ideas would demoralise the men; said he would engage to keep them out of trouble with a handspike. I let him take the helm, while the rest began thorough search, all keeping abreast, with lanterns; we left no corner unsearched. As there were only the big wooden boxes, there were no odd corners where a man could hide. Men much relieved when search over, and went back to work cheerfully. First mate scowled, but said nothing.

22 *July*.—Rough weather last three days, and all hands busy with sails—no time to be frightened. Men seem to have forgotten their dread. Mate cheerful again, and all on good terms. Praised men for work in bad weather. Passed Gib- **19**
raltar and out through Straits. All well.

24 *July*.—There seems some doom over this ship. Already a hand short, and entering on the Bay of Biscay with wild **20**
weather ahead, and yet last night another man lost—disappeared. Like the first, he came off his watch and was not seen again. Men all in a panic of fear; sent a round robin, asking to have double watch, as they fear to be alone. Mate violent. Fear there will be some trouble, as either he or the men will do some violence.

28 *July*.—Four days in hell, knocking about in a sort of maelstrom, and the wind a tempest. No sleep for any one. Men all worn out. Hardly know how to set a watch, since no one fit to go on. Second mate volunteered to steer and watch, and let men snatch a few hours' sleep. Wind abating; seas still terrific, but feel them less, as ship is steadier.

29 *July*.—Another tragedy. Had single watch to-night, as crew too tired to double. When morning watch came on deck could find no one except steersman. Raised outcry, and all came on deck. Thorough search, but no one found. Are now without second mate, and crew in a panic. Mate and I agreed to go armed henceforth and wait for any sign of cause.

30 *July*.—Last night. Rejoiced we are nearing England. Weather fine, all sails set. Retired worn out; slept soundly; awaked by mate telling me that both man of watch and steersman missing. Only self and mate and two hands left to work ship.

1 *August*.—Two days of fog, and not a sail sighted. Had hoped when in the English Channel to be able to signal for help or get in somewhere. Not having power to work sails, have to run before wind. Dare not lower, as could not raise them again. We seem to be drifting to some terrible doom. Mate now more demoralised than either of men. His stronger nature seems to have worked inwardly against himself. Men are beyond fear, working stolidly and patiently, with minds made up to worst. They are Russian, he Roumanian.

2 *August, midnight*.—Woke up from few minutes' sleep by hearing a cry, seemingly outside my port. Could see nothing in fog. Rushed on deck, and ran against mate. Tells me heard cry and ran, but no sign of man on watch. One more gone. Lord, help us! Mate says we must be past Straits of **21**
Dover, as in a moment of fog lifting he saw North Foreland, **22**
just as he heard the man cry out. If so we are now off in the
North Sea, and only God can guide us in the fog, which seems **23**
to move with us; and God seems to have deserted us.

3 *August*.—At midnight I went to relieve the man at the

19 *Gibraltar*. An area of the western Mediterranean Sea dominated by the Rock of Gibraltar, a British base and colony on the southern coast of Spain. Just opposite the strait lies the North African city of Tangier (see map, p. 336).

20 *Bay of Biscay*. A bay formed by the northern coast of Spain and the western coast of France extending from the island of Ushant on the coast of Finistère to Cape Ortegal on the north of Spanish Galicia. The bay is swept by strong northerly winds (see map, p. 336).

21 *Straits of Dover*. A narrow passage at the east end of the English Channel, its width is eighteen miles (see map, p. 337).

22 *North Foreland*. North Foreland (51° 24′ North Latitude, 1° 27′ East Longitude) is on the east coast of England between Margate and Broadstairs (see map, p. 337).

23 *North Sea*. The arm of the Atlantic Ocean between Great Britain and the continent of Europe.

wheel, but when I got to it found no one there. The wind was steady, and as we ran before it there was no yawing. I dared not leave it, so shouted for the mate. After a few seconds he rushed up on deck in his flannels. He looked wild-eyed and haggard, and I greatly fear his reason has given way. He came close to me and whispered hoarsely, with his mouth to my ear, as though fearing the very air might hear: "*It* is here; I know it, now. On the watch last night I saw It, like a man, tall and thin, and ghastly pale. It was in the bows, and looking out. I crept behind It, and gave It my knife; but the knife went through It, empty as the air." And as he spoke he took his knife and drove it savagely into space. Then he went on: "But It is here, and I'll find It. It is in the hold, perhaps, in one of those boxes. I'll unscrew them one by one and see. You work the helm." And, with a warning look and his finger on his lip, he went below. There was springing up a choppy wind, and I could not leave the helm. I saw him come out on deck again with a tool-chest and a lantern, and go down the forward hatchway. He is mad, stark, raving mad, and it's no use my trying to stop him. He can't hurt those big boxes: they are invoiced as "clay," and to pull them about is as harmless a thing as he can do. So here I stay, and mind the helm, and write these notes. I can only trust in God and wait till the fog clears. Then, if I can't steer to any harbour with the wind that is, I shall cut down sails and lie by, and signal for help. . . . .

It is nearly all over now. Just as I was beginning to hope that the mate would come out calmer—for I heard him knocking away at something in the hold, and work is good for him—there came up the hatchway a sudden, startled scream, which made my blood run cold, and up on the deck he came as if shot from a gun—a raging madman, with his eyes rolling and his face convulsed with fear. "Save me! save me!" he cried, and then looked round on the blanket of fog. His horror turned to despair, and in a steady voice he said: "You had better come too, captain, before it is too late. *He* is there. I know the secret now. The sea will save me from Him, and it is all that is left!" Before I could say a word, or move forward to seize him, he sprang on the bulwark and deliberately threw himself into the sea. I suppose I know the secret too, now. It was this madman who had got rid of the men one by one, and now he has followed them himself. God help me! How am I to account for all these horrors when I get to port? *When* I get to port! Will that ever be?

4 *August.*—Still fog, which the sunrise cannot pierce. I know there is sunrise because I am a sailor, why else I know not. I dared not go below, I dared not leave the helm; so here all night I stayed, and in the dimness of the night I saw It—Him! God forgive me, but the mate was right to jump overboard. It is better to die like a man; to die like a sailor in blue water no man can object. But I am captain, and I must not leave my ship. But I shall baffle this fiend or monster, for I shall tie my hands to the wheel when my strength begins to fail, and along with them I shall tie that which He—It!—dare not touch; and then, come good wind or

"I DARED NOT GO BELOW . . . SO HERE ALL NIGHT I STAYED."

foul, I shall save my soul, and my honour as a captain. I am growing weaker, and the night is coming on. If He can look me in the face again, I may not have time to act. . . . . If we are wrecked, mayhap this bottle may be found, and those who find it may understand; if not, ... well, then all men shall know that I have been true to my trust. God and the Blessed Virgin and the saints help a poor ignorant soul trying to do his duty. . . . .'

Of course the verdict was an open one. There is no evidence to adduce; and whether or not the man himself committed the murders there is now none to say. The folk hold almost universally here that the captain is simply a hero, and he is to be given a public funeral. Already it is arranged that his body is to be taken with a train of boats up the Esk for a piece and then brought back to Tate Hill Pier and up the Abbey steps; for he is to be buried in the churchyard on the cliff. The owners of more than a hundred boats have already given in their names as wishing to follow him to the grave.

No trace has ever been found of the great dog; at which there is much mourning, for, with public opinion in its present
state, he would, I believe, be adopted by the town. To- **24**
morrow will see the funeral; and so will end this one more
"mystery of the sea." **25**

24 *be adopted by the town.* This is a lovely notion—Dracula, as a great dog, turned into a town mascot.

25 *"mystery of the sea."* Stoker liked this phrase well enough to use it as the title of a later fiction (1902) in which "the beautiful American incognito heiress Marjory, who has been courted and won by Archie, a handsome young barrister, is about to be secretly married to him . . . [but] Archie is doomed to spend his wedding night alone, hacking with a pick-axe at the rock floor of a cave beside the sea." And so on.

26 *The funeral of the poor sea-captain.* An early description of such a parade of boats is to be found in *Early Voyages and Travels in the Levant*, edited by J. Theodore Bent. On page 155, in an extract from the diaries of Dr. John Covell, appears the following April 26, 1674, account of a sea funeral:

"*26th.* Put my dear Lord Harvey's body on board the *Centurion*. The great Cabin was hang'd and the floor cover'd with mourning; round about were fasten'd scutchions; the Steerage was hang'd likewise. My Lord's body was taken of the Dogger into the Centurion's long boat, there cover'd with a rich velvet Pal, bordered with white Sarsenet and satin. At the Head of the Corps was fixt a Hatchment, my Lord's armes, in a square frame standing on one of the corners. At the head of the boat was his six trumpeters and his drummer. The Advise's long boat tow'd it forward, and in it was his 6 Trumpeters likewise, and his drum, all sounding a dead march, went slowly forward in a round; the Consul's (Mr. Ricaut's) boat followed; after that many of the festoons in other boates. At its reception into the Centurion there was 3 voleyes of small shot and 30 Guns fired. The Advice fired 28; all the General ships and others in port fired, some 12, some 14, some 16 guns. Worthy Capt. Hill, who brought him out, fired every minute all the while we were going on the Dogger. The Body was put down into the hold, and a Cenotaph stood in the great cabbin, cover'd with the pall. The great Scutcheon displayed at the head six great tapers burning by in six great silver candlesticks. I gave away about 40 dwt. weights among the officers of the Centur., and sent a cask of 19 Meters of wine among the Seamen. We din'd aboard, treated civilly. The Consul brought flasques of Smyrna wine; Mr. Temple brought 20 flasques, and several fresh provisions. At 6 at night we all returned to Smyrna."

Stoker's sea captain is, of course, buried in the churchyard when the parade of boats is over. Burial at sea involves quite another ritual that is described with considerable feeling by Charles Nordhoff in his nineteenth-century account of *Sailor Life on Man of War and Merchant Vessel* (pp. 219–22). He writes:

"Shortly after we left Batavia, one of our lieutenants died very suddenly—and was, of course, buried at sea. This was not the first death on board, by several, but as this was the first and only occasion during our whole cruise in which the entire ceremonies provided for funeral occasions at sea were gone through with, it is a proper place in which to make some mention of them.

"The body of the deceased officer was laid out on trestles, on the half-deck, and covered over with the union jack, until the time came for committing it to the deep.

"When a sailor dies at sea, his corpse is sewed up in the hammock which has been until that time his

MINA MURRAY'S JOURNAL.

8 *August.*—Lucy was very restless all night, and I, too, could not sleep. The storm was fearful, and as it boomed loudly among the chimney-pots, it made me shudder. When a sharp puff came it seemed to be like a distant gun. Strangely enough, Lucy did not wake; but she got up twice and dressed herself. Fortunately, each time I awoke in time, and managed to undress her without waking her, and got her back to bed. It is a very strange thing, this sleep-walking, for as soon as her will is thwarted in any physical way, her intention, if there be any, disappears, and she yields herself almost exactly to the routine of her life.

Early in the morning we both got up and went down to the harbour to see if anything had happened in the night. There were very few people about, and though the sun was bright, and the air clear and fresh, the big, grim-looking waves, that seemed dark themselves because the foam that topped them was like snow, forced themselves in through the narrow mouth of the harbour—like a bullying man going through a crowd. Somehow I felt glad that Jonathan was not on the sea last night, but on land. But, oh, is he on land or sea? Where is he, and how? I am getting fearfully anxious about him. If I only knew what to do, and could do anything!

26 10 *August.*—The funeral of the poor sea-captain to-day was most touching. Every boat in the harbour seemed to be there, and the coffin was carried by captains all the way from Tate Hill Pier up to the churchyard. Lucy came with me, and we went early to our old seat, whilst the cortège of boats went up the river to the Viaduct and came down again. We had a lovely view, and saw the procession nearly all the way. The poor fellow was laid to rest quite near our seat, so that we stood on it when the time came and saw everything. Poor Lucy seemed much upset. She was restless and uneasy all the time, and I cannot but think that her dreaming at night is telling on her. She is quite odd in one thing: she will not admit to me that there is any cause for restlessness; or if there be, she does not understand it herself. There is an additional cause in that poor old Mr. Swales was found dead this morning on our seat, his neck being broken. He had evidently, as the doctor said, fallen back in the seat in some sort of fright, for there was a look of fear and horror on his face that the men said made them shudder. Poor dear old man! Perhaps he had seen Death with his dying eyes! Lucy is so sweet and sensitive that she feels influences more acutely than other people do. Just now she was quite upset by a little thing which I did not much heed, though I am myself very fond of animals. One of the men who come up here often to look for the boats was followed by his dog. The dog is always with him. They are both quiet persons, and I never saw the man angry, nor heard the dog bark. During
27 the service the dog would not come to its master, who was on the seat with us, but kept a few yards off, barking and howling. Its master spoke to it gently, and then harshly, and then

angrily; but it would neither come nor cease to make a noise. It was in a sort of fury, with its eyes savage, and all its hairs bristling out like a cat's tail when puss is on the war-path. Finally the man, too, got angry, and jumped down and kicked the dog, and then took it by the scruff of the neck and half dragged and half threw it on the tombstone on which the seat is fixed. The moment it touched the stone the poor thing became quiet and fell all into a tremble. It did not try to get away, but crouched down, quivering and cowering, and was in such a pitiable state of terror that I tried, though without effect, to comfort it. Lucy was full of pity, too, but she did not attempt to touch the dog, but looked at it in an agonised sort of way. I greatly fear that she is of too super-sensitive a nature to go through the world without trouble. She will be dreaming of this to-night, I am sure. The whole agglomeration of things—the ship steered into port by a dead man; his attitude, tied to the wheel with a crucifix and beads; the touching funeral; the dog, now furious and now in terror—will all afford material for her dreams.

I think it will be best for her to go to bed tired out physically, so I shall take her for a long walk by the cliffs **28**
to Robin Hood's Bay and back. She ought not to have much inclination for sleep-walking then.

ROBIN HOOD'S BAY, 1817.

bed, and now becomes his shroud. A couple of thirty-two-pound shot are enclosed, next to his feet, to bear the body down to the depths of the ocean, which is his grave.

"For our deceased officer, the carpenters constructed a plain deal coffin, the upper end of which was bored full of auger-holes, a very necessary precaution, as, had it been made tight, it would have swam upon the surface in place of sinking. In this, the corpse, dressed in full uniform, was placed, the lid screwed down, and the whole wrapped about with the union jack.

"At seven bells (half-past eleven), the mournful call of 'all hands to bury the dead' was heard, and the crew were gathered upon the upper deck, the marines paraded on the quarter-deck, with arms reversed, the ensign was lowered to half-mast, the officers mustered aft, with crape on their left arms, and all were hushed in silence, as beseemed a company about to commit a shipmate to the deep.

"The band, ranged upon the poop-deck, played that most impressive of dirges, 'the Dead March in Saul,' while, the officers acting as pall-bearers, a chosen band of seamen brought up to the gangway the bier upon which rested the remains of poor Lieutenant T—.

"The coffin was placed upon a broad plank, one end of which pointed overboard, and, the ship having been brought to, before, by backing the maintop-sail, the chaplain advanced, accompanied by the officers, and read the solemn and impressive funeral service of the Episcopal Church, provided for burials at sea.

"All was still, almost as death itself, and his low voice sounded clear and distinct fore and aft the decks. As he came to the close of the service, eight bells were struck, and, at the words, 'we now commit this body to the deep,' two gray-haired quartermasters reverently raised the inner end of the plank aloft—there was a momentary grating noise, a dull splash in the water—and all that was mortal of our deceased shipmate was gone to its long home.

"The marines now advanced to the gangway and fired a treble salute over the grave of the departed, and all was over. The boatswain 'piped down,' the maintopsail was filled, and we stood on our course."

27 *service the dog.* The behavior of the dog alerts us to Dracula's daytime presence in the suicide's grave.

28 *by the cliffs.* There were two ways to get to Robin Hood's Bay, a village some six miles from Whitby: one via the village of Hawkser, the other—the more direct way—the one that Lucy and Mina would take along the cliff "tops."

The village is still notable for its narrow streets and ancient houses seemingly piled on each other. "Nature," says the fifth edition of *Horne's Guide to Whitby* (p. 101), "nowhere provides a more pleasing variety of attractions to her devotees than she does in this neighborhood." In 1970, when I first visited the place, the village was as lovely as ever.

1 *a sweet little old-fashioned inn.* Perhaps at "A. W. Drewett, Fancy Bread & Biscuit Maker, & Confectioner," which, according to the fifth edition of *Horne's Guide to Whitby*, supplied "visitors . . . with Refreshments, Tea, Confectionery, &c."

ROBIN HOOD'S BAY.
A. W. DREWETT,
Fancy Bread & Biscuit Maker, & Confectioner,
FACING THE LIFEBOAT HOUSE.
Visitors supplied with Refreshments,
Tea, Confectionery, &c.

2 *the "New Woman."* The "new woman" is described by an as yet unliberated "old" woman in a February 6, 1892, *Illustrated London News* as follows:

"Home duties she has discarded as degrading to an educated woman, wifely respect she despises as the sign of craven submission to an inferior, children she dislikes as hindrances and nuisances, love is a dream fit only for lunatics and idiots. What she wants is freedom to do as she likes—the key of all the fields of life, not barring one. . . . She does not want to do anything immoral, but she wants to show that she can if she chooses . . . She cultivates her nerves and her biceps, plays cricket and golf, rows, rides and hunts . . . She would laugh to scorn the silly notion that only one man, and that her husband, should rejoice in her loveliness. . . .

CHAPTER VIII.

Mina Murray's Journal.

Same day, 11 *o'clock p.m.*—Oh, but I am tired! If it were not that I have made my diary a duty I should not open it to-night. We had a lovely walk. Lucy, after a while, was in gay spirits, owing, I think, to some dear cows who came nosing towards us in a field close to the lighthouse, and frightened the wits out of us. I believe we forgot everything, except, of course, personal fear, and it seemed to wipe the slate clean and give us a fresh start. We had a capital "severe
1 tea" at Robin Hood's Bay in a sweet little old-fashioned inn, with a bow-window right over the seaweed-covered rocks
2 of the strand. I believe we should have shocked the "New Woman" with our appetites. Men are more tolerant, bless them! Then we walked home with some, or rather many, stoppages to rest, and with our hearts full of a constant
3 dread of wild bulls. Lucy was really tired, and we intended to creep off to bed as soon as we could. The young curate came in, however, and Mrs. Westenra asked him to stay for
4 supper. Lucy and I had both a fight for it with the dusty miller; I know it was a hard fight on my part, and I am quite heroic. I think that some day the bishops must get together and see about breeding up a new class of curates, who don't take supper, no matter how they may be pressed to, and

THE "NEW WOMEN."

Maiden as she is, she knows to the last line all the hideous vice which abounds in large cities . . . any place rather than home, anything rather than home life, any exercise of virtue rather than respect for authority, that attention to duty, that modesty of habit, and that patient, sweet, and tranquil unselfishness which used to be the distinctive characteristics of the sex. . . . The two objects of her ambition are—to have plenty of 'oof', no matter by what means, and to be as much like a man as it is possible for a woman to make herself."

who will know when girls are tired. Lucy is asleep and breathing softly. She has more colour in her cheeks than usual, and looks, oh, so sweet. If Mr. Holmwood fell in love with her seeing her only in the drawing-room, I wonder what he would say if he saw her now. Some of the "New Women" writers will some day start an idea that men and women should be allowed to see each other asleep before proposing or accepting. But I suppose the New Woman won't condescend in future to accept; she will do the proposing herself. And a nice job she will make of it, too! There's some consolation in that. I am so happy to-night, because dear Lucy seems better. I really believe she has turned the corner, and that we are over her troubles with dreaming. I should be quite happy if I only knew if Jonathan . . . . God bless and keep him.

11 *August*, 3 *a.m.*—Diary again. No sleep now, so I may as well write. I am too agitated to sleep. We have had such an adventure, such an agonising experience. I fell asleep as soon as I had closed my diary. . . . Suddenly I became broad awake, and sat up, with a horrible sense of fear upon me, and of some feeling of emptiness around me. The room was dark, so I could not see Lucy's bed; I stole across and felt for her. The bed was empty. I lit a match, and found

3 *dread of wild bulls.* Because cattle were permitted to graze along the cliff tops.

"A CONSTANT DREAD OF WILD BULLS."

4 *dusty miller.* There is a plant called the Dusty Miller, but surely Stoker is not referring to it here. Clearly Mina means what we would call the sandman. The English dustman is sometimes credited with bringing sleep.

5 *diorama*. A miniature scene, usually in color, reproduced in three dimensions.

6 *St. Mary's Church*. The church was built by William de Percy in the twelfth century. It is still the parish church of Whitby. Today it boasts a peal of ten bells so that, says *Horne's Guide to Whitby* (71st edition) "from a camponologist's point of view, the installation is a perfect one. The bells have a very fine tone. . . ."

7 *seemed endless*. And well it might. The distance Mina ran from the West to the East Cliff is pretty nearly a mile, not counting the steps and the bridge.

that she was not in the room. The door was shut, but not
locked, as I had left it. I feared to wake her mother, who has
been more than usually ill lately, so threw on some clothes and
got ready to look for her. As I was leaving the room it struck
me that the clothes she wore might give me some clue to her
dreaming intention. Dressing-gown would mean house; dress,
outside. Dressing-gown and dress were both in their places.
"Thank God," I said to myself, "she cannot be far, as she is only
in her nightdress." I ran downstairs and looked in the sitting-
room. Not there! Then I looked in all the other open
rooms of the house, with an ever-growing fear chilling my
heart. Finally I came to the hall-door and found it open.
It was not wide open, but the catch of the lock had not
caught. The people of the house are careful to lock the
door every night, so I feared that Lucy must have gone out as
she was. There was no time to think of what might happen; a
vague, overmastering fear obscured all details. I took a big,
heavy shawl and ran out. The clock was striking one as I
was in the Crescent, and there was not a soul in sight.
I ran along the North Terrace, but could see no sign of the
white figure which I expected. At the edge of the West Cliff
above the pier I looked across the harbour to the East Cliff, in
the hope or fear—I don't know which—of seeing Lucy in our
favourite seat. There was a bright full moon, with heavy black,
driving clouds, which threw the whole scene into a fleeting
5 diorama of light and shade as they sailed across. For a moment or two I could see nothing, as the shadow of a cloud
6 obscured St. Mary's Church and all around it. Then as the
cloud passed I could see the ruins of the Abbey coming into
view; and as the edge of a narrow band of light as sharp
as a sword-cut moved along, the church and the churchyard became gradually visible. Whatever my expectation
was, it was not disappointed, for there, on our favourite seat, the
silver light of the moon struck a half-reclining figure, snowy
white. The coming of the cloud was too quick for me to see
much, for shadow shut down on light almost immediately; but
it seemed to me as though something dark stood behind the
seat where the white figure shone, and bent over it. What it
was, whether man or beast, I could not tell; I did not wait to
catch another glance, but flew down the steep steps to the
pier and along by the fish-market to the bridge, which was the
only way to reach the East Cliff. The town seemed as dead,
for not a soul did I see; I rejoiced that it was so, for I wanted
no witness of poor Lucy's condition. The time and distance
7 seemed endless, and my knees trembled and my breath came
laboured as I toiled up the endless steps to the Abbey. I
must have gone fast, and yet it seemed to me as if my feet
were weighted with lead, and as though every joint in my
body were rusty. When I got almost to the top I could see
the seat and the white figure, for I was now close enough to
distinguish it even through the spells of shadow. There was
undoubtedly something, long and black, bending over the half-
reclining white figure. I called in fright, "Lucy! Lucy!" and
something raised a head, and from where I was I could see a
white face and red, gleaming eyes. Lucy did not answer, and
I ran on to the entrance of the churchyard. As I entered, the

church was between me and the seat, and for a minute or so I lost sight of her. When I came in view again the cloud had passed, and the moonlight struck so brilliantly that I could see Lucy half reclining with her head lying over the back of the seat. She was quite alone, and there was not a sign of any living thing about.

When I bent over her I could see that she was still asleep. Her lips were parted, and she was breathing—not softly, as
usual with her, but in long, heavy gasps, as though striving to 8
get her lungs full at every breath. As I came close, she put up 9
her hand in her sleep and pulled the collar of her nightdress close round her throat. Whilst she did so there came a little
shudder through her, as though she felt the cold. I flung the 10
warm shawl over her, and drew the edges tight round her neck, for I dreaded lest she should get some deadly chill from the night air, unclad as she was. I feared to wake her all at once, so, in order to have my hands free that I might help her, I fastened the shawl at her throat with a big safety-pin; but I must have been clumsy in my anxiety and pinched or pricked her with it, for by-and-by, when her breathing became quieter, she put her hand to her throat again and moaned. When I had her carefully wrapped up I put my shoes on her feet, and then began very gently to wake her. At first she did not respond; but gradually she became more and more uneasy in her sleep, moaning and sighing occasionally. At last, as time was passing fast, and, for many other reasons, I wished to get her home at once, I shook her more forcibly, till finally she opened her eyes and awoke. She did not seem surprised to see me, as, of course, she did not realise all at once where she was. Lucy always wakes prettily, and even at such a time, when her body must have been chilled with cold, and her mind somewhat appalled at waking unclad in a churchyard at night, she did not lose her grace. She trembled a little, and clung to me; when I told her to come at once with me home she rose without a word, with the obedience of a child. As we passed along, the gravel hurt my feet, and Lucy noticed me wince. She stopped and wanted to insist upon my taking my shoes; but I would not. However, when we got to the pathway outside the churchyard, where there was a puddle of water remaining from the storm, I daubed my feet with mud, using each foot in turn on the other, so that as we went home no one, in case we should meet any one, should notice my bare feet.

Fortune favoured us, and we got home without meeting a soul. Once we saw a man, who seemed not quite sober, passing along a street in front of us; but we hid in a door till he had disappeared up an opening such as there are here, steep
little closes, or "wynds," as they call them in Scotland. My 11
heart beat so loud all the time that sometimes I thought I should faint. I was filled with anxiety about Lucy, not only for her health, lest she should suffer from the exposure, but for her reputation in case the story should get wind. When we got in, and had washed our feet, and had said a prayer of thankfulness together, I tucked her into bed. Before falling asleep she asked—even implored—me not to say a word to any one, even her mother, about her sleep-walking adventure. I

8 *long, heavy gasps.* Air hunger is a characteristic of anemia.

9 *she put up her hand . . . and pulled the collar of her nightdress close round her throat.* She begins almost instinctively to guard against anyone knowing her condition—even Mina.

10 *felt the cold.* A real symptom of anemia.

11 *closes, or "wynds."* A close is a narrow entry or alley, or a court to which it leads.

12 *benefited her.* Is this surprising? Not if we think of Dracula's visit to Lucy as the bridegroom's visit to his bride.

13 *Casino Terrace.* A curved street on the hill up to the Crescent.

14 *Spohr and Mackenzie.* Louis Spohr (1784–1859), a German violinist, was a prolific composer whose works include operas, choral and orchestral pieces, as well as a significant number of chamber music pieces. In addition to his achievements as a musician, Spohr is memorable because in 1804 he had the misfortune to lose a precious Guarnerius violin.

Sir Alexander Campbell Mackenzie, also a violinist, was born in Edinburgh in 1847 and lived well into the twentieth century until 1935. He wrote four operas, an operetta, and various cantatas and songs. In 1888 he was made the director of the Royal Academy of Music, which he guided for many years. Mackenzie was knighted in 1895, just a couple of years before *Dracula* was published.

hesitated at first to promise; but on thinking of the state of her mother's health, and how the knowledge of such a thing would fret her, and thinking, too, of how such a story might become distorted—nay, infallibly would—in case it should leak out, I thought it wiser to do so. I hope I did right. I have locked the door, and the key is tied to my wrist, so perhaps I shall not be again disturbed. Lucy is sleeping soundly; the reflex of the dawn is high and far over the sea. . . . .

Same day, noon.—All goes well. Lucy slept till I woke her, and seemed not to have even changed her side. The adventure of the night does not seem to have harmed her;
12 on the contrary, it has benefited her, for she looks better this morning than she has done for weeks. I was sorry to notice that my clumsiness with the safety-pin hurt her. Indeed, it might have been serious, for the skin of her throat was pierced. I must have pinched up a piece of loose skin and have transfixed it, for there are two little red points like pin-pricks, and on the band of her nightdress was a drop of blood. When I apologised and was concerned about it, she laughed and petted me, and said she did not even feel it. Fortunately it cannot leave a scar, as it is so tiny.

Same day, night.—We passed a happy day. The air was clear, and the sun bright, and there was a cool breeze. We took our lunch to Mulgrave Woods, Mrs. Westenra driving by the road and Lucy and I walking by the cliff-path and joining her at the gate. I felt a little sad myself, for I could not but feel how *absolutely* happy it would have been had Jonathan been with me. But there! I must only be patient. In the
13 evening we strolled in the Casino Terrace, and heard some
14 good music by Spohr and Mackenzie, and went to bed early. Lucy seems more restful than she has been for some time, and fell asleep at once. I shall lock the door and secure the key the same as before, though I do not expect any trouble to-night.

12 *August.*—My expectations were wrong, for twice during the night I was wakened by Lucy trying to get out. She seemed, even in her sleep, to be a little impatient at finding the door shut, and went back to bed under a sort of protest. I woke with the dawn, and heard the birds chirping outside of the window. Lucy woke, too, and, I was glad to see, was even better than on the previous morning. All her old gaiety of manner seemed to have come back, and she came and snuggled in beside me, and told me all about Arthur; I told her how anxious I was about Jonathan, and then she tried to comfort me. Well, she succeeded somewhat, for, though sympathy can't alter facts, it can help to make them more bearable.

13 *August.*—Another quiet day, and to bed with the key on my wrist as before. Again I awoke in the night, and found Lucy sitting up in bed, still asleep, pointing to the window. I got up quietly, and pulling aside the blind, looked out. It was brilliant moonlight, and the soft effect of the light over the sea and sky—merged together in one great, silent mystery—was beautiful beyond words. Between me and the moonlight flitted a great bat, coming and going in great, whirling circles.

Once or twice it came quite close, but was, I suppose, frightened at seeing me, and flitted away across the harbour towards the Abbey. When I came back from the window Lucy had lain down again, and was sleeping peacefully. She did not stir again all night.

14 *August.*—On the East Cliff, reading and writing all day. Lucy seems to have become as much in love with the spot as I am, and it is hard to get her away from it when it is time to come home for lunch or tea or dinner. This afternoon she made a funny remark. We were coming home for dinner, and had come to the top of the steps up from the West Pier and stopped to look at the view, as we generally do. The setting sun, low down in the sky, was just dropping behind Kettleness; the red light was thrown over on the East Cliff and the old Abbey, and seemed to bathe everything in a beautiful rosy glow. We were silent for a while, and suddenly Lucy murmured as if to herself:—

"His red eyes again! They are just the same." It was such an odd expression, coming *apropos* of nothing, that it quite startled me. I slewed round a little, so as to see Lucy well without seeming to stare at her, and saw that she was in a half-dreamy state, with an odd look on her face that I could not quite make out; so I said nothing, but followed her eyes, She appeared to be looking over at our own seat, whereon was a dark figure seated alone. I was a little startled myself, for it seemed for an instant as if the stranger had great eyes like burning flames; but a second look dispelled the illusion. The red sunlight was shining on the windows of St. Mary's Church behind our seat, and as the sun dipped there was just sufficient change in the refraction and reflection to make it appear as if the light moved. I called Lucy's attention to the peculiar effect, and she became herself with a start, but she looked sad all the same; it may have been that she was thinking of that terrible night up there. We never refer to it; so I said nothing, and we went home to dinner. Lucy had a headache and went early to bed. I saw her asleep, and went out for a little stroll myself; I walked along the cliffs to the westward, and was full of sweet sadness, for I was thinking of Jonathan. When coming home—it was then bright moonlight, so bright that, though the front of our part of the Crescent was in shadow, everything could be well seen—I threw a glance up at our window, and saw Lucy's head leaning out. I thought that perhaps she was looking out for me, so I opened my handkerchief and waved it. She did not notice or make any movement whatever. Just then, the moonlight crept round an angle of the building, and the light fell on the window. There distinctly was Lucy with her head lying up against the side of the window-sill and her eyes shut. She was fast asleep, and by her, seated on the window-sill, was something that looked like a good-sized bird. I was afraid she might get a chill, so I ran upstairs, but as I came into the room she was moving back to her bed, fast asleep, and breathing heavily; she was holding her hand to her throat, as though to protect it from cold.

I did not wake her, but tucked her up warmly; I have taken care that the door is locked and the window securely fastened.

She looks so sweet as she sleeps; but she is paler than is her wont, and there is a drawn, haggard look under her eyes which I do not like. I fear she is fretting about something. I wish I could find out what it is.

15 *August.*—Rose later than usual. Lucy was languid and tired, and slept on after we had been called. We had a happy surprise at breakfast. Arthur's father is better, and wants the marriage to come off soon. Lucy is full of quiet joy, and her mother is glad and sorry at once. Later on in the day she told me the cause. She is grieved to lose Lucy as her very own, but she is rejoiced that she is soon to have some one to protect her. Poor dear, sweet lady! She confided to me that she has got her death-warrant. She has not told Lucy, and made me promise secrecy; her doctor told her that within a few months, at most, she must die, for her heart is weakening. At any time, even now, a sudden shock would be almost sure to kill her. Ah, we were wise to keep from her the affair of the dreadful night of Lucy's sleep-walking.

17 *August.*—No diary for two whole days. I have not had the heart to write. Some sort of shadowy pall seems to be coming over our happiness. No news from Jonathan, and Lucy seems to be growing weaker, whilst her mother's hours are numbering to a close. I do not understand Lucy's fading away as she is doing. She eats well and sleeps well, and enjoys the fresh air; but all the time the roses in her
15 cheeks are fading, and she gets weaker and more languid day
by day; at night I hear her gasping as if for air. I keep the key of our door always fastened to my wrist at night, but she gets up and walks about the room, and sits at the open window. Last night I found her leaning out when I woke up, and when I tried to wake her I could not; she was in a faint. When I managed to restore her she was as weak as water, and cried silently between long, painful struggles for breath. When I asked her how she came to be at the window she shook her head and turned away. I trust her feeling ill may not be from that unlucky prick of the safety pin. I looked at her throat just now as she lay asleep, and the tiny wounds seem not to have healed. They are still open, and, if anything, larger than before, and the edges of them are faintly white. They are like little white dots with red centres. Unless they heal within a day or two, I shall insist on the doctor seeing about them.

16 *Letter, Samuel F. Billington & Son, Solicitors, Whitby, to*
17 *Messrs. Carter, Paterson & Co., London.*

"17 *August.*

"Dear Sirs,—

"Herewith please receive invoice of goods sent by Great Northern Railway. Same are to be delivered at Carfax, near
18, 19 Purfleet, immediately on receipt at goods station King's Cross.
The house is at present empty, but enclosed please find keys, all of which are labelled.

"You will please deposit the boxes, fifty in number, which form the consignment, in the partially ruined building forming part of the house and marked 'A' on rough diagram enclosed,

15 *and more languid.* Lucy's pallor and languor are very like the symptoms traditionally associated with falling in love.

16 Samuel F. Billington. A fictitious name.

17 *Messrs. Carter, Paterson & Co., London.* Among the scores of fictitious names of tradesmen and companies Stoker invented, these turn out to have been real. The cartage firm was founded on November 1, 1860, when "the partners set up in George Yard, Aldermanbury, with six carts and eight horses. Their business consisted largely of carting for the railways in the outer districts of London. . . . Although their main traffic was small parcels, delivered by horse van, they experimented with steam traction-engines for heavier loads. . . ." Which explains why Samuel F. Billington & Son, Solicitors, employed the firm to move the heavy boxes.

I am indebted to David Webb, A.L.A., for the news that "Carter Paterson's headquarters during the years 1887–1892 were in Goswell Road, E.C. 1., expanding from two adjacent buildings in 1887 to take up almost an entire block—nos. 122–130—in 1892."

18 *goods station.* Freight station.

19 *King's Cross.* A major railway terminal in north central London. Situated at the east terminus of Euston Road, approximately 1½ miles east of Regent's Park. (See chapter XVIII, note 17.)

Your agent will easily recognise the locality, as it is the ancient chapel of the mansion. The goods leave by the train at 9.30 to-night, and will be due at King's Cross at 4.30 to-morrow afternoon. As our client wishes the delivery made as soon as possible, we shall be obliged by your having teams ready at King's Cross at the time named and forthwith conveying the goods to destination. In order to obviate any delays possible through any routine requirements as to payment in your departments, we enclose cheque herewith for ten pounds (£10), receipt of which please acknowledge. Should the charge be less than this amount, you can return balance; if greater, we shall at once send cheque for difference on hearing from you. You are to leave the keys on coming away in the main hall of the house, where the proprietor may get them on his entering the house by means of his duplicate key.

"Pray do not take us as exceeding the bounds of business courtesy in pressing you in all ways to use the utmost expedition.

"We are, dear Sirs,
"Faithfully yours,
"SAMUEL F. BILLINGTON & SON.

Letter, Messrs. Carter, Paterson & Co., London, to Messrs. Billington & Son, Whitby.

"21 *August*.

"Dear Sirs,—

"We beg to acknowledge £10 received and to return cheque £1 17*s*. 9*d*., amount of overplus, as shown in receipted account herewith. Goods are delivered in exact accordance with instructions, and keys left in parcel in main hall, as directed.

"We are, dear Sirs,
"Yours respectfully,
"*Pro* CARTER, PATERSON & CO."

MINA MURRAY'S JOURNAL.

18 *August*.—I am happy to-day, and write sitting on the seat in the churchyard. Lucy is ever so much better. Last night she slept well all night, and did not disturb me once. The roses seem coming back already to her cheeks, though she is still sadly pale and wan-looking. If she were in any way anæmic I could understand it, but she is not. She is in gay spirits and full of life and cheerfulness. All the morbid reticence seems to have passed from her, and she has just reminded me, as if I needed any reminding, of *that* night, and that it was here, on this very seat, I found her asleep. As she told me she tapped playfully with the heel of her boot on the stone slab and said:—

"My poor little feet didn't make much noise then! I daresay poor old Mr. Swales would have told me that it was because I didn't want to wake up Geordie." As she was in such a communicative humour, I asked her if she had dreamed at all that night. Before she answered, that sweet, puckered look came into her forehead, which Arthur—I call him Arthur

20 Buda-Pesth. Buda-Pest is the name given to the sister cities, Buda and Pest, joined by "the most Western of splendid bridges" over the Danube. They became one municipality in 1873.

In Stoker's day Buda was a royal town of the kingdom of Hungary notable, among other things, for its thermal baths, some of which date back to the time of the Turkish dominion over the city. Cannon-making, type founding, and silk weaving were among Buda's chief industries.

Pest, larger and more important than Buda, served as the capital of Hungary and as a second residence for the emperor of the Austro-Hungarian empire. Pest had a fine academy of sciences and a national museum. The city was a center for the manufacture of heavy machinery, carriages, and gold and silver articles.

As the nineteenth century ended, the combined population of the two cities was upward of 400,000 people. (See map, p. 336.)

from her habit—says he loves; and, indeed, I don't wonder that he does. Then she went on in a half-dreaming kind of way, as if trying to recall it to herself:—

"I didn't quite dream; but it all seemed to be real. I only wanted to be here in this spot—I don't know why, for I was afraid of something—I don't know what. I remember, though I suppose I was asleep, passing through the streets and over the bridge. A fish leaped as I went by, and I leaned over to look at it, and I heard a lot of dogs howling—the whole town seemed as if it must be full of dogs all howling at once—as I went up the steps. Then I have a vague memory of something long and dark with red eyes, just as we saw in the sunset, and something very sweet and very bitter all around me at once; and then I seemed sinking into deep green water, and there was a singing in my ears, as I have heard there is to drowning men; and then everything seemed passing away from me; my soul seemed to go out from my body and float about the air. I seem to remember that once the West Lighthouse was right under me, and then there was a sort of agonising feeling, as if I were in an earthquake, and I came back and found you shaking my body. I saw you do it before I felt you."

Then she began to laugh. It seemed a little uncanny to me, and I listened to her breathlessly. I did not quite like it, and thought it better not to keep her mind on the subject, so we drifted on to other subjects, and Lucy was like her old self again. When we got home the fresh breeze had braced her up, and her pale cheeks were really more rosy. Her mother rejoiced when she saw her, and we all spent a very happy evening together.

19 *August.*—Joy, joy, joy! although not all joy. At last, news of Jonathan. The dear fellow has been ill; that is why he did not write. I am not afraid to think it or to say it, now that I know. Mr. Hawkins sent me on the letter, and wrote himself, oh, so kindly. I am to leave in the morning and to go over to Jonathan, and to help to nurse him if necessary, and to bring him home. Mr. Hawkins says it would not be a bad thing if we were to be married out there. I have cried over the good Sister's letter till I can feel it wet against my bosom, where it lies. It is of Jonathan, and must be next my heart, for he is *in* my heart. My journey is all mapped out, and my luggage ready. I am only taking one change of dress; Lucy will bring my trunk to London and keep it till I send for it, for it may be that . . . . I must write no more; I must keep it to say to Jonathan, my husband. The letter that he has seen and touched must comfort me till we meet.

Letter, Sister Agatha, Hospital of St. Joseph and Ste. Mary,
20 *Buda-Pesth, to Miss Wilhelmina Murray.*

"12 *August.*

"Dear Madam,—

"I write by desire of Mr. Jonathan Harker, who is himself not strong enough to write, though progressing well, thanks to God and St. Joseph and Ste. Mary. He has been under our care for nearly six weeks, suffering from a violent brain fever. He wishes me to convey his love, and to say that by this post I write for him to Mr. Peter Hawkins, Exeter, to say, with his dutiful respects, that he is sorry for his delay, and that all his work is completed. He will require some few weeks' rest in our sanatorium in the hills, but will then return. He wishes me to say that he has not sufficient money with him, and that he would like to pay for his staying here, so that others who need shall not be wanting for help.

"Believe me,

"Yours, with sympathy and all blessings,

"SISTER AGATHA.

"P.S.—My patient being asleep, I open this to let you know something more. He has told me all about you, and that you are shortly to be his wife. All blessings to you both! He has had some fearful shock—so says our doctor—and in his delirium his ravings have been dreadful; of wolves 21
and poison and blood; of ghosts and demons; and I fear to say of what. Be careful with him always that there may be nothing to excite him of this kind for a long time to come; the traces of such an illness as his do not lightly die away. We should have written long ago, but we knew nothing of his friends, and there was on him nothing that any one could understand. He came in the train from Klausenburg, and the guard was told by the station-master there that he rushed into the station shouting for a ticket for home. Seeing from his violent demeanour that he was English, they gave him a ticket for the furthest station on the way thither that the train reached.

"Be assured that he is well cared for. He has won all hearts by his sweetness and gentleness. He is truly getting on well, and I have no doubt will in a few weeks be all himself. But be careful of him for safety's sake. There are, I pray God and St. Joseph and Ste. Mary, many, many happy years for you both."

Dr. Seward's Diary.

19 *August.*—Strange and sudden change in Renfield last night. About eight o'clock he began to get excited and to sniff about as a dog does when setting. The attendant was struck by his manner, and knowing my interest in him, encouraged him to talk. He is usually respectful to the attendant, and at times servile; but to-night, the man tells me, he was quite haughty. Would not condescend to talk with him at all. All he would say was:—

"I don't want to talk to you: you don't count now; the 22
Master is at hand."

The attendant thinks it is some sudden form of religious mania which has seized him. If so, we must look out for squalls, for a strong man with homicidal and religious mania at once might be dangerous. The combination is a dreadful one. At nine o'clock I visited him myself. His attitude to me was the same as that to the attendant; in his sublime self-feeling the difference between myself and attendant seemed to him

21 *of wolves and poison.* How poison got into Harker's delirium is not clear. He has no experience of it in Castle Dracula.

22 "*. . . the Master is at hand.*" With this brusque announcement Renfield casts himself into the role of an anti-John-the-Baptist announcing the coming of the Anti-Christ.

The phrase "the Master is at hand," though suggestive, would not by itself be enough to justify the above comment; however, when, a couple of paragraphs later, Renfield's speech takes on a pseudobiblical lyricism, we know we are on the right track and a Bible search is in order.

23 *"The bride-maidens rejoice . . ."* Renfield's "bride-maidens" passage has been checked in an exhaustive concordance to the Bible, which shows that the phrase "coming of the bride" is nowhere in the Authorized Version; that "bride-maidens," with or without the hyphen is not listed either, though "bridegroom" and "bridechamber" both exist, as do "bondmaid," "handmaid," and "maidservant."

There *is* a passage in the New Testament that Renfield seems to be echoing, however. In the Gospel According to St. John (3:29) we read that "he that hath the bride is the bridegroom: but the friend of the bridegroom, which standeth and heareth him, rejoiceth greatly because of the bridegroom's voice . . ." The words are spoken by John the Baptist as part of a speech witnessing the coming of Christ.

In a footnote dealing with Renfield's speech in *A Dream of Dracula*, I wrote that "analogy lays traps for the unwary author. Did Stoker want Dracula cast as the radiant bride? In this book, I choose not to dwell on the question" (p. 314). Let me dwell a moment on the matter here. In Renfield's mind, certainly, the spiders are represented by the bride-maidens who are eclipsed by the coming of the bride. That is, the lesser joy is about to give way to the greater: the bride Dracula is coming and Renfield presumably is to be the groom. If my not-too-terribly tortured reasoning is sound, then Dracula's murderous visit to Renfield takes on the meaning of a macabre consummation of a monstrous wedding night.

24 *$C_2HCl_3O{\cdot}H_2O$!* Chloral hydrate, the ingredient of "knockout drops." According to the *Encyclopaedia Britannica*, an effective dose of chloral hydrate is perilously close to a lethal dose and is, therefore, dangerous to use. One or two grams will achieve sedation after ten or fifteen minutes, and a sleep lasting for five to eight hours.

Chloral hydrate is inexpensive, leaves no hangover, and is effective. If Seward took it on this occasion, he would be dishonoring Lucy by forgetting her.

as nothing. It looks like religious mania, and he will soon think that he himself is God. These infinitesimal distinctions between man and man are too paltry for an Omnipotent Being. How these madmen give themselves away! The real God taketh heed lest a sparrow fall; but the God created from human vanity sees no difference between an eagle and a sparrow. Oh, if men only knew!

For half an hour or more Renfield kept getting excited in greater and greater degree. I did not pretend to be watching him, but I kept strict observation all the same. All at once that shifty look came into his eyes which we always see when a madman has seized an idea, and with it the shifty movement of the head and back which asylum attendants come to know so well. He became quite quiet, and went and sat on the edge of his bed resignedly, and looked into space with lack-lustre eyes. I thought I would find out if his apathy were real or only assumed, and tried to lead him to talk of his pets, a theme which had never failed to excite his attention. At first he made no reply, but at length said testily:—

"Bother them all! I don't care a pin about them."

"What?" I said. "You don't mean to tell me you don't care about spiders?" (Spiders at present are his hobby, and the note-book is filling up with columns of small figures.) To this he answered enigmatically:—

23 "The bride-maidens rejoice the eyes that wait the coming of the bride; but when the bride draweth nigh, then the maidens shine not to the eyes that are filled."

He would not explain himself, but remained obstinately seated on his bed all the time I remained with him.

I am weary to-night and low in spirits. I cannot but think of Lucy, and how different things might have been. If I don't sleep at once, chloral, the modern Morpheus—
24 $C_2HCl_3O{\cdot}H_2O$! I must be careful not to let it grow into a habit. No, I shall take none to-night! I have thought of Lucy, and I shall not dishonour her by mixing the two. If need be, to-night shall be sleepless. . . . .

Glad I made the resolution; gladder that I kept to it. I had lain tossing about, and had heard the clock strike only twice, when the night-watchman came to me, sent up from the ward, to say that Renfield had escaped. I threw on my clothes and ran down at once; my patient is too dangerous a person to be roaming about. Those ideas of his might work out dangerously with strangers. The attendant was waiting for me. He said he had seen him not ten minutes before, seemingly asleep in his bed, when he had looked through the observation-trap in the door. His attention was called by the sound of the window being wrenched out. He ran back and saw his feet disappear through the window, and had at once sent up for me. He was only in his night-gear, and cannot be far off. The attendant thought it would be more useful to watch where he should go than to follow him, as he might lose sight of him whilst getting out of the building by the door. He is a bulky man, and couldn't get through the window. I am thin, so, with his aid, I got out, but feet foremost, and, as we were only a few feet above ground, landed unhurt. The attendant told me the patient had gone to the left and had taken a straight line, so I ran as quickly as I could. As I got through the belt of trees I saw a white figure scale the high wall which separates our grounds from those of the deserted house.

I ran back at once, and told the watchman to get three or four men immediately and follow me into the grounds of Carfax, in case our friend might be dangerous. I got a ladder myself, 25
and crossing the wall, dropped down on the other side. I could see Renfield's figure just disappearing behind the angle of the house, so I ran after him. On the far side of the house I found him pressed close against the old iron-bound oak door of the chapel. He was talking, apparently to some one, but I was afraid to go near enough to hear what he was saying, lest I might frighten him, and he should run off. Chasing an errant swarm of bees is nothing to following a
naked lunatic when the fit of escaping is upon him! After a 26
few minutes, however, I could see that he did not take note of anything around him, and so ventured to draw nearer to him—the more so as my men had now crossed the wall and were closing him in. I heard him say:—

"I am here to do Your bidding, Master. I am Your slave, and You will reward me, for I shall be faithful. I have worshipped You long and afar off. Now that You are near, I await Your commands, and You will not pass me by, will You, dear Master, in Your distribution of good things?"

He *is* a selfish old beggar anyhow. He thinks of the loaves 27
and fishes even when he believes he is in a Real Presence. His manias make a startling combination. When we closed in on him he fought like a tiger. He is immensely strong, and he was more like a wild beast than a man. I never saw a lunatic in such a paroxysm of rage before; and I hope I shall not again. It is a mercy that we have found out his strength and his danger in good time. With strength and determina-

AN EARLY STRAIT-WAISTCOAT.

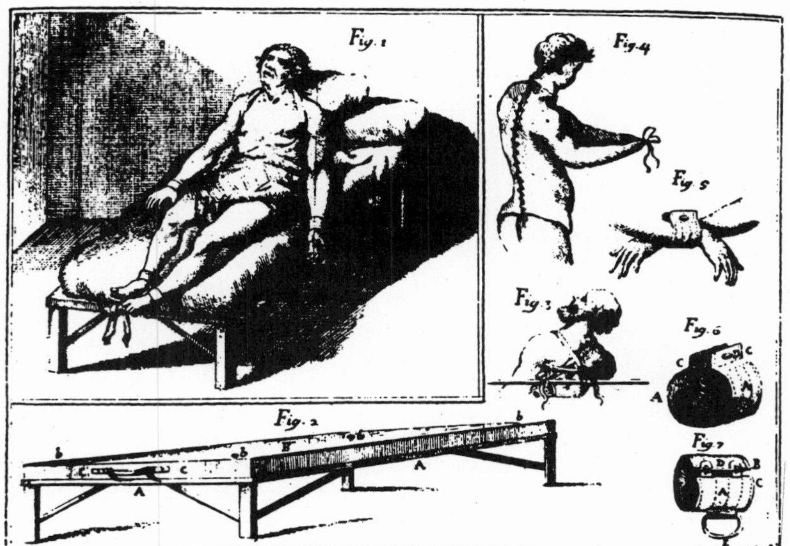

25 *I got a ladder.* Fifty-nine-year-old Renfield, imbued with the energy of madness, goes easily over the wall, while a slim twenty-nine-year-old Seward, who is merely unhappy, requires a ladder.

26 *naked lunatic.* Not many moments ago, Renfield was described as being in his nightgear. Perhaps for Victorian sensibilities that was naked enough.

27 *loaves and fishes.* The story of the loaves and fishes is told in all four of the Gospels: Matthew 15:32–39; Mark 6:37–44; Luke 9:12–17; and John 6:9–11. The version in Matthew reads:

32 Then Jesus called his disciples *unto him,* and said, I have compassion on the multitude, because they continue with me now three days, and have nothing to eat: and I will not send them away fasting, lest they faint in the way.

33 And his disciples say unto him, Whence should we have so much bread in the wilderness, as to fill so great a multitude?

34 And Jesus saith unto them, How many loaves have ye? And they said, Seven, and a few little fishes.

35 And he commanded the multitude to sit down on the ground.

36 And he took the seven loaves and the fishes, and gave thanks, and brake *them,* and gave to his disciples, and the disciples to the multitude.

37 And they did all eat, and were filled . . .

38 And they that did eat were four thousand men, beside women and children.

In the other Gospels the number of loaves and fishes is five and two respectively, and the number fed is given as five thousand.

tion like his, he might have done wild work before he was
28 caged. He is safe now at any rate. Jack Sheppard himself
29 couldn't get free from the strait-waistcoat that keeps him
restrained, and he's chained to the wall in the padded room. His cries are at times awful, but the silences that follow are more deadly still, for he means murder in every turn and movement.

Just now he spoke coherent words for the first time:—

"I shall be patient, Master. It is coming—coming—coming!"

So I took the hint, and came too. I was too excited to sleep, but this diary has quieted me, and I feel I shall get some sleep to-night.

28 *Jack Sheppard.* John Sheppard (1702–1724), an English criminal, was tried at the Old Bailey on August 13, 1724, and condemned to die. With his mistress's help, he escaped, but was rearrested on September 10. Handcuffed and chained to the floor of a Newgate cell, he escaped once more after climbing through the chimney to the room above, after which he made his way through five locked doors to the prison roof from which he managed to reach a nearby house. He was finally retaken on October 31. This time he did not escape.

Daniel Defoe wrote a fictitious account of Sheppard's life: *A Narrative of All the Robberies Escapes &c., of John Sheppard: Giving an Exact Description of the Manner of His Wonderful Escape from the Castle in Newgate, and of the Methods He Took Afterwards for His Security. Written by Himself During His Confinement in the Middle Stone Room, After His Being Retaken in Drury Lane.*

29 *strait-waistcoat.* In American English we would say "straitjacket."

No one is precisely sure who was the inventor of this device to restrain the mad, though David MacBride (1726–1778) has sometimes been given that credit because he was the first to describe the device in a textbook of medicine. His late-eighteenth-century description of it indicates that it has changed little since it first appeared in the treatment of the insane in the 1730s. MacBride writes that "these waistcoats are made of ticken, or some such strong stuff; are open at the back, and laced on like a pair of stays; the sleeves are made tight, and so long as to cover the ends of the fingers, and are there drawn close with a string, like a purse, by which contrivance the patient has no power of using his fingers; and when he is laid on his back in bed, and the arms brought across the chest, and fastened in that position, by tying the sleeve-strings fast round the waist, he has no power of his hands." MacBride adds that the physician will do well "to bear in mind, that all mad people are cowardly, and can be awed even by the menacing look of a very expressive countenance."

CHAPTER IX.

Letter, Mina Harker to Lucy Westenra.

"*Buda-Pesth, 24 August.*

"My dearest Lucy,—

"I know you will be anxious to hear all that has happened since we parted at the railway station at Whitby. Well, my dear, I got to Hull all right, and caught the boat to Hamburg, and 1
then the train on here. I feel that I can hardly recall anything of the journey, except that I knew I was coming to Jonathan, and, that as I should have to do some nursing, I had better get all the sleep I could. . . . . I found my dear one, oh, so thin and pale and weak-looking. All the resolution has gone out of his dear eyes, and that quiet dignity which I told you was in his face has vanished. He is only a wreck of himself, and he does not remember anything that has happened to him for a long time past. At least, he wants me to believe so, and I shall never ask. He has had some terrible shock, and I fear it might tax his poor brain if he were to try to recall it. Sister Agatha, who is a good creature and a born nurse, tells me that he raved of dreadful things whilst he was off his head. I wanted her to tell me what they were; but she would only cross herself, and say she would never tell; that the ravings of the sick were the secrets of God, and that if a nurse through her vocation should hear them, she should respect her trust. She is a sweet, good soul, and the next day, when she saw I was troubled, she opened up the subject again, and after saying that she could never mention what my poor dear raved about, added: 'I can tell you this much, my dear: that it was not about anything which he has done wrong himself; and you, as his wife to be, have no cause to be concerned. He has not forgotten you or what he owes to you. His fear was of great

1 *Hull . . . Hamburg.* Hull—also known as Kingston-upon-Hull—is described in the tenth edition of the *Encyclopaedia Britannica* (1888) as "a municipal and parliamentary borough" in the East Riding of Yorkshire. Hull was the third most important port of England in Stoker's day, a center of shipping to and from the Baltic ports, Denmark, Norway, Germany, and Holland. It had a population of more than 130,000 inhabitants and boasted a library of 40,000 volumes.

Hamburg was, and is, a flourishing German port city on the North Sea. In addition to its importance to European trade, nineteenth-century Hamburg figured significantly as the city of departure for the tide of emigrants that flowed from the Old to the New worlds. Between 1836 and 1874, more than 870,000 left Europe via Hamburg. (See map, p. 336.)

2 *chaplain and the Sisters.* Though we have indications that Jonathan Harker is not a Catholic, his marriage, at least, is performed by a chaplain in a Catholic hospital.

3 *an outward and visible sign.* This is good Catholic language. Any child that knows his catechism knows that "the sacraments are *outward* (visible) signs instituted by Christ *to give grace.*"

and terrible things, which no mortal can treat of.' I do believe the dear soul thought I might be jealous lest my poor dear should have fallen in love with any other girl. The idea of *my* being jealous about Jonathan! And yet, my dear, let me whisper, I felt a thrill of joy through me when I *knew* that no other woman was a cause of trouble. I am now sitting by his bedside, where I can see his face while he sleeps. He is waking! . . . . When he woke he asked me for his coat, as he wanted to get something from the pocket; I asked Sister Agatha, and she brought all his things. I saw that amongst them was his note-book, and was going to ask him to let me look at it—for I knew then that I might find some clue to his trouble—but I suppose he must have seen my wish in my eyes, for he sent me over to the window, saying he wanted to be quite alone for a moment. Then he called me back, and when I came he had his hand over the note-book, and he said to me very solemnly:—

"'Wilhelmina'—I knew then that he was in deadly earnest, for he has never called me by that name since he asked me to marry him—'you know, dear, my ideas of the trust between husband and wife: there should be no secret, no concealment. I have had a great shock, and when I try to think of what it is I feel my head spin round, and I do not know if it was all real or the dreaming of a madman. You know I have had brain fever, and that is to be mad. The secret is here, and I do not want to know it. I want to take up my life here, with our marriage.' For, my dear, we had decided to be married as soon as the formalities are complete. 'Are you willing, Wilhelmina, to share my ignorance? Here is the book. Take it and keep it, read it if you will, but never let me know; unless, indeed, some solemn duty should come upon me to go back to the bitter hours, asleep or awake, sane or mad, recorded here.' He fell back exhausted, and I put the book under his pillow, and kissed him. I have asked Sister Agatha to beg the Superior to let our wedding be this afternoon, and am waiting her reply. . . . .

"She has come and told me that the chaplain of the English mission church has been sent for. We are to be married in an hour, or as soon after as Jonathan awakes. . . . .

"Lucy, the time has come and gone. I feel very solemn, but very, very happy. Jonathan woke a little after the hour, and all was ready, and he sat up in bed, propped up with pillows. He answered his 'I will' firmly and strongly. I could hardly speak; my heart was so full that even those words seemed to choke me. The dear Sisters were so kind. Please God, I shall never, never forget them, nor the grave and sweet responsibilities I have taken upon me. I must tell you of my wedding
2 present. When the chaplain and the Sisters had left me alone with my husband—oh, Lucy, it is the first time I have written the words 'my husband'—left me alone with my husband, I took the book from under his pillow, and wrapped it up in white paper, and tied it with a little bit of pale blue ribbon which was round my neck, and sealed it over the knot with sealing-wax, and for my seal I used my wedding ring. Then I kissed it and showed it to my husband, and told him that I
3 would keep it so, and then it would be an outward and visible sign for us all our lives that we trusted each other; that I

would never open it unless it were for his own dear sake or for the sake of some stern duty. Then he took my hand in his, and oh, Lucy, it was the first time he took *his wife's* hand, and said that it was the dearest thing in all the wide world, and that he would go through all the past again to win it, if need be. The poor dear meant to have said a part of the past; but he cannot think of time yet, and I shall not wonder if at first he mixes up not only the month, but the year.

"Well, my dear, what could I say? I could only tell him that I was the happiest woman in all the wide world, and that I had nothing to give him except myself, my life, and my trust, and that with these went my love and duty for all the days of my life. And, my dear, when he kissed me, and drew me to him with his poor weak hands, it was like a very solemn 4
pledge between us. . . . .

"Lucy dear, do you know why I tell you all this? It is not only because it is all sweet to me, but because you have been, and are, very dear to me. It was my privilege to be your 5
friend and guide when you came from the schoolroom to prepare for the world of life. I want you to see now, and with the eyes of a very happy wife, whither duty has led me; so that in your own married life you too may be all happy as I am. My dear, please Almighty God, your life may be all it promises: a long day of sunshine, with no harsh wind, no forgetting duty, no distrust. I must not wish you no pain, for that can never be; but I do hope you will be *always* as happy as I am *now*. Good-bye, my dear. I shall post this at once, and, perhaps, write you very soon again. I must stop, for Jonathan is waking—I must attend to my husband!

"Your ever-loving

"MINA HARKER." 6

Letter, Lucy Westenra to Mina Harker.

"*Whitby*, 30 *August*.

"My dearest Mina,—

"Oceans of love and millions of kisses, and may you soon be in your own home with your husband. I wish you could be coming home soon enough to stay with us here. This strong air would soon restore Jonathan; it has quite restored me. I have an appetite like a cormorant, am full of life, and sleep well. You will be glad to know that I have quite given up walking in my sleep. I think I have not stirred out of my bed 7
for a week, that is when I once got into it at night. Arthur says I am getting fat. By the way, I forgot to tell you that Arthur is here. We have such walks and drives, and rides, and rowing, and tennis, and fishing together; and I love him more than ever. He *tells me* that he loves me more, but I doubt that, for at first he told me that he couldn't love me more than he did then. But this is nonsense. There he is, calling to me. So no more just at present from your loving

"LUCY.

"P.S.—Mother sends her love. She seems better, poor dear.

"P.P.S.—We are to be married on 28 September."

4 *his poor weak hands.* Jonathan's wedding day weakness is considerably insisted upon though, significantly enough, his wedding night is passed over in silence. A reader interested in the way Stoker's mind can handle a wedding night may care to see my discussion of *The Mystery of the Sea* in *A Dream of Dracula* (pp. 255–56). (See chapter VII, note 25.)

5 *your friend and guide . . . for the world of life.* This remark suggests that Mina may have been Lucy's schoolroom tutor as well as her friend.

Mina's relationship to Lucy has some fairly complex dimensions. We have seen that they were childhood intimates as well as schoolgirl companions. On the other hand, Mina, as an employed assistant schoolmistress, is on a lower social scale than her heiress friend. The same class distinction divides their respective fiancés.

6 *"Mina Harker."* The signature is a last piece of schoolgirl bravado as Mina flaunts her married name at a Lucy who displayed *her* three proposals so melodramatically.

7 *walking in my sleep.* Her previous sleepwalking, we must conclude, was in response to Dracula's gradual approach to Whitby. The vampire, it will be recalled, was buffeting the *Demeter* in the Atlantic between the twenty-fourth and twenty-eighth of July. It was on the twenty-sixth of July that Mina recorded that Lucy had resumed her old habit of sleepwalking. Since Dracula does not arrive in Whitby until 1:00 A.M. on the eighth of August, we have clear evidence that he is able to project his powers over long—very long—distances.

8 *even a full-grown cat will not tempt him.* Astonishing! Seward, on page 74, speculates on Renfield's progress from flies to spiders and so on up the scale of life and wonders whether as a scientist it would not "be worthwhile to complete the experiment"—that is, to permit Renfield ever larger victims. Here we have an indication that Seward, at least, is willing to undertake the experiment. There has been an offer first of a kitten, then of a full-grown cat! Here Renfield is sane enough to reject it, though he was eager for it earlier.

9 *"The unexpected always happens."* Modern collections of quotations show no trace of Disraeli as the author of this one. In H. L. Mencken's *A New Dictionary of Quotations*, the remark is noted as an "English proverb, not recorded before the nineteenth century." Benham's *Book of Quotations* says, laconically, "proverb. Source unknown."

Dr. Seward's Diary.

20 *August.*—The case of Renfield grows even more interesting. He has now so far quieted that there are spells of cessation from his passion. For the first week after his attack he was perpetually violent. Then one night, just as the moon rose, he grew quiet, and kept murmuring to himself: "Now I can wait; now I can wait." The attendant came to tell me, so I ran down at once to have a look at him. He was still in the strait-waistcoat and in the padded room, but the suffused look had gone from his face, and his eyes had something of their old pleading—I might almost say, "cringing"—softness. I was satisfied with his present condition, and directed him to be relieved. The attendants hesitated, but finally carried out my wishes without protest. It was a strange thing that the patient had humour enough to see their distrust, for, coming close to me, he said in a whisper, all the while looking furtively at them:—

"They think I could hurt you! Fancy *me* hurting *you*! The fools!"

It was soothing, somehow, to the feelings to find myself dissociated even in the mind of this poor madman from the others; but all the same I do not follow his thought. Am I to take it that I have anything in common with him, so that we are, as it were, to stand together; or has he to gain from me some good so stupendous that my well-being is needful to him? I must find out later on. To-night he will not speak. Even
8 the offer of a kitten or even a full-grown cat will not tempt him. He will only say: "I don't take any stock in cats. I have more to think of now, and I can wait; I can wait."

After a while I left him. The attendant tells me that he was quiet until just before dawn, and that then he began to get uneasy, and at length violent, until at last he fell into a paroxysm which exhausted him so that he swooned into a sort of coma.

. . . . Three nights has the same thing happened—violent all day, then quiet from moonrise to sunrise. I wish I could get some clue to the cause. It would almost seem as if there was some influence which came and went. Happy thought! We shall to-night play sane wits against mad ones. He escaped before without our help; to-night he shall escape with it. We shall give him a chance, and have the men ready to follow in case they are required. . . . .

9 23 *August.*—"The unexpected always happens." How well Disraeli knew life. Our bird when he found the cage open would not fly, so all our subtle arrangements went for nought. At any rate, we have proved one thing: that the spells of quietness last a reasonable time. We shall in future be able to ease his bonds for a few hours each day. I have given orders to the night attendant merely to shut him in the padded room, when once he is quiet, until an hour before sunrise. The poor soul's body will enjoy the relief even if his mind cannot appreciate it. Hark! The unexpected again! I am called; the patient has once more escaped.

Later.—Another night adventure. Renfield artfully waited until the attendant was entering the room to inspect. Then he dashed out past him and flew down the passage. I sent word for the attendants to follow. Again he went into the grounds of the deserted house, and we found him in the same place, pressed against the old chapel door. When he saw me he became furious, and had not the attendants seized him in time, he would have tried to kill me. As we were holding him a strange thing happened. He suddenly redoubled his efforts, and then as suddenly grew calm. I looked round instinctively, but could see nothing. Then I caught the patient's eye and followed it, but could trace nothing as it looked into the moonlit sky except a big bat, which was flapping its silent and ghostly way to the west. Bats usually wheel and flit about, but this one seemed to go straight on, as if it knew where it was bound for or had some intention of its own. The patient grew calmer every instant, and presently said:—

"You needn't tie me; I shall go quietly!" Without trouble we came back to the house. I feel there is something ominous in his calm, and shall not forget this night. . . . .

Lucy Westenra's Diary.

Hillingham, 24 *August*.—I must imitate Mina, and keep 10
writing things down. Then we can have long talks when we do meet. I wonder when it will be. I wish she were with me again, for I feel so unhappy. Last night I seemed to be dreaming again just as I was at Whitby. Perhaps it is the change of air, or getting home again. It is all dark and horrid to me, for I can remember nothing; but I am full of vague fear, and I feel so weak and worn out. When Arthur came to lunch he looked quite grieved when he saw me, and I hadn't the spirit to try to be cheerful. I wonder if I could sleep in mother's room to-night. I shall make an excuse and try.

25 *August*.—Another bad night. Mother did not seem to take to my proposal. She seems not too well herself, and doubtless she fears to worry me. I tried to keep awake, and succeeded for a while; but when the clock struck twelve it waked me from a doze, so I must have been falling asleep. There was a sort of scratching or flapping at the window, but I did not mind it, and as I remember no more, I suppose I must then have fallen asleep. More bad dreams. I wish I could remember them. This morning I am horribly weak. My face is ghastly pale, and my throat pains me. It must
be something wrong with my lungs, for I don't seem ever to 11
get air enough. I shall try to cheer up when Arthur comes, or else I know he will be miserable to see me so.

Letter, Arthur Holmwood to Dr. Seward.

"*Albemarle Hotel*, 31 *August*. 12

"My dear Jack,—

"I want you to do me a favour. Lucy is ill; that is, she has no special disease, but she looks awful, and is getting worse every day. I have asked her if there is any cause; I do not dare to ask her mother, for to disturb the poor lady's mind about her daughter in her present state of health would be fatal. Mrs. Westenra has confided to me that her doom is spoken —disease of the heart—though poor Lucy does not know it yet.

10 Hillingham. Presumably the Westenra family home in London. The name appears in no street guides either of Stoker's time or of the present day.

11 *with my lungs*. Lucy's symptoms are described with pretty fair accuracy here. Loss of blood does produce a quicker heartbeat and respiratory rate as the heart tries to circulate fewer red blood cells to the body. A normal respiratory rate is 14 to 16 breaths per minute. In Lucy's condition she is probably breathing 30 or 40 times per minute.

ALBEMARLE HOTEL.

12 "Albemarle Hotel." Reginald Colby (p. 160) tells us that "the best known of the Albemarle Street hotels was the Hotel Albemarle, the high gabled, mottled pink building which still stands at the corner of Albemarle Street and Piccadilly facing down St. James's Street. Originally Gordon's Hotel, where Byron and Nelson stayed, it became the Albemarle Hotel in 1858. Whistler made a well-known etching of St. James's Street, alive with hansoms, drawn from an upper window one June day in 1878. Sir Ernest George and Harold Peto rebuilt it in their *'François Premier'* style in 1889 with—a surprising innovation—the kitchens at the top of the house. Given the more fashionable sounding name of the 'Hotel Albemarle' it became the smartest hotel in the West End in the 'nineties, patronised by 'royalty, the diplomatic corps and the nobility'. Oscar Wilde used to frequent it at the height of his fame. A room and attendance cost 7s., lunch 4s. and dinner 7s. to quote the prices in Baedeker's *London* of 1898, and non-residents wishing to lunch or dine in the *Salle-à-Manger* were requested 'to leave their names at the Bureau beforehand.' "

The story goes that comedienne Lillie Langtry maintained a suite at the Albemarle "where she used to entertain, among others, the future Edward VII."

I am sure that there is something preying on my dear girl's mind. I am almost distracted when I think of her; to look at her gives me a pang. I told her I should ask you to see her, and though she demurred at first--I know why, old fellow—she finally consented. It will be a painful task for you, I know, old friend, but it is for *her* sake, and I must not hesitate to ask, or you to act. You are to come to lunch at Hillingham to-morrow, two o'clock, so as not to arouse any suspicion in Mrs. Westenra, and after lunch Lucy will take an opportunity of being alone with you. I shall come in for tea, and we can go away together; I am filled with anxiety, and want to consult with you alone as soon as I can after you have seen her. Do not fail!

"ARTHUR."

Telegram, Arthur Holmwood to Seward.

"1 *September.*

"Am summoned to see my father, who is worse. Am writing. Write me fully by to-night's post to Ring. Wire me if necessary."

Letter from Dr. Seward to Arthur Holmwood.

"2 *September.*

"My dear old fellow,—

"With regard to Miss Westenra's health, I hasten to let you know at once that in my opinion there is not any functional disturbance or any malady that I know of. At the same time, I am not by any means satisfied with her appearance; she is woefully different from what she was when I saw her last. Of course you must bear in mind that I did not have full opportunity of examination such as I should wish; our very friendship makes a little difficulty which not even medical science or custom can bridge over. I had better tell you exactly what happened, leaving you to draw, in a measure, your own conclusions. I shall then say what I have done and propose doing.

"I found Miss Westenra in seemingly gay spirits. Her mother was present, and in a few seconds I made up my mind that she was trying all she knew to mislead her mother and prevent her from being anxious. I have no doubt she guesses, if she does not know, what need of caution there is. We lunched alone, and as we all exerted ourselves to be cheerful, we got, as some kind of reward for our labours, some real cheerfulness amongst us. Then Mrs. Westenra went to lie down, and Lucy was left with me. We went into her boudoir, and till we got there her gaiety remained, for the servants were coming and going. As soon as the door was closed, however, the mask fell from her face, and she sank down into a chair with a great sigh, and hid her eyes with her hand. When I saw that her high spirits had failed, I at once took advantage of her reaction to make a diagnosis. She said to me very sweetly:—

"'I cannot tell you how I loathe talking about myself.' I reminded her that a doctor's confidence was sacred, but that you were grievously anxious about her. She caught on to my meaning at once, and settled that matter in a word. 'Tell

Arthur everything you choose. I do not care for myself, but all for him!' So I am quite free.

"I could easily see that she is somewhat bloodless, but I could not see the usual anæmic signs, and by a chance I was actually able to test the quality of her blood, for in opening a window which was stiff a cord gave way, and she cut her hand slightly with broken glass. It was a slight matter in itself, but it gave me an evident chance, and I secured a few drops of the blood and have analysed them. The qualitative analysis gives a quite 13 normal condition, and shows, I should infer, in itself a vigorous state of health. In other physical matters I was quite satisfied that there is no need for anxiety; but as there must be a cause somewhere, I have come to the conclusion that it must be something mental. She complains of difficulty in breathing satisfactorily at times, and of heavy, lethargic sleep, with dreams that frighten her, but regarding which she can remember nothing. She says that as a child she used to walk in her sleep, and that when in Whitby the habit came back, and that once she walked out in the night and went to the East Cliff, where Miss Murray found her; but she assures me that of late the habit has not returned. I am in doubt, and so have done the best thing I know of; I have written to my old friend and master, Professor Van Helsing, of Amsterdam, who knows as much about obscure diseases as any one in the world. I have asked him to come over, and as you told me that all things were to be at your charge, I have mentioned to him who you are and your relations to Miss Westenra. This, my dear fellow, is only in obedience to your wishes, for I am only too proud and happy to do anything I can for her. Van Helsing would, I know, do anything for me for a personal reason. So, no matter on what ground he comes, we must accept his wishes. He is a seemingly arbitrary man, but this is because he knows what he is talking about better than any one else. He is a philosopher and a metaphysician, and one of the most advanced scientists of his day; and he has, I believe, an absolutely open mind. This, with an iron nerve, a temper of the ice-brook, an indomitable resolution, self-command and toleration exalted from virtues to blessings, and the kindliest and truest heart that beats—these form his equipment for the noble work that he is doing for mankind—work both in theory and practice, for his views are as wide as his all-embracing sympathy. I tell you these facts that you may know why I have such confidence in him. I have asked him to come at once. I shall see Miss Westenra to-morrow again. She is to meet me at the Stores, so that I may not alarm her mother by too early a repetition of my call.

"Yours always,

"JOHN SEWARD."

Letter, Abraham Van Helsing, M.D., D.Ph., D.Lit., etc., etc., to Dr. Seward.

"*2 September.*

"My good Friend,—

"When I have received your letter I am already coming to you. By good fortune I can leave just at once, without wrong

13 *analysed them.* Seward, the lover, turns into Seward the doctor.

The "qualitative analysis" to which he subjected Lucy's blood could not have shown that she was in a vigorous state of health. Dr. Herman Schwartz writes: "Even qualitatively, her blood would have been paler because there would be fewer and smaller red blood cells."

Her disturbed dreams, on the other hand, may be a function of her blood loss since "anemia or any anoxic state . . . provokes active kaleidoscopic dreaming."

14 *the Great Eastern Hotel.* The Great Eastern Hotel (now called the Great Eastern Hotel and Albercorn Rooms) has been on its present site since 1860. The hotel is centrally located at a railhead for the boat trains to and from Harwich and Holland.

Later, Stoker either forgets that Van Helsing was to stay at the Great Eastern or chooses to have him change hotels, so that we find him (on p. 125) staying at the Berkeley.

to any of those who have trusted me. Were fortune other, then it were bad for those who have trusted, for I come to my friend when he call me to aid those he holds dear. Tell your friend that when that time you suck from my wound so swiftly the poison of the gangrene from that knife that our other friend, too nervous, let slip, you did more for him when he wants my aids and you call for them than all his great fortune could do. But it is pleasure added to do for him, your friend; it is to
14 you that I come. Have then rooms for me at the Great Eastern Hotel, so that I may be near to hand, and please it so arrange that we may see the young lady not too late on to-morrow, for it is likely that I may have to return here that night. But if need be I shall come again in three days, and stay longer if it must. Till then good-bye, my friend John.

"VAN HELSING."

Letter, Dr. Seward to Hon. Arthur Holmwood.

"3 *September.*

"My dear Art,—

"Van Helsing has come and gone. He came on with me to Hillingham, and found that, by Lucy's discretion, her mother was lunching out, so that we were alone with her. Van Helsing made a very careful examination of the patient. He is to report to me, and I shall advise you, for of course I was not present all the time. He is, I fear, much concerned, but says he must think. When I told him of our friendship and how you trust to me in the matter, he said: 'You must tell him all you think. Tell him what I think, if you can guess it, if you will. Nay, I am not jesting. This is no jest, but life and death, perhaps more.' I asked what he meant by that, for he was very serious. This was when we had come back to town, and he was having a cup of tea before starting on his return to Amsterdam. He would not give me any further clue. You must not be angry with him, Art, because his very reticence means that all his brains are working for her good. He will speak plainly enough when the time comes, be sure. So I told

him I would simply write an account of our visit, just as if I were doing a descriptive special article for *The Daily Telegraph.* He seemed not to notice, but remarked that the smuts in 15
London were not quite so bad as they used to be when he was a student here. I am to get his report to-morrow if he can possibly make it. In any case I am to have a letter.

"Well, as to the visit. Lucy was more cheerful than on the day I first saw her, and certainly looked better. She had lost something of the ghastly look that so upset you, and her breathing was normal. She was very sweet to the Professor (as she always is), and tried to make him feel at ease; though I could see that the poor girl was making a hard struggle for it. I believe Van Helsing saw it, too, for I saw the quick look under his bushy brows that I knew of old. Then he began to chat of all things, except ourselves and diseases, and with such an infinite geniality that I could see poor Lucy's pretence of animation merge into reality. Then, without any seeming change, he brought the conversation gently round to his visit, and suavely said:—

"'My dear young miss, I have the so great pleasure because you are much beloved. That is much, my dear, even were there that which I do not see. They told me you were down in the spirit, and that you were of a ghastly pale. To them I say: "Pouf!"' And he snapped his fingers at me and went on: 'But you and I shall show them how wrong they are. How can he'—and he pointed at me with the same look and gesture as that with which once he pointed me out to his class, on, or rather after, a particular occasion which he never fails to remind me of 16
—'know anything of a young ladies? He has his madmans to play with, and to bring them back to happiness and to those that love them. It is much to do, and, oh, but there are rewards, in that we can bestow such happiness. But the young ladies! He has no wife nor daughter, and the young do not tell themselves to the young, but to the old, like me, who have known so many sorrows and the causes of them. So, my dear, we will send him away to smoke the cigarette in the garden, whiles you and I have little talk all to ourselves.' I took the hint, and strolled about, and presently the Professor came to the window and called me in. He looked grave, but said: 'I have made careful examination, but there is no functional cause. With you I agree that there has been much blood lost; it has been, but is not. But the conditions of her are in no way anæmic. I have asked her to send me her maid, that I may ask just one or two question, that so I may not chance to miss nothing. I know well what she will say. And yet there is cause; there is always cause for everything. I must go back home and think. You must send to me the telegram every day; and if there be cause I shall come again. The disease—for not to be all well is a disease—interest me, and the sweet young dear, she interest me too. She charm me, and for 17
her, if not for you or disease, I come.'

"As I tell you, he would not say a word more, even when we were alone. And so now, Art, you know all I know. I shall keep stern watch. I trust your poor father is rallying. It must be a terrible thing to you, my dear old fellow, to be placed in such a position between two people who are both so dear to you. I know your idea of duty to your father, and

15 *the smuts.* Smog.

16 *never fails to remind me of.* Probably the gangrene sucking incident mentioned on page 110.

17 *She charm me.* This is the first, though not the last, time when Van Helsing's eye for the ladies is brought to our attention.

18 *Just before the stroke of noon.* Renfield's rages correspond to the times when Dracula's powers are limited.

you are right to stick to it; but, if need be, I shall send you word to come at once to Lucy; so do not be over-anxious unless you hear from me."

Dr. Seward's Diary.

4 *September.*—Zoophagous patient still keeps up our interest in him. He had only one outburst, and that was yesterday at
18 an unusual time. Just before the stroke of noon he began to grow restless. The attendant knew the symptoms, and at once summoned aid. Fortunately the men came at a run, and were just in time, for at the stroke of noon he became so violent that it took all their strength to hold him. In about five minutes, however, he began to get more and more quiet, and finally sank into a sort of melancholy, in which state he has remained up to now. The attendant tells me that his screams whilst in the paroxysm were really appalling; I found my hands full when I got in, attending to some of the other patients who were frightened by him. Indeed, I can quite understand the effect, for the sounds disturbed even me, though I was some distance away. It is now after the dinner-hour of the asylum, and as yet my patient sits in a corner brooding, with a dull, sullen, woe-begone look in his face, which seems rather to indicate than to show something directly. I cannot quite understand it.

Later.—Another change in my patient. At five o'clock I looked in on him, and found him seemingly as happy and contented as he used to be. He was catching flies and eating them, and was keeping note of his capture by making nail-marks on the edge of the door between the ridges of padding. When he saw me, he came over and apologised for his bad conduct, and asked me in a very humble, cringing way to be led back to his own room and to have his note-book again. I thought it well to humour him; so he is back in his room, with the window open. He has the sugar of his tea spread out on the window-sill, and is reaping quite a harvest of flies. He is not now eating them, but putting them into a box, as of old, and is already examining the corners of his room to find a spider. I tried to get him to talk about the past few days, for any clue to his thoughts would be of immense help to me; but he would not rise. For a moment or two he looked very sad, and said in a sort of far-away voice, as though saying it rather to himself than to me:—

"All over! all over! He has deserted me. No hope for me now unless I do it for myself!" Then suddenly turning to me in a resolute way, he said: "Doctor, won't you be very good to me and let me have a little more sugar? I think it would be good for me."

"And the flies?" I said.

"Yes! The flies like it, too, and I like the flies; therefore I like it." And there are people who know so little as to think that madmen do not argue. I procured him a double supply, and left him as happy a man as, I suppose, any in the world. I wish I could fathom his mind.

Midnight.—Another change in him. I had been to see Miss Westenra, whom I found much better, and had just returned, and was standing at our own gate looking at the sunset, when once more I heard him yelling. As his room is on this side of the house, I could hear it better than in the morning. It was a shock to me to turn from the wonderful smoky beauty of a sunset over London, with its lurid lights and inky shadows and all the marvellous tints that come on foul clouds even as on foul water, and to realise all the grim sternness of my own cold stone building, with its wealth of breathing misery, and my own desolate heart to endure it all. I reached him just as the sun was going down, and from his window saw the red disc sink. As it sank he became less and less frenzied; and just as it dipped he slid from the hands that held him, an inert mass, on the floor. It is wonderful, however, what intellectual recuperative power lunatics have, for within a few minutes he stood up quite calmly and looked around him. I signalled to the attendants not to hold him, for I was anxious to see what he would do. He went straight over to the window and brushed out the crumbs of sugar; then he took his fly-box and emptied it outside, and threw away the box; then he shut the window, and crossing over, sat down on his bed. All this surprised me, so I asked him: "Are you not going to keep flies any more?"

"No," said he; "I am sick of all that rubbish!" He certainly is a wonderfully interesting study. I wish I could get some glimpse of his mind or of the cause of his sudden passion. Stop; there may be a clue after all, if we can find
why to-day his paroxysms came on at high noon and at sunset. **19**
Can it be that there is a malign influence of the sun at periods **20**
which affects certain natures—as at times the moon does others? We shall see.

Telegram, Seward, London, to Van Helsing, Amsterdam.
"4 *September.*—Patient still better to-day."

Telegram, Seward, London, to Van Helsing, Amsterdam.

"5 *September.*—Patient greatly improved. Good appetite; sleeps naturally; good spirits; colour coming back."

Telegram, Seward, London, to Van Helsing, Amsterdam.

"6 *September.*—Terrible change for the worse. Come at once; do not lose an hour. I hold over telegram to Holmwood till have seen you."

19 *at high noon and at sunset.* The times when Dracula's power wanes and waxes—see page 213 where Dr. Van Helsing sets down the laws that govern Dracula's existence.

20 *a malign influence of the sun.* Seward's speculations about the sun's influences on human behavior continue into our own day. In 1937 Harlan True Stetson (p. 25), a writer on sunspots, observed that:

> "A sufficient number of observations have been made to show that there is a diurnal variation in the numbers of positive and negative ions in the air of the earth's surface. They have been found to rise near midday when the sun's radiation is strongest. They also show a seasonal rise, with the largest number occurring in the summer season, which would again appear to indicate that sunshine may be an important factor in their distribution.
>
> "If, now, changes in the character of sunshine, such as more or less ultraviolet light, affect the vitamin content of the human body with a consequent impact upon the sensitive endocrines, and if also it shall become established that changes in the atmospheric ions through some similar mysterious processes are accompanied by psychological changes and consequent mental outlook, we have a connecting chain whereby human behaviour could respond to the sunspot cycle."

CHAPTER X.

Letter, Dr. Seward to Hon. Arthur Holmwood.

"6 *September.*

"My dear Art,—

"My news to-day is not so good. Lucy this morning had gone back a bit. There is, however, one good thing which has arisen from it: Mrs. Westenra was naturally anxious concerning Lucy, and has consulted me professionally about her. I took advantage of the opportunity, and told her that my old master, Van Helsing, the great specialist, was coming to stay with me, and that I would put her in his charge conjointly with myself; so now we can come and go without alarming her unduly, for a shock to her would mean sudden death, and this, in Lucy's weak condition, might be disastrous to her. We are hedged in with difficulties, all of us, my poor old fellow; but, please God, we shall come through them all right. If any need I shall write, so that, if you do not hear from me, take it for granted that I am simply waiting for news. In haste,

"Yours ever,

"JOHN SEWARD."

Dr. Seward's Diary.

7 *September.*—The first thing Van Helsing said to me when we met at Liverpool Street was:—

"Have you said anything to our young friend the lover of her?"

"No," I said. "I waited till I had seen you, as I said in my telegram. I wrote him a letter simply telling him that you were coming, as Miss Westenra was not so well, and that I should let him know if need be."

"Right, my friend," he said, "quite right! Better he not

know as yet; perhaps he shall never know. I pray so; but if it be needed, then he shall know all. And, my good friend John, let me caution you. You deal with the madmen. All men are mad in some way or the other; and inasmuch as you deal discreetly with your madmen, so deal with God's madmen, too—the rest of the world. You tell not your madmen what you do nor why you do it; you tell them not what you think. So you shall keep knowledge in its place, where it may rest—where it may gather its kind around it and breed. You and I shall keep as yet what we know here, and here." He touched me on the heart and on the forehead, and then touched himself the same way. "I have for myself thoughts at the present. Later I shall unfold to you."

"Why not now?" I asked. "It may do some good; we may arrive at some decision." He stopped and looked at me, and said:—

"My friend John, when the corn is grown, even before it has ripened—while the milk of its mother-earth is in him, and the sunshine has not yet begun to paint him with his gold, the husbandman he pull the ear and rub him between his rough hands, and blow away the green chaff, and say to you: 'Look! he's good corn; he will make good crop when the time comes.'" I did not see the application, and told him so. For reply he reached over and took my ear in his hand and pulled it play- 1
fully, as he used long ago to do at lectures, and said: "The good husbandman tell you so then because he knows, but not till then. But you do not find the good husbandman dig up his planted corn to see if he grow; that is for the children who play at husbandry, and not for those who take it as of the work of their life. See you now, friend John? I have sown my corn, and Nature has her work to do in making it sprout; if he sprout at all, there's some promise; and I wait till the ear begins to swell." He broke off, for he evidently saw that I understood. Then he went on, and very gravely:—

"You were always a careful student, and your case-book was ever more full than the rest. You were only student then; now you are master, and I trust that good habit have not fail. Remember, my friend, that knowledge is stronger than memory, and we should not trust the weaker. Even if you have not kept the good practice, let me tell you that this case of our dear miss is one that may be—mind, I say *may be*—of such interest to us and others that all the rest may not make him kick the beam, as your peoples say. Take then good 2
note of it. Nothing is too small. I counsel you, put down in record even your doubts and surmises. Hereafter it may be of interest to you to see how true you guess. We learn from failure, not from success!"

When I described Lucy's symptoms—the same as before, but infinitely more marked—he looked very grave, but said nothing. He took with him a bag in which were many instruments and drugs, "the ghastly paraphernalia of our beneficial trade," as he once called, in one of his lectures, the equipment of a professor of the healing craft. When we were shown in, Mrs. Westenra met us. She was alarmed, but not nearly so much as I expected to find her. Nature in one of her beneficent moods has ordained that even death has some antidote to its own terrors. Here, in a case where any

1 *took my ear in his hand.* Annotating a joke is a dangerous business, but Stoker, in this paragraph, is being so outrageous that a footnote is one's only defense.

The center of the joke is a play on the word "ear": first the "husbandman he pull the ear and rub him." A moment later, Van Helsing does the same with Seward's ear so that there is a certain violence implicit in the line, "I wait till the ear begins to swell."

Nor is that all. Van Helsing's language echoes the biblical parable of the seed and the sower in which Jesus speaks of a sower who sows his seed and ". . . some fell by the way side . . . And some fell upon a rock . . . And some fell among thorns . . . And other fell on good ground, and sprang up, and bare fruit an hundredfold" (Luke 8:5–8).

Surely Stoker remembered that that parable ends with the sentence, "He that hath ears to hear, let him hear."

2 *kick the beam.* What Van Helsing is saying here in his pseudo Dutch-English is that Lucy's case, if it were laid on a balance scale, would outweigh in importance all other cases—hence, it would "kick the beam" of the scale.

3 *spiritual pathology.* We would say "psychology."

4 *"My God!" he said; "this is dreadful. . . ."* In an emergency Van Helsing loses his accent.

5 *". . . I would give the last drop of blood in my body for her."* In real life the hugger-mugger blood transfusions that follow would almost certainly kill both donor and patient, since no effort is made by Van Helsing or Seward to match blood types, which, in any event, they could not have known about until nearly three decades later.

shock may prove fatal, matters are so ordered that, from some cause or other, the things not personal—even the terrible change in her daughter to whom she is so attached—do not seem to reach her. It is something like the way Dame Nature gathers round a foreign body an envelope of some insensitive tissue which can protect from evil that which it would otherwise harm by contact. If this be an ordered selfishness, then we should pause before we condemn any one for the vice of egoism, for there may be deeper roots for its causes than we have knowledge of.

3 I used my knowledge of this phase of spiritual pathology, and laid down a rule that she should not be present with Lucy or think of her illness more than was absolutely required. She assented readily, so readily that I saw again the hand of Nature fighting for life. Van Helsing and I were shown up to Lucy's room. If I was shocked when I saw her yesterday, I was horrified when I saw her to-day. She was ghastly, chalkily pale; the red seemed to have gone even from her lips and gums, and the bones of her face stood out prominently; her breathing was painful to see or hear. Van Helsing's face grew set as marble, and his eyebrows converged till they almost touched over his nose. Lucy lay motionless and did not seem to have strength to speak, so for a while we were all silent. Then Van Helsing beckoned to me, and we went gently out of the room. The instant we had closed the door he stepped quickly along the passage to the next door, which was open. Then he pulled me quickly in with him and closed the door.

4 "My God!" he said; "this is dreadful. There is no time to be lost. She will die for sheer want of blood to keep the heart's action as it should be. There must be transfusion of blood at once. Is it you or me?"

"I am younger and stronger, Professor. It must be me."

"Then get ready at once. I will bring up my bag. I am prepared."

I went downstairs with him, and as we were going there was a knock at the hall-door. When we reached the hall the maid had just opened the door, and Arthur was stepping quickly in. He rushed up to me, saying in an eager whisper:—

"Jack, I was so anxious. I read between the lines of your letter, and have been in an agony. The dad was better, so I ran down here to see for myself. Is not that gentleman Dr. Van Helsing? I am so thankful to you, sir, for coming." When first the Professor's eye had lit upon him he had been angry at any interruption at such a time; but now, as he took in his stalwart proportions and recognised the strong young manhood which seemed to emanate from him, his eyes gleamed. Without a pause he said to him gravely as he held out his hand:—

"Sir, you have come in time. You are the lover of our dear miss. She is bad, very, very bad. Nay, my child, do not go like that." For he suddenly grew pale and sat down in a chair almost fainting. "You are to help her. You can do more than any that live, and your courage is your best help."

"What can I do?" asked Arthur hoarsely. "Tell me,
5 and I shall do it. My life is hers, and I would give the last drop of blood in my body for her." The Professor has a

strongly humorous side, and I could from old knowledge detect a trace of its origin in his answer:—

"My young sir, I do not ask so much as that—not the last!"

"What shall I do?" There was fire in his eyes, and his open nostril quivered with intent. Van Helsing slapped him on the shoulder. "Come!" he said. "You are a man, and it is a man we want. You are better than me, better than my friend John." Arthur looked bewildered, and the Professor went on by explaining in a kindly way:—

"Young miss is bad, very bad. She wants blood, and
blood she must have or die. My friend John and I have consulted; and we are about to perform what we call transfusion of
blood—to transfer from full veins of one to the empty veins 6
which pine for him. John was to give his blood, as he is the
more young and strong than me"—here Arthur took my hand
and wrung it hard in silence—"but, now you are here, you are
more good than us, old or young, who toil much in the world
of thought. Our nerves are not so calm and our blood not so 7
bright than yours!" Arthur turned to him and said:—

"If you only knew how gladly I would die for her you would understand——"

He stopped, with a sort of choke in his voice.

"Good boy!" said Van Helsing. "In the not-so-far-off you will be happy that you have done all for her you love. Come now and be silent. You shall kiss her once before it is done, but then you must go; and you must leave at my sign. Say no word to Madame; you know how it is with her! There must be no shock; any knowledge of this would be one. Come!"

We all went up to Lucy's room. Arthur by direction remained outside. Lucy turned her head and looked at us, but said nothing. She was not asleep, but she was simply too weak to make the effort. Her eyes spoke to us; that was all. Van Helsing took some things from his bag and laid them on a little table out of sight. Then he mixed a narcotic, and coming over to the bed, said cheerily:—

"Now, little miss, here is your medicine. Drink it off, like a good child. See, I lift you so that to swallow is easy. Yes." She had made the effort with success.

It astonished me how long the drug took to act. This, in
fact, marked the extent of her weakness. The time seemed
endless until sleep began to flicker in her eyelids. At last,
however, the narcotic began to manifest its potency; and she fell 8
into a deep sleep. When the Professor was satisfied he called
Arthur into the room, and bade him strip off his coat. Then
he added: "You may take that one little kiss whiles I bring
over the table. Friend John, help to me!" So neither of us
looked whilst he bent over her.

Van Helsing turning to me, said:—

"He is so young and strong and of blood so pure that we 9
need not defibrinate it."

Then with swiftness, but with absolute method, Van Helsing
performed the operation. As the transfusion went on some- 10
thing like life seemed to come back to poor Lucy's cheeks,
and through Arthur's growing pallor the joy of his face seemed
absolutely to shine. After a bit I began to grow anxious, for

6 *empty veins.* Veins are never empty. They are full of serum plus red blood cells.

7 *blood not so bright.* The brightest blood is dilute, *anemic blood.* On the other hand, adequate normal blood is dark.

8 *the narcotic began to manifest its potency.* Narcotics are for pain; narcoleptic drugs and hypnotics are for sleep.

9 "*. . . we need not defibrinate it.*" Fibrin is the clotting material in blood.

10 *performed the operation.* Did he transfuse the blood directly or use a receptacle?

11 *the loss of blood was telling on Arthur.* If the loss of blood was telling on Arthur, it would be because he had given Lucy more than two pints of his own blood. The healthy adult human body has four or five quarts of blood flowing in it. Modern blood-bank practice is to limit blood donations to one pint at prescribed intervals.

12 *port wine.* This is an old remedy for anemia. Port or port steeped in iron filings.

13 *trituration.* Rubbing, crushing, or bruising.

11 the loss of blood was telling on Arthur, strong man as he was. It gave me an idea of what a terrible strain Lucy's system must have undergone that what weakened Arthur only partially restored her. But the Professor's face was set, and he stood watch in hand and with his eyes fixed now on the patient and now on Arthur. I could hear my own heart beat. Presently he said in a soft voice: "Do not stir an instant. It is enough. You attend him; I will look to her." When all was over I could see how much Arthur was weakened. I dressed the wound and took his arm to bring him away, when Van Helsing spoke without turning round—the man seems to have eyes in the back of his head:—

"The brave lover, I think deserve another kiss, which he shall have presently." And as he had now finished his operation, he adjusted the pillow to the patient's head. As he did so the narrow black velvet band which she seems always to wear round her throat, buckled with an old diamond buckle which her lover had given her, was dragged a little up, and showed a red mark on her throat. Arthur did not notice it, but I could hear the deep hiss of indrawn breath which is one of Van Helsing's ways of betraying emotion. He said nothing at the moment, but turned to me, saying: "Now take down our brave
12 young lover, give him of the port wine, and let him lie down a while. He must then go home and rest, sleep much and eat much, that he may be recruited of what he has so given to his love. He must not stay here. Hold! a moment. I may take it, sir, that you are anxious of result. Then bring it with you that in all ways the operation is successful. You have saved her life this time, and you can go home and rest easy in mind that all that can be is. I shall tell her all when she is well; she shall love you none the less for what you have done. Good-bye."

When Arthur had gone I went back to the room. Lucy was sleeping gently, but her breathing was stronger; I could see the counterpane move as her breast heaved. By the bedside sat Van Helsing, looking at her intently. The velvet band again covered the red mark. I asked the Professor in a whisper:—

"What do you make of that mark on her throat?"

"What do you make of it?"

"I have not seen it yet," I answered, and then and there proceeded to loose the band. Just over the external jugular vein there were two punctures, not large, but not wholesome-looking. There was no sign of disease, but the edges were
13 white and worn-looking, as if by some trituration. It at once occurred to me that this wound, or whatever it was, might be the means of that manifest loss of blood; but I abandoned the idea as soon as formed, for such a thing could not be. The whole bed would have been drenched to a scarlet with the blood which the girl must have lost to leave such a pallor as she had before the transfusion.

"Well?" said Van Helsing.

"Well," said I, "I can make nothing of it." The Professor stood up. "I must go back to Amsterdam to-night," he said. "There are books and things there which I want. You must remain here all the night, and you must not let your sight pass from her."

"Shall I have a nurse?" I asked.

"We are the best nurses, you and I. You keep watch all

night; see that she is well fed, and that nothing disturbs her. You must not sleep all the night. Later on we can sleep, you and I. I shall be back so soon as possible. And then we may begin."

"May begin?" I said. "What on earth do you mean?"

"We shall see!" he answered as he hurried out. He came back a moment later and put his head inside the door, and said, with warning finger held up:—

"Remember, she is your charge. If you leave her, and harm befall, you shall not sleep easy hereafter!"

Dr. Seward's Diary—continued.

8 *September.*—I sat up all night with Lucy. The opiate worked itself off towards dusk, and she waked naturally; she looked a different being from what she had been before the operation. Her spirits even were good, and she was full of a happy vivacity, but I could see evidences of the absolute prostration which she had undergone. When I told Mrs. Westenra that Dr. Van Helsing had directed that I should sit up with her she almost pooh-poohed the idea, pointing out her daughter's renewed strength and excellent spirits. I was firm, however, and made preparations for my long vigil. When her maid had prepared her for the night I came in, having in the meantime had supper, and took a seat by the bedside. She did not in any way make objection, but looked at me gratefully whenever I caught her eye. After a long spell she seemed sinking off to sleep, but with an effort seemed to pull herself together and shook it off. This was repeated several times, with greater effort and with shorter pauses as the time moved on. It was apparent that she did not want to sleep, so I tackled the subject at once:—

"You do not want to go to sleep?"

"No; I am afraid."

"Afraid to go to sleep! Why so? It is the boon we all crave for."

"Ah, not if you were like me—if sleep was to you a presage of horror!"

"A presage of horror! What on earth do you mean?"

"I don't know; oh, I don't know. And that is what is so terrible. All this weakness comes to me in sleep; until I dread the very thought."

"But, my dear girl, you may sleep to-night. I am here watching you, and I can promise that nothing will happen."

"Ah, I can trust you!" I seized the opportunity, and said: "I promise you that if I see any evidence of bad dreams I will wake you at once."

"You will? Oh, will you really? How good you are to me. Then I will sleep!" And almost at the word she gave a deep sigh of relief, and sank back, asleep.

All night long I watched by her. She never stirred, but slept on and on in a deep, tranquil, life-giving, health-giving sleep. Her lips were slightly parted, and her breast rose and fell with the regularity of a pendulum. There was a smile on her face, and it was evident that no bad dreams had come to disturb her peace of mind.

In the early morning her maid came, and I left her in her

care and took myself back home, for I was anxious about many things. I sent a short wire to Van Helsing and to Arthur, telling them of the excellent result of the operation. My own work, with its manifold arrears, took me all day to clear off; it was dark when I was able to inquire about my zoophagous patient. The report was good: he had been quite quiet for the past day and night. A telegram came from Van Helsing at Amsterdam whilst I was at dinner, suggesting that I should be at Hillingham to-night, as it might be well to be at hand, and stating that he was leaving by the night mail and would join me early in the morning.

9 *September*.—I was pretty tired and worn out when I got to Hillingham. For two nights I had hardly had a wink of sleep, and my brain was beginning to feel that numbness which marks cerebral exhaustion. Lucy was up and in cheerful spirits. When she shook hands with me she looked sharply in my face and said:—

"No sitting up to-night for you. You are worn out. I am quite well again; indeed, I am; and if there is to be any sitting up, it is I who will sit up with you." I would not argue the point, but went and had my supper. Lucy came with me, and, enlivened by her charming presence, I made an excellent meal, and had a couple of glasses of the more than excellent port. Then Lucy took me upstairs, and showed me a room next her own, where a cosy fire was burning. "Now," she said, "you must stay here. I shall leave this door open and my door too. You can lie on the sofa, for I know that nothing would induce any of you doctors to go to bed whilst there is a patient above the horizon. If I want anything I shall call out, and you can come to me at once." I could not but acquiesce, for I was "dog-tired," and could not have sat up had I tried. So, on her renewing her promise to call me if she should want anything, I lay on the sofa, and forgot all about everything.

Lucy Westenra's Diary.

9 *September*.—I feel so happy to-night. I have been so miserably weak, that to be able to think and move about is like feeling sunshine after a long spell of east wind out of a steel sky. Somehow Arthur feels very, very close to me. I seem to feel his presence warm about me. I suppose it is that sickness and weakness are selfish things and turn our inner eyes and sympathy on ourselves, whilst health and strength give Love rein, and in thought and feeling he can wander where he wills. I know where my thoughts are. If Arthur only knew! My dear, my dear, your ears must tingle as you sleep, as mine do waking. Oh, the blissful rest of last night! How I slept, with that dear, good Dr. Seward watching me. And to-night I shall not fear to sleep, since he is close at hand and within call. Thank everybody for being so good to me! Thank God! Good-night, Arthur.

Dr. Seward's Diary.

10 *September*.—I was conscious of the Professor's hand on my head, and started awake all in a second. That is one of the things that we learn in an asylum, at any rate.

" And how is our patient ? "
" Well, when I left her, or rather when she left me," I
answered.
" Come, let us see," he said. And together we went into the
room.
The blind was down, and I went over to raise it gently,
whilst Van Helsing stepped, with his soft, cat-like tread, over
to the bed.
As I raised the blind, and the morning sunlight flooded the
room, I heard the Professor's low hiss of inspiration, and
knowing its rarity, a deadly fear shot through my heart. As I
passed over he moved back, and his exclamation of horror,
" Gott in Himmel ! " needed no enforcement from his agonised 14
face. He raised his hand and pointed to the bed, and his
iron face was drawn and ashen white. I felt my knees begin
to tremble.
There on the bed, seemingly in a swoon, lay poor Lucy,
more horribly white and wan-looking than ever. Even the
lips were white, and the gums seemed to have shrunken back 15
from the teeth, as we sometimes see in a corpse after a prolonged illness. Van Helsing raised his foot to stamp in anger,
but the instinct of his life and all the long years of habit stood
to him, and he put it down again softly. " Quick ! " he said.
" Bring the brandy." I flew to the dining-room, and returned
with the decanter. He wetted the poor white lips with it, and
together we rubbed palm and wrist and heart. He felt her
heart, and after a few moments of agonising suspense said :—
" It is not too late. It beats, though but feebly. All our
work is undone ; we must begin again. There is no young
Arthur here now ; I have to call on you yourself this time,
friend John." As he spoke, he was dipping into his bag and 16
producing the instruments for transfusion ; I had taken off
my coat and rolled up my shirt-sleeve. There was no possibility of an opiate just at present, and no need of one ; and so, 17
without a moment's delay, we began the operation. After a
time—it did not seem a short time either, for the draining 18
away of one's blood, no matter how willingly it be given, is
a terrible feeling—Van Helsing held up a warning finger.
" Do not stir," he said, " but I fear that with growing strength
she may wake ; and that would make danger, oh, so much
danger. But I shall precaution take. I shall give hypo-
dermic injection of morphia." He proceeded then, swiftly and 19
deftly, to carry out his intent. The effect on Lucy was not
bad, for the faint seemed to merge subtly into the narcotic
sleep. It was with a feeling of personal pride that I could see a
faint tinge of colour steal back into the pallid cheeks and lips.
No man knows till he experiences it, what it is to feel his own
life-blood drawn away into the veins of the woman he loves.

The Professor watched me critically. " That will do," he
said. " Already ?" I remonstrated. " You took a great deal
more from Art." To which he smiled a sad sort of smile as he
replied :—

" He is her lover, her *fiancé*. You have work, much work,
to do for her and for others ; and the present will suffice."

When we stopped the operation, he attended to Lucy, whilst
I applied digital pressure to my own incision. I laid down,
whilst I waited his leisure to attend to me, for I felt faint and a 20

14 *"Gott in Himmel!"* Van Helsing forsakes his Dutch for German. A literal Dutch translation of this would be *"God in de hemel!"*, though the more colloquial expression is *"O God!"* or *"Mijn God!"* for "Oh God!" and "My God!"

15 *the gums seemed to have shrunken back.* There is no medical reason for this.

16 *he was dipping into his bag.* Van Helsing is something of a medical boy scout who is prepared for any contingency. Here, a blood transfusion; later, sawing through iron bars; much later a trephining operation.

17 *and no need of one.* On the contrary, a mild analgesic would be useful here, since, in Stoker's day, transfusion needles were larger than they are now and induced considerable pain.

18 *the draining away of one's blood.* This is an exceptionally striking scene that lingers in the memory. Certainly it lingered in Lawrence Durrell's, who borrowed Stoker's phrasing and used it in a remarkable episode in *Balthazar* (p. 197), where the vampire's victim says proudly: "Until you have experienced it . . . you have no idea what it is like. To have one's blood sucked in darkness by someone one adores."

19 *". . . injection of morphia."* Nonsense! Again, . . .

20 *I felt faint and a little sick.* It is clear that the transfusion is an erotic gesture, and so Van Helsing understands it. Lucy is faint from *her* experience. Seward is faint from his. They have mingled their blood, and if Arthur knew, he would be jealous, as Van Helsing, a pander-come-lately, points out.

21 *a wife to nurse and look after you a bit.* Earlier, Lucy had felt Arthur's closeness to her because his blood flowed in her veins. Now Seward is cast in the role of surrogate husband.

little sick. By-and-by he bound up my wound, and sent me downstairs to get a glass of wine for myself. As I was leaving the room, he came after me, and half whispered:—

"Mind, nothing must be said of this. If our young lover should turn up unexpected, as before, no word to him. It would at once frighten him and enjealous him, too. There must be none. So!"

When I came back he looked at me carefully, and then said:—

"You are not much the worse. Go into the room, and lie on your sofa, and rest awhile; then have much breakfast, and come here to me."

I followed out his orders, for I knew how right and wise they were. I had done my part, and now my next duty was to keep up my strength. I felt very weak, and in the weakness lost something of the amazement at what had occurred. I fell asleep on the sofa, however, wondering over and over again how Lucy had made such a retrograde movement, and how she could have been drained of so much blood with no sign anywhere to show for it. I think I must have continued my wonder in my dreams, for, sleeping and waking, my thoughts always came back to the little punctures in her throat and the ragged, exhausted appearance of their edges—tiny though they were.

Lucy slept well into the day; and when she woke she was fairly well and strong, though not nearly so much so as the day before. When Van Helsing had seen her, he went out for a walk, leaving me in charge, with strict injunctions that I was not to leave her for a moment. I could hear his voice in the hall, asking the way to the nearest telegraph office.

Lucy chatted with me freely, and seemed quite unconscious that anything had happened. I tried to keep her amused and interested. When her mother came up to see her, she did not seem to notice any change whatever, but said to me gratefully:—

"We owe you so much, Dr. Seward, for all you have done, but you really must now take care not to overwork yourself.
21 You are looking pale yourself. You want a wife to nurse and look after you a bit; that you do!" As she spoke, Lucy turned crimson, though it was only momentarily, for her poor wasted veins could not stand for long such an unwonted drain to the head. The reaction came in excessive pallor as she turned imploring eyes on me. I smiled and nodded, and laid my finger on my lips; with a sigh, she sank back amid her pillows.

Van Helsing returned in a couple of hours, and presently said to me: "Now you go home, and eat much and drink enough. Make yourself strong. I stay here to-night, and I shall sit up with little miss myself. You and I must watch the case, and we must have none other to know. I have grave reasons. No, do not ask them; think what you will. Do not fear to think even the most not-probable. Good-night."

In the hall two of the maids came to me, and asked if they or either of them might not sit up with Miss Lucy. They implored me to let them; and when I said it was Dr. Van Helsing's wish that either he or I should sit up, they asked me quite piteously to intercede with the "foreign gentleman."

I was much touched by their kindness. Perhaps it is because I am weak at present, and perhaps because it was on Lucy's account, that their devotion was manifested; for over and over again have I seen similar instances of woman's kindness. I got back here in time for a late dinner; went my rounds—all well; and set this down whilst waiting for sleep. It is coming.

11 *September*.—This afternoon I went over to Hillingham. Found Van Helsing in excellent spirits, and Lucy much better. Shortly after I had arrived, a big parcel from abroad came for the Professor. He opened it with much impressment—assumed, of course—and showed a great bundle of white flowers.

"These are for you, Miss Lucy," he said.

"For me? Oh, Dr. Van Helsing!"

"Yes, my dear, but not for you to play with. These are medicines." Here Lucy made a wry face. "Nay, but they are not to take in a decoction or in nauseous form, so you need not snub that so charming nose, or I shall point out to my friend Arthur what woes he may have to endure in seeing so much beauty that he so loves so much distort. Aha, my pretty miss, that bring the so nice nose all straight again. This is medicinal, but you do not know how. I put him in your window, I make pretty wreath, and hang him round your neck, so that you sleep well. Oh yes! they, like the lotus
flower, make your trouble forgotten. It smell so like the 22
waters of Lethe, and of that fountain of youth that the Conquistodores sought for in the Floridas, and find him all too late."

Whilst he was speaking, Lucy had been examining the flowers and smelling them. Now she threw them down, saying, with half-laughter and half-disgust:—

"Oh, Professor, I believe you are only putting up a joke on
me. Why, these flowers are only common garlic." 23

To my surprise, Van Helsing rose up and said with all his sternness, his iron jaw set and his bushy eyebrows meeting:—

COMMON GARLIC.

22 *the waters of Lethe*. Lethe is a river in Hades whose waters are said to produce forgetfulness in the dead. Keats's *Ode on Melancholy* begins:

"No, no! go not to Lethe, neither twist
Wolf's-bane, tight-rooted, for its poisonous wine;"

23 ". . . *common garlic*." Garlic is richly and widely praised as a remedy for nearly all the ills of mankind. Emily Gerard tells us that in Saxon Transylvania "neither salt nor garlic should ever be given away, as with them the luck goes."

Of the plants that play a part in Saxon superstition, first and foremost is the fulsome garlic—not only employed against witches, but likewise regarded as a remedy in manifold illnesses and as an antidote against poison. Garlic put in the moneybag will prevent the witches from getting at it, in the stables will keep the milk from being abstracted, and while rubbed over the body will defend a person against the pest.

The Egyptians had so high a regard for garlic that they employed it when taking an oath. The tantrum-prone Israelites, complaining of their freedom in the desert, remembered "the fish, which we did eat in Egypt freely; the cucumbers, and the melons, and the leeks, and the onions, and the garlick" (Numbers 11:5). And the Talmud, too, praises garlic, saying that "five things are said of garlic: it satisfies, warms the body, makes the face shine, increases seminal fluid, and kills tape-worms. Some add that it fosters love and drives away enmity . . . by the feeling of comfort it engenders."

The Talmud, too, suggests garlic as a remedy for toothache and earache, though in the toothache remedy one is cautioned to take "care that the garlic does not touch the flesh lest it produce leprosy."

Pliny, an older authority, says of garlic (*Natural History*, pp. 31–35) that "it keeps off serpents and scorpions by its smell, and, as some have maintained, every kind of beast. It cures bites when drunk or eaten . . ." Pliny adds that a magnet, rubbed with garlic, will lose its power.

Richard Cavendish, in his *The Black Arts* (p. 254), tells us that "in classical times people who went to gather particularly powerful herbs were warned to go fast and be chaste, to wear white clothes or go naked, and sometimes to chew garlic, the smell of which would dismay the demonic forces they were likely to disturb."

Finally, in George Deaux's *The Black Death* (p. 148), there is the testimonial of "one maiden lady who was recently quoted on the occasion of her one hundredth birthday, as attributing her long life, but not her spinsterhood, to the fact that every day for the previous eighty years she had chewed up a large piece of garlic every morning."

24 *garlic . . . all the way from Haarlem.* In England garlic is still growing in the fields in September. One assumes, therefore, that blossoming garlic is more efficacious against vampires than the ordinary plant; hence the need to import the hothouse blooms from Haarlem.

25 *round the fireplace.* In case Dracula should enter as smoke or light beams.

26 *my fly, which was waiting.* A fly was a light public carriage for passengers.

27 *and sleep I want.* Well he may. The boat-train trip from Amsterdam to London was a minimum fourteen-hour experience. Though Van Helsing's precise age is not given, the round trip and its concomitant activity would have worn out a much younger man. In 1971 I followed in Van Helsing's footsteps. Despite modern conveniences and my comparative youth, it proved an exhausting journey—and I went only *one* way, from Amsterdam to London.

28 *like unshed tears.* This is another of those fine lyric sentences that give one a startled glimpse of Stoker's submerged poetic power.

"No trifling with me! I never jest! There is grim purpose in all I do; and I warn you that you do not thwart me. Take care, for the sake of others if not for your own." Then seeing poor Lucy scared, as she might well be, he went on more gently: "Oh, little miss, my dear, do not fear me. I only do for your good; but there is much virtue to you in those so common flower. See, I place them myself in your room. I make myself the wreath that you are to wear. But hush! no telling to others that make so inquisitive questions. We must obey, and silence is a part of obedience; and obedience is to bring you strong and well into loving arms that wait for you. Now sit still awhile. Come with me, friend John, and
24 you shall help me deck the room with my garlic, which is all the way from Haarlem, where my friend Vanderpool raise herb in his glass-houses all the year. I had to telegraph yesterday, or they would not have been here."

We went into the room, taking the flowers with us. The Professor's actions were certainly odd and not to be found in any pharmacopœia that I ever heard of. First he fastened up the windows and latched them securely; next, taking a handful of the flowers, he rubbed them all over the sashes, as though to ensure that every whiff of air that might get in would be laden with the garlic smell. Then with the wisp he rubbed all over the jamb of the door, above, below, and at
25 each side, and round the fireplace in the same way. It all seemed grotesque to me, and presently I said:—

"Well, Professor, I know you always have a reason for what you do, but this certainly puzzles me. It is well we have no sceptic here, or he would say that you were working some spell to keep out an evil spirit."

"Perhaps I am!" he answered quietly as he began to make the wreath which Lucy was to wear round her neck.

We then waited whilst Lucy made her toilet for the night, and when she was in bed he came and himself fixed the wreath of garlic round her neck. The last words he said to her were:—

"Take care you do not disturb it; and even if the room feel close, do not to-night open the window or the door."

"I promise," said Lucy, "and thank you both a thousand times for all your kindness to me! Oh, what have I done to be blessed with such friends?"

26 As we left the house in my fly, which was waiting, Van Helsing said:—

27 "To-night I can sleep in peace, and sleep I want—two nights of travel, much reading in the day between, and much anxiety on the day to follow, and a night to sit up, without to wink. To-morrow in the morning early you call for me, and we come together to see our pretty miss, so much more strong for my 'spell' which I have work. Ho! ho!"

He seemed so confident that I, remembering my own confidence two nights before and with the baneful result, felt awe and vague terror. It must have been my weakness that made me hesitate to tell it to my friend, but I felt it all the more,
28 like unshed tears.

CHAPTER XI.

Lucy Westenra's Diary.

12 *September.*—How good they all are to me. I quite love that dear Dr. Van Helsing. I wonder why he was so anxious about these flowers. He positively frightened me, he was so fierce. And yet he must have been right, for I feel comfort from them already. Somehow, I do not dread being alone to-night, and I can go to sleep without fear. I shall not mind any flapping outside the window. Oh, the terrible struggle that I have had against sleep so often of late; the pain of the sleeplessness, or the pain of the fear of sleep, with such unknown horrors as it has for me! How blessed are some people, whose lives have no fears, no dreads; to whom sleep is a blessing that comes nightly, and brings nothing but sweet dreams. Well, here I am to-night, hoping for sleep, and
lying like Ophelia in the play, with "virgin crants and maiden 1
strewments." I never liked garlic before, but to-night it is delightful! There is peace in its smell; I feel sleep coming already. Good-night, everybody.

Dr. Seward's Diary.

13 *September.*—Called at the Berkeley and found Van Helsing, 2
as usual, up to time. The carriage ordered from the hotel was waiting. The Professor took his bag, which he always brings with him now.

Let all be put down exactly. Van Helsing and I arrived at Hillingham at eight o'clock. It was a lovely morning; the bright sunshine and all the fresh feeling of early autumn seemed like the completion of nature's annual work. The leaves were turning to all kinds of beautiful colours, but had not yet begun to drop from the trees. When we entered we met Mrs. Westenra coming out of the morning

"LIKE OPHELIA."

1 *lying like Ophelia in the play.* Lucy is remembering Laertes's confrontation with the priest in the graveyard scene in *Hamlet* (Act V, Scene I, lines 249–57). Ophelia's body has been brought in to be buried and Laertes protests that it is being treated with insufficient ceremony. The priest replies:

"Her obsequies have been as far enlarg'd
As we have warranty: her death was doubtful,
And, but that great command o'ersways the order,
She should in ground unsanctified have lodg'd
Till the last trumpet; for charitable prayers,
Shards, flints, and pebbles should be thrown on her;
Yet here she is allow'd her virgin crants,
Her maiden strewments, and the bringing home
Of bell and burial."

There is a touching irony in Lucy's comparison of herself to Ophelia in this way. After all, Ophelia, in her "virgin crants" and "maiden strewments," was dead.

2 *called at the Berkeley.* Van Helsing stayed at a comfortable hotel. Charles Fornara, the general manager of the modern Berkeley, tells me that "there has only been one Berkeley Hotel in London for the past one hundred years."

In Stoker's day the Berkeley was at the corner of Berkeley Street and Piccadilly. The Berkeley may have had its origins in the Gloucester Coffee House, "where the mail coaches started on their journey to the west of England."

Van Helsing's single room in the off-season (August 1 to April 30) would have cost him six shillings per day, with two shillings extra for a hot or cold bath in the bathroom. Had he warmed himself, the charge would have been one shilling, sixpence additional in the bedroom. The famous Berkeley *diner du jour, à prix fixe* would have cost him ten shillings, sixpence. Lunch, *à prix fixe,* was four shillings. The Berkeley's restaurant, according to an 1898 Baedeker, was "frequented."

THE BERKELEY.

room. She is always an early riser. She greeted us warmly and said :—

"You will be glad to know that Lucy is better. The dear child is still asleep. I looked into her room and saw her, but did not go in, lest I should disturb her." The Professor smiled, and looked quite jubilant. He rubbed his hands together, and said :—

"Aha! I thought I had diagnosed the case. My treatment is working," to which she answered :—

"You must not take all the credit to yourself, doctor. Lucy's state this morning is due in part to me."

"How do you mean, ma'am?" asked the Professor.

"Well, I was anxious about the dear child in the night, and went into her room. She was sleeping soundly—so soundly that even my coming did not wake her. But the room was awfully stuffy. There were a lot of those horrible, strong-smelling flowers about everywhere, and she had actually a bunch of them round her neck. I feared that the heavy odour would be too much for the dear child in her weak state, so I took them all away and opened a bit of the window to let in a little fresh air. You will be pleased with her, I am sure."

She moved off into her boudoir, where she usually breakfasted early. As she had spoken, I watched the Professor's face, and saw it turn ashen grey. He had been able to retain his self-command whilst the poor lady was present, for he knew her state and how mischievous a shock would be; he actually smiled on her as he held open the door for her to pass into her room. But the instant she had disappeared he pulled me, suddenly and forcibly, into the dining-room and closed the door.

Then, for the first time in my life, I saw Van Helsing break down. He raised his hands over his head in a sort of mute despair, and then beat his palms together in a helpless way; finally he sat down on a chair, and putting his hands before his face, began to sob, with loud, dry sobs that seemed to come from the very racking of his heart. Then he raised his arms again, as though appealing to the whole universe. "God! God! God!" he said. "What have we done, what has this poor thing done, that we are so sore beset? Is there fate amongst us still, sent down from the pagan world of old, that such things must be, and in such way? This poor mother, all unknowing, and all for the best as she think, does such thing as lose her daughter body and soul; and we must not tell her, we must not even warn her, or she die, and then both die. Oh, how we are beset! How are all the powers of the devils against us!" Suddenly he jumped to his feet. "Come," he said, "come, we must see and act. Devils or no devils, or all the devils at once, it matters not; we fight him all the same." He went to the hall-door for his bag; and together we went up to Lucy's room. 3

Once again I drew up the blind, whilst Van Helsing went towards the bed. This time he did not start as he looked on the poor face with the same awful, waxen pallor as before. He wore a look of stern sadness and infinite pity.

"As I expected," he murmured, with that hissing inspiration of his which meant so much. Without a word he went and locked the door, and then began to set out on the little table the instruments for yet another operation of transfusion of blood. I had long ago recognised the necessity, and begun to take off my coat, but he stopped me with a warning hand. "No!" he said. "To-day you must operate. I shall provide. You are weakened already." As he spoke he took off his coat and rolled up his shirt-sleeve.

Again the operation; again the narcotic; again some return of colour to the ashy cheeks, and the regular breathing of healthy sleep. This time I watched whilst Van Helsing recruited himself and rested.

Presently he took an opportunity of telling Mrs. Westenra that she must not remove anything from Lucy's room without consulting him; that the flowers were of medicinal value, and that the breathing of their odour was a part of the system of cure. Then he took over the care of the case himself, saying that he would watch this night and the next and would send me word when to come.

After another hour Lucy waked from her sleep, fresh and bright and seemingly not much the worse for her terrible ordeal.

What does it all mean? I am beginning to wonder if my long habit of life amongst the insane is beginning to tell upon my own brain.

Lucy Westenra's Diary.

17 *September.*—Four days and nights of peace. I am getting so strong again that I hardly know myself. It is as if I had passed through some long nightmare, and had just awakened to see the beautiful sunshine and feel the fresh air of the morning around me. I have a dim half-remembrance of long, anxious times of waiting and fearing; darkness in which there was not even the pain of hope to make present distress more poignant; and then long spells of oblivion, and the rising back to life as a diver coming up through a great press of water. Since, however, Dr. Van Helsing has been with me, all this bad dreaming seems to have passed away; the noises

3 *Is there fate amongst us still.* Stoker is using the word in its most precise sense. The *Oxford English Dictionary* says that "the primary sense of the L.[atin] word [*fatum*] is a sentence or doom of the gods."

4 "The Pall Mall Gazette." A London daily newspaper whose specialty was human interest stories, especially interviews with "any politician, religionist, social reformer, man of science, artist, tradesman, rogue, madman, or any one else, who cared to advertise himself or his projects or pursuits, and in whom the public could be expected to take any interest." Thomas Bilder and his escaped wolf seem to fit the bill.

5 Zoological Gardens. The Zoological Gardens, in the northwest corner of Regent's Park, were open daily from 9:00 A.M. to sunset. Admission was (in Stoker's time) one shilling, except on Monday, when it was sixpence. Children were half price. In a more God-fearing age than ours, the zoo was closed on Sunday.

On summer Saturdays at 4:00 P.M. there was a military band concert at the zoo.

Visitors were cautioned not to get too close to the llamas "on account of [their] unpleasant expectorating propensities." The unpleasant odor of the monkey house was "judiciously disguised by numerous plants and flowers."

Readers of *Dracula* will want to know that unaccountably the zoo's bats were kept in the monkey house.

6 *behind the elephant-house.* Mr. Bilder's house, then, is about four hundred yards from his wolves, that being the distance, at the turn of the century, between the elephant house and the dens of the wolves and foxes.

7 *to his tea.* A British simple tea is usually served around 4:00 in the afternoon. High tea, a more complicated meal, is served at 6:00 P.M.

that used to frighten me out of my wits—the flapping against the windows, the distant voices which seemed so close to me, the harsh sounds that came from I know not where and commanded me to do I know not what—have all ceased. I go to bed now without any fear of sleep. I do not even try to keep awake. I have grown quite fond of the garlic, and a boxful arrives for me every day from Haarlem. To-night Dr. Van Helsing is going away, as he has to be for a day in Amsterdam. But I need not be watched; I am well enough to be left alone. Thank God for mother's sake, and dear Arthur's, and for all our friends who have been so kind! I shall not even feel the change, for last night Dr. Van Helsing slept in his chair a lot of the time. I found him asleep twice when I awoke; but I did not fear to go to sleep again, although the boughs or bats or something flapped almost angrily against the window-panes.

4 "*The Pall Mall Gazette,*" 18 *September.*

THE ESCAPED WOLF.

PERILOUS ADVENTURE OF OUR INTERVIEWER.

5 *Interview with the Keeper in the Zoological Gardens.*

After many inquiries and almost as many refusals, and perpetually using the words "Pall Mall Gazette" as a sort of talisman, I managed to find the keeper of the section of the Zoological Gardens in which the wolf department is included. Thomas Bilder lives in one of the cottages in the enclosure
6, 7 behind the elephant-house, and was just sitting down to his tea when I found him. Thomas and his wife are hospitable folk, elderly, and without children, and if the specimen I enjoyed of their hospitality be of the average kind, their lives must be pretty comfortable. The keeper would not enter on what he called "business" until the supper was over, and we were all satisfied. Then when the table was cleared, and he had lit his pipe, he said:—

"Now, sir, you can go on and arsk me what you want. You'll excoose me refoosin' to talk of perfeshunal subjects afore meals. I gives the wolves and the jackals and the hyenas in all our section their tea afore I begins to arsk them questions."

"How do you mean, ask them questions?" I queried, wishful to get him into a talkative humour.

"'Ittin' of them over the 'ead with a pole is one way; scratchin' of their hears is another, when gents as is flush wants a bit of a show-orf to their gals. I don't so much mind the fust—the 'ittin' with a pole afore I chucks in their dinner; but I waits till they've 'ad their sherry and kawffee, so to speak, afore I tries on with the ear-scratchin'. Mind you," he added philosophically, "there's a deal of the same nature in us as in them theer animiles. Here's you a-comin' and arskin' of me questions about my business, and I that grumpy-like that only for your bloomin' 'arf-quid I'd 'a' seen you blowed fust 'fore I'd answer. Not even when you arsked me sarcastic-like if I'd like you to arsk the Superintendent if you might arsk me questions. Without offence, did I tell yer to go to 'ell?"

"You did."

"An' when you said you'd report me for usin' of obscene language that was 'ittin' me over the 'ead; but the 'arf-quid made that all right. I weren't a-goin' to fight, so I waited for the food, and did with my 'owl as the wolves, and lions, and tigers does. But, Lor' love yer 'art, now that the old 'ooman has stuck a chunk of her tea-cake in me, an' rinsed me out with her bloomin' old teapot, and I've lit hup, you may scratch my ears for all you're worth, and won't git even a growl out of me. Drive along with your questions. I know what yer a-comin' at, that 'ere escaped wolf."

"Exactly. I want you to give me your view of it. Just tell me how it happened; and when I know the facts I'll get you to say what you consider was the cause of it, and how you think the whole affair will end."

"All right, guv'nor. This 'ere is about the 'ole story. That 'ere wolf what we called Bersicker was one of three grey **8**
ones that came from Norway to Jamrach's, which we bought **9**
off him four year ago. He was a nice well-behaved wolf, that never gave no trouble to talk of. I'm more surprised at 'im for wantin' to get out nor any other animile in the place. But, there, you can't trust wolves no more nor women."

"Don't you mind him, sir!" broke in Mrs. Tom, with a cheery laugh. "'E's got mindin' the animiles so long that blest if he ain't like a old wolf 'isself! But there ain't no 'arm in 'im."

"Well, sir, it was about two hours after feedin' yesterday **10**
when I first hear any disturbance. I was makin' up a litter in the monkey-house for a young puma which is ill; but when I heard the yelpin' and 'owlin' I kem away straight. There was Bersicker a-tearin' like a mad thing at the bars as if he wanted to get out. There wasn't much people about that day, and close at hand was only one man, a tall, thin chap, with a 'ook **11**
nose and a pointed beard, with a few white hairs runnin' **12**
through it. He had a 'ard, cold look and red eyes, and I took a sort of mislike to him, for it seemed as if it was 'im as they was hirritated at. He 'ad white kid gloves on 'is 'ands, and he pointed out the animiles to me and says: 'Keeper, these wolves seem upset at something.'

"Maybe it's you," says I, for I did not like the airs as he give 'isself. He didn't git angry, as I 'oped he would, but he smiled a kind of insolent smile, with a mouth full of white, sharp teeth. "Oh no, they wouldn't like me," 'e says.

"'Ow yes, they would,' says I, a-imitatin' of him. 'They always likes a bone or two to clean their teeth on about tea-time, which you 'as a bagful.'

"Well, it was a odd thing, but when the animiles see us a-talkin' they lay down, and when I went over to Bersicker he let me stroke his ears same as ever. That there man kem over, and blessed but if he didn't put in his hand and stroke the old wolf's ears too!

"'Tyke care, says I. 'Bersicker is quick.'

"'Never mind,' he says. 'I'm used to 'em!'

"Are you in the business yourself?' I says, tyking off my 'at,

"THAT 'ERE WOLF WHAT WE CALL BERSICKER."

8 *Bersicker.* Thomas Bilder's Cockney accent may hide the wolf's name, which is Berserker. (See chapter III, note 9, regarding Stoker's fondness for this name.)

9 *Jamrach's.* Jamrach was a well-known animal dealer.

10 *two hours after feedin'.* The beasts of prey were fed at 4:00 P.M., except in winter (November to February) when they had their meal at 3:00 P.M. Pelicans were fed at 2:30 P.M. and eagles at 3:30 P.M.

11 *only one man.* Once again we see Dracula moving about in daylight. The white kid gloves on the hands of the master of evil are a fine touch.

12 *white hairs runnin' through it.* Dracula's youth is not yet fully recovered. There is more blood to be let.

"THERE WAS BERSICKER A-TEARIN' LIKE A MAD THING AT THE BARS AS IF HE WANTED TO GET OUT."

for a man what trades in wolves, anceterer, is a good friend to 13
keepers.

"'No,' says he, 'not exactly in the business, but I 'ave made pets of several.' And with that he lifts his 'at as perlite as a lord, and walks away. Old Bersicker kep' a-lookin' arter 'im till 'e was out of sight, and then went and lay down in a corner, and wouldn't come hout the 'ole hevening. Well, larst night, so soon as the moon was hup, the wolves here all began a-'owling. There warn't nothing for them to 'owl at. There warn't no one near, except some one that was evidently a-callin' a dog somewheres out back of the gardings in the Park road. Once or twice I went out to see that all was right, and it was, and then the 'owling stopped. Just before twelve o'clock I just took a look round afore turnin' in, an', bust me, but when I kem opposite to old Bersicker's cage I see the rails broken and twisted about and the cage empty. And that's all I know for certing."

"Did any one else see anything?"

"One of our gard'ners was a-comin' 'ome about that time
from a 'armony, when he sees a big grey dog comin' out through 14
the garding 'edges. At least, so he says; but I don't give much for it myself, for if he did 'e never said a word about it to his missis when 'e got 'ome, and it was only after the escape of the wolf was made known, and we had been up all night a-huntin' of the Park for Bersicker, that he remembered seein' anything. My own belief was that the 'armony 'ad got into his 'ead."

"Now, Mr. Bilder, can you account in any way for the escape of the wolf?"

"Well, sir," he said, with a suspicious sort of modesty, "I think I can; but I don't know as 'ow you'd be satisfied with the theory."

"Certainly I shall. If a man like you, who knows the animals from experience, can't hazard a good guess at any rate, who is even to try?"

"Well then, sir, I accounts for it this way; it seems to me that 'ere wolf escaped—simply because he wanted to get out."

From the hearty way that both Thomas and his wife laughed at the joke I could see that it had done service before, and that the whole explanation was simply an elaborate sell. I couldn't cope in badinage with the worthy Thomas, but I thought I knew a surer way to his heart, so I said:—

"Now, Mr. Bilder, we'll consider that first half-sovereign worked off, and this brother of his is waiting to be claimed when you've told me what you think will happen."

"Right y'are, sir," he said briskly. "Ye'll excoose me, I know, for a-chaffin' of ye, but the old woman here winked at me, which was as much as telling me to go on."

"Well, I never!" said the old lady.

"My opinion is this: that 'ere wolf is a-'idin' of, somewheres. The gard'ner wot didn't remember said he was a-gallopin' northward faster than a horse could go; but I don't believe him, for, yer see, sir, wolves don't gallop no more nor dogs does, they not bein' built that way. Wolves is fine things in a storybook, and I dessay when they gets in packs and does be

13 *anceterer.* This is Cockney for "etcetera."

14 *'armony.* Glee club.

15 *my books.* Seward is doing his accounts.

chivyin' somethin' that's more afeared than they is they can make a devil of a noise and chop it up, whatever it is. But, Lor' bless you, in real life a wolf is only a low creature, not half so clever or bold as a good dog; and not half a quarter so much fight in 'im. This one ain't been used to fightin' or even to providin' for hisself, and more like he's somewhere round the Park a-'idin' an' a-shiverin' of, and, if he thinks at all, wonderin' where he is to get his breakfast from; or maybe he's got down some area and is in a coal-cellar. My eye, won't some cook get a rum start when she sees his green eyes a-shining at her out of the dark! If he can't get food he's bound to look for it, and mayhap he may chance to light on a butcher's shop in time. If he doesn't, and some nursemaid goes a-walkin' orf with a soldier, leavin' of the hinfant in the perambulator—well then I shouldn't be surprised if the census is one babby the less. That's all."

I was handing him the half-sovereign, when something came bobbing up against the window, and Mr. Bilder's face doubled its natural length with surprise.

"God bless me!" he said. "If there ain't old Bersicker come back by 'isself!"

He went to the door and opened it; a most unnecessary proceeding it seemed to me. I have always thought that a wild animal never looks so well as when some obstacle of pronounced durability is between us; a personal experience has intensified rather than diminished that idea.

After all, however, there is nothing like custom, for neither Bilder nor his wife thought any more of the wolf than I should of a dog. The animal itself was as peaceful and well-behaved as that father of all picture-wolves—Red Riding Hood's quondam friend, whilst moving her confidence in masquerade.

The whole scene was an unutterable mixture of comedy and pathos. The wicked wolf that for half a day had paralysed London and set all the children in the town shivering in their shoes, was there in a sort of penitent mood, and was received and petted like a sort of vulpine prodigal son. Old Bilder examined him all over with most tender solicitude, and when he had finished with his penitent said:—

"There, I knew the poor old chap would get into some kind of trouble; didn't I say it all along? Here's his head all cut and full of broken glass. 'E's been a-gettin' over some bloomin' wall or other. It's a shyme that people are allowed to top their walls with broken bottles. This 'ere's what comes of it. Come along, Bersicker."

He took the wolf and locked him up in a cage, with a piece of meat that satisfied, in quantity at any rate, the elementary conditions of the fatted calf, and went off to report.

I came off, too, to report the only exclusive information that is given to-day regarding the strange escapade at the Zoo.

Dr. Seward's Diary.

17 September.—I was engaged after dinner in my study
15 posting up my books, which, through press of other work

and the many visits to Lucy, had fallen sadly into arrear. Suddenly the door was burst open, and in rushed my patient, with his face distorted with passion. I was thunder-struck, for such a thing as a patient getting of his own accord into the Superintendent's study is almost unknown. Without an instant's pause he made straight at me. He had a dinner-knife in his hand, and, as I saw he was dangerous, I tried to keep the table between us. He was too quick and too strong for me, however; for before I could get my balance he had struck at me and cut my left wrist rather severely. Before he could strike again, however, I got in my right, and he was sprawling on his back on the floor. My wrist bled freely, and quite a little pool trickled on to the carpet. I saw that my friend was not intent on further effort, and occupied myself binding up my wrist, keeping a wary eye on the prostrate figure all the time. When the attendants rushed in, and we turned our attention to him, his employment positively sickened me. He was lying on his belly on the floor licking
up, like a dog, the blood which had fallen from my wounded **16**
wrist. He was easily secured, and, to my surprise, went with the attendants quite placidly, simply repeating over and over
again: "The blood is the life! the blood is the life!" **17**

I cannot afford to lose blood just at present: I have lost too much of late for my physical good, and then the prolonged strain of Lucy's illness and its horrible phases is telling on me. I am over-excited and weary, and I need rest, rest, rest. Happily Van Helsing has not summoned me, so I need not forego my sleep; to-night I could not well do without it.

Telegram, Van Helsing, Antwerp, to Seward, Carfax.

(Sent to Carfax, Sussex, as no county given; delivered late by twenty-two hours.)

"17 *September.* Do not fail to be at Hillingham to-night. If not watching all the time, frequently visit and see that flowers are as placed; very important; do not fail. Shall be with you as soon as possible after arrival."

Dr. Seward's Diary.

18 *September.*—Just off for train to London. The arrival of Van Helsing's telegram filled me with dismay. A whole night lost, and I know by bitter experience what may happen in a night. Of course it is possible that all may be well, but what *may* have happened? Surely there is some horrible doom hanging over us that every possible accident should thwart us in all we try to do. I shall take this cylinder with me, and
then I can complete my entry on Lucy's phonograph. **18**

Memorandum left by Lucy Westenra.

17 *September. Night.*—I write this and leave it to be seen, so that no one may by any chance get into any trouble through me. This is an exact record of what took place to-night. I feel I

16 *wounded wrist.* Renfield's behavior may be sickening, but it is worth remembering that Seward himself is something of a blood drinker, as we learned on page 110. Of course, Seward was sucking Van Helsing's poisoned blood, but in a fiction where blood drinking and blood transfusion have heavy implications, we need to notice every instance in which they occur.

17 *"The blood is the life! the blood is the life!"* Though Renfield is quick to quote Scripture here, his keepers might have reminded him that his doglike blood lapping is scripturally forbidden. "The blood *is* the life" comes from Deuteronomy 12:23, but the whole verse reads, "Only be sure that thou eat not the blood: for the blood *is* the life; and thou mayest not eat the life with the flesh."

Nor is this the only place in the Bible where blood drinking is prohibited:

Deuteronomy 12:16 says, "Only ye shall not eat the blood; ye shall pour it upon the earth as water."

Genesis 9:4 says, "But flesh with the life thereof, *which is* the blood thereof, shall ye not eat."

and Leviticus 17:11–12 says, "For the life of the flesh *is* in the blood: . . . Therefore I said unto the children of Israel, No soul of you shall eat blood, neither shall any stranger that sojourneth among you eat blood."

18 *Lucy's phonograph.* This is the first indication we have that Lucy, too, owns a dictating machine.

19 *simoom.* A hot, suffocating, sand-laden desert wind.

am dying of weakness, and have barely strength to write, but it must be done if I die in the doing.

I went to bed as usual, taking care that the flowers were placed as Dr. Van Helsing directed, and soon fell asleep.

I was waked by the flapping at the window, which had begun after that sleep-walking on the cliff at Whitby when Mina saved me, and which now I know so well. I was not afraid, but I did wish that Dr. Seward was in the next room—as Dr. Van Helsing said he would be—so that I might have called him. I tried to go to sleep, but could not. Then there came to me the old fear of sleep, and I determined to keep awake. Perversely sleep would try to come then when I did not want it; so, as I feared to be alone, I opened my door and called out: "Is there anybody there?" There was no answer. I was afraid to wake mother, and so closed my door again. Then outside in the shrubbery I heard a sort of howl like a dog's, but more fierce and deeper. I went to the window and looked out, but could see nothing, except a big bat, which had evidently been buffeting its wings against the window. So I went back to bed again, but determined not to go to sleep. Presently the door opened, and mother looked in; seeing by my moving that I was not asleep, came in, and sat by me. She said to me even more sweetly and softly than her wont:—

"I was uneasy about you, darling, and came in to see that you were all right."

I feared she might catch cold sitting there, and asked her to come in and sleep with me, so she came into bed, and lay down beside me; she did not take off her dressing gown, for she said she would only stay a while and then go back to her own bed. As she lay there in my arms, and I in hers, the flapping and buffeting came to the window again. She was startled and a little frightened, and cried out: "What is that?" I tried to pacify her, and at last succeeded, and she lay quiet; but I could hear her poor dear heart still beating terribly. After a while there was the low howl again out in the shrubbery, and shortly after there was a crash at the window, and a lot of broken glass was hurled on the floor. The window blind blew back with the wind that rushed in, and in the aperture of the broken panes there was the head of a great, gaunt grey wolf. Mother cried out in a fright, and struggled up into a sitting posture, and clutched wildly at anything that would help her. Amongst other things, she clutched the wreath of flowers that Dr. Van Helsing insisted on my wearing round my neck, and tore it away from me. For a second or two she sat up, pointing at the wolf, and there was a strange and horrible gurgling in her throat; then she fell over, as if struck with lightning, and her head hit my forehead and made me dizzy for a moment or two. The room and all round seemed to spin round. I kept my eyes fixed on the window, but the wolf drew his head back, and a whole myriad of little specks seemed to come blowing in through the broken window, and wheeling and circling round like the pillar of dust that travellers describe
19 when there is a simoom in the desert. I tried to stir, but there was some spell upon me, and dear mother's poor body, which seemed to grow cold already—for her dear heart had ceased to

beat—weighed me down; and I remembered no more for a while.

The time did not seem long, but very, very awful, till I recovered consciousness again. Somewhere near, a passing bell was tolling; the dogs all round the neighbourhood were howling; and in our shrubbery, seemingly just outside, a nightingale was singing. I was dazed and stupid with pain and terror and weakness, but the sound of the nightingale seemed like the voice of my dead mother come back to comfort me. The sounds seemed to have awakened the maids, too, for I could hear their bare feet pattering outside my door. I called to them, and they came in, and when they saw what had happened, and what it was that lay over me on the bed, they screamed out. The wind rushed in through the broken window, and the door slammed to. They lifted off the body of my dear mother, and laid her, covered up with a sheet, on the bed after I had got up. They were all so frightened and nervous that I directed them to go to the dining-room and have each a glass of wine. The door flew open for an instant **20**
and closed again. The maids shrieked, and then went in a body to the dining-room; and I laid what flowers I had on my dear mother's breast. When they were there I remembered what Dr. Van Helsing had told me, but I didn't like to remove them, and, besides, I would have some of the servants to sit up with me now. I was surprised that the maids did not come back. I called them, but got no answer, so I went to the dining-room to look for them.

My heart sank when I saw what had happened. They all four lay helpless on the floor, breathing heavily. The decanter of sherry was on the table half full, but there was a queer, acrid smell about. I was suspicious, and examined the decanter. It smelt of laudanum, and looking on the sideboard, **21**
I found that the bottle which mother's doctor uses for her —oh! did use—was empty. What am I to do? what am I to do? I am back in the room with mother. I cannot leave her, and I am alone, save for the sleeping servants, whom some one has drugged. Alone with the dead! I dare not go out, for I can hear the low howl of the wolf through the broken window.

The air seems full of specks, floating and circling in the draught from the window, and the lights burn blue and dim. What am I to do? God shield me from harm this night! I shall hide this paper in my breast, where they shall find it when they come to lay me out. My dear mother gone! It is time that I go too. Good-bye, dear Arthur, if I should not survive this night. God keep you, dear, and God help me!

"A NIGHTINGALE WAS SINGING."

20 *The door flew open for an instant and closed again.* As Dracula slips out to doctor the wine.

21 *laudanum.* A sedative hydroalcoholic solution containing either 1 percent morphine or 10 percent opium. Laudanum, in the nineteenth century, was easily available and widely used to calm the nerves. A carafe of laudanum at one's bedside table was not unusual.

CHAPTER XII.

Dr. Seward's Diary.

18 *September*.—I drove at once to Hillingham and arrived early. Keeping my cab at the gate, I went up the avenue alone. I knocked gently and rang as quietly as possible, for I feared to disturb Lucy or her mother, and hoped to only bring a servant to the door. After a while, finding no response, I knocked and rang again; still no answer. I cursed the laziness of the servants that they should lie abed at such an hour—for it was now ten o'clock—and so rang and knocked again, but more impatiently, but still without response. Hitherto I had blamed only the servants, but now a terrible fear began to assail me. Was this desolation but another link in the chain of doom which seemed drawing tight around us? Was it indeed a house of death to which I had come, too late? I knew that minutes, even seconds, of delay might mean hours of danger to Lucy, if she had had again one of those frightful relapses; and I went round the house to try if I could find by chance an entry anywhere.

I could find no means of ingress. Every window and door was fastened and locked, and I returned baffled to the porch. As I did so, I heard the rapid pit-pat of a swiftly driven horse's feet. They stopped at the gate, and a few seconds later I met Van Helsing running up the avenue. When he saw me, he gasped out:—

"Then it was you, and just arrived. How is she? Are we too late? Did you not get my telegram?"

I answered as quickly and coherently as I could that I had only got his telegram early in the morning and had not lost a minute in coming here, and that I could not make any one in the house hear me. He paused and raised his hat as he said solemnly:—

"Then I fear we are too late. God's will be done!" With his usual recuperative energy, he went on: "Come. If there be no way open to get in, we must make one. Time is all in all to us now."

We went round to the back of the house, where there was a kitchen window. The Professor took a small surgical saw from his case, and handing it to me, pointed to the iron bars which guarded the window. I attacked them at once and had very soon cut through three of them. Then with a long, 1
thin knife we pushed back the fastening of the sashes and opened the window. I helped the Professor in, and followed him. There was no one in the kitchen or in the servants' rooms, which were close at hand. We tried all the rooms as we went along, and in the dining-room, dimly lit by rays of light through the shutters, found four servant-women lying on the floor. There was no need to think them dead, for their stertorous breathing and the acrid smell of laudanum in the room left no doubt as to their condition. Van Helsing and I looked at each other, and as we moved away he said: "We can attend to them later." Then we ascended to 2
Lucy's room. For an instant or two we paused at the door to listen, but there was no sound that we could hear. With white faces and trembling hands, we opened the door gently, and entered the room.

How shall I describe what we saw? On the bed lay two women, Lucy and her mother. The latter lay farthest in, and she was covered with a white sheet, the edge of which had been blown back by the draught through the broken window, showing the drawn, white face, with a look of terror fixed upon it. By her side lay Lucy, with face white and still more drawn. The flowers which had been round her neck we found upon her mother's bosom, and her throat was bare, showing the two little wounds which we had noticed before, but looking horribly white and mangled. Without a word the Professor bent over the bed, his head almost touching poor Lucy's breast; then he gave a quick turn of his head, as of one who listens, and leaping to his feet, he cried out to me:—

"It is not yet too late! Quick! quick! Bring the brandy!"

I flew downstairs and returned with it, taking care to smell and taste it, lest it, too, were drugged like the decanter of sherry which I found on the table. The maids were still breathing, but more restlessly, and I fancied that the narcotic was wearing off. I did not stay to make sure, but returned to Van Helsing. He rubbed the brandy, as on another occasion, on her lips and gums and on her wrists and the palms of her hands. He said to me:—

"I can do this, all that can be at the present. You go wake those maids. Flick them in the face with a wet towel, and flick them hard. Make them get heat and fire and a warm bath. This poor soul is nearly as cold as that beside her. She will need be heated before we can do anything more."

I went at once, and found little difficulty in waking three of the women. The fourth was only a young girl, and the drug had evidently affected her more strongly, so I lifted her on the sofa and let her sleep. The others were dazed at first, but as

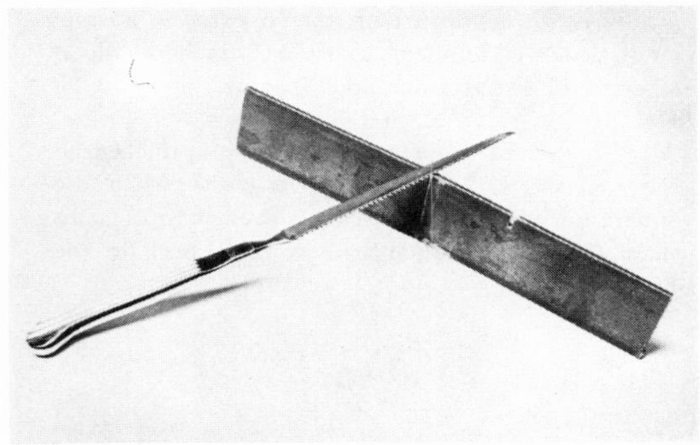

SURGICAL SAW AND IRON STRAP.

1 *soon cut through three of them.* An unlikely story. An energetic undergraduate, using a modern high carbon steel surgical saw against an iron strap one-eighth of an inch thick, was able to cut one-fourth of an inch into the strap in half an hour. Assuming that Seward was cutting into bars of modest thickness, three quarters of an inch per bar, the task of cutting three such bars should have taken five hours. This is to say nothing about the condition of the surgical saw which, in the modern experiment, was rendered nearly useless for iron bars, and absolutely useless for surgery.

On the other hand, Seward was desperate.

2 *we ascended to Lucy's room.* Since they ascended to her room, it is clear that her bedroom is on the second floor. Which makes for a mystery: How did Berserker, a *real* wolf (though no doubt inspired by Dracula), manage to crash his head through a second-story window?

More than likely, this is one of Stoker's oversights. Berserker's function is to break the window so that his master, equipped with occult powers, can get in. But that leaves us with another niggle: Van Helsing, later on, will instruct Lucy's friends on the characteristics of the vampire (p. 213). There they are told that the monster "may not enter anywhere at the first, unless there be some one of the household who bid him to come . . ." Berserker's forcible entry seems a violation of Van Helsing's dictum.

3 *the bath.* A warm bath for an extreme anemic could very well kill her because it distends the blood vessels and distracts the blood from the brain.

4 ". . . *Check to the King!*" According to the *Official Chess Handbook*, "the King is in check when the square on which it stands is attacked by an enemy man; the latter is then said to give check to the King."

remembrance came back to them they cried and sobbed in a hysterical manner. I was stern with them, however, and would not let them talk. I told them that one life was bad enough to lose, and that if they delayed they would sacrifice Miss Lucy. So, sobbing and crying, they went about their way, half clad as they were, and prepared fire and water. Fortunately, the kitchen and boiler fires were still alive, and there was no lack of hot water. We got a bath, and carried Lucy out as she was and placed her in it. Whilst we were busy chafing her limbs there was a knock at the hall-door. One of the maids ran off, hurried on some more clothes, and opened it. Then she returned and whispered to us that there was a gentleman who had come with a message from Mr. Holmwood. I bade her simply tell him that he must wait, for we could see no one now. She went away with the message, and, engrossed with our work, I clean forgot all about him.

I never saw in all my experience the Professor work in such deadly earnest. I knew—as he knew—that it was a stand-up fight with death, and in a pause told him so. He answered me in a way that I did not understand, but with the sternest look that his face could wear:—

"If that were all, I would stop here where we are now, and let her fade away into peace, for I see no light in life over her horizon." He went on with his work with, if possible, renewed and more frenzied vigour.

Presently we both began to be conscious that the heat was beginning to be of some effect. Lucy's heart beat a trifle more audibly to the stethoscope, and her lungs had a perceptible movement. Van Helsing's face almost beamed, and as
3 we lifted her from the bath and rolled her in a hot sheet to dry her he said to me:—
4 "The first gain is ours! Check to the King!"

We took Lucy into another room, which had by now been prepared, and laid her in bed and forced a few drops of brandy down her throat. I noticed that Van Helsing tied a soft silk handkerchief round her throat. She was still unconscious, and was quite as bad as, if not worse than, we had ever seen her.

Van Helsing called in one of the women, and told her to stay with her and not to take her eyes off her till we returned, and then beckoned me out of the room.

"We must consult as to what is to be done," he said as we descended the stairs. In the hall he opened the dining-room door, and we passed in, he closing the door carefully behind him. The shutters had been opened, but the blinds were already down, with that obedience to the etiquette of death which the British woman of the lower classes always rigidly observes. The room was, therefore, dimly dark. It was, however, light enough for our purposes. Van Helsing's sternness was somewhat relieved by a look of perplexity. He was evidently torturing his mind about something, so I waited for an instant, and he spoke:—

"What are we to do now? Where are we to turn for help? We must have another transfusion of blood, and that soon, or that poor girl's life won't be worth an hour's purchase. You are exhausted already; I am exhausted too. I fear to trust those women, even if they would have courage to submit. What are we to do for some one who will open his veins for her?"

"What's the matter with me, anyhow?"

The voice came from the sofa across the room, and its tones brought relief and joy to my heart, for they were those of Quincey Morris. Van Helsing started angrily at the first sound, but his face softened and a glad look came into his eyes as I cried out: "Quincey Morris!" and rushed towards him with outstretched hands.

"What brought you here?" I cried as our hands met.

"I guess Art is the cause."

He handed me a telegram:—

"Have not heard from Seward for three days, and am terribly anxious. Cannot leave. Father still in same condition. Send me word how Lucy is. Do not delay.—HOLMWOOD."

"I think I came just in the nick of time. You know you have only to tell me what to do."

Van Helsing strode forward and took his hand, looking him straight in the eyes as he said:—

"A brave man's blood is the best thing on this earth when a woman is in trouble. You're a man, and no mistake. Well, the devil may work against us for all he's worth, but God sends us men when we want them."

Once again we went through that ghastly operation. I have not the heart to go through with the details. Lucy had got a terrible shock, and it told on her more than before, for though plenty of blood went into her veins, her body did not respond to the treatment as well as on the other occasions. Her struggle back into life was something frightful to see and hear. However, the action of both heart and lungs improved, and Van Helsing made a subcutaneous injection of morphia, as before, and with good effect. Her faint became a profound slumber. The Professor watched whilst I went downstairs with Quincey Morris, and sent one of the maids to pay off one of the cabmen who were waiting. I left Quincey lying down after having a glass of wine, and told the cook to get ready a good breakfast. Then a thought struck me, and I went back to the room where Lucy now was. When I came softly in, I found Van Helsing with a sheet or two of note-paper in his hand. He had evidently read it, and was thinking it over as he sat with his hand to his brow. There was a look of grim satisfaction in his face, as of one who has had a doubt solved. He handed me the paper saying only: "It dropped from Lucy's breast when we carried her to the bath."

When I had read it, I stood looking at the Professor, and after a pause asked him: "In God's name, what does it all mean? Was she, or is she, mad; or what sort of horrible danger is it?" I was so bewildered that I did not know what to say more. Van Helsing put out his hand and took the paper, saying:—

"Do not trouble about it now. Forget it for the present. You shall know and understand it all in good time; but it will be later. And now what is it that you came to me to

5 in camera. A legal term meaning "in the judge's chambers." Otherwise, the phrase simply means "privately."

say?" This brought me back to fact, and I was all myself again.

"I came to speak about the certificate of death. If we do not act properly and wisely, there may be an inquest, and that paper would have to be produced. I am in hopes that we need have no inquest, for if we had it would surely kill poor Lucy, if nothing else did. I know, and you know, and the other doctor who attended her knows, that Mrs. Westenra had disease of the heart, and we can certify that she died of it. Let us fill up the certificate at once, and I shall take it myself to the registrar and go on to the undertaker."

"Good, oh my friend John! Well thought of! Truly Miss Lucy, if she be sad in the foes that beset her, is at least happy in the friends that love her. One, two, three, all open their veins for her, besides one old man. Ah yes, I know, friend John; I am not blind! I love you all the more for it! Now go."

In the hall I met Quincey Morris, with a telegram for Arthur telling him that Mrs. Westenra was dead; that Lucy also had been ill, but was now going on better; and that Van Helsing and I were with her. I told him where I was going, and he hurried me out, but as I was going said:—

"When you come back, Jack, may I have two words with you all to ourselves?" I nodded in reply and went out. I found no difficulty about the registration, and arranged with the local undertaker to come up in the evening to measure for the coffin and to make arrangements.

When I got back Quincey was waiting for me. I told him I would see him as soon as I knew about Lucy, and went up to her room. She was still sleeping, and the Professor seemingly had not moved from his seat at her side. From his putting his finger to his lips, I gathered that he expected her to wake before long and was afraid of forestalling nature. So I went down to Quincey and took him into the breakfast-room, where the blinds were not drawn down, and which was a little more cheerful, or rather less cheerless, than the other rooms. When we were alone, he said to me:—

"Jack Seward, I don't want to shove myself in anywhere where I've no right to be; but this is no ordinary case. You know I loved that girl and wanted to marry her; but, although that's all past and gone, I can't help feeling anxious about her all the same. What is it that's wrong with her? The Dutchman—and a fine old fellow he is; I can see that—said, that time you two came into the room, that you must have *another* transfusion of blood, and that both you and he were
5 exhausted. Now I know well that you medical men speak *in camera*, and that a man must not expect to know what they consult about in private. But this is no common matter, and, whatever it is, I have done my part. Is not that so?"

"That's so," I said, and he went on:—

"I take it that both you and Van Helsing had done already what I did to-day. Is not that so?"

"That's so."

"And I guess Art was in it too. When I saw him four days ago down at his own place he looked queer. I have not seen anything pulled down so quick since I was on the

Pampas and had a mare that I was fond of go to grass all in a 6
night. One of those big bats that they call vampires had got 7
at her in the night, and, what with his gorge and the vein left open, there wasn't enough blood in her to let her stand up, and I had to put a bullet through her as she lay. Jack, if you may tell me without betraying confidence, Arthur was the first; is not that so?" As he spoke the poor fellow looked terribly anxious. He was in a torture of suspense regarding the woman he loved, and his utter ignorance of the terrible mystery which seemed to surround her intensified his pain. His very heart was bleeding, and it took all the manhood of him—and there was a royal lot of it, too—to keep him from breaking down. I paused before answering, for I felt that I must not betray anything which the Professor wished kept secret; but already he knew so much, and guessed so much, that there could be no reason for not answering, so I answered in the same phrase: "That's so."

"And how long has this been going on?"

"About ten days."

"Ten days! Then I guess, Jack Seward, that that poor pretty creature that we all love has had put into her veins within that time the blood of four strong men. Man alive, her whole body wouldn't hold it." Then, coming close to me, he spoke in a fierce half-whisper: "What took it out?"

I shook my head. "That," I said, "is the crux. Van Helsing is simply frantic about it, and I am at my wits' end. I can't even hazard a guess. There has been a series of little circumstances which have thrown out all our calculations as to Lucy being properly watched. But these shall not occur again. Here we stay until all be well—or ill." Quincey held out his hand. "Count me in," he said. "You and the Dutchman will tell me what to do, and I'll do it."

When she woke late in the afternoon, Lucy's first movement was to feel in her breast, and, to my surprise, produced 8
the paper which Van Helsing had given me to read. The careful Professor had replaced it where it had come from, lest on waking she should be alarmed. Her eye then lit on Van Helsing and on me too, and gladdened. Then she looked round the room, and seeing where she was, shuddered; she gave a loud cry, and put her poor thin hands before her pale face. We both understood what that meant—that she had realised to the full her mother's death; so we tried what we could to comfort her. Doubtless sympathy eased her somewhat, but she was very low in thought and spirit, and wept silently and weakly for a long time. We told her that either or both of us would now remain with her all the time, and that seemed to comfort her. Towards dusk she fell into a doze. Here a very odd thing occurred. Whilst still asleep she took the paper from her breast and tore it in two. Van Helsing stepped over and took the pieces from her. All the same, however, she went on with the action of tearing, as though the material were still in her hands; finally she lifted her hands and opened them as though scattering the fragments. Van Helsing seemed surprised, and his brows gathered as if in thought, but he said nothing.

19 *September*.—All last night she slept fitfully, being always 9

6 *go to grass*. Among several meanings of "go to grass," the *Oxford English Dictionary* includes "to die; to be ruined."

7 *bats that they call vampires*. Quincey Morris's story is horrible and possible, but in its details unlikely. For one thing, the most common of the vampire bats, *Desmodus rotundus*, like the other two species of blood-drinking bats, is quite small. Professor William A. Wimsatt, in "Portrait of a Vampire," which appeared in *Ward's Natural Science Bulletin* (vol. 32, no. 2, Spring 1959, pp. 35–39, 62–63), observes that the nonbiologist seeing a vampire for the first time "is not infrequently disenchanted by its small size and far from formidable appearance. Mature adults weigh scarcely more than a large laboratory mouse (28–38 grams), and the wingspread does not exceed 14 inches."

Vampire bats are possible on the Pampas, since their habitat is the New World, chiefly in tropical climates, according to Professor Wimsatt, "extending from northeast and central Mexico south to Uruguay and northern Argentina, and including the coastal islands of the Caribbean." And vampire bats do prey on horses as well as other large domestic animals, but no single bat could have killed Morris's horse in the way he describes. When vampires kill large animals, the death results because several of the creatures have fed on it, returning frequently to the same wound.

Though vampire bats can and do attack humans, they do not necessarily take blood from the throat in Dracula's classic manner. Indeed, the vampire will bite where it can. Typically, humans are attacked in the extremities, those parts of the body being most frequently uncovered in sleep. Though it is ignominious to think of, the favorite biting place of the vampire is the exposed big toe.

Desmodus rotundus does have certain characteristics in common with Dracula: Like the Count, the vampire bat has a "fixed gaze . . . which . . . follows every movement with uncanny watchfulness"; the creature is swift, alert, and "when newly-caught is a savage, squealing animal, which bites viciously, and is capable of inflicting painful bleeding wounds." Like Dracula, it inflicts a characteristic wound, but not like the wounds described by Stoker. When the bat bites, "the biting action," says Professor Wimsatt, "tends to remove a small triangular 'divot' of flesh, leaving a cavity 1 or 2 mm. deep . . .", which induces profuse bleeding. Curiously enough, it makes of its highly specialized tongue a sort of inverted U tube, which it presses against the wound and draws the blood up through the underside of its tongue. "In effect," says Professor Wimsatt, [the vampire] "sucks its meal through a straw!"

Like Dracula, the vampire bat is a night feeder, being most active during three epochs of the night: from 7:00 to 9:00 P.M.; from 11:00 P.M. to 2:00 A.M.; and again between 4:00 and 6:00 A.M. The creature's high metabolic rate, combined with its liquid diet, makes the vampire a frequent urinator in flight.

8 *produced.* Undoubtedly a typo. Should read produce.

9 *19* September. There is a dating error here. It should read "20 *September*."

Seward's entry purports to be written at 1:00 A.M. on September 19. But he reports Lucy's death as happening at 8:00 or 9:00 o'clock on the morning of the day on which he writes his September 20 entry. And indeed, his present narrative is picked up in the September 20 record at 6:00 A.M., when he wakes Van Helsing and Arthur from the rest which, in this entry, he says they will take at 1:15 A.M.

10 *six o'clock.* This entry is made at 1:00 A.M. on the 20th. Arthur arrived at 6:00 P.M. on the 19th. He spends the night of the 19th and the morning of the 20th at Hillingham.

Seward's diary entry for September 20 (p. 146) tells us that Arthur's father is dead, but a time for that death is not given. Later, on the morning of the 20th, we are told (p. 149) that "Arthur had to be back the next day [the 21st] to attend at his father's funeral . . ." The elder Godalming, then, must have died sometime after 6:00 P.M. on the 18th. Given the events of the 20th, Arthur had to do some rather grim shuttling back and forth.

11 *an attack of gout.* Gout, the comic disease of literature, is not funny. It is a painful form of arthritis that can be so severe as to become deforming. While gout may be brought on by overindulgence in food and alcohol, there are many other precipitating factors: surgery, infection, a variety of medical treatments.

The chief symptoms of gout are acute pain in the extremities followed by inflammation and swelling. The pain may be so extraordinary that it becomes crushing.

12 *in my will.* The whole matter of Harker and Hawkins is rather awkwardly huddled together here.

afraid to sleep, and something weaker when she woke from it. The Professor and I took it in turns to watch, and we never left her for a moment unattended. Quincey Morris said nothing about his intention, but I knew that all night long he patrolled round and round the house.

When the day came, its searching light showed the ravages in poor Lucy's strength. She was hardly able to turn her head, and the little nourishment which she could take seemed to do her no good. At times she slept, and both Van Helsing and I noticed the difference in her, between sleeping and waking. Whilst asleep she looked stronger, although more haggard, and her breathing was softer; her open mouth showed the pale gums drawn back from the teeth, which thus looked positively longer and sharper than usual; when she woke the softness of her eyes evidently changed the expression, for she looked her own self, although a dying one. In the afternoon she asked for Arthur, and we telegraphed for him. Quincey went off to meet him at the station.

10 When he arrived it was nearly six o'clock, and the sun was setting full and warm, and the red light streamed in through the window and gave more colour to the pale cheeks. When he saw her, Arthur was simply choking with emotion, and none of us could speak. In the hours that had passed, the fits of sleep, or the comatose condition that passed for it, had grown more frequent, so that the pauses when conversation was possible were shortened. Arthur's presence, however, seemed to act as a stimulant; she rallied a little, and spoke to him more brightly than she had done since we arrived. He too pulled himself together, and spoke as cheerily as he could, so that the best was made of everything.

It is now nearly one o'clock, and he and Van Helsing are sitting with her. I am to relieve them in a quarter of an hour, and I am entering this on Lucy's phonograph. Until six o'clock they are to try to rest. I fear that to-morrow will end our watching, for the shock has been too great; the poor child cannot rally. God help us all.

Letter, Mina Harker to Lucy Westenra.

(Unopened by her.)

"17 *September.*

"My dearest Lucy,—

"It seems *an age* since I heard from you, or indeed since I wrote. You will pardon me, I know, for all my faults when you have read all my budget of news. Well, I got my husband back all right; when we arrived at Exeter there was a carriage
11 waiting for us, and in it, though he had an attack of gout, Mr. Hawkins. He took us to his own house, where there were rooms for us all nice and comfortable, and we dined together. After dinner Mr. Hawkins said:—

"'My dears, I want to drink your health and prosperity; and may every blessing attend you both. I know you both from children, and have, with love and pride, seen you grow up. Now I want you to make your home here with me. I have
12 left to me neither chick nor child; all are gone, and in my will I have left you everything.' I cried, Lucy dear, as

Jonathan and the old man clasped hands. Our evening was a very, very happy one.

"So here we are, installed in this beautiful old house, and from both my bedroom and drawing-room I can see the great elms of the cathedral close, with their great black stems standing out against the old yellow stone of the cathedral; and I can hear the rooks overhead cawing and cawing and chattering and gossiping all day, after the manner of rooks—and humans. I am busy, I need not tell you, arranging things and housekeeping. Jonathan and Mr. Hawkins are busy all day; for, now that Jonathan is a partner, Mr. Hawkins wants to tell him all about the clients.

"How is your dear mother getting on? I wish I could run up to town for a day or two to see you, dear, but I dare not go yet, with so much on my shoulders; and Jonathan wants looking after still. He is beginning to put some flesh on his bones again, but he was terribly weakened by the long illness; even now he sometimes starts out of his sleep in a sudden way and awakes all trembling until I can coax him back to his usual placidity. However, thank God, these occasions grow less frequent as the days go on, and they will in time pass away altogether, I trust. And now I have told you my news, let me ask yours. When are you to be married, and where, and who is to perform the ceremony, and what are you to wear, and is it to be a public or a private wedding? Tell me all about it, dear; tell me all about everything, for there is nothing which interests you which will not be dear to me. Jonathan asks me to send his 'respectful duty,' but I do not think that is good enough from the junior partner of the important firm of Hawkins & Harker; and so, as you love me, and he loves me, and I love you with all the moods and tenses of the verb, I send you simply his 'love' instead. Good-bye, my dearest Lucy, and all blessings on you.

"Yours,

"MINA HARKER."

Report from Patrick Hennessey, M.D., M.R.C.S., L.K.Q.C.P.I., etc., etc., to John Seward, M.D. 13

"20 *September.*

"My dear Sir,—

"In accordance with your wishes, I enclose report of the conditions of everything left in my charge. . . . . With regard to patient, Renfield, there is more to say. He has had another outbreak which might have had a dreadful ending, but which, as it fortunately happened, was unattended with any unhappy results. This afternoon a carrier's cart with two men made a call at the empty house whose grounds abut on ours—the house to which, you will remember, the patient twice ran away. The men stopped at our gate to ask the porter their way, as they were strangers. I was myself looking out of the study window, having a smoke after dinner, and saw one of them come up to the house. As he passed the window of Renfield's room, the patient began to rate him from within, and called him all the foul names he could lay his tongue to. The man, who seemed a decent fellow enough, contented himself by telling

13 Patrick Hennessey, M.D., M.R.C.S., L.K.Q.C.P.I. Doctor of Medicine; Member of the Royal College of Surgeons; Licentiate of the King's and Queen's College of Physicians, Ireland.

14 *'I'll fight for my Lord and Master!'* Renfield's violence is the clue that tells us Dracula is in one of these boxes. Note too that, heavy as the boxes are, the men have gotten to Carfax and back to the sanitarium, loaded, in half an hour. Quick work for English laborers at whom Stoker invariably pokes fun.

him to 'shut up for a foul-mouthed beggar,' whereon our man accused him of robbing him and wanting to murder him and said that he would hinder him if he were to swing for it. I opened the window and signed to the man not to notice, so he contented himself after looking the place over and making up his mind as to what kind of a place he had got to by saying: 'Lor' bless yer, sir, I wouldn't mind what was said to me in a bloomin' madhouse. I pity ye and the guv'nor for havin' to live in the house with a wild beast like that.' Then he asked his way civilly enough, and I told him where the gate of the empty house was; he went away, followed by threats and curses and revilings from our man. I went down to see if I could make out any cause for his anger, since he is usually such a well-behaved man, and except his violent fits nothing of the kind had ever occurred. I found him, to my astonishment, quite composed and most genial in his manner. I tried to get him to talk of the incident, but he blandly asked me questions as to what I meant, and led me to believe that he was completely oblivious of the affair. It was, I am sorry to say, however, only another instance of his cunning, for within half an hour I heard of him again. This time he had broken out through the window of his room, and was running down the avenue. I called to the attendants to follow me, and ran after him, for I feared he was intent on some mischief. My fear was justified when I saw the same cart which had passed before coming down the road, having on it some great wooden boxes. The men were wiping their foreheads, and were flushed in the face, as if with violent exercise. Before I could get up to him the patient rushed at them, and pulling one of them off the cart, began to knock his head against the ground. If I had not seized him just at the moment I believe he would have killed the man there and then. The other fellow jumped down and struck him over the head with the butt-end of his heavy whip. It was a terrible blow; but he did not seem to mind it, but seized him also, and struggled with the three of us, pulling us to and fro as if we were kittens. You know I am no light weight, and the others were both burly men. At first he was silent in his fighting; but as we began to master him, and the attendants were putting a strait-waistcoat on him, he began to shout: 'I'll frustrate them! They shan't rob
14 me! they shan't murder me by inches! I'll fight for my Lord and Master!' and all sorts of similar incoherent ravings. It was with very considerable difficulty that they got him back to the house and put him in the padded room. One of the attendants, Hardy, had a finger broken. However, I set it all right; and he is going on well.

"The two carriers were at first loud in their threats of actions for damages, and promised to rain all the penalties of the law on us. Their threats were, however, mingled with some sort of indirect apology for the defeat of the two of them by a feeble madman. They said that if it had not been for the way their strength had been spent in carrying and raising the heavy boxes to the cart they would have made short work of him. They gave as another reason for their defeat the extraordinary state of drouth to which they had been reduced by the dusty nature of their occupation and the reprehensible

distance from the scene of their labours of any place of public entertainment. I quite understood their drift, and after a stiff glass of grog, or rather more of the same, and with each a sovereign in hand, they made light of the attack, and swore that they would encounter a worse madman any day for the pleasure of meeting so 'bloomin' good a bloke' as your correspondent. I took their names and addresses, in case they might be needed. They are as follows:—Jack Smollet, of Dudding's Rents, King George's Road, Great Walworth, and **15, 16**
Thomas Snelling, Peter Parley's Row, Guide Court, Bethnal **17**
Green. They are both in the employment of Harris & Sons, Moving and Shipment Company, Orange Master's Yard, Soho. **18**

"I shall report to you any matter of interest occurring here, and shall wire you at once if there is anything of importance.

"Believe me, dear Sir,

"Yours faithfully,

"PATRICK HENNESSEY."

Letter, Mina Harker to Lucy Westenra.

(Unopened by her.)

"18 *September.*

"My dearest Lucy,—

"Such a sad blow has befallen us. Mr. Hawkins has died very suddenly. Some may not think it so sad for us, but we had both come to so love him that it really seems as though we had lost a father. I never knew either father or mother, so that the dear old man's death is a real blow to me. Jonathan is greatly distressed. It is not only that he feels sorrow, deep sorrow, for the dear, good man who has befriended him all his life, and now at the end has treated him like his own son and left him a fortune which to people of our modest bringing up is wealth beyond the dream of avarice, but Jonathan feels it on another account. He says the amount of responsibility which it puts upon him makes him nervous. He begins to doubt himself. I try to cheer him up, and *my* belief in *him* helps him to have a belief in himself. But it is here that the grave shock that he experienced tells upon him the most. Oh, it is too hard that a sweet, simple, noble, strong nature such as his—a nature which enabled him by our dear, good friend's aid to rise from clerk to master in a few years—should be so injured that the very **19**
essence of its strength is gone. Forgive me, dear, if I worry you with my troubles in the midst of your own happiness; but, Lucy dear, I must tell some one, for the strain of keeping up a brave and cheerful appearance to Jonathan tries me, and I have no one here that I can confide in. I dread coming up to London, as we must do the day after to-morrow; for poor Mr. Hawkins left in his will that he was to be buried in the grave with his father. As there are no relations at all, Jonathan will have to be chief mourner. I shall try to run over to see you, dearest, if only for a few minutes. Forgive me for troubling you. With all blessings,

"Your loving

"MINA HARKER."

15 *King George's Road.* According to Stoker, a street in Great Walworth, but it is not listed in Bartholomew's *Reference Atlas.* There is a King George's Avenue and a King George's Drive outside London. However, there *is* a St. George Street in Walworth.

16 *Great Walworth.* No listing as such in Bartholomew's *Atlas.* Referred to subsequently by Stoker as Walworth, a neighborhood in the Southwark district of south central London, located south of the Thames, approximately two miles southeast of Waterloo Station. (See map, pp. 340–41.)

17 *Bethnal Green.* A district of east central London, situated north of the Thames, northwest of the Isle of Dogs, and adjacent to the southwest edge of Victoria Park. (See map, pp. 340–41.)

18 *Soho.* A neighborhood of west central London, approximately one mile southeast of Regent's Park and one mile east of Hyde Park. Famous in the nineteenth century as a writers' and artists' quarter. (See map, pp. 340–41.)

19 *the very essence of its strength is gone.* Mina here takes note of a pervasive weakness in Harker. The reader, more than Mina (one assumes), has seen a good deal of Harker lying passive and supine: most notably, of course, in his nearly flirtatious lassitude in the presence of Dracula's women (p. 39); his swoon (p. 42); his doze (p. 45); and for a full six weeks he lay bedridden in Budapest (p. 99). Mina, on August 24, reports that he was "so thin and pale and weak-looking. . . . He is only a wreck of himself . . ." (p. 103). It is with this wreck that Mina spends her wedding night.

In all fairness, Stoker gives us plenty of reason to see Harker as, from time to time, a man of considerable resolution. The pattern of weakness noted here, however, is more revealing than the standard English masculinity Harker otherwise exhibits.

Dr. Seward's Diary.

20 *September.*—Only resolution and habit can let me make an entry to-night. I am too miserable, too low-spirited, too sick of the world and all in it, including life itself, that I would not care if I heard this moment the flapping of the wings of the angel of death. And he has been flapping those grim wings to some purpose of late—Lucy's mother and Arthur's father, and now . . . . Let me get on with my work.

I duly relieved Van Helsing in his watch over Lucy. We wanted Arthur to go to rest also, but he refused at first. It was only when I told him that we should want him to help us during the day, and that we must not all break down for want of rest, lest Lucy should suffer, that he agreed to go. Van Helsing was very kind to him. "Come, my child," he said; "come with me. You are sick and weak, and have had much sorrow and much mental pain, as well as that tax on your strength that we know of. You must not be alone; for to be alone is to be full of fears and alarms. Come to the drawing-room, where there is a big fire, and there are two sofas. You shall lie on one, and I on the other, and our sympathy will be comfort to each other, even though we do not speak, and even if we sleep." Arthur went off with him, casting back a longing look on Lucy's face, which lay on her pillow, almost whiter than the lawn. She lay quite still, and I looked round the room to see that all was as it should be. I could see that the Professor had carried out in this room, as in the other, his purpose of using the garlic; the whole of the window-sashes reeked with it, and round Lucy's neck, over the silk handkerchief which Van Helsing made her keep on, was a rough chaplet of the same odorous flowers. Lucy was breathing somewhat stertorously, and her face was at its worst, for the open mouth showed the pale gums. Her teeth, in the dim, uncertain light, seemed longer and sharper than they had been in the morning. In particular, by some trick of the light, the canine teeth looked longer and sharper than the rest. I sat down by her, and presently she moved uneasily. At the same moment there came a sort of dull flapping or buffeting at the window. I went over to it softly, and peeped out by the corner of the blind. There was a full moonlight, and I could see that the noise was made by a great bat, which wheeled round—doubtless attracted by the light, although so dim—and every now and again struck the window with its wings. When I came back to my seat I found that Lucy had moved slightly, and had torn away the garlic flowers from her throat. I replaced them as well as I could, and sat watching her.

Presently she woke, and I gave her food, as Van Helsing had prescribed. She took but a little, and that languidly. There did not seem to be with her now the unconscious struggle for life and strength that had hitherto so marked her illness. It struck me as curious that the moment she became conscious she pressed the garlic flowers close to her. It was certainly odd that whenever she got into that lethargic state, with the stertorous breathing, she put the flowers from her; but that when she waked she clutched them close. There was no possibility of making any mistake about this, for in the long hours that followed, she had many spells of sleeping and waking and repeated both actions many times.

At six o'clock Van Helsing came to relieve me. Arthur had then fallen into a doze, and he mercifully let him sleep on. When he saw Lucy's face I could hear the hissing indraw of his breath, and he said to me in a sharp whisper: "Draw up the blind; I want light!" Then he bent down, and, with his face almost touching Lucy's, examined her carefully. He removed the flowers and lifted the silk handkerchief from her throat. As he did so he started back, and I could hear his ejaculation, "Mein Gott!" as it was smothered in his throat. I bent over and looked too, and as I noticed some queer chill came over me.

The wounds on the throat had absolutely disappeared.

For fully five minutes Van Helsing stood looking at her, with his face at its sternest. Then he turned to me and said calmly:—

"She is dying. It will not be long now. It will be much difference, mark me, whether she dies conscious or in her sleep. Wake that poor boy, and let him come and see the last; he trusts us, and we have promised him."

I went to the dining-room and waked him. He was dazed for a moment, but when he saw the sunlight streaming in through the edges of the shutters he thought he was late, and expressed his fear. I assured him that Lucy was still asleep, but told him as gently as I could that both Van Helsing and I feared that the end was near. He covered his face with his hands, and slid down on his knees by the sofa, where he remained, perhaps a minute, with his head buried, praying, whilst his shoulders shook with grief. I took him by the hand and raised him up. "Come," I said, "my dear old fellow, summon all your fortitude; it will be best and easiest for *her*."

When we came into Lucy's room I could see that Van Helsing had, with his usual forethought, been putting matters straight and making everything look as pleasing as possible. He had even brushed Lucy's hair, so that it lay on the pillow in its usual sunny ripples. When we came into the room she opened her eyes, and seeing him, whispered softly:—

"Arthur! Oh, my love, I am so glad you have come!" He was stooping to kiss her, when Van Helsing motioned him back. "No," he whispered, "not yet! Hold her hand; it will comfort her more."

So Arthur took her hand and knelt beside her, and she looked her best, with all the soft lines matching the angelic beauty of her eyes. Then gradually her eyes closed, and she sank to sleep. For a little bit her breast heaved softly, and her breath came and went like a tired child's.

And then insensibly there came the strange change which I had noticed in the night. Her breathing grew stertorous, the mouth opened, and the pale gums, drawn back, made the teeth look longer and sharper than ever. In a sort of sleep-waking, vague, unconscious way she opened her eyes, which were now dull and hard at once, and said in a soft, voluptuous voice, such as I had never heard from her lips:—

"Arthur! Oh, my love, I am so glad you have come! Kiss me!" Arthur bent eagerly over to kiss her; but at that

20 *"I swear it!"* This is only the first of several oaths that will be taken. Here Van Helsing does the swearing. Later there will emerge a sort of chivalric band of warriors (including Mina) who are sworn to pursue the dragon Satan who has poisoned their lives.

21 *"We thought her dying whilst she slept . . ."* The relevant passages from Thomas Hood's poem "The Death-Bed" follow:

"We watched her breathing through the night,
Her breathing soft and low,
As in her breast the wave of life
Kept heaving to and fro.

"So silently we seemed to speak,
So slowly moved about,
As we had lent her half our powers
To eke her living out.

"Our very hopes belied our fears,
Our fears our hopes belied—
We thought her dying when she slept,
And sleeping when she died.

"For when the morn came dim and sad,
And chill with early showers,
Her quiet eyelids closed—she had
Another morn than ours!"

Another of Hood's poems—"The Dream of Eugene Aram"—had a major impact on Stoker's life when, in 1876, in Dublin, he had the momentous experience of hearing Henry Irving recite it. Stoker, in his *Personal Reminiscences of Henry Irving* (pp. 28–30), tells the story:

"And so after dinner he said he would like to recite for me Thomas Hood's poem 'The Dream of Eugene Aram.'

"That experience I shall never—can never—forget . . . such was Irving's commanding force, so great was the magnetism of his genius, so profound was the sense of his dominance that I sat spellbound. Outwardly I was as of stone . . . here was incarnate power, incarnate passion . . . Here was indeed Eugene Aram . . . After the climax of horror the Actor was able by art and habit to control himself to the narrative mood whilst he spoke a few concluding lines of the poem.

"Then he collapsed half fainting."

The reading had an effect on Stoker, too. He "burst into something like hysterics." From that moment on, the lives of both men were changed. They had, as Stoker put it, looked soul into soul. Two years later, Stoker followed Irving to London where he took up his duties as Irving's right-hand man. He played that role for twenty-seven years—until Irving's death.

instant Van Helsing, who, like me, had been startled by her voice, swooped upon him, and catching him by the neck with both hands, dragged him back with a fury of strength which I never thought he could have possessed, and actually hurled him almost across the room.

"Not for your life!" he said; "not for your living soul and hers!" And he stood between them like a lion at bay.

Arthur was so taken aback that he did not for a moment know what to do or say; and before any impulse of violence could seize him he realised the place and the occasion, and stood silent, waiting.

I kept my eyes fixed on Lucy, as did Van Helsing, and we saw a spasm as of rage flit like a shadow over her face; the sharp teeth champed together. Then her eyes closed, and she breathed heavily.

Very shortly after she opened her eyes in all their softness, and putting out her poor pale, thin hand, took Van Helsing's great brown one; drawing it to her, she kissed it. "My true friend," she said, in a faint voice, but with untellable pathos, "My true friend, and his! Oh, guard him, and give me peace!"

20 "I swear it!" said he solemnly, kneeling beside her and holding up his hand, as one who registers an oath. Then he turned to Arthur, and said to him: "Come, my child, take her hand in yours, and kiss her on the forehead, and only once.'

Their eyes met instead of their lips; and so they parted.

Lucy's eyes closed; and Van Helsing, who had been watching closely, took Arthur's arm, and drew him away.

And then Lucy's breathing became stertorous again, and all at once it ceased.

"It is all over," said Van Helsing. "She is dead!"

I took Arthur by the arm, and led him away to the drawing-room, where he sat down, and covered his face with his hands, sobbing in a way that nearly broke me down to see.

I went back to the room, and found Van Helsing looking at poor Lucy, and his face was sterner than ever. Some change had come over her body. Death had given back part of her beauty, for her brow and cheeks had recovered some of their flowing lines; even the lips had lost their deadly pallor. It was as if the blood, no longer needed for the working of the heart, had gone to make the harshness of death as little rude as might be.

21 "We thought her dying whilst she slept,
And sleeping when she died."

I stood beside Van Helsing, and said:—

"Ah well, poor girl, there is peace for her at last. It is the end!"

He turned to me, and said with grave solemnity:—

"Not so; alas! not so. It is only the beginning!"

When I asked him what he meant, he only shook his head and answered:—

"We can do nothing as yet. Wait and see."

CHAPTER XIII.

DR. SEWARD'S DIARY—*continued.*

THE funeral was arranged for the next succeeding day, so that Lucy and her mother might be buried together. I attended to all the ghastly formalities, and the urbane undertaker proved that his staff were afflicted—or blessed—with something of his own obsequious suavity. Even the woman who performed the last offices for the dead remarked to me, in a confidential, brother-professional way, when she had come out from the death-chamber:—

"She makes a very beautiful corpse, sir. It's quite a privilege to attend on her. It's not too much to say that she will do credit to our establishment!"

I noticed that Van Helsing never kept far away. This was possible from the disordered state of things in the household. There were no relatives at hand; and as Arthur had to be back the next day to attend at his father's funeral, we were unable to notify any one who should have been bidden. Under the circumstances, Van Helsing and I took it upon ourselves to examine papers, etc. He insisted upon looking over Lucy's papers himself. I asked him why, for I feared that he, being a foreigner, might not be quite aware of English legal requirements, and so might in ignorance make some unnecessary trouble. He answered me:—

"I know; I know. You forget that I am a lawyer as well as a doctor. But this is not altogether for the law. You knew that, when you avoided the coroner. I have more than him to avoid. There may be papers more—such as this."

As he spoke he took from his pocket-book the memorandum which had been in Lucy's breast, and which she had torn in her sleep.

"THE FUNERAL WAS ARRANGED."

"When you find anything of the solicitor who is for the late Mrs. Westenra, seal all her papers, and write him to-night. For me, I watch here in the room and in Miss Lucy's old room all night, and I myself search for what may be. It is not well that her very thoughts go into the hands of strangers."

I went on with my part of the work, and in another half-hour had found the name and address of Mrs. Westenra's solicitor and had written to him. All the poor lady's papers were in order; explicit directions regarding the place of burial were given. I had hardly sealed the letter, when, to my surprise, Van Helsing walked into the room, saying:—

"Can I help you, friend John? I am free, and if I may, my service is to you."

"Have you got what you looked for?" I asked, to which he replied:—

"I did not look for any specific thing. I only hoped to find, and find I have, all that there was—only some letters and a few memoranda, and a diary new begun. But I have them here, and we shall for the present say nothing of them. I shall see that poor lad to-morrow evening, and, with his sanction, I shall use some."

When we had finished the work in hand, he said to me:—

"And now, friend John, I think we may to bed. We want sleep, both you and I, and rest to recuperate. To-morrow we shall have much to do, but for the to-night there is no need of us. Alas!"

Before turning in we went to look at poor Lucy. The undertaker had certainly done his work well, for the room was
1 turned into a small *chapelle ardente*. There was a wilderness of beautiful white flowers, and death was made as little repulsive as might be. The end of the winding-sheet was laid over the face; when the Professor bent over and turned it gently back, we both started at the beauty before us, the tall wax candles showing a sufficient light to note it well. All Lucy's loveliness had come back to her in death, and the hours
2 that had passed, instead of leaving traces of "decay's effacing

1 chapelle ardente. A catafalque lighted up with candles.

2 *"decay's effacing fingers."* The phrase is from Byron's "Giaour." Byron is making an extended metaphor in which the nation Greece is seen as a newly dead person. He writes:

"He who hath bent him o'er the dead
Ere the first day of death is fled,
The first dark day of nothingness,
The last of danger and distress,
(Before Decay's effacing fingers
Have swept the lines where beauty lingers,)
And mark'd the mild angelic air,
The rapture of repose that's there,
The fix'd yet tender traits that streak
The languor of the placid cheek,
And—but for that sad shrouded eye,
That fires not, wins not, weeps not, now,
And but for that chill, changeless brow,
Where cold Obstruction's apathy
Appals the gazing mourner's heart,
As if to him it could impart
The doom he dreads, yet dwells upon;

Such is the aspect of this shore;
'Tis Greece, but living Greece no more!
So coldly sweet, so deadly fair,
We start, for soul is wanting there.
Hers is the loveliness in death,
That parts not quite with parting breath:"

The "Giaour" is interesting for another reason: it contains a famous vampire curse:

"But first on earth, as Vampyre sent
Thy corse shall from its tomb be rent;
Then ghastly haunt thy native place,
And suck the blood of all thy race;
There from thy *daughter*, *sister*, *wife*,
At midnight drain the stream of life;
Yet loathe the banquet, *which perforce*
Must feed thy livid living corse,"

Francis W. Frigout, Esq.,
Deputy Consul General, U.S.A.,
12, St. Helen's Place,
Bishopsgate Street,
London, E.C.

8th January, 1892

COPY			
For the funeral of the late Mrs. Virginia Dunning, aged 54 yrs. Died at Nelsons Hotel, Great Portland Street, London, W.1., Nov. 14th 1891. Delivered at the Royal Albert Docks 25th Nov 1891 for shipment to New York per National Line 'S.S.England' for transmission to San Francisco, California, U.S.A.			
5'10" x 20" Stout Elm Inner Coffin lined and ruffled fine cambric. Super Cambric Folding Sheet wool mattress and pillow. Stout Lead Coffin soldered complete. Lead plate with chased inscription for same. 4 men bearing in and removing remains to Mortuary Chapel. Hearse and one Carriage for removal. An English Oak Case with champhered lid and French polished plinth mounted with four pairs of solid polished brass handles. Brass angle plate. 2 illuminated brass crosses on lid. 8 large brass closing screws etc. Brass shield plate on Oak mount, engraved inscription. Serge wrapper for case and webbing. 6 men bearing in van. Strong deal packing case. Conveyance and pair removing remains to Royal Albert Dock. 8 assistants placing remains in same. Personal attendance throughout.	33	15	0
Consul General's Fee for Certificate and attendance at Nelsons Hotel	3	3	0
Certificate of Death.		2	7
Gratuity to Mortuary attendant.		2	6
Gratuity to men at Docks removing remains into shed.		4	0
	37	7	1
Van and 2 men moving personal effects from Nelsons Hotel to 48, High Street.		3	6
Warehousing same till January 8th 1892.		10	6
2 strong deal packing cases for same addressed to Mrs. Fannie A. Underhill, 1417a, Clay Street, San Francisco, California, U.S.A.	2	2	0
	£ 40	3	1d

A NINETEENTH-CENTURY FUNERAL EXPENSE ACCOUNT.

fingers," had but restored the beauty of life, till positively I could not believe my eyes that I was looking at a corpse.

The Professor looked sternly grave. He had not loved her as I had, and there was no need for tears in his eyes. He said to me: "Remain till I return," and left the room. He came back with a handful of wild garlic from the box waiting in the hall, but which had not been opened, and placed the flowers amongst the others on and around the bed. Then he took from his neck, inside his collar, a little golden crucifix, and placed it over the mouth. He restored the sheet to its place, and we came away.

I was undressing in my own room, when, with a premonitory tap at the door, he entered, and at once began to speak:—

"To-morrow I want you to bring me, before night, a set of post-mortem knives."

"Must we make an autopsy?" I asked.

"Yes, and no. I want to operate, but not as you think. Let me tell you now, but not a word to another. I want to cut off her head and take out her heart. Ah! you a surgeon, and so shocked! You, whom I have seen with no tremble of hand or heart, do operations of life and death that make the rest shudder. Oh, but I must not forget, my dear friend John, that you loved her; and I have not forgotten it, for it is I that shall operate, and you must only help. I would like to do it to-night, but for Arthur I must not; he will be free after his father's funeral to-morrow, and he will want to see her—to see *it*. Then, when she is coffined ready for the next day, you and I shall come when all sleep. We shall unscrew the coffin-lid, and shall do our operation; and then replace all, so that none know, save we alone."

"But why do it at all? The girl is dead. Why mutilate her poor body without need? And if there is no necessity for a post-mortem and nothing to gain by it—no good to her, to us, to science, to human knowledge—why do it? Without such it is monstrous."

For answer he put his hand on my shoulder, and said, with infinite tenderness:—

"Friend John, I pity your poor bleeding heart; and I love you the more because it does so bleed. If I could, I would take on myself the burden that you do bear. But there are things that you know not, but that you shall know, and bless me for knowing, though they are not pleasant things. John, my child, you have been my friend now many years, and yet did you ever know me to do any without good cause? I may err—I am but man; but I believe in all I do. Was it not for these causes that you send for me when the great trouble came? Yes! Were you not amazed, nay horrified, when I would not let Arthur kiss his love—though she was dying—and snatched him away by all my strength? Yes! And yet you saw how she thanked me, with her so beautiful dying eyes, her voice, too, so weak, and she kiss my rough old hand and bless me? Yes! And did you not hear me swear promise to her, that so she closed her eyes grateful? Yes!

"Well, I have good reason now for all I want to do. You have for many years trust me; you have believe me weeks past, when there be things so strange that you might have well doubt. Believe me yet a little, friend John. If you trust me

"I SAW ONE OF THE MAIDS PASS."

3 *"it is too late—or too early . . ."* There is something of a mystery here. Van Helsing placed the little gold crucifix over Lucy's mouth and arranged garlic flowers around her even though she was dead as a victim of the vampire. One would suppose that the spiritual damage to Lucy was already done, yet in Stoker's mythmaking, we are to understand that there was still more evil for Dracula to accomplish and that the theft of the crucifix enabled him to achieve it.

not, then I must tell what I think; and that is not perhaps well. And if I work—as work I shall, no matter trust or no trust—without my friend trust in me, I work with heavy heart and feel, oh! so lonely when I want all help and courage that may be!" He paused a moment and went on solemnly: "Friend John, there are strange and terrible days before us. Let us not be two, but one, that so we work to a good end. Will you not have faith in me?"

I took his hand, and promised him. I held my door open as he went away, and watched him go into his room and close the door. As I stood without moving, I saw one of the maids pass silently along the passage—she had her back towards me, so did not see me—and go into the room where Lucy lay. The sight touched me. Devotion is so rare, and we are so grateful to those who show it unasked to those we love. Here was a poor girl putting aside the terrors which she naturally had of death to go watch alone by the bier of the mistress whom she loved, so that the poor clay might not be lonely till laid to eternal rest. . . .

I must have slept long and soundly, for it was broad daylight when Van Helsing waked me by coming into my room. He came over to my bedside and said:—

"You need not trouble about the knives; we shall not do it."

"Why not?" I asked. For his solemnity of the night before had greatly impressed me.

3 "Because," he said sternly, "it is too late—or too early. See!" Here he held up the little golden crucifix. "This was stolen in the night."

"How, stolen," I asked in wonder, "since you have it now?"

"Because I get it back from the worthless wretch who stole it, from the woman who robbed the dead and the living. Her punishment will surely come, but not through me; she knew not altogether what she did, and thus unknowing, she only stole. Now we must wait."

He went away on the word, leaving me with a new mystery to think of, a new puzzle to grapple with.

The forenoon was a dreary time, but at noon the solicitor came: Mr. Marquand, of Wholeman, Sons, Marquand & Lidderdale. He was very genial and very appreciative of what we had done, and took off our hands all cares as to details. During lunch he told us that Mrs. Westenra had for some time expected sudden death from her heart, and had put her affairs in absolute order; he informed us that, with the exception of a certain entailed property of Lucy's father's which now, in default of direct issue, went back to a distant branch of the family, the whole estate, real and personal, was left absolutely to Arthur Holmwood. When he had told us so much he went on:—

"Frankly we did our best to prevent such a testamentary disposition, and pointed out certain contingencies that might leave her daughter either penniless or not so free as she should be to act regarding a matrimonial alliance. Indeed, we pressed the matter so far that we almost came into collision, for she asked us if we were or were not prepared to carry out her wishes. Of course, we had then no alternative but to accept. We were right in principle, and ninety-nine times out of a hundred we should have proved, by the logic of events, the accuracy of our judgment. Frankly, however, I must admit that in this case any other form of disposition would have rendered impossible the carrying out of her wishes. For by her predeceasing her daughter the latter would have come into possession of the property, and, even had she only survived her mother by five minutes, her property would, in case there were no will—and a will was a practical impossibility in such a case—have been treated at her decease as under intestacy. In which case Lord Godalming, though so dear a friend, would have had no claim in the world; and the inheritors, being remote, would not be likely to abandon their just rights, for sentimental reasons regarding an entire stranger. I assure you, my dear sirs, I am rejoiced at the result, perfectly rejoiced."

He was a good fellow, but his rejoicing at the one little part—in which he was officially interested—of so great a tragedy, was an object-lesson in the limitations of sympathetic understanding.

He did not remain long, but said he would look in later in the day and see Lord Godalming. His coming, however, had been a certain comfort to us, since it assured us that we should not have to dread hostile criticism as to any of our acts. Arthur was expected at five o'clock, so a little before that time we visited the death-chamber. It was so in very truth, for now both mother and daughter lay in it The undertaker, true to his craft, had made the best display he could of his goods, and there was a mortuary air about the place that lowered our spirits at once. Van Helsing ordered the former arrangement to be adhered to, explaining that, as Lord Godalming was coming very soon, it would be less harrowing to his feelings to see all that was left of his *fiancée* quite alone. The undertaker seemed shocked at his own stupidity, and exerted himself to restore things to the condition in which we left them the night before, so that when Arthur came such shocks to his feelings as we could avoid were saved.

Poor fellow! He looked desperately sad and broken; even his stalwart manhood seemed to have shrunk somewhat under the strain of his much-tried emotions. He had, I knew, been very genuinely and devotedly attached to his father; and to lose him, and at such a time, was a bitter blow to him. With me he was warm as ever, and to Van Helsing he was sweetly courteous; but I could not help seeing that there was some constraint with him. The Professor noticed it, too, and motioned me to bring him upstairs. I did so, and left him at the door of the room, as I felt he would like to be quite alone with her; but he took my arm and led me in, saying huskily:—

"You loved her too, old fellow; she told me all about it, and there was no friend had a closer place in her heart than you. I don't know how to thank you for all you have done for her. I can't think yet . . . ."

Here he suddenly broke down, and threw his arms round

my shoulders and laid his head on my breast, crying :—

"Oh, Jack! Jack! What shall I do? The whole of life seems gone from me all at once, and there is nothing in the wide world for me to live for."

I comforted him as well as I could. In such cases men do not need much expression. A grip of the hand, the tightening of an arm over the shoulder, a sob in unison, are expressions of sympathy dear to a man's heart. I stood still and silent till his sobs died away, and then I said softly to him :—

"Come and look at her."

Together we moved over to the bed, and I lifted the lawn from her face. God! how beautiful she was. Every hour seemed to be enhancing her loveliness. It frightened and amazed me somewhat; and as for Arthur, he fell a-trembling, and finally was shaken with doubt as with an ague. At last, after a long pause, he said to me in a faint whisper :—

"Jack, is she really dead?"

I assured him sadly that it was so, and went on to suggest —for I felt that such a horrible doubt should not have life for a moment longer than I could help—that it often happened that after death faces became softened and even resolved into their youthful beauty; that this was especially so when death had been preceded by any acute or prolonged suffering. It seemed to quite do away with any doubt, and, after kneeling beside the couch for a while and looking at her lovingly and long, he turned aside. I told him that that must be good-bye, as the coffin had to be prepared; so he went back and took her dead hand in his and kissed it, and bent over and kissed her forehead. He came away, fondly looking back over his shoulder at her as he came.

I left him in the drawing-room, and told Van Helsing that he had said good-bye; so the latter went to the kitchen to tell the undertaker's men to proceed with the preparations and to screw up the coffin. When he came out of the room again I told him of Arthur's question, and he replied :—

"I am not surprised. Just now I doubted for a moment myself!"

We all dined together, and I could see that poor Art was trying to make the best of things. Van Helsing had been silent all dinner-time, but when we had lit our cigars he said :—

"Lord——;" but Arthur interrupted him :—

"No, no, not that, for God's sake! not yet at any rate. Forgive me, sir: I did not mean to speak offensively; it is only because my loss is so recent."

The Professor answered very sweetly :—

"I only used that name because I was in doubt. I must not call you 'Mr.,' and I have grown to love you—yes, my dear boy, to love you—as Arthur."

Arthur held out his hand, and took the old man's warmly.

"Call me what you will," he said. "I hope I may always have the title of a friend. And let me say that I am at a loss for words to thank you for your goodness to my poor dear." He paused a moment, and went on: "I know that she understood your goodness even better than I do; and if I was rude or in any way wanting at that time you acted so—you remember"—the Professor nodded—"you must forgive me."

He answered with a grave kindness:—

"I know it was hard for you to quite trust me then, for to trust such violence needs to understand; and I take it that you do not—that you cannot—trust me now, for you do not yet understand. And there may be more times when I shall want you to trust when you cannot—and may not—and must not yet understand. But the time will come when your trust shall be whole and complete in me, and when you shall understand as though the sunlight himself shone through. Then you shall bless me from first to last for your own sake, and for the sake of others, and for her dear sake to whom I swore to protect."

"And, indeed, indeed, sir," said Arthur warmly, "I shall in all ways trust you. I know and believe you have a very noble heart, and you are Jack's friend, and you were hers. You shall do what you like."

The Professor cleared his throat a couple of times, as though about to speak, and finally said:—

"May I ask you something now?"

"Certainly."

"You know that Mrs. Westenra left you all her property?"

"No, poor dear; I never thought of it."

"And as it is all yours, you have a right to deal with it as you will. I want you to give me permission to read all Miss Lucy's papers and letters. Believe me, it is no idle curiosity. I have a motive of which, be sure, she would have approved. I have them all here. I took them before we knew that all was yours, so that no strange hand might touch them—no strange eye look through words into her soul. I shall keep them, if I may; even you may not see them yet, but I shall keep them safe. No word shall be lost; and in the good time I shall give them back to you. It's a hard thing I ask, but you will do it, will you not, for Lucy's sake?"

Arthur spoke out heartily, like his old self:—

"Dr. Van Helsing, you may do what you will. I feel that in saying this I am doing what my dear one would have approved I shall not trouble you with questions till the time comes."

The old Professor stood up as he said solemnly:—

"And you are right. There will be pain for us all; but it will not be all pain, nor will this pain be the last. We and you too—you most of all, my dear boy—will have to pass through the bitter water before we reach the sweet. But we must be brave of heart and unselfish, and do our duty, and all will be well!"

I slept on a sofa in Arthur's room that night. Van Helsing did not go to bed at all. He went to and fro, as if patrolling the house, and was never out of sight of the room where Lucy lay in her coffin, strewn with the wild garlic flowers, which sent, through the odour of lily and rose, a heavy, overpowering smell into the night.

Mina Harker's Journal.

22 *September.*—In the train to Exeter. Jonathan sleeping. It seems only yesterday that the last entry was made, and

4 *Hyde Park Corner.* Located at the southeast corner of Hyde Park in west central London. Intersected by Knightsbridge and Grosvenor Place. Approximately one-quarter mile west of Buckingham Palace (see map, pp. 340–41).

5 *the Row.* Probably Rotten Row, a track of approximately 1½ miles in Hyde Park reserved exclusively for riders.

6 *Piccadilly.* A thoroughfare in west central London. Begins at Piccadilly Circus and runs southwest approximately three quarters of a mile to Hyde Park Corner (see map, pp. 340–41).

7 *Giuliano's.* A search through the London post office directory for 1897 did not turn up any listing for Giuliano's.

HYDE PARK CORNER.

yet how much between then, in Whitby and all the world before me, Jonathan away and no news of him; and now, married to Jonathan, Jonathan a solicitor, a partner, rich, master of his business, Mr. Hawkins dead and buried, and Jonathan with another attack that may harm him. Some day he may ask me about it. Down it all goes. I am rusty in my shorthand—see what unexpected prosperity does for us—so it may be as well to freshen it up again with an exercise anyhow. . . . .

The service was very simple and very solemn. There were only ourselves and the servants there, one or two old friends of his from Exeter, his London agent, and a gentleman representing Sir John Paxton, the President of the Incorporated Law Society. Jonathan and I stood hand in hand, and we felt that our best and dearest friend was gone from us. . . . .

4 We came back to town quietly, taking a 'bus to Hyde Park Corner. Jonathan thought it would interest me to go into
5 the Row for a while, so we sat down; but there were very few people there, and it was sad-looking and desolate to see so many empty chairs. It made us think of the empty chair at
6 home; so we got up and walked down Piccadilly. Jonathan was holding me by the arm, the way he used to in old days before I went to school. I felt it very improper, for you can't go on for some years teaching etiquette and decorum to other girls without the pedantry of it biting into yourself a bit; but it was Jonathan, and he was my husband, and we didn't know anybody who saw us—and we didn't care if they did—so on we walked. I was looking at a very beautiful girl, in a big cart-
7 wheel hat, sitting in a victoria outside Giuliano's, when I felt Jonathan clutch my arm so tight that he hurt me, and he said under his breath: "My God!" I am always anxious about Jonathan, for I fear that some nervous fit may upset him again; so I turned to him quickly, and asked him what it was that disturbed him.

He was very pale, and his eyes seemed bulging out as, half in terror and half in amazement, he gazed at a tall, thin man, with a beaky nose and black moustache and pointed beard, 8 who was also observing the pretty girl. He was looking at her so hard that he did not see either of us, and so I had a good view of him. His face was not a good face; it was hard, and cruel, and sensual, and his big white teeth, that looked all the whiter because his lips were so red, were pointed like an animal's. Jonathan kept staring at him, till I was afraid he would notice. I feared he might take it ill, he looked so fierce and nasty. I asked Jonathan why he was disturbed, and he answered, evidently thinking that I knew as much about it as he did: "Do you see who it is?"

"No, dear," I said; "I don't know him; who is it?" His answer seemed to shock and thrill me, for it was said as if he did not know that it was to me, Mina, to whom he was speaking:—

"It is the man himself!"

The poor dear was evidently terrified at something—very greatly terrified; I do believe that if he had not had me to lean on and to support him he would have sunk down. He kept staring; a man came out of the shop with a small parcel, and gave it to the lady, who then drove off. The dark man kept his eyes fixed on her, and when the carriage moved up Piccadilly he followed in the same direction, and hailed a hansom. Jonathan kept looking after him, and said, as if to himself:—

"I believe it is the Count, but he has grown young. My God, if this be so! Oh, my God! my God! If I only knew! if I only knew!" He was distressing himself so much that I feared to keep his mind on the subject by asking him any questions, so I remained silent. I drew him away quietly, and he, holding my arm, came easily. We walked a little further, and then went in and sat for a while in the Green Park. It was a 9 hot day for autumn, and there was a comfortable seat in a shady place. After a few minutes' staring at nothing, Jonathan's eyes closed, and he went quietly into a sleep, with his head on my shoulder. I thought it was the best thing for him, so did not disturb him. In about twenty minutes he woke up, and said to me quite cheerfully:—

"Why, Mina, have I been asleep? Oh, do forgive me for being so rude. Come, and we'll have a cup of tea somewhere." He had evidently forgotten all about the dark stranger, as in his illness he had forgotten all that this episode had reminded him of. I don't like this lapsing into forgetfulness; it may make or continue some injury to the brain. I must not ask him, for fear I shall do more harm than good; but I must somehow learn the facts of his journey abroad. The time is come, I fear, when I must open that parcel and know what is written. Oh, Jonathan, you will, I know, forgive me if I do wrong, but it is for your own dear sake.

Later.—A sad home-coming in every way—the house empty of the dear soul who was so good to us; Jonathan still pale and dizzy under a slight relapse of his malady; and now a telegram from Van Helsing, whoever he may be:—

"You will be grieved to hear that Mrs. Westenra died five days ago, and that Lucy died the day before yesterday. They were both buried to-day."

8 *and pointed beard.* Mina's description of the vampire is less flattering to him than Jonathan Harker's first account of him. Harker called his nose "aquiline" (p. 21), while Mina says it is "beaky."

It should also be noted that here, once again, we see Dracula abroad in daylight. This will happen still another time in Stoker's story, though, interestingly enough, the film industry has taken it as dogma that a vampire can*not* stir abroad by day.

9 *Green Park.* A park of sixty acres opposite the east end of Hyde Park in west central London (see map, pp. 340–41).

Oh, what a wealth of sorrow in a few words! Poor Mrs. Westenra! poor Lucy! Gone, gone, never to return to us! And poor, poor Arthur, to have lost such sweetness out of his life! God help us all to bear our troubles.

Dr. Seward's Diary.

22 *September.*—It is all over. Arthur has gone back to Ring, and has taken Quincey Morris with him. What a fine fellow is Quincey! I believe in my heart of hearts that he suffered as much about Lucy's death as any of us; but he bore himself through it like a moral Viking. If America can go on breeding men like that, she will be a power in the world indeed. Van Helsing is lying down, having a rest preparatory to his journey. He goes over to Amsterdam to-night, but says he returns to-morrow night; that he only wants to make some arrangements which can only be made personally. He is to stop with me then, if he can; he says he has work to do in London which may take him some time. Poor old fellow! I fear that the strain of the past week has broken down even his iron strength. All the time of the burial he was, I could see, putting some terrible restraint on himself. When it was all over, we were standing beside Arthur, who, poor fellow, was speaking of his part in the operation where his blood had been transfused to his Lucy's veins; I could see Van Helsing's face grow white and purple by turns. Arthur was saying that he felt since then as if they two had been
10 really married, and that she was his wife in the sight of God. None of us said a word of the other operations, and none of us ever shall. Arthur and Quincey went away together to the station, and Van Helsing and I came on here. The moment we were alone in the carriage he gave way to a regular fit of hysterics. He has denied to me since that it was hysterics, and insisted that it was only his sense of humour asserting itself under very terrible conditions. He laughed till he cried, and I had to draw down the blinds lest any one should see us and misjudge; and then he cried till he laughed again; and laughed and cried together, just as a woman does. I tried to be stern with him, as one is to a woman under the circumstances; but it had no effect. Men and women are so different in manifestations of nervous strength or weakness! Then when his face grew grave and stern again I asked him why his mirth, and why at such a time. His reply was in a way characteristic of him, for it was logical and forceful and mysterious. He said:—

"Ah, you don't comprehend, friend John. Do not think that I am not sad, though I laugh. See, I have cried even when the laugh did choke me. But no more think that I am all sorry when I cry, for the laugh he come just the same. Keep it always with you that laughter who knock at your door and say, 'May I come in?' is not the true laughter. No! he is a king, and he come when and how he like. He ask no person; he choose no time of suitability. He say, 'I am here.' Behold, in example I grieve my heart out for that so sweet young girl; I give my blood for her, though I am old and worn; I give my time, my skill, my sleep; I let my other

10 *in the sight of God.* Van Helsing's hysterics point up the meaning of the various blood-takings and transfusions that occur in this book. Marriage, or a fusion of identities, or some sort of kinship is implied in every case.

Note, too, that Lucy is getting the wish she made when she cried, "Why can't they let a girl marry three men, or as many as want her, and save all this trouble?" (p. 62).

Van Helsing's laughter, seen charitably, is a hysteria brought on by great strain. In a less kindly light we see him here possessed by his familiar demon of tastelessness. Van Helsing, we will see, can be not only tasteless but sometimes downright brutal.

sufferers want that so she may have all. And yet I can laugh at her very grave—laugh when the clay from the spade of the sexton drop upon her coffin and say, 'Thud! thud!' to my heart, till it send back the blood from my cheek. My heart bleed for that poor boy—that dear boy, so of the age of mine own boy had I been so blessed that he live, and with his hair and eyes the same. There, you know now why I love him so. And yet when he say things that touch my husband-heart to the quick, and make my father-heart yearn to him as to no other man—not even to you, friend John, for we are more level in experiences than father and son—yet even at such moment King Laugh he come to me and shout and bellow in my ear, 'Here I am! here I am!' till the blood come dance back and bring some of the sunshine that he carry with him to my cheek. Oh, friend John, it is a strange world, a sad world, a world full of miseries, and woes, and troubles; and yet when King Laugh come he make them all dance to the tune he play. Bleeding hearts, and dry bones of the churchyard, and tears that burn as they fall—all dance together to the music that he make with that smileless mouth of him. And believe me, friend John, that he is good to come, and kind. Ah, we men and women are like ropes drawn tight with strain that pull us different ways. Then tears come; and, like the rain on the ropes, they brace us up, until perhaps the strain become too great, and we break. But King Laugh he come like the sunshine, and he ease off the strain again; and we bear to go on with our labour, what it may be."

I did not like to wound him by pretending not to see his idea; but, as I did not yet understand the cause of his laughter, I asked him. As he answered me his face grew stern, and he said in quite a different tone:—

"Oh, it was the grim irony of it all—this so lovely lady garlanded with flowers, that looked so fair as life, till one by one we wondered if she were truly dead; she laid in that so fine marble house in that lonely churchyard, where rest so many of her kin, laid there with the mother who loved her, and whom she loved; and that sacred bell going 'Toll! toll! toll!' so sad and slow; and those holy men, with the white garments of the angel, pretending to read books, and yet all the time their eyes never on the page; and all us with the bowed head. And all for what? She is dead; so! Is it not?"

"Well, for the life of me, Professor," I said, "I can't see anything to laugh at in all that. Why, your explanation makes it a harder puzzle than before. But even if the burial service was comic, what about poor Art and his trouble? Why, his heart was simply breaking."

"Just so. Said he not that the transfusion of his blood to her veins had made her truly his bride?"

"Yes, and it was a sweet and comforting idea for him."

"Quite so. But there was a difficulty, friend John. If so that, then what about the others? Ho, ho! Then this so sweet maid is a polyandrist, and me, with my poor wife dead to me, but alive by Church's law, though no wits, all gone—even I, who am faithful husband to this now-no wife, am bigamist."

11 *Hampstead Hill.* Not listed as such in Bartholomew's *Guide to London.* Hampstead Hill Gardens is a small street on the hill south of Hampstead Heath. The reference may be to this hill or to the heath itself, which, near Jack Straw's castle and the Spaniards, attains considerable elevation.

"I don't see where the joke comes in there either!" I said; and I did not feel particularly pleased with him for saying such things. He laid his hand on my arm, and said:—

"Friend John, forgive me if I pain. I showed not my feeling to others when it would wound, but only to you, my old friend, whom I can trust. If you could have looked into my very heart then when I want to laugh; if you could have done so when the laugh arrived; if you could do so now, when King Laugh have pack up his crown and all that is to him—for he go far, far away from me, and for a long, long time—maybe you would perhaps pity me the most of all."

I was touched by the tenderness of his tone, and asked why.

"Because I know!"

And now we are all scattered; and for many a long day loneliness will sit over our roofs with brooding wings. Lucy lies in the tomb of her kin, a lordly death-house in a lonely churchyard, away from teeming London; where the air is fresh,
11 and the sun rises over Hampstead Hill, and where wild flowers grow of their own accord.

So I can finish this diary; and God only knows if I shall ever begin another. If I do, or if I ever open this again, it will be to deal with different people and different themes; for here at the end, where the romance of my life is told, ere I go back to take up the thread of my life-work, I say sadly and without hope,

"FINIS."

"*The Westminster Gazette,*" 25 *September.*

A HAMPSTEAD MYSTERY.

The neighbourhood of Hampstead is just at present exercised with a series of events which seem to run on lines parallel to

HAMPSTEAD HEATH.

"THEY HAD BEEN WITH A 'BLOOFER LADY.'"

12 *the Heath.* A large public green of 240 acres on the northern perimeter of the neighborhood of Hampstead. It was once notorious for the presence of highwaymen. (See map, pp. 340–41.)

those of what was known to the writers of headlines as "The Kensington Horror," or "The Stabbing Woman," or "The Woman in Black." During the past two or three days several cases have occurred of young children straying from home or neglecting to return from their playing on the Heath. In all **12**
these cases the children were too young to give any properly intelligible account of themselves, but the consensus of their excuses is that they had been with a "bloofer lady." It has always been late in the evening when they have been missed, and on two occasions the children have not been found until early in the following morning. It is generally supposed in the neighbourhood that, as the first child missed gave as his reason for being away that a "bloofer lady" had asked him to come for a walk, the others had picked up the phrase and used it as occasion served. This is the more natural as the favourite game of the little ones at present is luring each other away by wiles. A correspondent writes us that to see some of the tiny tots pretending to be the "bloofer lady" is supremely funny. Some of our caricaturists might, he says, take a lesson in the irony of grotesque by comparing the reality and the picture. It is only in accordance with general principles of human nature that the "bloofer lady" should be the popular rôle at these *al fresco*

performances. Our correspondent naïvely says that even
13 Ellen Terry could not be so winningly attractive as some
of these grubby-faced little children pretend—and even imagine
themselves—to be.

There is, however, possibly a serious side to the question, for some of the children, indeed all who have been missed at night, have been slightly torn or wounded in the throat. The wounds seem such as might be made by a rat or a small dog, and although of not much importance individually, would tend to show that whatever animal inflicts them has a system or method of its own. The police of the division have been instructed to keep a sharp look-out for straying children, especially when very young, in and around Hampstead Heath, and for any stray dog which may be about.

"The Westminster Gazette," 25 September.

Extra Special.

THE HAMPSTEAD HORROR.

ANOTHER CHILD INJURED.

The "Bloofer Lady."

We have just received intelligence that another child, missed
last night, was only discovered late in the morning under a
14 furze bush at the Shooter's Hill side of Hampstead Heath,
which is, perhaps, less frequented than the other parts. It has
the same tiny wound in the throat as has been noticed in other
cases. It was terribly weak, and looked quite emaciated. It
too, when partially restored, had the common story to tell of
being lured away by the "bloofer lady."

ELLEN TERRY.

13 *Ellen Terry.* Ellen Terry (1847–1928), perhaps the greatest English actress of the nineteenth century, joined Sir Henry Irving, the greatest actor of his age, in a stage partnership at the Lyceum Theatre that lasted more than twenty years. Stoker, it will be remembered, was Irving's confidante and factotum for more than twenty-seven years in the management of the theatre. His work frequently brought him into contact with Ellen Terry whose close friend he became. Harry Ludlam, Stoker's biographer, describes how Stoker frequently read the manuscripts of plays for Ellen Terry and gave her critical advice on them—advice she did not always take.

Dame Ellen's stage career began when she was eight; she played Mamillius in Shakespeare's *The Winter's Tale.* Her most famous roles were Katharine, in *The Taming of the Shrew*, Portia in *The Merchant of Venice*, Lady Macbeth in *Macbeth*, and Juliet in *Romeo and Juliet*.

14 *Shooter's Hill.* Located, according to Bartholomew's *Guide to London*, in the Eltham district, several miles southeast of Hampstead Heath (see map, pp. 340–41).

CHAPTER XIV.

MINA HARKER'S JOURNAL.

23 *September*.—Jonathan is better after a bad night. I am so glad that he has plenty of work to do, for that keeps his mind off the terrible things; and oh, I am rejoiced that he is not now weighed down with the responsibility of his new position. I knew he would be true to himself, and now how proud I am to see my Jonathan rising to the height of his advancement and keeping pace in all ways with the duties that come upon him. He will be away all day till late, for he said he could not lunch at home. My household work is done, so I shall take his foreign journal, and lock myself up in my room and read it. . . . .

24 *September*.—I hadn't the heart to write last night; that terrible record of Jonathan's upset me so. Poor dear! How he must have suffered, whether it be true or only imagination. I wonder if there is any truth in it at all. Did he get his brain fever, and then write all those terrible things; or had he some cause for it all? I suppose I shall never know, for I dare not open the subject to him. . . . . And yet that man we saw yesterday! He seemed quite certain of him. . . . . Poor fellow! I suppose it was the funeral upset him and sent his mind back on some train of thought. . . . . He believes it all himself. I remember how on our wedding-day he said: "Unless some solemn duty come upon me to go back to the bitter hours, asleep or awake, mad or sane." There seems to be through it all some thread of continuity. . . . . That fearful Count was coming to London. . . . . 'If it should be, and he came to London, with its teeming millions.' . . . . There may be a solemn duty; and if it come we must not shrink from it. . . . . I shall be prepared. I shall get my

typewriter this very hour and begin transcribing. Then we shall be ready for other eyes if required. And if it be wanted; then, perhaps, if I am ready, poor Jonathan may not be upset, for I can speak for him and never let him be troubled or worried with it at all. If ever Jonathan quite gets over the nervousness he may want to tell me of it all, and I can ask him questions and find out things, and see how I may comfort him.

Letter, Van Helsing to Mrs. Harker.

"24 *September.*
(*Confidence.*)

"Dear Madam,—

"I pray you to pardon my writing, in that I am so far friend as that I sent to you sad news of Miss Lucy Westenra's death. By the kindness of Lord Godalming, I am empowered to read her letters and papers, for I am deeply concerned about certain matters vitally important. In them I find some letters from you, which show how great friends you were and how you love her. Oh, Madam Mina, by that love, I implore you, help me. It is for others' good that I ask—to redress great wrong, and to lift much and terrible troubles—that may be more great than you can know. May it be that I see you? You can trust me. I am friend of Dr. John Seward and of Lord Godalming (that was Arthur of Miss Lucy). I must keep it private for the present from all. I should come to Exeter to see you at once if you tell me I am privilege to come, and where and when. I implore your pardon, madam. I have read your letters to poor Lucy, and know how good you are and how your husband suffer; so I pray you, if it may be, enlighten him not, lest it may harm. Again your pardon, and forgive me.

"VAN HELSING."

Telegram, Mrs. Harker to Van Helsing.

"25 *September.*—Come to-day by quarter-past ten train if you can catch it. Can see you any time you call.

"WILHELMINA HARKER."

MINA HARKER'S JOURNAL.

25 *September.*—I cannot help feeling terribly excited as the time draws near for the visit of Dr. Van Helsing, for somehow I expect that it will throw some light upon Jonathan's sad experience; and as he attended poor dear Lucy in her last illness, he can tell me all about her. That is the reason of his coming; it is concerning Lucy and her sleep-walking, and not about Jonathan. Then I shall never know the real truth now! How silly I am. That awful journal gets hold of my imagination and tinges everything with something of its own colour. Of course it is about Lucy. That habit came back to the poor dear, and that awful night on the cliff must have made her ill.

I had almost forgotten in my own affairs how ill she was afterwards. She must have told him of her sleep-walking adventure on the cliff, and that I knew all about it; and now he wants me to tell him about it, so that he may understand. I hope I did right in not saying anything of it to Mrs. Westenra; I should never forgive myself if any act of mine, were it even a negative one, brought harm on poor dear Lucy. I hope, too, Dr. Van Helsing will not blame me; I have had so much trouble and anxiety of late that I feel I cannot bear more just at present.

I suppose a cry does us all good at times—clears the air as other rain does. Perhaps it was reading the journal yesterday that upset me, and then Jonathan went away this morning to stay away from me a whole day and night, the first time we have been parted since our marriage. I do hope the dear fellow will take care of himself, and that nothing will occur to upset him. It is two o'clock, and the doctor will be here soon now. I shall say nothing of Jonathan's journal unless he asks me. I am so glad I have type-written out my own journal, so that, in case he asks about Lucy, I can hand it to him; it will save much questioning.

Later.—He has come and gone. Oh, what a strange meeting, and how it all makes my head whirl round! I feel like one in a dream. Can it be all possible, or even a part of it? If I had not read Jonathan's journal first, I should never have accepted even a possibility. Poor, poor, dear Jonathan! How he must have suffered. Please the good God, all this may not upset him again. I shall try to save him from it; but it may be even a consolation and a help to him—terrible though it be and awful in its consequences—to know for certain that his eyes and ears and brain did not deceive him, and that it is all true. It may be that it is the doubt which haunts him; that when the doubt is removed, no matter which—waking or dreaming—may prove the truth, he will be more satisfied and better able to bear the shock. Dr. Van Helsing must be a good man as well as a clever one if he is Arthur's friend and Dr. Seward's, and if they brought him all the way from Holland to look after Lucy. I feel from having seen him that he *is* good and kind and of a noble nature. When he comes tomorrow I shall ask him about Jonathan; and then, please God, all this sorrow and anxiety may lead to a good end. I used to think I would like to practise interviewing; Jonathan's friend on "The Exeter News" told him that memory was everything in such work—that you must be able to put down exactly almost every word spoken, even if you had to refine some of it afterwards. Here was a rare interview; I shall try to record it *verbatim*.

It was half-past two o'clock when the knock came. I took my courage *à deux mains* and waited. In a few minutes Mary opened the door, and announced "Dr. Van Helsing." 1

I rose and bowed, and he came towards me; a man of medium height, strongly built, with his shoulders set back over a broad, deep chest and a neck well balanced on the trunk as the head is on the neck. The poise of the head strikes one at once as indicative of thought and power; the head is noble, well-sized, broad, and large behind the ears. The

1 *Mary.* This is Mary's first and only appearance in *Dracula.* The only words she speaks are "Dr. Van Helsing." Like all fleeting glimpses, this one is haunting. Was she tall or short? Young or old? Stoker created her with a stroke of the pen and then left her, a tantalizing presence on the page. And yet, she is the agent for a momentous meeting.

face, clean-shaven, shows a hard, square chin, a large, resolute, mobile mouth, a good-sized nose, rather straight, but with quick, sensitive nostrils, that seem to broaden as the big, bushy brows come down and the mouth tightens. The forehead is broad and fine, rising at first almost straight and then sloping back above two bumps or ridges wide apart; such a forehead that the reddish hair cannot possibly tumble over it, but falls naturally back and to the sides. Big, dark blue eyes are set widely apart, and are quick and tender or stern with the man's moods. He said to me:—

"Mrs. Harker, is it not?" I bowed assent.

"That was Miss Mina Murray?" Again I assented.

"It is Mina Murray that I came to see that was friend of that poor dear child Lucy Westenra. Madam Mina, it is on account of the dead I come."

"Sir," I said, "you could have no better claim on me than that you were a friend and helper of Lucy Westenra." And I held out my hand. He took it and said tenderly:—

"Oh, Madam Mina, I knew that the friend of that poor lily girl must be good, but I had yet to learn——" He finished his speech with a courtly bow. I asked him what it was that he wanted to see me about, so he at once began:—

"I have read your letters to Miss Lucy. Forgive me, but I had to begin to inquire somewhere, and there was none to ask. I know that you were with her at Whitby. She sometimes kept a diary—you need not look surprised, Madam Mina; it was begun after you had left, and was made in imitation of you—and in that diary she traces by inference certain things to a sleep-walking in which she puts down that you saved her. In great perplexity then I come to you, and ask you out of your so much kindness to tell me all of it that you remember."

"I can tell you, I think, Dr. Van Helsing, all about it."

"Ah, then you have good memory for facts, for details? It is not always so with young ladies."

"No, doctor, but I wrote it all down at the time. I can show it to you if you like."

"Oh, Madam Mina, I will be grateful; you will do me much favour." I could not resist the temptation of mystifying him a bit—I suppose it is some of the taste of the original apple that remains still in our mouths—so I handed him the shorthand diary. He took it with a grateful bow, and said:—

"May I read it?"

"If you wish," I answered as demurely as I could. He opened it, and for an instant his face fell. Then he stood up and bowed.

"Oh, you so clever woman!" he said. "I long knew that Mr. Jonathan was a man of much thankfulness; but see, his wife have all the good things. And will you not so much honour me and so help me as to read it for me? Alas! I know not the shorthand." By this time my little joke was over, and I was almost ashamed; so I took the typewritten copy from my workbasket and handed it to him.

"Forgive me," I said: "I could not help it; but I had been thinking that it was of dear Lucy that you wished to ask, and so that you might not have to wait—not on my account.

but because I know your time must be precious—I have written it out on the typewriter for you."

He took it, and his eyes glistened. "You are so good," he said. "And may I read it now? I may want to ask you some things when I have read."

"By all means," I said, "read it over whilst I order lunch; and then you can ask me questions whilst we eat." He bowed and settled himself in a chair with his back to the light, and became absorbed in the papers, whilst I went to see after lunch, chiefly in order that he might not be disturbed. When I came back I found him walking hurriedly up and down the room, his face all ablaze with excitement. He rushed up to me and took me by both hands.

"Oh, Madam Mina," he said, "how can I say what I owe to you? This paper is as sunshine. It opens the gate to me. I am daze, I am dazzle, with so much light; and yet clouds roll in behind the light every time. But that you do not, cannot, comprehend. Oh, but I am grateful to you, you so clever woman. Madam"—he said this very solemnly—"if ever Abraham Van Helsing can do anything for you or yours, I trust you will let me know. It will be pleasure and delight if I may serve you as a friend; as a friend, but all I have ever learned, all I can ever do, shall be for you and those you love. There are darknesses in life, and there are lights; you are one of the lights. You will have happy life and good life, and your husband will be blessed in you."

"But, doctor, you praise me too much, and—and you do not know me."

"Not know you—I, who am old, and who have studied all my life men and women; I, who have made my specialty the brain and all that belongs to him and all that follow from him! And I have read your diary that you have so goodly written for me, and which breathes out truth in every line. I, who have read your so sweet letter to poor Lucy of your marriage and your trust, not know you! Oh, Madam Mina, good women tell all their lives, and by day and by hour and by minute, such things that angels can read; and we men who wish to know have in us something of angels' eyes. Your husband is noble nature, and you are noble too, for you trust, and trust cannot be where there is mean nature. And your husband—tell me of him. Is he quite well? Is all that fever gone, and is he strong and hearty?" I saw here an opening to ask him about Jonathan, so I said:—

"He was almost recovered, but he has been greatly upset by Mr. Hawkins's death." He interrupted:—

"Oh yes, I know, I know. I have read your last two letters." I went on:—

"I suppose this upset him, for when we were in town on 2
Thursday last he had a sort of shock."

"A shock, and after brain fever so soon! That was not good. What kind of shock was it?"

"He thought he saw some one who recalled something terrible, something which led to his brain fever." And here the whole thing seemed to overwhelm me in a rush. The pity for Jonathan, the horror which he experienced, the whole fearful mystery of his diary, and the fear that has been brooding over me ever

2 *on Thursday last.* Mina, by naming the day on which she and Jonathan saw Dracula walking along Piccadilly, enables us to establish the calendar of events (see Appendix). Dracula's year, clearly, is one in which September 22 was a Thursday.

since, all came in a tumult. I suppose I was hysterical, for I threw myself on my knees and held up my hands to him, and implored him to make my husband well again. He took my hands and raised me up, and made me sit on the sofa, and sat by me; he held my hand in his, and said to me with, oh, such infinite sweetness:—

"My life is a barren and lonely one, and so full of work that I have not had much time for friendships; but since I have been summoned to here by my friend John Seward I have known so many good people and seen such nobility that I feel more than ever—and it has grown with my advancing years—the loneliness of my life. Believe me, then, that I come here full of respect for you, and you have given me hope—hope, not in what I am seeking of, but that there are good women still left to make life happy—good women, whose lives and whose truths may make good lesson for the children that are to be. I am glad, glad, that I may here be of some use to you; for if your husband suffer, he suffer within the range of my study and experience. I promise you that I will gladly do *all* for him that I can—all to make his life strong and manly, and your life a happy one. Now you must eat. You are overwrought and perhaps over-anxious. Husband Jonathan would not like to see you so pale; and what he like not where he love, is not to his good. Therefore for his sake you must eat and smile. You have told me all about Lucy, and so now we shall not speak of it, lest it distress. I shall stay in Exeter to-night, for I want to think much over what you have told me, and when I have thought I will ask you questions, if I may. And then, too, you will tell me of husband Jonathan's trouble so far as you can, but not yet. You must eat now; afterwards you shall tell me all."

After lunch, when we went back to the drawing-room, he said to me:—

"And now tell me all about him." When it came to speaking to this great, learned man, I began to fear that he would think me a weak fool, and Jonathan a madman—that journal is all so strange—and I hesitated to go on. But he was so sweet and kind, and he had promised to help, and I trusted him, so I said:—

"Dr. Van Helsing, what I have to tell you is so queer that you must not laugh at me or at my husband. I have been since yesterday in a sort of fever of doubt; you must be kind to me, and not think me foolish that I have even half believed some very strange things." He reassured me by his manner as well as his words when he said:—

"Oh, my dear, if you only knew how strange is the matter regarding which I am here, it is you who would laugh. I have learned not to think little of any one's belief, no matter how strange it be. I have tried to keep an open mind; and it is not the ordinary things of life that could close it, but the strange things, the extraordinary things, the things that make one doubt if they be mad or sane."

"Thank you, thank you, a thousand times! You have taken a weight off my mind. If you will let me, I shall give you a paper to read. It is long, but I have typewritten it out. It will tell you my trouble and Jonathan's. It is the copy of his journal when abroad, and all that happened. I dare not say anything of it; you will read for yourself and judge. And then when I see you, perhaps, you will be very kind and tell me what you think."

"I promise," he said as I gave him the papers; "I shall in the morning, so soon as I can, come to see you and your husband, if I may."

"Jonathan will be here at half-past eleven, and you must
come to lunch with us and see him then; you could catch 3
the quick 3.34 train, which will leave you at Paddington before 4
eight." He was surprised at my knowledge of the trains offhand, but he does not know that I have made up all the trains to and from Exeter, so that I may help Jonathan in case he is in a hurry.

So he took the papers with him and went away, and I sit here thinking—thinking I don't know what.

Letter (by hand), Van Helsing to Mrs. Harker.

"25 *September*, 6 *o'clock.*

"Dear Madam Mina,—

"I have read your husband's so wonderful diary. You may sleep without doubt. Strange and terrible as it is, it is *true*! I will pledge my life on it. It may be worse for others; but for him and you there is no dread. He is a noble fellow; and let me tell you from experience of men, that one who would do as he did in going down that wall and to that room—ay, and going a second time—is not one to be injured in permanence by a shock. His brain and his heart are all right; this I swear, before I have even seen him; so be at rest. I shall have much to ask him of other things. I am blessed that to-day I come to see you, for I have learn all at once so much that again I am dazzle—dazzle more than ever, and I must think.

"Yours the most faithful,

"ABRAHAM VAN HELSING."

Letter, Mrs. Harker to Van Helsing.

"25 *September*, 6.30 *p.m.*

"My dear Dr. Van Helsing,—

"A thousand thanks for your kind letter, which has taken a great weight off my mind. And yet, if it be true, what terrible things there are in the world, and what an awful thing if that man, that monster, be really in London! I fear to think. I
have this moment, whilst writing, had a wire from Jonathan,
saying that he leaves by the 6.25 to-night from Launceston and 5
will be here at 10.18, so that I shall have no fear to-night. Will you, therefore, instead of lunching with us, please come to breakfast at eight o'clock, if this be not too early for you? You can get away, if you are in a hurry, by the 10.30 train, which will bring you to Paddington by 2.35. Do not answer this, as I shall take it that, if I do not hear, you will come to breakfast.

"Believe me,

"Your faithful and grateful friend,

"MINA HARKER."

3 *you could catch the quick 3:34*. Mina keeps the train schedule in her head.

4 *Paddington*. A major railway terminal in west central London, approximately one-half mile north of Hyde Park and one mile southwest of Regent's Park (see map, pp. 340–41).

5 *Launceston*. A city in Cornwall about one hundred miles southwest of London (see map, p. 337).

Jonathan Harker's Journal.

26 *September*.—I thought never to write in this diary again, but the time has come. When I got home last night Mina had supper ready, and when we had supped she told me of Van Helsing's visit, and of her having given him the two diaries copied out, and of how anxious she has been about me. She showed me in the doctor's letter that all I wrote down was true. It seems to have made a new man of me. It was the doubt as to the reality of the whole thing that knocked me over. I felt impotent, and in the dark, and distrustful. But, now that I *know*, I am not afraid, even of the Count. He has succeeded after all, then, in his design in getting to London, and it was he I saw. He has got younger, and how? Van Helsing is the man to unmask him and hunt him out, if he is anything like what Mina says. We sat late, and talked it all over. Mina is dressing, and I shall call at the hotel in a few minutes and bring him over. . . . .

He was, I think, surprised to see me. When I came into the room where he was, and introduced myself, he took me by the shoulder, and turned my face round to the light, and said, after a sharp scrutiny:—

"But Madam Mina told me you were ill, that you had had a shock." It was so funny to hear my wife called "Madam Mina" by this kindly, strong-faced old man. I smiled, and said:—

"I *was* ill, I *have* had a shock; but you have cured me already."

"And how?"

"By your letter to Mina last night. I was in doubt, and then everything took a hue of unreality, and I did not know what to trust, even the evidence of my own senses. Not knowing what to trust, I did not know what to do; and so had only to keep on working in what had hitherto been the groove of my life. The groove ceased to avail me, and I mistrusted myself. Doctor, you don't know what it is to doubt everything, even yourself. No, you don't; you couldn't with eyebrows like yours." He seemed pleased, and laughed as he said:—

"So! You are physiognomist. I learn more here with each hour. I am with so much pleasure coming to you to breakfast; and, oh, sir, you will pardon praise from an old man, but you are blessed in your wife." I would listen to him go on praising Mina for a day, so I simply nodded and stood silent.

"She is one of God's women, fashioned by His own hand to show us men and other women that there is a heaven where we can enter, and that its light can be here on earth. So true, so sweet, so noble, so little an egoist—and that, let me tell you, is much in this age, so sceptical and selfish. And you, sir—I have read all the letters to poor Miss Lucy, and some of them speak of you, so I know you since some days from the knowing of others; but I have seen your true self since last night. You will give me your hand, will you not? And let us be friends for all our lives."

We shook hands, and he was so earnest and so kind that it made me quite choky.

"And now," he said, "may I ask you for some more help? I have a great task to do, and at the beginning it is to know. You can help me here. Can you tell me what went before your going to Transylvania? Later on I may ask more help, and of a different kind; but at first this will do."

"Look here, sir," I said, "does what you have to do concern the Count?"

"It does," he said solemnly.

"Then I am with you heart and soul. As you go by the 10.30 train, you will not have time to read them; but I shall get the bundle of papers. You can take them with you and read them in the train."

After breakfast I saw him to the station. When we were parting he said:—

"Perhaps you will come to town if I send to you, and take Madam Mina too.'

"We shall both come when you will," I said.

I had got him the morning papers and the London papers of the previous night, and while we were talking at the carriage window, waiting for the train to start, he was turning them over. His eye suddenly seemed to catch something in one of them, "The Westminster Gazette"—I knew it by the colour—and he grew quite white. He read something intently, groaning to himself: "Mein Gott! Mein Gott! So soon! so soon!" I do not think he remembered me at the moment. Just then the whistle blew, and the train moved off. This recalled him to himself, and he leaned out of the window and waved his hand, calling out: "Love to Madam Mina; I shall write so soon as ever I can."

Dr. Seward's Diary.

26 *September.*—Truly there is no such thing as finality.
Not a week since I said "Finis," and yet here I am starting 6
fresh again, or rather going on with the same record. Until this afternoon I had no cause to think of what is done. Renfield had become, to all intents, as sane as he ever was. He was already well ahead with his fly business; and he had just started in the spider line also; so he had not been of any trouble to me. I had a letter from Arthur, written on Sunday, and from it I gather that he is bearing up wonderfully well. Quincey Morris is with him, and that is much of a help, for he himself is a bubbling well of good spirits. Quincey wrote me a line too, and from him I hear that Arthur is beginning to recover something of his old buoyancy; so as to them all my mind is at rest. As for myself, I was settling down to my work with the enthusiasm which I used to have for it, so that I might fairly have said that the wound which poor Lucy left
on me was becoming cicatrised. Everything is, however, now 7
reopened; and what is to be the end God only knows. I have an idea that Van Helsing thinks he knows too, but he will only let out enough at a time to whet curiosity. He went to Exeter yesterday, and stayed there all night. To-day he

6 *Not a week since I said "Finis."* On page 160 where it closes the September 22 entry.

7 *cicatrised.* That is, scar tissue was forming.

8 *"Charcot has proved that . . ."* Jean-Martin Charcot (1825–1893), a French neurologist and pathologist of international reputation, made significant contributions to psychiatry in his studies on hypnotism. It was Charcot, working with women patients, who defined hypnosis as consisting of three stages: the cataleptic, the lethargic, and the somnambulistic. The cataleptic is the motionless, rigid state produced by the hypnotist using a sharp noise or a sudden light before the eyes; in the lethargic stage the subject appears to be asleep, though there is sound produced by the larynx and foam may appear in the subject's mouth; the somnambulistic state, following on the first two, is the one in which the subject's head droops and he appears to be asleep, though he answers questions freely. It is in this state that the hypnotist can most successfully impose suggestions on the subject.

Dr. Van Helsing, dealing with Mina, later, seems to go directly to the third stage with her.

CHARCOT EXAMINING A BRAIN.

came back, and almost bounded into the room at about half-past five o'clock, and thrust last night's "Westminster Gazette' into my hand.

"What do you think of that?" he asked as he stood back and folded his arms.

I looked over the paper, for I really did not know what he meant; but he took it from me and pointed out a paragraph about children being decoyed away at Hampstead. It did not convey much to me, until I reached a passage where it described small punctured wounds on their throats. An idea struck me, and I looked up. "Well?" he said.

"It is like poor Lucy's."

"And what do you make of it?"

"Simply that there is some cause in common. Whatever it was that injured her has injured them." I did not quite understand his answer:—

"That is true indirectly, but not directly."

"How do you mean, Professor?" I asked. I was a little inclined to take his seriousness lightly—for, after all, four days of rest and freedom from burning, harrowing anxiety does help to restore one's spirits—but when I saw his face, it sobered me. Never, even in the midst of our despair about poor Lucy, had he looked more stern.

"Tell me!" I said. "I can hazard no opinion. I do not know what to think, and I have no data on which to found a conjecture."

"Do you mean to tell me, friend John, that you have no suspicion as to what poor Lucy died of; not after all the hints given, not only by events, but by me?"

"Of nervous prostration following on great loss or waste of blood."

"And how the blood lost or waste?" I shook my head. He stepped over and sat down beside me, and went on:—

"You are clever man, friend John; you reason well, and your wit is bold; but you are too prejudiced. You do not let your eyes see nor your ears hear, and that which is outside your daily life is not of account to you. Do you not think that there are things which you cannot understand, and yet which are; that some people see things that others cannot? But there are things old and new which must not be contemplate by men's eyes, because they know—or think they know—some things which other men have told them. Ah, it is the fault of our science that it wants to explain all; and if it explain not, then it says there is nothing to explain. But yet we see around us every day the growth of new beliefs, which think themselves new; and which are yet but the old, which pretend to be young—like the fine ladies at the opera. I suppose now you do not believe in corporeal transference. No? Nor in materialisation. No? Nor in astral bodies. No? Nor in the reading of thought. No? Nor in hypnotism——"

8 "Yes," I said. "Charcot has proved that pretty well." He smiled as he went on: "Then you are satisfied as to it. Yes? And of course then you understand how it act, and can follow the mind of the great Charcot—alas that he is no more!—into the very soul of the patient that he influence. No? Then, friend John, am I to take it that you simply

OLD PARR, BY RUBENS.

accept fact, and are satisfied to let from premise to conclusion be a blank? No? Then tell me—for I am student of the brain—how you accept the hypnotism and reject the thought-reading. Let me tell you, my friend, that there are things done to-day in electrical science which would have been deemed unholy by the very men who discovered electricity—who would themselves not so long before have been burned as wizards. There are always mysteries in life. Why was it
that Methuselah lived nine hundred years, and 'Old Parr' one **9**
hundred and sixty-nine, and yet that poor Lucy, with four men's blood in her poor veins, could not live even one day?
For, had she live one more day, we could have save her. **10**
Do you know all the mystery of life and death? Do you **11**
know the altogether of comparative anatomy, and can say wherefore the qualities of brutes are in some men, and not in others? Can you tell me why, when other spiders die small
and soon, that one great spider lived for centuries in the tower **12**
of the old Spanish church and grew and grew, till, on descending, he could drink the oil of all the church lamps? Can you tell me why in the Pampas, ay and elsewhere, there are bats that come at night and open the veins of cattle and horses and suck dry their veins; how in some islands of the Western seas there are bats which hang on the trees all day,

VAMPIRE BAT.

9 *'Old Parr.'* "Old Parr" was a British legend in his lifetime, which was said to be very long. Patrick M. McGrady, Jr., in his *The Youth Doctors* (New York: Ace Publishing Co., 1968, p. 26), says that Old Parr was "pointed out for centuries as an example of a clean-living old gentleman from the country who might have lived forever except for an unfortunate sojourn to corrupting high-living London," where he was brought so that the earl of Arundel could present him to King Charles I. It makes a fine tale, but, unfortunately, McGrady adds that "recent investigation has revealed that the Thomas Parr born in 1484 was probably at least two generations removed from the Thomas Parr who died in 1635." Parr's alleged longevity was, according to Paul Niehans, the rejuvenator, the effect of "his heavy and well developed testicles."

There exists a fine portrait of "Old Parr" by Rubens.

10 *we could have save her.* One would like to know how.

11 *the mystery of life and death?* This question launches Van Helsing into a speech that echoes God's voice in the whirlwind: "Who *is* this that darkeneth counsel by words without knowledge?" The rest of that remarkable chapter (Job 38) deserves rereading.

12 *that one great spider.* So far, I can find no trace of this prodigy.

Spiders, as Van Helsing properly points out, are not usually long-lived, though male spiders die sooner than females who outlive them by several weeks. In any case, a year-old spider of either sex is already living on borrowed time.

On the other hand, Willis J. Gertsch (p. 505) tells us that "the more primitive true spiders often live more than a single year . . . Dr. Lucien Berland kept a female *filistatid* for ten years. It is probable that all ancestral spiders were longer-lived, and that one of the sacrifices of the modern true spider for the many advantages it enjoys is a drastic reduction in life span . . . Exceeding all other spiders in length of life are the large tarantulas. Dr. Baerg has kept a female tarantula for more than 20 years and believes that 25 or 30 years probably represents the normal age for females."

THE TORTOISE.

13 *why the tortoise lives more long.* The long life of the tortoise is both traditional and true. In a table of longevity that appears in Alex Comfort's *The Biology of Senescence*, the shortest-lived of the tortoises, *Testudo marginata*, has a twenty-eight-year life-span. The oldest is *Testudo sumeiri*, which lives to be 152 years or more. Some seven varieties of tortoise survive to the age of one hundred.

Pliny thought highly of the medical value of the tortoise which he believed was useful in curing epilepsy and warding off magic. Its blood would cure a toothache and was an antidote to the poison of spiders and snakes.

that those who have seen describe as like giant nuts or pods, and that when the sailors sleep on the deck, because that it is hot, flit down on them, and then—and then in the morning are found dead men, white as even Miss Lucy was?"

"Good God, Professor!" I said, starting up. "Do you mean to tell me that Lucy was bitten by such a bat; and that such a thing is here in London in the nineteenth century?" He waved his hand for silence, and went on:—

13 "Can you tell me why the tortoise lives more long than generations of men; why the elephant goes on and on till he have seen dynasties; and why the parrot never die only of bite of cat or dog or other complaint? Can you tell me why men believe in all ages and places that there are some few who live on always if they be permit; that there are men and women who cannot die? We all know—because science has vouched for the fact—that there have been toads shut up in rocks for thousands of years, shut in one so small hole that only hold him since the youth of the world. Can you tell me how the Indian fakir can make himself to die and have been buried, and his grave sealed and corn sowed on it, and the corn reaped and be cut and sown and reaped and cut again, and then men come and take away the unbroken seal, and that there lie the Indian fakir, not dead, but that rise up and walk amongst them as before?" Here I interrupted him. I was getting bewildered; he so crowded on my mind his list of nature's eccentricities and possible impossibilities that my imagination was getting fired. I had a dim idea that he was teaching me some lesson, as long ago he used to do in his study at Amsterdam; but he used then to tell me the thing, so that I could have the object of thought in mind all the time. But now I was without this help, yet I wanted to follow him, so I said:—

"Professor, let me be your pet student again. Tell me the thesis, so that I may apply your knowledge as you go on. At

"WHY THE ELEPHANT GOES ON AND ON."

present I am going in my mind from point to point as a mad man, and not a sane one, follows an idea. I feel like a novice blundering through a bog in a mist, jumping from one tussock to another in the mere blind effort to move on without knowing where I am going."

"That is good image," he said. "Well, I shall tell you. My thesis is this: I want you to believe."

"To believe what?"

"To believe in things that you cannot. Let me illustrate.
I heard once of an American who so defined faith: 'that 14
which enables us to believe things which we know to be untrue.' For one, I follow that man. He meant that we shall have an open mind, and not let a little bit of truth check the rush of a big truth, like a small rock does a railway truck. We get the small truth first. Good! We keep him, and we value him; but all the same we must not let him think himself all the truth in the universe."

"Then you want me not to let some previous conviction injure the receptivity of my mind with regard to some strange matter. Do I read your lesson aright?"

"Ah, you are my favourite pupil still. It is worth to teach you. Now that you are willing to understand, you have taken the first step to understand. You think then that those so small holes in the children's throats were made by the same that made the hole in Miss Lucy?'

"I suppose so." He stood up and said solemnly:—

"Then you are wrong. Oh, would it were so! but alas! no. It is worse, far, far worse."

"In God's name, Professor Van Helsing, what do you mean?" I cried.

He threw himself with a despairing gesture into a chair, and placed his elbows on the table, covering his face with his hands as he spoke:—

"They were made by Miss Lucy!"

14 *an American who so defined faith*. Which American? Was it Mark Twain whose epigraph to chapter XII of *Following the Equator* reads (p. 132): "There are those who scoff at the schoolboy, calling him frivolous and shallow. Yet it was the schoolboy who said, 'Faith is believing what you know ain't so.'" Twain ascribes the remark to *Pudd'nhead Wilson's New Calendar*.

Or was it William James, who put the matter more elegantly in his *Will to Believe*, writing of his title essay that it is "in justification of faith, or defence of our right to adopt a believing attitude in religious matters, in spite of the fact that our merely logical intellect may not have been coerced."

Twain's book appeared in 1897, the same year as *Dracula*. *The Will to Believe*, published in the same year, has, however, an 1896 copyright date. This suggests James as the more likely source of the idea, if not the quotation.

Twain becomes the likelier candidate if we consider that he and Stoker met in London well before the publication of *Dracula*. Henry W. Fischer, in his book *Abroad With Mark Twain and Eugene Field* (New York: N. L. Brown, 1922), tells us that the two men discussed witchcraft "before a motley crowd of litterateurs at Brown's Hotel, London. 'Fine,' said Bram Stoker [to Twain], 'tell us some more; I have a short story on witchcraft in hand.'" (p. 174).

Professor Sholom Kahn of the Hebrew University in Jerusalem, writing in his unpublished *Mark Twain's "Mysterious Stranger"* (p. 311), asserts that Stoker's remark "was undoubtedly referring to *Dracula* published in 1897."

CHAPTER XV.

Dr. Seward's Diary—*continued.*

For a while sheer anger mastered me; it was as if he had during her life struck Lucy on the face. I smote the table hard and rose up as I said to him:—

"Dr. Van Helsing, are you mad?" He raised his head and looked at me, and somehow the tenderness of his face calmed me at once. "Would I were!" he said. "Madness were easy to bear compared with truth like this. Oh, my friend, why, think you, did I go so far round, why take so long to tell you so simple a thing? Was it because I hate you and have hated you all my life? Was it because I wished to give you pain? Was it that I wanted, now so late, revenge for that time when you saved my life, and from a fearful death? Ah no!"

"Forgive me," said I. He went on:—

"My friend, it was because I wished to be gentle in the breaking to you, for I know you have loved that so sweet lady. But even yet I do not expect you to believe. It is so hard to accept at once any abstract truth, that we may doubt such to be possible when we have always believed the 'no' of it; it is more hard still to accept so sad a concrete truth, and of such a one as Miss Lucy. To-night I go to prove it. Dare you come with me?"

This staggered me. A man does not like to prove such a truth; Byron excepted from the category, jealousy.

1 "And prove the very truth he most abhorred."

He saw my hesitation, and spoke:—

"The logic is simple, no madman's logic this time, jumping from tussock to tussock in a misty bog. If it be not true, then proof will be relief; at worst it will not harm. If it be true!

1 "*And prove the very truth he most abhorred.*" The line, slightly misquoted, is from Byron's *Don Juan*, Canto I, stanza 139, line 1112.

This is a remarkable allusion to be popping into Stoker's mind at this point in his narrative. The scene in *Don Juan* has an outraged husband "with torches, friends, and servants in great number," breaking into his wife Dona Julia's bedchamber "to prove himself the thing he most abhorr'd." Adultery was Byron's subject as some hideous manifestation of sexuality is Stoker's.

Ah, there is the dread; yet very dread should help my cause, for in it is some need of belief. Come, I tell you what I propose: first, that we go off now and see that child in the hospital. Dr. Vincent, of the North Hospital, where the 2
papers say the child is, is friend of mine, and I think of yours since you were in class at Amsterdam. He will let two scientists see his case, if he will not let two friends. We shall tell him nothing, but only that we wish to learn. And then——"

"And then?" He took a key from his pocket and held it up. "And then we spend the night, you and I, in the churchyard where Lucy lies. This is the key that lock the tomb. I had it from the coffin-man to give to Arthur." My heart sank within me, for I felt that there was some fearful ordeal before us. I could do nothing, however, so I plucked up what heart I could and said that we had better hasten, as the afternoon was passing. . . . .

We found the child awake. It had had a sleep and taken some food, and altogether was going on well. Dr. Vincent took the bandage from its throat, and showed us the punctures. There was no mistaking the similarity to those which had been on Lucy's throat. They were smaller, and the edges looked fresher; that was all. We asked Vincent to what he attributed them, and he replied that it must have been a bite of some animal, perhaps a rat; but, for his own part, he was inclined to think that it was one of the bats which are so numerous on the northern heights of London. "Out of so many harmless ones," he said, "there may be some wild specimen from the South of a more malignant species. Some sailor may have brought one home, and it managed to escape; or even from the Zoological Gardens a young one may have got loose, or one be bred there from a vampire. These things do occur, you know. Only ten days ago a wolf got out, and was, I believe, traced up in this direction. For a week after, the children were playing nothing but Red Riding Hood on the Heath and in every alley in the place until this 'bloofer lady' scare came along, since when it has been quite a gala-time with them. Even this poor little mite, when he woke up today, asked the nurse if he might go away. When she asked him why he wanted to go, he said he wanted to play with the 'bloofer lady.'"

"I hope," said Van Helsing, "that when you are sending the child home you will caution its parents to keep strict watch over it. These fancies to stray are most dangerous; and if the child were to remain out another night, it would probably be fatal. But in any case I suppose you will not let it away for some days?"

"Certainly not, not for a week at least; longer if the wound is not healed."

Our visit to the hospital took more time than we had reckoned on, and the sun had dipped before we came out. When Van Helsing saw how dark it was, he said:—

"There is no hurry. It is more late than I thought. Come, let us seek somewhere that we may eat, and then we shall go on our way."

We dined at "Jack Straw's Castle" along with a little crowd of 3
bicyclists and others who were genially noisy. About ten

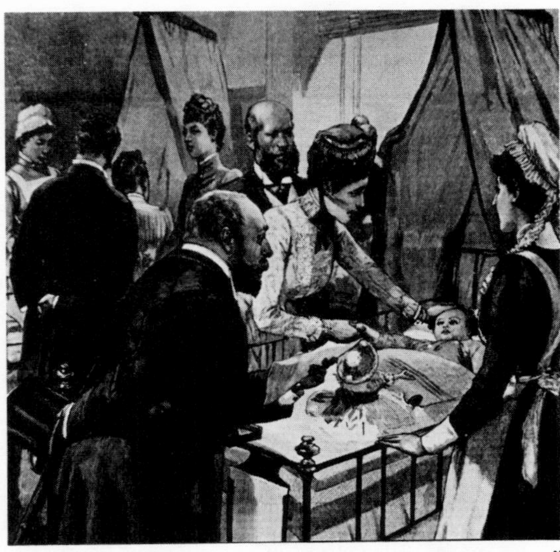

"WE GO OFF NOW AND SEE THAT CHILD IN THE HOSPITAL."

2 *North Hospital.* Probably North London Hospital, Gower Street, West London.

JACK STRAW'S CASTLE, A CONTEMPORARY PHOTOGRAPH.

3 *"Jack Straw's Castle."* A public inn on North End Way on Hampstead Heath. Situated at the point where Spaniards Road and North End Way converge. Now spelled without the apostrophe.

"WE REACHED THE WALL OF THE CHURCHYARD, WHICH WE CLIMBED OVER."

4 *mix-up as to locality.* The mix-up continues. In 1970 I tried to follow Seward and Van Helsing's footsteps to the graveyard in which Lucy was buried. Guided by friendly, if incredulous, drinkers at a pub called "The Spaniards" (see note 7), I finally found a graveyard that was within easy walking distance from that fine hostelry. It was the graveyard of St. John's Church in Church Row, just south of the West Heath. There are, however, other cemeteries in the vicinity of Hampstead Heath. If, as Seward tells us, the cemetery he and Van Helsing reached was so isolated that they met fewer and fewer people, then St. John's Church is an unlikely locality, situated as it is in a densely populated area.

o'clock we started from the inn. It was then very dark, and the scattered lamps made the darkness greater when we were once outside their individual radius. The Professor had evidently noted the road we were to go, for he went on unhesitatingly;
4 but, as for me, I was in quite a mix-up as to locality. As we went further, we met fewer and fewer people, till at last we were somewhat surprised when we met even the patrol of horse police going their usual suburban round. At last we reached the wall of the churchyard, which we climbed over. With some little difficulty—for it was very dark, and the whole place seemed so strange to us—we found the Westenra tomb. The Professor took the key, opened the creaky door, and standing back, politely, but quite unconsciously, motioned me to precede him. There was a delicious irony in the offer, in the courtliness of giving preference on such a ghastly occasion. My companion followed me quickly, and cautiously drew the door to, after carefully ascertaining that the lock was a falling, and not a spring, one. In the latter case we should have been in a bad plight. Then he fumbled in his bag, and taking out a match-box and a piece of candle, proceeded to make a light. The tomb in the day-time, and when wreathed with fresh flowers, had looked grim and gruesome enough; but now, some days afterwards, when the flowers hung lank and dead, their whites turning to rust and their greens to browns; when the spider and the beetle had resumed their accustomed dominance; when time-discoloured stone, and dust-encrusted mortar, and rusty, dank iron, and tarnished brass, and clouded silver-plating gave back the feeble glimmer of a candle, the effect was more miserable and sordid than could have been imagined. It conveyed irresistibly the idea that life—animal life—was not the only thing which could pass away.

Van Helsing went about his work systematically. Holding his candle so that he could read the coffin plates, and so

THE LEAD COFFIN.

holding it that the sperm dropped in white patches which congealed as they touched the metal, he made assurance of Lucy's coffin. Another search in his bag, and he took out a turnscrew.

"What are you going to do?" I asked.

"To open the coffin. You shall yet be convinced." Straightway he began taking out the screws, and finally lifted off the lid, showing the casing of lead beneath. The sight was almost too much for me. It seemed to be as much an affront to the dead as it would have been to have stripped off her clothing in her sleep whilst living; I actually took hold of his hand to stop him. He only said: "You shall see," and again fumbling in
his bag, took out a tiny fret-saw. Striking the turnscrew through 5
the lead with a swift downward stab, which made me wince, he made a small hole, which was, however, big enough to admit the point of the saw. I had expected a rush of gas from the week-old corpse. We doctors, who have had to study our dangers, have to become accustomed to such things, and I drew back towards the door. But the Professor never stopped for a moment; he sawed down a couple of feet along one side of the lead coffin, and then across, and down the other side. Taking the edge of the loose flange, he bent it back towards the foot of the coffin, and holding up the candle into the aperture, motioned to me to look.

I drew near and looked. The coffin was empty.

It was certainly a surprise to me, and gave me a considerable shock, but Van Helsing was unmoved. He was now more sure than ever of his ground, and so emboldened to proceed in his task. "Are you satisfied now, friend John?" he asked.

I felt all the dogged argumentativeness of my nature awake within me as I answered him:—

"I am satisfied that Lucy's body is not in that coffin; but that only proves one thing."

"And what is that, friend John?"

"That it is not there."

"That is good logic," he said, "so far as it goes. But how do you—how can you—account for it not being there?"

"Perhaps a body-snatcher," I suggested. "Some of the undertaker's people may have stolen it." I felt that I was speaking folly, and yet it was the only real cause which I could suggest. The Professor sighed. "Ah well!" he said, "we must have more proof. Come with me."

He put on the coffin-lid again, gathered up all his things and placed them in the bag, blew out the light, and placed the candle also in the bag. We opened the door, and went out. Behind us he closed the door and locked it. He handed me the key, saying: "Will you keep it? You had better be assured." I laughed—it was not a very cheerful laugh, I am

5 *turnscrew.* A screwdriver.

BRANCH OF A YEW.

6 *yew-tree.* As well as providing the wood for the famous longbows of England, the yew is the familiar graveyard tree of literature.

7 *near the "Spaniards."* The "Spaniards" is a pub near Hampstead Heath, which is still open for business, still thriving. The street before the old building is so narrow that traffic can move in only one direction at a time.

The "Spaniards" was a gathering place for the "No Popery" rioters of 1780.

THE SPANIARDS.

bound to say—as I motioned him to keep it. "A key is nothing," I said; "there may be duplicates; and anyhow it is not difficult to pick a lock of that kind." He said nothing, but put the key in his pocket. Then he told me to watch at one side of the churchyard whilst he would watch at the other.
6 I took up my place behind a yew-tree, and I saw his dark figure move until the intervening headstones and trees hid it from my sight.

It was a lonely vigil. Just after I had taken my place I heard a distant clock strike twelve, and in time came one and two. I was chilled and unnerved, and angry with the Professor for taking me on such an errand and with myself for coming. I was too cold and too sleepy to be keenly observant, and not sleepy enough to betray my trust; so altogether I had a dreary, miserable time.

Suddenly, as I turned round, I thought I saw something like a white streak, moving between two dark yew-trees at the side of the churchyard farthest from the tomb; at the same time a dark mass moved from the Professor's side of the ground, and hurriedly went towards it. Then I too moved; but I had to go round headstones and railed-off tombs, and I stumbled over graves. The sky was overcast, and somewhere far off an early cock crew. A little way off, beyond a line of scattered juniper-trees, which marked the pathway to the church, a white, dim figure flitted in the direction of the tomb. The tomb itself was hidden by trees, and I could not see where the figure disappeared. I heard the rustle of actual movement where I had first seen the white figure, and coming over, found the Professor holding in his arms a tiny child. When he saw me he held it out to me, and said:—

"Are you satisfied now?"

"No," I said, in a way that I felt was aggressive.

"Do you not see the child?"

"Yes, it is a child, but who brought it here? And is it wounded?" I asked.

"We shall see," said the Professor, and with one impulse we took our way out of the churchyard, he carrying the sleeping child.

When we had got some little distance away, we went into a clump of trees, and struck a match, and looked at the child's throat. It was without a scratch or scar of any kind.

"Was I right?" I asked triumphantly.

"We were just in time," said the Professor thankfully.

We had now to decide what we were to do with the child, and so consulted about it. If we were to take it to a police-station we should have to give some account of our movements during the night; at least, we should have had to make some statement as to how we had come to find the child. So finally we decided that we would take it to the Heath, and when we heard a policeman coming, would leave it where he could not fail to find it; we would then seek our way home as quickly as we could. All fell out well. At the edge of Hampstead Heath we heard a policeman's heavy tramp, and laying the child on the pathway, we waited and watched until he saw it as he flashed his lantern to and fro. We heard his exclamation of astonishment, and then we went away silently. By good chance
7 we got a cab near the "Spaniards," and drove to town.

I cannot sleep, so I make this entry. But I must try to get a few hours' sleep, as Van Helsing is to call for me at noon. He insists that I shall go with him on another expedition.

27 *September*.—It was two o'clock before we found a suitable opportunity for our attempt. The funeral held at noon was all completed, and the last stragglers of the mourners had taken themselves lazily away, when, looking carefully from behind a clump of alder-trees, we saw the sexton lock the gate after him. We knew then that we were safe till morning did we desire it; but the Professor told me that we should not want more than an hour at most. Again I felt that horrid sense of the reality of things, in which any effort of imagination seemed out of place; and I realised distinctly the perils of the law which we were incurring in our unhallowed work. Besides, I felt it was all so useless. Outrageous as it was to open a leaden coffin, to see if a woman dead nearly a week were really dead, it now seemed the height of folly to open the tomb again, when we knew, from the evidence of our own eyesight, that the coffin was empty. I shrugged my shoulders, however, and rested silent, for Van Helsing had a way of going on his own road, no matter who remonstrated. He took the key, opened the vault, and again courteously motioned me to precede. The place was not so gruesome as last night, but oh, how unutterably mean-looking when the sunshine streamed in. Van Helsing walked over to Lucy's coffin, and I followed. He bent over and again forced back the leaden flange; and then a shock of surprise and dismay shot through me.

There lay Lucy, seemingly just as we had seen her the night before her funeral. She was, if possible, more radiantly beautiful than ever; and I could not believe that she was dead. The lips were red, nay redder than before; and on the cheeks was a delicate bloom.

"Is this a juggle?" I said to him.

"Are you convinced now?" said the Professor in response, and as he spoke he put over his hand, and in a way that made me shudder, pulled back the dead lips and showed the white teeth.

"See," he went on, "see, they are even sharper than before. With this and this"—and he touched one of the canine teeth and that below it—"the little children can be bitten. Are you of belief now, friend John?" Once more, argumentative hostility woke within me. I *could* not accept such an overwhelming idea as he suggested; so, with an attempt to argue of which I was even at the moment ashamed, I said:—

"She may have been placed here since last night."

"Indeed? That is so, and by whom?"

"I do not know. Some one has done it."

"And yet she has been dead one week. Most peoples in that time would not look so." I had no answer for this, so was silent. Van Helsing did not seem to notice my silence; at any rate, he showed neither chagrin nor triumph. He was looking intently at the face of the dead woman, raising the eyelids and looking at the eyes, and once more opening the lips and examining the teeth. Then he turned to me and said:—

"Here, there is one thing which is different from all recorded: here is some dual life that is not as the common. She was

8 *was buried alive.* The accidental burial of the dead is frequently cited as contributing to the legendry of the vampire. In my book, *A Dream of Dracula*, we read:

> "Reasonable men want reasonable explanations for phenomena that apparently defy reason, and vampires have had their share of being explained on *this* side of the supernatural. Bodies unnaturally well preserved in their graves have been referred to soil conditions that retarded decay. A favorite way of dealing with the risen dead, or those found in their coffin with their shrouds chewed or blood on their lips, has been to decide that these were examples of unfortunates prematurely put into their graves. And there are burial traditions that are meant to provide against such accidents. The wake is one such custom; . . . Sometimes the dead are provided with a bell by which they may signal that an error has been made . . ." (pp. 126–27).

Edgar Allan Poe's "Fall of the House of Usher" turns on such a macabre accident.

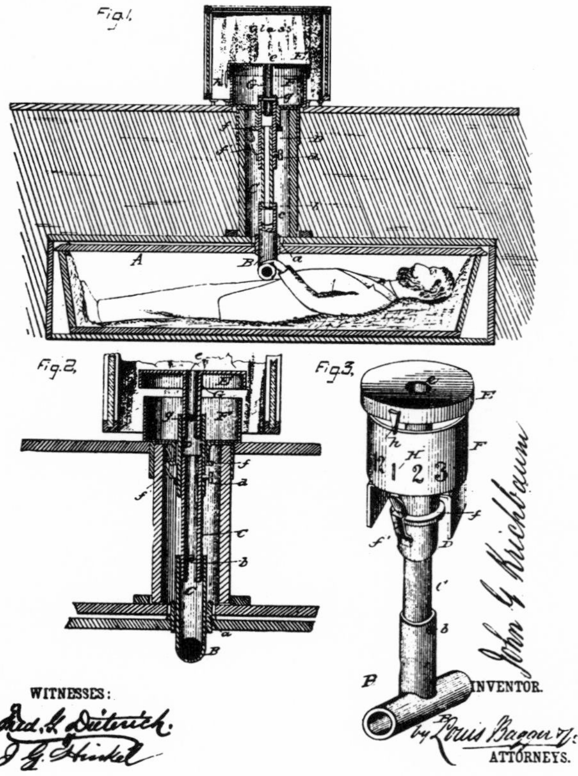

KRICHBAUM'S DEVICE FOR INDICATING LIFE IN BURIED PERSONS, PATENT SKETCH, 1882.

bitten by the vampire when she was in a trance, sleep-walking—oh, you start; you do not know that, friend John, but you shall know it all later—and in trance could he best come to take more blood. In trance she died, and in trance she is Un-Dead, too. So it is that she differ from all other. Usually when the Un-Dead sleep at home"—as he spoke he made a comprehensive sweep of his arm to designate what to a vampire was "home"—"their face show what they are, but this so sweet that was when she not Un-Dead she go back to the nothings of the common dead. There is no malign there, see, and so it make hard that I must kill her in her sleep." This turned my blood cold, and it began to dawn upon me that I was accepting Van Helsing's theories; but if she were really dead, what was there of terror in the idea of killing her? He looked up at me, and evidently saw the change in my face, for he said almost joyously:—

"Ah, you believe now?"

I answered: "Do not press me too hard all at once. I am willing to accept. How will you do this bloody work?"

"I shall cut off her head and fill her mouth with garlic, and I shall drive a stake through her body." It made me shudder to think of so mutilating the body of the woman whom I had loved. And yet the feeling was not so strong as I had expected. I was, in fact, beginning to shudder at the presence of this being, this Un-Dead, as Van Helsing called it, and to loathe it. Is it possible that love is all subjective, or all objective?

I waited a considerable time for Van Helsing to begin, but he stood as if wrapped in thought. Presently he closed the catch of his bag with a snap, and said:—

"I have been thinking, and have made up my mind as to what is best. If I did simply follow my inclining I would do now, at this moment, what is to be done; but there are other things to follow, and things that are thousand times more difficult in that them we do not know. This is simple. She have yet no life taken, though that is of time; and to act now would be to take danger from her for ever. But then we may have to want Arthur, and how shall we tell him of this? If you, who saw the wounds on Lucy's throat, and saw the wounds so similar on the child's at the hospital; if you, who saw the coffin empty last night and full to-day with a woman who have not change only to be more rose and more beautiful in a whole week after she die—if you know of this and know of the white figure last night that brought the child to the churchyard, and yet of your own senses you did not believe, how, then, can I expect Arthur, who know none of those things, to believe? He doubted me when I took him from her kiss when she was dying. I know he has forgiven me because in some mistaken idea I have done things that prevent him say good-bye as he ought; and he may think that in some more mistaken idea
8 this woman was buried alive; and that in most mistake of all we have killed her. He will then argue back that it is we, mistaken ones, that have killed her by our ideas; and so he will be much unhappy always. Yet he never can be sure; and that is the worst of all. And he will sometimes think that she he loved was buried alive, and that will paint his dreams with horrors of what she must have suffered; and, again, he will

think that we may be right, and that his so beloved was, after all, an Un-Dead. No! I told him once, and since then I learn much. Now, since I know it is all true, a hundred thousand times more do I know that he must pass through the bitter waters to reach the sweet. He, poor fellow, must have one hour that will make the very face of heaven grow black to him; then we can act for good all round and send him peace. My mind is made up. Let us go. You return home for to-night to your asylum, and see that all be well. As for me, I shall spend the night here in this churchyard in my own way. To-morrow night you will come to me to the Berkeley Hotel at ten of the clock. I shall send for Arthur to come too, and also that so fine young man of America that gave his blood. Later we shall all have work to do. I come with you so far as Piccadilly and there dine, for I must be back here before the sun set."

So we locked the tomb and came away, and got over the wall of the churchyard, which was not much of a task, and drove back to Piccadilly.

Note left by Van Helsing in his portmanteau, Berkeley Hotel, directed to John Seward, M.D.

(Not delivered.)

"27 *September.*

"Friend John,—

"I write this in case anything should happen. I go alone to watch in that churchyard. It pleases me that the Un-Dead, Miss Lucy, shall not leave to-night, that so on the morrow night she may be more eager. Therefore I shall fix some things she like not—garlic and a crucifix—and so seal up the door of the tomb. She is young as Un-Dead, and will heed. Moreover, these are only to prevent her coming out; they may not prevail on her wanting to get in; for then the Un-Dead is desperate, and must find the line of least resistance, whatsoever it may be. I shall be at hand all the night from sunset till after the sunrise, and if there be aught that may be learned I shall learn it. For Miss Lucy, or from her, I have no fear; but that other to whom is there that she is Un-Dead, he have now the power to seek her tomb and find shelter. He is cunning, as I know from Mr. Jonathan and from the way that all along he have fooled us when he played with us for Miss Lucy's life, and we lost; and in many ways the Un-Dead are strong. He have always the strength in his hand of twenty men; even we four who gave our strength to Miss Lucy it also is all to him. Besides, he can summon his wolf and I know not what. So if it be that he come thither on this night he shall find me; but none other shall—until it be too late. But it may be that he will not attempt the place. There is no reason why he should; his hunting ground is more full of game than the churchyard where the Un-Dead woman sleep, and one old man watch.

"Therefore I write this in case . . . . Take the papers that are with this, the diaries of Harker and the rest, and read them, and then find this great Un-Dead, and cut off his head and burn his heart or drive a stake through it, so that the world may rest from him.

"If it be so, farewell.

"VAN HELSING."

9 *to find that Van Helsing was mad.* Again, the concern for sanity.

10 *grave duty.* No doubt this is another of Van Helsing's macabre puns.

11 *'buy a pig in a poke.'* A folk phrase meaning to acquire something without looking at it first. The word "poke" means a pocket or small pack.

Dr. Seward's Diary.

28 *September.*—It is wonderful what a good night's sleep will do for one. Yesterday I was almost willing to accept Van Helsing's monstrous ideas; but now they seem to start out lurid before me as outrages on common sense. I have no doubt that he believes it all. I wonder if his mind can have become in any way unhinged. Surely there must be *some* rational explanation of all these mysterious things. Is it possible that the Professor can have done it himself? He is so abnormally clever that if he went off his head he would carry out his intent with regard to some fixed idea in a wonderful way. I am loath to think it, and indeed it would be almost as
9 great a marvel as the other to find that Van Helsing was mad; but anyhow I shall watch him carefully. I may get some light on the mystery.

29 *September, morning.* . . . . Last night, at a little before ten o'clock, Arthur and Quincey came into Van Helsing's room; he told us all that he wanted us to do, but especially addressing himself to Arthur, as if all our wills were centred in his. He began by saying that he hoped we would all come
10 with him too, "for," he said, "there is a grave duty to be done there. You were doubtless surprised at my letter?" This query was directly addressed to Lord Godalming.

"I was. It rather upset me for a bit. There has been so much trouble around my house of late that I could do without any more. I have been curious, too, as to what you mean. Quincey and I talked it over; but the more we talked, the more puzzled we got, till now I can say for myself that I'm about up a tree as to any meaning about anything."

"Me, too," said Quincey Morris laconically.

"Oh," said the Professor, "then you are nearer the beginning, both of you, than friend John here, who has to go a long way back before he can even get so far as to begin."

It was evident that he recognised my return to my old doubting frame of mind without my saying a word. Then, turning to the other two, he said with intense gravity:—

"I want your permission to do what I think good this night. It is, I know, much to ask; and when you know what it is I propose to do you will know, and only then, how much. Therefore may I ask that you promise me in the dark, so that afterwards, though you may be angry with me for a time—I must not disguise from myself the possibility that such may be—you shall not blame yourselves for anything."

"That's frank anyhow," broke in Quincey. "I'll answer for the Professor. I don't quite see his drift, but I swear he's honest; and that's good enough for me."

"I thank you, sir," said Van Helsing proudly. "I have done myself the honour of counting you one trusting friend, and such endorsement is dear to me." He held out a hand, which Quincey took.

Then Arthur spoke out:—

11 "Dr. Van Helsing, I don't quite like to 'buy a pig in a poke,' as they say in Scotland, and if it be anything in which my honour as a gentleman or my faith as a Christian is concerned, I cannot make such a promise. If you can assure me that what you intend does not violate either of these

two, then I give my consent at once; though, for the life of me, I cannot understand what you are driving at."

"I accept your limitation," said Van Helsing, "and all I ask of you is that if you feel it necessary to condemn any act of mine, you will first consider it well and be satisfied that it does not violate your reservations."

"Agreed!" said Arthur; "that is only fair. And now that the *pourparlers* are over, may I ask what it is we are to do?"

"I want you to come with me, and to come in secret, to the churchyard at Kingstead." **12**

Arthur's face fell as he said in an amazed sort of way:—

"Where poor Lucy is buried?" The Professor bowed. Arthur went on: "And when there?"

"To enter the tomb!" Arthur stood up.

"Professor, are you in earnest; or is it some monstrous joke? Pardon me, I see that you are in earnest." He sat down again, but I could see that he sat firmly and proudly, as one who is on his dignity. There was silence until he asked again:—

"And when in the tomb?"

"To open the coffin."

"This is too much!" he said, angrily rising again. "I am willing to be patient in all things that are reasonable; but in this—this desecration of the grave—of one who——" He fairly choked with indignation. The Professor looked pityingly at him.

"If I could spare you one pang, my poor friend," he said, "God knows I would. But this night our feet must tread in thorny paths; or later, and for ever, the feet you love must walk in paths of flame!"

Arthur looked up with set, white face and said:—

"Take care, sir, take care!"

"Would it not be well to hear what I have to say?" said Van Helsing. "And then you will at least know the limit of my purpose. Shall I go on?"

"That's fair enough," broke in Morris.

After a pause Van Helsing went on, evidently with an effort:—

"Miss Lucy is dead; is it not so? Yes! Then there can be no wrong to her. But if she be not dead——"

Arthur jumped to his feet.

"Good God!" he cried. "What do you mean? Has there been any mistake; has she been buried alive?" He groaned in anguish that not even hope could soften.

"I did not say she was alive, my child; I did not think it. I go no further than to say that she might be Un-Dead."

"Un-Dead! Not alive! What do you mean? Is this all a nightmare, or what is it?"

"There are mysteries which men can only guess at, which age by age they may solve only in part. Believe me, we are now on the verge of one. But I have not done. May I cut off the head of dead Miss Lucy?"

"Heavens and earth, no!" cried Arthur in a storm of passion. "Not for the wide world will I consent to any mutilation of her dead body. Dr. Van Helsing, you try me too far. What have I done to you that you should torture

12 *Kingstead.* No churchyard by this name existed in Victorian London.

me so? What did that poor, sweet girl do that you should want to cast such dishonour on her grave? Are you mad that speak such things, or am I mad that listen to them? Don't dare to think more of such a desecration; I shall not give my consent to anything you do. I have a duty to do in protecting her grave from outrage; and, by God, I shall do it!"

Van Helsing rose up from where he had all the time been seated, and said, gravely and sternly:—

"My Lord Godalming, I, too, have a duty to do, a duty to others, a duty to you, a duty to the dead; and, by God, I shall do it! All I ask you now is that you come with me, that you look and listen; and if when later I make the same request you do not be more eager for its fulfilment even than I am, then—then I shall do my duty, whatever it may seem to me. And then, to follow of your Lordship's wishes, I shall hold myself at your disposal to render an account to you, when and where you will." His voice broke a little, and he went on with a voice full of pity:—

"But, I beseech you, do not go forth in anger with me. In a long life of acts which were often not pleasant to do, and which sometimes did wring my heart, I have never had so heavy a task as now. Believe me that if the time comes for you to change your mind towards me, one look from you will wipe away all this so sad hour, for I would do what a man can to save you from sorrow. Just think. For why should I give myself so much of labour and so much of sorrow? I have come here from my own land to do what I can of good; at the first to please my friend John, and then to help a sweet young lady, whom, too, I came to love. For her—I am ashamed to say so much, but I say it in kindness—I gave what you gave: the blood of my veins; I gave it, I, who was not, like you, her lover, but only her physician and her friend. I gave to her my nights and days—before death, after death; and if my death can do her good even now, when she is the dead Un-Dead, she shall have it freely." He said this with a very grave, sweet pride, and Arthur was much affected by it. He took the old man's hand and said in a broken voice:—

"Oh, it is hard to think of it, and I cannot understand; but at least I shall go with you and wait."

CHAPTER XVI.

Dr. Seward's Diary—*continued.*

It was just a quarter before twelve o'clock when we got into the churchyard over the low wall. The night was dark, with occasional gleams of moonlight between the rents of the heavy clouds that scudded across the sky. We all kept somehow close together, with Van Helsing slightly in front as he led the way. When we had come close to the tomb I looked well at Arthur, for I feared that the proximity to a place laden with so sorrowful a memory would upset him; but he bore himself well. I took it that the very mystery of the proceeding was in some way a counteractent to his grief. The Professor unlocked the door, and seeing a natural hesitation amongst us for various reasons, solved the difficulty by entering first himself. The rest of us followed, and he closed the door. He then lit a dark lantern and pointed to the coffin. Arthur stepped forward hesitatingly; Van Helsing said to me:—

"You were with me here yesterday. Was the body of Miss Lucy in that coffin?"

"It was." The Professor turned to the rest, saying:—

"You hear; and yet there is one who does not believe with me." He took his screwdriver and again took off the lid of the coffin. Arthur looked on, very pale but silent; when the lid was removed he stepped forward. He evidently did not know that there was a leaden coffin, or, at any rate, had not thought of it. When he saw the rent in the lead, the blood rushed to his face for an instant, but as quickly fell away again, so that he remained of a ghastly whiteness; he was still silent. Van Helsing forced back the leaden flange, and we all looked in and recoiled.

The coffin was empty!

For several minutes no one spoke a word. The silence was broken by Quincey Morris:—

"Professor, I answered for you. Your word is all I want. I wouldn't ask such a thing ordinarily—I wouldn't so dishonour you as to imply a doubt; but this is a mystery that goes beyond any honour or dishonour. Is this your doing?"

"I swear to you by all that I hold sacred that I have not removed nor touched her. What happened was this: Two

1 *wafer-like biscuit*. Father William Quinn, of the Canon Law Office of the Archdiocese of San Francisco, advises me that this procedure is, in terms of Church doctrine, absolutely impermissible since, in Catholic belief, the sanctified wafer *is* the Body of Christ Himself. The Host, therefore, may not be used in any profane way, no matter how exalted the end in view.

nights ago my friend Seward and I came here—with good purpose, believe me. I opened that coffin, which was then sealed up, and we found it, as now, empty. We then waited, and saw something white come through the trees. The next day we came here in day-time, and she lay there. Did she not, friend John?"

"Yes."

"That night we were just in time. One more so small child was missing, and we find it, thank God, unharmed amongst the graves. Yesterday I came here before sundown, for at sundown the Un-Dead can move. I waited here all the night till the sun rose, but I saw nothing. It was most probable that it was because I had laid over the clamps of those doors garlic, which the Un-Dead cannot bear, and other things which they shun. Last night there was no exodus, so to-night before the sundown I took away my garlic and other things. And so it is we find this coffin empty. But bear with me. So far there is much that is strange. Wait you with me outside, unseen and unheard, and things much stranger are yet to be. So"—here he shut the dark slide of his lantern—"now to the outside." He opened the door, and we filed out, he coming last and locking the door behind him.

Oh! but it seemed fresh and pure in the night air after the terror of that vault. How sweet it was to see the clouds race by, and the passing gleams of the moonlight between the scudding clouds crossing and passing—like the gladness and sorrow of a man's life; how sweet it was to breathe the fresh air, that had no taint of death and decay; how humanising to see the red lighting of the sky beyond the hill, and to hear far away the muffled roar that marks the life of a great city. Each in his own way was solemn and overcome. Arthur was silent, and was, I could see, striving to grasp the purpose and the inner meaning of the mystery. I was myself tolerably patient, and half inclined again to throw aside doubt and to accept Van Helsing's conclusions. Quincey Morris was phlegmatic in the way of a man who accepts all things, and accepts them in the spirit of cool bravery, with hazard of all he has to stake. Not being able to smoke, he cut himself a good-sized plug of tobacco and began to chew. As to Van Helsing, he was employed in a definite way. First he took from his bag
1 a mass of what looked like thin, wafer-like biscuit, which was carefully rolled up in a white napkin; next he took out a double-handful of some whitish stuff, like dough or putty. He crumbled the wafer up fine and worked it into the mass between his hands. This he then took, and rolling it into thin strips, began to lay them into the crevices between the door and its setting in the tomb. I was somewhat puzzled at this, and being close, asked him what it was that he was doing. Arthur and Quincey drew near also, as they too were curious. He answered:—

"I am closing the tomb, so that the Un-Dead may not enter."

"And is that stuff you have put there going to do it?" asked Quincey. "Great Scott! Is this a game?"

"It is."

"What is that which you are using?" This time the question was by Arthur. Van Helsing reverently lifted his hat as he answered:—

"The Host. I brought it from Amsterdam. I have an Indul- 2
gence." It was an answer that appalled the most sceptical of us, and we felt individually that in the presence of such earnest purpose as the Professor's, a purpose which could thus use the to him most sacred of things, it was impossible to distrust. In respectful silence we took the places assigned to us close round the tomb, but hidden from the sight of any one approaching. I pitied the others, especially Arthur. I had myself been apprenticed by my former visits to this watching horror; and yet I, who had up to an hour ago repudiated the proofs, felt my heart sink within me. Never did tombs look so ghastly white; never did cypress, or yew, or juniper so seem the embodiment of funereal gloom; never did tree or grass wave or rustle so ominously; never did bough creak so mysteriously; and never did the far-away howling of dogs send such a woeful presage through the night.

There was a long spell of silence, a big, aching void, and then from the Professor a keen "S-s-s-s!" He pointed; and far down the avenue of yews we saw a white figure advance—a dim white figure, which held something dark at its breast. The figure stopped, and at the moment a ray of moonlight fell between the masses of driving clouds and showed in
startling prominence a dark-haired woman, dressed in the 3
cerements of the grave. We could not see the face, for it was bent down over what we saw to be a fair-haired child. There was a pause and a sharp little cry, such as a child gives in sleep, or a dog as it lies before the fire and dreams. We were starting forward, but the Professor's warning hand, seen by us as he stood behind a yew-tree, kept us back; and then as we looked the white figure moved forwards again. It was now near enough for us to see clearly, and the moonlight still held. My own heart grew cold as ice, and I could hear the gasp of Arthur, as we recognised the features of Lucy Westenra. Lucy Westenra, but yet how changed. The sweetness was
turned to adamantine, heartless cruelty, and the purity to 4
voluptuous wantonness. Van Helsing stepped out, and, obedient to his gesture, we all advanced too; the four of us ranged in a line before the door of the tomb. Van Helsing raised his lantern and drew the slide; by the concentrated light that fell on Lucy's face we could see that the lips were crimson with fresh blood, and that the stream had trickled over her chin and stained the purity of her lawn death-robe.

We shuddered with horror. I could see by the tremulous light that even Van Helsing's iron nerve had failed. Arthur was next to me, and if I had not seized his arm and held him up, he would have fallen.

When Lucy—I call the thing that was before us Lucy because it bore her shape—saw us she drew back with an angry snarl, such as a cat gives when taken unawares; then her eyes ranged over us. Lucy's eyes in form and colour; but Lucy's eyes unclean and full of hell-fire, instead of the pure, gentle orbs we knew. At that moment the remnant of my love passed into hate and loathing; had she then to be killed, I could have done it with savage delight. As she looked, her eyes blazed with unholy light, and the face became wreathed with a voluptuous smile. Oh, God, how it

2 ". . . *Indulgence.*" All that the Indulgence can grant to Van Helsing is a remission of temporal punishment for a sin he had committed and that was already forgiven. The Indulgence, which is a sort of "payment" from the Treasury of Grace, cannot be given for sins about to be committed.

Father Quinn, of the preceding note, says of Van Helsing's "Indulgence," that he "cannot conceive of anyone giving it."

3 *dark-haired woman.* Though Lucy is described here as dark-haired, on page 147 Van Helsing is described as having "brushed Lucy's hair, so that it lay on the pillow in its usual sunny ripples." If Lucy were indeed blonde, then the early scene between Harker and the three vampires in Transylvania becomes even more intriguing. There, the most beautiful of the three has "great, wavy masses of golden hair," and Harker says of her that "I seemed somehow to know her face, and to know it in connection with some dreamy fear . . . (p. 39.)"

THE FEAST OF BLOOD. 82[illegible]

It was no dream. It was no vision of a too excited fancy, for until those palpable sounds, and that most fearfully palpable form crossed his sight, he was rather inclined to go the other way, and to fancy what the sexton had reported was nothing but a delusion of his overwrought brain. Oh, that he could but for one brief moment have found himself deceived.

"Speak!" he gasped; "speak! speak!"

There was no reply.

"I conjure you, I pray you though the sound of your voice should hurl me to perdition—I implore you, speak."

things that had ensued regarding the after death condition of that fair girl.

The noise increased each moment, and finally there was a sudden crash.

"She comes! she comes!" gasped Ringwood.

He grasped the front of the pulpit with a frantic violence, and then slowly and solemnly there crossed his excited vision a figure all clothed in white. Yes, white flowing vestments, and he knew by their fashion that they were not worn by the living, and that it was some inhabitant of the tomb that he now looked upon.

He did not see the face. No, that for a time was hidden from him, but his heart told him who it was. Yes, it was his Clara.

All was silent, and the figure in white moved on slowly but surely towards the door of the church, but ere it passed out, it turned for a moment, as if for the very purpose of removing from the mind of Ringwood any lingering doubt as to its identity.

He then saw the face, oh, so well-known, u t so pale. It was Clara Crofton!

"'Tis she! 'tis she!" was all he could say.

It seemed, too, as if some crevice in the clouds had opened at the moment, in order that he should with an absolute certainty see the countenance of that solemn figure, and then all was more than usually silent again. The door closed, and the figure was gone.

He rose in the pulpit, and clasped his

"A DARK-HAIRED WOMAN, DRESSED IN THE CEREMENTS OF THE GRAVE." FROM *VARNEY THE VAMPYRE.*

4 *the purity to voluptuous wantonness.* Here, as on her deathbed (see p. 147), Lucy, as a consequence of the vampire taint, is described as a sexually aroused woman. The reader will have noticed that for poor Lucy death and vampirism are her best cosmeticians.

5 *tingling of glass.* Lucy's sweet voice here recalls the "silvery, musical laugh" of the three voluptuous women at Dracula's castle (see p. 39). In both cases we have the tingling of glass as a comparison.

6 *the coils of Medusa's snakes.* I have described Medusa's metamorphosis elsewhere: "The story goes like this: Medusa, proud of her youth and beauty, and tossing, a trifle arrogantly, her marvelous sunburst hair, walked one day into the temple of Athena where she attracted the attention of the sea god Poseidon. Poseidon, enchanted by her grace, her style, her dancer's movements, made passionate advances to her. It is not surprising that Medusa yielded to his passion. Her mistake was that she yielded right there on the spot. Right *in* Athena's temple . . .

"The displeasure of a goddess can be horrid. There Medusa was, lovely and young and proud of her golden hair—lying in the very bliss of love—when she heard what at first seemed a distant, slithering sound; and then a nearer hiss of serpents sprouting in her hair . . . and the agonizing change began, seething and scalding, as the woman was slowly twisted into the monster we have seen: serpent-haired, boar-tusked, scaly skinned, brassy, and cold." (pp. 53–55 of *Monsters*)

made me shudder to see it! With a careless motion, she flung to the ground, callous as a devil, the child that up to now she had clutched strenuously to her breast, growling over it as a dog growls over a bone. The child gave a sharp cry, and lay there moaning. There was a cold-bloodedness in the act which wrung a groan from Arthur; when she advanced to him with outstretched arms and a wanton smile, he fell back and hid his face in his hands.

She still advanced, however, and with a languorous, voluptuous grace, said:—

"Come to me, Arthur. Leave these others and come to me. My arms are hungry for you. Come, and we can rest together. Come, my husband, come!"

There was something diabolically sweet in her tones—some-
5 thing of the tingling of glass when struck—which rang through the brains even of us who heard the words addressed to another. As for Arthur, he seemed under a spell; moving his hands from his face, he opened wide his arms. She was leaping for them, when Van Helsing sprang forward and held between them his little golden crucifix. She recoiled from it, and, with a suddenly distorted face, full of rage, dashed past him as if to enter the tomb.

When within a foot or two of the door, however, she stopped as if arrested by some irresistible force. Then she turned, and her face was shown in the clear burst of moonlight and by the lamp, which had now no quiver from Van Helsing's iron nerves. Never did I see such baffled malice on a face; and never, I trust, shall such ever be seen again by mortal eyes. The beautiful colour became livid, the eyes seemed to throw out sparks of hell-fire, the brows were wrinkled as though the
6 folds of the flesh were the coils of Medusa's snakes, and the lovely, blood-stained mouth grew to an open square, as in the passion masks of the Greeks and Japanese. If ever a face meant death—if looks could kill—we saw it at that moment.

And so for full half a minute, which seemed an eternity, she remained between the lifted crucifix and the sacred closing of her means of entry. Van Helsing broke the silence by asking Arthur:—

"Answer me, oh my friend! Am I to proceed in my work?"

Arthur threw himself on his knees, and hid his face in his hands, as he answered:—

"Do as you will, friend; do as you will. There can be no horror like this ever any more!" and he groaned in spirit. Quincey and I simultaneously moved towards him, and took his arms. We could hear the click of the closing lantern as Van Helsing held it down; coming close to the tomb, he began to remove from the chinks some of the sacred emblem which he had placed there. We all looked on in horrified amazement as we saw, when he stood back, the woman, with a corporeal body as real at the moment as our own, pass in through the interstice where scarce a knife-blade could have gone. We all felt a glad sense of relief when we saw the Professor calmly restoring the strings of putty to the edges of the door.

When this was done, he lifted the child and said:—

" . . . THE CHILD THAT UP TO NOW SHE HAD CLUTCHED STRENUOUSLY TO HER BREAST, GROWLING OVER IT AS A DOG GROWLS OVER A BONE."

"Come now, my friends; we can do no more till to-morrow. There is a funeral at noon, so here we shall all come before long after that. The friends of the dead will all be gone by two, and when the sexton lock the gate we shall remain. Then there is more to do; but not like this of to-night. As for this little one, he is not much harm, and by to-morrow night he shall be well. We shall leave him where the police will find him, as on the other night; and then to home." Coming close to Arthur, he said:—

"My friend Arthur, you have had sore trial; but after, when you will look back, you will see how it was necessary. You are now in the bitter waters, my child. By this time to-morrow you will, please God, have passed them, and have drunk of the sweet waters; so do not mourn overmuch. Till then I shall not ask you to forgive me."

Arthur and Quincey came home with me, and we tried to cheer each other on the way. We had left the child in safety, and were tired; so we all slept with more or less reality of sleep.

29 *September, night.*—A little before twelve o'clock we three—Arthur, Quincey Morris, and myself—called for the Professor. It was odd to notice that by common consent we had all put on black clothes. Of course, Arthur wore black, for he was in deep mourning, but the rest of us wore it by instinct. We got to the churchyard by half-past one, and strolled about, keeping out of official observation, so that when the gravediggers had completed their task and the sexton, under the belief that every one had gone, had locked the gate, we had the place all to ourselves. Van Helsing, instead of his little black bag, had with him a long leather one, something like a cricketing bag; it was manifestly of fair weight.

When we were alone and had heard the last of the footsteps die out up the road, we silently, and as if by ordered intention, followed the Professor to the tomb. He unlocked the door, and we entered, closing it behind us. Then he took from his bag the lantern, which he lit, and also two wax candles, which, when lighted, he stuck, by melting their own ends, on other coffins, so that they might give light sufficient to work by. When he again lifted the lid off Lucy's coffin we all looked—Arthur trembling like an aspen—and saw that the body lay there in all its death-beauty. But there was no love in my own heart, nothing but loathing for the foul Thing which had taken Lucy's shape without her soul. I could see even Arthur's face grow hard as he looked. Presently he said to Van Helsing:—

"Is this really Lucy's body, or only a demon in her shape?"

"It is her body, and yet not it. But wait a while, and you shall see her as she was, and is."

She seemed like a nightmare of Lucy as she lay there; the pointed teeth, the bloodstained, voluptuous mouth—which it made one shudder to see—the whole carnal and unspiritual appearance, seeming like a devilish mockery of Lucy's sweet purity. Van Helsing, with his usual methodicalness, began taking the various contents from his bag and placing them ready for use. First he took out a soldering iron and

some plumbing solder, and then a small oil-lamp, which gave out, when lit in a corner of the tomb, gas which burned at fierce heat with a blue flame; then his operating knives, which he placed to hand; and last a round wooden stake, 7
some two and a half or three inches thick and about three feet long. One end of it was hardened by charring in the fire, and was sharpened to a fine point. With this stake came a heavy hammer, such as in households is used in the coal-cellar for breaking the lumps. To me, a doctor's preparations for work of any kind are stimulating and bracing, but the effect of these things on both Arthur and Quincey was to cause them a sort of consternation. They both, however, kept their courage, and remained silent and quiet.

When all was ready, Van Helsing said:—

"Before we do anything, let me tell you this; it is out of the lore and experience of the ancients and of all those who have studied the powers of the Un-Dead. When they become such, there comes with the change the curse of immortality; they cannot die, but must go on age after age adding new victims and multiplying the evils of the world; for all that die from the preying of the Un-Dead become themselves Un-Dead, and prey on their kind. And so the circle goes on ever widening, like as the ripples from a stone thrown in the water. Friend Arthur, if you had met that kiss which you know of before poor Lucy die; or again, last night when you open your arms to her, you would in time, when you had died, have become *nosferatu*, as they call it in Eastern Europe, and 8
would all time make more of those Un-Deads that so have fill us with horror. The career of this so unhappy dear lady is but just begun. Those children whose blood she suck are not as yet so much the worse; but if she live on, Un-Dead, more and more they lose their blood, and by her power over them they come to her; and so she draw their blood with that so wicked mouth. But if she die in truth, then all cease; the tiny wounds of the throats disappear, and they go back to their plays unknowing ever of what has been. But of the most blessed of all, when this now Un-Dead be made to rest as true dead, then the soul of the poor lady whom we love shall again be free. Instead of working wickedness by night and growing more debased in the assimilation of it by day, she shall take her place with the other Angels. So that, my friend, it will be a blessed hand for her that shall strike the blow that sets her free. To this I am willing; but is there none amongst us who has a better right? Will it be no joy to think of hereafter in the silence of the night when sleep is not: 'It was my hand that sent her to the stars; it was the hand of him that loved her best; the hand that of all she would herself have chosen, had it been to her to choose'? Tell me if there be such a one amongst us?"

We all looked at Arthur. He saw, too, what we all did, the infinite kindness which suggested that his should be the hand which would restore Lucy to us as a holy, and not an unholy, memory; he stepped forward and said bravely, though his hand trembled, and his face was as pale as snow:—

"My true friend, from the bottom of my broken heart I thank you. Tell me what I am to do, and I shall not falter!" Van Helsing laid a hand on his shoulder, and said:—

7 *round wooden stake.* In Tod Browning's film of *Dracula*, this scene is only hinted at on screen. After 1958, when Hammer Films released *The Horror of Dracula*, the staking of female vampires became a staple for explicit color photography in subsequent vampire films. Strangely enough, no film has ever shown a stake of quite the monstrous proportions that Stoker describes. The photograph shows a pretty accurate model of the stake made for me by a federal judge who chopped down a young oak for the sake of this research.

8 nosferatu. A Romanian word meaning "not dead."

9 *He looked like a figure of Thor*. Thor is, of course, the name of the Norse god of thunder whose weapon was a hammer, and consequently a symbol of great strength. When we remember how shadowy a character Godalming has been, this sudden access of power as he destroys the woman he loves gives one pause.

In Baring-Gould's *A Book of Folk-Lore*, there is a piquant note on Thor:

"Thor the Thunderer has left us his name in Thursday. According to Scandinavian belief he is red-bearded, and his hammer that he flings is the thunderbolt. A gentleman wrote to me in 1890:—

"It was in the autumn of 1857 or 1858 that I had taken some quinine to a lad who lived with his old grandmother. On my next visit the old dame scornfully refused another bottle, and said she 'knowed on a soight better cure for the ague than yon mucky stuff.' With that she took me round to the bottom of the bed and showed me three horse-shoes nailed there with a hammer placed crosswise upon them. On my expressing incredulity, she waxed wroth, and said: 'Naay, lad, it's a chawm. I tak's t' mell (hammer) i' moy left haun and I mashys they shoon throice, and Oi sez, sez Oi:—

Feyther, Son, an' Holi Ghoast,
Naale the divil to this poast!
Throice I stroikes with holy crook,
Won for God, an' won for Wod, an' won for Lok!

Theen, laad, whin the old un comes to shak him he wean't nivver git past you; you'ull fin' him saafe as t' church steaple.'

"Could there be confusion worse confounded than this? The Holy Trinity invoked, and in the same breath God, Woden, and Loki—the very spirit of evil; and the Holy Crook and Thor's hammer treated as one and the same thing.

Yours faithfully,
B. M. Heanley.

Upton Grey Vicarage, Winchfield."

"Clearly here God takes the place of Thor; and the Triad—Thor, Woden, and Loki—are equal with the Father, Son, and Holy Ghost."

For our purposes we need to recognize that the nailing of the devil to the post is a version of the staking of the vampire.

The fusion of Christian and Norse symbols makes for a macaronic theology, but so, for that matter, does the lore of the vampire.

Arthur, if Montague Summers is right, is not following the vampire killing rules. Summers tells us that "it is highly important that the body of the Vampire should be transfixed by a single blow, for two blows would restore it to life. This curious idea is almost universally found in tradition and folklore."

"Brave lad! A moment's courage, and it is done. This stake must be driven through her. It will be a fearful ordeal—be not deceived in that—but it will be only a short time, and you will then rejoice more than your pain was great; from this grim tomb you will emerge as though you tread on air. But you must not falter when once you have begun. Only think that we, your true friends, are round you, and that we pray for you all the time."

"Go on," said Arthur hoarsely. "Tell me what I am to do."

"Take this stake in your left hand, ready to place the point over the heart, and the hammer in your right. Then when we begin our prayer for the dead—I shall read him, I have here the book, and the others shall follow—strike in God's name, that so all may be well with the dead that we love, and that the Un-Dead pass away."

Arthur took the stake and the hammer, and when once his mind was set on action his hands never trembled nor even quivered. Van Helsing opened his missal and began to read, and Quincey and I followed as well as we could. Arthur placed the point over the heart, and as I looked I could see its dint in the white flesh. Then he struck with all his might.

The Thing in the coffin writhed; and a hideous, blood-curdling screech came from the opened red lips. The body shook and quivered and twisted in wild contortions; the sharp white teeth champed together till the lips were cut, and the mouth was smeared with a crimson foam. But Arthur never
9 faltered. He looked like a figure of Thor as his untrembling arm rose and fell, driving deeper and deeper the mercy-bearing stake, whilst the blood from the pierced heart welled and spurted up around it. His face was set, and high duty seemed to shine through it; the sight of it gave us courage, so that our voices seemed to ring through the little vault.

And then the writhing and quivering of the body became less, and the teeth ceased to champ, and the face to quiver. Finally it lay still. The terrible task was over.

The hammer fell from Arthur's hand. He reeled and would have fallen had we not caught him. The great drops of sweat sprang out on his forehead, and his breath came in broken gasps. It had indeed been an awful strain on him; and had he not been forced to his task by more than human considerations he could never have gone through with it. For a few minutes we were so taken up with him that we did not look towards the coffin. When we did, however, a murmur of startled surprise ran from one to the other of us. We gazed so eagerly that Arthur rose, for he had been seated on the ground, and came and looked too; and then a glad, strange light broke over his face and dispelled altogether the gloom of horror that lay upon it.

There, in the coffin lay no longer the foul Thing that we had so dreaded and grown to hate that the work of her destruction was yielded as a privilege to the one best entitled to it, but Lucy as we had seen her in her life, with her face of unequalled sweetness and purity. True that there were there, as we had seen them in life, the traces of care and pain and waste; but these were all dear to us, for they marked her truth to what we knew. One and all we felt that the holy calm that lay like sunshine over the wasted face and form was only an earthly token and symbol of the calm that was to reign for ever.

Van Helsing came and laid his hand on Arthur's shoulder, and said to him :—

"And now, Arthur, my friend, dear lad, am I not forgiven?"

The reaction of the terrible strain came as he took the old man's hand in his, and raising it to his lips, pressed it, and said :—

"Forgiven! God bless you that you have given my dear one her soul again, and me peace." He put his hands on the Professor's shoulder, and laying his head on his breast, cried for a while silently, whilst we stood unmoving. When he raised his head Van Helsing said to him :—

"And now, my child, you may kiss her. Kiss her dead lips if you will, as she would have you to, if for her to choose. For she is not a grinning devil now—not any more a foul Thing for all eternity. No longer she is the devil's Un-Dead. She is God's true dead, whose soul is with Him!"

Arthur bent and kissed her, and then we sent him and Quincey out of the tomb; the Professor and I sawed the top off the stake, leaving the point of it in the body. Then we cut off the head and filled the mouth with garlic. We soldered up the leaden coffin, screwed on the coffin-lid, and gathering up our belongings, came away. When the Professor locked the door he gave the key to Arthur. **10**

Outside the air was sweet, the sun shone, and the birds sang, and it seemed as if all nature were tuned to a different pitch. There was gladness and mirth and peace everywhere, for we were at rest ourselves on one account, and we were glad, though it was with a tempered joy.

Before we moved away Van Helsing said :—

"Now, my friends, one step of our work is done, one the most harrowing to ourselves. But there remains a greater task: to find out the author of all this our sorrow and to stamp him out. I have clues which we can follow; but it is a long task, and a difficult, and there is danger in it, and pain. Shall you not all help me? We have learned to believe, all of us—is it not so? And since so, do we not see our duty? Yes! And do we not promise to go on to the bitter end?"

Each in turn, we took his hand, and the promise was made. Then said the Professor as we moved off :—

"Two nights hence you shall meet with me and dine together at seven of the clock with friend John. I shall entreat two others, two that you know not as yet; and I shall be ready to all our work show and our plans unfold. Friend John, you come with me home, for I have much to consult about, and you can help me. To-night I leave for Amsterdam, but shall return to-morrow night. And then begins our great quest. But first I shall have much to say, so that you may know what is to do and to dread. Then our promise shall be made to each other anew; for there is a terrible task before us, and once our feet are on the ploughshare, we must not draw back." **11**

R. E. L. Masters and Edward Lea, contemporary sex crime researchers, describe (pp. 148–49) the murderous practice of Peter Kurten, "the Dusseldorf Monster," who "would continue to stab his victims until he experienced orgasm . . ." The authors add unnecessarily "that [they] see here an obvious parallel to the act of coitus . . ."

The Lucy staking episode takes place the day after her wedding was scheduled.

The literary antecedent for this scene may be found in the German tale, *The Mysterious Stranger* (1860), where the situation is somewhat reversed. There a young woman drives three long nails into the heart of the vampire while the knight, Woislaw, recites "the credo in a loud voice."

10 *gave the key to Arthur.* One wonders why. Is it simply because Arthur is now Lucy's heir? Or is there a macabre suggestion that Arthur is likely to visit the tomb again?

11 "*. . . we must not draw back.*" Surely Van Helsing is giving us a loose rendering of Luke 9:62, where Jesus, speaking to a hesitant would-be disciple, says: "No man, having put his hand to the plough, and looking back, is fit for the kingdom of God."

CHAPTER XVII.

Dr. Seward's Diary—*continued.*

When we arrived at the Berkeley Hotel, Van Helsing found a telegram waiting for him:—

"Am coming up by train. Jonathan at Whitby. Important news.—Mina Harker."

The Professor was delighted. "Ah, that wonderful Madam Mina," he said, "pearl among women! She arrive, but I cannot stay. She must go to your house, friend John. You must meet her at the station. Telegraph her *en route*, so that she may be prepared."

When the wire was despatched he had a cup of tea; over it he told me of a diary kept by Jonathan Harker when abroad, and gave me a typewritten copy of it, as also of Mrs. Harker's diary at Whitby. "Take these," he said, "and study them well. When I have returned you will be master of all the facts, and we can then better enter on our inquisition. Keep them safe, for there is in them much of treasure. You will need all your faith, even you who have had such an experience as that of to-day. What is here told," he laid his hand heavily and gravely on the packet of papers as he spoke, "may be the beginning of the end to you and me and many another; or it may sound the knell of the Un-Dead who walk the earth. Read all, I pray you, with the open mind; and if you can add in any way to the story here told do so, for it is all-important. You have kept diary of all these so strange things; is it not so? Yes! Then we shall go through all these together when that we meet." He then made ready for his departure, and shortly after

"WE TOOK THE UNDERGROUND."

1 *Liverpool Street.* A major passenger terminal in central London, located at the intersection of Liverpool Street and Bishopsgate (see map, pp. 340–41).

2 *Fenchurch Street.* There is a railway terminal on Fenchurch Street in central London (see map, pp. 340–41).

drove off to Liverpool Street. I took my way to Paddington, 1
where I arrived about fifteen minutes before the train came in.

The crowd melted away, after the bustling fashion common to arrival platforms; and I was beginning to feel uneasy, lest I might miss my guest, when a sweet-faced, dainty-looking girl stepped up to me, and, after a quick glance, said: "Dr. Seward, is it not?"

"And you are Mrs. Harker!" I answered at once; whereupon she held out her hand.

"I knew you from the description of poor dear Lucy; but——" She stopped suddenly, and a quick blush overspread her face.

The blush that rose to my own cheeks somehow set us both at ease, for it was a tacit answer to her own. I got her luggage, which included a typewriter, and we took the
Underground to Fenchurch Street, after I had sent a wire to 2
my housekeeper to have a sitting-room and bedroom prepared at once for Mrs. Harker.

In due time we arrived. She knew, of course, that the place was a lunatic asylum, but I could see that she was unable to repress a slight shudder when we entered.

She told me that, if she might, she would come presently to my study, as she had much to say. So here I am finishing my entry in my phonograph diary whilst I await her. As yet I have not had the chance of looking at the papers which Van Helsing left with me, though they lie open before me. I must get her interested in something, so that I may have an opportunity of reading them. She does not know how precious time is, or what a task we have in hand. I must be careful not to frighten her. Here she is!

Mina Harker's Journal.

29 *September.*—After I had tidied myself, I went down to Dr. Seward's study. At the door I paused a moment, for I thought I heard him talking with some one. As, however, he had pressed me to be quick, I knocked at the door, and on his calling out, "Come in," I entered.

3 *I felt quite excited over it.* Strange that Mina has never seen a phonograph since, as we were told in chapter XI, her intimate friend Lucy has one that Dr. Seward uses to complete an entry in *his* journal.

To my intense surprise, there was no one with him. He was quite alone, and on the table opposite him was what I knew at once from the description to be a phonograph. I had never seen one, and was much interested.

"I hope I did not keep you waiting," I said; "but I stayed at the door as I heard you talking, and thought there was some one with you."

"Oh," he replied, with a smile, "I was only entering my diary."

"Your diary?" I asked him in surprise.

"Yes," he answered. "I keep it in this." As he spoke he
3 laid his hand on the phonograph. I felt quite excited over it, and blurted out:—

"Why, this beats even shorthand! May I hear it say something?"

"Certainly," he replied with alacrity, and stood up to put it in train for speaking. Then he paused, and a troubled look overspread his face.

"The fact is," he began awkwardly, "I only keep my diary in it; and as it is entirely—almost entirely—about my cases, it may be awkward—that is, I mean"—— He stopped, and I tried to help him out of his embarrassment:—

"You helped to attend dear Lucy at the end. Let me hear how she died; for all that I can know of her, I shall be very grateful. She was very, very dear to me."

To my surprise, he answered, with a horrorstruck look in his face:—

"Tell you of her death? Not for the wide world!"

"Why not?" I asked, for some grave, terrible feeling was coming over me. Again he paused, and I could see that he was trying to invent an excuse. At length he stammered out:—

"You see, I do not know how to pick out any particular part of the diary." Even while he was speaking an idea dawned upon him, and he said with unconscious simplicity, in a different voice, and with the naïveté of a child: "That's quite true, upon my honour. Honest Indian!" I could not but smile, at which he grimaced. "I gave myself away that time!" he said. "But do you know that, although I have kept the diary for months past, it never once struck me how I was going to find any particular part of it in case I wanted to look it up?" By this time my mind was made up that the diary of a doctor who attended Lucy might have something to add to the sum of our knowledge of that terrible Being, and I said boldly:—

"Then, Dr. Seward, you had better let me copy it out for you on my typewriter." He grew to a positively deathly pallor as he said:—

"No! no! no! For all the world, I wouldn't let you know that terrible story!"

Then it was terrible; my intuition was right! For a moment I thought, and as my eyes ranged the room, unconsciously looking for something or some opportunity to aid me, they lit on the great batch of typewriting on the table. His eyes caught the look in mine, and, without his thinking, followed their direction. As they saw the parcel he realised my meaning.

"You do not know me." I said. "When you have read those papers—my own diary and my husband's also, which I have typed—you will know me better. I have not faltered in giving every thought of my own heart in this cause; but, of course, you do not know me—yet; and I must not expect you to trust me so far."

He is certainly a man of noble nature; poor dear Lucy was right about him. He stood up and opened a large drawer, in which were arranged in order a number of hollow cylinders of metal covered with dark wax, and said:—

"You are quite right. I did not trust you because I did not know you. But I know you now; and let me say that I should have known you long ago. I know that Lucy told you of me; she told me of you too. May I make the only atonement in my power? Take the cylinders and hear them—the first half-dozen of them are personal to me, and they will not horrify you; then you will know me better. Dinner will by then be ready. In the meantime I shall read over some of these documents, and shall be better able to understand certain things." He carried the phonograph himself up to my sitting-room and adjusted it for me. Now I shall learn something pleasant, I am sure; for it will tell me the other side of a true love episode of which I know one side already. . . . .

Dr. Seward's Diary.

29 *September.*—I was so absorbed in that wonderful diary of Jonathan Harker and that other of his wife that I let the time run on without thinking. Mrs. Harker was not down when the maid came to announce dinner, so I said: "She is possibly tired; let dinner wait an hour;" and I went on with my work. I had just finished Mrs. Harker's diary, when she came in. She looked sweetly pretty, but very sad, and her eyes were flushed with crying. This somehow moved me much. Of late I have had cause for tears, God knows! but the relief of them was denied me; and now the sight of those sweet eyes, brightened with recent tears, went straight to my heart. So I said as gently as I could:—

"I greatly fear I have distressed you."

"Oh no, not distressed me," she replied, "but I have been more touched than I can say by your grief. That is a wonderful machine, but it is cruelly true. It told me, in its very tones, the anguish of your heart. It was like a soul crying out to almighty God. No one must hear them spoken ever again! See, I have tried to be useful. I have copied out the words on my typewriter, and none other need now hear your heart beat, as I did."

"No one need ever know, shall ever know," I said in a low voice. She laid her hand on mine and said very gravely:—

"Ah, but they must!"

"Must! But why?" I asked.

"Because it is a part of the terrible story, a part of poor dear Lucy's death and all that led to it; because in the struggle which we have before us to rid the earth of this terrible monster we must have all the knowledge and all the help which we can get. I think that the cylinders which you gave me contained more than you intended me to know; but I can see

4 *I put the forked metal to my ears.* The reference, of course, is to the earphones that accompanied the machine.

5 *case-bottle.* A bottle, specially designed to fit a traveling case.

that there are in your record many lights to this dark mystery. You will let me help, will you not? I know all up to a certain point; and I see already, though your diary only took me to 7 September, how poor Lucy was beset, and how her terrible doom was being wrought out. Jonathan and I have been working day and night since Professor Van Helsing saw us. He is gone to Whitby to get more information, and he will be here to-morrow to help us. We need have no secrets amongst us; working together and with absolute trust, we can surely be stronger than if some of us were in the dark." She looked at me so appealingly, and at the same time manifested such courage and resolution in her bearing, that I gave in at once to her wishes. "You shall," I said, "do as you like in the matter. God forgive me if I do wrong! There are terrible things yet to learn of; but if you have so far travelled on the road to poor Lucy's death, you will not be content, I know, to remain in the dark. Nay, the end—the very end—may give you a gleam of peace. Come, there is dinner. We must keep one another strong for what is before us; we have a cruel and dreadful task. When you have eaten you shall learn the rest, and I shall answer any questions you ask—if there be anything which you do not understand, though it was apparent to us who were present."

MINA HARKER'S JOURNAL.

29 *September.*—After dinner I came with Dr. Seward to his study. He brought back the phonograph from my room, and I took my typewriter. He placed me in a comfortable chair, and arranged the phonograph so that I could touch it without getting up, and showed me how to stop it in case I should want to pause. Then he very thoughtfully took a chair, with his back to me, so that I might be as free as possible, and began to
4 read. I put the forked metal to my ears and listened.

When the terrible story of Lucy's death, and—and all that followed, was done, I lay back in my chair powerless. Fortunately I am not of a fainting disposition. When Dr. Seward saw me he jumped up with a horrified exclamation,
5 and hurriedly taking a case-bottle from a cupboard, gave me some brandy, which in a few minutes somewhat restored me. My brain was all in a whirl, and only that there came through all the multitude of horrors, the holy ray of light that my dear, dear Lucy was at last at peace, I do not think I could have borne it without making a scene. It is all so wild, and mysterious, and strange that if I had not known Jonathan's experience in Transylvania I could not have believed. As it was, I didn't know what to believe, and so got out of my difficulty by attending to something else. I took the cover off my typewriter, and said to Dr. Seward:—

"Let me write this all out now. We must be ready for Dr. Van Helsing when he comes. I have sent a telegram to Jonathan to come on here when he arrives in London from Whitby. In this matter dates are everything, and I think that if we get all our material ready, and have every item put in chronological order, we shall have done much. You tell me that Lord Godalming and Mr. Morris are coming too. Let us be able to tell them when they come." He accordingly set the

phonograph at a slow pace, and I began to typewrite from the 6
beginning of the seventh cylinder. I used manifold, and so took three copies of the diary, just as I had done with all the rest. It was late when I got through, but Dr. Seward went about his work of going his round of the patients; when he had finished he came back and sat near me, reading, so that I did not feel too lonely whilst I worked. How good and thoughtful he is; the world seems full of good men—even if there *are* monsters in it. Before I left him I remembered what Jonathan put in his diary of the Professor's perturbation at reading something in an evening paper at the station at Exeter; so, seeing that Dr. Seward keeps his newspapers, I borrowed the files of "The Westminster Gazette" and "The Pall Mall Gazette," and took them to my room. I remember how much "The Dailygraph" and "The Whitby Gazette," of which I had made cuttings, helped us to understand the terrible events at Whitby when Count Dracula landed, so I shall look through the evening papers since then, and perhaps I shall get some new light. I am not sleepy, and the work will help to keep me quiet.

6 *at a slow pace*. This was not a good idea. To set the cylinder speed at "a slow pace" would ensure distortion of the voice.

Dr. Seward's Diary.

30 *September*.—Mr. Harker arrived at nine o'clock. He had got his wife's wire just before starting. He is uncommonly clever, if one can judge from his face, and full of energy. If his journal be true—and judging by one's own wonderful experiences, it must be—he is also a man of great nerve. That going down to the vault a second time was a remarkable piece of daring. After reading his account of it I was prepared to meet a good specimen of manhood, but hardly the quiet, business-like gentleman who came here to-day.

Later.—After lunch Harker and his wife went back to their own room, and as I passed a while ago I heard the click of the typewriter. They are hard at it. Mrs. Harker says that they are knitting together in chronological order every scrap of evidence they have. Harker has got the letters between the consignee of the boxes at Whitby and the carriers in London who took charge of them. He is now reading his wife's typescript of my diary. I wonder what they make out of it. Here he is. . . . .

Strange that it never struck me that the very next house might be the Count's hiding-place! Goodness knows that we had enough clues from the conduct of the patient Renfield! The bundle of letters relating to the purchase of the house were with the typescript. Oh, if we had only had them earlier we might have saved poor Lucy! Stop; that way madness lies! Harker has gone back, and is again collating his material. He says that by dinner-time they will be able to show a whole connected narrative. He thinks that in the meantime I should see Renfield, as hitherto he has been a sort of index to the coming and going of the Count. I hardly see this yet, but when I get at the dates I suppose I shall. What a good thing that Mrs. Harker put my cylinders into type! We never could have found the dates otherwise. . . . .

I found Renfield sitting placidly in his room with his hands folded, smiling benignly. At the moment he seemed as sane as any one I ever saw. I sat down and talked with him on a lot of subjects, all of which he treated naturally. He then, of his own accord, spoke of going home, a subject he has never mentioned to my knowledge during his sojourn here. In fact, he spoke quite confidently of getting his discharge at once. I believe that, had I not had the chat with Harker and read the letters and the dates of his outbursts, I should have been prepared to sign for him after a brief time of observation. As it is, I am darkly suspicious. All those outbreaks were in some way linked with the proximity of the Count. What then does this absolute content mean? Can it be that his instinct is satisfied as to the vampire's ultimate triumph? Stay; he is himself zoophagous, and in his wild ravings outside the chapel door of the deserted house he always spoke of "master." This all seems confirmation of our idea. However, after a while I came away; my friend is just a little too sane at present to make it safe to probe him too deep with questions. He might begin to think, and then—! So I came away. I mistrust these quiet moods of his; so I have given the attendant a hint to look closely after him, and to have a strait-waistcoat ready in case of need.

Jonathan Harker's Journal.

29 *September, in train to London.*—When I received Mr. Billington's courteous message that he would give me any information in his power, I thought it best to go down to Whitby and make, on the spot, such inquiries as I wanted. It was now my object to trace that horrid cargo of the Count's to its place in London. Later, we may be able to deal with it. Billington junior, a nice lad, met me at the station, and brought me to his father's house, where they had decided that I must stay the night. They are hospitable, with true Yorkshire hospitality: give a guest everything, and leave him free to do as he likes. They all knew that I was busy, and that my stay was short, and Mr. Billington had ready in his office all the papers concerning the consignment of boxes. It gave me almost a turn to see again one of the letters which I had seen on the Count's table before I knew of his diabolical plans. Everything had been carefully thought out, and done systematically and with precision. He seemed to have been prepared for every obstacle which might be placed by accident in the way of his intentions being carried out. To use an Americanism, he had "taken no chances," and the absolute accuracy with which his instructions were fulfilled, was simply the logical result of his care. I saw the invoice, and took note of it: "Fifty cases of common earth, to be used for experimental purposes." Also the copy of letter to Carter Paterson, and their reply; of both of these I got copies. This was all the information Mr. Billington could give me, so I went down to the port and saw the coastguards, the Customs officers and the harbour-master. They had all something to say of the strange entry of the ship, which is already taking its place in local tradition; but no one could add to the simple description "Fifty cases of common earth." I then saw the station-master, who kindly put me in communication

with the men who had actually received the boxes. Their tally was exact with the list, and they had nothing to add except that the boxes were "main and mortal heavy," and that shifting them was dry work. One of them added that it was hard lines that there wasn't any gentleman "such-like as yourself, squire," to show some sort of appreciation of their efforts in a liquid form; another put in a rider that the thirst then generated was such that even the time which had elapsed had not completely allayed it. Needless to add, I took care before leaving to lift, for ever and adequately, this source of reproach.

30 *September*.—The station-master was good enough to give me a line to his old companion the station-master at King's Cross, so that when I arrived there in the morning I was able to ask him about the arrival of the boxes. He, too, put me at once in communication with the proper officials, and I saw that their tally was correct with the original invoice. The opportunities of acquiring an abnormal thirst had been here limited; a noble use of them had, however, been made, and again I was compelled to deal with the result in an *ex post facto* manner.

From thence I went on to Carter in Paterson's central office, where I met with the utmost courtesy. They looked up the transaction in their day-book and letter-book, and at once telephoned to their King's Cross office for more details. 7
By good fortune, the men who did the teaming were waiting for work, and the official at once sent them over, sending also by one of them the way-bill and all the papers connected with the delivery of the boxes at Carfax. Here again I found the tally agreeing exactly; the carriers' men were able to supplement the paucity of the written words with a few details. These were, I shortly found, connected almost solely with the dusty nature of the job, and of the consequent thirst engendered in the operators. On my affording an opportunity, through the medium of the currency of the realm, of the allaying, at a later period, this beneficent evil, one of the men remarked:—

"That 'ere 'ouse, guv'nor, is the rummiest I ever was in. Blyme! but it ain't been touched sence a hundred years. There was dust that thick in the place that you might have slep' on it without 'urtin' of yer bones; an' the place was that neglected that yer might 'ave smelled ole Jerusalem in it. But the ole chapel—that took the cike, that did! Me and my mate, we thort we wouldn't never git out quick enough. Lor', I wouldn't take less nor a quid a moment to stay there arter dark."

Having been in the house, I could well believe him; but if he knew what I know, he would, I think, have raised his terms.

Of one thing I am now satisfied: that *all* the boxes which arrived at Whitby from Varna in the *Demeter* were safely deposited in the old chapel of Carfax. There should be fifty of them there, unless any have since been removed—as from Dr. Seward's diary I fear.

I shall try to see the carter who took away the boxes from Carfax when Renfield attacked them. By following up this clue we may learn a good deal.

Later.—Mina and I have worked all day, and we have put all the papers into order.

7 *telephoned*. The telephone, invented in 1876, was just coming into popular use in the 1890s.

8 *he is true grit, and he improves under strain.* Eric Partridge's *A Dictionary of Slang and Unconventional English* cites "clear grit." Both "grit" and "sand" used about someone's character imply courage, stamina, or spirit.

Mina Harker's Journal.

30 *September.*—I am so glad that I hardly know how to contain myself. It is, I suppose, the reaction from the haunting fear which I have had: that this terrible affair and the reopening of his old wound might act detrimentally on Jonathan. I saw him leave for Whitby with as brave a face as I could, but I was sick with apprehension. The effort has, however, done him good. He was never so resolute, never so strong, never so full of volcanic energy, as at present. It is just as that
8 dear, good Professor Van Helsing said: he is true grit, and he improves under strain that would kill a weaker nature. He came back full of life and hope and determination; we have got everything in order for to-night. I feel myself quite wild with excitement. I suppose one ought to pity any thing so hunted as is the Count. That is just it: this Thing is not human—not even beast. To read Dr. Seward's account of poor Lucy's death, and what followed, is enough to dry up the springs of pity in one's heart.

Later.—Lord Godalming and Mr. Morris arrived earlier than we expected. Dr. Seward was out on business, and had taken Jonathan with him, so I had to see them. It was to me a painful meeting, for it brought back all poor dear Lucy's hopes of only a few months ago. Of course they had heard Lucy speak of me, and it seemed that Dr. Van Helsing, too, has been quite "blowing my trumpet," as Mr. Morris expressed it. Poor fellows, neither of them is aware that I know all about the proposals they made to Lucy They did not quite know what to say or do, as they were ignorant of the amount of my knowledge; so they had to keep on neutral subjects. However, I thought the matter over, and came to the conclusion that the best thing I could do would be to post them in affairs right up to date. I knew from Dr. Seward's diary that they had been at Lucy's death—her real death—and that I need not fear to betray any secret before the time. So I told them, as well as I could, that I had read all the papers and diaries, and that my husband and I, having typewritten them, had just finished putting them in order. I gave them each a copy to read in the library. When Lord Godalming got his and turned it over—it does make a pretty good pile—he said:—

"Did you write all this, Mrs. Harker?"

I nodded, and he went on:—

"I don't quite see the drift of it; but you people are all so good and kind, and have been working so earnestly and so energetically, that all I can do is to accept your ideas blindfold and try to help you. I have had one lesson already in accepting facts that should make a man humble to the last hour of his life. Besides, I know you loved my poor Lucy——" Here he turned away and covered his face with his hands. I could hear the tears in his voice. Mr. Morris, with instinctive delicacy, just laid a hand for a moment on his shoulder, and then walked quietly out of the room. I suppose there is something in woman's nature that makes a man free to break down before her and express his feelings on the tender or emotional side without feeling it derogatory to his manhood;

for when Lord Godalming found himself alone with me he sat down on the sofa and gave way utterly and openly. I sat down beside him and took his hand. I hope he didn't think it forward of me, and that if he ever thinks of it afterwards he never will have such a thought. There I wrong him; I *know* he never will—he is too true a gentleman. I said to him, for I could see that his heart was breaking :—

"I loved dear Lucy, and I know what she was to you, and what you were to her. She and I were like sisters; and now she is gone, will you not let me be like a sister to you in your trouble? I know what sorrows you have had, though I cannot measure the depth of them. If sympathy and pity can help in your affliction, won't you let me be of some little service—for Lucy's sake?"

In an instant the poor dear fellow was overwhelmed with grief. It seemed to me that all that he had of late been suffering in silence found a vent at once. He grew quite hysterical,
and raising his open hands, beat his palms together in a perfect 9
agony of grief. He stood up and then sat down again, and the tears rained down his cheeks. I felt an infinite pity for him, and opened my arms unthinkingly. With a sob he laid his head on my shoulder, and cried like a wearied child, whilst he shook with emotion.

We women have something of the mother in us that makes us rise above smaller matters when the mother-spirit is invoked; I felt this big, sorrowing man's head resting on me, as though it were that of the baby that some day may lie on my bosom, and I stroked his hair as though he were my own child. I never thought at the time how strange it all was.

After a little bit his sobs ceased, and he raised himself with an apology, though he made no disguise of his emotion. He told me that for days and nights past—weary days and sleepless night—he had been unable to speak with any one, as a man must speak in his time of sorrow. There was no woman whose sympathy could be given to him, or with whom, owing to the terrible circumstance with which his sorrow was surrounded, he could speak freely. "I know now how I suffered," he said, as he dried his eyes, "but I do not know even yet—and none other can ever know—how much your sweet sympathy has been to me to-day. I shall know better in time; and believe me that, though I am not ungrateful now, my gratitude will grow with my understanding. You will let me be like a brother, will you not, for all our lives—for dear Lucy's sake?"

"For dear Lucy's sake," I said as we clasped hands. "Ay, and for your own sake," he added, "for if a man's esteem and gratitude are ever worth the winning, you have
won mine to-day. If ever the future should bring to you a 10
time when you need a man's help, believe me, you will not call in vain. God grant that no such time may ever come to you to break the sunshine of your life; but if it should ever come, promise me that you will let me know." He was so earnest, and his sorrow was so fresh, that I felt it would comfort him, so I said :—

"I promise."

As I came along the corridor I saw Mr. Morris looking out

9 *beat his palms together.* Dr. Van Helsing beats *his* palms together in this same curious fashion when he finds that Lucy's mother has removed the garlic blossoms meant to protect Lucy from the vampire. (See chapter XI, page 126.) Both men are reduced to sobs, though Van Helsing's grief is described as "a sort of mute despair," while Godalming's is "a perfect agony of grief."

10 *If ever the future should bring.* This is preparation for Godalming's role as banker of the expedition against Dracula later in the book.

Godalming's promise to Mina echoes a similar promise Dr. Seward made to Lucy on page 60. Seward, too, is described as taking Lucy's hands in his, the way Godalming takes Mina's. Curiously enough, though Quincey Morris also has a heartfelt scene with Lucy (p. 62), Morris makes no grand promises to her on that occasion.

11 *"I wish I could comfort all who suffer from the heart . . ."* So now Mina takes over and becomes everyone's bride, including, in time, Dracula's.

What we have here is a matronly parallel to the scene in which Lucy receives three proposals, accepts one, and wishes she could accept all.

of a window. He turned as he heard my footsteps. "How is Art?" he said. Then noticing my red eyes, he went on: "Ah, I see you have been comforting him. Poor old fellow! he needs it. No one but a woman can help a man when he is in trouble of the heart; and he had no one to comfort him."

He bore his own trouble so bravely that my heart bled for him. I saw the manuscript in his hand, and I knew that when he read it he would realise how much I knew; so I said to him:—

11 "I wish I could comfort all who suffer from the heart. Will you let me be your friend, and will you come to me for comfort if you need it? You will know, later on, why I speak." He saw that I was in earnest, and stooping, took my hand, and raising it to his lips, kissed it. It seemed but poor comfort to so brave and unselfish a soul, and impulsively I bent over and kissed him. The tears rose in his eyes, and there was a momentary choking in his throat; he said quite calmly:—

"Little girl, you will never regret that true-hearted kindness, so long as ever you live!" Then he went into the study to his friend.

"Little girl!"—the very words he had used to Lucy, and oh, but he proved himself a friend!

CHAPTER XVIII.

Dr. Seward's Diary.

30 *September.*—I got home at five o'clock, and found that Godalming and Morris had not only arrived, but had already studied the transcript of the various diaries and letters which Harker and his wonderful wife had made and arranged. Harker had not yet returned from his visit to the carriers' men, of whom Dr. Hennessey had written to me. Mrs. Harker gave us a cup of tea, and I can honestly say that, for the first time since I have lived in it, this old house seemed like *home*. 1
When we had finished, Mrs. Harker said:—

"Dr. Seward, may I ask a favour? I want to see your patient, Mr. Renfield. Do let me see him. What you have said of him in your diary interests me so much!" She looked so appealing and so pretty that I could not refuse her, and there was no possible reason why I should; so I took her with me. When I went into the room, I told the man that a lady would like to see him; to which he simply answered: "Why?"

"She is going through the house, and wants to see every one in it," I answered. "Oh, very well," he said; "let her come in, by all means; but just wait a minute till I tidy up the place." His method of tidying was peculiar: he simply swallowed all the flies and spiders in the boxes before I could stop him. It was quite evident that he feared, or was jealous of, some interference. When he had got through his disgusting task, he said cheerfully: "Let the lady come in," and sat down on the edge of his bed with his head down, but with his eyelids raised so that he could see her as she entered. For a moment I thought that he might have some homicidal intent; I remembered how quiet he had been just

1 *this old house seemed like* home. After Lucy's death the survivors become more and more one family. Seward's appreciation of Mina's tea, like Godalming weeping on her bosom, emphasizes her role as the common mother-bride of them all.

2 ". . . *errors of* non causæ *and* ignoratio elenchi." Legal Latin for "there is not a reason" and "ignorance of the charge," respectively.

before he attacked me in my own study, and I took care to stand where I could seize him at once if he attempted to make a spring at her. She came into the room with an easy gracefulness which would at once command the respect of any lunatic—for easiness is one of the qualities mad people most respect. She walked over to him, smiling pleasantly, and held out her hand.

"Good-evening, Mr. Renfield," said she. "You see, I know you, for Dr. Seward has told me of you." He made no immediate reply, but eyed her all over intently with a set frown on his face. This look gave way to one of wonder, which merged in doubt; then, to my intense astonishment, he said:—

"You're not the girl the doctor wanted to marry, are you? You can't be, you know, for she's dead." Mrs. Harker smiled sweetly as she replied:—

"Oh no! I have a husband of my own, to whom I was married before I ever saw Dr. Seward, or he me. I am Mrs. Harker."

"Then what are you doing here?"

"My husband and I are staying on a visit with Dr. Seward."

"Then don't stay."

"But why not?" I thought that this style of conversation might not be pleasant to Mrs. Harker, any more than it was to me, so I joined in:—

"How did you know I wanted to marry any one?" His reply was simply contemptuous, given in a pause in which he turned his eyes from Mrs. Harker to me, instantly turning them back again:—

"What an asinine question!"

"I don't see that at all, Mr. Renfield," said Mrs. Harker, at once championing me. He replied to her with as much courtesy and respect as he had shown contempt to me:—

"You will, of course, understand, Mrs. Harker, that when a man is so loved and honoured as our host is, everything regarding him is of interest in our little community. Dr. Seward is loved not only by his household and his friends, but even by his patients, who, being some of them hardly in mental equilibrium, are apt to distort causes and effects. Since I myself have been an inmate of a lunatic asylum, I cannot but notice that the sophistic tendencies of some of its
2 inmates lean towards the errors of *non causæ* and *ignoratio elenchi*." I positively opened my eyes at this new development. Here was my own pet lunatic—the most pronounced of his type that I had ever met with—talking elemental philosophy, and with the manner of a polished gentleman. I wonder if it was Mrs. Harker's presence which had touched some chord in his memory. If this new phase was spontaneous, or in any way due to her unconscious influence, she must have some rare gift or power.

We continued to talk for some time; and, seeing that he was seemingly quite reasonable, she ventured, looking at me questioningly as she began, to lead him to his favourite topic. I was again astonished, for he addressed himself to the question with the impartiality of the completest sanity; he even took himself as an example when he mentioned certain things.

"Why, I myself am an instance of a man who had a strange belief. Indeed, it was no wonder that my friends were alarmed, and insisted on my being put under control. I used to fancy that life was a positive and perpetual entity, and that by consuming a multitude of live things, no matter how low in the scale of creation, one might indefinitely prolong life. At times I held the belief so strongly that I actually tried to take human life. The doctor here will bear me out that on one occasion I tried to kill him for the purpose of strengthening my vital powers by the assimilation with my own body of his life through the medium of his blood—relying, of course, upon
the Scriptural phrase, 'For the blood is the life.' Though, 3
indeed, the vendor of a certain nostrum has vulgarised the 4
truism to the very point of contempt. Isn't that true, doctor?" I nodded assent, for I was so amazed that I hardly knew what to either think or say; it was hard to imagine that I had seen him eat up his spiders and flies not five minutes before. Looking at my watch, I saw that I should go to the station to meet Van Helsing, so I told Mrs. Harker that it was time to leave. She came at once, after saying pleasantly to Mr. Renfield: "Good-bye, and I hope I may see you often, under auspices pleasanter to yourself," to which, to my astonishment, he replied:—

"Good-bye, my dear. I pray God I may never see your sweet face again. May He bless and keep you!"

When I went to the station to meet Van Helsing I left the boys behind me. Poor Art seemed more cheerful than he has been since Lucy first took ill, and Quincey is more like his own bright self than he has been for many a long day.

Van Helsing stepped from the carriage with the eager nimbleness of a boy. He saw me at once, and rushed up to me, saying:—

"Ah, friend John, how goes all? Well? So! I have been busy, for I come here to stay if need be. All affairs are settled with me, and I have much to tell. Madam Mina is with you? Yes. And her so fine husband? And Arthur and my friend Quincey, they are with you, too? Good!"

As I drove to the house I told him of what had passed, and of how my own diary had come to be of some use through Mrs. Harker's suggestion; at which the Professor interrupted me:—

"Ah, that wonderful Madam Mina! She has man's brain—a brain that a man should have were he much gifted—and woman's heart. The good God fashioned her for a purpose, believe me, when He made that so good combination. Friend John, up to now fortune has made that woman of help to us; after to-night she must not have to do with this so terrible affair. It is not good that she run a risk so great. We men are determined—nay, are we not pledged?—to destroy this monster; but it is no part for a woman. Even if she be not harmed, her heart may fail her in so much and so many horrors; and hereafter she may suffer—both in waking, from her nerves, and in sleep, from her dreams. And, besides, she
is young woman and not so long married; there may be other 5
things to think of some time, if not now. You tell me she has wrote all, then she must consult with us; but to-morrow she say good-bye to this work, and we go alone." I agreed

3 *'For the blood is the life.'* In Seward's entry for September 17, we have seen Renfield, after an outburst of violence, finally quieted by his attendants to whom he repeats over and over again: "The blood is the life! the blood is the life!" (See chapter XI, note 17.)

4 *a certain nostrum.* The nostrum to which Renfield refers is surely "Hughes's Blood Pills," which, in an advertising brochure that accompanied the remedy, claimed that:

"The Blood being therefore the Life of the living Body, it stands to reason that if it is poisoned, you poison the whole system, and eventually destroy the life of the man. When the blood is chilled, or distempered through breathing impure air, unhealthy food, etc., it at once gets disturbed, and breeds disease in some form or other. This is the cause of Blast, Scurvy, Piles, Boils, King's Evil, Swollen Glands, Inflammation of the Eyes and Lids, Pains in the Sides, Back, and Kidneys, Cough, Bronchitis, Pleurisy, Rheumatism, Wounds in the Legs and Different Parts of the Body, all Scorbutic Affections, Cancer, Pimples on the Face, Neck, etc., and all Skin Eruptions, Chilliness, Headache, Indigestion, Fullness after Meals, Dyspepsia, Vomiting, Loss of Appetite, Consumption, Toothache, Neuralgia, Fits, St. Vitus's Dance, all Liver Complaints, Costiveness, Yellow Jaundice, Depression of Spirits, Stitches in the Sides, Fevers, Epidemics, Plagues, Gout, Nerve Diseases, Lumbago, Erysipelas, all kinds of Inflammation, and most Chest Diseases.

"The noted Pills, 'Hughes's Blood Pills,' act directly upon the Blood and Juices of all parts of the system, which they Strengthen and Purify. By so doing the Liver, Kidneys, Heart, Lungs, Stomach, Bowels, Brain and Nerves are renewed and toned to such a degree that their functions are perfectly performed, securing to the man healthy days."

The usual dose, according to the authors of the British Medical Association publication *Secret Remedies* (1909), was "one or two pills at night, or one three times a day." *Secret Remedies* gives the formula for the nostrum as follows:

"Aloes	0.7 grain
Jalap resin	0.2 "
Powdered chinchona bark	0.3 "
Powdered ginger	0.2 "
Oil of cloves	Trace

In one pill."

The pills were made in Wales and sold for one shilling, one and one-half pence for a box of thirty.

5 *there may be other things to think of some time.* Van Helsing is thinking of the probable effects on her child if Mina should become pregnant.

heartily with him, and then I told him what we had found in his absence: that the house which Dracula had bought was the very next one to my own. He was amazed, and a great concern seemed to come on him. "Oh that we had known it before!" he said, "for then we might have reached him in time to save poor Lucy. However, 'the milk that is spilt cries not out afterwards,' as you say. We shall not think of that, but go on our way to the end." Then he fell into a silence that lasted till we entered my own gateway. Before we went to prepare for dinner he said to Mrs. Harker:—

"I am told, Madam Mina, by my friend John that you and your husband have put up in exact order all things that have been, up to this moment."

"Not up to this moment, Professor," she said impulsively, "but up to this morning."

"But why not up to now? We have seen hitherto how good light all the little things have made. We have told our secrets, and yet no one who has told is the worse for it."

Mrs. Harker began to blush, and taking a paper from her pocket, she said:—

"Dr. Van Helsing, will you read this, and tell me if it must go in. It is my record of to-day. I too have seen the need of putting down at present everything, however trivial; but there is little in this except what is personal. Must it go in?" The Professor read it over gravely, and handed it back, saying:—

"It need not go in if you do not wish it; but I pray that it may. It can but make your husband love you the more, and all us, your friends, more honour you—as well as more esteem and love." She took it back with another blush and a bright smile.

And so now, up to this very hour, all the records we have are complete and in order. The Professor took away one copy to study after dinner, and before our meeting, which is fixed for nine o'clock. The rest of us have already read everything; so when we meet in the study we shall all be informed as to facts, and can arrange our plan of battle with this terrible and mysterious enemy.

Mina Harker's Journal.

30 *September.*—When we met in Dr. Seward's study two hours after dinner, which had been at six o'clock, we unconsciously formed a sort of board or committee. Professor Van Helsing took the head of the table, to which Dr. Seward motioned him as he came into the room. He made me sit next to him on his right, and asked me to act as secretary; Jonathan sat next to me. Opposite us were Lord Godalming, Dr. Seward, and Mr. Morris—Lord Godalming being next the Professor, and Dr. Seward in the centre. The Professor said:—

"I may, I suppose, take it that we are all acquainted with the facts that are in these papers." We all expressed assent, and he went on:—

"Then it were, I think good that I tell you something of the kind of enemy with which we have to deal. I shall then make known to you something of the history of this man, which has been ascertained for me. So we then can discuss how we shall act, and can take our measure according.

"There are such beings as vampires; some of us have evidence that they exist. Even had we not the proof of our own unhappy experience, the teachings and the records of the past give proof enough for sane peoples. I admit that at the first I was sceptic. Were it not that through long years I have train myself to keep an open mind, I could not have believe until such time as that fact thunder on my ear. 'See! see! I prove; I prove.' Alas! Had I known at the first what now I know—nay, had I even guess at him—one so precious life had been spared to many of us who did love her. But that is gone; and we must so work, that other poor souls perish not, whilst we can save. The *nosferatu* do not die like the bee when he sting once. He is only stronger; and being stronger, have yet more power to work evil. This vampire which is amongst us is of himself so strong in person as twenty men; he is of cunning more than mortal, for his cunning be the growth of ages; he have still the aids of necromancy, which is, as his etymology imply, the divination by the dead, and all the dead that he can come nigh to are for him at command; he is brute, and more than brute: he is devil in callous, and the heart of him is not; he can, within limitations, appear at will when, and where, and in any of the forms that are to him; he can, within his range, direct the elements: the storm, the fog, the thunder; he can command all the meaner things: the rat, and the owl, and the bat—the moth, and the fox, and the wolf; he can grow and become small; and he can at times vanish and come unknown.
How then are we to begin our strife to destroy him? How 6
shall we find his where; and having found it, how can we destroy? My friends, this is much; it is a terrible task that we undertake, and there may be consequence to make the brave shudder. For if we fail in this our fight he must surely win: and then where end we? Life is nothings; I heed him not. But to fail here, is not mere life or death. It is that we become as him; that we henceforward become foul things of the night like him—without heart or conscience, preying on the bodies and the souls of those we love best. To us for ever are the gates of heaven shut; for who shall open them to us again? We go on for all time abhorred by all; a blot on the face of God's sunshine; an arrow in the side of Him who died for man. But we are face to face with duty; and in such case must we shrink? For me, I say, no; but then I am old, and life, with his sunshine, his fair places, his song of birds, his music, and his love, lie far behind. You others are young. Some have seen sorrow; but there are fair days yet in store. What say you?"

Whilst he was speaking Jonathan had taken my hand. I feared, oh so much, that the appalling nature of our danger was overcoming him when I saw his hand stretch out; but it was life to me to feel its touch—so strong, so self-reliant, so

6 *How shall we find his where.* No doubt this locution is merely Van Helsing's Dutchism, but Stoker, who spent nearly thirty years in the theatre, may have remembered the duke of France's gracious words to Cordelia:

> "Fairest Cordelia, that art most rich, being poor;
> . . . .
> Thee and thy virtues here I seize upon:
> Not all the dukes of waterish Burgundy
> Shall buy this unpriz'd precious maid of me.
> Bid them farewell, Cordelia, though unkind:
> Thou losest here, a better where to find."
>
> (*King Lear*, Act I, Scene I, lines 253–64)

7 *Chersonese.* A Greek peninsula (Thrace) just west of the Hellespont.

resolute. A brave man's hand can speak for itself; it does not even need a woman's love to hear its music.

When the Professor had done speaking my husband looked in my eyes, and I in his; there was no need for speaking between us.

"I answer for Mina and myself," he said.

"Count me in, Professor," said Mr. Quincey Morris, laconically as usual.

"I am with you," said Lord Godalming, "for Lucy's sake, if for no other reason."

Dr. Seward simply nodded. The Professor stood up and, after laying his golden crucifix on the table, held out his hand on either side. I took his right hand, and Lord Godalming his left; Jonathan held my right with his left and stretched across to Mr. Morris. So as we all took hands our solemn compact was made. I felt my heart icy cold, but it did not even occur to me to draw back. We resumed our places, and Dr. Van Helsing went on with a sort of cheerfulness which showed that the serious work had begun. It was to be taken as gravely, and in as businesslike a way, as any other transaction of life:—

"Well, you know what we have to contend against; but we, too, are not without strength. We have on our side power of combination—a power denied to the vampire kind; we have resources of science; we are free to act and think; and the hours of the day and the night are ours equally. In fact, so far as our powers extend, they are unfettered, and we are free to use them. We have self-devotion in a cause, and an end to achieve which is not a selfish one. These things are much.

"Now let us see how far the general powers arrayed against us are restrict, and how the individual cannot. In fine, let us consider the limitations of the vampire in general, and of this one in particular.

"All we have to go upon are traditions and superstitions. These do not at the first appear much, when the matter is one of life and death—nay of more than either life or death. Yet must we be satisfied; in the first place because we have to be—no other means is at our control—and secondly, because, after all, these things—tradition and superstition—are everything. Does not the belief in vampires rest for others—though not, alas! for us—on them? A year ago which of us would have received such a possibility, in the midst of our scientific, sceptical, matter-of-fact nineteenth century? We even scouted a belief that we saw justified under our very eyes. Take it, then, that the vampire, and the belief in his limitations and his cure, rest for the moment on the same base. For, let me tell you, he is known everywhere that men have been. In old Greece, in old Rome; he flourish in
7 Germany all over, in France, in India, even in the Chersonese; and in China, so far from us in all ways, there even is he, and the peoples fear him at this day. He have follow the wake of the berserker Icelander, the devil-begotten Hun, the Slav, the Saxon, the Magyar. So far, then, we have all we may act upon; and let me tell you that very much of the beliefs are justified by what we have seen in our own so unhappy experience. The vampire live on, and cannot die by mere passing of the time; he can flourish when that he can

fatten on the blood of the living. Even more, we have seen amongst us that he can even grow younger; that his vital faculties grow strenuous, and seem as though they refresh themselves when his special pabulum is plenty. But he cannot flourish without this diet; he eat not as others. Even friend Jonathan, who lived with him for weeks, did never see him to eat, never! He throws no shadow; he make in the mirror no reflect, as again Jonathan observe. He has the strength of many in his hand—witness again Jonathan when he shut the door against the wolfs, and when he help him from the diligence too. He can transform himself to wolf, as we gather from the ship arrival in Whitby, when he tear open the dog; he can be as bat, as Madam Mina saw him on the window at Whitby, and as friend John saw him fly from this so near house, and as my friend Quincey saw him at the window of Miss Lucy. He can come in mist which he create—that noble ship's captain proved him of this; but, from what we know, the distance he can make this mist is limited, and it can only be round himself. He come on moonlight rays as elemental dust—as again Jonathan saw those sisters in the castle of Dracula. He become so small—we ourselves saw Miss Lucy, ere she was at peace, slip through a hairbreadth space at the tomb door. He can, when once he find his way, come out from anything or into anything, no matter how close it be bound or even fused up with fire —solder you call it. He can see in the dark—no small power this, in a world which is one half shut from the light. Ah, but hear me through. He can do all these things, yet he is not free. Nay; he is even more prisoner than the slave of the galley, than the madman in his cell. He cannot go where he lists; he who is not of nature has yet to obey some of nature's laws—why we know not. He may not enter anywhere at the first, unless there be some one of the household who bid him to come; though afterwards he can come as he please. His power ceases, as does that of all evil things, at the coming of the day. Only at certain times can he have limited freedom. If he be not at the place whither he is
bound, he can only change himself at noon or at exact sunrise **8**
or sunset. These things are we told, and in this record of ours we have proof by inference. Thus, whereas he can do as he will within his limit, when he have his earth-home, his coffin home, his hell-home, the place unhallowed, as we saw when he went to the grave of the suicide at Whitby; still at other time he can only change when the time come. It is said, too, that he can only pass running water at the slack or the flood of the tide. Then there are things which so afflict him that he has no power, as the garlic that we know of; and as for things sacred, as this symbol, my crucifix, that was amongst us even now when we resolve, to them he is nothing, but in their presence he take his place far off and silent with respect. There are others, too, which I shall tell you of, lest
in our seeking we may need them. The branch of wild rose **9**
on his coffin keep him that he move not from it; a sacred bullet fired into the coffin kill him so that he be true dead; and as for the stake through him, we know already of its peace; or the cut-off head that giveth rest. We have seen it with our eyes.

8 *at noon or at exact sunrise or sunset.* We see now why it was that Renfield's pattern of violence took the form that it did. His periods of excitement corresponded to the times of change in Dracula's day.

9 *The branch of wild rose.* In the language of flowers, the wild rose represents simplicity and modesty and can mean "I shall follow you everywhere!"

The rose, for obvious reasons, stands for beauty. In Greek mythology the rose was first made of the transformed body of a dead nymph, which Chloris, the deity of flowers, revived. Aphrodite presented the rose to Eros, the young god of love.

The antivampire properties of the wild rose may take their origin from the rose's general association with Christ. The true wild rose is rare in the Holy Land, but Christian tradition identifies it with the Rose of Sharon, which stands for Jesus who says: "*I am* the rose of Sharon, *and* the lily of the valleys" (Song of Songs 2:1).

Emily Gerard, in her *Land Beyond the Forest* (p. 186), tells us that in Transylvania "it is also very usual to lay the thorny branch of a wild rose bush across the body [of a dead person] to prevent it leaving the coffin."

"HE MUST, INDEED, HAVE BEEN THAT VOIVODE DRACULA."

"Thus when we find the habitation of this man-that-was, we
can confine him to his coffin and destroy him, if we obey
10 what we know. But he is clever. I have asked my friend
Arminius, of Buda-Pesth University, to make his record; and,
from all the means that are, he tell me of what he has been.
He must, indeed, have been that Voivode Dracula who won
his name against the Turk, over the great river on the very
frontier of Turkey-land. If it be so, then was he no common
man; for in that time, and for centuries after, he was spoken of
as the cleverest and the most cunning, as well as the bravest
11 of the sons of the 'land beyond the forest.' That mighty
brain and that iron resolution went with him to his grave, and
are even now arrayed against us. The Draculas were, says
Arminius, a great and noble race, though now and again were
scions who were held by their coevals to have had dealings with
12 the Evil One. They learned his secrets in the Scholomance,
13 amongst the mountains over Lake Hermanstadt, where the
devil claims the tenth scholar as his due. In the records are
such words as 'stregoica'—witch, 'ordog,' and 'pokol'—
Satan and hell; and in one manuscript this very Dracula is
14 spoken of as 'wampyr,' which we all understand too well.
There have been from the loins of this very one great men
and good women, and their graves make sacred the earth
where alone this foulness can dwell. For it is not the least of
its terrors that this evil thing is rooted deep in all good; in
15 soil barren of holy memories it cannot rest."
16 Whilst they were talking Mr. Morris was looking steadily
at the window, and he now got up quietly, and went out
of the room. There was a little pause, and then the Professor
went on:—

"And now we must settle what we do. We have here
much data, and we must proceed to lay out our campaign.
We know from the inquiry of Jonathan that from the castle
17 to Whitby came fifty boxes of earth, all of which were delivered
at Carfax; we also know that at least some of these boxes have
been removed. It seems to me, that our first step should be
to ascertain whether all the rest remain in the house beyond
that wall where we look to-day; or whether any more have been
removed. If the latter, we must trace——"

Here we were interrupted in a very startling way. Outside
18 the house came the sound of a pistol-shot; the glass of the
window was shattered with a bullet, which, ricochetting from
the top of the embrasure, struck the far wall of the room.
I am afraid I am at heart a coward, for I shrieked out. The
men all jumped to their feet; Lord Godalming flew over to
the window and threw up the sash. As he did so we heard
Mr. Morris's voice without:—

"Sorry! I fear I have alarmed you. I shall come in and tell you about it." A minute later he came in and said:—

"It was an idiotic thing of me to do, and I ask your pardon, Mrs. Harker, most sincerely; I fear I must have frightened you terribly. But the fact is that whilst the Professor was talking there came a big bat and sat on the window-sill. I have got such a horror of the damned brutes from recent events that I cannot stand them, and I went out to have a shot, as I have been doing of late of evenings whenever I have seen one. You used to laugh at me for it then, Art."

10 *my friend Arminius.* Harry Ludlam, Stoker's biographer, asserts that "Count Dracula began to stir in his tomb" on an evening in 1890 when Arminius Vambery, a professor of Oriental languages at the University of Budapest, "came to supper [with Stoker and others] in the Beefsteak Room. . . . Vambery, who wrote twelve languages, spoke sixteen, and knew twenty, had been to Central Asia, following after centuries in the track of Marco Polo. He was full of experiences fascinating to hear, and spoke of places where mystery and intense superstition still reigned. Places like Transylvania."

Vambery, according to Ludlam, enlarged Stoker's understanding of the historical Dracula, Vlad Ţepeş, or Vlad the Impaler.

Professors Florescu and McNally, in *In Search of Dracula,* while they repeat the tale of Arminius Vambery's help to Stoker, add that "unfortunately, no correspondence between Vambery and Stoker can be found today. Moreover, a search through all of the professor's published writings fails to reveal any comments on Vlad, Dracula, or vampires."

It does, however, seem likely that "my friend Arminius" is a compliment to the Hungarian.

11 *'land beyond the forest.'* Literally, Transylvania.

12 *Scholomance.* Stoker may have seen Emily Gerard's Victorian account of the Scholomance in her *Land Beyond the Forest* (p. 198):

"As I am on the subject of thunder-storms, I may as well here mention the *scholomance,* or school, supposed to exist somewhere in the heart of the mountains, and where the secrets of nature, the language of animals, and all magic spells are taught by the devil in person. Only ten scholars are admitted at a time, and when the course of learning has expired, and nine of them are released to return to

"Did you hit it?" asked Dr. Van Helsing.

"I don't know; I fancy not, for it flew away into the wood." Without saying any more he took his seat, and the Professor began to resume his statement:—

"We must trace each of these boxes; and when we are ready, we must either capture or kill this monster in his lair; or we must, so to speak, sterilise the earth, so that no more he can seek safety in it. Thus in the end we may find him in his form of man between the hours of noon and sunset, and so engage with him when he is at his most weak.

"And now for you, Madam Mina, this night is the end until all be well. You are too precious to us to have such risk. When we part to-night, you no more must question. We shall tell you all in good time. We are men, and are able to bear; but you must be our star and our hope, and we shall act all the more free that you are not in the danger, such as we are."

All the men, even Jonathan, seemed relieved; but it did not seem to me good that they should brave danger and, perhaps, lessen their safety—strength being the best safety—through care of me; but their minds were made up, and, though it was a bitter pill for me to swallow, I could say nothing, save to accept their chivalrous care of me.

Mr. Morris resumed the discussion:—

"As there is no time to lose, I vote we have a look at his house right now. Time is everything with him; and swift action on our part may save another victim."

I own that my heart began to fail me when the time for action came so close, but I did not say anything, for I had a greater fear that if I appeared as a drag or a hindrance to their work, they might even leave me out of their counsels altogether. They have now gone off to Carfax, with means to get into the house.

Manlike, they have told me to go to bed and sleep; as if a woman can sleep when those she loves are in danger! I shall lie down and pretend to sleep, lest Jonathan have added anxiety about me when he returns.

"THERE CAME A BIG BAT AND SAT ON THE WINDOW-SILL."

their homes, the tenth scholar is detained by the devil as payment, and, mounted upon an *ismeju*, or dragon, becomes henceforward the devil's aide-de-camp, and assists him in 'making the weather'—that is, preparing the thunder-bolts."

13 *Lake Hermanstadt.* According to Emily Gerard in her *Land Beyond the Forest*, "a small lake, immeasurably deep, and lying high up in the mountains to the south of Hermanstadt, is supposed to be the caldron where is brewed the thunder, under whose water the dragon lies sleeping in fair weather. Roumanian peasants anxiously warn the traveller to beware of throwing a stone into this lake, lest it should wake the dragon and provoke a thunderstorm."

Miss Gerard also tells us that the inhabitants of Hermanstadt are reputed to be the descendants of those children who followed the Pied Piper as he took his revenge against the pinchpenny burghers of Hamelin. (See map, p. 335.)

14 *spoken of as 'wampyr.'* There is a pamphlet in German about the monstrous deeds of Vlad the Impaler dated 1491. Professors Florescu and McNally tell us that "although the pamphlet does not describe Dracula as a *'wampyr,'* it does call him a cruel tyrant and *wütrich*, an old German term for 'berserker.' This presumably was Stoker's cue for transforming Dracula into a vampire."

15 *". . . soil barren of holy memories it cannot rest."* Van Helsing's remark raises an interesting question since it implies that Dracula, though allied with the Devil, is yet capable of Christian hope for his own salvation. Later, as we shall see, the vampire, who carries his boxes of hallowed soil with him, will turn out to have been both prudent and provident.

It is a very old Christian tradition to bury the dead in consecrated ground, though there is no Church dogma that requires such burial. Dracula, clinging to his consecrated soil, is behaving like a proper Christian.

The holiness of Dracula's soil creates problems for us, however. Why, if it is already sacred, is it subsequently necessary to "cleanse" it by making it even more sacred? (See chapter XXII, note 14.)

16 *looking steadily at the window.* Quincey Morris is a frequent window gazer. Presumably, this is part of his frontier American heritage. Stoker, no doubt, meant the trait to imply a huntsman's alertness. Ironically enough, this man of action rarely accomplishes anything.

17 *delivered.* Via King's Cross Station in London. (See chapter VIII, note 19.)

18 *a pistol-shot.* Quincey, the rambunctious American, and official bat-watcher of the group, bangs away with his six-shooter endangering his friends. As he says a moment later, "It was an idiotic thing of me to do."

19 *the Windham.* A club for gentlemen "connected with each other by a common bond of literary or personal acquaintance." The club was founded by Lord Nugent and housed in a former residence of William Windham.

20 *burnt rum punch.* One recipe, though probably not the elder Godalming's, appears in *The Art of British Cooking* by Theodora FitzGibbon. Here it is:

"5 lemons
½ pound lump sugar
1 piece of cinnamon stick
2 cups water
1 bottle rum

Rub lemons with the lumps of sugar until you have removed all the yellow zest. Put the lemony sugar into a saucepan with the lemon juice and the cinnamon stick; pour over the water and bring just to a boil. See that the lumps of sugar dissolve. Then add the rum, heat up, but do not boil, for fear of destroying the strength of the rum. Remove the cinnamon stick and serve hot."

21 *Derby night.* The famous Derby horse race was founded in 1780 by the twelfth earl of Derby. The race is run at Epsom on the Wednesday before, or the second Wednesday after, Whitsunday.

22 *into the Union.* Texas was admitted to the Union on December 29, 1845. Renfield's projection about the Pole and the Tropics has come true now that Hawaii and Alaska are both states of the Union.

23 *Monroe doctrine.* The doctrine promulgated in the first administration (1817–1821) of President James Monroe, which, in effect, warned the European Powers not to meddle in or attempt to control the destiny of the Spanish-American states in the Western Hemisphere. The Monroe Doctrine remained United States foreign policy for more than seventy years from 1823 to 1895.

Dr. Seward's Diary.

1 *October*, 4 *a.m.*—Just as we were about to leave the house, an urgent message was brought to me from Renfield to know if I would see him at once, as he had something of the utmost importance to say to me. I told the messenger to say that I would attend to his wishes in the morning; I was busy just at the moment. The attendant added:—

"He seems very importunate, sir. I have never seen him so eager. I don't know but what, if you don't see him soon, he will have one of his violent fits." I knew the man would not have said this without some cause, so I said: "All right; I'll go now;" and I asked the others to wait a few minutes for me, as I had to go and see my "patient."

"Take me with you, friend John," said the Professor. "His case in your diary interested me much, and it had bearing, too, now and again on *our* case. I should much like to see him, and especial when his mind is disturbed."

"May I come also?" asked Lord Godalming.

"Me too?" said Quincey Morris. I nodded, and we all went down the passage together.

We found him in a state of considerable excitement, but far more rational in his speech and manner than I had ever seen him. There was an unusual understanding of himself, which was unlike anything I had ever met with in a lunatic; and he took it for granted that his reasons would prevail with others entirely sane. We all four went into the room, but none of the others at first said anything. His request was that I would at once release him from the asylum and send him home. This he backed up with arguments regarding his complete recovery, and adduced his own existing sanity. "I appeal to your friends," he said; "they will, perhaps, not mind sitting in judgment on my case. By the way, you have not introduced me." I was so much astonished, that the oddness of introducing a madman in an asylum did not strike me at the moment; and, besides, there was a certain dignity in the man's manner, so much of the habit of equality, that I at once made the introduction: "Lord Godalming; Professor Van Helsing; Mr. Quincey Morris, of Texas; Mr. Renfield." He shook hands with each of them, saying in turn:—

"Lord Godalming, I had the honour of seconding your
19 father at the Windham; I grieve to know, by your holding
the title, that he is no more. He was a man loved and
honoured by all who knew him; and in his youth was, I
20 have heard, the inventor of a burnt rum punch, much
21 patronised on Derby night. Mr. Morris, you should be proud
22 of your great state. Its reception into the Union was a
precedent which may have far-reaching effects hereafter, when
the Pole and the Tropics may hold allegiance to the Stars
and Stripes. The power of Treaty may yet prove a vast engine
23 of enlargement, when the Monroe doctrine takes its true
place as a political fable. What shall any man say of his
pleasure at meeting Van Helsing? Sir, I make no apology for
dropping all forms of conventional prefix. When an individual
has revolutionised therapeutics by his discovery of the continuous evolution of brain-matter, conventional forms are

unfitting, since they would seem to limit him to one of a class. You, gentlemen, who by nationality, by heredity, or by the possession of natural gifts, are fitted to hold your respective places in the moving world, I take to witness that I am as sane as at least the majority of men who are in full possession of their liberties. And I am sure that you, Dr. Seward, humanitarian and medico-jurist as well as scientist, will deem it a moral duty to deal with me as one to be considered as under exceptional circumstances." He made this last appeal with a courtly air of conviction which was not without its own charm.

I think we were all staggered. For my own part, I was under the conviction. despite my knowledge of the man's character and history, that his reason had been restored; and I felt under a strong impulse to tell him that I was satisfied as to his sanity, and would see about the necessary formalities for his release in the morning. I thought it better to wait, however, before making so grave a statement, for of old I knew the sudden changes to which this particular patient was liable. So I contented myself with making a general statement that he appeared to be improving very rapidly; that I would have a longer chat with him in the morning, and would then see what I could do in the direction of meeting his wishes. This did not at all satisfy him, for he said quickly:—

"But I fear, Dr. Seward, that you hardly apprehend my wish. I desire to go at once—here—now—this very hour—this very moment, if I may. Time presses, and in our implied agreement with the old scytheman it is of the essence of the contract. I am sure it is only necessary to put before so admirable a practitioner as Dr. Seward so simple, yet so momentous a wish, to ensure its fulfilment." He looked at me keenly, and seeing the negative in my face, turned to the others, and scrutinised them closely. Not meeting any sufficient response, he went on:—

"Is it possible that I have erred in my supposition?"

"You have," I said frankly, but at the same time, as I felt, brutally. There was a considerable pause, and then he said slowly:—

"Then I suppose I must only shift my ground of request. Let me ask for this concession—boon, privilege, what you will. I am content to implore in such a case, not on personal grounds, but for the sake of others. I am not at liberty to give you the whole of my reasons; but you may, I assure you, take it from me that they are good ones, sound and unselfish, and springing from the highest sense of duty. Could you look, sir, into my heart, you would approve to the full the sentiments which animate me. Nay, more, you would count me amongst the best and truest of your friends." Again he looked at us all keenly. I had a growing conviction that this sudden change of his entire intellectual method was but yet another form or phase of his madness, and so determined to let him go on a little longer, knowing from experience that he would, like all lunatics, give himself away in the end. Van Helsing was gazing at him with a look of the utmost intensity, his bushy eyebrows almost meeting with the fixed concentration of his look. He said to Renfield in a tone which did not surprise me at the time, but only when I thought of it afterwards—for it was as of one addressing an equal :—

"Can you not tell frankly your real reason for wishing to be free to-night? I will undertake that if you will satisfy even me —a stranger, without prejudice, and with the habit of keeping an open mind—Dr. Seward will give you, at his own risk and on his own responsibility, the privilege you seek." He shook his head sadly, and with a look of poignant regret on his face. The Professor went on :—

"Come, sir, bethink yourself. You claim the privilege of reason in the highest degree, since you seek to impress us with your complete reasonableness. You do this, whose sanity we have reason to doubt, since you are not yet released from medical treatment for this very defect. If you will not help us in our effort to choose the wisest course, how can we perform the duty which you yourself put upon us? Be wise, and help us; and if we can we shall aid you to achieve your wish." He still shook his head as he said :—

"Dr. Van Helsing, I have nothing to say. Your argument is complete, and if I were free to speak I should not hesitate a moment; but I am not my own master in the matter. I can only ask you to trust me. If I am refused, the responsibility does not rest with me." I thought it was now time to end the scene, which was becoming too comically grave, so I went towards the door, simply saying :—

"Come, my friends, we have work to do. Good-night."

As, however, I got near the door, a new change came over the patient. He moved towards me so quickly that for the moment I feared that he was about to make another homicidal attack. My fears, however, were groundless, for he held up his two hands imploringly, and made his petition in a moving manner. As he saw that the very excess of his emotion was militating against him, by restoring us more to our old relations, he became still more demonstrative. I glanced at Van Helsing, and saw my conviction reflected in his eyes; so I became a little more fixed in my manner, if not more stern, and motioned to him that his efforts were unavailing. I had previously seen something of the same constantly growing excitement in him when he had to make some request of which at the time he had thought much, such, for instance, as when he wanted a cat; and I was prepared to see the collapse into the same sullen acquiescence on this occasion. My expectation was not realised, for, when he found that his appeal would not be successful, he got into quite a frantic condition. He threw himself on his knees, and held up his hands, wringing them in plaintive supplication, and poured forth a torrent of entreaty, with the tears rolling down his cheeks and his whole face and form expressive of the deepest emotion :—

"Let me entreat you, Dr. Seward, oh, let me implore you, to let me out of this house at once. Send me away how you will and where you will; send keepers with me with whips and chains; let them take me in a strait-waistcoat, manacled and leg-ironed, even to a gaol; but let me go out of this. You don't know what you do by keeping me here. I am speaking from the depths of my heart—of my very soul. You don't know whom you wrong, or how; and I may not tell. Woe is me! I may not tell. By all you hold sacred—by all you hold dear—by your love that is lost—by your hope that lives—for the sake of the Almighty, take me out of this and save my soul from guilt! Can't you hear me, man? Can't you understand? Will you never learn? Don't you know that I am sane and earnest now; that I am no lunatic in a mad fit, but a sane man fighting for his soul? Oh, hear me! hear me! Let me go! let me go! let me go!"

I thought that the longer this went on the wilder he would get, and so would bring on a fit; so I took him by the hand and raised him up.

"Come," I said sternly, "no more of this; we have had quite enough already. Get to your bed and try to behave more discreetly."

He suddenly stopped and looked at me intently for several moments. Then, without a word, he rose and moving over, sat down on the side of the bed. The collapse had come, as on former occasions, just as I had expected.

When I was leaving the room, last of our party, he said to me in a quiet, well-bred voice :— **24**

"You will, I trust, Dr. Seward, do me the justice to bear in mind, later on, that I did what I could to convince you to-night."

24 *in a quiet, well-bred voice.* We are not told what it is that has made Renfield suddenly sane, though it is reasonable to suppose that his concern for Mina is an important element in his recovery. It may be, too, that, having seen the Wicked One steady and whole has dissipated the more trivial miasmas of insanity.

CHAPTER XIX.

Jonathan Harker's Journal.

1 *October*, 5 *a.m.*—I went with the party to the search with an easy mind, for I think I never saw Mina so absolutely strong and well. I am so glad that she consented to hold back and let us men do the work. Somehow, it was a dread to me that she was in this fearful business at all; but now that her work is done, and that it is due to her energy and brains and foresight that the whole story is put together in such a way that every point tells, she may well feel that her part is finished, and that she can henceforth leave the rest to us. We were, I think, all a little upset by the scene with Mr. Renfield. When we came away from his room we were silent till we got back to the study. Then Mr. Morris said to Dr. Seward:—

"Say, Jack, if that man wasn't attempting a bluff, he is about the sanest lunatic I ever saw. I'm not sure, but I believe that he had some serious purpose, and if he had, it was pretty rough on him not to get a chance." Lord Godalming and I were silent, but Dr. Van Helsing added:—

"Friend John, you know more of lunatics than I do, and I'm glad of it, for I fear that if it had been to me to decide I would before that last hysterical outburst have given him free. But we live and learn, and in our present task we must take no chance, as my friend Quincey would say. All is best as they are." Dr. Seward seemed to answer them both in a dreamy kind of way:—

"I don't know but that I agree with you. If that man had been an ordinary lunatic I would have taken my chance of
1 trusting him; but he seems so mixed up with the Count in an indexy kind of way that I am afraid of doing anything wrong by helping his fads. I can't forget how he prayed with almost equal fervour for a cat, and then tried to tear my throat out

1 *in an indexy kind of way.* Dr. Seward has not yet been able to link what Van Helsing has said about a vampire's behavior at sunrise and noon (p. 213) with his own observations of Renfield's periods of excitement.

with his teeth. Besides, he called the Count 'lord and master,' and he may want to get out to help him in some diabolical way. That horrid thing has the wolves and the rats and his own kind to help him, so I suppose he isn't above trying to use a respectable lunatic. He certainly did seem earnest, though. I only hope we have done what is best. These things, in conjunction with the wild work we have in hand, help to unnerve a man." The Professor stepped over, and laying his hand on his shoulder, said in his grave, kindly way:—

"Friend John, have no fear. We are trying to do our duty in a very sad and terrible case; we can only do as we deem best. What else have we to hope for, except the pity of the good God?" Lord Godalming had slipped away for a few minutes, but he now returned. He held up a little silver whistle as he remarked:—

"That old place may be full of rats, and if so, I've got an antidote on call." Having passed the wall, we took our way to the house, taking care to keep in the shadows of the trees on the lawn when the moonlight shone out. When we got to the porch the Professor opened his bag and took out a lot of things, which he laid on the step, sorting them into four little groups, evidently one for each. Then he spoke:—

"My friends, we are going into a terrible danger, and we need arms of many kinds. Our enemy is not merely spiritual. Remember that he has the strength of twenty men, and that, though our necks or our windpipes are of the common kind—and therefore breakable or crushable—his are not amenable to mere strength. A stronger man, or a body of men more strong in all than him, can at certain times hold him; but yet they cannot hurt him as we can be hurt by him. We must, therefore, guard ourselves from his touch. Keep this near your heart"—as he spoke he lifted a little silver crucifix and held it out to me, I being nearest to him—"put these flowers round your neck"—here he handed to me a wreath of withered garlic blossoms—"for other enemies more mundane, this revolver and this knife; and for aid in all, these so small electric lamps, which you can fasten to your breast; and for all, and above all at the last, this, which we must not desecrate needless." This was a portion of sacred wafer, which he put in an envelope and handed to me. Each of the others was similarly equipped. "Now," he said, "friend John, where are the skeleton keys? If so that we can open the door, we need not break house by the window, as before at Miss Lucy's."

Dr. Seward tried one or two skeleton keys, his mechanical dexterity as a surgeon standing him in good stead. Presently he got one to suit; after a little play back and forward the bolt yielded, and, with a rusty clang, shot back. We pressed on the door, the rusty hinges creaked, and it slowly opened. It was startlingly like the image conveyed to me in Dr. Seward's diary of the opening of Miss Westenra's tomb; I fancy that the same idea seemed to strike the others, for with one accord they shrank back. The Professor was the first to move forward, and stepped into the open door.

2 "In manus tuas, Domine!" "Into thy hand, oh Lord." See Luke 23:46, where we read: "And when Jesus had cried with a loud voice, he said, Father, into thy hands I commend my spirit: and having said thus, he gave up the ghost."

3 *gloated.* This is a strange use of the word "gloated," which, normally, is the past tense of the verb "to gloat." Stoker may have written "bloated" which would make the "g" a typographer's error.

The Rider Edition of *Dracula* (1912), on which the Arrow Edition is based, has "glutted," which seems a good emendation.

4 *intensified its loathesomeness.* Stoker was haunted by such odors. Compare this to his later, even more explicit description of the smell in the serpent's hole in *The Lair of the White Worm*, where he writes (p. 117): "[The smell] was like nothing that Adam had ever met with. He compared it with all the noxious experiences he had ever had—the drainage of war hospitals, of slaughterhouses, the refuse of dissecting rooms—the sourness of chemical waste and the poisonous effluvium of the bilge of a water-logged ship whereon a multitude of rats had been drowned."

In fairness to Stoker, it should be noted that Montague Summers in *The Vampire: His Kith and Kin* (p. 179) asserts that bad breath is a vampire characteristic: "His [the vampire's] breath is unbearably fetid and rank with corruption, the stench of the charnel."

2 "*In manus tuas, Domine!*" he said, crossing himself as he passed over the threshold. We closed the door behind us, lest when we should have lit our lamps we should possibly attract attention from the road. The Professor carefully tried the lock, lest we might not be able to open it from within should we be in a hurry making our exit. Then we all lit our lamps and proceeded on our search.

The light from the tiny lamps fell in all sorts of odd forms, as the rays crossed each other, or the opacity of our bodies threw great shadows. I could not for my life get away from the feeling that there was some one else amongst us. I suppose it was the recollection, so powerfully brought home to me by the grim surroundings, of that terrible experience in Transylvania. I think the feeling was common to us all, for I noticed that the others kept looking over their shoulders at every sound and every new shadow, just as I felt myself doing.

The whole place was thick with dust. The floor was seemingly inches deep, except where there were recent footsteps, in which on holding down my lamp I could see marks of hobnails where the dust was caked. The walls were fluffy and heavy with dust, and in the corners were masses of spiders' webs, whereon the dust had gathered till they looked like old tattered rags as the weight had torn them partly down. On a table in the hall was a great bunch of keys, with a time-yellowed label on each. They had been used several times, for on the table were several similar rents in the blanket of dust, similar to that exposed when the Professor lifted them. He turned to me and said:—

"You know this place, Jonathan. You have copied maps of it, and you know at least more than we do. Which is the way to the chapel?" I had an idea of its direction, though on my former visit I had not been able to get admission to it; so I led the way, and after a few wrong turnings found myself opposite a low, arched oaken door, ribbed with iron bands. "This is the spot," said the Professor as he turned his lamp on a small map of the house, copied from the file of my original correspondence regarding the purchase. With a little trouble we found the key on the bunch and opened the door. We were prepared for some unpleasantness, for as we were opening the door a faint, malodorous air seemed to exhale through the gaps, but none of us ever expected such an odour as we encountered. None of the others had met the Count at all at close quarters, and when I had seen him he was either in the fasting stage of his existence in his rooms or,
3 when he was gloated with fresh blood, in a ruined building open to the air; but here the place was small and close, and the long disuse had made the air stagnant and foul. There was an earthy smell, as of some dry miasma, which came through the fouler air. But as to the odour itself, how shall I describe it? It was not alone that it was composed of all the ills of mortality and with the pungent, acrid smell of blood, but it seemed as though corruption had become itself corrupt. Faugh! it sickens me to think of it. Every breath exhaled by that monster seemed to have clung to the place
4 and intensified its loathsomeness.

Under ordinary circumstances such a stench would have

brought our enterprise to an end; but this was no ordinary case, and the high and terrible purpose in which we were involved gave us a strength which rose above merely physical considerations. After the involuntary shrinking consequent on the first nauseous whiff, we one and all set about our work as though that loathsome place were a garden of roses.

We made an accurate examination of the place, the Professor saying as we began :—

"The first thing is to see how many of the boxes are left; we must then examine every hole and corner and cranny, and see if we cannot get some clue as to what has become of the rest." A glance was sufficient to show how many remained, for the great earth chests were bulky, and there was no mistaking them.

There were only twenty-nine left out of the fifty! Once I got a fright, for, seeing Lord Godalming suddenly turn and look out of the vaulted door into the dark passage beyond, I looked too, and for an instant my heart stood still. Somewhere, looking out from the shadow, I seemed to see the high lights of the Count's evil face, the ridge of the nose, the red eyes, the red lips, the awful pallor. It was only for a moment, for, as Lord Godalming said, "I thought I saw a face, but it was only the shadows," and resumed his inquiry, I turned my lamp in the direction, and stepped into the passage. There was no sign of any one; and as there were no corners, no doors, no aperture of any kind, but only the solid walls of the passage, there could be no hiding-place even for *him*. I took 5
it that fear had helped imagination, and said nothing.

A few minutes later I saw Morris step suddenly back from a corner, which he was examining. We all followed his movements with our eyes, for undoubtedly some nervousness was growing on us, and we saw a whole mass of phosphorescence, which twinkled like stars. We all instinctively drew back. The whole place was becoming alive with rats. 6

For a moment or two we stood appalled, all save Lord Godalming, who was seemingly prepared for such an emergency. Rushing over to the great iron-bound oaken door, which Dr. Seward had described from the outside, and which I had seen myself, he turned the key in the lock, drew the huge bolts, and swung the door open. Then, taking his little silver whistle from his pocket, he blew a low, shrill call. It was answered from behind Dr. Seward's house by the yelping of dogs, and after about a minute three 7
terriers came dashing round the corner of the house. Unconsciously we had all moved towards the door, and as we moved I noticed that the dust had been much disturbed: the boxes which had been taken out had been brought this way. But even in the minute that had elapsed the number of the rats had vastly increased. They seemed to swarm over the place all at once, till the lamplight, shining on their moving dark bodies and glittering, baleful eyes, made the place look like a bank of earth set with fireflies. The dogs dashed on, but at the threshold suddenly stopped and snarled, and then, simultaneously lifting their noses, began to howl in most lugubrious fashion. The rats were multiplying in thousands, and we moved out.

5 *even for* him. Harker has forgotten how in chapter III (p. 42) the vampire sisters "simply seemed to fade into the rays of the moonlight and pass out through the window . . ."

He has also forgotten Dr. Van Helsing's lecture on the attributes of the vampire (p. 213) where Van Helsing says: "He can, when once he find his way, come out from anything or into anything, no matter how close it be bound . . ."

6 *alive with rats.* These would have to be Norway rats, since the native British black rat was all but extinct in the British Isles by the end of the nineteenth century, according to Charles Gould in his *Mythical Monsters* (1886).

Rats and mice were said to be related to death. Christina Hole, in her *English Folklore* (pp. 84–89), says that "sometimes the soul would leave the body during sleep, and in such cases it often took the form of a mouse or a bee. . . . Both rats and mice were thought to have foreknowledge of disaster. If all the rats suddenly left a house it was a sign the building was unsound and would fall."

A commonplace of folk wisdom has it that rats will leave a sinking ship, and Miss Hole cites several instances of the truth of the adage.

Stoker did not need to go very far afield for the imagery of this scene. Browning's *Pied Piper of Hamelyn* no doubt sufficed.

Charles Gould reports that "the ancient work Chin-y-king speaks of [a rat which equals an elephant in size] in these terms: 'There is in the depths of the north a rat which weighs as much as a thousand pounds; its flesh is very good for those who are heated.' "

Stoker was either haunted by rats or else he recognized their special power in works of terror. They appear with great effectiveness in the posthumous collection of his tales called *Dracula's Guest*, particularly in "The Judge's House," but elsewhere in that volume as well.

7 *three terriers.* Probably "black-and-tan" terriers. These terriers were such skillful rat killers that bets were placed on the time it took them to kill a certain number of rats. The *World Encyclopedia of Dogs* cites one terrier that killed one hundred rats in six minutes and thirty-two seconds.

Lord Godalming lifted one of the dogs, and carrying him in, placed him on the floor. The instant his feet touched the ground he seemed to recover his courage, and rushed at his natural enemies. They fled before him so fast that before he had shaken the life out of a score, the other dogs, who had by now been lifted in in the same manner, had but small prey ere the whole mass had vanished.

With their going it seemed as if some evil presence had departed, for the dogs frisked about and barked merrily as they made sudden darts at their prostrate foes, and turned them over and over and tossed them in the air with vicious shakes. We all seemed to find our spirits rise. Whether it was the purifying of the deadly atmosphere by the opening of the chapel door, or the relief which we experienced by finding ourselves in the open I know not; but most certainly the shadow of dread seemed to slip from us like a robe, and the occasion of our coming lost something of its grim significance, though we did not slacken a whit in our resolution. We closed the outer door and barred and locked it, and bringing the dogs with us, began our search of the house. We found nothing throughout except dust in extraordinary proportions, and all untouched save for my own footsteps when I had made my first visit. Never once did the dogs exhibit any symptom of uneasiness, and even when we returned to the chapel they frisked about as though they had been rabbit-hunting in a summer wood.

The morning was quickening in the east when we emerged from the front. Dr. Van Helsing had taken the key of the hall-door from the bunch, and locked the door in orthodox fashion, putting the key into his pocket when he had done.

"So far," he said, "our night has been eminently successful. No harm has come to us such as I feared might be, and yet we have ascertained how many boxes are missing. More than all do I rejoice that this, our first—and perhaps our most difficult and dangerous—step has been accomplished without the bringing thereinto our most sweet Madam Mina or troubling her waking or sleeping thoughts with sights and sounds and smells of horror which she might never forget. One lesson, too, we have learned, if it be allowable to argue *a particulari*: that the brute beasts which are to the Count's command are yet themselves not amenable to his spiritual power; for look, these rats that would come to his call, just as from his castle top he summon the wolves to your going and to that poor mother's cry, though they come to him, they run pell-mell from the so little dogs of my friend Arthur. We have other matters before us, other dangers, other fears; and that monster—he has not used his power over the brute world for the only or the last time to-night. So be it that he has gone elsewhere. Good! It has given us opportunity to cry 8
'check' in some ways in this chess game, which we play for the stake of human souls. And now let us go home. The dawn is close at hand, and we have reason to be content with our first night's work. It may be ordained that we have many

". . . WE SAW A WHOLE MASS OF PHOSPHORESCENCE WHICH TWINKLED LIKE STARS. WE ALL INSTINCTIVELY DREW BACK. THE PLACE WAS BECOMING ALIVE WITH RATS."

8 *to cry 'check.'* See the other chess reference in chapter XII, note 4.

9 *Renfield's room.* Renfield's moaning, the distant screaming, and Mina's pallor and soft breathing make an ironic *obbligato,* emphasizing how far from "eminently successful" the night has been for the forces of good.

10 *for a woman to bear.* The absurd male belief in the weakness of the female compounds Harker's disaster. He and the other men repeatedly underestimate Mina's strength.

11 *might be worse.* Concealment, as it turns out, *is* worse. It may be argued that Van Helsing's long reticence about the facts in Lucy's case helped to precipitate her disaster, too.

12 *our work is to be a sealed book.* The decision *not* to share their confidences with Mina will have heavy consequences.

nights and days to follow, if full of peril; but we must go on, and from no danger shall we shrink."

The house was silent when we got back, save for some poor creature who was screaming away in one of the distant wards,
9 and a low, moaning sound from Renfield's room. The poor wretch was doubtless torturing himself, after the manner of the insane, with needless thoughts of pain.

I came tiptoe into our own room, and found Mina asleep, breathing so softly that I had to put my ear down to hear it. She looks paler than usual. I hope the meeting to-night has not upset her. I am truly thankful that she is to be left out of our future work, and even of our deliberations. It is too
10 great a strain for a woman to bear. I did not think so at first, but I know better now. Therefore I am glad that it is settled. There may be things which would frighten her to
11 hear; and yet to conceal them from her might be worse than to tell her if once she suspected that there was any con-
12 cealment. Henceforth our work is to be a sealed book to her, till at least such time as we can tell her that all is finished, and the earth free from a monster of the nether world. I daresay it will be difficult to begin to keep silence after such confidence as ours; but I must be resolute, and to-morrow I shall keep dark over to-night's doings, and shall refuse to speak of anything that has happened. I rest on the sofa, so as not to disturb her.

1 *October, later.*—I suppose it was natural that we should have all overslept ourselves, for the day was a busy one, and the night had no rest at all. Even Mina must have felt its exhaustion, for though I slept till the sun was high, I was awake before her, and had to call two or three times before she awoke. Indeed, she was so sound asleep that for a few seconds she did not recognise me, but looked at me with a sort of blank terror, as one looks who has been waked out of a bad dream. She complained a little of being tired, and I let her rest till later in the day. We now know of twenty-one boxes having been removed, and if it be that several were taken in any of these removals we may be able to trace them all. Such will, of course, immensely simplify our labour, and the sooner the matter is attended to the better. I shall look up Thomas Snelling to-day.

Dr. Seward's Diary.

1 *October.*—It was towards noon when I was awakened by the Professor walking into my room. He was more jolly and cheerful than usual, and it is quite evident that last night's work has helped to take some of the brooding weight off his mind. After going over the adventure of the night he suddenly said:—

"Your patient interests me much. May it be that with you I visit him this morning? Or if that you are too occupy, I can go alone if it may be. It is a new experience to me to find a lunatic who talk philosophy, and reason so sound." I had some work to do which pressed, so I told him that if he would go alone I would be glad, as then I should not have to keep him waiting; so I called an attendant and gave him the necessary instructions. Before the Professor left the room I cautioned him against getting any false impression from my patient. "But," he answered, "I want him to talk of himself and of his delusion as to consuming live things. He said to Madam Mina, as I see in your diary of yesterday, that he had once had such a belief. Why do you smile, friend John?"

"Excuse me," I said, "but the answer is here." I laid my hand on the type-written matter. "When our sane and learned lunatic made that very statement of how he *used* to consume life, his mouth was actually nauseous with the flies and spiders which he had eaten just before Mrs. Harker entered the room." Van Helsing smiled in turn. "Good!" he said. "Your memory is true, friend John. I should have remembered. And yet it is this very obliquity of thought and memory which makes mental disease such a fascinating study. Perhaps I may gain more knowledge out of the folly of this madman than I shall from the teaching of the most wise. Who knows?" I went on with my work, and before long was through that in hand. It seemed that the time had been very short indeed, but there was Van Helsing back in the study. "Do I interrupt?" he asked politely as he stood at the door.

"Not at all," I answered. "Come in. My work is finished, and I am free. I can go with you now, if you like."

"It is needless; I have seen him!"

"Well?"

"I fear that he does not appraise me at much. Our interview was short. When I entered his room he was sitting on a stool in the centre, with his elbows on his knees, and his face was the picture of sullen discontent. I spoke to him as cheerfully as I could, and with such a measure of respect as I could assume. He made no reply whatever. "Don't you know me?" I asked. His answer was not reassuring: "I know you well enough; you are the old fool Van Helsing. I wish you would take yourself and your idiotic brain theories somewhere else. Damn all thick-headed Dutchmen!" Not a word more would he say, but sat in his implacable sullenness as indifferent to me as though I had not been in the room at all. Thus departed for this time my chance of much learning from this so clever lunatic; so I shall go, if I may, and cheer myself with a few happy words with that sweet soul Madam Mina. Friend John, it does rejoice me unspeakable that she is no more to be pained, no more to be worried, with our terrible things. Though we shall much miss her help, it is better so."

"I agree with you with all my heart," I answered earnestly, for I did not want him to weaken in this matter. "Mrs. Harker is better out of it. Things are quite bad enough for us, all men of the world, and who have been in many tight places in our time; but it is no place for a woman, and if she had remained in touch with the affair, it would in time infallibly have wrecked her."

So Van Helsing has gone to confer with Mrs. Harker and Harker; Quincey and Art are all out following up the clues as to the earth-boxes. I shall finish my round of work, and we shall meet to-night.

Mina Harker's Journal.

1 *October.*—It is strange to me to be kept in the dark as I

13 *low-spirited to-day.* Mina, the morning after the Count's first nuptial visit, is depressed, and guilt-ridden, unlike Lucy, who, it will be remembered, slept well for the first time in many weeks (p. 94). Surely this is because Mina is a married woman.

am to-day; after Jonathan's full confidence for so many years, to see him manifestly avoid certain matters, and those the most vital of all. This morning I slept late after the fatigues of yesterday, and though Jonathan was late too, he was the earlier. He spoke to me before he went out, never more sweetly or tenderly, but he never mentioned a word of what had happened in the visit to the Count's house. And yet he must have known how terribly anxious I was. Poor dear fellow! I suppose it must have distressed him even more than it did me. They all agreed that it was best that I should not be drawn further into this awful work, and I acquiesced. But to think that he keeps anything from me! And now I am crying like a silly fool, when I *know* it comes from my husband's great love and from the good, good wishes of those other strong men. . . . .

That has done me good. Well, some day Jonathan will tell me all; and lest it should ever be that he should think for a moment that I kept anything from him, I still keep my journal as usual. Then if he has feared of my trust I shall show it to him, with every thought of my heart put down for his dear
13 eyes to read. I feel strangely sad and low-spirited to-day. I suppose it is the reaction from the terrible excitement.

Last night I went to bed when the men had gone, simply because they told me to. I didn't feel sleepy, and I did feel full of devouring anxiety. I kept thinking over everything that has been ever since Jonathan came to see me in London, and it all seems like a horrible tragedy, with fate pressing on relentlessly to some destined end. Everything that one does seems, no matter how right it may be, to bring on the very thing which is most to be deplored. If I hadn't gone to Whitby, perhaps poor dear Lucy would be with us now. She hadn't taken to visiting the churchyard till I came, and if she hadn't come there in the day-time with me she wouldn't have walked there in her sleep; and if she hadn't gone there at night and asleep, that monster couldn't have destroyed her as he did. Oh, why did I ever go to Whitby? There now, crying again! I wonder what has come over me to-day. I must hide it from Jonathan, for if he knew that I had been crying twice in one morning—I, who never cried on my own account, and whom he has never caused to shed a tear—the dear fellow would fret his heart out. I shall put a bold face on, and if I do feel weepy, he shall never see it. I suppose it is one of the lessons that we poor women have to learn. . . . .

I can't quite remember how I fell asleep last night. I remember hearing the sudden barking of the dogs and a lot of queer sounds, like praying on a very tumultuous scale, from Mr. Renfield's room, which is somewhere under this. And then there was silence over everything, silence so profound that it startled me, and I got up and looked out of the window. All was dark and silent, the black shadows thrown by the moonlight seeming full of a silent mystery of their own. Not a thing seemed to be stirring, but all to be grim and fixed as death or fate; so that a thin streak of white mist, that crept with almost imperceptible slowness across the grass towards the house, seemed to have a sentience and a vitality of its own. I think that the digression of my thoughts must have done me good, for when I got back to bed I found a lethargy creeping over me. I lay a while, but could not quite sleep, so I got out and looked out of the window again. The mist was spreading, and was now close up to the house, so that I could see it lying thick against the wall, as though it were stealing up to the windows. The poor man was more loud than ever, and though I could not distinguish a word he said, I could in some way recognise in his tones some passionate entreaty on his part. Then there was the sound of a struggle, and I knew that the attendants were dealing with him. I was so frightened that I crept into bed, and pulled the clothes over my head, putting my fingers in my ears. I was not then a bit sleepy, at least so I thought; but I must have fallen asleep, for, except dreams, I do not remember anything until the morning, when Jonathan woke me. I think that it took me an effort and a little time to realise where I was, and that it was Jonathan who was bending over me. My dream was very peculiar, and was almost typical of the way that waking thoughts become merged in, or continued in, dreams.

I thought that I was asleep, and waiting for Jonathan to come back. I was very anxious about him, and I was powerless to act; my feet, and my hands, and my brain were weighted, so that nothing could proceed at the usual pace. And so I slept uneasily and thought. Then it began to dawn upon me that the air was heavy, and dank, and cold. I put back the clothes from my face, and found, to my surprise, that all was dim around me. The gas-light which I had left lit for Jonathan, but turned down, came only like a tiny red spark through the fog, which had evidently grown thicker and poured into the room. Then it occurred to me that I had shut the window before I had come to bed. I would have got out to make certain on the point, but some leaden lethargy seemed to chain my limbs and even my will. I lay still and endured; that was all. I closed my eyes, but could still see through my eyelids. (It is wonderful what tricks our dreams play us, and how conveniently we can imagine.) The mist grew thicker and thicker, and I could see now how it came in, for I could see it like smoke—or with the white energy of boiling water—pouring in, not through the window, but through the joinings of the door. It got thicker and thicker, till it seemed as if it became concentrated into a sort of pillar of cloud in the room, through the top of which I could see the light of the gas shining like a red eye. Things began to whirl through my brain just as the cloudy column was now whirling in the room, and through it all came the scriptural words "a pillar of cloud by day and of fire by night." Was it indeed 14
some such spiritual guidance that was coming to me in my sleep? But the pillar was composed of both the day and the night-guiding, for the fire was in the red eye, which at the thought got a new fascination for me; till, as I looked, the fire divided, and seemed to shine on me through the fog like two red eyes, such as Lucy told me of in her momentary mental wandering when, on the cliff, the dying sunlight struck the windows of St. Mary's Church. Suddenly the horror burst upon me that it was thus that Jonathan had seen those awful women growing into reality through the whirling mist in the

14 "*. . . of cloud by day and of fire by night.*" The pillar of cloud by day and fire by night are described in Exodus 40:34–38 as follows:

> "Then a cloud covered the tent of the congregation, and the glory of the Lord filled the tabernacle.
>
> "And Moses was not able to enter into the tent of the congregation, because the cloud abode thereon, and the glory of the Lord filled the tabernacle.
>
> "And when the cloud was taken up from over the tabernacle, the children of Israel went onward in all their journeys:
>
> "But if the cloud were not taken up, then they journeyed not till the day that it was taken up.
>
> "For the cloud of the Lord *was* upon the tabernacle by day, and fire was on it by night, in the sight of all the house of Israel, throughout all their journeys."

At this point there is an exquisite confusion in Mina's dream. Dracula's cloud and fire present themselves to her as hints of a "spiritual guidance," but as her dream fades, instead of God's face, it is the demon's that emerges from the mist and fire.

The erotic content of this scene is unavoidable. Mina is overwhelmed by a lassitude similar to that of her husband Jonathan upon encountering the three women. Like Jonathan, though she "lay still and endured," she also peeps out from behind closed eyelashes at the demon lover advancing in the mist.

moonlight, and in my dream I must have fainted, for all became black darkness. The last conscious effort which imagination made was to show me a livid white face bending over me out of the mist. I must be careful of such dreams, for they would unseat one's reason if there were too much of them. I would get Dr. Van Helsing or Dr. Seward to prescribe something for me which would make me sleep, only that I fear to alarm them. Such a dream at the present time would become woven into their fears for me. To-night I shall strive hard to sleep naturally. If I do not, I shall to-morrow night get them to give me a dose of chloral; that cannot hurt me for once, and it will give me a good night's sleep. Last night tired me more than if I had not slept at all.

2 October, 10 *p.m.*—Last night I slept, but did not dream. I must have slept soundly, for I was not waked by Jonathan coming to bed; but the sleep has not refreshed me, for to-day I feel terribly weak and spiritless. I spent all yesterday trying to read, or lying down dozing. In the afternoon Mr. Renfield asked if he might see me. Poor man, he was very gentle, and when I came away he kissed my hand and bade God bless me. Some way it affected me much; I am crying when I think of him. This is a new weakness, of which I must be careful. Jonathan would be miserable if he knew I had been crying. He and the others were out until dinner-time, and they all came in tired. I did what I could to brighten them up, and I suppose that the effort did me good, for I forgot how tired I was. After dinner they sent me to bed, and all went off to smoke together, as they said, but I knew that they wanted to tell each other of what had occurred to each during the day; I could see from Jonathan's manner that he had something important to communicate. I was not so sleepy as I should have been; so before they went I asked Dr. Seward to give me a little opiate of some kind, as I had not slept well the night before. He very kindly made me up a sleeping draught, which he gave to me, telling me that it would do me no harm, as it was very mild. . . . . I have taken it, and am waiting for sleep, which still keeps aloof. I hope I have not done wrong, for as sleep begins to flirt with me, a new fear comes: that I may have been foolish in thus depriving myself of the power of waking. I might want it. Here comes sleep. Good-night.

CHAPTER XX.

JONATHAN HARKER'S JOURNAL.

1 *October, evening.*—I found Thomas Snelling in his house at Bethnal Green, but unhappily he was not in a condition to remember anything. The very prospect of beer which my expected coming had opened to him had proved too much, and he had begun too early on his expected debauch. I learned, however, from his wife, who seemed a decent, poor soul, that he was only the assistant to Smollet, who of the two mates was the responsible person. So off I drove to Walworth, and found Mr. Joseph Smollet at home and in his shirt-sleeves, taking a late tea out of a saucer. He is a decent, intelligent fellow, distinctly a good, reliable type of workman, and with a headpiece of his own. He remembered all about the incident of the boxes, and from a wonderful dog's-eared notebook, which he produced from some mysterious receptacle about the seat of his trousers, and which had hieroglyphical entries in thick, half-obliterated pencil, he gave me the destinations of the boxes. There were, he said, six in the cartload
which he took from Carfax and left at 197, Chicksand Street, 1
Mile End New Town, and another six which he deposited at 2
Jamaica Lane, Bermondsey. If then the Count meant to 3, 4
scatter these ghastly refuges of his over London, these places were chosen as the first of delivery, so that later he might distribute more fully. The systematic manner in which this was done made me think that he could not mean to confine himself to two sides of London. He was now fixed on the far east of the northern shore, on the east of the southern shore, and on the south. The north and west were surely never meant to be
left out of his diabolical scheme—let alone the City itself and 5

1 *197, Chicksand Street.* This street did exist at the time Stoker was writing, but the street numbers ended at sixty-seven.

2 *Mile End New Town.* A neighborhood of east central London.

Mile End Road is a continuation of Whitechapel Road in the Whitechapel district of London. In Stoker's day it was a neighborhood chiefly inhabited by artisans. It was in Whitechapel that an earlier Arnold Toynbee died while lecturing to an audience of London workingmen. (See map, pp. 340–41.)

3 *Jamaica Lane.* David Webb of the Bishopsgale Foundation informs me that at the end of the nineteenth century London had a Jamaica Place, Jamaica Road, and a Jamaica Street, Bermondsey; but no Jamaica Lane.

4 *Bermondsey.* A commercial and shipping district in south central London that was famous for its tanneries, glue factories, and wool warehouses (see map, pp. 340–41).

5 *the City.* The self-governing nucleus of central London. A center of business and commerce (see map, pp. 340–41).

6 *Pincher's Alley.* Not in Baedeker's guide to London.

"THE VERY HEART OF FASHIONABLE LONDON."

the very heart of fashionable London in the south-west and west. I went back to Smollet, and asked him if he could tell us if any other boxes had been taken from Carfax.

He replied :—

"Well, guv'nor, you've treated me wery 'an'some"—I had given him half a sovereign—"an' I'll tell yer all I know. I heeard a man by the name of Bloxam say four nights ago in
6 the 'Are an' 'Ounds, in Pincher's Alley, as 'ow he an' his mate 'ad 'ad a rare dusty job in a old 'ouse at Purfleet. There ain't a-many such jobs as this 'ere, an' I'm thinkin' that maybe Sam Bloxam could tell ye summut." I asked if he could tell me where to find him. I told him that if he could get me the address it would be worth another half-sovereign to him. So he gulped down the rest of his tea and stood up, saying that he was going to begin the search then and there. At the door he stopped, and said :—

"Look 'ere, guv'nor, there ain't no sense in me a-keepin' you 'ere. I may find Sam soon, or I mayn't; but anyhow he ain't like to be in a way to tell ye much to-night. Sam is a rare one when he starts on the booze. If you can give me a envelope with a stamp on it, and put yer address on it, I'll find out where Sam is to be found and post it ye to-night. But ye'd better be up arter 'im soon in the mornin', or maybe ye won't ketch 'im; for Sam gets off main early, never mind the booze the night afore."

This was all practical, so one of the children went off with a penny to buy an envelope and a sheet of paper, and to keep the change. When she came back, I addressed the envelope and stamped it, and when Smollet had again faithfully promised to post the address when found, I took my way to home. We're on the track anyhow. I am tired to-night, and want sleep. Mina is fast asleep, and looks a little too pale; her eyes look as though she had been crying. Poor dear, I've no doubt it frets her to be kept in the dark, and it may make her doubly anxious about me and the others. But it is best as it is. It is better to be disappointed and worried in such a way now than to have her nerve broken. The doctors were quite right to insist on her being kept out of this dreadful business. I must be firm, for on me this particular burden of silence must rest. I shall not ever enter on the subject with her under any circumstances. Indeed, it may not be a hard task, after all, for she herself has become reticent on the subject, and has not spoken of the Count or his doings ever since we told her of our decision.

2 *October, evening.*—A long and trying and exciting day. By the first post I got my directed envelope with a dirty scrap of paper enclosed, on which was written with a carpenter's pencil in a sprawling hand :—

"Sam Bloxam, Korkrans, 4, Poters Cort, Bartel Street, Walworth. Arsk for the depite."

I got the letter in bed, and rose without waking Mina. She looked heavy and sleepy and pale, and far from well. I determined not to wake her, but that, when I should return from this new search, I would arrange for her going back to Exeter. I think she would be happier in our own home, with her daily tasks to interest her, than in being here amongst us and in ignorance. I only saw Dr. Seward for a moment, and told him where I was off to, promising to come back and tell the rest so soon as I should have found out anything. I drove to Walworth and found, with some difficulty, Potter's Court. Mr. 7
Smollet's spelling misled me, as I asked for Poter's Court instead of Potter's Court. However, when I had found the court, I had no difficulty in discovering Corcoran's lodging-house. When I asked the man who came to the door for the "depite," he shook his head, and said: "I dunno 'im. There ain't no such a person 'ere; I never 'eard of 'im in all my bloomin' days. Don't believe there ain't nobody of that kind livin' 'ere or anywheres." I took out Smollet's letter, and as I read it it seemed to me that the lesson of the spelling of the name of the court might guide me. "What are you?" I asked.

"I'm the depity," he answered. I saw at once that I was on the right track; phonetic spelling had again misled me. A half-crown tip put the deputy's knowledge at my disposal, and I learned that Mr. Bloxam, who had slept off the remains of his beer on the previous night at Corcoran's, had left for his work at Poplar at five o'clock that morning. He could not 8
tell me where the place of work was situated, but he had a vague idea that it was some kind of a "new-fangled ware'us;" and with this slender clue I had to start for Poplar. It was twelve o'clock before I got any satisfactory hint of such a building, and this I got at a coffee-shop, where some workmen were having their dinner. One of these suggested that there was being erected at Cross Angel Street a new "cold storage" building; and as this suited the condition of a "new-fangled ware'us," I at once drove to it. An interview with a surly gatekeeper and a surlier foreman, both of whom were appeased with coin of the realm, put me on the track of Bloxam; he was sent for on my suggesting that I was willing to pay his day's wages to his foreman for the privilege of asking him a few questions on a private matter. He was a smart enough

7 *Potter's Court.* A fictitious address.

WORKING-CLASS HOUSING, LONDON.

8 *Poplar.* An industrial and shipping district in east London, directly north of the Isle of Dogs (see map, pp. 340–41).

9 *old feller, with a white moustache.* Dracula has aged considerably in little less than one week. On September 22, Mina Harker reports seeing him as "a tall, thin man, with a beaky nose and black moustache and pointed beard . . . (see chapter XIII, note 8). We may account for the change in Dracula if we recall that Lucy, his first source of nourishment in England, died on September 20; and that he did not take first blood from Mina until September 30 (see p. 230). The point, then, is that Dracula, when Samuel Bloxam helped him with his boxes, was, as it were, between feedings. The date, according to Joseph Smollet's account, would be September 27.

10 *Piccadilly Circus.* The northeast terminus of Piccadilly. Regent Street, Shaftesbury Avenue, Coventry Street, Haymarket, and Piccadilly converge here. Center of shops, hotels, clubs, theatres (see map, pp. 340–41).

11 *Junior Constitutional.* A conservative club located at 101, Piccadilly. Ronald Firbank was one of its members. (See map, pp. 340–41.)

fellow, though rough of speech and bearing. When I had promised to pay for his information and given him an earnest, he told me that he had made two journeys between Carfax and a house in Piccadilly, and had taken from this house to the latter nine great boxes—"main heavy ones"—with a horse and cart hired by him for this purpose. I asked him if he could tell me the number of the house in Piccadilly, to which he replied :—

"Well, guv'nor, I forgits the number, but it was only a few doors from a big white church or somethink of the kind, not long built. It was a dusty old 'ouse, too, though nothin' to the dustiness of the 'ouse we tooked the bloomin' boxes from."

"How did you get into the houses if they were both empty?"

"There was the old party what engaged me a-waitin' in the 'ouse at Purfleet. He 'elped me to lift the boxes and put them in the dray. Curse me, but he was the strongest chap I
9 ever struck, an' him a old feller, with a white moustache, one that thin you would think he couldn't throw a shadder."

How this phrase thrilled through me!

"Why, 'e took up 'is end o' the boxes like they was pounds of tea, and me a-puffin' an' a-blowin' afore I could up-end mine anyhow—an' I'm no chicken, neither."

"How did you get into the house in Piccadilly?" I asked.

"He was there too. He must 'a' started off and got there afore me, for when I rung of the bell he kem an' opened the door 'isself an' 'elped me to carry the boxes into the 'all."

"The whole nine?" I asked.

"Yus; there was five in the first load an' four in the second. It was main dry work, an' I don't so well remember 'ow I got 'ome." I interrupted him :—

"Were the boxes left in the hall?"

"Yus; it was a big 'all, an' there was nothin' else in it." I made one more attempt to further matters :—

"You didn't have any key?"

"Never used no key nor nothink. The old gent, he opened the door 'isself an' shut it again when I druv off. I don't remember the last time—but that was the beer."

"And you can't remember the number of the house?"

"No, sir. But ye needn't have no difficulty about that. It's a 'igh 'un with a stone front with a bow on it, an' 'igh steps up to the door. I know them steps, 'avin' 'ad to carry the boxes up with three loafers what come round to earn a copper. The old gent give them shillin's, an' they seein' they got so much, they wanted more; but 'e took one of them by the shoulder and was like to throw 'im down the steps, till the lot of them went away cussin'." I thought that with this description I could find the house, so, having paid my friend for his information, I started off for Piccadilly. I had gained a new painful experience: the Count could, it was evident, handle the earth-boxes himself. If so, time was precious; for, now that he had achieved a certain amount of distribution, he could, by choosing his own time, complete the task unob-
10 served. At Piccadilly Circus I discharged my cab, and walked
11 westward; beyond the Junior Constitutional I came across the house described, and was satisfied that this was the next

of the lairs arranged by Dracula. The house looked as though it had been long untenanted. The windows were encrusted with dust, and the shutters were up. All the framework was black with time, and from the iron the paint had mostly scaled away. It was evident that up to lately there had been a large notice-board in front of the balcony; it had, however, been roughly torn away, the uprights which had supported it still remaining. Behind the rails of the balcony I saw there were some loose boards, whose raw edges looked white. I would have given a good deal to have been able to see the notice-board intact, as it would, perhaps, have given some clue to the ownership of the house. I remembered my experience of the investigation and purchase of Carfax, and I could not but feel that if I could find the former owner there might be some means discovered of gaining access to the house.

There was at present nothing to be learned from the Piccadilly side, and nothing could be done; so I went round to the back to see if anything could be gathered from this quarter. The mews were active, the Piccadilly houses being mostly in occupation. I asked one or two of the grooms and helpers whom I saw round if they could tell me anything about the empty house. One of them said that he heard it had lately been taken, but he couldn't say from whom. He told me, however, that up to very lately there had been a notice-board
of "For sale" up, and that perhaps Mitchell, Sons, & Candy, **12**
the house agents, could tell me something, as he thought he remembered seeing the name of that firm on the board. I did not wish to seem too eager, or to let my informant know or guess too much, so, thanking him in the usual manner, I strolled away. It was now growing dusk, and the autumn night was closing in, so I did not lose any time. Having learned the address of Mitchell, Sons, & Candy from a
directory at the Berkeley, I was soon at their office in Sack- **13**
ville Street.

The gentleman who saw me was particularly suave in manner, but uncommunicative in equal proportion. Having once told me that the Piccadilly house—which throughout our interview he called a "mansion"—was sold, he considered my business as concluded. When I asked who had purchased it, he opened his eyes a thought wider, and paused a few seconds before replying:—

"It is sold, sir."

"Pardon me," I said, with equal politeness, "but I have a special reason for wishing to know who purchased it."

Again he paused longer, and raised his eyebrows still more. "It is sold, sir," was again his laconic reply.

"Surely," I said, "you do not mind letting me know so much."

"But I do mind," he answered. "The affairs of their clients are absolutely safe in the hands of Mitchell, Sons, & Candy." This was manifestly a prig of the first water, and there was no use arguing with him. I thought I had best meet him on his own ground, so I said:—

"Your clients, sir, are happy in having so resolute a guardian of their confidence. I am myself a professional man." Here I handed him my card. "In this instance I am not prompted by curiosity; I act on the part of Lord Godal-

12 *Mitchell, Sons, & Candy.* No such firm existed in London—at least not in the period that Stoker lived there (1878–1912).

13 *Sackville Street.* A street just west of Piccadilly Circus, connecting Piccadilly and Vigo Street (see map, pp. 340–41).

14 *Aërated Bread Company.* A chain of tea shops still extant in England.

ming, who wishes to know something of the property which was, he understood, lately for sale." These words put a different complexion on affairs. He said :—

"I would like to oblige you if I could, Mr. Harker, and especially would I like to oblige his lordship. We once carried out a small matter of renting some chambers for him when he was the Honourable Arthur Holmwood. If you will let me have his lordship's address I will consult the House on the subject, and will, in any case, communicate with his lordship by to-night's post. It will be a pleasure if we can so far deviate from our rules as to give the required information to his lordship."

I wanted to secure a friend, and not to make an enemy, so I thanked him, gave the address at Dr. Seward's, and came away. It was now dark, and I was tired and hungry. I got
14 a cup of tea at the Aërated Bread Company and came down to Purfleet by the next train.

I found all the others at home. Mina was looking tired and pale, but she made a gallant effort to be bright and cheerful ; it wrung my heart to think that I had had to keep anything from her and so caused her inquietude. Thank God, this will be the last night of her looking on at our conferences, and feeling the sting of our not showing our confidence. It took all my courage to hold to the wise resolution of keeping her out of our grim task. She seems somehow more reconciled ; or else the very subject seems to have become repugnant to her, for when any accidental allusion is made she actually shudders. I am glad we made our resolution in time, as with such a feeling as this, our growing knowledge would be torture to her.

I could not tell the others of the day's discovery till we were alone ; so after dinner—followed by a little music to save appearances even amongst ourselves—I took Mina to her room and left her to go to bed. The dear girl was more affectionate with me than ever, and clung to me as though she would detain me ; but there was much to be talked of and I came away. Thank God, the ceasing of telling things has made no difference between us.

When I came down again I found the others all gathered round the fire in the study. In the train I had written my diary so far, and simply read it off to them as the best means of letting them get abreast of my own information ; when I had finished Van Helsing said :—

"This has been a great day's work, friend Jonathan. Doubtless we are on the track of the missing boxes. If we find them all in that house, then our work is near the end. But if there be some missing, we must search until we find them. Then shall we make our final *coup*, and hunt the wretch to his real death." We all sat silent awhile and all at once Mr. Morris spoke :—

"Say ! how are we going to get into that house ?"

"We got into the other" answered Lord Godalming quickly.

"But, Art, this is different. We broke house at Carfax, but we had night and a walled park to protect us. It will be a mighty different thing to commit burglary in Piccadilly, either by day or night. I confess I don't see how we are going to get in unless that agency duck can find us a key of some sort ;

perhaps we shall know when you get his letter in the morning." Lord Godalming's brows contracted, and he stood up and walked about the room. By-and-by he stopped and said, turning from one to another of us:—

"Quincey's head is level. This burglary business is getting serious; we got off once all right; but we have now a rare job on hand—unless we can find the Count's key basket."

As nothing could well be done before morning, and as it would be at least advisable to wait till Lord Godalming should hear from Mitchell's, we decided not to take any active step before breakfast time. For a good while we sat and smoked, discussing the matter in its various lights and bearings; I took the opportunity of bringing this diary right up to the moment. I am very sleepy and shall go to bed. . . .

Just a line. Mina sleeps soundly and her breathing is regular. Her forehead is puckered up into little wrinkles, as though she thinks even in her sleep. She is still too pale, but does not look so haggard as she did this morning. To-morrow will, I hope, mend all this; she will be herself at home in Exeter. Oh, but I am sleepy!

Dr. Seward's Diary.

1 *October.*—I am puzzled afresh about Renfield. His moods change so rapidly that I find it difficult to keep touch of them, and as they always mean something more than his own well-being, they form a more than interesting study. This morning, when I went to see him after his repulse of Van Helsing, his manner was that of a man commanding destiny. He was, in fact, commanding destiny—subjectively. He did not really care for any of the things of mere earth; he was in the clouds and looked down on all the weaknesses and wants of us poor mortals. I thought I would improve the occasion and learn something, so I asked him:—

"What about the flies these times?" He smiled on me in quite a superior sort of way—such a smile as would have become
the face of Malvolio—as he answered me:— **15**

"The fly, my dear sir, has one striking feature: its wings are typical of the aërial powers of the psychic faculties. The
ancients did well when they typified the soul as a butterfly!" **16**

I thought I would push his analogy to its utmost logically, so I said quickly:—

"Oh, it is a soul you are after now, is it?" His madness foiled his reason, and a puzzled look spread over his face as, shaking his head with a decision which I had but seldom seen in him, he said:—

"Oh no, oh no! I want no souls. Life is all I want." Here he brightened up; "I am pretty indifferent about it at present. Life is all right; I have all I want. You must get a new patient, doctor, if you wish to study zoophagy!"

This puzzled me a little, so I drew him on:—

"Then you command life; you are a god I suppose?" He smiled with an ineffably benign superiority.

"Oh no! Far be it from me to arrogate to myself the attributes of the Deity. I am not even concerned in His especially spiritual doings. If I may state my intellectual posi-

MALVOLIO CROSS-GARTERED.

15 *the face of Malvolio.* Malvolio is Olivia's priggish steward in Shakespeare's *Twelfth Night*.

The allusion is to Act III, scene IV, in which Malvolio grins like an idiot as he follows the instructions of a letter he mistakenly believes to be from Olivia. The letter (Act II, Scene V) advises him that "if thou entertainest my love, let it appear in thy smiling . . ."

"THE FLY, MY DEAR SIR."

16 "*. . . the soul as a butterfly!*" The Oxford *Dictionary of Modern Greek* defines the word *psyche* as soul, heat, energy, and finally, butterfly. The idea is well known. Coleridge writes:

"The butterfly the ancient Grecians made
The soul's fair emblem, and its only name—
But of the soul, escaped the slavish trade
Of mortal life! For in this earthly frame
Ours is the reptile's lot—much toil, much blame—
Manifold motions making little speed,
And to deform and kill the things whereon we
feed."

In W. J. Holland's *The Butterfly Book*, there is an unsettling reference to butterflies (p. 299), which is apt here. He writes:

"The lepidopterous insects in general, soon after they emerge from the pupa state, and commonly during their first flight, discharge some drops of a red-colored fluid, more or less intense in different species, which, in some instances, where their numbers have been considerable, have produced the appearance of a 'shower of blood,' as this natural phenomenon is sometimes called.

"Showers of blood have been recorded by historians and poets as preternatural—have been considered in the light of prodigies, and regarded, where they have happened, as fearful prognostics of impending evil."

17 *". . . in the position which Enoch occupied spiritually!"*

Enoch was the father of Methuselah. If Enoch is said to walk with God, then the suggestion is that Renfield walks with the devil. The Bible says of Enoch (Genesis 5:21–24):

"And Enoch lived sixty and five years, and begat Methuselah:

And Enoch walked with God after he begat Methuselah three hundred years, and begat sons and daughters:

And all the days of Enoch were three hundred sixty and five years:

And Enoch walked with God: and he *was* not; for God took him."

18 *unconscious cerebration*. See chapter VI, note 27.

tion I am, so far as concerns things purely terrestrial, some-
17 what in the position which Enoch occupied spiritually!" This was a poser to me. I could not at the moment recall Enoch's appositeness; so I had to ask a simple question, though I felt that by so doing I was lowering myself in the eyes of the lunatic:—

"And why with Enoch?"

"Because he walked with God." I could not see the analogy, but did not like to admit it; so I harked back to what he had denied:—

"So you don't care about life and you don't want souls. Why not?" I put my question quickly and somewhat sternly, on purpose to disconcert him. The effort succeeded; for an instant he unconsciously relapsed into his old servile manner, bent low before me, and actually fawned upon me as he replied:—

"I don't want any souls, indeed, indeed! I don't. I couldn't use them if I had them; they would be no manner of use to me. I couldn't eat them or——" he suddenly stopped and the old cunning look spread over his face, like a wind sweep on the surface of the water. "And doctor, as to life, what is it after all? When you've got all you require, and you know that you will never want, that is all. I have friends—good friends—like you Dr. Seward;" this was said with a leer of inexpressible cunning, "I know that I shall never lack the means of life!"

I think that through the cloudiness of his insanity he saw some antagonism in me, for he at once fell back on the last refuge of such as he—a dogged silence. After a short time I saw that for the present it was useless to speak to him. He was sulky, and so I came away.

Later in the day he sent for me. Ordinarily I would not have come without special reason, but just at present I am so interested in him that I would gladly make an effort. Besides, I am glad to have anything to help to pass the time. Harker is out, following up clues; and so are Lord Godalming and Quincey. Van Helsing sits in my study poring over the record prepared by the Harkers; he seems to think that by accurate knowledge of all details he will light upon some clue. He does not wish to be disturbed in the work, without cause. I would have taken him with me to see the patient, only I thought that after his last repulse he might not care to go again. There was also another reason: Renfield might not speak so freely before a third person as when he and I were alone.

I found him sitting out in the middle of the floor on his stool, a pose which is generally indicative of some mental energy on his part. When I came in, he said at once, as though the question had been waiting on his lips:—

"What about souls?" It was evident then that my sur-
18 mise had been correct. Unconscious cerebration was doing its work, even with the lunatic. I determined to have the matter out. "What about them yourself?" I asked. He did not reply for a moment but looked all round him, and up and down, as though he expected to find some inspiration for an answer.

"I don't want any souls!" he said in a feeble, apologetic way. The matter seemed preying on his mind, and so I determined to use it—to "be cruel only to be kind." So I said:— 19

"You like life, and you want life?"

"Oh yes! but that is all right; you needn't worry about that!"

"But," I asked, "how are we to get the life without getting the soul also?" This seemed to puzzle him, so I followed it up:—

"A nice time you'll have some time when you're flying out there, with the souls of thousands of flies and spiders and birds and cats buzzing and twittering and miauing all round you. You've got their lives, you know, and you must put up with their souls!" Something seemed to affect his imagination, for he put his fingers to his ears and shut his eyes, screwing them up tightly just as a small boy does when his face is being soaped. There was something pathetic in it that touched me; it also gave me a lesson, for it seemed that before me was a child—only a child, though the features were worn, and the stubble on the jaws was white. It was evident that he was undergoing some process of mental disturbance, and, knowing how his past moods had interpreted things seemingly foreign to himself, I thought I would enter into his mind as well as I could and go with him. The first step was to restore confidence, so I asked him, speaking pretty loud so that he would hear me through his closed ears:—

"Would you like some sugar to get your flies round again!" He seemed to wake up all at once, and shook his head. With a laugh he replied:—

"Not much! flies are poor things, after all!" After a pause he added "But I don't want their souls buzzing round me, all the same."

"Or spiders" I went on.

"Blow spiders! What's the use of spiders? There isn't anything in them to eat or"—he stopped suddenly, as though reminded of a forbidden topic.

"So, so!" I thought to myself, "this is the second time he has suddenly stopped at the word 'drink'; what does it mean?" Renfield seemed himself aware of having made a lapse, for he hurried on, as though to distract my attention from it:—

"I don't take any stock at all in such matters. 'Rats and 20
mice and such small deer' as Shakespeare has it 'chicken-feed of the larder' they might be called. I'm past all that sort of nonsense. You might as well ask a man to eat molecules with a pair of chop-sticks, as to try to interest me about the lesser carnivora, when I know of what is before me."

"I see," I said. "You want big things that you can make your teeth meet in? How would you like to breakfast on elephant?"

"What ridiculous nonsense you are talking!" He was getting too wide awake, so I thought I would press him hard. "I wonder," I said reflectively, "what an elephant's soul is like!"

The effect I desired was obtained, for he at once fell from his high-horse and became a child again.

"I don't want an elephant's soul, or, any soul at all!" he

19 *"be cruel only to be kind."* The line is from Shakespeare's *Hamlet* (Act III, Scene IV).

20 *'Rats and mice and such small deer.'* The line is from Shakespeare's *King Lear* (Act III, Scene IV, line 144), but actually reads "mice and rats and such small deer." Note that deer means animals here.

One wonders if Stoker remembered that the verse is spoken by Edgar, *pretending* to be mad in his role as poor Tom, and that Tom claims to eat "the swimming frog, the toad, the tadpole, the wall-newt, and the water . . . [and] when the foul fiend rages, eats cow-dung for sallets; swallows the old rat and the ditch-dog" (lines 134–37). Immediately after his speech about the rats and mice, Edgar adds, ". . . peace, thou fiend!" and later, "the prince of darkness is a gentleman" (lines 146–48).

said. For a few moments he sat despondently. Suddenly he jumped to his feet, with his eyes blazing and all the signs of intense cerebral excitement. "To hell with you and your souls!" he shouted. "Why do you plague me about souls. Haven't I got enough to worry, and pain, and distract me already, without thinking of souls!" He looked so hostile that I thought he was in for another homicidal fit, so I blew my whistle. The instant, however, that I did so he became calm, and said apologetically:—

"Forgive me, Doctor; I forgot myself. You do not need any help. I am so worried in my mind that I am apt to be irritable. If you only knew the problem I have to face, and that I am working out, you would pity, and tolerate, and pardon me. Pray do not put me in a strait-waistcoat. I want to think and I cannot think freely when my body is confined. I am sure you will understand!" He had evidently self-control; so when the attendants came I told them not to mind, and they withdrew. Renfield watched them go; when the door was closed he said, with considerable dignity and sweetness:—

"Dr. Seward you have been very considerate towards me. Believe me that I am very very grateful to you!" I thought it well to leave him in this mood, and so I came away. There is certainly something to ponder over in this man's state. Several points seem to make what the American interviewer calls "a story," if one could only get them in proper order. Here they are:—

Will not mention "drinking."

Fears the thought of being burdened with the "soul" of anything.

Has no dread of wanting "life" in the future.

Despises the meaner forms of life altogether, though he dreads being haunted by their souls.

Logically all these things point one way! he has assurance of some kind that he will acquire some higher life. He dreads the consequence—the burden of a soul. Then it is a human life he looks to!

And the assurance—?

Merciful God! the Count has been to him, and there is some new scheme of terror afoot!

Later.—I went after my round to Van Helsing and told him my suspicion. He grew very grave; and, after thinking the matter over for a while asked me to take him to Renfield. I did so. As we came to the door we heard the lunatic within singing gaily, as he used to do in the time which now seems so long ago. When we entered we saw with amazement that he had spread out his sugar as of old; the flies, lethargic with the autumn, were beginning to buzz into the room. We tried to make him talk of the subject of our previous conversation, but he would not attend. He went on with his singing, just as though we had not been present. He had got a scrap of paper and was folding it into a note book. We had to come away as ignorant as we went in.

His is a curious case indeed; we must watch him to-night.

A PICCADILLY HOUSE.

Letter, Mitchell, Sons and Candy to Lord Godalming.

"1 *October.*

"My Lord,

"We are at all times only too happy to meet your wishes. We beg, with regard to the desire of your Lordship, expressed by Mr. Harker on your behalf, to supply the following information concerning the sale and purchase of No. 347, Piccadilly. The original vendors are the executors of the late Mr. Archibald Winter-Suffield. The purchaser is a foreign nobleman, Count de Ville, who effected the purchase himself paying the purchase money in notes 'over the counter,' if your Lordship will pardon us using so vulgar an expression. Beyond this we know nothing whatever of him.

"We are, my Lord,
"Your Lordship's humble servants,
"MITCHELL, SONS & CANDY."

Dr. Seward's Diary.

2 *October.*—I placed a man in the corridor last night, and told him to make an accurate note of any sound he might hear from Renfield's room, and gave him instructions that if there should be anything strange he was to call me. After dinner, when we had all gathered round the fire in the study—Mrs. Harker having gone to bed—we discussed the attempts and discoveries of the day. Harker was the only one who had any result, and we are in great hopes that his clue may be an important one.

Before going to bed I went round to the patient's room and looked in through the observation trap. He was sleeping soundly, and his heart rose and fell with regular respiration.

21 *I sometimes think we must be all mad and that we shall wake to sanity in strait-waistcoats.* Of all the characters in this book, Seward comes closest to having a complex personality. He has the nineteenth century's faith in progress at the same time as he is prone to the sort of personal depression that comes from a confusion about one's self and one's motives. Throughout, he is doggedly honest and frequently ineffectual.

This morning the man on duty reported to me that a little after midnight he was restless and kept saying his prayers somewhat loudly. I asked him if that was all; he replied that it was all he heard. There was something about his manner so suspicious that I asked him point blank if he had been asleep. He denied sleep, but admitted to having "dozed" for a while. It is too bad that men cannot be trusted unless they are watched.

To-day Harker is out following up his clue, and Art and Quincey are looking after horses. Godalming thinks that it will be well to have horses always in readiness, for when we get the information which we seek there will be no time to lose. We must sterilize all the imported earth between sunrise and sunset; we shall thus catch the Count at his weakest, and without a refuge to fly to. Van Helsing is off to the British Museum looking up some authorities on ancient medicine. The old physicians took account of things which their followers do not accept, and the Professor is searching for witch and demon cures which may be useful to us later.

21 I sometimes think we must be all mad and that we shall wake to sanity in strait-waistcoats.

Later.—We have met again. We seem at last to be on the track, and our work of to-morrow may be the beginning of the end. I wonder if Renfield's quiet has anything to do with this. His moods have so followed the doings of the Count, that the coming destruction of the monster may be carried to him in some subtle way. If we could only get some hint as to what passed in his mind, between the time of my argument with him to-day and his resumption of fly-catching, it might afford us a valuable clue. He is now seemingly quiet for a spell . . . . Is he? —— that wild yell seemed to come from his room . . . .

The attendant came bursting into my room and told me that Renfield had somehow met with some accident. He had heard him yell; and when he went to him found him lying on his face on the floor, all covered with blood. I must go at once. . . . .

CHAPTER XXI.

Dr. Seward's Diary.

3 *October.*—Let me put down with exactness all that happened, as well as I can remember it, since last I made an entry. Not a detail that I can recall must be forgotten; in all calmness I must proceed.

When I came to Renfield's room I found him lying on the floor on his left side in a glittering pool of blood. When I went to move him, it became at once apparent that he had received some terrible injuries; there seemed none of that unity of purpose between the parts of the body which marks even lethargic sanity. As the face was exposed I could see that it was horribly bruised, as though it had been beaten against the floor—indeed it was from the face wounds that the pool of blood originated. The attendant who was kneeling beside the body said to me as we turned him over:—

"I think, sir, his back is broken. See, both his right arm 1
and leg and the whole side of his face are paralysed." How such a thing could have happened puzzled the attendant beyond measure. He seemed quite bewildered, and his brows were gathered in as he said:—

"I can't understand the two things. He could mark his face like that by beating his own head on the ground. I saw a
young woman do it once at the Eversfield Asylum before any- 2
one could lay hands on her. And I suppose he might have broke his back by falling out of bed, if he got in an awkward kink. But for the life of me I can't imagine how the two things occurred. If his back was broke, he couldn't beat his head; and if his face was like that before the fall out of bed, there would be marks of it." I said to him:—

"Go to Dr. Van Helsing, and ask him to kindly come

1 *his back is broken.* "It is absolute madness to turn someone over if you suspect a spinal injury," writes my medical correspondent Dr. Herman Schwartz.

2 *Eversfield Asylum.* The name of the asylum appears to be an invention.

here at once. I want him without an instant's delay." The man ran off, and within a very few minutes the Professor, in his dressing gown and slippers, appeared. When he saw Renfield on the ground, he looked keenly at him a moment and then turned to me. I think he recognized my thought in my eyes, for he said very quietly, manifestly for the ears of the attendant :—

"Ah, a sad accident! He will need very careful watching, and much attention. I shall stay with you myself; but I shall first dress myself. If you will remain I shall in a few minutes join you."

The patient was now breathing stertorously, and it was easy to see that he had suffered some terrible injury. Van Helsing returned with extraordinary celerity, bearing with him a surgical case. He had evidently been thinking and had his mind made up; for, almost before he looked at the patient, he whispered to me :—

"Send the attendant away. We must be alone with him when he becomes conscious, after the operation." So I said :—

"I think that will do now, Simmons. We have done all that we can at present. You had better go your round, and Dr. Van Helsing will operate. Let me know instantly if there be anything unusual anywhere."

The man withdrew, and we went into a strict examination of the patient. The wounds of the face were superficial; the real injury was a depressed fracture of the skull, extending right up through the motor area. The Professor thought a moment and said :—

"We must reduce the pressure and get back to normal con-
3 ditions, as far as can be; the rapidity of the suffusion shows the terrible nature of his injury. The whole motor area seems affected. The suffusion of the brain will increase quickly, so
4 we must trephine at once or it may be too late." As he was speaking there was a soft tapping at the door. I went over and opened it and found in the corridor without, Arthur and Quincey in pyjamas and slippers: the former spoke :—

"I heard your man call up Dr. Van Helsing and tell him of an accident. So I woke Quincey, or rather called for him as he was not asleep. Things are moving too quickly and too strangely for sound sleep for any of us these times. I've been thinking that to-morrow night will not see things as they have been. We'll have to look back—and forward a little more than we have done. May we come in?" I nodded, and held the door open till they had entered; then I closed it again. When Quincey saw the attitude and state of the patient, and noted the horrible pool on the floor, he said softly :—

"My God! what has happened to him? Poor, poor devil!" I told him briefly, and added that we expected he would recover consciousness after the operation—for a short time at all events. He went at once and sat down on the edge of the bed, with Godalming beside him; we all watched in patience.

"We shall wait," said Van Helsing, "just long enough to
5 fix the best spot for trephining, so that we may most quickly

3 *the suffusion.* Renfield may have a cortical edema, a swelling of the brain with pressure on the cranial nerves and brain cells with consequent stroke, confusion, or seizures.

There is a neuromotor area in the frontal lobe of the brain in which motor activity for the rest of the body originates. Renfield's fracture may be impinging on this motor area.

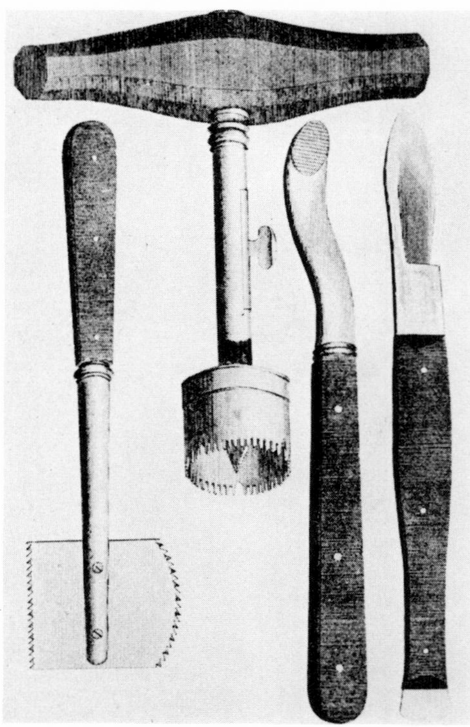

INSTRUMENTS USED IN TREPHINATION: *FROM LEFT TO RIGHT:* HEY'S SAW, TREPHINE, ELEVATOR, AND SCALPEL.

4 *we must trephine at once.* In a trephining operation the skull is opened with a surgical instrument called a trephine. The trephine works something like a hollow, sawtoothed drill, and, indeed, in its earlier forms was very like a brace and bit and required two hands to manipulate it. The trephining operation is usually performed for removal of an intracranial tumor, to relieve intracranial pressure, or to drain a brain abscess.

Trephination, as it is also called, was an operation performed as long ago as Paleolithic times.

5 *the best spot.* It would be virtually impossible to tell from observation what that spot should be. Usually a cluster of burr holes is made, rather than one. In any case, the more time that elapses with the pressure of hemorrhage, the greater the damage to the brain.

and perfectly remove the blood clot; for it is evident that the hæmorrhage is increasing."

The minutes during which we waited passed with fearful slowness. I had a horrible sinking in my heart, and from Van Helsing's face I gathered that he felt some fear or apprehension as to what was to come. I dreaded the words that Renfield might speak. I was positively afraid to think; but the conviction of what was coming was on me, as I have read of men who have heard the death-watch. The poor man's breathing came in uncertain gasps. Each instant he seemed as though he would open his eyes and speak; but then would follow a prolonged stertorous breath, and he would relapse into a more fixed insensibility. Inured as I was to sick beds and death, this suspense grew, and grew upon me. I could almost hear the beating of my own heart; and the blood surging through my temples sounded like blows from a hammer. The silence finally became agonising. I looked at my companions, one after another, and saw from their flushed faces and damp brows that they were enduring equal torture. There was a nervous suspense over us all, as though overhead some dread bell would peal out powerfully when we should least expect it.

At last there came a time when it was evident that the patient was sinking fast; he might die at any moment. I looked up at the Professor and caught his eyes fixed on mine. His face was sternly set as he spoke:—

"There is no time to lose. His words may be worth many lives; I have been thinking so, as I stood here. It may be there is a soul at stake! We shall operate just above the ear."

Without another word he made the operation. For a few 6
moments the breathing continued to be stertorous. Then there came a breath so prolonged that it seemed as though it would tear open his chest. Suddenly his eyes opened, and became fixed in a wild, helpless stare. This was continued for a few moments; then it softened into a glad surprise, and from the lips came a sigh of relief. He moved convulsively, and as he did so, said:—

"I'll be quiet, Doctor. Tell them to take off the strait-waistcoat. I have had a terrible dream, and it has left me so weak that I cannot move. What's wrong with my face? it feels all swollen, and it smarts dreadfully." He tried to turn his head; but even with the effort his eyes seemed to grow glassy again, so I gently put it back. Then Van Helsing said in a quiet grave tone:—

"Tell us your dream, Mr. Renfield." As he heard the voice his face brightened through its mutilation, and he said:—

"That is Dr. Van Helsing. How good it is of you to be here. Give me some water, my lips are dry; and I shall try to tell you. I dreamed"—he stopped and seemed fainting, I called quietly to Quincey—"The brandy—it is in my study—quick!" He flew and returned with a glass, the decanter of brandy and a carafe of water. We moistened the parched lips, and the patient quickly revived. It seemed however that his poor injured brain had been working in the interval, for, when he was quite conscious, he looked at me piercingly

6 *he made the operation*. Without an anesthetic! This is the second operation without an anesthetic (see chapter X, note 17).

7 "*. . . but not where He was!*" Stoker, determined that his reader should lose none of the religious implications of Dracula's meeting with Renfield, begins here to capitalize the personal pronouns referring to Him, though it will be seen (as in the paragraph below) that he is not entirely consistent.

8 *the 'Death's-head moth!'* In addition to its forbidding name, the death's-head moth is notable for its power of squeaking. P. Martin Duncan, in *The Transformation of Insects* (p. 204), writes that "this gift, combined with the sombre hues of the sphinx, and the presence of the death's head upon its back, have surrounded the moths with much mysterious dread, and there are many people in the most civilised and learned countries in the world that are heartily afraid of them. They are said to be a sign of bad luck, and are supposed to precede a death in the house . . . The squeaking appears to be connected in some way or other with a small membranous capsule, which is situated on either side of the body at the base of the abdomen, and which is covered with some hairs that can be made to vibrate. The fondness of the moth for honey leads it into bee-hives, and it is most remarkable that the insect should know that honey is to be got there. The bees, moreover, do not rush upon the robber, but employ every artifice to shut it out or wall it up."

Ornella Volta reports that the *Acherontia atropos*, in addition to its strange cry, "nourishes itself on an alkaline vegetable (very much resembling dead fish) that has a narcotic action comparable to that of morphine."

with an agonised confusion which I shall never forget, and said :—

"I must not deceive myself; it was no dream, but all a grim reality." Then his eyes roved round the room; as they caught sight of the two figures sitting patiently on the edge of the bed he went on :—

"If I were not sure already, I would know from them." For an instant his eyes closed—not with pain or sleep but voluntarily, as though he were bringing all his faculties to bear; when he opened them he said, hurriedly, and with more energy than he had yet displayed :—

"Quick, Doctor, quick. I am dying! I feel that I have but a few minutes; and then I must go back to death—or worse! Wet my lips with brandy again. I have something that I must say before I die; or before my poor crushed brain dies anyhow. Thank you! It was that night after you left me, when I implored you to let me go away. I couldn't speak then, for I felt my tongue was tied; but I was as sane then, except in that way, as I am now. I was in an agony of despair for a long time after you left me; it seemed hours. Then there came a sudden peace to me. My brain seemed to become cool again, and I realized where I was.
7 I heard the dogs bark behind our house, but not where He was!" As he spoke Van Helsing's eyes never blinked, but his hand came out and met mine and gripped it hard. He did not, however, betray himself; he nodded slightly, and said: "Go on," in a low voice. Renfield proceeded :—

"He came up to the window in the mist, as I had seen him often before; but he was solid then—not a ghost, and his eyes were fierce like a man's when angry. He was laughing with his red mouth; the sharp white teeth glinted in the moonlight when he turned to look back over the belt of trees, to where the dogs were barking. I wouldn't ask him to come in at first, though I knew he wanted to—just as he had wanted all along. Then he began promising me things—not in words but by doing them." He was interrupted by a word from the Professor :—

"How?"

"By making them happen; just as he used to send in the flies when the sun was shining. Great big fat ones with steel and sapphire on their wings; and big moths, in the night, with skull and cross-bones on their backs." Van Helsing nodded to him as he whispered to me unconsciously :—

8 "The *Acherontia atropos of the Sphinges*—what you call the 'Death's-head moth!'" The patient went on without stopping.

"Then he began to whisper: 'Rats, rats, rats! Hundreds, thousands, millions of them, and every one a life; and dogs to eat them, and cats too. All lives! all red blood, with years of life in it; and not merely buzzing flies!' I laughed at him, for I wanted to see what he could do. Then the dogs howled, away beyond the dark trees in His house. He beckoned me to the window. I got up and looked out, and He raised his hands, and seemed to call out without using any words. A dark mass spread over the grass, coming on like the shape of a flame of fire; and then He moved the mist to the right and left, and I could see that there

"THE 'DEATH'S-HEAD MOTH!'"

were thousands of rats with their eyes blazing red—like His, only smaller. He held up his hand, and they all stopped; and I thought He seemed to be saying: 'All these lives will I give 9
you, ay, and many more and greater, through countless ages, if you will fall down and worship me!' And then a red cloud, like the colour of blood, seemed to close over my eyes; and before I knew what I was doing, I found myself opening the sash and saying to Him: 'Come in, Lord and Master!' The rats were all gone, but He slid into the room through the sash, though it was only open an inch wide—just as the Moon herself has often come in through the tiniest crack, and has stood before me in all her size and splendour."

His voice was weaker, so I moistened his lips with the brandy again, and he continued; but it seemed as though his memory had gone on working in the interval for his story was further advanced. I was about to call him back to the point, but Van Helsing whispered to me: "Let him go on. Do not interrupt him; he cannot go back, and may-be could not proceed at all if once he lost the thread of his thought." He proceeded:—

"All day I waited to hear from him, but he did not send me anything, not even a blow-fly, and when the moon got up I was pretty angry with him. When he slid in through the window, though it was shut, and did not even knock, I got mad with him. He sneered at me, and his white face looked out of the mist with his red eyes gleaming, and he went on as though he owned the whole place, and I was no one. He 10
didn't even smell the same as he went by me. I couldn't hold him. I thought that, somehow, Mrs. Harker had come into the room."

The two men sitting on the bed stood up and came over

9 *'All these lives will I give you . . .'* This scene, and some of the language describing it, echoes the Temptation of Christ by Satan in the wilderness. In the fourth chapter of the Gospel According to St. Matthew we read: "Then was Jesus led up of the Spirit into the wilderness to be tempted of the devil. . . . Again, the devil taketh him up into an exceeding high mountain, and sheweth him all the kingdoms of the world, and the glory of them; . . . Then saith Jesus unto him, Get thee hence, Satan: for it is written, Thou shalt worship the Lord thy God, and him only shalt thou serve."

10 *He didn't even smell the same.* Because Mina's blood now flows in his veins. Note, too, the change in Mina.

11 *I grabbed it tight.* Since, theologically speaking, everything is topsy-turvy in the allegory of Renfield and Dracula, we are permitted to see this scene as the dark analogue of Jacob wrestling with the angel of the Lord (Genesis 32:24–25):

"And Jacob was left alone; and there wrestled a man with him until the breaking of the day.

"And when he saw that he prevailed not against him, he touched the hollow of his thigh; and the hollow of Jacob's thigh was out of joint, as he wrestled with him."

In Jacob's case the wrestling produced good for himself and the people of Israel. In a spiritual sense, Renfield too emerges from this combat victorious.

12 *He slipped through it.* Apparently through the mist.

13 *"Should we disturb her?"* Quincey chooses a poor moment for Victorian priggery. Fortunately, Van Helsing's continental common sense prevails.

standing behind him so that he could not see them, but where they could hear better. They were both silent, but the Professor started and quivered; his face, however, grew grimmer and sterner still. Renfield went on without noticing:—

"When Mrs. Harker came in to see me this afternoon she wasn't the same; it was like tea after the teapot had been watered." Here we all moved, but no one said a word; he went on:—

"I didn't know that she was here till she spoke; and she didn't look the same. I don't care for the pale people; I like them with lots of blood in them, and hers had all seemed to have run out. I didn't think of it at the time; but when she went away I began to think, and it made me mad to know that He had been taking the life out of her." I could feel that the rest quivered, as I did; but we remained otherwise still. "So when He came to-night I was ready for
11 Him. I saw the mist stealing in, and I grabbed it tight. I had heard that madmen have unnatural strength; and as I knew I was a madman—at times anyhow—I resolved to use my power. Ay, and He felt it too, for He had to come out of the mist to struggle with me. I held tight; and I thought I was going to win, for I didn't mean Him to take any more of her life, till I saw His eyes. They burned into me, and my
12 strength became like water. He slipped through it, and when I tried to cling to Him, He raised me up and flung me down. There was a red cloud before me, and a noise like thunder, and the mist seemed to steal away under the door." His voice was becoming fainter and his breath more stertorous. Van Helsing stood up instinctively.

"We know the worst now," he said. "He is here, and we know his purpose. It may not be too late. Let us be armed—the same as we were the other night, but lose no time; there is not an instant to spare." There was no need to put our fear, nay our conviction, into words—we shared them in common. We all hurried and took from our rooms the same things that we had when we entered the Count's house. The Professor had his ready, and as we met in the corridor he pointed to them significantly as he said:—

"They never leave me; and they shall not till this unhappy business is over. Be wise also, my friends. It is no common enemy that we deal with. Alas! alas! that that dear Madam Mina should suffer." He stopped; his voice was breaking, and I do not know if rage or terror predominated in my own heart.

Outside the Harkers' door we paused. Art and Quincey held back, and the latter said:—

13 "Should we disturb her?"

"We must," said Van Helsing grimly. "If the door be locked, I shall break it in."

"May it not frighten her terribly? It is unusual to break into a lady's room!" Van Helsing said solemnly.

"You are always right; but this is life and death. All chambers are alike to the doctor; and even were they not they are all as one to me to-night. Friend John, when I turn the handle, if the door does not open, do you put your shoulder down and shove; and you too, my friends. Now!"

He turned the handle as he spoke, but the door did not yield. We threw ourselves against it; with a crash it burst open, and we almost fell headlong into the room. The Professor did actually fall, and I saw across him as he gathered himself up from hands and knees. What I saw appalled me. I felt my hair rise like bristles on the back of my neck, and my heart seemed to stand still.

The moonlight was so bright that through the thick yellow 14
blind the room was light enough to see. On the bed beside
the window lay Jonathan Harker, his face flushed and breath- 15
ing heavily as though in a stupor. Kneeling on the near
edge of the bed facing outwards was the white-clad figure of
his wife. By her side stood a tall, thin man, clad in black.
His face was turned from us, but the instant we saw we all
recognised the Count—in every way, even to the scar on his 16
forehead. With his left hand he held both Mrs. Harker's
hands, keeping them away with her arms at full tension; his
right hand gripped her by the back of the neck, forcing her 17
face down on his bosom. Her white nightdress was smeared
with blood, and a thin stream trickled down the man's bare breast which was shown by his torn-open dress. The attitude of the two had a terrible resemblance to a child forcing a kitten's nose into a saucer of milk to compel it to drink. As we burst into the room, the Count turned his face, and the hellish look that I had heard described seemed to leap into it. His eyes flamed red with devilish passion; the great nostrils of the white aquiline nose opened wide and quivered at the edge; and the white sharp teeth, behind the full lips of the blood dripping mouth, champed together like those of a wild beast. With a wrench, which threw his victim back upon the bed as though hurled from a height, he turned and sprang at us. But by this time the Professor had gained his feet, and was holding towards him the envelope which contained the Sacred Wafer. The Count suddenly stopped, just as poor Lucy had done outside the tomb, and cowered back. Further and further back he cowered, as we, lifting our crucifixes, advanced. The moonlight suddenly failed, as a great black cloud sailed across the sky; and when the gaslight sprang up under Quincey's match, we saw nothing but a faint vapour. This, as we looked, trailed under the door, which with the recoil from its bursting open, had swung back to its old position. Van Helsing, Art, and I moved forward to Mrs. Harker, who by this time had drawn her breath and with it had given a scream so wild, so ear-piercing, so despairing that it seems to me now that it will ring in my ears till my dying day. For a few seconds she lay in her helpless attitude and disarray. Her face was ghastly, with a pallor which was accentuated by the blood which smeared her lips and cheeks and chin; from her throat trickled a thin stream of blood. Her eyes were mad with terror. Then she put before her face her poor crushed hands, which bore on their whiteness the red mark of the Count's terrible grip, and from behind them came a low desolate wail which made the terrible scream seem only the

14 *The moonlight was so bright.* This extraordinary scene is crammed with implications, nearly all of them sexual. As sheer stagecraft, it bears comparison with the moment in Castle Dracula where Harker, flat on his back, peeps out at the three beautiful brides of Dracula more than half hoping that they will do their worst. In that scene, it will be remembered, it is Dracula who bursts into the room precisely like an outraged father-husband-lover to prevent the longed-for consummation. Here a full Victorian committee, representing the supine Harker, is in time to create scandal, if not *interruptus.*

Just what *is* going on here? A vengeful cuckoldry? A *ménage à trois?* Mutual oral sexuality? The impregnation of Mina? Stoker, no doubt, would be horrified by these suggestions and yet each of them is in some way valid. No wonder Mina cries out against herself "Unclean, unclean!" and vows not to touch or kiss Jonathan Harker again.

15 *lay Jonathan Harker.* Jonathan is frequently seen as either passive, supine, or enfeebled. Here he is all three. See Mina's reference to Harker's weakness in her letter to Lucy on page 103.

16 *scar on his forehead.* If Dracula's face was "turned from us," it is hard to see how they could recognize the scar on the Count's forehead. A moment later Stoker corrects himself and we see that "the Count turned his face."

17 *her face down on his bosom.* If Dracula is, as I have urged, an aspect of the anti-Christ in Stoker's allegory, then this scene between him and Mina has some resemblance to the mythical relationship between the pelican and its young. The pelican, it will be remembered, was fabled to care for its offspring by opening a vein in its bosom from which the young birds drank. Medieval writers made of the pelican a convenient emblem for Christ's passion. Much later, Shakespeare makes Lear refer to the legend of the pelican and the way it nourishes its young. Speaking of his wicked daughters, Regan and Goneril, the old king says (Act III, Scene IV, lines 72–76):

> ". . . . . . nothing could have subdu'd nature
> To such a lowness but his unkind daughters.
> Is it the fashion that discarded fathers
> Should have thus little mercy on their flesh?
> Judicious punishment! 'twas this flesh begot
> Those pelican daughters."

quick expression of an endless grief. Van Helsing stepped forward and drew the coverlet gently over her body, whilst Art, after looking at her face for an instant despairingly, ran out of the room. Van Helsing whispered to me:—

"Jonathan is in a stupor such as we know the Vampire can produce. We can do nothing with poor Madam Mina for a few moments till she recovers herself; I must wake him!" He dipped the end of a towel in cold water and with it began to flick him on the face, his wife all the while holding her face between her hands and sobbing in a way that was heart-breaking to hear. I raised the blind, and looked out of the window. There was much moonshine; and as I looked I could see Quincey Morris run across the lawn and hide himself in the
shadow of a great yew tree. It puzzled me to think why he **18**
was doing this; but at the instant I heard Harker's quick exclamation as he woke to partial consciousness, and turned to the bed. On his face, as there might well be, was a look of wild amazement. He seemed dazed for a few seconds, and then full consciousness seemed to burst upon him all at once, and he started up. His wife was aroused by the quick movement, and turned to him with her arms stretched out, as though to embrace him; instantly, however, she drew them in again, and putting her elbows together, held her hands before her face, and shuddered till the bed beneath her shook.

"In God's name what does this mean?" Harker cried out, "Dr. Seward, Dr. Van Helsing, what is it? What has happened? What is wrong? Mina, dear, what is it? What does that blood mean? My God, my God! has it come to
this!" and, raising himself to his knees, he beat his hands **19**
wildly together. "Good God help us! help her! oh, help her!" With a quick movement he jumped from bed, and began to pull on his clothes,—all the man in him awake at the need for instant exertion. "What has happened? Tell me all about it?" he cried without pausing. "Dr. Van Helsing, you love Mina, I know. Oh, do something to save her. It cannot have gone too far yet. Guard her while I look for *him*!" His wife, through her terror and horror and distress, saw some sure danger to him; instantly forgetting her own grief, she seized hold of him and cried out:—

"No! no! Jonathan, you must not leave me. I have suffered enough to-night, God knows, without the dread of his harming you. You must stay with me. Stay with these friends who will watch over you!" Her expression became frantic as she spoke; and, he yielding to her, she pulled him down sitting on the bed side, and clung to him fiercely.

Van Helsing and I tried to calm them both. The Professor held up his little golden crucifix, and said with wonderful calmness:—

"Do not fear, my dear. We are here; and whilst this is close to you no foul thing can approach. You are safe for to-night; and we must be calm and take counsel together." She shuddered and was silent, holding down her head on her husband's breast. When she raised it, his white night-robe was stained with blood where her lips had touched, and where the thin open wound in her neck had sent forth drops. The instant she saw it she drew back, with a low wail, and whispered, amidst choking sobs:—

"THE COUNT SUDDENLY STOPPED . . . AND COWERED BACK."

18 *a great yew tree.* Lucy, in her graveyard scene, moves down an avenue of yews. (See p. 189 as well as chapter XV, note 6, on yews.)

19 *he beat his hands wildly together.* This means of showing grief is very like Van Helsing's hand-clapping display of hysteria on page 124, and Lord Godalming's on page 205.

20 *"Unclean, unclean! . . ."* Mina echoes the Victorian (and not yet wholly altered) masculine view that the rape victim was morally stained by the violent embrace she endured. Though Jonathan Harker rejects the notion, the rest of the action of the book is predicated on its force. Mina has been stained, spotted. Everything that follows is a chronicle of how the spots on Mina's soul are cleansed. Because she has been washed in the Blood of the Beast, she must be washed again in the Blood of the Lamb.

The cry "unclean, unclean" echoes that of the leper about whom the Bible tells us (Leviticus 13:45, 46): "And the leper in whom the plague *is*, his clothes shall be rent, and his head bare, and he shall put a covering upon his upper lip, and shall cry, Unclean, unclean." And, "All the days wherein the plague *shall be* in him he shall be defiled; he *is* unclean: he shall dwell alone; without the camp *shall* his habitation *be*."

In the Middle Ages, too, the isolation of the leper was complete. In *The Medieval Hospitals of England* (pp. 68–69) we read that:

"After separation the fate of the outcast is irrevocably sealed. Remembering the exhortation, he must never frequent places of public resort, nor eat and drink with the sound; he must not speak to them unless they are on the windward side, nor may he touch infants or young folk. Henceforth his signal is the clapper, by which he gives warning of his approach and draws attention to his request. This instrument consisted of tablets of wood, attached at one end with leather thongs, which made a loud click when shaken. In England, a bell was often substituted for this dismal rattle. Stow and Holinshed refer to the 'clapping of dishes and ringing of bels' by the lazar. The poor creature of shocking appearance . . . holds in his one remaining hand a bell. His piteous cry is 'Sum good, my gentyll mayster, for God sake.' . . ."

21 *and his eyes blazed.* Compare this description with that of Dracula and Mina on page 249. Harker and the vampire are given similarly passionate countenances and busy hands. In both, quite different, situations, Mina's position is the same, though it is in her husband's arms that she sobs.

A LEPER

20 "Unclean, unclean! I must touch him or kiss him no more. Oh, that it should be that it is I who am now his worst enemy, and whom he may have most cause to fear." To this he spoke out resolutely:—

"Nonsense, Mina. It is a shame to me to hear such a word. I would not hear it of you; and I shall not hear it from you. May God judge me by my deserts, and punish me with more bitter suffering than even this hour, if by any act or will of mine anything ever come between us!" He put out his arms and folded her to his breast; and for a while she lay there sobbing. He looked at us over her bowed head, with eyes that blinked damply above his quivering nostrils; his mouth was set as steel. After a while her sobs became less frequent and more faint, and then he said to me, speaking with a studied calmness which I felt tried his nervous power to the utmost:—

"And now, Dr. Seward, tell me all about it. Too well I know the broad fact; tell me all that has been." I told him exactly what had happened, and he listened with
21 seeming impassiveness; but his nostrils twitched and his eyes blazed as I told how the ruthless hands of the Count had held his wife in that terrible and horrid position, with her mouth to the open wound in his breast. It interested me, even at that moment, to see, that, whilst the face of white set passion

worked convulsively over the bowed head, the hands tenderly and lovingly stroked the ruffled hair. Just as I had finished, Quincey and Godalming knocked at the door. They entered in obedience to our summons. Van Helsing looked at me questioningly. I understood him to mean if we were to take advantage of their coming to divert if possible the thoughts of the unhappy husband and wife from each other and from themselves; so on nodding acquiescence to him he asked them what they had seen or done. To which Lord Godalming answered:—

"I could not see him anywhere in the passage, or in any of our rooms. I looked in the study but, though he had been there, he had gone. He had however——" He stopped suddenly looking at the poor drooping figure on the bed. Van Helsing said gravely:—

"Go on friend Arthur. We want here no more concealments. Our hope now is in knowing all. Tell freely!" So Art went on:—

"He had been there, and though it could only have been for a few seconds, he made rare hay of the place. All the manuscript had been burned, and the blue flames were flickering amongst the white ashes; the cylinders of your phonograph too were thrown on the fire, and the wax had helped the flames." Here I interrupted. "Thank God there is the other copy in the safe!" His face lit for a moment, but fell again as he went on: "I ran down stairs then, but could see no sign of him. I looked into Renfield's room; but there was no trace there except——!" Again he paused. "Go on," said Harker hoarsely; so he bowed his head and moistening his lips with his tongue, added: "except that the poor fellow is dead." Mrs. Harker raised her head, looking from one to the other of us as she said solemnly:—

"God's will be done!" I could not but feel that Art was 22
keeping back something; but, as I took it that it was with a purpose, I said nothing. Van Helsing turned to Morris and asked:—

"And you, friend Quincey, have you any to tell?"

"A little," he answered. "It may be much eventually, but at present I can't say. I thought it well to know if possible where the Count would go when he left the house. I
did not see him; but I saw a bat rise from Renfield's win- 23
dow, and flap westward. I expected to see him in some shape go back to Carfax; but he evidently sought some other lair

"I SAW A BAT RISE FROM RENFIELD'S WINDOW."

22 *"God's will be done!"* Mina's pious comment is all the requiem that a long-suffering Renfield will have.

23 *I saw a bat.* Quincey, the window-watcher, at last has something to report.

He will not be back to night; for the sky is reddening in the east, and the dawn is close. We must work to-morrow!"

He said the latter words through his shut teeth. For a space of perhaps a couple of minutes there was silence, and I could fancy that I could hear the sound of our hearts beating; then Van Helsing said, placing his hand very tenderly on Mrs. Harker's head:—

"And now, Madam Mina—poor, dear, dear Madam Mina—tell us exactly what happened. God knows that I do not want that you be pained; but it is need that we know all. For now more than ever has all work to be done quick and sharp, and in deadly earnest. The day is close to us that must end all, if it may so be; and now is the chance that we may live and learn."

The poor, dear lady shivered, and I could see the tension of her nerves as she clasped her husband closer to her and bent her head lower and lower still on his breast. Then she raised her head proudly, and held out one hand to Van Helsing who took it in his, and, after stooping and kissing it reverently, held it fast. The other hand was locked in that of her husband, who held his other arm thrown round her protectingly. After a pause in which she was evidently ordering her thoughts, she began:—

"I took the sleeping draught which you had so kindly given me, but for a long time it did not act. I seemed to become more wakeful, and myriads of horrible fancies began to crowd in upon my mind—all of them connected with death, and vampires; with blood, and pain, and trouble." Her husband involuntarily groaned as she turned to him and said lovingly: "Do not fret, dear. You must be brave and strong, and help me through the horrible task. If you only knew what an effort it is to me to tell of this fearful thing at all, you would understand how much I need your help. Well, I saw I must try to help the medicine to its work with my will, if it was to do me any good, so I resolutely set myself to sleep. Sure enough sleep must soon have come to me, for I remember no more. Jonathan coming in had not waked me, for he lay by my side when next I remember. There was in the room the same thin white mist that I had before noticed. But I forget now if you know of this; you will find it in my diary which I shall show you later. I felt the same vague terror which had come to me before, and the same sense of some presence. I turned to wake Jonathan, but found that he slept so soundly that it seemed as if it was he who had taken the sleeping draught, and not I. I tried, but I could not wake him. This caused me a great fear, and I looked around terrified. Then indeed, my heart sank within me: beside the bed, as if he had stepped out of the mist—or rather as if the mist had turned into his figure, for it had entirely disappeared—stood a tall, thin man, all in black. I knew him at once from the descriptions of the others. The waxen face; the high aquiline nose, on which the light fell in a thin white line; the parted red lips, with the sharp white teeth showing between; and the red eyes that I had seemed to see in the sunset on the windows of St. Mary's Church at Whitby. I knew, too, the red scar on his forehead where Jonathan had struck him. For an instant my heart stood still, and I would have screamed out, only that I was paralysed. In the pause he spoke in a sort of keen, cutting, whisper, pointing as he spoke to Jonathan :—

'"Silence! If you make a sound I shall take him and dash his brains out before your very eyes.' I was appalled and was too bewildered to do or say anything. With a mocking smile, he placed one hand upon my shoulder and, holding me tight, bared my throat with the other, saying as he did so: 'First, a little refreshment to reward my exertions. You may as well be
quiet; it is not the first time, or the second, that your veins have **24**
appeased my thirst!' I was bewildered, and, strangely enough,
I did not want to hinder him. I suppose it is a part of the **25**
horrible curse that such is, when his touch is on his victim. And oh, my God, my God, pity me! He placed his reeking lips upon my throat!" Her husband groaned again. She clasped his hand harder, and looked at him pityingly, as if he were the injured one, and went on :—

"I felt my strength fading away, and I was in a half swoon. **26**
How long this horrible thing lasted I know not; but it seemed that a long time must have passed before he took his foul, awful, sneering mouth away. I saw it drip with the fresh blood!" The remembrance seemed for a while to overpower her, and she drooped and would have sunk down but for her husband's sustaining arm. With a great effort she recovered herself and went on :—

"Then he spoke to me mockingly, 'And so you, like the others, would play your brains against mine. You would help these men to hunt me and frustrate me in my designs! You know now, and they know in part already, and will know in full before long, what it is to cross my path. They should have kept their energies for use closer to home. Whilst they played wits against me—against me who commanded nations, and intrigued for them, and fought for them, hundreds of years before they were born—I was countermining them. And
you, their best beloved one, are now to me, flesh of my flesh; **27**
blood of my blood; kin of my kin; my bountiful wine-press **28**
for a while; and shall be later on my companion and my helper. You shall be avenged in turn; for not one of them but shall minister to your needs. But as yet you are to be punished for what you have done. You have aided in thwarting me; now you shall come to my call. When my brain says "Come!" to you, you shall cross land or sea to do my bidding; and to that end this!' With that he pulled open his shirt, and with
his long sharp nails opened a vein in his breast. When the **29**
blood began to spurt out, he took my hands in one of his, holding them tight, and with the other seized my neck and pressed my mouth to the wound, so that I must either suffocate or swallow some of the—Oh my God! my God! what have I done? What have I done to deserve such a fate, I who have tried to walk in meekness and righteousness all my days. God pity me! Look down on a poor soul in worse than mortal peril; and in mercy pity those to whom she is dear!" Then she began to rub her lips as though to cleanse them from pollution.

As she was telling her terrible story, the eastern sky began to quicken, and everything became more and more clear. Harker

24 *it is not the first time, or the second.* The first visit was the night of the 30th. The second on October 1. This, then, on October 2, is the third.

25 *I did not want to hinder him.* Mina acknowledges (as did Jonathan in the presence of the three beautiful vampires in Transylvania) the attractive fascination of the monster.

26 *I was in a half swoon.* Jonathan, in a similar moment, was "in a languorous ecstasy" (see chapter III, p. 41).

27 *flesh of my flesh.* Stoker seems anxious for us to understand the blood exchange between Mina and Dracula as a parodic version of the Christian marriage ceremony. The phrase "flesh of my flesh" appears early in Genesis when Adam, waking out of the sleep into which God cast him, and finding the newly created Eve beside him says, "This *is* now bone of my bones, and flesh of my flesh: she shall be called Woman, because she was taken out of man. Therefore shall a man leave his father and his mother, and shall cleave unto his wife: and they shall be one flesh" (Genesis 2:23–24).

In the Roman Catholic marriage ceremony, we read: "So also ought men to love their wives as their own bodies . . . for we are members of His body, of His flesh, and of His bones. . . . For this cause shall a man leave his father and mother, and shall cleave to his wife; and they shall be two in one flesh."

Orson Welles, in his Mercury Theater radio production of *Dracula* (July 1, 1938), has Dracula repeating these words to Mina on board the *Demeter* en route to Transylvania, producing the effect of an eerie wedding flight.

28 *my bountiful wine-press.* The reader with a long memory will recall Paget's description of Transylvanian winemaking cited in chapter I, note 31. It sheds a particularly cruel light on this speech.

29 *opened a vein in his breast.* Assuming that Dracula has *extraordinarily* sharp fingernails, the likeliest vein he could open would be the superficial intercostal. How he managed to close a spurting vein again is quite another question for which I propose no answer at all.

was still and quiet; but over his face, as the awful narrative went on, came a grey look which deepened and deepened in the morning light, till when the first red streak of the coming dawn shot up, the flesh stood darkly out against the whitening hair.

We have arranged that one of us is to stay within call of the unhappy pair till we can meet together and arrange about taking action.

Of this I am sure: the sun rises to-day on no more miserable house in all the great round of its daily course.

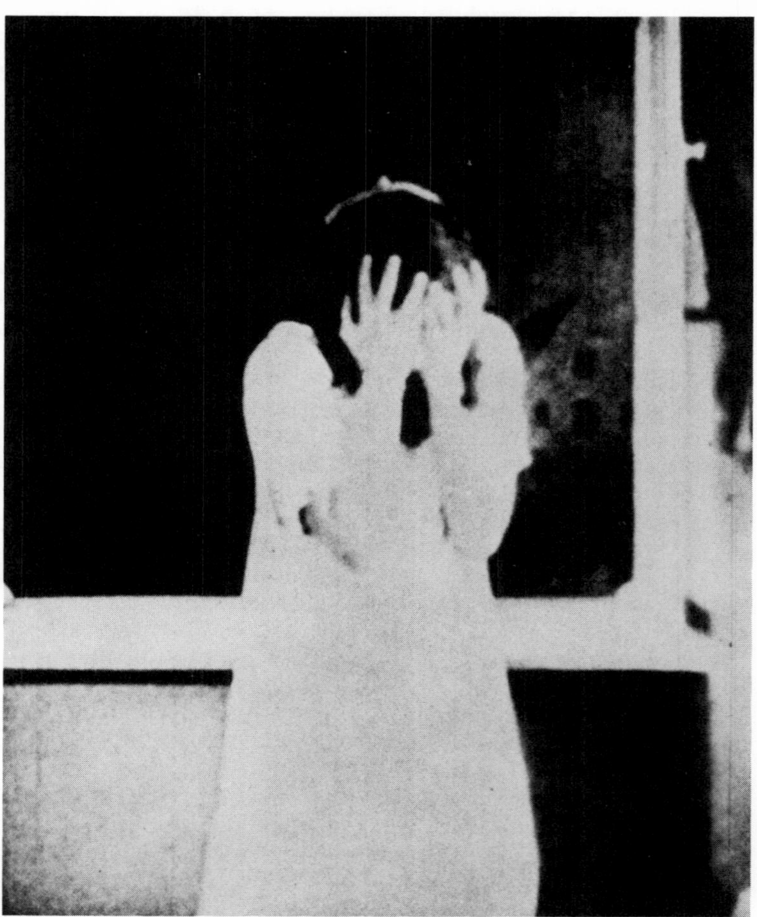

"OH MY GOD! MY GOD!"

CHAPTER XXII.

JONATHAN HARKER'S JOURNAL.

3 *October.*—As I must do something or go mad, I write this diary. It is now six o'clock, and we are to meet in the study in half an hour and take something to eat; for Dr. Van Helsing and Dr. Seward are agreed that if we do not eat we cannot work our best. Our best will be, God knows, required to-day. I must keep writing at every chance, for I dare not stop to think. All, big and little, must go down; perhaps at the end the little things may teach us most. The teaching, big or little, could not have landed Mina or me anywhere worse than we are to-day. However, we must trust and hope. Poor Mina told me just now, with the tears running down her dear cheeks, that it is in trouble and trial that our faith is tested—that we must keep on trusting; and that God will aid us up to the end. The end! oh my God! what end? . . . . . To work! To work!

When Dr. Van Helsing and Dr. Seward had come back from seeing poor Renfield, we went gravely into what was to be done. First, Dr. Seward told us that when he and Dr. Van Helsing had gone down to the room below they had found Renfield lying on the floor, all in a heap. His face was all bruised and crushed in, and the bones of the neck were broken.

Dr. Seward asked the attendant who was on duty in the passage if he had heard anything. He said that he had been
sitting down—he confessed to half dozing—when he heard 1
loud voices in the room, and then Renfield had called out
loudly several times, "God! God! God!" After that there was 2
a sound of falling, and when he entered the room he found him lying on the floor, face down, just as the doctors had seen him,

1 *half dozing.* Again, an employee is incompetent.

2 *"God! God! God!"* Renfield's apotheosis echoes Christ's last words, "My God, My God, why hast thou forsaken me?" (Matthew 27:46.)

3 *nothing . . . should be kept from her*. A very sensible conclusion, very tardily arrived at. One could argue that, beginning with Professor Van Helsing's secrecy, all the catastrophes of the book so far have come about because of unshared confidences.

4 "*. . . after what has happened?*" Translated from Van Helsing's Dutch-English, this means "Are you not afraid that you may be a vampire?"

5 *but least of all by your own*. First, of course, because Catholic Van Helsing regards suicide as a mortal sin; and second, because, according to folk tradition, a suicide risks turning into a vampire.

Van Helsing asked if he had heard "voices" or "a voice," and he said he could not say; that at first it had seemed to him as if there were two, but as there was no one in the room it could have been only one. He could swear to it, if required, that the word "God" was spoken by the patient. Dr. Seward said to us, when we were alone, that he did not wish to go into the matter; the question of an inquest had to be considered, and it would never do to put forward the truth, as no one would believe it. As it was, he thought that on the attendant's evidence he could give a certificate of death by misadventure in falling from bed. In case the coroner should demand it, there would be a formal inquest, necessarily to the same result.

When the question began to be discussed as to what should be our next step, the very first thing we decided was that
3 Mina should be in full confidence; that nothing of any sort—no matter how painful—should be kept from her. She herself agreed as to its wisdom, and it was pitiful to see her so brave and yet so sorrowful, and in such a depth of despair. "There must be no more concealment," she said, "Alas! we have had too much already. And besides there is nothing in all the world that can give me more pain than I have already endured—than I suffer now! Whatever may happen, it must be of new hope or of new courage to me!" Van Helsing was, looking at her fixedly as she spoke, and said, suddenly but quietly:—

"But dear Madam Mina are you not afraid; not for your-
4 self, but for others from yourself, after what has happened?" Her face grew set in its lines, but her eyes shone with the devotion of a martyr as she answered:—

"Ah no! for my mind is made up!"

"To what?" he asked gently, whilst we were all very still; for each in our own way we had a sort of vague idea of what she meant. Her answer came with direct simplicity, as though she were simply stating a fact:—

"Because if I find in myself—and I shall watch keenly for it—a sign of harm to any that I love, I shall die!"

"You would not kill yourself?" he asked, hoarsely.

"I would; if there were no friend who loved me, who would save me such a pain, and so desperate an effort!" She looked at him meaningly as she spoke. He was sitting down; but now he rose and came close to her and put his hand on her head as he said solemnly:

"My child, there is such an one if it were for your good. For myself I could hold it in my account with God to find such an euthanasia for you, even at this moment if it were best. Nay, were it safe! But my child——" for a moment he seemed choked, and a great sob rose in his throat; he gulped it down and went on:—

"There are here some who would stand between you and death. You must not die. You must not die by any hand;
5 but least of all by your own. Until the other, who has fouled your sweet life, is true dead you must not die; for if he is still with the quick Un-dead, your death would make you even as he is. No, you must live! You must struggle and strive to live, though death would seem a boon unspeakable. You must fight Death himself, though he come to you in pain or in joy; by the day, or the night; in safety or in peril! On your

living soul I charge you that you do not die—nay nor think of death—till this great evil be past." The poor dear grew white as death, and shook and shivered, as I have seen a quicksand 6
shake and shiver at the incoming of the tide. We were all silent; we could do nothing. At length she grew more calm and turning to him said, sweetly, but oh! so sorrowfully, as she held out her hand:—

"I promise you, my dear friend, that if God will let me live, I shall strive to do so; till, if it may be in His good time, this horror may have passed away from me." She was so good and brave that we all felt that our hearts were strengthened to work and endure for her, and we began to discuss what we were to do. I told her that she was to have all the papers in the safe, and all the papers or diaries and phonographs we might hereafter use; and was to keep the record as she had done before. She was pleased with the prospect of anything to do —if "pleased" could be used in connection with so grim an interest.

As usual Van Helsing had thought ahead of everyone else, and was prepared with an exact ordering of our work.

"It is perhaps well" he said "that at our meeting after our
visit to Carfax we decided not to do anything with the earth- 7
boxes that lay there. Had we done so, the Count must have guessed our purpose, and would doubtless have taken measures in advance to frustrate such an effort with regard to the others; but now he does not know our intentions. Nay more, in all probability, he does not know that such a power exists to us as can sterilize his lairs, so that he cannot use them as of old. We are now so much further advanced in our knowledge as to their disposition, that, when we have examined the house in Piccadilly, we may track the very last of them. To-day, then, is ours; and in it rests our hope. The sun that rose on our sorrow this morning guards us in its
course. Until it sets to-night, that monster must retain what- 8
ever form he now has. He is confined within the limitations of his earthly envelope. He cannot melt into thin air nor disappear through cracks or chinks or crannies. If he go through a door-way, he must open the door like a mortal. And so we have this day to hunt out all his lairs and sterilize them. So we shall, if we have not yet catch him and destroy him, drive him to bay in some place where the catching and the destroying shall be, in time, sure." Here I started up for I could not contain myself at the thought that the minutes and seconds so preciously laden with Mina's life and happiness were flying from us, since whilst we talked action was possible. But Van Helsing held up his hand warningly. "Nay, friend Jonathan," he said, "in this, the quickest way home is the longest way, so your proverb say. We shall all act, and act with desperate quick, when the time has come. But think, in all probable the key of the situation is in that house in Piccadilly. The Count may have many houses which he has bought. Of them he will have deeds of purchase, keys and other things. He will have paper that he write on; he will have his book of cheques. There are many belongings that he must have somewhere; why not in this place so central, so quiet, where he come and go by the front or the back at all hour, when in the very vast

6 *I have seen a quicksand.* Such a quicksand plays an important part in the narrative of Wilkie Collins's *The Moonstone*, a work that, as earlier noted, provided a structural model for *Dracula*.

7 *visit to Carfax.* Before dawn on October 1, as recorded in Jonathan Harker's October 1 entry (chapter XIX, pp. 220–26).

8 *must retain whatever form.* Stoker, in this paragraph, is inventing as much folklore as he is remembering. The lore of the vampire is neither consistent nor dogmatic and varies from country to country—and in some countries, from place to place. Though Van Helsing acknowledges that "all we have to go upon are traditions and superstitions," he proceeds to act as if they were fixed and systematic. (See chapter XVIII, pp. 212–13.)

This impulse to make law out of lore is very powerful and finds its most vivid expression in the film industry's treatment of the vampire.

9 *'stop the earths.'* A term taken from the practice in fox hunting of closing up possible burrows, or holes, in which a pursued fox might take refuge in the course of the hunt.

"WE RUN DOWN OUR OLD FOX."

of the traffic there is none to notice. We shall go there and search that house; and when we learn what it holds, then we
9 do what our friend Arthur call, in his phrases of hunt 'stop the earths' and so we run down our old fox—so? is it not?"

"Then let us come at once," I cried, "we are wasting the precious, precious time!" The Professor did not move, but simply said:—

"And how are we to get into that house in Piccadilly?"

"Any way!" I cried. "We shall break in if need be."

"And your police; where will they be, and what will they say?"

I was staggered; but I knew that if he wished to delay he had a good reason for it. So I said, as quietly as I could:—

"Don't wait more than need be; you know, I am sure, what torture I am in."

"Ah, my child, that I do; and indeed there is no wish of me to add to your anguish. But just think, what can we do, until all the world be at movement. Then will come our time. I have thought and thought, and it seems to me that the simplest way is the best of all. Now we wish to get into the house, but we have no key; is it not so?" I nodded.

"Now suppose that you were, in truth, the owner of that house, and could not still get it; and think there was to you no conscience of the housebreaker, what would you do?"

"I should get a respectable locksmith, and set him to work to pick the lock for me."

"And your police, they would interfere, would they not?"

"Oh, no! not if they knew the man was properly employed."

"Then," he looked at me keenly as he spoke, "all that is in doubt is the conscience of the employer, and the belief of your policemen as to whether or no that employer has a good conscience or a bad one. Your police must indeed be zealous men and clever—oh so clever!—in reading the heart, that they trouble themselves in such matter. No, no, my friend Jonathan, you go take the lock off a hundred empty house in this your London, or of any city in the world; and if you do

it as such things are rightly done, and at the time such things are rightly done, no one will interfere. I have read of a gentleman who owned a so fine house in your London, and when he went for months of summer to Zwitzerland and lock up his house, some burglar came and broke window at back and got in. Then he went and made open the shutters in front and walk out and in through the door, before the very eyes of the police. Then he have an auction in that house, and advertise it, and put up big notice: and when the day come he sell off by a great auctioneer all the goods of that other man who own them. Then he go to a builder, and he sell him that house, making an agreement that he pull it down and take all away within a certain time. And your police and other authority help him all they can. And when that owner come back from his holiday in Zwitzerland he find only an empty hole where his house had been. This was all done *en règle*; and in our work we shall be *en règle* too. We shall not **10**
go so early that the policeman who have then little to think of, shall deem it strange; but we shall go after ten o'clock when there are many about, and when such things would be done were we indeed owners of the house."

10 en règle. According to rule. In order.

I could not but see how right he was, and the terrible despair of Mina's face became relaxed a thought; there was hope in such good counsel. Van Helsing went on:—

"When once within that house we may find more clues; at any rate some of us can remain there whilst the rest find the other places where there be more earth-boxes—at Bermondsey and Mile End."

Lord Godalming stood up. "I can be of some use here" he said. "I shall wire to my people to have horses and carriages where they will be most convenient."

"Look here, old fellow," said Morris, "it is a capital idea to have all ready in case we want to go horsebacking; but don't you think that one of your snappy carriages with its heraldic adornments in a byeway of Walworth or Mile End would attract too much attention for our purposes? It seems to me that we ought to take cabs when we go south or east; and even leave them somewhere near the neighbourhood we are going to."

"Friend Quincey is right!" said the Professor. "His head is what you call in plane with the horizon. It is a difficult thing that we go to do, and we do not want no peoples to watch us if so it may."

Mina took a growing interest in everything, and I was rejoiced to see that the exigency of affairs was helping her to forget for a time the terrible experience of the night. She was very, very pale—almost ghastly, and so thin that her lips were drawn away, showing her teeth in somewhat of prominence. I did not mention this last, lest it should give her needless pain; but it made my blood run cold in my veins to think of what had occurred with poor Lucy when the Count had sucked her blood. As yet there was no sign of the teeth growing sharper; but the time as yet was short, and there was time for fear.

When we came to the discussion of the sequence of our efforts and of the disposition of our forces, there were new sources of doubt. It was finally agreed that before starting for

11 *last night he banqueted heavily.* Van Helsing's remark is unbelievably cruel, but by now the reader may be accustomed to his lapses of taste. (See the King Laugh episode, chapter XIII, pp. 158–60.) Still, this is an unforgivable remark that a saintly Mina is nevertheless able to forgive.

Piccadilly we should destroy the Count's lair close at hand. In case he should find it out too soon, we should thus be still ahead of him in our work of destruction; and his presence in his purely material shape, and at his weakest, might give us some new clue.

As to the disposal of forces, it was suggested by the Professor that, after our visit to Carfax, we should all enter the house in Piccadilly; that the two doctors and I should remain there, whilst Lord Godalming and Quincey found the lairs at Walworth and Mile End and destroyed them. It was possible, if not likely, the Professor urged, that the Count might appear in Piccadilly during the day, and that if so we might be able to cope with him then and there. At any rate we might be able to follow him in force. To this plan I strenuously objected, in so far as my going was concerned, for I said that I intended to stay and protect Mina. I thought that my mind was made up on the subject; but Mina would not listen to my objection. She said that there might be some law matter in which I could be useful; that amongst the Count's papers might be some clue which I could understand out of my experience in Transylvania; and that, as it was, all the strength we could muster was required to cope with the Count's extraordinary power. I had to give in, for Mina's resolution was fixed; she said that it was the last hope for *her* that we should all work together. "As for me," she said, "I have no fear. Things have been as bad as they can be; and whatever may happen must have in it some element of hope or comfort. Go my husband! God can, if He wishes it, guard me as well alone as with any one present." So I started up crying out: "Then in God's name let us come at once, for we are losing time. The Count may come to Piccadilly earlier than we think."

"Not so!" said Van Helsing holding up his hand.

"But why?" I asked.

"Do you forget," he said, with actually a smile, "that
11 last night he banqueted heavily, and will sleep late?"

Did I forget! shall I ever—can I ever! Can any of us ever forget that terrible scene! Mina struggled hard to keep her brave countenance; but the pain overmastered her and she put her hands before her face, and shuddered whilst she moaned. Van Helsing had not intended to recall her frightful experience. He had simply lost sight of her and her part in the affair in his intellectual effort. When it struck him what he had said, he was horrified at his thoughtlessness and tried to comfort her. "Oh Madam Mina," he said, "dear, dear Madam Mina, alas! that I of all who so reverence you, should have said anything so forgetful. These stupid old lips of mine and this stupid old head do not deserve so; but you will forget it, will you not?" He bent low beside her as he spoke; she took his hand, and looking at him through her tears, said hoarsely:—

"No, I shall not forget, for it is well that I remember; and with it I have so much in memory of you that is sweet, that I take it all together. Now, you must all be going soon. Breakfast is ready, and we must all eat that we may be strong."

Breakfast was a strange meal to us all. We tried to be

cheerful and encourage each other, and Mina was the brightest and most cheerful of us. When it was over, Van Helsing stood up and said :—

"Now, my dear friends, we go forth to our terrible enterprise. Are we all armed, as we were on that night when first we visited our enemy's lair; armed against ghostly as well as carnal attack?" We all assured him. "Then it is well. Now Madam Mina, you are in any case *quite* safe here until the sunset; and before then we shall return—if——We shall return! But before we go let me see you armed against personal attack. I have myself, since you came down, prepared your chamber by the placing of the things of which we know, so that He may not enter. Now let me guard yourself. On your forehead I touch this piece of Sacred Wafer in the name of the Father, the Son, and ——"

There was a fearful scream which almost froze our hearts to hear. As he had placed the Wafer on Mina's forehead, it had 12
seared it—had burned into the flesh as though it had been a piece of white-hot metal. My poor darling's brain told her the significance of the fact as quickly as her nerves received the pain of it; and the two so overwhelmed her that her overwrought nature had its voice in that dreadful scream. But the words to her thought came quickly; the echo of the scream had not ceased to ring on the air when there came the reaction, and she sank on her knees on the floor in an agony of abasement. Pulling her beautiful hair over her face, as the leper of old his mantle, she wailed out :—

"Unclean! Unclean! Even the Almighty shuns my polluted flesh! I must bear this mark of shame upon my forehead until the Judgment Day." They all paused. I had thrown myself beside her in an agony of helpless grief, and putting my arms around held her tight. For a few minutes our sorrowful hearts beat together, whilst the friends around us turned away their eyes that ran tears silently. Then Van Helsing turned and said gravely; so gravely that I could not help feeling that he was in some way inspired, and was stating things outside himself :—

"It may be that you may have to bear that mark till God himself see fit, as He most surely shall, on the Judgment Day to redress all wrongs of the earth and of His children that He has placed thereon. And oh, Madam Mina, my dear, my dear, may we who love you be there to see, when that red scar, the sign of God's knowledge of what has been, shall pass away and leave your forehead as pure as the heart we know. For so surely as we live, that scar shall pass away when God sees right to lift the burden that is hard upon us. Till then we bear our Cross, as His Son did in obedience to His will. It may be that we are chosen instruments of His good pleasure, and that we ascend to His bidding as that other through stripes and shame; through tears and blood; through doubts and fears, and all that makes the difference between God and man."

There was hope in his words, and comfort; and they made for resignation. Mina and I both felt so, and simultaneously we each took one of the old man's hands and bent over and kissed it. Then without a word we all knelt down together,

12 *As he had placed the Wafer on Mina's forehead.* The branding of Mina is, to borrow Stoker's language, the outward and visible sign of her unwilling commerce with the devil. Of course, it is also Dracula's revenge against Harker for the mark the young solicitor put on Dracula's forehead when he wielded the shovel against him (chapter IV, p. 54). See also chapter XXI, note 20, where the idea of Mina's moral stain is discussed.

13 *true to each other.* At this point the narrative, which has been an implicit Christian allegory, becomes nearly explicit. The men are seen as chivalric knights pledged to heroic deeds for the sake of Mina's salvation.

Here, perhaps more than in any other place, Mina's name may have emblematic meaning. Spelled backwards, it almost achieves the Latin *anima*, or soul.

14 *in sacred earth.* I have thus far been unable to find any folkloric or historic antecedent for this poignant idea. It appears to be Stoker's own invention, serving to emphasize how intimately evil is allied to good. There is a certain flush of Manichaeanism in the idea, one that is probably far from Stoker's intention. It is hard to believe that Stoker meant to hold God responsible for the invention of evil.

15 *laid it reverently on the earth.* Not for a devout Catholic. The Host, which represents the Risen Body and Blood of Christ, is intended as food for the soul. As Van Helsing uses it, the Wafer would decay. This is precisely *not* a reverential use of the Host. (See chapter XVI, note 1.)

13 and, all holding hands, swore to be true to each other. We men pledged ourselves to raise the veil of sorrow from the head of her whom, each in his own way, we loved; and we prayed for help and guidance in the terrible task which lay before us.

It was then time to start. So I said farewell to Mina, a parting which neither of us shall forget to our dying day; and we set out.

To one thing I have made up my mind: if we find out that Mina must be a vampire in the end, then she shall not go into that unknown and terrible land alone. I suppose it is thus that in old times one vampire meant many; just as their
14 hideous bodies could only rest in sacred earth, so the holiest love was the recruiting sergeant for their ghastly ranks.

We entered Carfax without trouble and found all things the same as on the first occasion. It was hard to believe that amongst so prosaic surroundings of neglect and dust and decay there was any ground for such fear as already we knew. Had not our minds been made up, and had there not been terrible memories to spur us on, we could hardly have proceeded with our task. We found no papers, or any sign of use in the house; and in the old chapel the great boxes looked just as we had seen them last. Dr. Van Helsing said to us solemnly as we stood before them:—

"And now, my friends, we have a duty here to do. We must sterilise this earth, so sacred of holy memories, that he has brought from a far distant land for such fell use. He has chosen this earth because it has been holy. Thus we defeat him with his own weapon, for we make it more holy still. It was sanctified to such use of man, now we sanctify it to God." As he spoke he took from his bag a screw-driver and a wrench, and very soon the top of one of the cases was thrown open. The earth smelled musty and close; but we did not somehow seem to mind, for our attention was concentrated on the Professor. Taking from his box a piece of the Sacred Wafer
15 he laid it reverently on the earth, and then shutting down the lid began to screw it home, we aiding him as he worked.

One by one we treated in the same way each of the great boxes, and left them as we had found them to all appearance; but in each was a portion of the Host.

When we closed the door behind us, the Professor said solemnly:—

"So much is already done. If it may be that with all the others we can be so successful, then the sunset of this evening may shine on Madam Mina's forehead all white as ivory and with no stain!"

As we passed across the lawn on our way to the station to catch our train we could see the front of the asylum. I looked eagerly, and in the window of my own room saw Mina. I waved my hand to her, and nodded to tell that our work there was successfully accomplished. She nodded in reply to show that she understood. The last I saw, she was waving her hand in farewell. It was with a heavy heart that we sought the station and just caught the train, which was steaming in as we reached the platform.

I have written this in the train.

Piccadilly, 12.30 *o'clock*.—Just before we reached Fenchurch Street Lord Godalming said to me:

"Quincey and I will find a locksmith. You had better not come with us in case there should be any difficulty; for under the circumstances it wouldn't seem so bad for us to break into an empty house. But you are a solicitor and the Incorporated **16**
Law Society might tell you that you should have known better." I demurred as to my not sharing any danger even of odium, but he went on: "Besides, it will attract less attention if there are not too many of us. My title will make it all right with the locksmith, and with any policeman that may come along. You had better go with Jack and the Professor and stay in the Green Park, somewhere in sight of the house; and when you see the door opened and the smith has gone away, do you all come across. We shall be on the look out for you, and shall let you in."

"The advice is good!" said Van Helsing, so we said no more. Godalming and Morris hurried off in a cab, we following in another. At the corner of Arlington Street our contingent got out and strolled into the Green Park. My heart beat as I saw the house on which so much of our hope was centred, looming up grim and silent in its deserted condition amongst its more lively and spruce-looking neighbours. We sat down on a bench within good view, and began to smoke cigars so as to attract as little attention as possible. The minutes seemed to pass with leaden feet as we waited for the coming of the others.

At length we saw a four-wheeler drive up. Out of it, in leisurely fashion, got Lord Godalming and Morris; and down from the box descended a thick-set working man with his rush-woven basket of tools. Morris paid the cabman, who touched his hat and drove away. Together the two ascended the steps, and Lord Godalming pointed out what he wanted done. The workman took off his coat leisurely and hung it on one of the spikes of the rail, saying something to a policeman who just then sauntered along. The policeman nodded acquiescence, and the man kneeling down placed his bag beside him. After searching through it, he took out a selection of tools which he proceeded to lay beside him in orderly fashion. Then he stood up, looked into the keyhole, blew into it, and, turning to his employers, made some remark. Lord Godalming smiled, and the man lifted a good sized bunch of keys; selecting one of them, he began to probe the lock, as if feeling his way with it. After fumbling about for a bit he tried a second, and then a third. All at once the door opened under a slight push from him, and he and the two others entered the hall. We sat still; my own cigar burnt furiously, but Van Helsing's went cold altogether. We waited patiently as we saw the workman come out and bring in his bag. Then he held the door partly open, steadying it with his knees, whilst he fitted a key to the lock. This he finally handed to Lord Godalming, who took out his purse and gave him something. The man touched his hat, took his bag, put on his coat and departed; not a soul took the slightest notice of the whole transaction.

When the man had fairly gone, we three crossed the street and knocked at the door. It was immediately opened by

16 *Incorporated Law Society*. The British counterpart of the American Bar Association.

17 *the East and the South.* There were twenty-nine boxes at Carfax and there are eight here. Fourteen still need to be accounted for.

This paragraph comes close to creating some human sympathy for Dracula, the lonely bachelor in barren rented rooms who covers his writing materials in thin wrapping paper, but forgets to empty out his bloody washbasin.

Quincey Morris, beside whom stood Lord Godalming lighting a cigar.

"The place smells so vilely," said the latter as we came in. It did indeed smell vilely—like the old chapel at Carfax—and with our previous experience it was plain to us that the Count had been using the place pretty freely. We moved to explore the house, all keeping together in case of attack; for we knew we had a strong and wily enemy to deal with, and as yet we did not know whether the Count might not be in the house. In the dining-room, which lay at the back of the hall, we found eight boxes of earth. Eight boxes only out of the nine which we sought! Our work was not over, and would never be until we should have found the missing box. First we opened the shutters of the window which looked out across a narrow stone flagged yard at the blank face of a stable, pointed to look like the front of a miniature house. There were no windows in it, so we were not afraid of being overlooked. We did not lose any time in examining the chests. With the tools which we had brought with us we opened them, one by one, and treated them as we had treated those others in the old chapel. It was evident to us that the Count was not at present in the house, and we proceeded to search for any of his effects.

After a cursory glance at the rest of the rooms, from basement to attic, we came to the conclusion that the dining-room contained any effects which might belong to the Count; and so we proceeded to minutely examine them. They lay in a sort of orderly disorder on the great dining-room table. There were title deeds of the Piccadilly house in a great bundle; deeds of the purchase of the houses at Mile End and Bermondsey; notepaper, envelopes, and pens and ink. All were covered up in thin wrapping paper to keep them from the dust. There were also a clothes brush, a brush and comb, and a jug and basin—the latter containing dirty water which was reddened as if with blood. Last of all was a little heap of keys of all sorts and sizes, probably those belonging to the other houses. When we had examined this last find, Lord Godalming and Quincey Morris taking accurate notes of the
17 various addresses of the houses in the East and the South, took with them the keys in a great bunch, and set out to destroy the boxes in these places. The rest of us are, with what patience we can, waiting their return—or the coming of the Count.

CHAPTER XXIII.

Dr. Seward's Diary.

3 *October*.—The time seemed terribly long whilst we were waiting for the coming of Godalming and Quincey Morris. The Professor tried to keep our minds active by using them all the time. I could see his beneficent purpose, by the side glances which he threw from time to time at Harker. The poor fellow is overwhelmed in a misery that is appalling to see. Last night he was a frank, happy-looking man, with strong youthful face, full of energy, and with dark brown hair. To-day he is
a drawn, haggard old man, whose white hair matches well with 1
the hollow burning eyes and grief-written lines of his face. His energy is still intact; in fact he is like a living flame. This may yet be his salvation, for, if all go well, it will tide him over the despairing period; he will then, in a kind of way, wake again to the realities of life. Poor fellow, I thought my own trouble was bad enough, but his——! The Professor knows this well enough, and is doing his best to keep his mind active. What he has been saying was, under the circumstances, of absorbing interest. So well as I can remember, here it is:—

"I have studied, over and over again since they came into 2
my hands, all the papers relating to this monster; and the more I have studied, the greater seems the necessity to utterly stamp him out. All through there are signs of his advance; not only of his power, but of his knowledge of it. As I learned from the researches of my friend Arminius of Buda-Pesth, he was in life a most wonderful man. Soldier, statesman, and alchemist—which latter was the highest development of the science-knowledge of his time. He had a mighty brain, a learning beyond compare, and a heart that knew no fear and
no remorse. He dared even to attend the Scholomance, and 3
there was no branch of knowledge of his time that he did not essay. Well, in him the brain powers survived the physical death; though it would seem that memory was not all complete. In some faculties of mind he has been, and is, only a child; but he is growing, and some things that were childish at the first are now of man's stature. He is experimenting, and doing it well; and if it had not been that we have crossed his path he would be yet—he may be yet if we fail—the

1 *a drawn, haggard old man.* He looks, in fact, remarkably the way Dracula himself once looked. Harker's "old age" forms a symbol of a singular subtlety. As if it had been given to him to encounter an aspect of himself in Transylvania with which he was doomed to merge.

In the course of the novel he and Dracula, pivoting around Mina, whom they both love, slowly change place and form. It is a strange transformation in which, *via* Mina, Harker has been weakened by a succubus, who in turn nourishes her incubus, the ever more youthful Dracula.

It will be seen too that, except for the final moments of the fiction, Harker becomes increasingly more supine as Dracula grows more active.

2 *"I have studied . . ."* The speech that follows is nearly accent-free.

3 *Scholomance.* See chapter XVIII, note 12.

4 *father or furtherer of a new order of beings.* It would be worth much to know how long it takes for the devil's get to come to term. For the sake of my pet notion that the mark on Mina's forehead is the visible sign of her pregnancy by Dracula, the time should be thirteen months—the number that actually passed before her baby was born. I regret to say that Anton La Vey, San Francisco's resident Satanist, tells me that the devil's children by mortals spend the usual nine months *in utero.* Arturo Graf, in a fine chapter in his book *The Story of the Devil,* says: "We have seen that the devils, in either a natural or an unnatural manner were capable of procreation; and since they were numberless, it is not to be wondered at if the number of their children was immense. Jordanes, the historian of the Goths, in the fourth century, declares that the Huns were born of the union of horrible witches with incubi; and during the whole period of the Middle Ages, there was a decided tendency to regard all deformed and misshapen children as the offspring of the Devil . . . Attila, the Scourge of God, was a son of the Devil, according to some; according to others, the son of a mastiff.

"Not only did the devil beget—he also loved and there are stories of his anguish in love's toils.

"One final note: women who experienced it, report that the devil's sperm is cold as ice."

5 Festina lente. Make haste slowly.

6 *telegraph boy.* This is perhaps the speediest service in the history of the telegraph—fifteen minutes from the time Mina sights Dracula to the moment when her message is hand-delivered.

4 father or furtherer of a new order of beings, whose road must lead through Death, not Life."

Harker groaned and said, "And this is all arrayed against my darling! But how is he experimenting? The knowledge may help us to defeat him!"

"He has all along, since his coming, been trying his power, slowly but surely; that big child-brain of his is working. Well for us, it is, as yet, a child-brain; for had he dared, at the first, to attempt certain things he would long ago have been beyond our power. However, he means to succeed, and a man who has centuries before him can afford to wait and to go
5 slow. *Festina lente* may well be his motto."

"I fail to understand," said Harker wearily. "Oh, do be more plain to me! Perhaps grief and trouble are dulling my brain." The Professor laid his hand tenderly on his shoulder as he spoke:—

"Ah, my child, I will be plain. Do you not see how, of late, this monster has been creeping into knowledge experimentally. How he has been making use of the zoophagous patient to effect his entry into friend John's home; for your Vampire, though in all afterwards he can come when and how he will, must at the first make entry only when asked thereto by an inmate. But these are not his most important experiments. Do we not see how at the first all these so great boxes were moved by others. He knew not then but that must be so. But all the time that so great child-brain of his was growing, and he began to consider whether he might not himself move the box. So he begin to help; and then, when he found that this be all-right, he try to move them all alone. And so he progress, and he scatter these graves of him; and none but he know where they are hidden. He may have intend to bury them deep in the ground. So that he only use them in the night, or at such time as he can change his form, they do him equal well; and none may know these are his hiding place! But, my child, do not despair: this knowledge come to him just too late! Already all of his lairs but one be sterilize as for him; and before the sunset this shall be so. Then he have no place where he can move and hide. I delayed this morning that so we might be sure. Is there not more at stake for us than for him? Then why we not be even more careful than him? By my clock it is one hour, and already, if all be well, friend Arthur and Quincey are on their way to us. To-day is our day, and we must go sure, if slow, and lose no chance. See! there are five of us when those absent ones return."

Whilst he was speaking we were startled by a knock at the
6 hall door, the double postman's knock of the telegraph boy. We all moved out to the hall with one impulse, and Van Helsing, holding up his hand to us to keep silence, stepped to the door and opened it. The boy handed in a despatch. The Professor closed the door again and, after looking at the direction, opened it and read it aloud.

"Look out for D. He has just now, 12.45, come from Carfax hurriedly and hastened towards the south. He seems to be going the round and may want to see you: Mina."

There was a pause, broken by Jonathan Harker's voice:—

"Now, God be thanked, we shall soon meet!" Van Helsing turned to him quickly and said:—

"God will act in His own way and time. Do not fear, and do not rejoice as yet; for what we wish for at the moment may be our undoings."

"I care for nothing now," he answered hotly, "except to wipe out this brute from the face of creation. I would sell my soul to do it!"

"Oh hush, hush, my child!" said Van Helsing, "God does not purchase souls in this wise; and the Devil, though he may purchase, does not keep faith. But God is merciful and just, and knows your pain and your devotion to that dear Madam Mina. Think you, how her pain would be doubled, did she but hear your wild words. Do not fear any of us; we are all devoted to this cause, and to-day shall see the end. The time is coming for action; to-day this Vampire is limit to the powers of man, and till sunset he may not change. It will take him time to arrive here—see it is twenty minutes past one—and there are yet some times before he can hither come, be he never so quick. What we must hope for is that my Lord Arthur and Quincey arrive first."

About half an hour after we had received Mrs. Harker's telegram, there came a quiet resolute knock at the hall door. It was just an ordinary knock, such as is given hourly by thousands of gentlemen, but it made the Professor's heart and mine beat loudly. We looked at each other, and together moved out into the hall; we each held ready to use our various
armaments—the spiritual in the left hand, the mortal in the 7
right. Van Helsing pulled back the latch, and, holding the door half open, stood back, having both hands ready for action. The gladness of our hearts must have shown upon our faces when on the step, close to the door, we saw Lord Godalming and Quincey Morris. They came quickly in and closed the door behind them, the former saying, as they moved along the hall:—

"It is all right. We found both places; six boxes in each, 8
and we destroyed them all!"

"Destroyed?" asked the Professor.

"For him!" We were silent for a minute, and then Quincey said:—

"There's nothing to do but to wait here. If, however, he doesn't turn up by five o'clock, we must start off; for it won't do to leave Mrs. Harker alone after sunset."

"He will be here before long now," said Van Helsing, who had been consulting his pocket-book. "*Nota bene*, in Madam's telegram he went south from Carfax, that means he went to cross the river, and he could only do so at slack of tide, which should be something before one o'clock. That he went south has a meaning for us. He is as yet only suspicious; and he went from Carfax first to the place where he would suspect interference least. You must have been at Bermondsey only a short time before him. That he is not here already shows that he went to Mile End next. This took him some time; for he would then have to be carried over the river in some way. Believe me, my friends, we shall not have long to wait now. We should have ready some plan of attack,

7 *the mortal in the right.* Symbolically, one would have expected the order to be reversed: the mortal weapons in the left hand and the spiritual in the right. Stoker here was faced with the pragmatic problem that his heroes, no matter how deeply they were involved in religious allegory, were likely to be right-handed.

8 *six boxes in each.* The tally of boxes so far accounted for is: 29 at Carfax, 8 at Piccadilly, 6 at Mile End, 6 at Walworth (Bermondsey), for a total of 49.

so that we may throw away no chance. Hush, there is no time now. Have all your arms! Be ready!' He held up a warning hand as he spoke, for we all could hear a key softly inserted in the lock of the hall door.

I could not but admire, even at such a moment, the way in which a dominant spirit asserted itself. In all our hunting parties and adventures in different parts of the world, Quincey
9 Morris had always been the one to arrange the plan of action, and Arthur and I had been accustomed to obey him implicitly. Now, the old habit seemed to be renewed instinctively. With a swift glance round the room, he at once laid out our plan of attack, and, without speaking a word, with a gesture, placed us each in position. Van Helsing, Harker, and I were just behind the door so that when it was opened the Professor could guard it whilst we two stepped between the incomer and the door. Godalming behind and Quincey in front stood just out of sight ready to move in front of the window. We waited in a suspense that made the seconds pass with nightmare slowness. The slow, careful steps came along the hall; the Count was evidently prepared for some surprise—at least he feared it.

Suddenly with a single bound he leaped into the room, winning a way past us before any of us could raise a hand to stay him. There was something so panther-like in the movement—something so unhuman, that it seemed to sober us all from the shock of his coming. The first to act was Harker, who, with a quick movement, threw himself before the door leading into the room in the front of the house. As the Count saw us, a horrible sort of snarl passed over his face, showing the eye-teeth long and pointed; but the evil smile as quickly passed into a cold stare of lion-like disdain. His expression again changed, as, with a single impulse, we all advanced upon him. It was a pity that we had not some better organised plan of attack, for even at the moment I wondered what we were to do. I did not myself know whether our lethal weapons would avail us anything. Harker
10 evidently meant to try the matter, for he had ready his great Kukri knife, and made a fierce and sudden cut at him. The blow was a powerful one; only the diabolical quickness of the Count's leap back saved him. A second less and the trenchant blade had shorne through his heart. As it was, the point just cut the cloth of his coat, making a wide gap whence a bundle of bank-notes and a stream of gold fell out. The expression of the Count's face was so hellish, that for a moment I feared for Harker, though I saw him throw the terrible knife aloft again for another stroke. Instinctively I moved forward with a protective impulse, holding the crucifix and wafer in my left hand. I felt a mighty power fly along my arm; and it was without surprise I saw that the monster cower back before a similar movement made spontaneously by each one of us. It would be impossible to describe the expression of hate and baffled malignity—of anger and hellish rage—which came over the Count's face. His waxen hue became greenish-yellow by
11 the contrast of his burning eyes, and the red scar on the
12 forehead showed on the pallid skin like a palpitating wound.
The next instant, with a sinuous dive he swept under Harker's

9 *the plan of action.* Quincey may be a master planner but Stoker forgets what his master plan is, as we see a little farther down the page, when we learn that "it was a pity that we had not some better organised plan of attack . . ."

10 *great Kukri knife.* The kukri knife is the preferred combat weapon of the Gurkhas of Nepal. The Gurkhas were famous fighting troops in the British army in preindependence India. Frederick Wilkinson, in *Swords and Daggers* (p. 72), says that "traditionally, a Ghurka never sheaths his *kukri* without first drawing blood with it and this custom is still observed by many of these fine warriors of Nepal."

An initiation rite for a Gurkha warrior required him to show his prowess by beheading a young bullock with his kukri knife with a single blow.

11 *the red scar on the forehead.* The scar, put there by Harker's wild swing with the shovel in Transylvania (p. 54), has been fully avenged, in kind. Mina's scar, made by the Wafer, is, of course, Dracula's revenge. Both of them now carry the mark of Cain.

12 *like a palpitating wound.* As vivid as the mark on Mina's forehead.

arm, ere his blow could fall, and, grasping a handful of the money from the floor, dashed across the room, threw himself 13
at the window. Amid the crash and glitter of the falling glass, he tumbled into the flagged area below. Through the sound of the shivering glass I could hear the "ting" of the gold, as some of the sovereigns fell on the flagging.

We ran over and saw him spring unhurt from the ground. He, rushing up the steps, crossed the flagged yard, and pushed open the stable door. There he turned and spoke to us:—

"You think to baffle me, you——with your pale faces all in a row, like sheep in a butcher's. You shall be sorry yet, each one of you! You think you have left me without a place to rest; but I have more. My revenge is just begun! I spread it over centuries, and time is on my side. Your girls that you all love are mine already; and through them you and others shall yet be mine—my creatures, to do my bidding and to be my jackals when I want to feed. Bah!" With a contemptuous sneer, he passed quickly through the door, and we heard the rusty bolt creak as he fastened it behind him. A door beyond opened and shut. The first of us to speak was the Professor, as, realising the difficulty of following him through the stable, we moved towards the hall.

"We have learnt something—much! Notwithstanding his brave words, he fears us; he fear time, he fear want! For if not, why he hurry so? His very tone betray him, or my ears deceive. Why take that money? You follow quick. You are hunters of wild beast, and understand it so. For me, I make sure that nothing here may be of use to him, if so that he return." As he spoke he put the money remaining into his pocket; took the title-deeds in the bundle as Harker had left them; and swept the remaining things into the open fireplace where he set fire to them with a match.

Godalming and Morris had rushed out into the yard, and Harker had lowered himself from the window to follow the Count. He had, however, bolted the stable door; and by the time they had forced it open there was no sign of him. Van Helsing and I tried to make inquiry at the back of the house; but the mews was deserted and no one had seen him depart.

It was now late in the afternoon, and sunset was not far off. We had to recognise that our game was up; with heavy hearts we agreed with the Professor when he said:—

"Let us go back to Madam Mina—poor, poor, dear Madam Mina. All we can do just now is done; and we can there, at least, protect her. But we need not despair. There is but one more earth-box, and we must try to find it; when that is done all may yet be well." I could see that he spoke as bravely as he could to comfort Harker. The poor fellow was quite broken down; now and again he gave a low groan which he could not suppress—he was thinking of his wife.

With sad hearts we came back to my house, where we found Mrs. Harker waiting us, with an appearance of cheerfulness which did honour to her bravery and unselfishness.

13 *threw himself at the window.* Berserker, the wolf (chapter XI, pp. 134–35), smashed a window to provide entry for Dracula. Here the Count smashes his own way out. In both places there is plenty of falling glass. Note that Dracula came in by the door, proving that he is not obedient to the Law of Hell as Goethe's Mephistopheles has given it to us (in MacIntyre's translation of Faust, p. 95).

> "O, that's just one of those things: a law for spirits
> and demons—where they steal in they must go out."

14 *Oh that I could give any idea of the scene.* Here and on the following page is Victorian bathetic at its worst. This is the sort of stuff that made Virginia Woolf (in *Orlando*) characterize the age as "wet." Let the reader's courage not fail him. Patience or an extra handkerchief, or both, will get him past this slough of feeling.

When she saw our faces, her own became as pale as death; for a second or two her eyes were closed as if she were in secret prayer; and then she said cheerfully :—

"I can never thank you all enough. Oh, my poor darling!" as she spoke, she took her husband's grey head in her hands and kissed it—"Lay your poor head here and rest it. All will yet be well, dear! God will protect us if He so will it in His good intent." The poor fellow only groaned. There was no place for words in his sublime misery.

We had a sort of perfunctory supper together, and I think it cheered us all up somewhat. It was, perhaps, the mere animal heat of food to hungry people—for none of us had eaten anything since breakfast—or the sense of companionship may have helped us; but anyhow we were all less miserable, and saw the morrow as not altogether without hope. True to our promise, we told Mrs. Harker everything which had passed; and although she grew snowy white at times when danger had seemed to threaten her husband, and red at others when his devotion to her was manifested, she listened bravely and with calmness. When we came to the part where Harker had rushed at the Count so recklessly, she clung to her husband's arm, and held it tight as though her clinging could protect him from any harm that might come. She said nothing, however, till the narration was all done, and matters had been brought right up to the present time. Then without letting go her husband's hand she stood up amongst us and
14 spoke. Oh that I could give any idea of the scene; of that sweet, sweet, good, good woman in all the radiant beauty of her youth and animation, with the red scar on her forehead of which she was conscious, and which we saw with grinding of our teeth—remembering whence and how it came; her loving kindness against our grim hate; her tender faith against all our fears and doubting; and we, knowing that so far as symbols went, she with all her goodness and purity and faith, was outcast from God.

"Jonathan," she said, and the word sounded like music on her lips it was so full of love and tenderness, "Jonathan dear, and you all my true, true friends, I want you to bear something in mind through all this dreadful time. I know that you must fight—that you must destroy even as you destroyed the false Lucy so that the true Lucy might live hereafter; but it is not a work of hate. That poor soul who has wrought all this misery is the saddest case of all. Just think what will be his joy when he too is destroyed in his worser part that his better part may have spiritual immortality. You must be pitiful to him too, though it may not hold your hands from his destruction."

As she spoke I could see her husband's face darken and draw together, as though the passion in him were shrivelling his being to its core. Instinctively the clasp on his wife's hand grew closer, till his knuckles looked white. She did not flinch from the pain which I knew she must have suffered, but looked at him with eyes that were more appealing than ever. As she stopped speaking he leaped to his feet, almost tearing his hand from hers as he spoke :—

"May God give him into my hand just for long enough to

destroy that earthly life of him which we are aiming at. If beyond it I could send his soul for ever and ever to burning hell I would do it!"

"Oh, hush! oh, hush! in the name of the good God. Don't say such things, Jonathan, my husband; or you will crush me with fear and horror. Just think, my dear—I have been thinking all this long, long day of it—that... perhaps... some day... I too may need such pity; and that some other like you—and with equal cause for anger—may deny it to me! Oh my husband! my husband, indeed I would have spared you such a thought had there been another way; but I pray that God may not have treasured your wild words, except as the heart-broken wail of a very loving and sorely stricken man. Oh God, let these poor white hairs go in evidence of what he has suffered, who all his life has done no wrong, and on whom so many sorrows have come."

We men were all in tears now. There was no resisting them, and we wept openly. She wept too, to see that her sweeter counsels had prevailed. Her husband flung himself on his knees beside her, and putting his arms round her, hid his face in the folds of her dress. Van Helsing beckoned to us and we stole out of the room, leaving the two loving hearts alone with their God.

Before they retired the Professor fixed up the room against any coming of the Vampire, and assured Mrs. Harker that she might rest in peace. She tried to school herself to the belief, and, manifestly for her husband's sake, tried to seem content. It was a brave struggle; and was, I think and believe, not without its reward. Van Helsing had placed at hand a bell which either of them was to sound in case of any emergency. When they had retired, Quincey, Godalming, and I arranged that we should sit up, dividing the night between us, and watch over the safety of the poor stricken lady. The first watch falls to Quincey, so the rest of us shall be off to bed as soon as we can. Godalming has already turned in, for his is the second watch. Now that my work is done I, too, shall go to bed.

Jonathan Harker's Journal.

3—4 *October, close to midnight.*—I thought yesterday would never end. There was over me a yearning for sleep, in some sort of blind belief that to wake would be to find things changed, and that any change must now be for the better. Before we parted, we discussed what our next step was to be, but we could arrive at no result. All we knew was that one earth-box remained, and that the Count alone knew where it was. If he chooses to lie hidden, he may baffle us for years; and in the meantime!—the thought is too horible, I dare not think of it even now. This I know: that if ever there was a woman who was all perfection, that one is my poor wronged darling. I love her a thousand times more for her sweet pity of last night, a pity that made my own hate of the monster seem despicable. Surely God will not permit the world to be the poorer by the loss of such a creature. This is hope to me. We are all drifting reefwards now, and faith is our only anchor. Thank God! Mina is sleeping, and sleeping without

15 *a deeper meaning.* What that meaning might be remains a sore puzzle to this editor.

dreams. I fear what her dreams might be like, with such terrible memories to ground them in. She has not been so calm, within my seeing, since the sunset. Then, for a while, there came over her face a repose which was like spring after the blasts of March. I thought at the time that it was the softness of the red sunset on her face, but somehow now I
15 think it has a deeper meaning. I am not sleepy myself, though I am weary—weary to death. However, I must try to sleep; for there is to-morrow to think of, and there is no rest for me until . . . .

Later.—I must have fallen asleep, for I was awaked by Mina, who was sitting up in bed, with a startled look on her face. I could see easily, for we did not leave the room in darkness; she had placed a warning hand over my mouth, and now she whispered in my ear:—

"Hush! there is someone in the corridor!" I got up softly, and, crossing the room, gently opened the door.

Just outside, stretched on a mattress lay Mr. Morris, wide awake. He raised a warning hand for silence as he whispered to me:—

"Hush! go back to bed; it is all right. One of us will be here all night. We don't mean to take any chances!"

His look and gesture forbade discussion, so I came back and told Mina. She sighed, and positively a shadow of a smile stole over her poor, pale face as she put her arms round me and said softly:—

"Oh, thank God for good brave men!" With a sigh she sank back again to sleep. I write this now as I am not sleepy, though I must try again.

4 *October, morning.*—Once again during the night I was wakened by Mina. This time we had all had a good sleep, for the grey of the coming dawn was making the windows into sharp oblongs, and the gas flame was like a speck rather than a disc of light. She said to me hurriedly:—

"Go, call the Professor. I want to see him at once."

"Why?" I asked.

"I have an idea. I suppose it must have come in the night, and matured without my knowing it. He must hypnotise me before the dawn, and then I shall be able to speak. Go quick, dearest; the time is getting close." I went to the door. Dr. Seward was resting on the mattress, and, seeing me, he sprang to his feet.

"Is anything wrong?" he asked, in alarm.

"No," I replied; "but Mina wants to see Dr. Van Helsing at once."

"I will go," he said, and hurried into the Professor's room.

In two or three minutes later Van Helsing was in the room in his dressing-gown, and Mr. Morris and Lord Godalming were with Dr. Seward at the door asking questions. When the Professor saw Mina a smile—a positive smile ousted the anxiety of his face; he rubbed his hands as he said:—

"Oh, my dear Madam Mina, this is indeed a change. See! friend Jonathan, we have got our dear Madam Mina, as of old, back to us to day!" Then turning to her, he said, cheerfully: "And what am I do for you? For at this hour you do not want me for nothings."

"I want you to hypnotise me!" she said. "Do it before the dawn, for I feel that then I can speak, and speak freely. Be quick, for the time is short!" Without a word he motioned her to sit up in bed.

Looking fixedly at her, he commenced to make passes in front of her, from over the top of her head downward, with each hand in turn. Mina gazed at him fixedly for a few minutes, during which my own heart beat like a trip hammer, for I felt that some crisis was at hand. Gradually her eyes closed, and she sat, stock still; only by the gentle heaving of her bosom could one know that she was alive. The Professor made a few more passes and then stopped, and I could see that his forehead was covered with great beads of perspiration. Mina opened her eyes; but she did not seem the same woman. There was a far-away look in her eyes, and her voice had a sad dreaminess which was new to me. Raising his hand to impose silence, the Professor motioned to me to bring the others in. They came on tip-toe, closing the door behind them, and stood at the foot of the bed, looking on. Mina appeared not to see them. The stillness was broken by Van Helsing's voice speaking in a low level tone which would not break the current of her thoughts:—

"Where are you?" The answer came in a neutral way:—

"I do not know. Sleep has no place it can call its own.' **16**

For several minutes there was silence. Mina sat rigid, and the Professor stood staring at her fixedly; the rest of us hardly dared to breathe. The room was growing lighter; without taking his eyes from Mina's face, Dr. Van Helsing motioned me to pull up the blind. I did so, and the day seemed just upon us. A red streak shot up, and a rosy light seemed to diffuse itself through the room. On the instant the Professor spoke again:—

"Where are you now?" The answer came dreamily, but with intention; it were as though she were interpreting something. I have heard her use the same tone when reading her shorthand notes.

"I do not know. It is all strange to me!"

"What do you see?"

"I can see nothing; it is all dark."

"What do you hear?" I could detect the strain in the Professor's patient voice.

"The lapping of water. It is gurgling by, and little waves leap. I can hear them on the outside."

"Then you are on a ship?" We all looked at each other, trying to glean something each from the other. We were afraid to think. The answer came quick:—

"Oh, yes!"

"What else do you hear?"

"The sound of men stamping overhead as they run about. There is the creaking of a chain, and the loud tinkle as the check of the capstan falls into the rachet."

"What are you doing?"

"I am still—oh, so still. It is like death!" The voice faded away into a deep breath as of one sleeping, and the open eyes closed again.

By this time the sun had risen, and we were all in the full light of day. Dr. Van Helsing placed his hands on Mina's

16 ". . . *Sleep has no place it can call its own.*" A line of extraordinary beauty.

17 *or slack tide.* As Van Helsing informed us in his lecture on the traits and characteristics of the vampire (chapter XVIII, p. 213).

18 *said sorrowfully.* Again, one is forced to wonder at Van Helsing's behavior toward Mina. This is not the first time that he has caused her acute anguish by being unnecessarily forthright. (See chapter XXII, p. 262, the "Do you forget . . ." episode.)

shoulders, and laid her head down softly on her pillow. She lay like a sleeping child for a few moments, and then, with a long sigh, awoke and stared in wonder to see us all around her. "Have I been talking in my sleep?" was all she said. She seemed, however, to know the situation without telling; though she was eager to know what she had told. The Professor repeated the conversation, and she said:—

"Then there is not a moment to lose: it may not be yet too late!" Mr. Morris and Lord Godalming started for the door but the Professor's calm voice called them back:—

"Stay, my friends. That ship wherever it was, was weighing anchor whilst she spoke. There are many ships weighing anchor at the moment in your so great Port of London. Which of them is it that you seek? God be thanked that we have once again a clue, though whither it may lead us we know not. We have been blind somewhat; blind after the manner of men, since when we can look back we see what we might have seen looking forward if we had been able to see what we might have seen! Alas! but that sentence is a puddle; is it not? We can know now what was in the Count's mind when he seize that money, though Jonathan's so fierce knife put him in the danger that even he dread. He meant escape. Hear me, ESCAPE! He saw that with but one earth-box left, and a pack of men following like dogs after a fox, this London was no place for him. He have take his last earth-box on board a ship, and he leave the land. He think to escape, but no! we follow him. Tally Ho! as friend Arthur would say when he put on his red frock! Our old fox is wily; oh! so wily and we must follow with wile. I too am wily and I think his mind in a little while. In meantime we may rest and in peace, for there are waters between us which he do not want to pass, and which he could not if he would—unless the ship were to touch the land, and then only
17 at full or slack tide. See, and the sun is just rose, and all day to sunset is to us. Let us take bath, and dress, and have breakfast which we all need, and which we can eat comfortable since he be not in the same land with us." Mina looked at him appealingly as she asked:—

"But why need we seek him further, when he is gone away from us?" He took her hand and patted it as he replied:—

"Ask me nothings as yet. When we have breakfast, then I answer all questions." He would say no more, and we separated to dress.

After breakfast Mina repeated her question. He looked at
18 her gravely for a minute and then said sorrowfully:—

"Because my dear, dear Madam Mina, now more than ever must we find him even if we have to follow him to the jaws of Hell!" She grew paler as she asked faintly:—

"Why?"

"Because," he answered solemnly, "he can live for centuries, and you are but mortal woman. Time is now to be dreaded—since once he put that mark upon your throat."

I was just in time to catch her as she fell forward in a faint.

CHAPTER XXIV.

DR. SEWARD'S PHONOGRAPH DIARY, SPOKEN BY VAN HELSING.

THIS to Jonathan Harker.

You are to stay with your dear Madam Mina. We shall go to make our search—if I can call it so, for it is not search but knowing, and we seek confirmation only. But do you stay and take care of her to-day. This is your best and most holiest office. This day nothing can find him here. Let me tell you that so you will know what we four know already, for I have tell them. He, our enemy, have gone away; he have gone back to his Castle in Transylvania. I know it so well, as if a great hand of fire wrote it on the wall. He have 1
prepare for this in some way, and that last earth-box was ready to ship somewheres. For this he took the money; for this he hurry at the last, lest we catch him before the sun go down. It was his last hope, save that he might hide in the tomb that he think poor Miss Lucy, being as he thought like him, keep open to him. But there was not of time. When that fail he make straight for his last resource—his last earthwork I might say did I wish *double entente.* He is clever, oh so clever! he know that his game here was finish; and so he decide he go back home. He find ship going by the route he came, and he go in it. We go off now to find what ship, and whither bound; when we have discover that, we come back and tell you all. Then we will comfort you and poor dear Madam Mina with new hope. For it will be hope when you think it over: that all is not lost. This very creature that we pursue, he take hundreds of years to get so far as London; and yet in one day, when we know of the

1 *a great hand of fire wrote it on the wall.* The writing on the wall was the work of God's hand. What it wrote was *Mene, Mene, Tekel, Upharsin,* and it was a message of doom to wicked Belshazzar (Daniel 5:5, 5:25). The message was not, however, written in fire.

disposal of him we drive him out. He is finite, though he is powerful to do much harm and suffers not as we do. But we are strong, each in our purpose; and we are all more strong together. Take heart afresh dear husband of Madam Mina. This battle is but begun, and in the end we shall win —so sure as that God sits on high to watch over His children. Therefore be of much comfort till we return.

VAN HELSING.

Jonathan Harker's Journal.

4 *October.*—When I read to Mina, Van Helsing's message in the phonograph, the poor girl brightened up considerably. Already the certainty that the Count is out of the country has given her comfort; and comfort is strength to her. For my own part, now that this horrible danger is not face to face with us, it seems almost impossible to believe in it. Even my own terrible experiences in Castle Dracula seem like a long-
2 forgotten dream. Here in the crisp autumn air in the bright sunlight—

Alas! how can I disbelieve! In the midst of my thought my eye fell on the red scar on my poor darling's white forehead. Whilst that lasts, there can be no disbelief. And afterwards the very memory of it will keep faith crystal clear. Mina and I fear to be idle, so we have been over all the diaries again and again. Somehow, although the reality seems greater each time, the pain and the fear seem less. There is something of a guiding purpose manifest throughout, which is comforting. Mina says that perhaps we are the instruments of ultimate good. It may be! I shall try to think as she does. We have never spoken to each other yet of the future. It is better to wait till we see the Professor and the others after their investigations.

The day is running by more quickly than I ever thought a day could run for me again. It is now three o'clock.

Mina Harker's Journal.

5 *October*, 5 *p.m.*—Our meeting for report. Present: Professor Van Helsing, Lord Godalming, Dr. Seward, Mr. Quincey Morris, Jonathan Harker, Mina Harker.

Dr. Van Helsing described what steps were taken during the day to discover on what boat and whither bound Count Dracula made his escape:—

"As I knew that he wanted to get back to Transylvania, I felt sure that he must go by the Danube mouth; or by somewhere in the Black Sea, since by that way he come. It was a
3 dreary blank that was before us. *Omne ignotum pro magnifico;* and so with heavy hearts we start to find what ships leave for the Black Sea last night. He was in sailing ship, since Madam Mina tell of sails being set. These not so important as to go in your list of the shipping in the *Times*, and so we go, by suggestion of my Lord Godalming, to your Lloyd's, where are note of all ships that sail, however so small. There we find that only one Black-Sea-bound ship go out
4 with the tide. She is the *Czarina Catherine*, and she sail

2 *in the crisp autumn air*. We are reminded that it is autumn. The story began in spring.

3 Omne ignotum pro magnifico. "That which is not known is wonderful." Van Helsing is quoting from Chapter 30 of Tacitus's *Agricola*, but precisely to what purpose is not clear. Tacitus cites Agricola, the Roman governor in Britain, as saying: "The very seclusion and remoteness of our glory here in Britain, the mystery lent by distance, has protected us by magnifying our prestige."

4 *the* Czarina Catherine. Again, though there is no record of a ship named the Czarina Catherine in Lloyd's *Registry*, there was one sailing vessel named the *Czarina* that sailed out of Sands Point, New York. The *Czarina* was built in Humboldt Bay, California. She was 116′ long, 30′ 6″ in breadth, 10′ 6″ in depth, and weighed 230 tons. Her skipper's name was C. Schmalz. Lloyd's *Registry* for 1896 and 1897 also shows two steam vessels named *Czarina* and *Czaritsa* respectively.

Stoker's choice of a name for the ship that is to bear Dracula homeward is interesting. Catherine the Second, empress of Russia, was so notoriously active sexually that even the *Encyclopaedia Britannica* notes that she "became and remained perfectly immoral in her sexual relations to men. The scandalous chronicle of her life was the commonplace of all Europe."

The ship that carried the vampire *to* England, it will be remembered, was the *Demeter*. (See chapter VII, note 10.)

THE LONDON DOCKS.

from Doolittle's Wharf for Varna, and thence on to other 5, 6
parts and up the Danube. 'Soh!' said I, 'this is the ship whereon is the Count.' So off we go to Doolittle's Wharf, and there we find a man in an office of wood so small that the man look bigger than the office. From him we inquire of the goings of the *Czarina Catherine.* He swear much, and he red face and loud of voice, but he good fellow all the same; and when Quincey give him something from his pocket which crackle as he roll it up, and put it in a so small bag which he have hid deep in his clothing, he still better fellow and humble servant to us. He come with us, and ask many men who are rough and hot; these be better fellows too when they have been no more
thirsty. They say much of blood and bloom and of others 7
which I comprehend not, though I guess what they mean; but nevertheless they tell us all things which we want to know.

"They make known to us among them, how last after- 8
noon at about five o'clock comes a man so hurry. A tall man, thin and pale, with high nose and teeth so white, and eyes that seem to be burning. That he be all in black,
except that he have a hat of straw which suit not him or 9

5 *Doolittle's Wharf.* Doolittle's Wharf appears neither in the London City Directory nor on any London map of Stoker's day.

6 *Varna.* In the nineteenth century, Varna (43°12′ North Latitude, 27°56′ East Longitude) was still a fortified town on the Bulgarian Black Sea coast. Its population was a mixture of Greeks, Bulgarians, Turks, Jews, and gypsies. (See map, p. 335.)

7 *of blood and bloom.* Stoker, at this point, reiterates a crude pun in which his central theme of blood is parodied by the ship captain's use of the word blood as a profane reference in the following paragraph.

8 *how last afternoon at about five o'clock.* Since we are reading Mina's October 5 entry, Van Helsing's reference makes precise the beginning of Dracula's flight to the east: October 4 at about five o'clock.

But we seem to have some confusion in the dates of the entries. We are here in an October 5 entry. If Mina, in her hypnotic trance, made contact with Dracula in a ship going out to sea on the *morning* of October 4, as Jonathan's journal for that date shows, then the events described here must have taken place on the afternoon of October 3 and not "last afternoon at about five o'clock [October 4]."

Either Mina's or Jonathan's immediately preceding date of entry is mistaken.

9 *hat of straw.* Dracula's straw hat is another of Stoker's masterful touches. The disordered King Vampire, in flight, is shorn of his dignity as he is made to run.

the time. That he scatter his money in making quick inquiry as to what ship sails for the Black Sea and for where. Some took him to the office and then to the ship, where he
10 will not go aboard but halt at shore end of gang-plank, and ask that the captain come to him. The captain come, when told that he will be pay well; and though he swear much at the first he agree to term. Then the thin man go and some one tell him where horse and cart can be hired. He go there, and soon he come again, himself driving cart on which is a great box; this he himself lift down, though it take several to put it on truck for the ship. He give much talk to captain as to how and where his box is to be place; but the captain like it not and swear at him in many tongues, and tell him that if he like he can come and see where it shall be. But he say 'no;' that he come not yet, for that he have much to do. Whereupon the captain tell him that he had better be quick—with blood—for that his ship will leave the place—of blood—before the turn of the tide—with blood. Then the thin man smile, and say that of course he must go when he think fit; but he will be surprise if he go quite so soon. The captain swear again, polyglot, and the thin man make him bow, and thank him, and say that he will so far intrude on his kindness as to come aboard before the sailing. Final the captain, more red than ever, and in more tongues, tell him that he doesn't want no Frenchmen—with bloom upon them and also with blood—in his ship—with blood on her also. And so, after asking where there might be close at hand a shop where he might purchase ship forms, he departed.

"No one knew where he went 'or bloomin' well cared,' as they said, for they had something else to think of—well with blood again; for it soon became apparent to all that the *Czarina Catherine* would not sail as was expected. A thin mist began to creep up from the river, and it grew, and grew; till soon a dense fog enveloped the ship and all around her. The captain swore polyglot—very polyglot—polyglot with bloom and blood; but he could do nothing. The water rose and rose; and he began to fear that he would lose the tide altogether. He was in no friendly mood, when just at full tide, the thin man came up the gang-plank again and asked to see where his box had been stowed. Then the captain replied that he wished that he and his box—old and with much bloom and blood—were in hell. But the thin man did not be offend, and went down with the mate and saw where it was place, and came up and stood awhile on deck in fog. He must have come off by himself, for none notice him. Indeed they thought not of him; for soon the fog begin to melt away, and all was clear again. My friends of the thirst and the language that was of bloom and blood laughed, as they told how the captain's swears exceeded even his usual polyglot, and was more than ever full of picturesque, when on questioning other mariners who were on movement up and down on the river that hour, he found that few of them had seen any of fog at all, except where it lay round the wharf. However the ship went out on the ebb tide; and was doubtless by morning far down the river mouth. She was by then, when they told us, well out to sea.

10 *gang-plank*. Because, as we have learned from Van Helsing (p. 213), he can only pass running water at the slack or the flood of the tide.

"And so my dear Madam Mina, it is that we have to rest for a time, for our enemy is on the sea, with the fog at his command, on his way to the Danube mouth. To sail a ship takes time, go she never so quick; and when we start we go on land more quick, and we meet him there. Our best hope is **11**
to come on him when in the box between sunrise and sunset; for then he can make no struggle, and we may deal with him as we should. There are days for us, in which we can make ready our plan. We know all about where he go; for we have seen the owner of the ship, who have shown us invoices and all papers that can be. The box we seek is to be landed in Varna, and to be given to an agent, one Ristics who will there present his credentials; and so our merchant friend will have done his part. When he ask if there be any wrong, for that so, he can telegraph and have inquiry made at Varna, we say 'no;' for what is to be done is not for police or of the customs. It must be done by us alone and in our own way."

When Dr. Van Helsing had done speaking, I asked him if it were certain that the Count had remained on board the ship. He replied: "We have the best proof of that: your own evidence, when in the hypnotic trance this morning." I asked him again if it were really necessary that they should pursue the Count, for oh! I dread Jonathan leaving me, and I know that he would surely go if the others went. He answered in growing passion, at first quietly. As he went on, however, he grew more angry and more forceful, till in the end we could not but see wherein was at least some of that personal dominance which made him so long a master amongst men:—

"Yes it is necessary—necessary—necessary! For your sake in the first, and then for the sake of humanity. This monster has done much harm already, in the narrow scope where he find himself, and in the short time when as yet he was only as a body groping his so small measure in darkness and not knowing. All this have I told these others; you, my dear Madam Mina, will learn it in the phonograph of my friend John, or in that of your husband. I have told them how the measure of leaving his own barren land—barren of peoples—and coming to a new land where life of man teems till they are like the multitude of standing corn, was the work of centuries. Were another of the Un-Dead, like him, to try to do what he has done, perhaps not all the centuries of the world that have been, or that will be, could aid him. With this one, all the forces of nature that are occult and deep and strong must have worked together in some wondrous way. The very place, where he have been alive, Un-Dead for all these centuries, is full of strangeness of the geologic and chemical world. There are deep caverns and **12**
fissures that reach none know whither. There have been volcanoes, some of whose openings still send out waters of strange properties, and gases that kill or make to vivify. Doubtless, there is something magnetic or electric in some of these combinations of occult forces which work for physical life in strange way; and in himself were from the first some great qualities. In a hard and warlike time he was celebrate that he have more iron nerve, more subtle brain, more braver heart, than any man. In him some vital principle

11 *on land more quick.* If the land route was quicker, why did Dracula choose the slower sea route home? Probably because by sea he could obviate the dangers of discovery in the frequent customs inspections that overland travel would have entailed. Perhaps, too, his supernatural powers, suitable enough for modifying the speed of sailing vessels, were insufficient to affect the pace of steam railways.

12 *geologic and chemical world.* Stoker here wants to rationalize Dracula's powers by ascribing them to "forces of nature." Fortunately, this excursion into scientism is brief and we are soon back to a diabolic Dracula.

13 *whose very existence would defame Him.* A curious remark, since, according to Stoker's fiction, Dracula *does* exist. What does this do to God's fame?

14 *knights of the Cross.* Again, Stoker is insistent that the hunt for Dracula is a form of crusade.

15 *on his own ground.* Van Helsing echoes Dracula himself (chapter III, p. 31). Of course, he has read Jonathan's journal.

A TURKISH WARRIOR.

have in strange way found their utmost; and as his body keep strong and grow and thrive, so his brain grow too. All this without that diabolic aid which is surely to him; for it have to yield to the powers that come from, and are, symbolic of good. And now this is what he is to us. He have infect you—oh forgive me, my dear, that I must say such; but it is for good of you that I speak. He infect you in such wise, that even if he do no more, you have only to live—to live in your own old, sweet way; and so in time, death, which is of man's common lot and with God's sanction, shall make you like to him. This must not be! We have sworn together that it must not. Thus are we ministers of God's own wish: that the world, and men for
13 whom His Son die, will not be given over to monsters, whose very existence would defame Him. He have allowed us to
14 redeem one soul already, and we go out as the old knights of the Cross to redeem more. Like them we shall travel towards the sunrise; and like them, if we fall, we fall in good cause." He paused and I said:—

"But will not the Count take his rebuff wisely? Since he has been driven from England, will he not avoid it, as a tiger does the village from which he has been hunted?"

"Aha!" he said, "your simile of the tiger good, for me, and I shall adopt him. Your man-eater, as they of India call the tiger who has once taste blood of the human, care no more for other prey, but prowl unceasing till he get him. This that we hunt from our village is a tiger, too, a man-eater, and he never cease to prowl. Nay in himself he is not one to retire and stay afar. In his life, his living life,
15 he go over the Turkey frontier and attack his enemy on his own ground; he be beaten back, but did he stay? No! He come again, and again, and again. Look at his persistence and endurance. With the child-brain that was to him he have long since conceive the idea of coming to a great city. What does he do? He find out the place of all the world most of promise for him. Then he deliberately set himself down to prepare for the task. He find in patience just how is his strength, and what are his powers. He study new tongues. He learn new social life; new environment of old ways, the politic, the law, the finance, the science, the habit of a new land and a new people who have come to be since he was. His glimpse that he have had, whet his appetite only and enkeen his desire. Nay, it help him to grow as to his brain; for it all prove to him how right he was at the first in his surmises. He have done this alone; all alone! from a ruin tomb in a forgotten land. What more may he not do when the greater world of thought is open to him. He that can smile at death, as we know him; who can flourish in the midst of diseases that kill off whole peoples. Oh! if such an one was to come from God, and not the Devil, what a force for good might he not be in this old world of ours. But we are pledged to set the world free. Our toil must be in silence, and our efforts all in secret; for in this enlightened age, when men believe not even what they see, the doubting of wise men would be his greatest strength. It would be at once his sheath and his armour, and

others. I shall try to open the subject with him.

Later.—When the Professor came in, we talked over the state of things. I could see that he had something on his mind which he wanted to say, but felt some hesitancy about broaching the subject. After beating about the bush a little, he said suddenly:—

"Friend John, there is something that you and I must talk 18
of alone, just at the first at any rate. Later, we may have to take the others into our confidence;" then he stopped, so I waited; he went on:—

"Madam Mina, our poor, dear Madam Mina is changing." A cold shiver ran through me to find my worst fears thus endorsed. Van Helsing continued:—

"With the sad experience of Miss Lucy, we must this time be warned before things go too far. Our task is now in reality more difficult than ever, and this new trouble makes every hour of the direst importance. I can see the characteristics of the vampire coming in her face. It is now but very, very slight; but it is to be seen if we have eyes to notice without to prejudge. Her teeth are some sharper, and at times her eyes are more hard. But these are not all, there is to her the silence now often; as so it was with Miss Lucy. She did not speak, even when she wrote that which she wished to be known later. Now my fear is this. If it be that she can, by our hypnotic trance, tell what the Count see and hear, is it not more true that he who have hypnotise her first, and who have drink of her very blood and make her drink of his, should, if he will, compel her mind to disclose to him that which she know?" I nodded acquiescence; he went on:—

"Then, what we must do is to prevent this; we must keep
her ignorant of our intent, and so she cannot tell what she know 19
not. This is a painful task! Oh! so painful that it heartbreak me to think of; but it must be. When to-day we meet, I must tell her that for reason which we will not to speak she must not more be of our council, but be simply guarded by us." He wiped his forehead, which had broken out in profuse perspiration at the thought of the pain which he might have to inflict upon the poor soul already so tortured. I knew that it would be some sort of comfort to him if I told him that I also had come to the same conclusion; for at any rate it would take away the pain of doubt. I told him, and the effect was as I expected.

It is now close to the time of our general gathering. Van Helsing has gone away to prepare for the meeting, and his painful part of it. I really believe his purpose is to be able to pray alone.

Later.—At the very outset of our meeting a great personal relief was experienced by both Van Helsing and myself. Mrs. Harker had sent a message by her husband to say that she would not join us at present, as she thought it better that we should be free to discuss our movements without her presence to embarrass us. The Professor and I looked at each other for an instant, and somehow we both seemed relieved. For my own part, I thought that if Mrs. Harker realised the danger herself, it was much pain as well as much danger averted. Under the circumstances we agreed, by a questioning look and

18 *talk of alone.* Once again there is a question of confidence. From this moment on, the two doctors, in choosing not to confide their medical suspicions, split themselves off from the other men.

19 *what she know not.* Now Mina is to be isolated from the counsels of the band. Since lack of candor (particularly Van Helsing's at the beginning) has played a strong part in producing Lucy's and Mina's catastrophe, one would have supposed the two physicians had learned their lesson.

20 *Winchesters.* The Winchester rifle was first made in 1866. It takes its name from Oliver F. Winchester (1810–1880), its manufacturer.

21 *Tobolsk.* A city in west Siberia. A market center for fish, furs, sawmills, shipyards (see map, p. 336).

22 *dishonour to science.* Some sort of joke on Quincey's level head is intended here. It escapes me.

23 *one meeting.* This must be a printer's error; it should read "our meeting."

answer, with finger on lip, to preserve silence of our suspicions, until we should have been able to confer alone again. We went at once into our Plan of Campaign. Van Helsing roughly put the facts before us first:—

"The *Czarina Catherine* left the Thames yesterday morning. It will take her at the quickest speed she has ever made at least three weeks to reach Varna; but we can travel overland to the same place in three days. Now, if we allow for two days less for the ship's voyage, owing to such weather influences as we know that the Count can bring to bear; and if we allow a whole day and night for any delays which may occur to us, then we have a margin of nearly two weeks. Thus, in order to be quite safe, we must leave here on 17th at latest. Then we shall at any rate be in Varna a day before the ship arrives, and able to make such preparations as may be necessary. Of course we shall all go armed—armed against evil things, spiritual as well as physical." Here Quincey Morris added:—

"I understand that the Count comes from a wolf country, and it may be that he shall get there before us. I propose
20 that we add Winchesters to our armament. I have a kind of belief in a Winchester when there is any trouble of that sort around. Do you remember Art, when we had the pack after
21 us at Tobolsk? What wouldn't we have given then for a repeater apiece!"

"Good!" said Van Helsing, "Winchesters it shall be. Quincey's head is level at all times, but most so when there is
22 to hunt, though my metaphor be more dishonour to science than wolves be of danger to man. In the meantime we can do nothing here; and as I think that Varna is not familiar to any of us, why not go there more soon? It is as long to wait here as there. To-night and to-morrow we can get ready, and then, if all be well, we four can set out on our journey."

"We four?" said Harker interrogatively, looking from one to another of us.

"Of course!" answered the Professor quickly, "You must remain to take care of your so sweet wife!" Harker was silent for awhile and then said in a hollow voice:—

"Let us talk of that part of it in the morning. I want to consult with Mina." I thought that now was the time for Van Helsing to warn him not to disclose our plans to her; but he took no notice. I looked at him significantly and coughed. For answer he put his finger on his lip and turned away.

Jonathan Harker's Journal.

23 5 *October, afternoon.*—For some time after one meeting this morning I could not think. The new phases of things leave my mind in a state of wonder which allows no room for active thought. Mina's determination not to take any part in the discussion set me thinking; and as I could not argue the matter with her, I could only guess. I am as far as ever from a solution now. The way the others received it, too, puzzled me; the last time we talked of the subject we agreed that there was to be no more concealment of anything amongst us. Mina is sleeping now, calmly and sweetly like a little child.

Her lips are curved and her face beams with happiness. **24**
Thank God there are such moments still for her.

Later.—How strange it all is. I sat watching Mina's happy sleep, and came as near to being happy myself as I suppose I shall ever be. As the evening drew on, and the earth took its shadows from the sun sinking lower, the silence of the room grew more and more solemn to me. All at once Mina opened her eyes, and looking at me tenderly, said:—

"Jonathan, I want you to promise me something on your word of honour. A promise made to me, but made holily in God's hearing, and not to be broken though I should go down on my knees and implore you with bitter tears. Quick, you must make it to me at once."

"Mina," I said, "a promise like that, I cannot make at once. I may have no right to make it."

"But, dear one," she said, with such spiritual intensity that
her eyes were like pole stars, "it is I who wish it; and it is **25**
not for myself. You can ask Dr. Van Helsing if I am not right; if he disagrees you may do as you will. Nay more, if you all agree, later, you are absolved from the promise."

"I promise!" I said, and for a moment she looked supremely happy; though to me all happiness for her was denied by the red scar on her forehead. She said:—

"Promise me that you will not tell me anything of the plans formed for the campaign against the Count. Not by word, or inference, or implication; not at any time whilst this remains to me!" and she solemnly pointed to the scar. I saw that she was in earnest, and said solemnly:—

"I promise!" and as I said it I felt that from that instant a door had been shut between us.

Later, midnight.—Mina has been bright and cheerful all the evening. So much so that all the rest seemed to take courage, as if infected somewhat with her gaiety; as a result even I myself felt as if the pall of gloom which weighs us down were somewhat lifted. We all retired early. Mina is now sleeping like a little child; it is a wonderful thing that her faculty of sleep remains to her in the midst of her terrible trouble. Thank God for it, for then at least she can forget her care. Perhaps her example may affect me as her gaiety did to-night. I shall try it. Oh! for a dreamless sleep.

6 *October, morning.*—Another surprise. Mina woke me **26**
early, about the same time as yesterday, and asked me to bring Dr. Van Helsing. I thought that it was another occasion for hypnotism, and without question went for the Professor. He had evidently expected some such call, for I found him dressed in his room. His door was ajar, so that he could hear the opening of the door of our room. He came at once; as he passed into the room, he asked Mina if the others might come too.

"No," she said quite simply, "it will not be necessary. You can tell them just as well. I must go with you on your journey."

Dr. Van Helsing was as startled as I was. After a moment's pause he asked:—

"But why?"

24 *beams with happiness.* As Dracula recedes farther from her.

25 *pole stars.* The pole star is Polaris, which is indeed an exceedingly bright star. Polaris is the prime navigational star.

26 *6 October, morning.* The error in dating persists. It was Jonathan who reported the first hypnotic session as October 4 (chapter XXIII, p. 274). Now, on the morning of the 6th, he refers to "yesterday."

27 *her soul is true.* And yet, there is the chilling possibility of a doubt: How do we know that her impulse to join the men is not a piece of Dracula-directed intrigue? If she can be useful to her men in the state of hypnosis, it may have occurred to Dracula that she might be equally useful to him—in the same way—whether they confide in her or not. After all, it was she who, in her hypnotic trance, found his box in the *Czarina Catherine.*

28 *asked Mr. Morris.* He is still "Mr." Morris to Jonathan who is not one of the three comrades: Godalming, Seward, Morris. They are moneyed gentlemen, while Jonathan has been, until recently, no more than a solicitor's clerk.

29 *a thousand men looking on.* In the event, as we shall see, there were many fewer than a thousand.

Lest Quincey Morris's language here sound like the easy bluster of a *Miles Gloriosus*, it should be pointed out that his high-hearted speech is in the best tradition of Texas courage in which language and action are both grander than life. Here, for example, are excerpts from a letter written by William Barret Travis who commanded the Alamo on the day (February 28, 1836) when that fort was overrun and almost all of its inhabitants slain:

Commandant of the Alamo,
Bejar, Feb'y 24th 1836.

To the People of Texas and all Americans in the world.

Fellow citizens and compatriots—I am besieged, by a thousand or more of the Mexicans under Santa Anna. I have sustained a continual Bombardment and cannonade for 24 hours and have not lost a man. The enemy has demanded a surrender at discretion, otherwise, the garrison are to be put to the sword, if the fort is taken. I have answered the demand with a cannon shot, and our flag still waves proudly from the walls. *I shall never surrender or retreat.* . . . I am determined to sustain myself as long as possible and die like a soldier who never forgets what is due to his own honor and that of his country. VICTORY OR DEATH.

William Barret Travis,
Lt. Col. comdt.

"You must take me with you. I am safer with you, and you shall be safer too."

"But why, dear Madam Mina? You know that your safety is our solemnest duty. We go into danger, to which you are, or may be, more liable than any of us from—from circumstances—things that have been." He paused embarrassed.

As she replied, she raised her finger and pointed to her forehead:—

"I know. That is why I must go. I can tell you now, whilst the sun is coming up; I may not be able again. I know that when the Count wills me I must go. I know that if he tells me to come in secret, I must come by wile; by any device to hoodwink—even Jonathan." God saw the look that she turned on me as she spoke, and if there be indeed a Recording Angel that look is noted to her everlasting honour. I could only clasp her hand. I could not speak; my emotion was too great for even the relief of tears. She went on:—

"You men are brave and strong. You are strong in your numbers, for you can defy that which would break down the human endurance of one who had to guard alone. Besides, I may be of service, since you can hypnotise me and so learn that which even I myself do not know." Dr. Van Helsing said very gravely:—

"Madam Mina you are, as always, most wise. You shall with us come; and together we shall do that which we go forth to achieve." When he had spoken, Mina's long spell of silence made me look at her. She had fallen back on her pillow asleep; she did not even wake when I had pulled up the blind and let in the sunlight which flooded the room. Van Helsing motioned to me to come with him quietly. We went to his room, and within a minute Lord Godalming, Dr. Seward, and Mr. Morris were with us also. He told them what Mina had said, and went on:—

"In the morning we shall leave for Varna. We have now
27 to deal with a new factor: Madam Mina. Oh, but her soul is true. It is to her an agony to tell us so much as she has done; but it is most right, and we are warned in time. There must be no chance lost, and in Varna we must be ready to act the instant when that ship arrives."

28 "What shall we do exactly?" asked Mr. Morris laconically. The Professor paused before replying:—

"We shall at the first board that ship; then, when we have identified the box, we shall place a branch of the wild rose on it. This we shall fasten, for when it is there none can emerge; so at least says the superstition. And to superstition must we trust at the first; it was man's faith in the early, and it have its root in faith still. Then, when we get the opportunity that we seek, when none are near to see, we shall open the box, and—and all will be well."

"I shall not wait for any opportunity," said Morris. "When I see the box I shall open it and destroy the monster, though
29 there were a thousand men looking on, and if I am to be wiped out for it the next moment!" I grasped his hand instinctively and found it as firm as a piece of steel. I think he understood my look; I hope he did.

"Good boy," said Dr. Van Helsing. "Brave boy. Quincey

is all man, God bless him for it. My child, believe me none of us shall lag behind or pause from any fear. I do but say what we may do—what we must do. But, indeed, indeed we cannot say what we shall do. There are so many things which may happen, and their ways and their ends are so various that until the moment we may not say. We shall all be armed, in all ways; and when the time for the end has come, our effort shall not be lack. Now let us to-day put all our affairs in order. Let all things which touch on others dear to us, and who on us depend, be complete; for none of us can tell what, or when, or how, the end may be." As for me, my own affairs are regulate; and as I have nothing else to do, I shall go make arrangement for the travel. I shall have all tickets and so forth for our journey."

There was nothing further to be said, and we parted. I shall now settle up all my affairs of earth, and be ready for whatever may come. . . . **30**

Later.—It is all done; my will is made, and all complete. Mina if she survive is my sole heir. If it should not be so, then the others who have been so good to us shall have remainder.

It is now drawing towards the sunset; Mina's uneasiness calls my attention to it. I am sure that there is something on her mind which the time of exact sunset will reveal. These occasions are becoming harrowing times for us all, for each sunrise and sunset opens up some new danger—some new pain, which, however, may in God's will be means to a good end. I write all these things in the diary since my darling must not hear them now; but if it may be that she can see them again, they shall be ready."

She is calling to me.

30 *whatever may come.* The solemnity is pretty heavy here—as if they were readying themselves for their own deaths.

CHAPTER XXV.

Dr. Seward's Diary.

11 *October, Evening.*—Jonathan Harker has asked me to note this, as he says he is hardly equal to the task, and he wants an exact record kept.

I think that none of us were surprised when we were asked to see Mrs. Harker a little before the time of sunset. We have of late come to understand that sunrise and sunset are to her times of peculiar freedom; when her old self can be manifest without any controlling force subduing or restraining her, or inciting her to action. This mood or condition begins some half hour or more before actual sunrise or sunset, and lasts till either the sun is high, or whilst the clouds are still aglow with the rays streaming above the horizon. At first there is a sort of negative condition, as if some tie were loosened, and then the absolute freedom quickly follows; when however the freedom ceases the change-back or relapse comes quickly, preceded only by a spell of warning silence.

To-night, when we met she was somewhat constrained, and bore all the signs of an internal struggle. I put it down myself to her making a violent effort at the earliest instant she could do so. A very few minutes, however, gave her complete control of herself; then, motioning her husband to sit beside her on the sofa where she was half reclining, she made the rest of us bring chairs up close. Taking her husband's hand in hers began :—

"We are all here together in freedom, for perhaps the last time! I know, dear; I know that you will always be with me to the end." This was to her husband whose hand had, as we could see, tightened upon hers. "In the morning we go out upon our task, and God alone knows what may be in store for any of us. You are going to be so good to me as to take me with you. I know that all that brave earnest men can do for a poor weak woman, whose soul perhaps is lost—no, no, not yet, but is at any rate at stake—you will do. But you must remember that I am not as you are. There is a poison in my blood, in my soul, which may destroy me; which must destroy me, unless some relief comes to us. Oh, my friends, you know as well as I do, that my soul is at stake; and though I know there is one way out for me, you must not and I must not take it!" She looked appealingly to us all in turn, beginning and ending with her husband.

"What is that way?" asked Van Helsing in a hoarse voice. "What is that way, which we must not—may not—take?"

"That I may die now, either by my own hand or that of another, before the greater evil is entirely wrought. I know, and you know, that were I once dead you could and would set free my immortal spirit, even as you did my poor Lucy's. Were death, or the fear of death, the only thing that stood in the way I would not shrink to die here, now, amidst the friends who love me. But death is not all. I cannot believe that to die in such a case, when there is hope before us and a bitter task to be done, is God's will. Therefore, I on my part, give up here the certainty of eternal rest, and go out into the dark where may be the blackest things that the world or the nether world holds!" We were all silent, for we knew instinctively that this was only a prelude. The faces of the others were set, and Harker's grew ashen grey; perhaps he guessed better than any of us what was coming. She continued:—

"This is what I can give into the hotch-pot." I could not 1
but note the quaint legal phrase which she used in such a place, and with all seriousness. "What will each of you give? Your lives I know," she went on quickly, "that is easy for brave men. Your lives are God's, and you can give them back to Him; but what will you give to me?" She looked again questioningly, but this time avoided her husband's face. Quincey seemed to understand; he nodded, and her face lit up. "Then I shall tell you plainly what I want, for there must be no doubtful matter in this connection between us now. You must promise me, one and all—even you my beloved husband—that, should the time come, you will kill me."

"What is that time?" The voice was Quincey's, but it was low and strained.

"When you shall be convinced that I am so changed that it is better that I die that I may live. When I am thus dead in the flesh, then you will, without a moment's delay, drive a stake through me and cut off my head; or do whatever else may be wanting to give me rest!"

Quincey was the first to rise after the pause. He knelt down before her and taking her hand in his said solemnly:—

"I'm only a rough fellow, who hasn't, perhaps, lived as a man should to win such a distinction, but I swear to you by all that I hold sacred and dear that, should the time ever come, I shall not flinch from the duty that you have set us. And I promise you, too, that I shall make all certain, for if I am only doubtful I shall take it that the time has come!"

1 *hotch-pot*. A legal term meaning "the bringing together of shares or properties in order to divide them equally, especially when they are to be divided among the children of a parent dying intestate."

2 *"My true friend!"* Lucy's words on *her* deathbed. (See chapter XII, p. 148.)

3 *him that loves me best.* This time, as Mina knows, she is echoing Van Helsing's words to Godalming as they prepare to drive the stake into Lucy's heart. (See chapter XVI, p. 193.)

2 "My true friend!" was all she could say amid her fast-falling tears, as, bending over, she kissed his hand.

"I swear the same, my dear Madam Mina!" said Van Helsing.

"And I!" said Lord Godalming, each of them in turn kneeling to her to take the oath. I followed, myself. Then her husband turned to her, wan-eyed and with a greenish pallor which subdued the snowy whiteness of his hair, and asked:—

"And must I, too, make such a promise, oh, my wife?"

"You too, my dearest," she said, with infinite yearning of pity in her voice and eyes. "You must not shrink. You are nearest and dearest and all the world to me; our souls are knit into one, for all life and all time. Think dear, that there have been times when brave men have killed their wives and their womenkind, to keep them from falling into the hands of the enemy. Their hands did not falter any the more because those that they loved implored them to slay them. It is men's duty towards those whom they love, in such times of sore trial! And oh, my dear, if it is to be that I must meet
3 death at any hand, let it be at the hand of him that loves me best. Dr. Van Helsing, I have not forgotten your mercy in poor Lucy's case to him who loved"—she stopped with a flying blush, and changed her phrase—"to him who had best right to give her peace. If that time shall come again, I look to you to make it a happy memory of my husband's life that it was his loving hand which set me free from the awful thrall upon me."

"Again I swear!" came the Professor's resonant voice. Mrs. Harker smiled, positively smiled, as with a sigh of relief she leaned back and said:—

"And now one word of warning, a warning which you must never forget: this time, if it ever come, may come quickly and unexpectedly, and in such case you must lose no time in using your opportunity. At such a time I myself might be—nay! if the time ever comes, *shall* be—leagued with your enemy against you."

"One more request;" she became very solemn as she said this, "it is not vital and necessary like the other, but I want you to do one thing for me, if you will." We all acquiesced, but no one spoke; there was no need to speak:—

"I want you to read the Burial Service." She was interrupted by a deep groan from her husband; taking his hand in hers, she held it over her heart, and continued. "You must read it over me some day. Whatever may be the issue of all this fearful state of things, it will be a sweet thought to all or some of us. You, my dearest, will I hope read it, for then it will be in your voice in my memory for ever—come what may!"

"But oh, my dear one," he pleaded, "death is afar off from you."

"Nay," she said, holding up a warning hand. "I am deeper in death at this moment than if the weight of an earthly grave lay heavy upon me!"

"Oh, my wife, must I read it?" he said, before he began.

"It would comfort me, my husband!" was all she said; and he began to read when she had got the book ready.

"How can I—how could any one—tell of that strange scene, its solemnity, its gloom, its sadness, its horror; and, withal, its sweetness. Even a sceptic, who can see nothing but a travesty of bitter truth in anything holy or emotional, would have been melted to the heart had he seen that little group of loving and devoted friends kneeling round that stricken and sorrowing lady; or heard the tender passion of her husband's voice, as in tones so broken with emotion that often he had to pause, he read the simple and beautiful
service for the Burial of the Dead. I—I cannot go on— 4
words—and—v-voice—f-fail m-me!" 5

She was right in her instinct. Strange as it all was, bizarre as it may hereafter seem even to us who felt its potent influence at the time, it comforted us much; and the silence, which showed Mrs. Harker's coming relapse from her freedom of soul, did not seem so full of despair to any of us as we had dreaded.

Jonathan Harker's Journal.

15 *October. Varna.*—We left Charing Cross on the morning 6, 7
of the 12th, got to Paris the same night, and took the places
secured for us in the Orient Express. We travelled night and 8
day, arriving here at about five o'clock. Lord Godalming went to the Consulate to see if any telegram had arrived for him, whilst the rest of us came on to this hotel—the Odessus. The journey may have had incidents; I was, however, too eager to get on, to care for them. Until the *Czarina Catherine* comes into port there will be no interest for me in anything in the wide world. Thank God! Mina is well, and looks to be getting stronger; her colour is coming back. She sleeps a great deal; throughout the journey she slept nearly all the time. Before sunrise and sunset, however, she is very wakeful and alert; and it has become a habit for Van Helsing to hypnotise her at such times. At first, some effort was needed, and he had to make many passes; but now, she seems to yield at once, as if by habit, and scarcely any action is needed. He seems to have power at these particular moments to simply will, and her thoughts obey him. He always asks her what she can see and hear. She answers to the first:—

"Nothing; all is dark." And to the second:—

"I can hear the waves lapping against the ship, and the water rushing by. Canvas and cordage strain and masts and yards creak. The wind is high—I can hear it in the shrouds, and the bow throws back the foam." It is evident that the *Czarina Catherine* is still at sea, hastening on her way to Varna. Lord Godalming has just returned. He had four telegrams, one each day since we started, and all to the same effect: that the *Czarina Catherine* had not been reported to

4 *service for the Burial of the Dead.* The Order for the Burial of the Dead, as it is contained in the Church of England Book of Common Prayer, is indeed a moving and impressive service. In the poignantly archaic style of Edward the VI's time, it begins:

"*The priest metyng the Corps at the Churche style, shall say: Or the priestes and clerkes shall sing, and so goe either into the Churche, or towardes the graue.*

"I am the resurrecciō and the life (sayth the Lord): he that beleueth in me, yea though he were dead, yet shall he liue. And whosoeuer lyueth and beleueth in me: shall not dye for euer (John 11).

"I know that my redemer lyueth, and that I shall ryse out of the yearth in the last daye, and shalbe couered again with my skinne and shall see God in my flesh: yea and I myselfe shall beholde hym, not with other but with these same iyes (Job 19).

"We brought nothyng into this worlde, neyther may we carye any thyng out of this worlde. The Lord geueth, and the Lord taketh awaie. Euen as it pleaseth the Lorde, so cummeth thynges to passe: blessed be the name of the Lorde" (Timothy I:6; Job 1).

The service continues through various stages of grandeur and grief and devotion and concludes with this passage from John 6:

"Jesus saied to his disciples and to the Jewes: Al that the father geueth me, shall come to me: and he that cometh to me, I cast not away. For I came down from heauen: not to do that I wil, but that he wil, which hath sente me. And this is the fathers wyll which hath sente me, that of all which he hath geuē me, I shal lose nothing: but raise them up again at the last day. And this is the wil of him that sent me: that euery one which seeth the sonne and beleueth on him, haue euerlasting life: And I wil raise him up at the laste daye."

The service is long and solemn. Held over a still living woman, one can well believe that the effect on the listeners was shattering.

5 "*. . . f-fail m-me!*" How the diary entry manages to stammer is a piquant literary mystery that is better left unsolved.

6 *15* October. Varna. Presumable hour of arrival, 10:30 A.M.

7 *Charing Cross.* A railway terminal in west London, situated on the Strand just east of Trafalgar Square (see map, pp. 340–41).

8 *the Orient Express.* J. H. Price, editor of Cook's Continental Timetable, writes to say that the Orient Express from Paris to Varna (until 1894) had to cross the Danube by ferry between Giurgiu and

Ruse (Ruschuk) where passengers had to catch another train from Ruse to Varna. After 1894, the train went from Paris to the Black Sea coast via the Feteşti bridge across the Danube. There never was a through train from Paris to Varna.

Mr. Price writes: "The train ran twice weekly, leaving Paris Est at 7:08 P.M. or thereabouts (the time varied slightly over the years) on Tuesday and Friday . . ."

The date of Mina's entry (October 15) suggests that the journey from London to Varna took 3½ days. The scheduled time from Paris to Varna was just about three days. If we assume that the travelers left London *very* early on the morning of the 12th, then their arrival at 5:00 A.M. on the 15th seems reasonable—if perfect connections were made all the way (an unlikely assumption, however, especially considering Jonathan Harker's journey from London the last time). (See chapter I, note 20.)

The modern timetable for the journey:

London-Paris	6	hours
Paris-Belgrade	31	hours
Belgrade-Sofia	8	hours
Sofia-Varna	9½	hours
Waiting times	5	hours (two in Belgrade; three in Sofia)
Total time	59½	hours

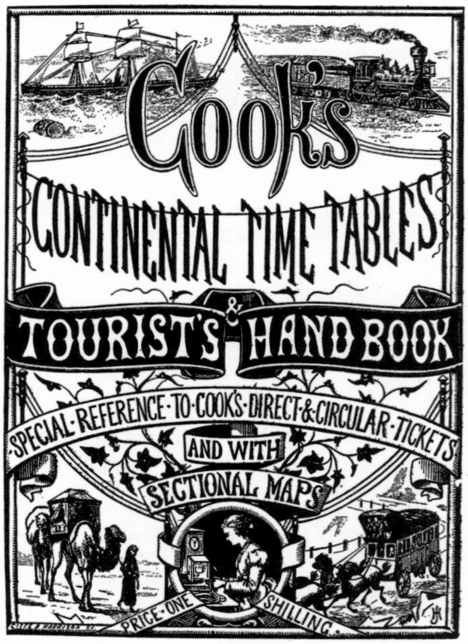

9 *Lloyd's.* Lloyd's of London, probably the most famous insurance corporation in the world, now comprises some three hundred individual syndicates. The house was founded in the late seven-

9 Lloyd's from anywhere. He had arranged before leaving London that his agent should send him every day a telegram saying if the ship had been reported. He was to have a message even if she were not reported, so that he might be sure that there was a watch being kept at the other end of the wire.

We had dinner and went to bed early. To-morrow we are to see the Vice-Consul, and to arrange, if we can, about getting on board the ship as soon as she arrives. Van Helsing says that our chance will be to get on board between sunrise and sunset. The Count, even if he takes the form of a bat, cannot cross the running water of his own volition, and so cannot leave the ship. As he dare not change to man's form without suspicion—which he evidently wishes to avoid—he must remain in the box. If, then, we can come on board after sunrise, he is at our mercy; for we can open the box and make sure of him, as we did of poor Lucy, before he wakes. What mercy he shall get from us will not count for much. We think that we shall not have much trouble with officials or the seamen. Thank God! this is the country where bribery can do anything, and we are well supplied with money. We have only to make sure that the ship cannot come into port between sunset and sunrise without our being warned, and we shall be safe. Judge Moneybag will settle this case, I think!

16 *October.*—Mina's report still the same: lapping waves and rushing water, darkness and favouring winds. We are evidently in good time, and when we hear of the *Czarina Catherine* we shall be ready. As she must pass the Dardanelles we are sure to have some report.

. . . . . .

17 *October.*—Everything is pretty well fixed now, I think, to welcome the Count on his return from his tour. Godalming told the shippers that he fancied that the box sent aboard might contain something stolen from a friend of his, and got a half consent that he might open it at his own risk. The owner gave him a paper telling the Captain to give him every facility in doing whatever he chose on board the ship, and also a similar authorisation to his agent at Varna. We have seen the agent, who was much impressed with Godalming's kindly manner to him, and we are all satisfied that whatever he can do to aid our wishes will be done. We have already arranged what to do in case we get the box open. If the Count is there, Van Helsing and Seward will cut off his head at once and drive a stake through his heart. Morris and Godalming and I shall prevent interference, even if we have to use the arms which we shall have ready. The Professor says that if we can so treat the Count's body, it will soon after fall into dust. In such case there would be no evidence against us, in case any suspicion of murder were aroused. But even if it were not, we should stand or fall by our act and perhaps some day this very script may be evidence to come between some of us and a rope. For myself, I should take the chance only too thankfully if it were to come. We mean to leave no stone unturned to carry out our intent. We have arranged with

certain officials that the instant the *Czarina Catherine* is seen, we are to be informed by a special messenger.

24 *October*.—A whole week of waiting. Daily telegrams to Godalming, but only the same story: "Not yet reported." Mina's morning and evening hypnotic answer is unvaried: lapping waves, rushing water, and creaking masts.

Telegram, October 24th.

Rufus Smith, Lloyd's, London, to Lord Godalming, care of H.B.M. Vice-Consul, Varna. **10**

"*Czarina Catherine* reported this morning from Darda- **11**
nelles."

Dr. Seward's Diary.

25 *October*.—How I miss my phonograph! To write diary with a pen is irksome to me; but Van Helsing says I must. We were all wild with excitement yesterday when Godalming got his telegram from Lloyd's. I know now what men feel in battle when the call to action is heard. Mrs. Harker, alone of our party, did not show any signs of emotion. After all, it is not strange that she did not; for we took special care not to let her know anything about it, and we all tried not to show any excitement when we were in her presence. In old days she would, I am sure, have noticed, no matter how we might have tried to conceal it; but in this way she is greatly changed during the past three weeks. The lethargy grows upon her, and though she seems strong and well, and is getting back some of her colour, Van Helsing and I are not satisfied. We talk of her often; we have not, however, said a word to the others. It would break poor Harker's heart—certainly his nerve—if he knew that we had even a suspicion on the subject. Van Helsing examines, he tells me, her teeth very carefully, whilst she is in the hypnotic condition, for he says that so long as they do not begin to sharpen there is no active danger of a
change in her. If this change should come, it would be **12**
necessary to take steps! . . . . We both know what those steps would have to be, though we do not mention our thoughts to each other. We should neither of us shrink from the task—awful though it be to contemplate. "Euthanasia" is is an excellent and a comforting word! I am grateful to whoever invented it.

It is only about 24 hours' sail from the Dardanelles to here, at the rate the *Czarina Catherine* has come from London. She should therefore arrive some time in the morning; but as she cannot possibly get in before then, we are all about to retire early. We shall get up at one o'clock, so as to be ready.

25 *October, Noon*.—No news yet of the ship's arrival. Mrs. Harker's hypnotic report this morning was the same as usual, so it is possible that we may get news at any moment. We men are all in a fever of excitement, except Harker, who is calm; his hands are as cold as ice, and an hour ago I found him
whetting the edge of the great Ghoorka knife which he now **13**
always carries with him. It will be a bad look out for the Count

teenth century. G. M. Trevelyan in his *English Social History* tells us that "Edward Lloyd . . . was . . . a coffee house keeper in Lombard Street in the reign of Queen Anne. To his house merchants came for the latest information and for the personal intercourse and advice necessary for all transactions . . . Before the end of the Queen's reign, Lloyd had set up a pulpit for auctions and for reading out shipping news."

Lloyd's is a byword for fiscal responsibility and for its willingness to insure (on payment of sufficient premium) almost anything.

10 H.B.M. Her Britannic Majesty.

11 ". . . *this morning from Dardanelles*." Dracula's journey lasted twenty days *to* the Dardanelles. If we add "24 hours' sail from the Dardanelles to here" (p. 295), Van Helsing's prediction (p. 286) of the time it should have taken is precisely fulfilled.

12 *If this change should come.* But in Seward's diary of October 5, twenty days ago (p. 285), we read that "her teeth are some sharper, and at times her eyes are more hard." Perhaps Van Helsing means if they get any sharper. It may be that Seward, or Stoker, is being careless.

13 *Ghoorka.* The modern spelling is Gurkha. It is the name given to the warriors of north India who use the kukri knife. (See chapter XXIII, note 10 and illustration, on the kukri knife.)

14 27 October, Noon. Two days later than expected.

15 *Galatz.* Galatz, a Romanian Black Sea port, is some 130 miles north east of Bucharest by rail. Our band of travelers would have found that the main thoroughfares were paved, and the streets lighted with gas, and the quays with electricity. Among other signs of progress, Galatz boasted a fine prison. (See map, p. 335.)

if the edge of that "Kúkri" ever touches his throat, driven by that stern, ice-cold hand!

Van Helsing and I were a little alarmed about Mrs. Harker to-day. About noon she got into a sort of lethargy which we did not like; although we kept silence to the others, we were neither of us happy about it. She had been restless all the morning, so that we were at first glad to know that she was sleeping. When, however, her husband mentioned casually that she was sleeping so soundly that he could not wake her, we went to her room to see for ourselves. She was breathing naturally and looked so well and peaceful that we agreed that the sleep was better for her than anything else. Poor girl, she has so much to forget that it is no wonder that sleep, if it brings oblivion to her, does her good.

Later.—Our opinion was justified, for when after a refreshing sleep of some hours she woke up, she seemed brighter and better than she has been for days. At sunset she made the usual hypnotic report. Wherever he may be in the Black Sea, the Count is hurrying to his destination. To his doom I trust!

26 *October.*—Another day and no tidings of the *Czarina Catherine.* She ought to be here by now. That she is still journeying *somewhere* is apparent, for Mrs. Harker's hypnotic report at sunrise was still the same. It is possible that the vessel may be lying by, at times, for fog; some of the steamers which came in last evening reported patches of fog both to north and south of the port. We must continue our watching, as the ship may now be signalled any moment.

14 27 *October, Noon.*—Most strange; no news yet of the ship we wait for. Mrs. Harker reported last night and this morning as usual: "lapping waves and rushing water," though she added that "the waves were very faint." The telegrams from London have been the same: "no further report." Van Helsing is terribly anxious, and told me just now that he fears the Count is escaping us. He added significantly:—

"I did not like that lethargy of Madam Mina's. Souls and memories can do strange things during trance." I was about to ask him more, but Harker just then came in, and he held up a warning hand. We must try to-night, at sunset, to make her speak more fully when in her hypnotic state.

28 *October.*—Telegram. *Rufus Smith, London, to Lord Godalming, care of H.B.M. Vice-Consul, Varna.*

15 "*Czarina Catherine* reported entering Galatz at one o'clock to-day."

Dr. Seward's Diary.

28 *October.*—When the telegram came announcing the arrival in Galatz I do not think it was such a shock to any of us as might have been expected. True, we did not know whence, or how, or when, the bolt would come; but I think we all expected that something strange would happen. The delay of arrival

at Varna made us individually satisfied that things would not be just as we had expected; we only waited to learn where the change would occur. None the less, however, was it a surprise. I suppose that nature works on such a hopeful basis that we believe against ourselves that things will be as they ought to be, not as we should know that they will be. Transcendentalism is a beacon to the angels, even if it be
a will-o'-the-wisp to man. It was an odd experience, and **16**
we all took it differently. Van Helsing raised his hands over his head for a moment, as though in remonstrance with the Almighty; but he said not a word, and in a few seconds stood up with his face sternly set. Lord Godalming grew very pale, and sat breathing heavily. I was myself half stunned and looked in wonder at one after another. Quincey Morris
tightened his belt with that quick movement which I knew so **17**
well; in our old wandering days it meant "action." Mrs. Harker grew ghastly white, so that the scar on her forehead seemed to burn, but she folded her hands meekly and looked up in prayer. Harker smiled—actually smiled—the dark bitter smile of one who is without hope; but at the same time his action belied his words, for his hands instinctively sought the hilt of the great Kukri knife and rested there. "When does the next train start for Galatz?" said Van Helsing to us generally.

"At 6.30 to morrow morning!" We all stared, for the answer came from Mrs. Harker.

"How on earth do you know?" said Art.

"You forget—or perhaps you do not know, though Jonathan does and so does Dr. Van Helsing—that I am the train fiend. At home in Exeter I always used to make up the time-tables, so as to be helpful to my husband. I found it so useful sometimes, that I always make a study of the time-tables now. I **18**
knew that if anything were to take us to Castle Dracula we should go by Galatz, or at any rate through Bucharest, so I learned the times very carefully. Unhappily there are not many to learn, as the only train to-morrow leaves as I say."

"Wonderful woman!" murmured the Professor.

"Can't we get a special?" asked Lord Godalming. Van Helsing shook his head: "I fear not. This land is very different from your's or mine; even if we did have a special, it would probably not arrive as soon as our regular train. Moreover we have something to prepare. We must think. Now let us organize. You, friend Arthur, go to the train and get the tickets and arrange that all be ready for us to go in the morning. Do you, friend Jonathan, go to the agent of the ship and get from him letters to the agent in Galatz, with authority to make search the ship just as it was here. Morris Quincey, you see the Vice-Consul, and get his aid with his fellow in Galatz and all he can do to make our way smooth, so that no times be lost when over the Danube. John will stay with Madam Mina and me, and we shall consult. For so if time be long you may be delayed; and it will not matter when the sun set, since I am here with Madam to make report."

"And I," said Mrs. Harker brightly, and more like her old self than she had been for many a long day, "shall try

16 *a will-o'-the-wisp to man.* This is a sentence whose meaning is obscure, though Stoker may be saying simply that angels, who are already transcendant beings, are better able to see God's light than men, who are confused and baffled by their own corporeality.

17 *which I knew so well.* This is the first instance we have of Quincey's belt-tightening habits.

"AT HOME IN EXETER."

18 *a study of the time-tables.* Jonathan too, like Mina, has an abiding interest in trains. At the moment when he makes his resolution to escape from Dracula's castle he cries out, "And then away for home! away to the quickest and nearest train!" (chapter IV, p. 56). Stoker, it should be recalled, was the manager of Henry Irving's Lyceum Theatre Company. In that capacity he was often called on to plan the itinerary for an acting company that would play thirty provincial towns in five months, a task that made him familiar with railroad timetables.

19 *troubled glance.* The doctors are remembering their secret anxieties about Dracula's power over Mina. (See chapter XXIV, p. 285.)

to be of use in all ways, and shall think and write for you as I used to do. Something is shifting from me in some strange way, and I feel freer than I have been of late!" The three younger men looked happier at the moment as they seemed to realise the significance of her words; but Van Helsing and I, turning to each other, met each a grave
19 and troubled glance. We said nothing at the time however.

When the three men had gone out to their tasks Van Helsing asked Mrs. Harker to look up the copy of the diaries and find him the part of Harker's journal at the Castle. She went away to get it; when the door was shut upon her he said to me:—

"We mean the same! speak out!"

"There is some change. It is a hope that makes me sick, for it may deceive us."

"Quite so. Do you know why I asked her to get the manuscript?"

"No!" said I, "unless it was to get an opportunity of seeing me alone."

"You are in part right, friend John, but only in part. I want to tell you something. And oh, my friend, I am taking a great—a terrible—risk; but I believe it is right. In the moment when Madam Mina said those words that arrest both our understanding, an inspiration come to me. In the trance of three days ago the Count sent her his spirit to read her mind; or more like he took her to see him in his earth-box in the ship with water rushing, just as it go free at rise and set of sun. He learn then that we are here; for she have more to tell in her open life with eyes to see and ears to hear than he, shut, as he is, in his coffin-box. Now he make his most effort to escape us. At present he want her not. He is sure with his so great knowledge that she will come at his call; but he cut her off—take her, as he can do, out of his own power, that so she come not to him. Ah! there I have hope that our man-brains that have been of man so long and that have not lost the grace of God, will come higher than his child-brain that lie in his tomb for centuries, that grow not yet to our stature, and that do only work selfish and therefore small. Here comes Madam Mina; not a word to her of her trance! She know it not; and it would overwhelm her and make despair just when we want all her hope, all her courage; when most we want all her great brain which is trained like man's brain, but is of sweet woman and have a special power which the Count give her, and which he may not take away altogether—though he think not so. Hush! let me speak, and you shall learn. Oh John, my friend, we are in awful straits. I fear, as I never feared before. We can only trust the good God. Silence! here she comes!"

I thought that the Professor was going to break down and have hysterics, just as he had when Lucy died, but with a great effort he controlled himself and was at perfect nervous poise when Mrs. Harker tripped into the room, bright and happy-looking and, in the doing of work, seemingly forgetful of her misery. As she came in, she handed a number of sheets of typewriting to Van Helsing. He looked over them gravely, his face brightening up as he read. Then holding the pages between his finger and thumb he said:—

"Friend John, to you with so much of experience already—and you too, dear Madam Mina, that are young,—here is a lesson: do not fear ever to think. A half thought has been buzzing often in my brain, but I fear to let him loose his wings. Here now, with more knowledge, I go back to where that half-thought come from, and I find that he be no half-thought at all; that be a whole thought, though so young that he is not yet strong to use his little wings. Nay, like the "Ugly
Duck" of my friend Hans Andersen, he be no duck-thought 20
at all, but a big swan-thought that sail nobly on big wings, when the time come for him to try them. See I read here what Jonathan have written:—

"That other of his race who, in a later age, again and again, brought his forces over The Great River into Turkey Land; who, when he was beaten back, came again, and again, and again, though he had to come alone from the bloody field where his troops were being slaughtered, since he knew that he alone could ultimately triumph."

What does this tell us? Not much? no! The Count's child-thought see nothing; therefore he speak so free. Your man-thought see nothing; my man-thought see nothing, till just now. No! But there comes another word from some one who speak without thought because she too know not what it mean—what it *might* mean. Just as there are elements which rest, yet when in nature's course they move on their way and they touch—then pouf! and there comes a flash of light, heaven's wide, that blind and kill and destroy some; but that show up all earth below for leagues and leagues. Is it not so? Well, I shall explain. To begin, have you ever study the philosophy of crime. 'Yes' and 'No.' You, John, yes; for it is a study of insanity. You, no, Madam Mina; for crime touch you not—not but once. Still, your mind works true, and argues not
a particulari ad universale. There is this peculiarity in crimi- 21
nals. It is so constant, in all countries and at all times, that even police, who know not much from philosophy, come to know it empirically, that *it is*. That is to be empiric. The criminal always work at one crime—that is the true criminal who seems predestinate to crime, and who will of none other. This criminal has not full man-brain. He is clever and cunning and resourceful; but he be not of man-stature as to brain. He be of child-brain in much. Now this criminal of ours is predestinate to crime also; he too have child-brain, and it is of the child to do what he have done. The little bird, the little fish, the little animal learn not by principle, but empirically; and when he learn to do, then there is to him the ground
to start from to do more. '*Dos pou sto*,' said Archimedes. 22
"Give me a fulcrum, and I shall move the world!' To do once, is the fulcrum whereby child-brain become man-brain; and until he have the purpose to do more, he continue to do the same again every time, just as he have done before! Oh, my dear, I see that your eyes are opened, and that to you the lightning flash show all the leagues," for Mrs. Harker began to clap her hands, and her eyes sparkled. He went on:—

"Now you shall speak. Tell us two dry men of science what you see with those so bright eyes." He took her hand and held it whilst she spoke. His finger and thumb closed on

20 *my friend Hans Andersen.* Hans Christian Andersen (1805–1875), a Danish author who is most familiar for having collected and retold the fairy tales that are associated with his name.

21 a particulari ad universale. From the particular to the universal.

22 'Dos pou sto.' The line in Archimedes' *Geometra* reads "*Dos moi pou stō Kai tēn gēn kinēsō.*" Or, "Give me a place to stand and I will move the earth."

23 *Nordau.* Max Nordau (1849–1923), a Hungarian physician, novelist, and Zionist leader, wrote a strange book entitled *Degeneration* (1892–93), in which he undertook to show that there was a close relationship between genius and moral degeneracy.

24 *Lombroso.* Cesare Lombroso (1836–1909) is sometimes called the father of modern criminology. He is still remembered for his belief that there existed among the human species the type of born criminal who was a throwback to his primordial ancestors.

The criminal type, according to Lombroso in *Criminal Man*, had a low cranial capacity, a retreating forehead, a thick-boned skull, tufted, crispy hair, and large ears. He was also inordinately sensual, lazy, impulsive, and vain, and able to endure pain.

It will be seen that Mina, referring to Lombroso here, is merely providing the reader with the name of the theorist whom Van Helsing follows in *his* description of Dracula.

A glance at Harker's description of Dracula in chapter II, pp. 21–22, lets us see that there, too, Lombroso (p. 15) is being closely followed.

Harker writes: "His [the Count's] face was . . . aquiline, with high bridge of the thin nose and peculiarly arched nostrils . . ."

Lombroso: "[The criminal's] nose on the contrary . . . is often aquiline like the beak of a bird of prey."

Harker: "His eyebrows were very massive, almost meeting over the nose . . ."

Lombroso: "The eyebrows are bushy and tend to meet across the nose."

Harker: ". . . his ears were pale and at the tops extremely pointed . . ."

Lombroso: "with a protuberance on the upper part of the posterior margin . . . a relic of the pointed ear . . ."

25 *"Seventy-two only . . ."* It is hard to know whether Stoker means us to admire Van Helsing's sangfroid. A man who can kiss a woman's hand even as he counts her pulse ought to raise questions of confidence.

26 *as the great Psalmist says.* The Psalmist says it in a variety of ways:

Psalms 7:15 "He made a pit, and digged it, and is fallen into the ditch *which* he made."

Psalms 9:15 "The heathen are sunk down in the pit *that* they made: in the net which they hid is their own foot taken."

Psalms 9:16 ". . . the wicked is snared in the work of his own hands."

Psalms 57:6 "They have prepared a net for my steps; my soul is bowed down: they have digged a pit before me, into the midst whereof they are fallen *themselves*. Selah."

Psalms 141:10 "Let the wicked fall into their own nets, whilst I withal escape."

her pulse, as I thought instinctively and unconsciously, as she spoke:—

23 "The Count is a criminal and of criminal type. Nordau
24 and Lombroso would so classify him, and *quâ* criminal he is of imperfectly formed mind. Thus, in a difficulty he has to seek resource in habit. His past is a clue, and the one page of it that we know—and that from his own lips—tells that once before, when in what Mr. Morris would call a 'tight place,' he went back to his own country from the land he had tried to invade, and thence, without losing purpose, prepared himself for a new effort. He came again, better equipped for his work; and won. So he came to London to invade a new land. He was beaten, and when all hope of success was lost, and his existence in danger, he fled back over the sea to his home; just as formerly he had fled back over the Danube from Turkey land."

"Good, good! oh, you so clever lady?" said Van Helsing, enthusiastically, as he stooped and kissed her hand. A moment later he said to me, as calmly as though we had been having a sick room consultation:—

25 "Seventy-two only; and in all this excitement. I have hope." Turning to her again, he said with keen expectation:—

"But go on. Go on! there is more to tell if you will. Be not afraid; John and I know. I do in any case, and shall tell you if you are right. Speak, without fear!"

"I will try to; but you will forgive me if I seem egotistical."

"Nay! fear not, you must be egotist, for it is of you that we think."

"Then, as he is criminal he is selfish; and as his intellect is small and his action is based on selfishness, he confines himself to one purpose. That purpose is remorseless. As he fled back over the Danube, leaving his forces to be cut to pieces, so now he is intent on being safe, careless of all. So, his own selfishness frees my soul somewhat of the terrible power which he acquired over me on that dreadful night. I felt it, Oh! I felt it. Thank God, for His great mercy! My soul is freer than it has been since that awful hour; and all that haunts me is a fear lest in some trance or dream he may have used my knowledge for his ends." The Professor stood up:—

"He has so used your mind; and by it he has left us here in Varna, whilst the ship that carried him rushed through enveloping fog up to Galatz, where, doubtless, he had made preparation for escaping from us. But his child-mind only saw so far; and it may be that, as ever is in God's Providence, the very thing that the evil doer most reckoned on for his selfish good, turns out to be his chiefest harm. The hunter is
26 taken in his own snare, as the great Psalmist says. For now that he think he is free from every trace of us all, and that he has escaped us with so many hours to him, then his selfish child-brain will whisper him to sleep. He think, too, that as he cut himself off from knowing your mind, there can be no
27 knowledge of him to you; there is where he fail! That terrible baptism of blood which he give you makes you free to go to him in spirit, as you have as yet done in your times of freedom, when the sun rise and set. At such times you go by my

volition and not by his; and this power to good of you and others, you have won from your suffering at his hands. This is now all more precious that he know it not, and to guard himself have even cut himself off from his knowledge of our where. We, however, are not all selfish, and we believe that God is with us through all this blackness, and these many dark hours. We shall follow him; and we shall not flinch; even if we peril ourselves that we become like him. Friend John, this has been a great hour; and it have done much to advance us on our way. You must be scribe and write him all down, so that when the others return from their work you can give it to them; then they shall know as we do."

And so I have written it whilst we wait their return, and Mrs. Harker has written with her typewriter all since she brought the MS. to us.

27 *That terrible baptism of blood.* This dark analogy is to the Christian concept of being "washed in the blood of the lamb," a baptism that produces salvation. But Mina, as she knows, has been baptized in the blood of goat-footed Satan.

CHAPTER XXVI.

Dr. Seward's Diary.

29 *October.*—This is written in the train from Varna to Galatz. Last night we all assembled a little before the time of sunset. Each of us had done his work as well as he could; so far as thought, and endeavour, and opportunity go, we are prepared for the whole of our journey, and for our work when we get to Galatz. When the usual time came round Mrs. Harker prepared herself for her hypnotic effort; and after
1 a longer and more strenuous effort on the part of Van Helsing than has been usually necessary, she sank into the trance. Usually she speaks on a hint; but this time the Professor had to ask her questions, and to ask them pretty resolutely, before we could learn anything; at last her answer came:—

"I can see nothing; we are still; there are no waves lapping, but only a steady swirl of water softly running against the hawser. I can hear men's voices calling, near and far, and the roll and creak of oars in the rowlocks. A gun is fired somewhere; the echo of it seems far away. There is tramping of feet overhead, and ropes and chains are dragged along. What is this? There is a gleam of light; I can feel the air blowing upon me."

Here she stopped. She had risen, as if impulsively, from where she lay on the sofa, and raised both her hands, palms upwards, as if lifting a weight. Van Helsing and I looked at each other with understanding. Quincey raised his eyebrows slightly and looked at her intently, whilst Harker's hand instinctively closed round the hilt of his kúkri. There was a long pause. We all knew that the time when she could speak was passing; but we felt that it was useless to say any-

1 *more strenuous effort.* Because, we are to understand, she is being drawn ever deeper into Dracula's power.

thing. Suddenly she sat up, and, as she opened her eyes, said sweetly :—

"Would none of you like a cup of tea? You must all be so tired!" We could only make her happy, and so acquiesced. She bustled off to get tea; when she had gone Van Helsing said :—

"You see, my friends. *He* is close to land: he has left his earth-chest. But he has yet to get on shore. In the night he may lie hidden somewhere; but if he be not carried on shore, or if the ship do not touch it, he cannot achieve the land. In such case he can, if it be in the night, change his form and can jump or fly on shore, as he did at Whitby. But if the day come before he get on shore, then, unless he be carried he cannot escape. And if he be carried, then the customs men may discover what the box contains. Thus, in fine, if he escape not on shore to-night, or before dawn, there will be the whole day lost to him. We may then arrive in time; for if he escape not at night we shall come on him in daytime, boxed up and at our mercy; for he dare not be his true self, awake and visible, lest he be discovered."

There was no more to be said, so we waited in patience until the dawn; at which time we might learn more from Mrs. Harker.

Early this morning we listened, with breathless anxiety, for her response in her trance. The hypnotic stage was even longer in coming than before; and when it came the time remaining until full sunrise was so short that we began to despair. Van Helsing seemed to throw his whole soul into the effort; at last, in obedience to his will she made reply :—

"All is dark. I hear lapping water, level with me, and some creaking as of wood on wood." She paused, and the red sun shot up. We must wait till to-night.

And so it is that we are travelling towards Galatz in an agony of expectation. We are due to arrive between two and three in the morning; but already, at Bucharest, we are three **2**
hours late, so we cannot possibly get in till well after sun-up. Thus we shall have two more hypnotic messages from Mrs. Harker; either or both may possibly throw more light on what is happening.

Later.—Sunset has come and gone. Fortunately it came at a time when there was no distraction; for had it occurred whilst we were at a station, we might not have secured the necessary calm and isolation. Mrs. Harker yielded to the hypnotic influence even less readily than this morning. I am in fear that her power of reading the Count's sensations may die away, just when we want it most. It seems to me that her imagination is beginning to work. Whilst she has been in the trance hitherto she has confined herself to the simplest of facts. If this goes on it may ultimately mislead us. If I thought that the Count's power over her would die away equally with her power of knowledge it would be a happy thought; but I am afraid that it may not be so. When she did speak, her words were enigmatical :—

"Something is going out; I can feel it pass me like a cold wind. I can hear, far off, confused sounds—as of men talking in strange tongues, fierce-falling water, and the howling of

2 *Bucharest.* At the end of the nineteenth century, when Seward and his companions were in Bucharest, it had a population of 250,000 people. The ninth edition of the *Encyclopaedia Britannica* says of the city that it had picturesque churches and many trees. Bucharest's streets were irregular, poorly paved, or not paved at all. In summer public transportation was by means of 500 *droshkis;* in winter a similar number of sledges took their place.

Our travelers would have been pleased to know that an English company had recently built Bucharest's first tramway system. Count Dracula, for his part, was no doubt pleased to know that more than 20,000 Transylvanians held civil service positions in Bucharest.

Ironically enough, for our delayed travelers, the word "Bucharest" means "city of joy." (See map, p. 335.)

3 *any foreign language.* This is a gentle dig at Quincey, the provincial American.

wolves." She stopped and a shudder ran through her, increasing in intensity for a few seconds, till, at the end, she shook as though in a palsy. She said no more, even in answer to the Professor's imperative questioning. When she woke from the trance, she was cold, and exhausted, and languid; but her mind was all alert. She could not remember anything, but asked what she had said; when she was told, she pondered over it deeply, for a long time and in silence.

30 *October*, 7 *a.m.*—We are near Galatz now, and I may not have time to write later. Sunrise this morning was anxiously looked for by us all. Knowing of the increasing difficulty of procuring the hypnotic trance Van Helsing began his passes earlier than usual. They produced no effect, however, until the regular time when she yielded with a still greater difficulty, only a minute before the sun rose. The Professor lost no time in his questioning; her answer came with equal quickness:—

"All is dark. I hear water swirling by, level with my ears, and the creaking of wood on wood. Cattle low far off. There is another sound, a queer one like—" she stopped and grew white, and whiter still.

"Go on; Go on! Speak, I command you!" said Van Helsing in an agonized voice. At the same time there was despair in his eyes, for the risen sun was reddening even Mrs. Harker's pale face. She opened her eyes, and we all started as she said, sweetly and seemingly with the utmost unconcern:—

"Oh Professor why ask me to do what you know I can't? I don't remember anything." Then, seeing the look of amazement on our faces, she said, turning from one to the other with a troubled look:—

"What have I said? What have I done? I know nothing, only that I was lying here, half asleep, and I heard you say 'go on! speak, I command you!' It seemed so funny to hear you order me about, as if I were a bad child!"

"Oh, Madam Mina" he said, sadly, "it is proof, if proof be needed, of how I love and honour you, when a word for your good, spoken more earnest than ever, can seem so strange because it is to order her whom I am proud to obey!"

The whistles are sounding; we are nearing Galatz. We are on fire with anxiety and eagerness.

Mina Harker's Journal.

30 *October.*—Mr. Morris took me to the hotel where our rooms had been ordered by telegraph, he being the one who
3 could best be spared, since he does not speak any foreign language. The forces were distributed much as they had been at Varna, except that Lord Godalming went to the Vice-Consul as his rank might serve as an immediate guarantee of some sort to the official, we being in extreme hurry. Jonathan and the two doctors went to the shipping agent to learn particulars of the arrival of the *Czarina Catherine.*

Later.—Lord Godalming has returned. The Consul is away, and the Vice-Consul sick; so the routine work has been

attended to by a clerk. He was very obliging, and offered to
do anything in his power.

Jonathan Harker's Journal.

30 *October.*—At nine o'clock Dr. Van Helsing, Dr. Seward,
and I called on Messrs. Mackenzie & Steinkoff, the agents of 4
the London firm of Hapgood. They had received a wire from
London, in answer to Lord Godalming's telegraphed request,
asking them to show us any civility in their power. They were
more than kind and courteous, and took us at once on board
the *Czarina Catherine* which lay at anchor out in the river
harbour. There we saw the Captain, Donelson by name, who 5
told us of his voyage. He said that in all his life he had never
had so favourable a run.

"Man!" he said, "but it made us afeard, for we expeckit
that we should have to pay for it wi' some rare piece o' ill
luck, so as to keep up the average. It's no canny to run frae 6
London to the Black Sea wi' a wind ahint ye, as though the 7
Deil himself were blawin' on yer sail for his ain purpose. An'
a' the time we could no speer a thing. Gin we were nigh a 8, 9
ship, or a port, or a headland, a fog fell on us and travelled
wi' us, till when after it had lifted and we looked out, the deil
a thing could we see. We ran by Gibraltar wi'oot bein' able to
signal; an' till we came to the Dardanelles and had to wait to
get our permit to pass, we never were within hail o' aught. At
first I inclined to slack off sail and beat about till the fog was
lifted; but whiles, I thocht that if the Deil was minded to get 10
us into the Black Sea quick, he was like to do it whether we
would or no. If we had a quick voyage it would be no to our
miscredit wi' the owners, or no hurt to our traffic; an' the Old 11
Mon who had served his ain purpose wad be decently grateful
to us for no hinderin' him." This mixture of simplicity and
cunning, of superstition and commercial reasoning, aroused
Van Helsing, who said:—

"Mine friend, that Devil is more clever than he is thought
by some; and he know when he meet his match!" The
skipper was not displeased with the compliment, and went
on:—

"When we got past the Bosphorus the men began to
grumble; some o' them, the Roumanians, came and asked me
to heave overboard a big box which had been put on board by
a queer lookin' old man just before we had started frae
London. I had seen them speer at the fellow, and put out
their twa fingers when they saw him, to guard against the evil
eye. Man! but the supersteetion of foreigners is pairfectly
rideeculous! I sent them aboot their business pretty quick;
but as just after a fog closed in on us, I felt a wee bit as they
did anent something, though I wouldn't say it was agin the bit 12, 13
box. Well, on we went, and as the fog didn't let up for five
days I joost let the wind carry us; for if the Deil wanted to
get somewheres—well, he would fetch it up a'reet. An' if he
didn't, well we'd keep a sharp look out anyhow. Sure enuch,
we had a fair way and deep water all the time; and two days 14
ago, when the mornin' sun came through the fog, we found

4 *Messrs. Mackenzie & Steinkoff, the agents of the London firm of Hapgood.* Neither Mackenzie nor Steinkoff is listed in the London city directories of Stoker's day, and no such firm as Hapgood existed in London either.

5 *Donelson by name.* With Donelson's Scottish, we now have six accents in the novel: Dracula's Romanian-modified English; Van Helsing's Dutch; Quincey Morris's American; various workingmen's Cockney; the Yorkshire speech of Whitby; and now Donelson's Scottish. Except for Dracula's speech, which is not presented as accented for very long, the speech mannerisms are used for comic effect, though in Van Helsing's case, the effect is often merely bizarre.

6 *canny.* Skill.

7 *ahint.* Behind.

8 *speer.* See.

9 *Gin.* When.

10 *but whiles.* But then.

11 *an' the Old Mon.* The devil.

12 *"anent."* About.

13 *agin.* Regarding.

14 *two days ago.* They entered the mouth of the Danube, then, on October 28.

"I HAD TO ARGY WI' THEM ABOOT IT WI' A HANDSPIKE."

15 *handspike*. A bar used as a lever.

16 *masel'*. Myself.

17 *a Hebrew of rather the Adelphi Theatre type*. That is to say, a caricature. In a Baedeker's *London* for 1898, we read: "Royal Adelphi Theatre, 411 Strand (N.Side), near Bedford Street. Melodramas and

ourselves just in the river opposite Galatz. The Roumanians were wild, and wanted me right or wrong to take out the box and fling it in the river. I had to argy wi' them aboot it wi' a
15 handspike; an' when the last o' them rose off the deck, wi' his head in his hand, I had convinced them that, evil eye or no evil eye, the property and the trust of my owners were better in my hands than in the river Danube. They had, mind ye, taken the box on the deck ready to fling in, and as it was marked Galatz *viâ* Varna, I thocht I'd let it lie till we discharged in the port an' get rid o't athegither. We didn't do much clearin' that day, an' had to remain the nicht at anchor; but in the mornin', braw an' airly, an hour before sun-up, a man came aboard wi' an order, written to him from England, to receive a box marked for one Count Dracula. Sure enuch the matter was one ready to his hand. He had his papers a' reet, an' glad I was to be rid o' the dam thing, for I was beginnin'
16 masel' to feel uneasy at it. If the Deil did have any luggage aboord the ship, I'm thinkin' it was nane ither than that same!

"What was the name of the man who took it?" asked Dr. Van Helsing with restrained eagerness.

"I'll be tellin' ye quick!" he answered, and, stepping down to his cabin, produced a receipt signed "Immanuel Hildesheim." Burgen-strasse 16 was the address. We found out that this was all the Captain knew; so with thanks we came away.

17 We found Hildesheim in his office, a Hebrew of rather the Adelphi Theatre type, with a nose like a sheep, and a fez. His arguments were pointed with specie—we doing the punctuation—and with a little bargaining he told us what he knew. This turned out to be simple but important. He had received a letter from Mr. de Ville of London, telling him to receive, if possible before sunrise so as to avoid customs, a box which would arrive at Galatz in the *Czarina Catherine*. This he was to give in charge to a certain Petrof Skinsky, who dealt with the Slovaks who traded down the river to the port. He had been paid for his work by an English bank note, which had been duly cashed for gold at the Danube International Bank. When Skinsky had come to him, he had taken him to the ship and handed over the box, so as to save porterage. That was all he knew.

We then sought for Skinsky, but were unable to find him. One of his neighbours, who did not seem to bear him any affection, said that he had gone away two days before, no one knew whither. This was corroborated by his landlord who had received by messenger the key of the house together with the
18 rent due, in English money. This had been between ten and eleven o'clock last night. We were at a standstill again.

Whilst we were talking one came running and breathlessly gasped out that the body of Skinsky had been found inside the wall of the churchyard of St. Peter, and that the throat had been torn open as if by some wild animal. Those we had been speaking with ran off to see the horror, the women crying out "This is the work of a Slovak!" We hurried away lest we should have been in some way drawn into the affair, and so detained.

As we came home we could arrive at no definite conclusion. We were all convinced that the box was on its way, by water, to somewhere; but where that might be we would have to discover. With heavy hearts we came home to the hotel to Mina.

When we met together, the first thing was to consult as to taking Mina again into our confidence. Things are getting desperate, and it is at least a chance, though a hazardous one. As a preliminary step, I was released from my promise to her.

"I FEEL SO GRATEFUL TO THE MAN WHO INVENTED THE 'TRAVELLER'S' TYPEWRITER."

Mina Harker's Journal.

30 *October, evening.*—They were so tired and worn out and
dispirited that there was nothing to be done till they had some
rest; so I asked them all to lie down for half an hour whilst I
should enter everything up to the moment. I feel so grateful
to the man who invented the "Traveller's" typewriter, and to **19**
Mr. Morris for getting this one for me. I should have felt
quite astray doing the work if I had to write with a pen. . . .

It is all done; poor dear, dear Jonathan, what he must have suffered, what must he be suffering now. He lies on the sofa hardly seeming to breathe, and his whole body appears in collapse. His brows are knit; his face is drawn with pain. Poor fellow, maybe he is thinking, and I can see his face all wrinkled up with the concentration of his thoughts. Oh! if I could only help at all. . . . I shall do what I can. . . .

I have asked Dr. Van Helsing, and he has got me all the
papers that I have not yet seen. . . . Whilst they are resting, **20**
I shall go over all carefully, and perhaps I may arrive at some
conclusion. I shall try to follow the Professor's example, and
think without prejudice on the facts before me. . . .

I do believe that under God's providence I have made a

farces. Stalls 10s. 6d., dress circle 6s., upper circle 4s. and 3s., pit 2s. 6d., gallery 1s."

The Adelphi was not far from the Lyceum Theatre where Stoker spent much of his adult life as confidante to Sir Henry Irving and as actor-manager of the theatre.

This casual bit of anti-Semitism on Stoker's part is certainly too bad, but it is not unusual in a nineteenth-century British gentleman. When it came to serious politics, Stoker joined other intellectuals of his day in protesting the mistreatment of Jews in Russia in 1905.

18 *between ten and eleven.* On October 29.

19 *who invented the "Traveller's" typewriter.* I have been unable to identify a "Traveller's" typewriter; but if Mina means a portable, then she is probably talking about the Blickensderfer typewriter which, according to G. Tilghman Richards's *The History and Development of Typewriters*, was "the first true portable." On the other hand, since portability is a relative matter, Mina may have been using the Columbia Type-writer that appeared in 1885 and weighed less than six pounds and was priced at five pounds, five shillings.

By the end of the nineteenth century, the typewriter had established itself as an indispensable writing tool.

Mina, who is a speed typist, undoubtedly used one of a bewildering variety of touch typing systems that existed in her day. It was not until well past 1890 that the so-called Universal system triumphed over its competitors.

The Universal, or QWERTY, arrangement is the one that has come down to our own time. Michael H. Adler, author of *The Writing Machine*, tells us (p. 205) that there are two explanations for the origin of the QWERTY arrangement of typewriter keys: (1) it was "developed empirically as a means of overcoming type-bar clash in . . . early machines"; (2) that it came about because "of the manufacturer's desire to make the salesman's job easier for him: since he had to demonstrate the machine to skeptical clients, placing the letters of the word 'typewriter' on the same line made them easier for him to find, with corresponding increases in his typing speed . . . and volume of sales."

The chief competitor of the Universal keyboard was the one called Ideal. The Ideal system displayed a configuration of keys that spelled DHIATENSOR and was based on the fact that more than 70 percent of English words are composed of these ten letters.

20 *that I have not yet seen.* Mina's fortitude is beyond belief.

21 *octroi officers.* Tax collection officials.

discovery. I shall get the maps and look over them. . . .

I am more than ever sure that I am right. My new conclusion is ready, so I shall get our party together and read it. They can judge it; it is well to be accurate, and every minute is precious.

Mina Harker's Memorandum.

(Entered in her Journal.)

Ground of inquiry.—Count Dracula's problem is to get back to his own place.

(*a*) He must be *brought back* by some one. This is evident; for had he power to move himself as he wished he could go either as man, or wolf, or bat, or in some other way. He evidently fears discovery or interference, in the state of helplessness in which he must be—confined as he is between dawn and sunset in his wooden box.

(*b*) *How is he to be taken?*—Here a process of exclusions may help us. By road, by rail, by water?

1. *By Road.*—There are endless difficulties, especially in leaving a city.

(*x*) There are people; and people are curious, and investigate. A hint, a surmise, a doubt as to what might be in the box, would destroy him.

21 (*y*) There are, or there might be, customs and octroi officers to pass.

(*z*) His pursuers might follow. This is his greatest fear; and in order to prevent his being betrayed he has repelled, so far as he can, even his victim—me!

2. *By Rail.*—There is no one in charge of the box. It would have to take its chance of being delayed; and delay would be fatal, with enemies on the track. True, he might escape at night; but what would he be, if left in a strange place with no refuge that he could fly to. This is not what he intends; and he does not mean to risk it.

3. *By Water.*—Here is the safest way, in one respect, but with most danger in another. On the water he is powerless except at night; even then he can only summon fog and storm and snow and his wolves. But were he wrecked, the living water would engulf him, helpless; and he would indeed be lost. He could have the vessel drive to land; but if it were unfriendly land, wherein he was not free to move, his position would still be desperate.

We know from the record that he was on the water; so what we have to do is to ascertain *what* water.

The first thing is to realise exactly what he has done as yet; we may, then, get a light on what his later task is to be.

Firstly.—We must differentiate between what he did in London as part of his general plan of action, when he was pressed for moments and had to arrange as best he could.

Secondly we must see, as well as we can surmise it from the facts we know of, what he has done here.

As to the first, he evidently intended to arrive at Galatz,

and sent invoice to Varna to deceive us lest we should ascertain his means of exit from England; his immediate and sole purpose then was to escape. The proof of this, is the letter of instructions sent to Immanuel Hildesheim to clear and take away the box *before sunrise.* There is also the instruction to Petrof Skinsky. These we must only guess at; but there must have been some letter or message, since Skinsky came to Hildesheim.

That, so far, his plans were successful we know. The *Czarina Catherine* made a phenomenally quick journey—so much so that Captain Donelson's suspicions were aroused;
but his superstition united with his canniness played the 22
Count's game for him, and he ran with his favouring wind through fogs and all till he brought up blindfold at Galatz. That the Count's arrangements were well made, has been proved. Hildesheim cleared the box, took it off, and gave it to Skinsky. Skinsky took it—and here we lose the trail. We only know that the box is somewhere on the water, moving along. The customs and the octroi, if there be any, have been avoided.

Now we come to what the Count must have done after his arrival—*on land*, at Galatz.

The box was given to Skinsky before sunrise. At sunrise
the Count could appear in his own form. Here, we ask why 23
Skinsky was chosen at all to aid in the work? In my husband's diary, Skinsky is mentioned as dealing with the Slovaks
who trade down the river to the port; and the man's remark, 24
that the murder was the work of a Slovak, showed the general feeling against his class. The Count wanted isolation.

My surmise is, this: that in London the Count decided to get back to his Castle by water, as the most safe and secret way. He was brought from the Castle by Szgany, and probably they delivered their cargo to Slovaks who took the boxes to Varna, for there they were shipped for London. Thus the Count had knowledge of the persons who could arrange this
service. When the box was on land, before sunrise or 25
after sunset, he came out from his box, met Skinsky and instructed him what to do as to arranging the carriage of the box up some river. When this was done, and he knew
that all was in train, he blotted out his traces, as he thought, 26
by murdering his agent.

I have examined the map and find that the river most
suitable for the Slovaks to have ascended is either the Pruth 27
or the Sereth. I read in the typescript that in my trance I heard cows low and water swirling level with my ears and the creaking of wood. The Count in his box, then, was on a river in an open boat—propelled probably either by oars or poles, for the banks are near and it is working against stream. There would be no such sound if floating down stream.

Of course it may not be either the Sereth or the Pruth, but we may possibly investigate further. Now of these two, the Pruth is the more easily navigated, but the Sereth is,
at Fundu, joined by the Bistritza which runs up round the 28
Borgo pass. The loop it makes is manifestly as close to Dracula's Castle as can be got by water."

22 *his canniness.* According to Stoker, Captain Donelson must be canny because he is a Scotsman.

23 *in his own form.* But in a weakened condition, according to the characteristics and traits of the vampire as Dr. Van Helsing gives them in chapter XVIII, page 213.

24 *the man's remark.* An error. On page 306 Stoker wrote: ". . . the women crying out 'This is the work of a Slovak!' "

25 *before sunrise or after sunset.* It was, according to Captain Donelson, an hour before sunrise. (See p. 306.)

26 *all was in train.* The plan was in motion, as in the French idiom *en train de,* meaning in the process of, or under way.

27 *is either the Pruth or the Sereth.* The Prut flows from the Carpathian Mountains into the Danube, forming the boundary between Moldavia and Bessarabia (since World War II between Romania and Russia). The Siret also flows into the Danube from the Carpathians. The Bistrita joins the Siret below Baku. (See map, p. 335.)

28 *Fundu.* Fundu, as such, does not appear on any of the maps consulted in half a dozen reputable and heavy atlases. Stoker may have seen a "Fundu-Moldovei," which appears (in the Pergamon *Atlas,* p. 170) to be about ten miles east of the Bistrita River and an equal distance west of Cimpulung Moldovenesc, approximately at the 47°N parallel.

From this point on in the narrative, the reader who wants to follow the action on a map runs into some difficulty because there appears to be more than one Bistrita River. The one that flows into the Siret, and which our travelers take, is also called the Golden Bistrita. Farther north and west, and quite close to the Borgo Pass, there is a lesser Bistrita River. It may be that Stoker confused the two as this editor, for a long time, did.

29 *where he perish.* Because the vampire cannot abide running water. See Van Helsing's description of the powers and the limitations of the vampire in chapter XVIII, p. 213.

Mina Harker's Journal—continued.

When I had done reading, Jonathan took me in his arms and kissed me. The others kept shaking me by both hands, and Dr. Van Helsing said:—

"Our dear Madam Mina is once more our teacher. Her eyes have seen where we were blinded. Now we are on the track once again, and this time we may succeed. Our enemy is at his most helpless; and if we can come on him by day, on the water, our task will be over. He has a start, but he is powerless to hasten, as he may not leave his box lest those who carry him may suspect; for them to suspect would be to prompt them to throw him in the stream
29 where he perish. This he knows, and will not. Now men, to our Council of War; for, here and now, we must plan what each and all shall do."

"I shall get a steam launch and follow him," said Lord Godalming.

"And I, horses to follow on the bank lest by chance he land," said Mr. Morris.

"Good!" said the Professor, "both good. But neither must go alone. There must be force to overcome force if need be; the Slovak is strong and rough, and he carries rude arms." All the men smiled, for amongst them they carried a small arsenal. Said Mr. Morris:—

"I have brought some Winchesters; they are pretty handy in a crowd, and there may be wolves. The Count, if you remember, took some other precautions; he made some requisitions on others that Mrs. Harker could not quite hear or understand. We must be ready at all points." Dr. Seward said:—

"I think I had better go with Quincey. We have been accustomed to hunt together, and we two, well armed, will be a match for whatever may come along. You must not be alone Art. It may be necessary to fight the Slovaks, and a chance thrust—for I don't suppose these fellows carry guns—would undo all our plans. There must be no chances, this time; we shall not rest until the Count's head and body have been separated, and we are sure that he cannot re-incarnate." He looked at Jonathan as he spoke, and Jonathan looked at me. I could see that the poor dear was torn about in his mind. Of course he wanted to be with me; but then the boat service would, most likely, be the one which would destroy the... the...the...Vampire. (Why did I hesitate to write the word?) He was silent awhile, and during his silence Dr. Van Helsing spoke:—

"Friend Jonathan, this is to you for twice reasons. First, because you are young and brave and can fight, and all energies may be needed at the last; and again that it is your right to destroy him—that—which has wrought such woe to you and yours. Be not afraid for Madam Mina; she will be my care, if I may. I am old. My legs are not so quick to run as once; and I am not used to ride so long or to pursue as need be, or to fight with lethal weapons. But I can be of other service; I can fight in other way. And I can die, if need be, as well as younger men. Now let me say that what

I would is this: while you, my Lord Godalming, and friend Jonathan go in your so swift little steamboat up the river, and whilst John and Quincey guard the bank where perchance he might be landed, I will take Madam Mina right into the heart of the enemy's country. Whilst the old fox is tied in his box, floating on the running stream whence he cannot escape to land—where he dares not raise the lid of his coffin-box lest his Slovak carriers should in fear leave him to perish—we shall go in the track where Jonathan went,—from Bistritz over the Borgo, and find our way to the Castle of Dracula. Here, Madam Mina's hypnotic power will surely help, and we shall find our way—all dark and unknown otherwise—after the first sunrise when we are near that fateful place. There is much to be done, and other places to be made sanctify, so that that nest of vipers be obliterated." Here Jonathan interrupted him hotly:—

"Do you mean to say, Professor Van Helsing, that you would bring Mina, in her sad case and tainted as she is with that devil's illness, right into the jaws of his death-trap? Not for the world! Not for Heaven or Hell!" He became almost speechless for a minute, and then went on:—

"Do you know what the place is? Have you seen that awful den of hellish infamy—with the very moonlight alive with grisly shapes, and every speck of dust that whirls in the wind a devouring monster in embryo? Have you felt the Vampire's lips upon your throat?" Here he turned to me, and as his eyes lit on my forehead, he threw up his arms with a cry: "Oh, my God, what have we done to have this terror upon us!" and he sank down on the sofa in a collapse of misery. The Professor's voice, as he spoke in clear, sweet tones, which seemed to vibrate in the air, calmed us all:—

"Oh my friend, it is because I would save Madam Mina from that awful place that I would go. God forbid that I should take her into that place. There is work—wild work—to be done there, that her eyes may not see. We men here, all save Jonathan, have seen with their own eyes what is to be done before that place can be purify. Remember that we are in terrible straits. If the Count escape us this time—and he is strong and subtle and cunning—he may choose to sleep him for a century; and then in time our dear one"—he took my hand—"would come to him to keep him company, and would be as those others that you, Jonathan, saw. You have told us of their gloating lips; you heard their ribald laugh as they clutched the moving bag that the Count threw to them. You shudder; and well may it be. Forgive me that I make you so much pain, but it is necessary. My friend, is it not a dire need for the which I am giving, if need me, my life? If it **30** were that anyone went into that place to stay, it is I who would have to go, to keep them company."

"Do as you will;" said Jonathan, with a sob that shook him all over, "We are in the hands of God!"

Later.—"Oh, it did me good to see the way that these brave men worked. How can women help loving men when they are so earnest, and so true, and so brave! And, too, it made me think of the wonderful power of money! What can it not do when it is properly applied; and what might it do

". . . MY LORD GODALMING, AND FRIEND JONATHAN GO . . . UP THE RIVER."

30 *if need me, my life?* This is Van Helsing Dutch. But later editions have corrected this line to read "if need be" (Arrow Books), and "possibly" (Heritage Press).

when basely used. I felt so thankful that Lord Godalming is
rich, and that both he and Mr. Morris, who also has plenty of
money, are willing to spend it so freely. For if they did not,
our little expedition could not start, either so promptly or so
well equipped, as it will within another hour. It is not three
hours since it was arranged what part each of us was to do;
31 and now Lord Godalming and Jonathan have a lovely steam
32 launch, with steam up ready to start at a moment's notice.
Dr. Seward and Mr. Morris have half a dozen beautiful horses,
well appointed. We have all the maps and appliances of various
kinds that can be had. Professor Van Helsing and I are to
33 leave by the 11.40 train to-night for Veresti, where we are to
get a carriage to drive to the Borgo Pass. We are bringing a
good deal of ready money, as we are to buy a carriage and
horses. We shall drive ourselves, for we have no one whom
we can trust in the matter. The Professor knows something of
a great many languages, so we shall get on all right. We have
all got arms, even for me a large-bore revolver; Jonathan
would not be happy unless I was armed like the rest. Alas!
I cannot carry one arm that the rest do; the scar on my forehead forbids that. Dear Dr. Van Helsing comforts me by
telling me that I am fully armed as there may be wolves; the
weather is getting colder every hour, and there are snow-flurries which come and go as warnings.

Later.—It took all my courage to say good-bye to my darling. We may never meet again. Courage, Mina! the Professor is looking at you keenly; his look is a warning. There must be no tears now—unless it may be that God will let them fall in gladness.

Jonathan Harker's Journal.

October 30. *Night.*—I am writing this in the light from the
furnace door of the steam launch; Lord Godalming is firing
up. He is an experienced hand at the work, as he has had
for years a launch of his own on the Thames, and another on the
34 Norfolk Broads. Regarding our plans, we finally decided that
Mina's guess was correct, and that if any waterway was chosen
for the Count's escape back to his Castle, the Sereth and then
the Bistritza at its junction, would be the one. We took it,
that somewhere about the 47th degree, north latitude, would
be the place chosen for the crossing the country between the
35 river and the Carpathians. We have no fear in running at
good speed up the river at night; there is plenty of water, and
the banks are wide enough apart to make steaming, even in
the dark, easy enough. Lord Godalming tells me to sleep for
a while, as it is enough for the present for one to be on watch.
But I cannot sleep—how can I with the terrible danger hanging
over my darling, and her going out into that awful place. . . .
My only comfort is that we are in the hands of God. Only
for that faith it would be easier to die than to live, and so be
quit of all the trouble. Mr. Morris and Dr. Seward were off
on their long ride before we started; they are to keep up the
right bank, far enough off to get on higher lands where they can
see a good stretch of river and avoid the following of its curves.
They have, for the first stages, two men to ride and lead their

31 *steam launch.* As the novel rushes to its close, Stoker seems to be having a fit of symmetrical recall. At the opening of the book Jonathan Harker told us that he crossed "the most Western of splendid bridges over the Danube" (p. 1). What is interesting here is that Count Széchenyi, the same count who designed the bridge, was also the man who introduced steam navigation on the Danube. The details of the bridge and the information about the steamboats are on facing pages (pp. 220–21) of Paget's *Hungary and Transylvania*.

32 *at a moment's notice.* This is hasty shopping indeed.

33 *Veresti. Stieler's Hand-Atlas* shows a Veresci just a few miles north of the 47° N. latitude that Harker mentions below as "the place chosen for the crossing the country between the river and the Carpathians." From Veresci to the Borgo Pass, over rough country, would be some ninety miles.

34 *Norfolk Broads.* An area on the southeast coast of England, just north of Norwich. (See map, p. 337.)

35 *and the Carpathians.* At Dorna-Watra (Vatra-Dornei). (See map, p. 335.)

spare horses—four in all, so as not to excite curiosity. When they dismiss the men, which shall be shortly, they shall themselves look after the horses. It may be necessary for us to join forces; if so they can mount our whole party. One of the saddles has a movable horn, and can be easily adapted for 36
Mina, if required.

It is a wild adventure we are on. Here, as we are rushing along through the darkness, with the cold from the river seeming to rise up and strike us; with all the mysterious voices of the night around us, it all comes home. We seem to be drifting into unknown places and unknown ways; into a whole world of dark and dreadful things. Godalming is shutting the furnace door. . . .

31 *October.*—Still hurrying along. The day has come, and Godalming is sleeping. I am on watch. The morning is bitterly cold; the furnace heat is grateful, though we have heavy fur coats. As yet we have passed only a few open boats, but none of them had on board any box or package of anything like the size of the one we seek. The men were scared every time we turned our electric lamp on them, and fell on their knees and prayed.

1 *November, evening.*—No news all day; we have found nothing of the kind we seek. We have now passed into the Bistritza; and if we are wrong in our surmise our chance is gone. We have overhauled every boat, big and little. Early this morning, one crew took us for a Government boat, and treated us accordingly. We saw in this a way of smoothing matters, so at Fundu, where the Bistritza runs into the Sereth,
we got a Roumanian flag which we now fly conspicuously. 37
With every boat which we have overhauled since then this trick has succeeded; we have had every deference shown to us, and not once any objection to whatever we chose to ask or do. Some of the Slovaks tell us that a big boat passed them, going at more than usual speed as she had a double crew on board. This was before they came to Fundu, so they could not tell us whether the boat turned into the Bistritza or continued on up the Sereth. At Fundu we could not hear of any such boat, so she must have passed there in the night. I am feeling very sleepy; the cold is perhaps beginning to tell upon me, and nature must have rest some time. Godalming insists that he shall keep the first watch. God bless him for all his goodness to poor dear Mina and me.

2 *November, morning.*—It is broad daylight. That good fellow would not wake me. He says it would have been a sin to, for I slept so peacefully and was forgetting my trouble. It seems brutally selfish of me to have slept so long, and let him watch all night; but he was quite right. I am a new man this morning; and, as I sit here and watch him sleeping, I can do all that is necessary both as to minding the engine, steering, and keeping watch. I can feel that my strength and energy are coming back to me. I wonder where Mina is now, and Van Helsing. They should have got to Veresti about noon on Wednesday. It would take them some time to get the carriage and horses; so if they had started and travelled hard, they would be about now at the Borgo Pass. God guide and help them! I am afraid to think what may happen. If we could

36 *a movable horn.* Presumably so that, as a Victorian lady, Mina may ride sidesaddle and not in the gross masculine way, astride.

37 *we got a Roumanian flag.* The flag our travelers hoisted had three vertical stripes, blue, yellow, and red. The blue stripes form the fly, the part of the flag farthest from the point of suspension.

38 *Strasba.* I have traced the course of the Bistrita River north from Baku in a variety of atlases without finding any Strasba. There is a Straja (47° N. latitude, 25° E. longitude). (See map, p. 335.)

only go faster! but we cannot; the engines are throbbing and doing their utmost. I wonder how Dr. Seward and Mr. Morris are getting on. There seem to be endless streams running down from the mountains into this river, but as none of them are very large—at present, at all events, though they are terrible doubtless in winter and when the snow melts—the horsemen may not have met much obstruction. I hope that
38 before we get to Strasba we may see them; for if by that time we have not overtaken the Count, it may be necessary to take counsel together what to do next.

Dr. Seward's Diary.

2 *November.*—Three days on the road. No news, and no time to write it if there had been, for every moment is precious. We have had only the rest needful for the horses; but we are both bearing it wonderfully. Those adventurous days of ours are turning up useful. We must push on; we shall never feel happy till we get the launch in sight again.

3 *November.*—We heard at Fundu that the launch had gone up the Bistritza. I wish it wasn't so cold. There are signs of snow coming; and if it falls heavy it will stop us. In such case we must get a sledge and go on, Russian fashion.

4 *November.*—To-day we heard of the launch having been detained by an accident when trying to force a way up the rapid. The slovak boats get up all right, by aid of a rope, and steering with knowledge. Some went up only a few hours before. Godalming is an amateur fitter himself, and evidently it was he who put the launch in trim again. Finally, they got up the Rapids all right, with local help, and are off on the chase afresh. I fear that the boat is not any better for the accident; the peasantry tell us that after she got upon the smooth water again, she kept stopping every now and again so long as she was in sight. We must push on harder than ever; our help may be wanted soon.

Mina Harker's Journal.

31 *October.*—Arrived at Veresti at noon. The Professor tells me that this morning at dawn he could hardly hypnotize me at all, and that all I could say was: "dark and quiet." He is off now buying a carriage and horses. He says that he will later on try to buy additional horses, so that we may be able to change them on the way. We have something more than 70 miles before us. The country is lovely, and most interesting; if only we were under different conditions, how delightful it would be to see it all. If Jonathan and I were driving through it alone what a pleasure it would be. To stop and see people, and learn something of their life, and to fill our minds and memories with all the colour and picturesqueness of the whole wild, beautiful country and the quaint people! But, alas!—

Later.—Dr. Van Helsing has returned. He has got the carriage and horses; we are to have some dinner, and to start in an hour. The landlady is putting us up a huge basket of provisions; it seems enough for a company of soldiers. The Professor encourages her, and whispers to me that it may be a week before we can get any good food again. He has been shopping too, and has sent home such a wonderful lot of fur coats and wraps, and all sorts of warm things. There will not be any chance of our being cold.

We shall soon be off. I am afraid to think what may happen to us. We are truly in the hands of God. He alone knows what may be, and I pray Him, with all the strength of my sad and humble soul, that He will watch over my beloved husband; that whatever may happen, Jonathan may know that I loved him and honoured him more than I can say, and that my latest and truest thought will be always for him.

CHAPTER XXVII.

Mina Harker's Journal.

1 *November.*—All day long we have travelled, and at a good speed. The horses seem to know that they are being kindly treated, for they go willingly their full stage at best speed. We have now had so many changes and find the same thing so constantly that we are encouraged to think that the journey will be an easy one. Dr. Van Helsing is laconic; he tells the
1 farmers that he is hurrying to Bistritz, and pays them well to
make the exchange of horses. We get hot soup, or coffee, or
2 tea; and off we go. It is a lovely country; full of beauties of
all imaginable kinds, and the people are brave, and strong, and simple, and seem full of nice qualities. They are *very, very* superstitious. In the first house where we stopped, when the woman who served us saw the scar on my forehead, she crossed herself and put out two fingers towards me, to keep off the evil eye. I believe they went to the trouble of putting an extra amount of garlic into our food; and I can't abide garlic. Ever since then I have taken care not to take off my hat or veil, and so have escaped their suspicions. We are travelling fast, and as we have no driver with us to carry tales, we go ahead of scandal; but I daresay that fear of the evil eye will follow hard behind us all the way. The Professor seems tireless; all day he would not take any rest, though he made me sleep for a long spell. At sunset time he hypnotized me, and he says that I answered as usual "darkness, lapping water and creaking wood;" so our enemy is still on the river. I am afraid to think of Jonathan, but somehow I have now no fear for him, or for myself. I write this whilst we wait in a farmhouse for the horses to be got ready. Dr.

1 *to Bistritz.* But there is never any mention of getting there. This is not surprising since the only roads from northern Verecsi to the Borgo Pass go via Gura-Humorului, Campulung, and Vatra-Dornei. (See map, p. 335.)

2 *It is a lovely country; full of beauties.* From this point in the narrative, and for the next ten pages, it will be seen that Stoker is so intent on balancing his opening and closing action that he not only makes Mina and Dr. Van Helsing retrace Jonathan's route to Dracula's castle, but he also distributes Jonathan's experiences (and sometimes Jonathan's very language) between them. Mina and Van Helsing travel, like Jonathan, through beautiful, very cold country. The peasants make the sign of the evil eye against Mina; Dr. Van Helsing sleeps through part of his journey, and, of course, Mina through much of hers.

Van Helsing is sleeping. Poor dear, he looks very tired and old and grey, but his mouth is set as firmly as a conqueror's; even in his sleep he is instinct with resolution. When we have well started I must make him rest whilst I drive. I shall tell him that we have days before us, and he must not break down when most of all his strength will be needed . . . . All is ready; we are off shortly.

2 *November, morning.*—I was successful, and we took turns driving all night; now the day is on us, bright though cold. There is a strange heaviness in the air—I say heaviness for want of a better word; I mean that it oppresses us both. It is very cold, and only our warm furs keep us comfortable. At dawn Van Helsing hypnotised me; he says I answered "darkness, creaking wood and roaring water," so the river is changing as they ascend. I do hope that my darling will not run an chance of danger—more than need be; but we are in God' hands.

2 *November, night.*—All day long driving. The country gets wilder as we go, and the great spurs of the Carpathians, which at Veresti seemed so far from us and so low on the horizon, now seem to gather round us and tower in front. We both seem in good spirits; I think we make an effort each to cheer the other; in the doing so we cheer ourselves. Dr. Van Helsing says that by morning we shall reach the Borgo Pass. The houses are very few here now, and the Professor says that the last horses we got will have to go on with us, as we may not be able to change. He got two in addition to the two we changed, so that now we have a rude four-in-hand. The dear horses are patient and good, and they give us no trouble. We are not worried with other travellers, and so even I can drive. We shall get to the Pass in daylight; we do not want to arrive before. So we take it easy, and have each a long rest in turn. Oh, what will to-morrow bring to us? We go to seek the place where my poor darling suffered so much. God grant that we may be guided aright, and that He will deign to watch over my husband and those dear to us both, and who are in such deadly peril. As for me, I am not worthy in His sight. Alas! I am unclean to His eyes, and shall be until He may deign to let me stand forth in His sight as one of those who have not incurred His wrath. 3

"THE COUNTRY GETS WILDER AS WE GO."

3 *incurred His wrath.* It is extraordinarily tempting to speculate about the cause (or causes) of Mina's self-accusation. What has she done to incur God's wrath? The best clue to the source of her guilt, of course, is her confession (on p. 255) that when Dracula first drank her blood, she "was bewildered, and, strangely enough, . . . did not want to hinder him."

Though Mina, even this late into the narrative, is still pious, still able to breathe a brief prayer to God, it is also clear that she has a growing sense of her deepening attachment to Dracula. From here on, as Dr. Van Helsing fears, Mina drifts away from being God's creature more and more closely toward being the devil's own.

Memorandum by Abraham Van Helsing.

4 *November.*—This to my old and true friend John Seward, M.D., of Purfleet, London, in case I may not see him. It may explain. It is morning, and I write by a fire which all the night I have kept alive—Madam Mina aiding me. It is cold, cold; so cold that the grey heavy sky is full of snow, which when it falls will settle for all winter as the ground is hardening to receive it. It seems to have affected Madam Mina; she has been so heavy of head all day that she was not like herself. She sleeps, and sleeps, and sleeps! She, who is usual so alert, have done literally nothing all the day;

4 *the end of the world.* For his part, Jonathan wrote (p.12) that, as the pass opened out on the eastern side, "it seemed as though the mountain range had separated two atmospheres . . ."

she even have lost her appetite. She make no entry into her little diary, she who write so faithful at every pause. Something whisper to me that all is not well. However, to-night she is more *vif.* Her long sleep all day have refresh and restore her, for now she is all sweet and bright as ever. At sunset I try to hypnotise her, but alas! with no effect; the power has grown less and less with each day, and to-night it fail me altogether. Well, God's will be done—whatever it may be, and whithersoever it may lead!

Now to the historical, for as Madam Mina write not in her stenography, I must, in my cumbrous old fashion, that so each day of us may not go unrecorded.

We got to the Borgo Pass just after sunrise yesterday morning. When I saw the signs of the dawn I got ready for the hypnotism. We stopped our carriage, and got down so that there might be no disturbance. I made a couch with furs, and Madam Mina, lying down, yield herself as usual, but more slow and more short time than ever, to the hypnotic sleep. As before, came the answer: "darkness and the swirling of water." Then she woke, bright and radiant, and we go on our way and soon reach the Pass. At this time and place she become all on fire with zeal; some new guiding power be in her manifested, for she point to a road and say:—

"This is the way."

"How know you it?" I ask.

"Of course I know it," she answer, and with a pause, add: "Have not my Jonathan travel it and wrote of his travel?"

At first I think somewhat strange, but soon I see that there be only one such by-road. It is used but little, and very different from the coach road from the Bukovina to Bistritz, which is more wide and hard, and more of use.

So we came down this road; when we meet other ways—not always were we sure that they were roads at all, for they be neglect and light snow have fallen—the horses know and they only. I give rein to them, and they go on so patient. By-and-by we find all the things which Jonathan have note in that wonderful diary of him. Then we go on for long, long hours and hours. At the first, I tell Madam Mina to sleep; she try, and she succeed. She sleep all the time; till at the last, I feel myself to suspicious grow, and attempt to wake her. But she sleep on, and I may not wake her though I try. I do not wish to try too hard lest I harm her; for I know that she have suffer much, and sleep at times be all-in-all to her. I think I drowse myself, for all of sudden I feel guilt, as though I have done something; I find myself bolt up, with the reins in my hand, and the good horses go along jog, jog, just as ever. I look down and find Madam Mina still sleep. It is now not far off sunset time, and over the snow the light of the sun flow in big yellow flood, so that we throw great long shadow on where the mountain rise so steep. For we are going up, and up; and all is oh! so wild
4 and rocky, as though it were the end of the world.

Then I arouse Madam Mina. This time she wake with not much trouble, and then I try to put her to hypnotic sleep. But she sleep not, being as though I were not. Still I try

the snow, and all was for a time in a great twilight—I took out the horses and fed them in what shelter I could. Then I make a fire; and near it I make Madam Mina, now awake and more charming than ever, sit comfortable amid her rugs. I got ready food: but she would not eat, simply saying that she had not hunger. I did not press her, knowing her unavailingness. But I myself eat, for I must needs now be strong for all. Then, with the fear on me of what might be, I drew a ring so big for her comfort, round where Madam 6
Mina sat; and over the ring I passed some of the wafer, and I broke it fine so that all was well guarded. She sat still all the time—so still as one dead; and she grew whiter and ever whiter till the snow was not more pale; and no word she said. But when I drew near, she clung to me, and I could know that the poor soul shook her from head to feet with a tremor that was pain to feel. I said to her presently, when she had grown more quiet:—

"Will you not come over to the fire?" for I wished to make a test of what she could. She rose obedient, but when she have made a step she stopped, and stood as one stricken.

"Why not go on?" I asked. She shook her head, and, coming back, sat down in her place. Then, looking at me with open eyes, as of one waked from sleep, she said simply:—

"I cannot!" and remained silent. I rejoiced, for I knew that what she could not, none of those that we dreaded could. Though there might be danger to her body, yet her soul was safe!

Presently the horses began to scream, and tore at their tethers till I came to them and quieted them. When they did feel my hands on them, they whinnied low as in joy, and licked at my hands and were quiet for a time. Many times through the night did I come to them, till it arrive to the cold hour when all nature is at lowest; and every time my coming was with quiet of them. In the cold hour the fire began to die, and I was about stepping forth to replenish it, for now the snow came in flying sweeps and with it a chill mist. Even in the dark there was a light of some kind, as there ever is over snow; and it seemed as though the snow-flurries and the wreaths of mist took shape as of women with trailing garments. All was in dead, grim silence only that the horses whinnied and cowered, as if in terror of the worst. I began to fear—horrible fears; but then came to me the sense of safety in that ring wherein I stood. I began, too, to think that my imaginings were of the night, and the gloom, and the unrest that I have gone through, and all the terrible anxiety. It was as though my memories of all Jonathan's horrid experience were befooling me; for the snow flakes and the mist began to wheel and circle round, till I could get as though a shadowy glimpse of those women that would have kissed him. And then the horses cowered lower and lower, and moaned in terror as men do in pain. Even the madness of fright was not to them, so that they could break away. I feared for my dear Madam Mina when these weird figures drew near and circled round. I looked at her, but she sat calm, and smiled at me; when I would have stepped to

"... SUCH A CASTLE AS JONATHAN TELL OF IN HIS DIARY."

SORCERER WITHIN A RING.

6 *I drew a ring.* "Casting the circle" is a standard practice among magicians or witches. So the witch in Faust (Act I, "The Witch's Kitchen Scene") obeys Mephistopheles's request to "draw your circle and speak your spells, and let him have a good full cup," as she prepares the brew of youth for Faust. MacIntyre's translation (p. 197) of *Faust*.

Stewart Farrar, writing as a professed witch in his book *What Witches Do* (p. 51), tells us that:

"Every witch must learn: how to cast a Magic Circle. The Circle has a double function: concentration and protection. It has been used in witchcraft, magic and occult ceremonial down the ages. Its first cousins are the church, the mosque, and the synagogue, and its ancestors are Stonehenge, Avebury, and other such places in many lands.

"In its concentration aspect, it symbolizes the relationship between Microcosm and Macrocosm. It is, at the same time, infinity and the focus within infinity. As a protection against hostile psychic forces, it is the Akashic Egg [the egg containing the spiritual ether], the consecrated sanctuary, the barrier set up by ritualized (and therefore amplified) will.

"When it is a question of evoking and handling entities which might otherwise be too powerful to control, the Circle combines concentration and protection . . .

"The sceptic will argue that the Magic Circle is merely a psychological aid; but even on that level it is a valid and effective one. The church is just as much a man-made environment as the Circle, yet most men find it easier to attune themselves to the infinite within its walls, and the Law of Sanctuary expresses a fundamental human attitude. Man feels both holier and safer on consecrated ground, even though it is only he who has declared it sacred, by whatever criterion he may recognize."

Dr. Van Helsing, of course, is not a witch. However, as a secular person handling consecrated material as a protection against demonic or psychic forces, he is certainly practicing "white" magic.

the fire to replenish it, she caught me and held me back, and whispered, like a voice that one hears in a dream, so low it was :—

"No ! No ! Do not go without. Here you are safe !" I turned to her, and looking in her eyes, said :—

" But you ? It is for you that I fear ! whereat she laughed —a laugh, low and unreal, and said :—

" Fear for *me* ! Why fear for me ? None safer in all the world from them than I am," and as I wondered at the meaning of her words, a puff of wind made the flame leap up, and I see the red scar on her forehead. Then, alas ! I knew. Did I not, I would soon have learned, for the wheeling figures of mist and snow came closer, but keeping ever without the Holy circle. Then they began to materialise, till—if God have not take away my reason, for I saw it through my eyes—there were before me in actual flesh the same three women that Jonathan saw in the room, when they would have kissed his throat. I knew the swaying round forms, the bright hard eyes, the white teeth, the ruddy colour, the voluptuous lips. They smiled ever at poor dear Madam Mina ; and as their laugh came through the silence of the night, they twined their arms and pointed to her, and said in those so sweet tingling tones that Jonathan said were of the intolerable sweetness of the water-glasses :—

"Come, sister. Come to us. Come ! Come !" In fear I turned to my poor Madam Mina, and my heart with gladness leapt like flame ; for oh ! the terror in her sweet eyes, the repulsion, the horror, told a story to my heart that was all of hope. God be thanked she was not, yet, of them. I seized some of the firewood which was by me, and holding out some of the Wafer, advanced on them towards the fire. They drew back before me, and laughed their low horrid laugh. I fed the fire, and feared them not ; for I knew that we were safe within our protections. They could not approach me, whilst so armed, nor Madam Mina whilst she remained within the ring, which she could not leave no more than they could enter. The horses had ceased to moan, and lay still on the ground ; the snow fell on them softly, and they grew whiter. I knew that there was for the poor beasts no more of terror.

And so we remained till the red of the dawn began to fall through the snow-gloom. I was desolate and afraid, and full of woe and terror ; but when that beautiful sun began to climb the horizon life was to me again. At the first coming of the dawn the horrid figures melted in the whirling mist and snow ; the wreaths of transparent gloom moved away towards the castle, and were lost.

Instinctively, with the dawn coming, I turned to Madam Mina, intending to hypnotise her ; but she lay in a deep and sudden sleep, from which I could not wake her. I tried to hypnotise through her sleep, but she made no response, none at all ; and the day broke. I fear yet to stir. I have made my fire and have seen the horses, they are all dead. To-day I have much to do here, and I keep waiting till the sun is up high ; for there may be places where I must go, where that sunlight, though snow and mist obscure it, will be to me a safety.

I will strengthen me with breakfast, and then I will to my terrible work. Madam Mina still sleeps; and, God be thanked! she is calm in her sleep. . . .

Jonathan Harker's Journal.

4 *November, evening.*—The accident to the launch has been a terrible thing for us. Only for it we should have overtaken the boat long ago; and by now my dear Mina would have been free. I fear to think of her, off on the wolds near that horrid place. We have got horses, and we follow on the track. I note this whilst Godalming is getting ready. We have our arms. The Szgany must look out if they mean fight. Oh, if only Morris and Seward were with us. We must only hope! If I write no more Good bye, Mina! God bless and keep you.

Dr. Seward's Diary.

5 *November.*—With the dawn we saw the body of Szgany before us dashing away from the river with their leiter-waggon. They surrounded it in a cluster, and hurried along as though beset. The snow is falling lightly and there is a strange excitement in the air. It may be our own excited feelings, but the depression is strange. Far off I hear the howling of wolves; the snow brings them down from the mountains, and there are dangers to all of us, and from all sides. The horses are nearly ready, and we are soon off. We ride to death of some one. God alone knows who, or where, or what, or when, or how it may be. . . .

Dr. Van Helsing's Memorandum.

5 *November, afternoon.*—I am at least sane. Thank God for that mercy at all events, though the proving it has been dreadful. When I left Madam Mina sleeping within the Holy circle, I took my way to the castle. The blacksmith hammer which I took in the carriage from Veresti was useful; though the doors were all open I broke them off the rusty hinges, lest some ill-intent or ill-chance should close them, so that being entered I might not get out. Jonathan's bitter experience served me here. By memory of his diary 7 I found my way to the old chapel, for I knew that here my work lay. The air was oppressive; it seemed as if there was some sulphurous fume, which at times made me dizzy. Either there was a roaring in my ears or I heard afar off the howl of wolves. Then I bethought me of my dear Madam Mina, and I was in terrible plight. The dilemma had me between his horns. Her, I had not dare to take into this place, but left safe from the Vampire in that Holy circle; and yet even there would be the wolf! I resolve me that my work lay here, and that as to the wolves we must submit, if it were God's Will. At any rate it was only death and freedom beyond. So did I choose for her. Had it but been for myself the choice had been easy; the maw of the wolf were better to rest in than the grave of the

7 *experience served me here.* Van Helsing has in mind Jonathan Harker's experience in Dracula's castle. (See chapter II, p. 28.)

Vampire! So I make my choice to go on with my work.

I knew that there were at least three graves to find—graves that are inhabit; so I search, and search, and I find one of them. She lay in her Vampire sleep, so full of life and voluptuous beauty that I shudder as though I have come to do murder. Ah, I doubt not that in old time, when such things were, many a man who set forth to do such a task as mine, found at the last his heart fail him, and then his nerve. So he delay, and delay, and delay, till the mere beauty and the fascination of the wanton Un-dead have hypnotise him; and he remain on, and on, till sunset come, and the Vampire sleep be over. Then the beautiful eyes of the fair woman open and look love, and the voluptuous mouth present to a kiss—and man is weak. And there remain one more victim in the Vampire fold; one more to swell the grim and grisly ranks of the Un-dead! . . . .

There is some fascination, surely, when I am moved by the mere presence of such an one, even lying as she lay in a tomb fretted with age and heavy with the dust of centuries, though there be that horrid odour such as the lairs of the Count have had. Yes, I was moved—I, Van Helsing, with all my purpose and with my motive for hate—I was moved to a yearning for delay which seemed to paralyse my faculties and to clog my very soul. It may have been that the need of natural sleep, and the strange oppression of the air were beginning to overcome me. Certain it was that I was lapsing into sleep, the open-eyed sleep of one who yields to a sweet fascination, when there came through the snow-stilled air a long, low wail, so full of woe and pity that it woke me like the sound of a clarion. For it was the voice of my dear Madam Mina that I heard.

Then I braced myself again to my horrid task, and found by wrenching away tomb-tops one other of the sisters, the other dark one. I dared not pause to look on her as I had on her sister, lest once more I should begin to be enthrall; but I go on searching until, presently, I find in a high great tomb as if made to one much beloved that other fair sister which, like Jonathan I had seen to gather herself out of the atoms of the mist. She was so fair to look on, so radiantly beautiful, so exquisitely voluptuous, that the very instinct of man in me, which calls some of my sex to love and to protect one of hers, made my head whirl with new emotion. But God be thanked, that soul-wail of my dear Madam Mina had not died out of my ears; and, before the spell could be wrought further upon me, I had nerved myself to my wild work. By this time I had searched all the tombs in the chapel, so far as I could tell; and as there had been only three of these Un-Dead phantoms around us in the night, I took it that there were no more of active Un-Dead existent. There was one great tomb more lordly than all the rest; huge it was, and nobly proportioned. On it was but one word

DRACULA.

This then was the Un-Dead home of the King-Vampire, to whom so many more were due. Its emptiness spoke eloquent to make certain what I knew. Before I began to restore these women to their dead selves through my awful work, I laid in Dracula's tomb some of the Wafer, and so banished him from it, Un-Dead, for ever.

Then began my terrible task, and, I dreaded it. Had it been but one, it had been easy, comparative. But three! To begin twice more after I had been through a deed of horror; for if it was terrible with the sweet Miss Lucy, what would it not be with these strange ones who had survived through centuries, and who had been strengthened by the passing of the years; who would, if they could, have fought for their foul lives. . . .

Oh, my friend John, but it was butcher work; had I not been nerved by thoughts of other dead, and of the living over whom hung such a pall of fear, I could not have gone on. I tremble and tremble even yet, though till all was over, God be thanked, my nerve did stand. Had I not seen the repose in the first face, and the gladness that stole over it just ere the final dissolution came, as realisation that the soul had been won, I could not have gone further with my butchery. I could not have endured the horrid screeching as the stake drove home; the plunging of writhing form, and lips of bloody foam. I should have fled in terror and left my work undone. But it is over! And the poor souls, I can pity them now and weep, as I think of them placid each in her full sleep of death, for a short moment ere fading. For, friend John, hardly had my knife severed the head of each, before the whole body began to melt away and crumble into its native dust, as though the death that should have come centuries agone had at last assert himself and say at once and loud "I am here!"

Before I left the castle I so fixed its entrances that never more can the Count enter there Un-Dead.

When I stepped into the circle where Madam Mina slept, she woke from her sleep, and, seeing me, cried out in pain that I had endured too much.

"Come!" she said, "Come away from this awful place! Let us go to meet my husband who is, I know, coming towards us." She was looking thin and pale and weak; but her eyes were pure and glowed with fervour. I was glad to see her paleness and her illness, for my mind was full of the fresh horror of that ruddy vampire sleep.

And so with trust and hope, and yet full of fear, we go eastward to meet our friends—and *him*—whom Madam Mina tell me that she *know* are coming to meet us.

Mina Harker's Journal.

6 *November*.—It was late in the afternoon when the Professor and I took our way towards the east whence I knew Jonathan was coming. We did not go fast, though the way was steeply downhill, for we had to take heavy rugs and wraps with us; we dared not face the possibility of being left without warmth in the cold and the snow. We had to take some of our provisions too, for we were in a perfect desolation, and, so far as we could see through the snow-fall, there was not even the sign of a habitation. When we had gone about a mile, I was tired with the heavy walking and sat down to rest. Then we looked back and saw where the clear line of Dracula's

castle cut the sky; for we were so deep under the hill whereon it was set that the angle of perspective of the Carpathian mountains was far below it. We saw it in all its grandeur, perched a thousand feet on the summit of a sheer precipice, and with seemingly a great gap between it and the steep of the adjacent mountain on any side. There was something wild and uncanny about the place. We could hear the distant howling of wolves. They were far off, but the sound, even though coming muffled through the deadening snowfall, was full of terror. I knew from the way Dr. Van Helsing was searching about that he was trying to seek some strategic point, where we would be less exposed in case of attack. The rough roadway still led downwards; we could trace it through the drifted snow.

In a little while the Professor signalled to me, so I got up and joined him. He had found a wonderful spot, a sort of natural hollow in a rock, with an entrance like a doorway between two boulders. He took me by the hand and drew me in: "See!" he said, "here you will be in shelter; and if the wolves do come I can meet them one by one." He brought in our furs, and made a snug nest for me, and got out some provisions and forced them upon me. But I could not eat; to even try to do so was repulsive to me, and, much as I would have liked to please him, I could not bring myself to the attempt. He looked very sad, but did not reproach me. Taking his field-glasses from the case, he stood on the top of the rock, and began to search the horizon. Suddenly he called out:—

'Look! Madam Mina, look! look!" I sprang up and stood beside him on the rock; he handed me his glasses and pointed. The snow was now falling more heavily, and swirled about fiercely, for a high wind was beginning to blow. However there were times when there were pauses between the snow flurries and I could see a long way round. From the height where we were it was possible to see a great distance; and far off, beyond the white waste of snow, I could see the river lying like a black ribbon in kinks and curls as it wound its way. Straight in front of us and not far off—in fact so near that I wondered we had not noticed before—came a group of mounted men hurrying along. In the midst of them was a cart, a long leiter-waggon which swept from side to side, like a dog's tail wagging, with each stern inequality of the road. Outlined against the snow as they were, I could see from the men's clothes that they were peasants or gypsies of some kind.

On the cart was a great square chest. My heart leaped as I saw it, for I felt that the end was coming. The evening was now drawing close, and well I knew that at sunset the Thing, which was till then imprisoned there, would take new freedom and could in any of many forms elude all pursuit. In fear I turned to the Professor; to my consternation, however, he was not there. An instant later, I saw him below me. Round the rock he had drawn a circle, such as we had found shelter in last night. When he had completed it he stood beside me again, saying:—

"At least you shall be safe here from *him!*" He took

". . . A LONG LEITER-WAGGON WHICH SWEPT FROM SIDE TO SIDE, LIKE A DOG'S TAIL WAGGING . . ."

the glasses from me, and at the next lull of the snow swept the whole space below us. "See," he said, "they come quickly; they are flogging the horses, and galloping as hard as they can." He paused and went on in a hollow voice:—

"They are racing for the sunset. We may be too late. God's will be done!" Down came another blinding rush of driving snow, and the whole landscape was blotted out. It soon passed, however, and once more his glasses were fixed on the plain. Then came a sudden cry:—

"Look! Look! Look! See, two horsemen follow fast, coming up from the south. It must be Quincey and John. Take the glass. Look, before the snow blots it all out!" I took it and looked. The two men might be Dr. Seward and Mr. Morris. I knew at all events that neither of them was Jonathan. At the same time I *knew* that Jonathan was not far off; looking around I saw on the north side of the coming party two other men, riding at break-neck speed. One of them I knew was Jonathan, and the other I took, of course, to be Lord Godalming. They, too, were pursuing the party with the cart. When I told the Professor he shouted in glee like a schoolboy, and, after looking intently till a snowfall made sight impossible, he laid his Winchester rifle ready for use against the boulder at the opening of our shelter. "They are all converging," he said. "When the time comes we shall have the gypsies on all sides." I got out my revolver ready to hand, for whilst we were speaking the howling of wolves came louder and closer. When the snowstorm abated a moment we looked again. It was strange to see the snow falling in such heavy flakes close to us, and beyond, the sun shining more and more brightly as it sank down towards the far mountain tops. Sweeping the glass all around us I could see here and there dots moving singly and in twos and threes and larger numbers—the wolves were gathering for their prey.

Every instant seemed an age whilst we waited. The wind came now in fierce bursts, and the snow was driven with fury as it swept upon us in circling eddies. At times we could not see an arm's length before us; but at others as the hollow-sounding wind swept by us, it seemed to clear the air-space around us so that we could see afar off. We had of late been so accustomed to watch for sunrise and sunset, that we knew with fair accuracy when it would be; and we knew that before long the sun would set.

It was hard to believe that by our watches it was less than an hour that we waited in that rocky shelter before the various bodies began to converge close upon us. The wind came now with fiercer and more bitter sweeps, and more steadily from the north. It seemingly had driven the snow clouds from us, for, with only occasional bursts, the snow fell. We could distinguish clearly the individuals of each party, the pursued and the pursuers. Strangely enough those pursued did not seem to realize, or at least to care, that they were pursued; they seemed, however, to hasten with redoubled speed as the sun dropped lower and lower on the mountain tops.

Closer and closer they drew. The Professor and I crouched down behind our rock, and held our weapons ready; I could see that he was determined that they should not pass. One and all were quite unaware of our presence.

All at once two voices shouted out to: "Halt!" One was my Jonathan's, raised in a high key of passion; the other Mr. Morris' strong resolute tone of quiet command. The gypsies may not have known the language, but there was no mistaking the tone, in whatever tongue the words were spoken. Instinctively they reined in, and at the instant Lord Godalming and Jonathan dashed up at one side and Dr. Seward and Mr. Morris on the other. The leader of the gypsies, a splendid looking fellow who sat his horse like a centaur, waved them back, and in a fierce voice gave to his companions some word to proceed. They lashed the horses which sprang forward; but the four men raised their Winchester rifles, and in an unmistakeable way commanded them to stop. At the same moment Dr. Van Helsing and I rose behind the rock and pointed our weapons at them. Seeing that they were surrounded the men tightened their reins and drew up. The leader turned to them and gave a word at which every man of the gipsy party drew what weapon he carried, knife or pistol, and held himself in readiness to attack. Issue was joined in an instant.

The leader, with a quick movement of his rein, threw his horse out in front, and pointing first to the sun—now close down on the hill tops—and then to the castle, said something which I did not understand. For answer, all four men of our party threw themselves from their horses and dashed towards the cart. I should have felt terrible fear at seeing Jonathan in such danger, but that the ardour of battle must have been upon me as well as the rest of them; I felt no fear, but only a wild, surging desire to do something. Seeing the quick movement of our parties, the leader of the gypsies gave a command; his men instantly formed round the cart in a sort of undisciplined endeavour, each one shouldering and pushing the other in his eagerness to carry out the order.

In the midst of this I could see that Jonathan on one side of the ring of men, and Quincey on the other, were forcing a way to the cart; it was evident that they were bent on finishing their task before the sun should set. Nothing seemed to stop or even to hinder them. Neither the levelled weapons or the flashing knives of the gypsies in front, or the howling of the wolves behind, appeared to even attract their attention. Jonathan's impetuosity, and the manifest singleness of his purpose, seemed to overawe those in front of him; instinctively they cowered aside and let him pass. In an instant he had jumped upon the cart, and, with a strength which seemed incredible, raised the great box, and flung it over the wheel to the ground. In the meantime, Mr. Morris had had to use force to pass through his side of the ring of Szgany. All the time I had been breathlessly watching Jonathan I had, with the tail of my eye, seen him pressing desperately forward, and had seen the knives of the gypsies flash as he won a way through them, and they cut at him. He had parried with his great bowie knife, and at first I thought that he too had come through in safety; but as he sprang beside Jonathan, who had by now jumped from the cart, I could see that with his left hand

8 *he was clutching at his side.* There is an irony here in the way Quincey Morris is mortally wounded wielding his great bowie knife.

James Bowie (1799–1836), who is credited with inventing the knife that bears his name, died of knife wounds (March 6, 1836) sustained while fighting off attacking Mexican soldiers in the famous defense of the Alamo. His death, too, like Quincey's, was reported by a woman, a survivor of the massacre at the Alamo, the wife of a Texas lieutenant who, says T. R. Fehrenbach (p. 214), along with a Negro, "was spared expressly at Santa Anna's [the Mexican general's] orders. [She] saw Bowie's body tossed aloft on a dozen bayonets."

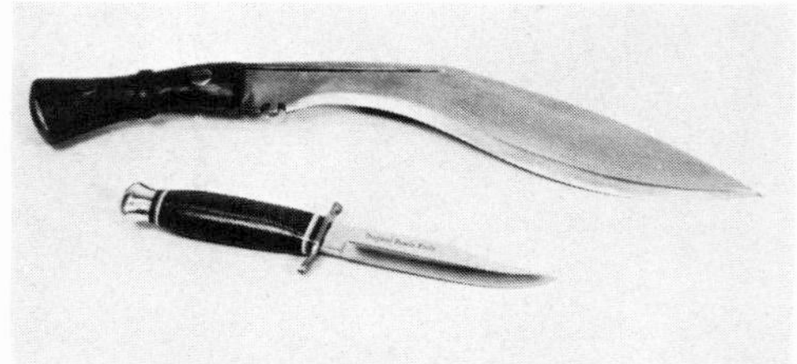

THE KUKRI AND THE BOWIE.

9 *bowie knife.* This is a moment of international cooperation as the American wields a frontiersman's knife and the Englishman swings his great kukri.

10 *shouted to the horsemen not to desert them.* Mina, until now, has not been able to understand what the gypsies say to each other.

8 he was clutching at his side, and that the blood was spurting through his fingers. He did not delay notwithstanding this, for as Jonathan, with desperate energy, attacked one end of the chest, attempting to prize off the lid with his great kukri knife, he attacked the other frantically with his bowie. Under the efforts of both men the lid began to yield; the nails drew with a quick screeching sound, and the top of the box was thrown back.

By this time the gypsies, seeing themselves covered by the Winchesters, and at the mercy of Lord Godalming and Dr. Seward, had given in and made no further resistance. The sun was almost down on the mountain tops, and the shadows of the whole group fell long upon the snow. I saw the Count lying within the box upon the earth, some of which the rude falling from the cart had scattered over him. He was deathly pale, just like a waxen image, and the red eyes glared with the horrible vindictive look which I knew too well.

As I looked, the eyes saw the sinking sun, and the look of hate in them turned to triumph.

But, on the instant, came the sweep and flash of Jonathan's great knife. I shrieked as I saw it shear through the throat;
9 whilst at the same moment Mr. Morris's bowie knife plunged into the heart.

It was like a miracle; but before our very eyes, and almost in the drawing of a breath, the whole body crumbled into dust and passed from our sight.

I shall be glad as long as I live that even in that moment of final dissolution, there was in the face a look of peace, such as I never could have imagined might have rested there.

The Castle of Dracula now stood out against the red sky, and every stone of its broken battlements was articulated against the light of the setting sun.

The gypsies, taking us as in some way the cause of the extraordinary disappearance of the dead man, turned, without a word, and rode away as if for their lives. Those who were
10 unmounted jumped upon the leiter-wagon and shouted to the horsemen not to desert them. The wolves, which had withdrawn to a safe distance, followed in their wake, leaving us alone.

Mr. Morris, who had sunk to the ground, leaned on his elbow, holding his hand pressed to his side; the blood still gushed through his fingers. I flew to him, for the Holy circle did not now keep me back; so did the two doctors. Jonathan knelt behind him and the wounded man laid back his head on his shoulder. With a sigh he took, with a feeble effort, my hand in that of his own which was unstained. He must have seen the anguish of my heart in my face, for he smiled at me and said:—

"I am only too happy to have been of any service! Oh, God!" he cried suddenly, struggling up to a sitting posture and pointing to me, "It was worth for this to die! Look! look!"

The sun was now right down upon the mountain top, and the red gleams fell upon my face, so that it was bathed in rosy light. With one impulse the men sank on their knees and a deep and earnest "Amen" broke from all as their eyes fol-

". . . BUT BEFORE OUR VERY EYES, AND ALMOST IN THE DRAWING OF A BREATH, THE WHOLE BODY CRUMBLED INTO DUST AND PASSED FROM OUR SIGHT."

Sätty©75

lowed the pointing of his finger as the dying man spoke:—

"Now God be thanked that all has not been in vain! See! the snow is not more stainless than her forehead! The curse has passed away!"

And, to our bitter grief, with a smile and in silence, he died, a gallant gentleman.

NOTE.

"OUR BOY'S BIRTHDAY."

Seven years ago we all went through the flames; and the happiness of some of us since then is, we think, well worth the pain we endured. It is an added joy to Mina and to me that our boy's birthday is the same day as that on which Quincey Morris died. His mother holds, I know, the secret belief that some of our brave friend's spirit has passed into him. His bundle of names links all our little band of men together; but we call him Quincey.

In the summer of this year we made a journey to Transylvania, and went over the old ground which was, and is, to us so full of vivid and terrible memories. It was almost impossible to believe that the things which we had seen with our own eyes and heard with our own ears were living truths. Every trace of all that had been was blotted out. The castle stood as before, reared high above a waste of desolation.

When we got home we got to talking of the old time—which we could all look back on without despair, for Godalming and Seward are both happily married. I took the papers from the safe where they have been ever since our return so long ago. We were struck with the fact, that in all the mass of material of which the record is composed, there is hardly one authentic document; nothing but a mass of type-writing, except the later note-books of Mina and Seward and myself, and Van Helsing's memorandum. We could hardly ask any one, even did we wish to, to accept these as proofs of so wild a story. Van Helsing summed it all up as he said, with our boy on his knee:—

"We want no proofs; we ask none to believe us! This boy will some day know what a brave and gallant woman his mother is. Already he knows her sweetness and loving care; later on he will understand how some men so loved her, that they did dare much for her sake."

JONATHAN HARKER.

APPENDIXES

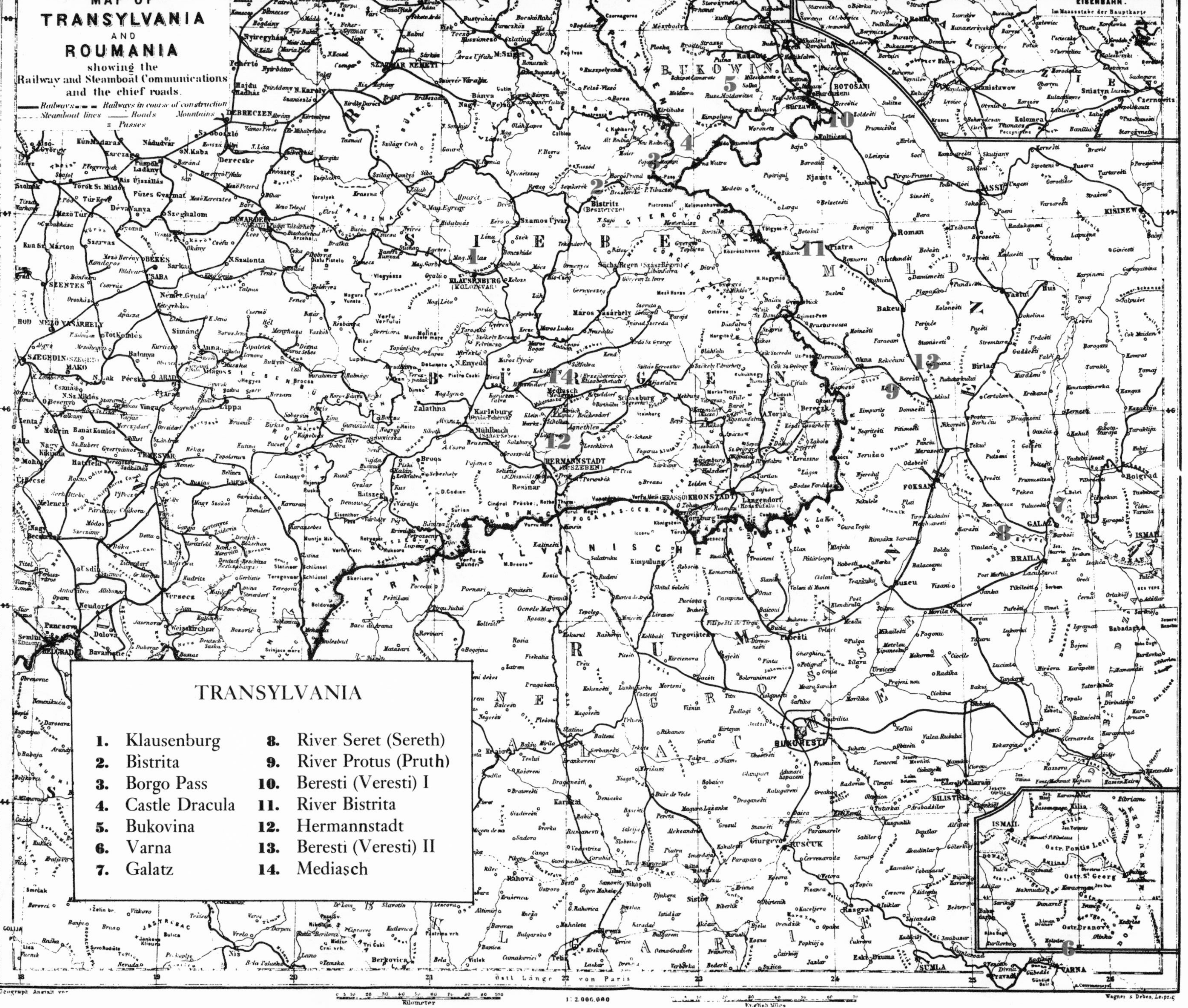
MAP OF
TRANSYLVANIA
AND
ROUMANIA
showing the
Railway and Steamboat Communications
and the chief roads.
Railways — Railways in course of construction
Steamboat lines — Roads — Mountains
Passes
TRANSYLVANIA
1. Klausenburg
2. Bistrita
3. Borgo Pass
4. Castle Dracula
5. Bukovina
6. Varna
7. Galatz
8. River Seret (Sereth)
9. River Protus (Pruth)
10. Beresti (Veresti) I
11. River Bistrita
12. Hermannstadt
13. Beresti (Veresti) II
14. Mediasch
1:2.000.000
Östl. Länge von Paris
Kilometer
English Miles
Wagner & Debes, Leipzig

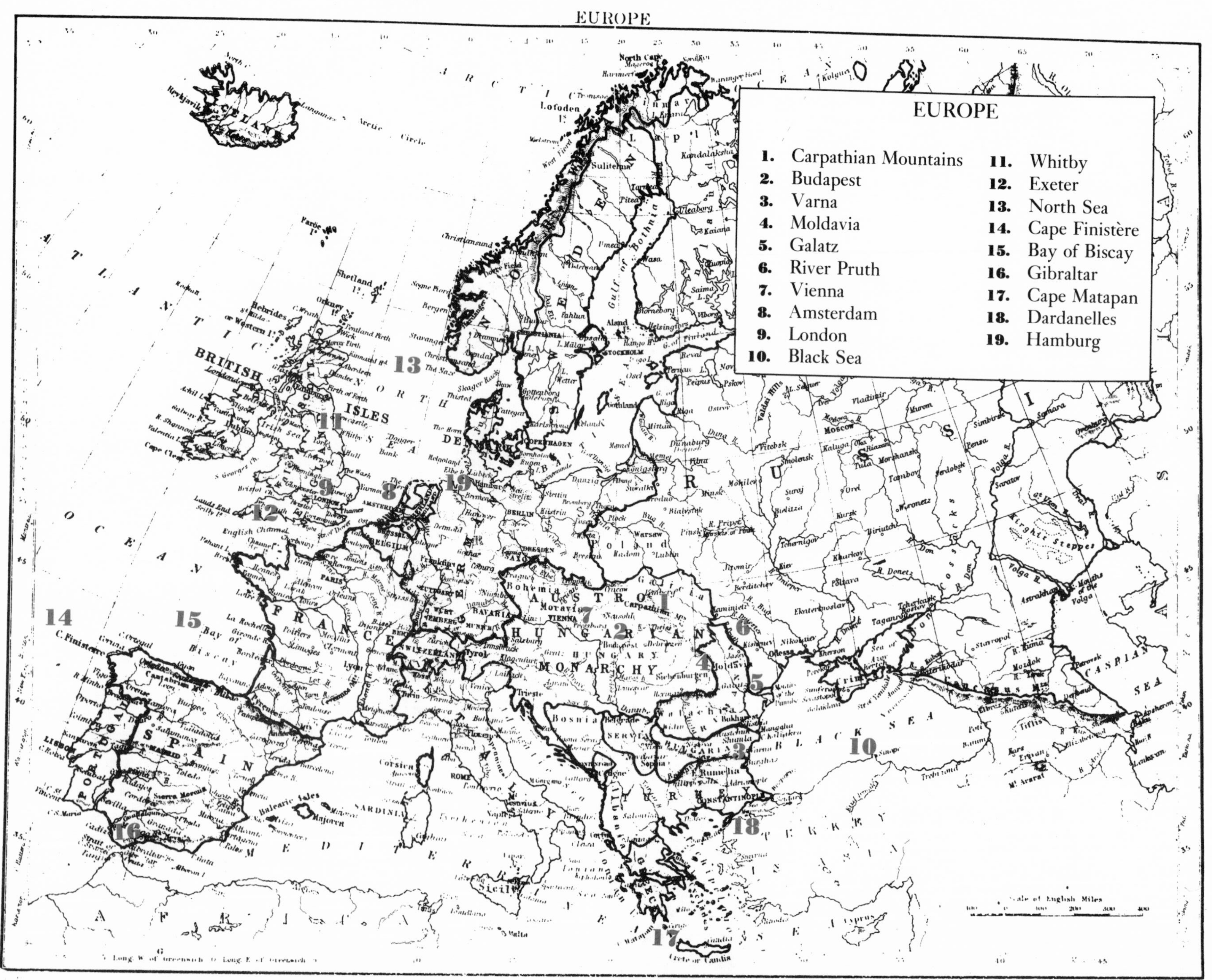
EUROPE
1. Carpathian Mountains
2. Budapest
3. Varna
4. Moldavia
5. Galatz
6. River Pruth
7. Vienna
8. Amsterdam
9. London
10. Black Sea
11. Whitby
12. Exeter
13. North Sea
14. Cape Finistère
15. Bay of Biscay
16. Gibraltar
17. Cape Matapan
18. Dardanelles
19. Hamburg

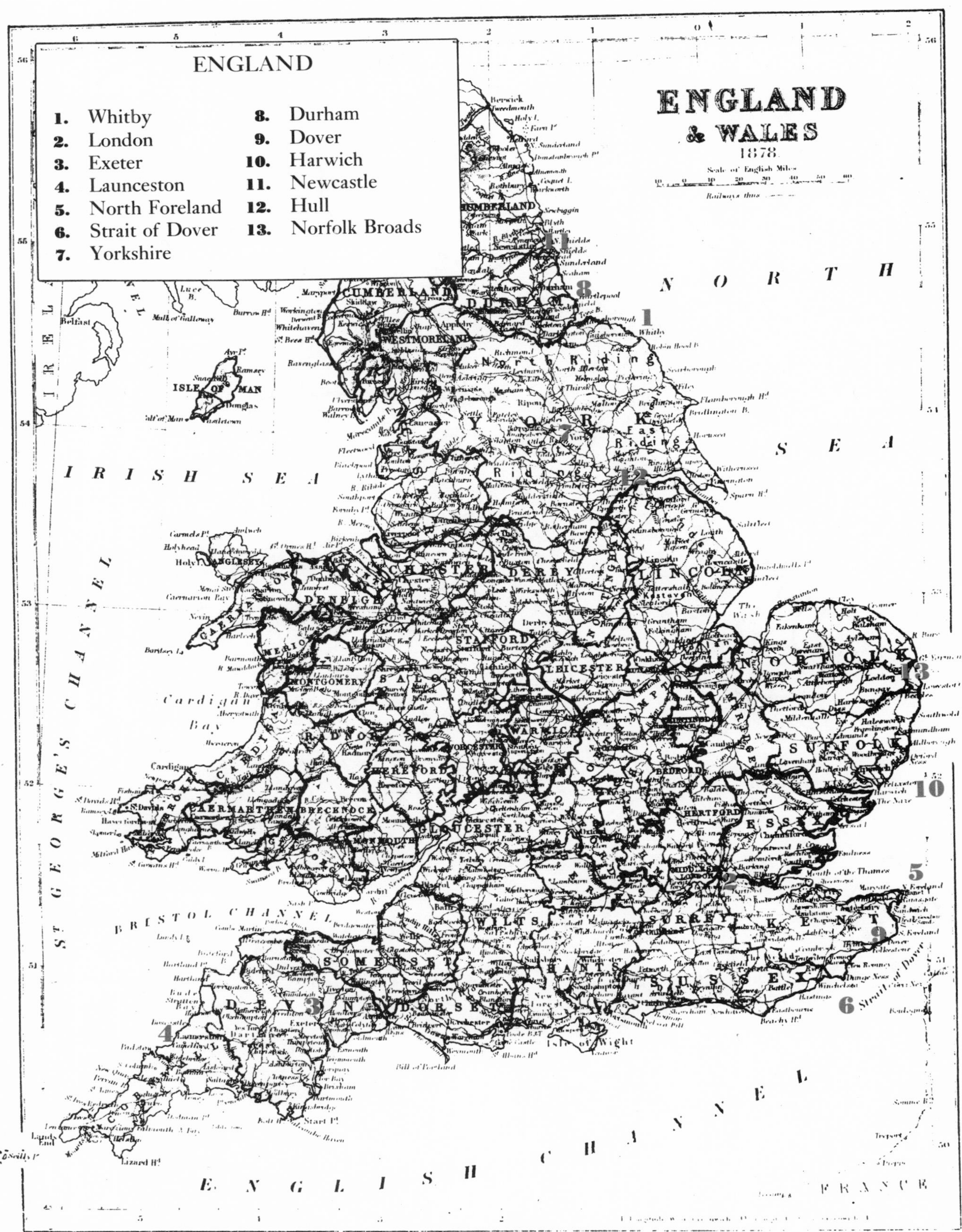
ENGLAND
1. Whitby
2. London
3. Exeter
4. Launceston
5. North Foreland
6. Strait of Dover
7. Yorkshire
8. Durham
9. Dover
10. Harwich
11. Newcastle
12. Hull
13. Norfolk Broads
ENGLAND & WALES
1878
NORTH SEA
IRISH SEA
ST GEORGE'S CHANNEL
BRISTOL CHANNEL
ENGLISH CHANNEL
FRANCE

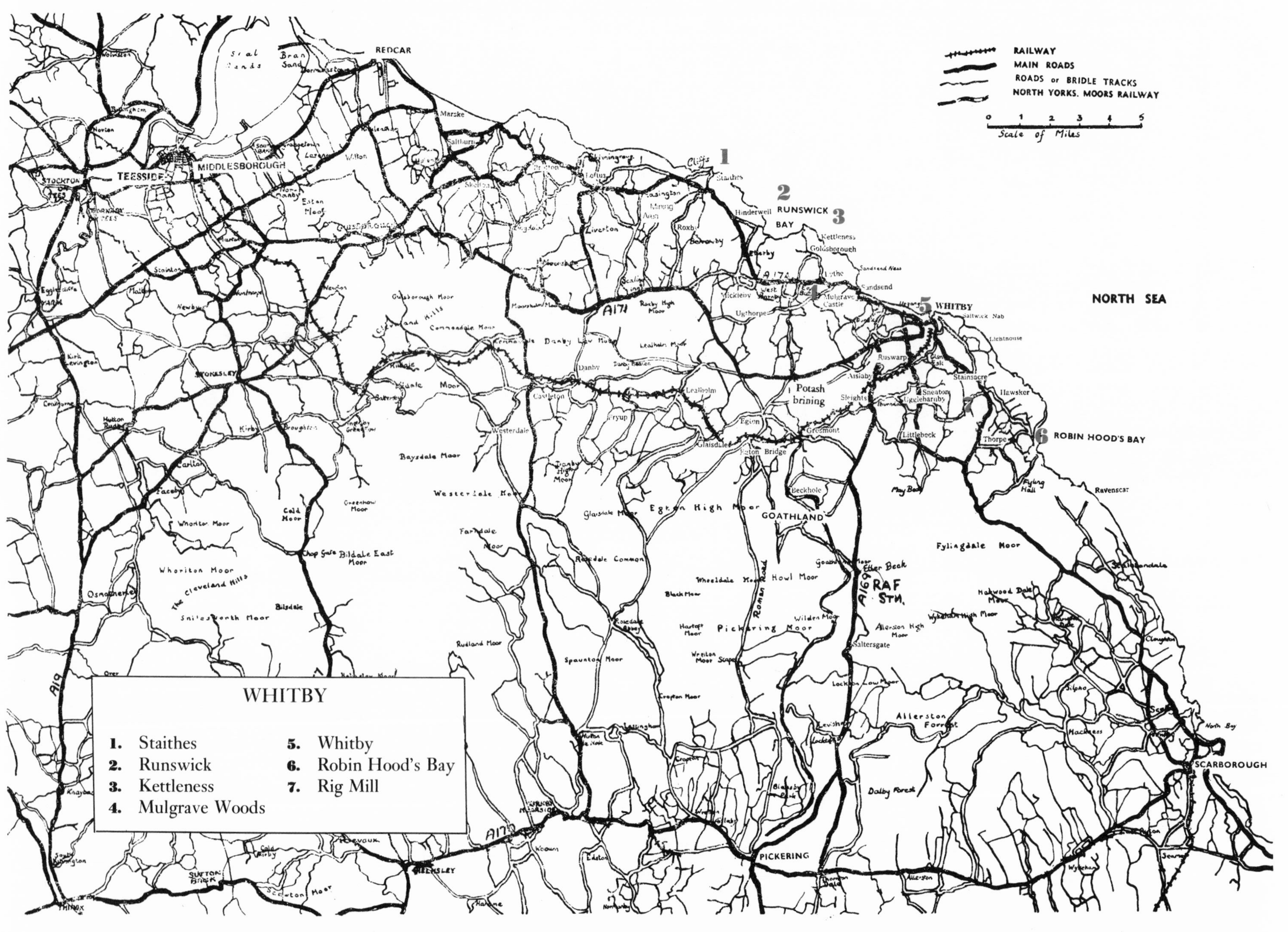

WHITBY

1. Staithes
2. Runswick
3. Kettleness
4. Mulgrave Woods
5. Whitby
6. Robin Hood's Bay
7. Rig Mill

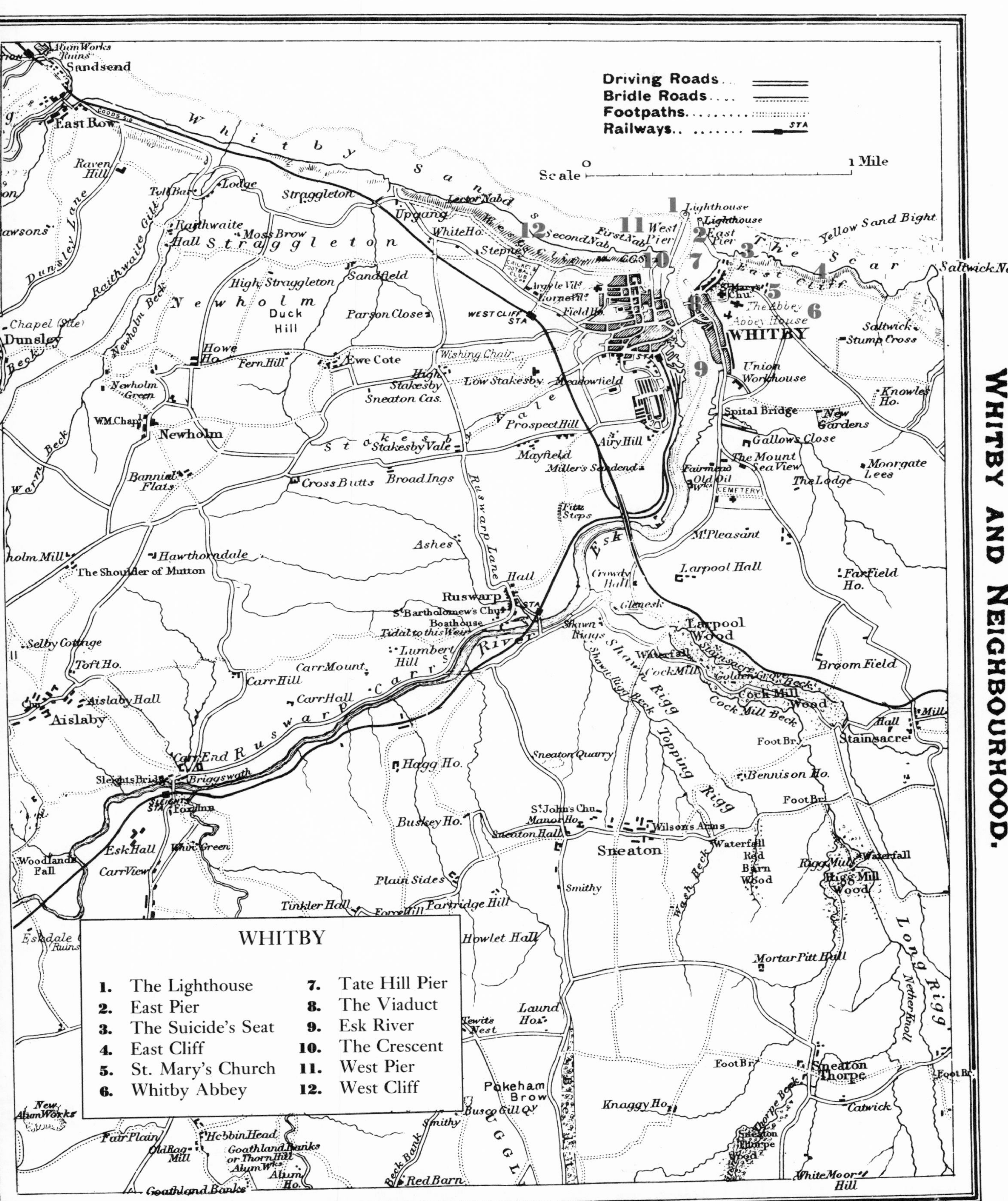
WHITBY AND NEIGHBOURHOOD.
Driving Roads
Bridle Roads
Footpaths
Railways
STA
Scale 0 1 Mile
WHITBY
1. The Lighthouse
2. East Pier
3. The Suicide's Seat
4. East Cliff
5. St. Mary's Church
6. Whitby Abbey
7. Tate Hill Pier
8. The Viaduct
9. Esk River
10. The Crescent
11. West Pier
12. West Cliff
Sandsend
East Row
Raven Hill
Whitby Sands
Straggleton
Upgang
Newholm
Duck Hill
Dunsley
Sneaton Cas.
Stakesby Vale
Cross Butts
Broad Ings
Ruswarp Lane
Ashes
Hawthorndale
The Shoulder of Mutton
Ruswarp
St. Bartholomew's Chu.
Carr Hill
Carr Hall
Aislaby Hall
Aislaby
Sleights Bridge
Esk Hall
Carr View
Woodlands Pall
WHITBY
Saltwick Nab
Yellow Sand Bight
Union Workhouse
Spital Bridge
Gallows Close
The Mount
Sea View
The Lodge
Moorgate Lees
Cemetery
Mt. Pleasant
Larpool Hall
Larpool Wood
Far Field Ho.
Broom Field
Cock Mill Wood
Stainsacre
Bennison Ho.
Sneaton Quarry
Topping Rigg
Hagg Ho.
Buskey Ho.
St. John's Chu.
Sneaton Hall
Wilson's Arms
Sneaton
Red Barn Wood
Rigg Mill Wood
Plain Sides
Tinkler Hall
Partridge Hill
Howlet Hall
Laund Ho.
Mortar Pitt Hall
Long Rigg
Nether Knoll
Sneaton Thorpe
Catwick
Pokeham Brow
Knaggy Ho.
Fair Plain
Hobbin Head
Goathland Banks
Red Barn
White Moor Hill

PARLIAMENT
HILL
FIELDS
Vale of Health
HOLLOWAY
KENTISH TOWN
PRIMROSE HILL
CAMDEN TOWN
REGENT'S PARK
Zoological Gardens
Botanic Gardens
ST. PANCRAS STA.
PENTONVILLE
MARYLEBONE
TOTTENHAM COURT ROAD
NEW OXFORD ST.
HYDE PARK
Serpentine
KNIGHTSBRIDGE
PICCADILLY
GREEN PARK
Buckingham Palace
ST. JAMES'S PARK
BIRD CAGE WALK
CONSTITUTION HILL
WESTMINSTER
VICTORIA STA.
Houses of Parliament
WESTMINSTER BRIDGE
LAMBETH BRIDGE
WATERLOO BRIDGE
Charing Cr. Sta.
Chelsea Hospital
LUPUS STREET
VAUXHALL BRIDGE
UPPER KENNINGTON LANE
1
2
3
4
5
6
7
8
9
10
11
12
17
19
22
24

LONDON
1. Piccadilly
2. Albemarle Hotel
3. Hyde Park
4. Hyde Park Corner
5. Rotten Row
6. Berkeley Hotel
7. Sackville Street (the office of Mitchell, Sons, & Candy)
8. Piccadilly Circus
9. Soho
10. British Museum
11. King's Cross Station
12. Charing Cross Station
13. The City
14. Walworth
15. Bermondsey
16. Liverpool Street Station
17. Zoological Gardens
18. Chatham Street
19. Paddington Station
20. Fenchurch Street Station
21. Mile End
22. Arlington Street
23. Bethnal Green
24. Green Park
25. Poplar
Abney Park Cemetery
Stoke Newington
Hackney Marsh
Low Leyton Marsh
Victoria Park
Stepney
Limehouse
London Docks
West India Docks
Upper Pool
Lower Pool
Limehouse Reach
Liverpool St. Sta.
Bermondsey
Isle of Dogs

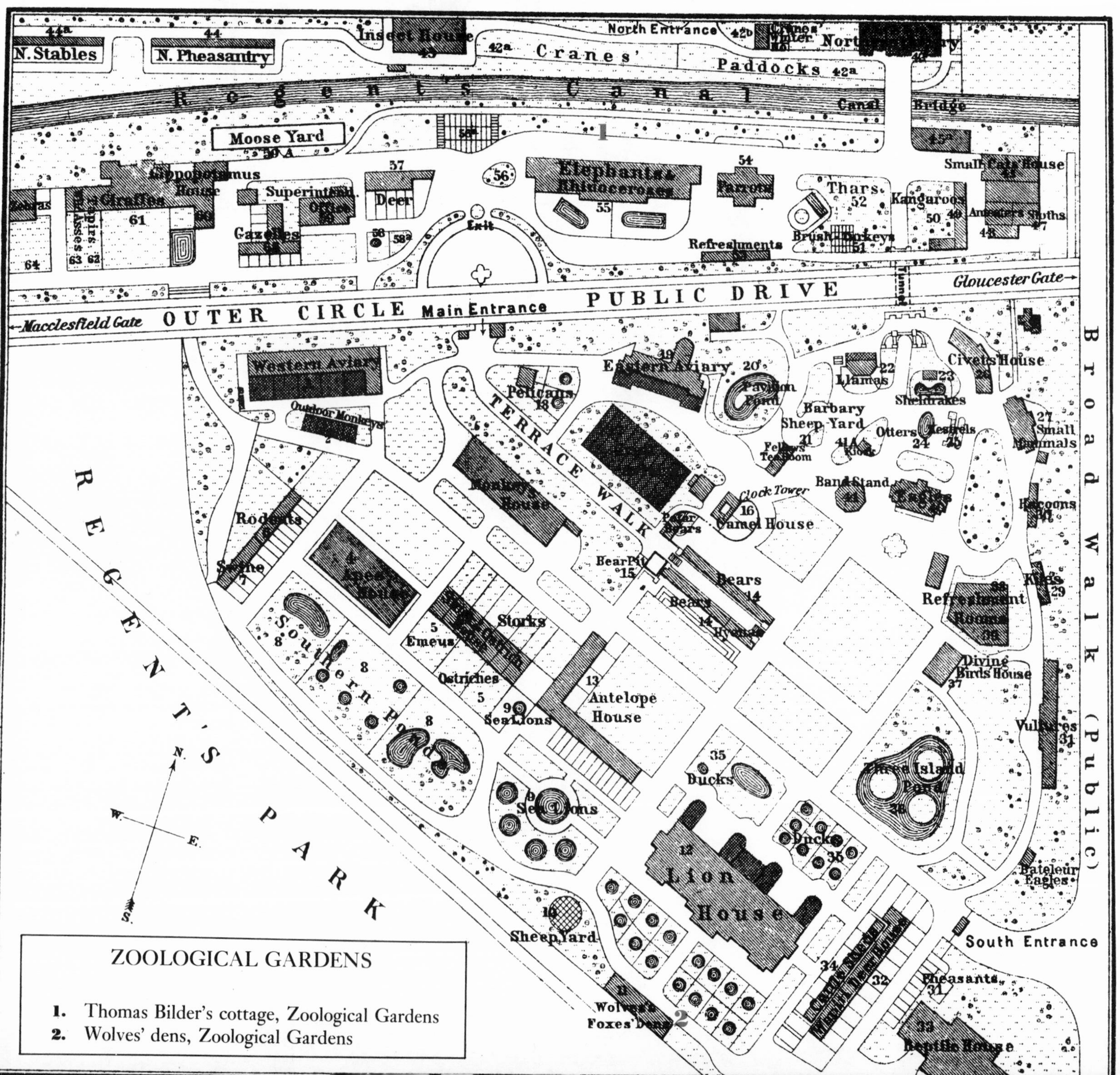

ZOOLOGICAL GARDENS

1. Thomas Bilder's cottage, Zoological Gardens
2. Wolves' dens, Zoological Gardens

CALENDAR OF EVENTS • 1887

1887 is a probable date for the events in this book, but a reader is cautioned not to believe in it too precisely. Any five-year period before or after 1887 will do to account for the phases of the moon as Stoker has given them to us.

MAY

● New Moon ◐ First Quarter ○ Full Moon ◑ Last Quarter

Sunday	Monday	Tuesday	Wednesday	Thursday	Friday	Saturday
1 Jonathan Harker departs Munich 8:35 P.M. SR: 4:41 SS: 7:04 ●	**2** Harker arrives Klausenburg; stays the night. SR: 4:41 SS: 7:04 ●	**3** Harker arrives Bistrita; stays at Golden Krone Hotel; makes first journal entry. SR: 4:48 SS: 7:07 ◐	**4** Harker leaves by coach for Castle Dracula; arrives at 2 A.M. (?) the following morning. SR: 4:44 SS: 7:10 ◐	**5** St. George's Day. Harker becomes acquainted with Dracula. SR: 4:44 SS: 7:10 ◐	**6** SR: 4:44 SS: 7:10 ◐	**7** SR: 4:40 SS: 7:13 ◐
8 Harker realizes he is a prisoner. SR: 4:40 SS: 7:13 ◐	**9** Mina Murray's first communication to Lucy Westenra. SR: 4:37 SS: 7:16 ◐	**10** SR: 4:37 SS: 7:16 ◐	**11** Harker watches Dracula crawl face-down over the castle wall. SR: 4:37 SS: 7:16 ○	**12** SR: 4:33 SS: 7:19 ○	**13** SR: 4:33 SS: 7:19 ○	**14** SR: 4:31 SS: 7:22 ○
15 Harker enters the forbidden room and encounters the three beautiful vampires. SR: 4:31 SS: 7:22 ○	**16** SR: 4:31 SS: 7:22 ○	**17** SR: 4:29 SS: 7:25 ◑	**18** Dracula asks Harker to write three misleading letters to England dated June 12, June 19, and June 29. SR: 4:29 SS: 7:25 ◑	**19** SR: 4:26 SS: 7:28 ◑	**20** SR: 4:26 SS: 7:28 ◑	**21** SR: 4:26 SS: 7:28 ◑
22 SR: 4:23 SS: 7:30 ◑	**23** SR: 4:21 SS: 7:33 ◑	**24** Lucy is proposed to three times in one day, and accepts Arthur Holmwood. SR: 4:21 SS: 7:33 ◑	**25** Dr. Seward makes his first entry on Renfield, the madman. SR: 4:21 SS: 7:33 ◑	**26** SR: 4:21 SS: 7:33 ●	**27** SR: 4:21 SS: 7:33 ●	**28** Harker tries to smuggle letters out with the gypsies. SR: 4:18 SS: 7:38 ●
29 SR: 4:18 SS: 7:38 ●	**30** SR: 4:18 SS: 7:38 ●	**31** Harker discovers his personal effects are gone. SR: 4:18 SS: 7:38 ●				

JUNE

● New Moon ◐ First Quarter ○ Full Moon ◑ Last Quarter

Sunday	Monday	Tuesday	Wednesday	Thursday	Friday	Saturday
			1 SR: 4:18 SS: 7:38 ●	**2** SR: 4:17 SS: 7:38 ◐	**3** SR: 4:15 SS: 7:42 ◐	**4** SR: 4:15 SS: 7:42 ◐
5 Renfield begins to catch and eat flies. SR: 4:15 SS: 7:42 ◐	**6** SR: 4:15 SS: 7:42 ◐	**7** SR: 4:13 SS: 7:45 ◐	**8** SR: 4:13 SS: 7:45 ◐	**9** SR: 4:13 SS: 7:45 ◐	**10** SR: 4:13 SS: 7:45 ○	**11** SR: 4:13 SS: 7:45 ○
12 SR: 4:13 SS: 7:48 ○	**13** SR: 4:13 SS: 7:48 ○	**14** SR: 4:13 SS: 7:48 ○	**15** SR: 4:13 SS: 7:48 ○	**16** SR: 4:13 SS: 7:48 ○	**17** Slovaks deliver large empty boxes to Castle Dracula. SR: 4:13 SS: 7:50 ◑	**18** Renfield turns his attention to spiders. SR: 4:13 SS: 7:50 ◑
19 SR: 4:13 SS: 7:50 ◑	**20** SR: 4:13 SS: 7:50 ◑	**21** SR: 4:13 SS: 7:50 ◑	**22** SR: 4:14 SS: 7:51 ◑	**23** Dracula leaves the castle dressed in Harker's clothes, and returns with a child for the three beautiful vampire women. SR: 4:14 SS: 7:51 ◑	**24** The bereft mother is killed in the courtyard of Castle Dracula by wolves. SR: 4:14 SS: 7:51 ●	**25** Harker climbs along the castle wall to Dracula's room, thence to the cellar where he finds Dracula inert in a box. SR: 4:14 SS: 7:51 ●
26 SR: 4:14 SS: 7:51	**27** SR: 4:16 SS: 7:51	**28** SR: 4:16 SS: 7:51	**29** SR: 4:16 SS: 7:51	**30** Harker again seeks out Dracula in his box, and gashes Dracula's forehead with a spade. SR: 4:16 SS: 7:51		

Sunday	Monday	Tuesday	Wednesday	Thursday	Friday	Saturday
					1 Renfield eats a blow-fly. SR: 3:43 SS: 8:21	**2** SR: 3:44 SS: 8:21
3 SR: 3:45 SS: 8:22	**4** SR: 3:46 SS: 8:22	**5** SR: 3:46 SS: 8:22	**6** The Schooner *Demeter* departs Varna. SR: 3:46 SS: 8:22	**7** SR: 3:49 SS: 8:21	**8** Renfield captures a sparrow, to which he feeds flies and spiders. He begins to collect a colony of birds. SR: 3:51 SS: 8:20	**9** SR: 3:51 SS: 8:19
10 SR: 3:52 SS: 8:19	**11** The *Demeter* enters the Bosphorus. SR: 3:53 SS: 8:17	**12** The *Demeter* clears the Dardanelles. SR: 3:54 SS: 8:17	**13** The *Demeter* passes Cape Matapan. SR: 3:55 SS: 8:16	**14** SR: 3:56 SS: 8:15	**15** SR: 3:57 SS: 8:14	**16** A man disappears from the *Demeter*. SR: 3:58 SS: 8:13
17 A tall thin man is seen on board. SR: 4:00 SS: 8:11	**18** SR: 4:01 SS: 8:10	**19** Renfield asks Dr. Seward for a kitten, and is refused. SR: 4:03 SS: 8:09	**20** Renfield eats his colony of sparrows. SR: 4:04 SS: 8:08	**21** SR: 4:05 SS: 8:06	**22** The *Demeter* passes Gibraltar. SR: 4:06 SS: 8:05	**23** SR: 4:07 SS: 8:04
24 Mina arrives Whitby. Another sailor lost on the *Demeter*. SR: 4:09 SS: 8:03	**25** SR: 4:11 SS: 8:02	**26** Mina receives the false letter written by Jonathan on May 18. Lucy begins walking in her sleep. SR: 4:12 SS: 8:01	**27** Lucy walks in her sleep. SR: 4:13 SS: 7:59	**28** The *Demeter* weathers heavy storms; the men are exhausted. SR: 4:15 SS: 7:58	**29** A third deckhand disappears from the *Demeter*. SR: 4:17 SS: 7:55	**30** Two more men disappear from the *Demeter*. SR: 4:20 SS: 7:53
31 SR: 4:21 SS: 7:51						

AUGUST

● New Moon ◐ First Quarter ○ Full Moon ◑ Last Quarter

Sunday	Monday	Tuesday	Wednesday	Thursday	Friday	Saturday
	1 Whitby. Old Mr. Swales discusses death with Mina and Lucy. *Demeter* in English Channel. SR: 4:22 SS: 7:49 ◐	**2** The *Demeter* passes the Strait of Dover. A sixth crew member disappears. SR: 4:23 SS: 7:48 ◐	**3** Aboard the *Demeter* a seventh sailor disappears. Later this day, the mate jumps overboard. SR: 4:24 SS: 7:47 ◐	**4** Last entry log of the *Demeter*. Captain ties himself to the wheel. Prepared to die like a man. SR: 4:25 SS: 7:43 ◐	**5** SR: 4:27 SS: 7:44 ◐	**6** The *Demeter is* sighted off Whitby. SR: 4:29 SS: 7:42 ◐
7 A great storm strikes Whitby. The *Demeter* is beached. A dog is seen leaping from the ship. Dracula takes refuge in the suicide's grave. SR: 4:31 SS: 7:40 ◐	**8** SR: 4:32 SS: 7:38 ○	**9** SR: 4:34 SS: 7:36 ○	**10** Whitby. The captain of the *Demeter* is buried. Mr. Swales dies of a broken neck, the result of a fall. He is Dracula's first British victim. SR: 4:35 SS: 7:31 ○	**11** Whitby. Lucy sleepwalks to the "suicide's seat" on the East Cliff. Dracula drinks her blood for the first time. SR: 4:37 SS: 7:32 ○	**12** SR: 4:38 SS: 7:30 ○	**13** SR: 4:40 SS: 7:28 ○
14 Whitby. Dracula, in the form of a bat, takes Lucy's blood again. SR: 4:41 SS: 7:26 ○	**15** SR: 4:42 SS: 7:24 ◑	**16** SR: 4:44 SS: 7:22 ◑	**17** SR: 4:46 SS: 7:20 ◑	**18** Fifty boxes of earth from the *Demeter* are delivered to Carfax, Purfleet, near London. SR: 4:48 SS: 7:18 ◑	**19** Whitby. Mina receives word of Jonathan from Sister Agatha in Budapest. SR: 4:49 SS: 7:16 ◑	**20** Purfleet. Renfield escapes for the first time. He is peculiarly agitated and runs toward Carfax before being captured. SR: 4:50 SS: 7:13 ◑
21 SR: 4:52 SS: 7:11 ◑	**22** SR: 4:54 SS: 7:09 ●	**23** Purfleet. Renfield escapes again. SR: 4:56 SS: 7:08 ●	**24** Mina and Jonathan married in Budapest. SR: 4:57 SS: 7:06 ●	**25** SR: 4:54 SS: 7:05 ●	**26** SR: 5:01 SS: 7:03 ●	**27** SR: 5:03 SS: 7:00 ●
28 SR: 5:05 SS: 6:57	**29** SR: 5:07 SS: 6:55	**30** SR: 5:08 SS: [illegible]	**31** Hillingham. Arthur Holmwood asks Dr. Seward to examine Lucy. SR: 5:10 SS: [illegible]			

SEPTEMBER — New Moon ◐ First Quarter ○ Full Moon ◑ Last Quarter

Sunday	Monday	Tuesday	Wednesday	Thursday	Friday	Saturday
				1 SR: 5:12 SS: 6:48	**2** Dr. Seward writes to Dr. Van Helsing requesting help in his treatment of Lucy. SR: 5:13 SS: 6:46	**3** Van Helsing arrives, examines Lucy, and leaves. SR: 5:15 SS: 6:44
4 Lucy appears to improve. SR: 5:16 SS: 6:42	**5** SR: 5:17 SS: 6:39	**6** Lucy suddenly becomes worse. SR: 5:19 SS: 6:37	**7** Van Helsing supervises the first transfusion to Lucy. (Donor: Arthur Holmwood.) SR: 5:21 SS: 6:34	**8** SR: 5:23 SS: 6:31	**9** SR: 5:24 SS: 6:29	**10** Lucy receives the second transfusion. (Donor: John Seward.) SR: 5:26 SS: 6:27
11 SR: 5:28 SS: 6:25	**12** SR: 5:29 SS: 6:23	**13** Lucy receives the third transfusion. (Donor: Dr. Van Helsing.) SR: 5:30 SS: 6:20	**14** SR: 5:31 SS: 6:18	**15** SR: 5:33 SS: 6:16	**16** SR: 5:35 SS: 6:14	**17** The wolf Berserker escapes from the zoo. Later, he breaks a window at Hillingham frightening Mrs. Westenra to death, and provides Dracula with entry to Lucy. Renfield attacks Seward and licks his spilled blood. SR: 5:37 SS: 6:11
18 Lucy receives the fourth transfusion. (Donor: Quincey Morris.) Mr. Hawkins dies. SR: 5:39 SS: 6:09	**19** Lord Godalming, Arthur's father, dies; Arthur assumes the title. SR: 5:41 SS: 6:06	**20** Lucy dies 6:30 A.M. (?) Renfield escapes and attacks workmen removing two boxes of earth from Carfax. SR: 5:42 SS: 6:04	**21** Arthur's father is buried. SR: 5:43 SS: 6:01	**22** Dracula, looking younger, is seen in Hyde Park by the Harkers. Lucy is buried in a churchyard near Hampstead Heath. SR: 5:45 SS: 5:59	**23** On Hampstead Heath children are lured and bitten by the beautiful "Bloofer" lady. Mina reads Jonathan's journal. SR: 5:47 SS: 5:56	**24** SR: 5:48 SS: 5:54
25 Van Helsing meets Mina and reads Jonathan's journal. SR: 5:50 SS: 5:51	**26** Van Helsing and Seward visit Lucy's tomb at night and find it empty. Van Helsing meets Jonathan Harker. SR: 5:52 SS: 5:49	**27** Van Helsing and Seward visit the tomb by daylight, and find Lucy "more radiantly beautiful than ever" in her coffin. SR: 5:54 SS: 5:47	**28** Van Helsing, Seward, Godalming, and Morris visit the tomb at night. They see Lucy walking with a child. Lucy and Arthur were to have been married today. SR: 5:56 SS: 5:45	**29** Van Helsing, Seward, Godalming, and Morris visit the tomb at night. Godalming drives stake through Lucy's heart. Mina meets Seward; they exchange diaries. SR: 5:57 SS: 5:43	**30** Dracula takes first blood from Mina who believes she has had only a bad dream. SR: 5:59 SS: 5:40	

OCTOBER

● New Moon ◐ First Quarter ○ Full Moon ◑ Last Quarter

Sunday	Monday	Tuesday	Wednesday	Thursday	Friday	Saturday
						1 Renfield astounds Mina, Jonathan, Morris, Van Helsing, and Seward by his apparent sanity. The men break into Carfax and search the chapel. SR: 6:00 SS: 5:38 ◐
2 Dracula breaks Renfield's back: crushes skull. Van Helsing operates. Renfield dies. Mina and Dracula drink each other's blood. Mark on Mina's forehead. SR: 6:02 SS: 5:36 ◐	**3** Van Helsing, Seward, Harker, Godalming, and Morris confront Dracula at 347 Piccadilly. Dracula escapes. SR: 6:04 SS: 5:34 ◐	**4** SR: 6:06 SS: 5:31 ◐	**5** Dracula leaves for Varna on the *Czarina Catherine* at high tide, at 12:55 A.M. SR: 6:08 SS: 5:28 ◐	**6** SR: 6:04 SS: 5:31 ○	**7** SR: 6:05 SS: 5:30 ○	**8** SR: 6:06 SS: 5:28 ○
9 SR: 6:07 SS: 5:26 ○	**10** SR: 6:09 SS: 5:24 ○	**11** SR: 6:10 SS: 5:22 ○	**12** The Harkers, Morris, Godalming, Seward, and Van Helsing leave London in pursuit of Dracula. They board the Orient Express in Paris and arrive in Varna three days later. SR: 6:11 SS: 5:21 ◑	**13** SR: 6:12 SS: 5:19 ◑	**14** SR: 6:14 SS: 5:17 ◑	**15** The group arrives in Varna. They wait for news of Dracula. SR: 6:15 SS: 5:15 ◑
16 SR: 6:17 SS: 5:13 ◑	**17** SR: 6:18 SS: 5:12 ◑	**18** SR: 6:19 SS: 5:10 ◑	**19** SR: 6:21 SS: 5:08 ●	**20** SR: 6:22 SS: 5:06 ●	**21** SR: 6:23 SS: 5:05 ●	**22** SR: 6:25 SS: 5:04 ●
23 SR: 6:26 SS: 5:02 ● **30** They arrive in Galatz. Godalming and Harker set off upriver in a steam launch. Morris and Seward set out on horseback. Mina and Van Helsing leave by train for Verecski. SR: 6:35	**24** SR: 6:27 SS: 5:00 ● **31** Mina and Van Helsing arrive at Verecski. Van Helsing buys a carriage and horses. SR: 6:36	**25** SR: 6:29	**26** SR: 6:30	**27** SR: 6:31	**28** They learn that the *Czarina Catherine* has been diverted to Galatz. SR: 6:32	**29** They travel by train from Varna to Galatz. SR: 6:33

Sunday	Monday	Tuesday	Wednesday	Thursday	Friday	Saturday
		1 SR: 6:36 SS: 4:51 ◐	2 SR: 6:37 SS: 4:50 ◐	3 SR: 6:38 SS: 4:49 ◐	4 SR: 6:39 SS: 4:47 ○	5 Mina and Van Helsing reach the Borgo Pass. SR: 6:40 SS: 4:46 ○
6 Their launch being disabled, Harker and Godalming take up the pursuit on horseback. SR: 6:42 SS: 4:45 ○	7 Mina and Van Helsing arrive in the vicinity of Castle Dracula. Van Helsing encloses Mina in a holy circle. The three female vampires appear and invite Mina to follow. Later: Van Helsing drives stakes through their hearts. SR: 6:43 SS: 4:43 ○	8 The wagon bearing Dracula approaches the castle, pursued by Seward, Morris, Jonathan, Harker, and Godalming. After a fight in which Morris dies, Jonathan kills Dracula at 4:42 P.M.—sunset! SR: 6:45 SS: 4:42 ○	9	10	11	12
13	14	15	16	17	18	19
20	21	22	23	24	25	26
27	28	29	30			

Dracula Onstage

Dracula, in one form or another, is present on only sixty-two pages (of a total of 390) in the original edition of the novel. His appearances are charted below. For the reader's convenience, the pages where Dracula appears in this edition are given in parentheses.

Chapter Number	Page Numbers (inclusive)	No. of Pages in Chapter	No. of Pages in which Dracula is Present	Page Numbers of Original Edition (and this edition)	Mode of Appearance
I	1–14	14	5	10,11,12,13,14 (13,14,16,17)	As the coach driver.
II	15–27	13	12	15 (19)	As the coach driver.
				16,17,18,19,20, 21,22,23,24,25, 26 (20,21,22,23, 24,25,26,27,28)	As the Count.
III	28–40	13	9	29,30,31,32,33, 34,35,39,40 (29, 30,31,33,34,35, 36,37,41)	As the Count.
IV	41–54	14	9	42,43,44,45,49, 50,51,52,53 (44, 45,46,47,50,52, 53,54)	As the Count.
V	55–63	9	0		
VI	64–76	13	0		
VII	77–90	14	1	81 (81)	As the dog who* leaps ashore from the *Demeter* when it arrives in Whitby.

*"that" or "who"? A puzzle for grammarians. If the dog is only a dog, then "that"; if Dracula, then "who"; if Dracula *in* the dog, then *?*

Chapter Number	Page Numbers (inclusive)	No. of Pages in Chapter	No. of Pages in which Dracula is Present	Page Numbers of Original Edition (and this edition)	Mode of Appearance
			3	84,86,87 (84,86, 87)	Described in the log of the *Demeter*.
VIII	91–105	15	1	93 (92)	Seen by Mina as something tall and dark standing behind Lucy.
				96 (94)	As a bat.
			1	100 (98)	Described by Lucy as "something long and dark with red eyes."
IX	106–119	14	1	111 (107)	As a bat.
X	120–134	15	0		
XI	135–147	13	1	145 (134)	As a bat.
XII	148–165	18	1	162 (146)	As a bat.
XIII	166–181	16	2	175,176 (156, 157)	As the Count.
XIV	182–197	16	0		
XV	198–211	14	0		
XVI	212–222	11	0		
XVII	223–236	14	0		
XVIII	237–253	14	1	247 (214)	As a bat.
XIX	254–266	13	1	258 (223)	As the Count.
XX	267–281	15	0		
XXI	282–296	15	7	293 (253)	As a bat.
				286,287,289, 290,294,295, 296 (246,247, 248,249,254, 255)	As the Count.
XXII	297–309	13	0		
XXIII	310–323	14	3	314,315,316 (270,271)	As the Count.
XXIV	324–338	15	0		
XXV	339–353	15	0		
XXVI	354–371	18	0		
XXVII	372–390	19	1	388 (330)	As the Count.

Selected Filmography

Stoker's Count Dracula, it is now abundantly clear, is destined to lead a life of ghastly immortality on the screen. Since 1922, when F. W. Murnau's thinly disguised version of *Dracula* appeared in Germany, there have been dozens of films purporting to deal with Stoker's elegant monster, as well as literally hundreds of others in which less glamorous vampires, male and female, have appeared. The film industry long ago recognized that there was as much gold as there was blood in "the Dracula matter," and ground out one profitable horror movie after another. A list of Dracula film titles, then, is hardly a roll call of great film achievement, though here and there a masterpiece, a near-masterpiece, or a movie with great moments in it shows suddenly luminous in the long file of refurbished clichés. Nevertheless, the image of the Count stalking his victims through scenes in which blood lust and lust are commingled has been so powerfully emblematic that even the worst of the films contributes something to our understanding of the film lore of the vampire, and the fascination it holds for the contemporary imagination. The list that follows is not intended to be either complete or critical. It is meant simply to call attention to those films (not necessarily the best) that mark the significant changes in the evolving image of the vampire as he is perceived by, and as he reflects, the contemporary imagination.

---

*Readers interested in extensive and critical lists of vampire films may wish to see the useful Filmography that appears on page 216 of *In Search of Dracula* (Raymond T. McNally and Radu Florescu). Issues number 19 and 21 of *Photon Magazine* taken together are even more extensive, though less critical in their coverage of the vampire genre. The most thoughtful essay of the vampire in film is still Jean-Claude Michel's "*Les Vampires à l'ecran*" in *L'Écran Fantastique*, second series, number 2, Paris, 1971.

Date	Title	Director	Studio	With Performances By
†1922	*Nosferatu*	F. W. Murnau	Prana (Germany)	Max Schreck (Count Orlok)
†1931	*Dracula*	Tod Browning	Universal (U.S.)	Bela Lugosi (Count Dracula)
1936	*Dracula's Daughter*	Lambert Hillyer	Universal (U.S.)	Gloria Holden (Countess Zaleska)
1943	*Son of Dracula*	Robert Siodmak	Universal (U.S.)	Lon Chaney, Jr. (Count Alucard)
1945	*House of Dracula*	Erle C. Kenton	Universal (U.S.)	John Carradine (Count Dracula)
1958	*The Return of Dracula*	Paul Landres	United Artists (U.S.)	Francis Lederer (Count Dracula-Bellac Gordal)
†1958	*The Horror of Dracula*	Terence Fisher	Hammer (Great Britain)	Christopher Lee (Count Dracula)
1960	*The Brides of Dracula*	Terence Fisher	Hammer (Great Britain)	David Peel (Baron Meinster)
1965	*Dracula—Prince of Darkness*	Terence Fisher	Hammer (Great Britain)	Christopher Lee (Count Dracula)
1966	*Billy the Kid vs. Dracula*	William Beaudine	Circle Productions (U.S.)	John Carradine (Count Dracula)
†1967	*The Fearless Vampire Killers*	Roman Polanski	Cadre-M.G.M. (France–U.S.)	Ferdy Mayne (Count Von Krolock)
1969	*The Blood of Dracula's Castle*	Al Adamson	Crown-International (U.S.)	Alex d'Arcy (Count Dracula), John Carradine (George, the butler)
1970	*Taste the Blood of Dracula*	Peter Sandy	Hammer-Warner Pathé (Great Britain)	Christopher Lee (Count Dracula)
†1972	*Vampir*	Pedro Portabella	Films 59 (Spain)	Christopher Lee (Count Dracula)
†1973	*Blacula*	William Crain	American International	William Marshall (Count Dracula)
†1974	*Dracula*	Andy Warhol Paul Morrissey	Carlo Ponti - Braunsberg Rassam Productions	Udo Kier (Count Dracula)

†The best of the films are indicated by this mark.

English-language and Foreign Editions of *Dracula*

BRITISH EDITIONS

Date	*Publisher*	*Place of Publication*
1897	A. Constable and Co.	Westminster
1901	A. Constable and Co.	Westminster
1904	A. Constable and Co.	Westminster
1912	W. Rider and Co. (Popular edition)	London
1916	W. Rider and Co.	London
1920	A. Constable and Co.	Westminster
1921	W. Rider and Co.	London
1931	W. Rider and Co. (Crown edition)	London
1947	W. Rider and Co. (Crown edition)	London
1949	W. Rider and Co. (Crown edition)	London
1954	Arrow Books	London
1966	Jarrolds	London

AMERICAN EDITIONS

Date	*Publisher*	*Place of Publication*
1899	Doubleday, McClure and Co.	New York
1901	A. Wessels (A special limited edition)	New York
1909	Doubleday, Page and Co.	New York
191_*	W. R. Caldwell (International Adventure Library, Three Owls Edition)	New York
1913	Doubleday, Page and Co.	Garden City
1917	Doubleday, Page and Co.	Garden City
1919	Doubleday, Page and Co.	Garden City
1920	Doubleday, Page and Co.	Garden City
1927	Doubleday, Page and Co.	Garden City
1927	Doubleday, Page and Co. (Lambskin Library Edition)	Garden City
1928	Doubleday, Page and Co. (The Sundial Library Edition)	Garden City
1928	Grosset and Dunlap	New York
1930	Grosset and Dunlap (Illustrated with scenes from Tod Browning's film *Dracula*, produced by Carl Laemmle, Jr.)	New York
1932	Modern Library	New York
1959	Garden City Books	Garden City
1965	Heritage Press (With a foreword by Anthony Boucher. Illustrated with wood engravings by Felix Hoffman)	New York
196_*	Modern Library	New York
1970	Dodd, Mead and Co. (With illustrations of the author and the setting of the story. Introduction by James Nelson)	New York
1973	Garden City Publishing Co. (An edition with *Dracula* and *Frankenstein*)	Garden City

*No certain date is given for this edition in the National Union catalogue or in the Library of Congress catalogue.

FOREIGN EDITIONS

Date	*Publisher*	*Place of Publication*
Gaelic (Irish)		
1933	Oifig Díolta Foillseacháin Rialtais (Tr. Seán Ó Cuirrín)	Dublin
French		
1946	Les Editions des Quatre Vents (Tr. Eve and Lucie Paul-Marguerite)	
1968	Lavallois-Perret (Tr. Lucienne Molitor, with a preface and bibliography by Gilbert Sigaux. Illustrated)	Paris
Italian		
1959	Longanesi Co. (Tr. Adriana Pellegrini)	Milan
1966	Longanesi Co. (Tr. Adriana Pellegrini)	Milan
Spanish		
1966	Molino (Tr. unknown)	Madrid
German		
1967	Carl Hanser Verlag (Tr. Stasi Kull)	Munich

BIBLIOGRAPHY

A note of caution about the Bibliography, which is necessarily a grabbag of sorts. Most of the books listed were consulted in order to find answers to a host of unrelated questions posed by details of Stoker's text. The list does not, therefore, make any coherent statement about vampires, the historical Dracula, or about Bram Stoker. Starred items are those that will prove useful to a reader interested in pursuing any of these matters. For the rest, the books listed make a testimonial to Stoker's pack-rat mind which, while it was engaged in making a masterpiece, was also busy stuffing its pages with helter-skelter references to all sorts of things.

For the reader's interest I list the various editions of *Dracula* that have appeared.

Adler, Michael H. *The Writing Machine.* London: George Allen & Unwin, Ltd., 1974.

Allen, Glover Morrill. *Bats.* New York: Dover Publications, 1939.

Ambrose, Gordon, and Newbold, George. *A Handbook of Medical Hypnosis.* London: Bailliere, Tindall and Cox, 1959.

Andree's Hand-Atlas. Bielefeld and Leipsig: Verlag von Velhagen und Klasing, 1913.

Arey, Leslie Brainerd. *Developmental Anatomy—A Textbook and Laboratory Manual of Embryology.* Philadelphia and London: W. B. Saunders Company, 1965.

*Babinger, Franz. *Mehmed der Eroberer: Seine Zeit.* Munich: F. Bruckmann, 1959.

Baedeker, Karl. *Austria–Handbook for Travellers.* London: Dulau and Co., 1897.

———. *London and Its Environs–Handbook for Travellers.* 7th rev. ed. London: Dulau and Co., 1889.

Baltimore Catechism No. 2. New rev. ed. Helped by Rt. Rev. Msgr. Michael A. McGuire, pastor of the Church of St. Francis of Rome, Bronx, N.Y. San Francisco: Benziger Brothers, Inc., 1962.

*Baring-Gould, Rev. Sabine. *A Book of Folk-Lore.* London: Collin's Clear Type Press, n.d.

*———. *The Book of Werewolves.* London: Smith-Elder and Co., 1965.

Bartholomew's Reference Atlas of Greater London. 11th ed. Edinburgh: John Bartholomew and Son, Ltd., The Geographical Institute, 1961.

Battcock, Gregory, ed. *The New American Cinema, A Critical Anthology.* New York: A Dutton Paperback Original, 1967.

Benham, Sir Henry. *Benham's Book of Quotations.* New York: G. P. Putnam's Sons, n.d.

Bentham, William G. *The Laws of Scientific Hand Reading.* New York: Duell, Sloan and Pearce, 1966.

Bickmore, D. P., and Shaw, M. A., planned and directed. *The Atlas of Britain and Northern Ireland.* Oxford: Clarendon Press, 1963.

Binding, G. J. *Everything You Want to Know about Garlic.* New York: Pyramid Books, 1970.

*Birkhead, Edith. *The Tale of Terror.* London: Russell and Russell, 1963.

Black, Henry Campbell. *Black's Law Dictionary.* 3rd ed. St. Paul, Minnesota: West Publishing Co., 1968.

Blum, R. and E. *The Dangerous House, The Love of Crisis and Mystery in Rural Greece.* New York: Charles Scribner's Sons, 1970.

Bodge, Sir E. A. Wallis, tr. *The Book of the Dead.* New York: Dover Publications, 1969.

Booth, Charles. *Life and Labour of the People in London.* 3rd ed. London and New York: The Macmillan Co., 1902–1903.

Bourne, Henry R. *English Newspapers.* New York: Russell and Russell, 1966.

*Brereton, Austin. *The Life of Henry Irving.* London and New York: Longmans, Green and Co., 1908.

Brion, Marcel. *Attila, Scourge of God.* London: Cassell, 1929.

Brown, Raymond Lamont. *A Book of Superstitions.* New York: Taplinger Publishing Co., 1970.

Bryan, William J., Jr., M.D. *Religious Aspects of Hypnosis.* Springfield, Illinois: Charles C. Thomas, 1962.

Bucknill, John Charles, and Tuke, Daniel H. *A Manual of Psychological Medicine.* New York and London: Hafner Publishing Co., 1968.

Burton, Sir Richard F. *The Book of the Thousand Nights and a Night.* Vol. 1. New York: privately printed by the Burton Club, n.d.

Byron, Lord George Gordon. *Complete Poetical Works.* New York: Houghton Mifflin, 1905.

*Calmet, Augustine. *The Phantom World.* London: Richard Bentley, 1850.

Calverton, V. F., and Schmalhausen, S. D., eds. *Sex in Civilization.* Garden City, New York: Garden City Publishing Co., 1929.

Capote, Truman. *In Cold Blood.* New York: A Signet Book, 1965.

*Carmouche, Pierre. *Le Vampire.* Paris: Chez J. N. Barba Libraire, 1820.

Cavendish, Richard. *The Black Arts.* New York: G. P. Putnam's Sons, 1967.

Cirker, Blanche, ed. *Thomas Bewick and His School: 1800 Woodcuts.* New York: Dover Publications, 1962.

Citizen's Atlas of the World. Edinburgh: John Bartholomew and Sons, Ltd., 1952.

Clay, Rotha Mary. *The Mediaeval Hospitals of England.* New York: Barnes & Noble, Inc., 1966.

Clemens, Samuel L. *Following the Equator–A Journey Around the World.* Vol. I. New York and London: Harper and Brothers, 1897 and 1899.

Cohen, Daniel. *A Modern Look at Monsters.* New York: Dodd, Mead & Co., 1970.

Colby, Reginald. *Mayfair–A Town within London.* South Brunswick, New Jersey: A. S. Barnes, 1967.

Coles, Paul. *The Ottoman Impact on Europe.* London: Thames and Hudson, 1968.

*Collins, Charles M. *A Feast of Blood.* New York: Avon Books, 1967.

Comfort, Alex. *The Biology of Senescence.* New York: Rinehart and Co., Inc., 1956.

Connoly, John. *The Construction and Government of Lunatic Asylums.* London: Dawson's of Pall Mall, 1968.

*Craig, Gordon. *Henry Irving.* New York and Toronto: Longmans, Green and Co., 1930.

Crowley, R. and E. *New Acronyms and Initialisms.* Detroit, Michigan: Gale Research, 1969.

Culbreth, David R., M.D. *A Manual of Materia Medica and Pharmacology.* 7th ed. Philadelphia: Lea & Febiger, 1927.

Davis, William Stearns. *A Short History of the Near East.* New York: The Macmillan Co., 1922.

*Deane, Hamilton, and Balderston, John. *Dracula: The Vampire Play in Three Acts.* New York: Samuel French, Inc., 1960.

Deaux, George. *The Black Death.* London: Hamish Hamilton, 1969.

de Vries, Leonard. *Victorian Advertisements.* London: John Murray, 1968.

Dingwall, Eric J., ed. *Abnormal Hypnotic Phenomena.* Vol. IV. New York: Barnes & Noble, Inc., 1968.

Doré, Gustave, and Jerrold, Blanchard. *London: A Pilgrimage.* New York: Dover Publications, 1970.

Duncan, P. Martin. *The Transformation (or Metamorphoses) of Insects.* London and New York: Cassel, Petter, Galpin, 1882.

Earle, Arthur Scott. *Surgery in America: From the Colonial Era to the Twentieth Century, Selected Writings.* Philadelphia: W. B. Saunders Company, 1965.

Eichler, Lillian. *Customs of Mankind.* New York: Garden City Publishing Co., 1924.

*Eisler, Robert. *Man into Wolf.* New York: Philosophical Library, 1952.

Eliot, Valerie, ed. *T. S. Eliot/The Waste Land–A Facsimile and Transcript of the Original Drafts.* New York: Harcourt Brace Jovanovich, 1971.

Estabrooks, George H. *Hypnotism.* London: Museum Press, 1959.

Eversley, Lord, and Chirol, Sir Valentine. *The Turkish Empire from 1288 to 1914.* London: T. Fisher Unwin, Ltd., 1923.

*Ewers, Hanns Heinz. *Vampir. Ein Verwilderter Roman.* Munich: George Müller Verlag, 1921.

*Faivre, Tony. *Les Vampires.* Paris: Eric Losfeld, 1962.

Farrar, Stewart. *What Witches Do.* New York: Coward, McCann & Geoghegan, Inc., 1971.

Fehrenbach, T. R. *Lone Star.* New York: Macmillan, 1968.

FitzGibbon, Theodora. *The Art of British Cooking.* New York: Doubleday & Co., Inc., 1965.

Fliess Robert. *Ego and Body-Ego.* New York: Schulte Publishing Co., 1961.

*Florescu, Radu, and McNally, Raymond T. *In Search of Dracula.* Greenwich, Connecticut: New York Graphic Society, 1972.

Forster, Edward Seymour, ed., tr. *The Turkish Letters of Ogier Ghislain de Busbecq.* New York: Twain Publishers, 1968.

Freud, Sigmund. *General Psychological Theories,* Philip Rieff, ed. New York: Crowell Collier, 1963.

Funk, Charles Earl. *A Hog on Ice and Other Curious Expressions.* New York: Harper and Brothers 1948.

Gaer, Joseph. *The Lore of the Old Testament.* Boston: Little, Brown and Company, 1951.

Gale, Frederick C. *Mortuary Science.* Springfield, Illinois: Charles C. Thomas, 1961.

Garst, Doris Shannon. *James Bowie and His Famous Knife.* New York: Julian Messner, 1955.

Gasquet, Abbot. *The Greater Abbeys of England.* London: Chatto and Windus, 1908.

Geographer's A to Z Street Atlas of London, The. London: Geographer's Map Co., Ltd., n.d.

*Gerard, E. *The Land Beyond the Forest*. New York: Harper and Bros., 1888.

Gertsch, Willis J. *American Spiders*. New York: D. Van Nostrand Co., Inc., 1949.

Gibson, Right Reverend E.C.S. *The First and Second Prayer Books of Edward VI*. New York: Everyman Library, Dutton, 1964.

*Gifford, Denis. *Movie Monsters*. London: Studio Vista, 1969.

Gifford, Edward S. *The Evil Eye: Studies in the Folklore of Vision*. New York: The Macmillan Co., 1958.

Gill, Merton M. *Hypnosis and Related States*. New York: International University Press, 1959.

———, and Brenman, Margaret. *Hypnosis and Related States*. New York: International Universities Press, Inc., 1959.

Goethe, Johann Wolfgang von. *Faust*. Translated by Carlyle F. MacIntyre. Norfolk, Connecticut: New Directions, 1941.

Goodall, G. and Treharne, R., eds. *Muir's Atlas of Ancient and Classical History*. New York: Barnes & Noble, Inc., 1961.

Gould, Charles. *Mythical Monsters*. London: W. H. Allen and Co., 1886.

Govani, Laura E., and Hayes, Janice E. *Drugs and Nursing Implications*. 2nd ed. New York: Meredith Corporation, 1971.

Graf, Arturo. *The Story of the Devil*. Translated by Edward Noble Stone. New York: The Macmillan Co., 1931.

Graham, Harvey. *The Story of Surgery*. New York: Doubleday, Doran and Co., Inc., 1936.

Grant, Sir Alexander, and Lushington, E. L., eds. *Philosophical Works of the Late James Frederick Ferrier*. Vol. II—*Lectures on Greek Philosophy*. New ed. Edinburgh and London: William Blackwood and Sons, 1883.

Grieve, M. *A Modern Herbal*. New York–London: Hafner Publishing, Inc., 1967.

Guillain, Charles, M.D. *J.-M. Charcot–His Life–His Work*. Edited and translated by Pearce Bailey. New York: Paul B. Hoeber, Inc.—Medical Book Department of Harper Bros., 1959.

Habensein, Robert W., and Lamers, William M. *The History of American Funeral Directing*. Milwaukee, Wisconsin: Bulfin Printers, 1962.

*Haining, Peter, ed. *Midnight People*. New York: Popular Library, 1968.

Halasz, Zoltan. *Hungarian Wine through the Ages*. Translated by István Farkas and Éva Rácz. Budapest: Corvina Press, 1962.

Hall, Florence Howe. *Social Customs*. Boston: L. C. Page and Company, Inc., 1911.

Hall, Frederick T. *Pedigree of the Devil*. New York: Criterion Books, 1969.

Hall, J. K.; Zilboorg, Gregory; and Bunker, Henry Alden. *One Hundred Years of American Psychiatry*. New York: Columbia University Press, 1944.

Harkness, Kenneth. *Official Chess Handbook*. New York: David McKay Company, Inc., 1967.

Heiberg, J. L., ed. Archimedes' *Geometra*. Translated by D. C. Macgregor. London: Oxford University Press, H. L. Milford, 1922.

Hemans, Mrs. Felicia. *Poems*. Hartford: Edward Hopkins, 1827.

Henriques, Fernando. *Modern Sexuality*. Vol. III. *Prostitution and Society*. London: Macgibbon and Kee, 1968.

Herriot, Edouard. *Eastward from Paris*. London: Victor Gollancz, Ltd., 1934.

Higgins, Lois Lundell, and Fitzpatrick, Edward A. *Criminology and Crime Prevention*. Milwaukee: Bruce Publishing Co., 1958.

Hind, A. M. *A History of Engraving and Etching*. New York: Dover Publications, 1963.

———. *An Introduction to a History of Woodcut*. Boston: Houghton Mifflin, 1935.

Holden, Harold M. *Noses*. New York: World Publishing Company, 1950.

Hole, Christina. *English Folklore*. 2nd ed. rev. London: B. T. Batsford, Ltd., 1945.

Holland, W. J. *The Butterfly Book*. Garden City: Doubleday, Page and Co., 1916.

Horne's Guide to Whitby. 5th ed. Whitby: Horne and Son, 1897.

Hunter, Richard, and Macalpine, Ida, eds. *Three Hundred Years of Psychiatry, 1536–1860*. London: Oxford University Press, 1963.

Ingersoll, Ernest. *Dragons and Dragon Lore*. New York: Payson and Clarke, Ltd., 1928.

Jacobs, Jay. *The Horizon Book of Great Cathedrals*. New York: American Heritage Publishing Co., Inc., 1968.

James, Henry. *The American*. (Chiltern Library Edition). London: John Lehman, 1949.

James, William. *Varieties of Religious Experience*. New York: The New American Library, Inc., 1958.

———. *The Will to Believe and Other Essays in Popular Philosophy*. New York, London, and Bombay: Longmans, Green and Co., 1897.

*Jerome, Joseph. *Montague Summers: A Memoire*. London: Cecil and Amelia Wolf, 1965.

Jerrold, Walter, ed. *The Complete Poetical Works of Thomas Hood*. New York: Henry Frowde, 1906.

Johnson, Stowers. *Gay Bulgaria*. London: Robert Hale, Ltd., 1964.

*Jones, Ernest. *On the Nightmare*. New York: Liveright Publishing Corp., 1951.

Jones, Kathleen. *Mental Health and Social Policy 1845–1959*. London: Routledge and Kegan Paul, 1960.

Jung, C. G. *Psychiatric Studies*. New York: Pantheon Books, Inc., 1957.

*Katz, Leon. *Dracula: Sabbat*. Copyright by Leon Katz, 1970.

*Knowlson, T. Sharper. *Origins of Popular Superstitions and Customs*. London: T. Werner Laurie, Ltd., 1934.

Kracauer, Siegfried. *From Caligari to Hitler*. Princeton, New Jersey: Princeton University Press, 1966.

*Krauss, F. S. Dr. *Volksglaube und Religiöserbrauch der süd Slaven*. Münster: Druck und Verlag der Aschendorffschen Buchhandlung, 1890.

Krutch, Joseph Wood. *Herbal*. New York: G. P. Putnam's Sons, 1965.

Lefebvre, Rev. Gaspar, O.S.B. *Catholic Liturgy*. St. Louis: B. Herder Book Co., 1954.

Legman, G. *The Horn Book: Studies in Erotic Folklore and Bibliography*. New Hyde Park, New York: University Books, 1964.

Leigh, Denis, M.D., F.R.C.P. *The Historical Development of British Psychiatry*. Vol. I. New York: Pergamon Press, 1961.

List of the Streets and Places within the Administrative County of London, with alterations since 1856. London: London City Council, 1929.

Lombroso, Cesare. *Crime, Its Causes and Remedies*. Translated by Henry P. Horton. Boston: Little, Brown and Company, 1918.

Lombroso-Ferrero, Gina. *Criminal Man*. New York: G. P. Putnam's Sons, 1911.

Lowe, Thompson R. *The History of the Devil*. London: Broadway House, 1929.

*Ludlam, Harry. *A Biography of Dracula*. London: W. Foulsham and Co., 1962.

Lyght, Charles E., ed. *The Merck Manual of Diagnosis and Therapy*. 11th ed. Rahway, New Jersey: Merck, Sharp and Dohme Research Laboratories, 1966.

McCarthy, L. A. *Hungary, A Short History*. Chicago: Aldine Publishing Co., 1962.

*Martin, Betsy W. D., ed. *The Nine Dragon Screen*. London: The China Society, 1965.

Masters, Anthony. *Natural History of the Vampire*. New York: G. P. Putnam's Sons, 1972.

Masters, R. E. L., and Lea, Edward. *Sex Crimes in History*. New York: Julian Press, Inc., 1963.

*Mayo, Herbert, M.D. *Letters on the Truths Contained in Popular Superstitions*. Edinburgh: Blackwood, 1849.

*Mistler, Jean. *La Symphonie Inachevée*. Paris: Editions du Rocher, 1950.

Mortimer-Granville. *Sleep and Sleeplessness*. Boston: S. E. Cassino, 1881.

Nagel's Encyclopedia Guide–Bulgaria. Geneva, Switzerland: Nagel Publishers, 1968.

Nordhoff, Charles. *Sailor Life on Man of War and Merchant Vessel*. New York: Dodd, Mead & Co., 1883.

*O'Donnell, Elliott. *Werewolves*. New York: Longvue Press, 1965.

Oesterreich, T. K. *Possession, Demoniacal and Other Among Primitive Races*. Translated by D. Ibberson. New Hyde Park, N.Y.: University Books, 1966.

*Paget, John. *Hungary and Transylvania*. Philadelphia: Lea and Blanchard, 1850.

Park, Roswell. *The Evil Eye: Thanatology and Other Essays*. Boston: Gorham Press, 1912.

Pergamon World Atlas. Pergamon Press. Warsaw: Blish Scientific Institute, 1968.

Pickering, James Sayre. *The Stars Are Yours*. Rev. ed. New York: The Macmillan Co., 1953.

Pike, Edward Royston. *Human Documents in the Age of the Forsytes*. New York: Praeger, 1970.

*Polidori, John. *The Vampyre: A Tale*. London: Sherwood, Neely and Jones, 1819.

*Prest, Thomas Presket. *Varney the Vampyre*. New York: Arno Press in cooperation with McGrath Publishing Co., 1971.

*Ronay, Gabriel. *The Truth About Dracula*. New York: Stein & Day, 1972.

*Rudorff, Raymond. *The Dracula Archives*. New York: Arbor House (World), 1971.

Rugoff, Milton. *Prudery and Passion*. New York: G. P. Putnam's Sons, 1971.

Rydberg, Viktor. *Teutonic Mythology*. New York: Dover Publications, 1966.

*Scarborough, Dorothy. *The Supernatural in Modern English Fiction*. New York: Octagon Books, 1967.

Schevill, Ferdinand. *The History of the Balkan Peninsula*. 2nd ed. New York: Harcourt, Brace and Co., 1933.

Schwoebel, Robert. *The Shadow of the Crescent*. New York: St. Martin's Press, 1967.

Scott, Sir Walter. *Marmion Canto from the Complete Works of Sir Walter Scott*. Boston: Houghton Mifflin, 1900.

Shelley, Mary. *Frankenstein*. New York: E. P. Dutton and Co., Inc., 1961.

Skinner, Charles M. *Myths and Legends of Flowers, Trees, Fruits and Plants*. Philadelphia and London: J. B. Lippincott, 1911.

Smith, Wayland. *Eros Denied*. New York: Grove Press, 1964.

Sorell, Walter. *The Story of the Human Hand*. Indianapolis: The Bobbs-Merrill Co., 1967.

Steffan, Guy T., and Pratt, Willis W., eds. Byron's *Don Juan*. Vol. II. Austin: University of Texas Press, 1957.

Stetson, Harlan True. *Sunspots and Their Effects*. New York: Whittlesey House, 1937.

Stieler's Hand-Atlas. Gotha: Justus Perthes, 1922.

*Stoker, Bram. *Dracula*. London: Constable and Co., 1897.

*———. *Dracula's Guest*. London: Jarrold, 1966.

*———. *The Gates of Life*. New York: Cupples and Lean, 1908.

*———. *The Jewel of the Seven Stars*. London: Jarrold, 1966.

*———. *Lair of the White Worm*. London: Jarrold, 1966. (First published 1911.)

*———. *The Mystery of the Sea*. New York: Doubleday, Page, 1902.

*———. *Personal Reminiscences of Henry Irving*. 2 vols. New York: The Macmillan Co., 1906.

*———. *The Watter's Mou'*. Westminster: A. Constable and Co., 1895.

Strange, Jack Roy. *Abnormal Psychology*. New York: McGraw-Hill, 1965.

*Sturgeon, Theodore. *Some of Your Blood*. London: Sphere Books, Ltd., 1961.

*Summers, Montague. *The Gothic Guest*. London: Russell and Russell, 1964.

*———. *The Vampire: His Kith and Kin*. New Hyde Park: University Books, 1960.

*———. *The Vampire in Europe*. New York: University Books, 1968.

Surtees, R. S. *The Analysis of the Hunting Field*. New York: Abercrombie and Fitch, 1966.

Sylva, Carmen, and Strettell, Alma. *Legends from River and Mountain*. London: George Allen, 1896.

Talkington, Perry C., and Bloss, Charles L., eds. *Evolving Concepts in Psychiatry*. New York: Grune and Stratton, 1969.

Tarr, László. *The History of the Carriage*. Translated by Elizabeth Hoch. London: Vision Press Ltd. Budapest: Corvina Press, 1969.

Teutsch, Friedrich. *Die Siebenbürger Sachsen*. Leipzig: Verlag von K. F. Koehler, 1916.

Thomas, Frederick. *The Evil Eye*. London: John Murray, 1895.

Thompson, C. J. S. *The Hand of Destiny*. Detroit: Singing Tree Press, 1967.

Thrupp, George A. *The History of Coaches*. Amsterdam, Holland: Meridian Publishing Co., 1969.

Timbs, John F. S. A. *Curiosities of London*. London: Longmans, Green, Reader, and Dyer, 1868.

*Tolstoi, Aleksei. *Vampires*. Translated by Fedor Nikanov. New York: Hawthorne Books, 1969.

*Turgenev, Ivan. *Dream Tales and Prose Poems*. Translated by Constance Garnett. London: The Macmillan Co., 1906.

*Varma, Devendra P. *The Gothic Flame*. London: Arthur Barker, Ltd., 1957.

*Viereck, George Sylvester. *The House of the Vampire*. New York: Moffat, Yard and Co., 1907.

*Volta, Ornella. *The Vampire*. Translated by Raymond Rudorff. London: Tandem Books, 1965.

Vuia, Romulus. *Le Village Roumain de Transylvanie et du Banat* (Extrait de *La Transylvanie*). Bucarest, 1937.

Walker, Mrs. *Untrodden Paths in Roumania*. London: Chapman and Hall, Ltd., 1888.

White, T. H. *A Book of Beasts,* being a translation from *A Latin Bestiary of the Twelfth Century*. New York: G. P. Putnam's Sons, 1954.

Wilkinson, Frederick. *Swords and Daggers*. London: Wardlock and Co., Ltd., 1967.

Wlislocki, Heinrich von, Dr. *Märchen und Sagen*. Berlin: Nicolaische Verlags-Buchhandlung, 1886.

*Wolf, Leonard. *A Dream of Dracula*. Boston-Toronto: Little, Brown and Company, 1972.

———. *Monsters*. San Francisco: Straight Arrow Books, 1974.

*Wright, Dudley. *Vampires and Vampirism*. London: W. Rider and Son, Ltd., 1924.

Young, Wayland. *Eros Denied*. New York: Grove Press, 1964.

Zarek, Otto. *The History of Hungary*. Translated by H. S. H. Prince Peter Wolkonsky. London: Selwyn and Blount, 1939.

Ziegler, Philip. *The Black Death*. New York: John Day Co., 1969.

INDEX

Briefly annotated cities and London streets are not listed in this index. *Page numbers in italics indicate illustrations.*